EXPLICITLY YOURS

THE COMPLETE SERIES

◆

Possession

Domination

Provocation

Obsession

◆

JESSICA HAWKINS

Editing by Elizabeth London Editing
Proofreading by Tracy Seybold
Cover Design © Okay Creations.
Cover Photos © Shutterstock Contributors
Kiuikson & Fotoduki

ISBN: 0997869151
ISBN-13: 978-0-9978691-5-6

TITLES BY JESSICA HAWKINS

LEARN MORE AT JESSICAHAWKINS.NET/BOOKS

WHITE MONARCH SERIES

VIOLENT DELIGHTS
VIOLENT ENDS
VIOLENT TRIUMPHS

RIGHT WHERE I WANT YOU

SOMETHING IN THE WAY SERIES

SOMETHING IN THE WAY
SOMEBODY ELSE'S SKY
MOVE THE STARS
LAKE + MANNING

SLIP OF THE TONGUE
THE FIRST TASTE
YOURS TO BARE

EXPLICITLY YOURS SERIES

POSSESSION
DOMINATION
PROVOCATION
OBSESSION

THE CITYSCAPE SERIES

COME UNDONE
COME ALIVE
COME TOGETHER

Possession

EXPLICITLY YOURS ♦ BOOK ONE

JESSICA HAWKINS

Chapter One

Each night started with the flip of a switch. Hey Joe's neon OPEN sign flickered and hummed to life. Lola's watch read 5:59 P.M., but time had no place on the Sunset Strip. Johnny wiped down the wraparound bar with the efficiency of someone who did it more often than he brushed his own teeth.

"Opening at goddamn six o'clock," Quartz said, shuffling in. "You ever heard some people like to drink their lunch?"

"But if we opened earlier, you wouldn't get to say that every night," Lola said.

Quartz's whiskey on the rocks already sat in front of his regular stool. "Bad enough you're going to cut me off in eight hours. When's Mitch going to wake up and open his bar at a decent hour?"

"Don't think he'll be getting to that," Johnny muttered. "Your tab's hit its max, Quartz. Need you to pay that tonight."

"But if I did, you'd never get to say that."

"I'm serious." Johnny kept the whiskey bottle in his hand, ready to refill Quartz's glass. "You see anybody walking through the door? This isn't back in the day. Look around."

Quartz made a point of twisting on his seat. "Looks like the same old trough I've been drinking out of since '67."

"The point is, you want a bar to come to every night, need to help keep us in business."

Lola shook her head quickly at Johnny.

"What?" Johnny asked, leaving the bottle on the bar to serve another customer. "They'll find out at some point."

Lola ducked under the hatch and came up behind the bar. "Don't listen to him," she said to Quartz, taking Johnny's rag and picking up where he left off.

Quartz put the rest of his drink back with a jerk of his head. "Never do. Figured out years ago that your boyfriend's ponytail holder is cutting off the circulation to his brain."

"He gets crabby when business is slow," Lola said. "Mitch's been breathing down his neck about bad sales."

Two more regulars came in and took their seats next to Quartz. Lola served them and stood back as they grumbled about their wives, bosses, and neighbors. At least, those were the typical topics. She wasn't actually listening because she was watching Johnny at the opposite end of the bar. For the third night in a row, he checked the bulbs on a string of busted Christmas lights that'd been up for nine months.

"Why don't you just buy new lights?" Lola asked.

"Because these ones are fine, babe. There's only one broken bulb. I just need to find it." The lights were even smaller in his sizeable hands. He raised his brows at her. "You going to trade me in for a newer model the day you figure out my one flaw?"

Lola smiled. "After nine years, you must keep it pretty well hidden, whatever it is." Before she'd even finished the sentence, a car engine revved out front. And then another. An ear-splitting racket nearly shook the building.

Quartz swiveled around on his barstool. "They trying to wake the dead?" he yelled.

"Nah. Just get some attention," Johnny said. "Ignore them."

Fumes seeped through the open door, clouding the room. Lola spent five or more nights a week at Hey Joe, the place she considered her second home. The staff and the patrons were her family. So when a lone beer drinker in the corner booth glared at her, she went to see what the commotion was about.

It was dark out. People roamed down the Strip's sidewalk. An electric-blue Subaru was parallel parked out front. The owner, who couldn't have been much older than eighteen, honked at her.

"We've got customers inside," she called over the noise. "Take it somewhere else."

He hit the gas again. Behind him sat a black Nissan with red rims and a matching spoiler. The driver turned his music up so loud the sidewalk vibrated.

Lola went to the curb. With a rag from her apron pocket, she waved away exhaust fumes. It took one well-placed, swift kick of her Converse to put a dent in the Subaru's fender. "I said—"

The driver gaped. "What the—?"

"Get the fuck lost!"

He jumped out and came around the hood toward her. Lola braced herself for an argument, but he stopped mid-step and looked up.

"You heard the lady," Johnny said from behind her. "Don't make me call your mommy."

"Look what she did to my car." The kid pointed at the dent. "That's a brand-new paint job."

"She's done worse to men twice your size," Johnny said. Some people by the door snickered.

"But—"

"Look, kid," Johnny said. "Something you should know about this little stretch of the Strip—we don't call the cops. We handle our own business."

The boy flipped them off with both hands but returned to his car.

Johnny squeezed Lola's shoulders. "Can't go around kicking people's cars, babe."

She glanced back at him. "He started it."

Even with affection in his brown, gold-flecked eyes, the look he gave her was louder than any words.

"Aw, come on," Lola said. "I'm not the one who threatened to *handle* him."

"Why do you say it like that?" He tucked a loose strand of his long hair behind his ear and half smiled. "Think I can't take a couple punks?"

"Oh, I know you could. I also know that you, Jonathan Pace, are all talk."

Johnny winked. "Not when it comes to my lady."

With a kiss on the back of her head, he left Lola standing at the curb. She slung the towel over her shoulder. The two cars took the pavement in a fury of screech and burn, and what followed was a rare moment of silence. Sunset Strip was always busy, but every year the crowd at Hey Joe thinned a little more.

Lola turned to go back inside. Everyone had cleared the sidewalk except one man, who was watching her. He stood by the door with a hip slightly cocked and his long arms straight at his sides, as if he'd been passing by and hadn't meant to stop. Even in the dark, she was struck by his movie-star good looks—chocolate-colored hair styled into a neat wave, a jaw so sharp it could cut metal. She might've guessed he'd accidentally wandered over from a film premiere on Hollywood Boulevard, except that he was too buttoned up and stiff.

"You lost?" she asked.

He straightened his back. "What gives you that impression?"

"If you're looking for happy hour," she said, pointing west noncommittally, "try a few blocks down."

"There's no happy hour here?" He checked the lit, orange sign on the roof. "At Hey Joe?"

"Not the kind you're looking for."

He touched the perfectly done red knot of his tie. "It's the suit, isn't it? I look out of place."

She moved closer, pulled by the deep lull of his voice. The LED beer logos in the window turned the lingering smoke multi-colored. His deep-set eyes were dark, his jaw abrupt in all its angles. She had to tilt her head back to look up at him. His attractiveness sank its teeth in her, more obvious with every passing second. "Not just the suit."

"What then?" He ran his fingers through his stiff, rust-colored hair. He had so much of it that the gesture made some strands stand on end. "That better?"

It was that he was too much—his green, almond-shaped, watchful eyes, and his tall, straight back. He didn't match the carefree laughs and imperfect postures of the people inside the bar. He turned them into commoners, with their round faces, round eyes, round bellies. It was that until that moment, she'd thought she knew what it meant to get butterflies.

But she couldn't say those things. "We just don't see a lot of suits at this end."

"You work here?" he asked.

Lola stuck her hands in the pockets of her apron. "Not like I wear this thing to make a fashion statement."

His loud laugh almost startled her. When he stopped, it echoed. He looked from her neck down, everywhere and all at once, as if he might reach out and touch her. His perusal made her feel exposed, and she was glad her apron subdued the cropped T-shirt and leather pants underneath it.

"You really did a number on that car," he said, his eyes back at her face.

Lola didn't embarrass easily, but there was no denying the sudden warmth in her cheeks. Wherever this man came from, people didn't kick cars there. "You must think I'm a real class act."

"Doesn't matter what I think."

"I guess that's a yes then." She shrugged, because he was right—he was a stranger. She did things like that all the time in front of customers, new and old. Then again, none of them had ever given her butterflies.

He turned his head toward the door so his profile, straight and clean like his suit, was backlit by the sign. A face as handsome as his almost seemed predatorily arranged to disarm prey. "That was your boyfriend?"

"Who, Johnny?"

He looked back at her. "Ponytail and Zeppelin T-shirt. Big guy."

She shifted on her feet. "How do you know he's not my husband?"

"You aren't wearing a ring."

She balled her hands, which were still in her apron. The man stared at her longer than was appropriate, but she wasn't ready to look away. That was why she had to. "I should get back to work."

He nodded. "So should I."

She glanced around the block. There weren't any offices nearby.

Before she could ask, he said, "I was actually on my way in for a drink with some colleagues. I'm here on business."

"Here?" she asked. "This bar?"

He turned and pulled open the door. "This very one. After you, Miss…?"

Light slivered onto the sidewalk. From the bar came a soundtrack of snapping pool balls, glass bottoms on tabletops, men arguing. "Lola," she said, then amended, "Lola Winters" because he looked like a man who dealt in last names.

"Lola." He smiled up to his dusky-green eyes. "Beau Olivier. Nice to meet you."

She didn't move right away. She liked the closeness of him. "Sounds French, but you don't."

"I'm not. My father was," he said. "I grew up here."

"Was?"

"He passed away."

"I'm sorry," Lola said.

"It was a long time ago. *C'est la vie.*"

"C'est la vie," she repeated.

He looked at her expectantly. For a moment, she'd forgotten they were about to go inside. She cleared her throat and walked through the door. Hey Joe's interior was booths mutilated by cigarette burns older than Lola, and black and muddied-white checkered linoleum flooring. A neon-pink mud flap girl watched over the crowd from behind the stage. They were things Lola only thought about once in a while when she considered reupholstering, replacing or removing them. But she thought about them then.

"What can I get you?" she asked over her shoulder as she walked.

"Scotch, neat."

"Preference?"

"Macallan if you've got it."

She stooped behind the bar. "That isn't on special, Beau," she teased.

He smiled again. "I like the way you say my name."

"Yeah, well. So does Johnny."

Beau joined two other men at the bar—the ones who'd snickered on the sidewalk earlier. They were younger than Beau, younger than Lola even, in T-shirts and flannels, jeans and sneakers. She wouldn't have looked twice at them if they'd come in without Beau.

Lola made his drink, glancing at him from under her lashes. He'd loosened his tie. She noticed things about him she hadn't in the dark—the early shadow of stubble forming on his cleft chin, fine lines around his eyes, dimples that hugged his smile like parentheses. He'd called Johnny big, but Beau likely surpassed him in height.

Beau walked back to her end of the bar. She gave him his Scotch.

"Is it just me, or does alcohol taste better on a Friday?" he asked.

"See those guys?" She nodded at Quartz and the others posted in their usual spot. "Tastes the same every day of the week to them." She watched them as if looking through a window into her life. It didn't matter the day, their conversations ran a loop of the same topics. That kind of thing was standard around there. "Bottomless glasses, arguing about bullshit. I still don't know how they function day to day when they're here drinking four, five nights a week."

She turned back to Beau. He'd been staring at her profile and flinched when she caught him, but he didn't look away. He lowered his drink on the bar.

"What?" she asked, busying her hands by filling the sink with dirty glasses.

"Nothing."

"Not nothing." She turned on the faucet and squeezed dish soap into the water. "I've seen that look before."

"I don't doubt that."

She glanced up. "Looks like that lead to trouble."

"Probably. I'm not good at keeping my opinion to myself, though."

She paused. Warm water rose up her forearms. Instinct told her to ignore the comment. She'd done a good job of staying out of trouble since coming to Hey Joe. It'd been a while since anyone besides Johnny had looked at her that way, though. With some hesitation, she asked, "What's your opinion?"

He squinted at her. "You move around this bar like you've been doing it for years. But something doesn't quite click. I'm wondering how you got here."

"That's easy," she said. "On two legs."

"Then what keeps you here?"

They stared at each other. He didn't look as though he expected an answer, and that was good. She wasn't going to give him one—it was none of his business.

"You think you have me figured out in ten minutes?" Lola asked.

"That's ten minutes longer than it takes me for most people." Beau kept his eyes on her face. "And that has my attention."

"Is it hard to get your attention?"

"It's harder to keep it," he said, without even a threat in his voice that he might take his attention away. Even though neither of them moved, it was as if they were getting closer and closer. "But you, Lola, you're—"

"We're low on change," Johnny said, turning the corner from the back office. "Can you do a bank run Monday?"

Lola plunged her hands deeper into the hot water and fumbled for the sponge. "Sure," she said and wiped her brow with her forearm. "Yeah. I have to make the deposit anyway."

Johnny looked from Lola to Beau.

"This is Beau," she said. "Apparently my little show out front made him thirsty."

Johnny nodded once and shook Beau's hand. "Johnny. Welcome."

"This your bar?"

"Nah. I just manage it with Lola."

"She's modest," he said. "She didn't say she was a manager."

"*Assistant* manager to my *boyfriend*." She looked at Beau's empty glass. "Guess you needed that drink. Another?"

Beau reached inside his jacket and took out his wallet. "Looks like it'll be one of those nights. Let me guess…cash only?"

Lola nodded and refilled his drink.

He put some bills on the bar and gestured toward the men he'd arrived with. "For our first round. Everything they order goes on my tab."

Johnny blatantly stared at the cash-stuffed, dark leather wallet in Beau's hand.

"Do they work for you?" Lola asked.

"Not yet. But I want to show them a good time."

"So you brought them here?" she asked, raising her eyebrows. Hey Joe could definitely be a good time, but it was a lot of other things too, like rough around the edges.

"This is the type of place where they're comfortable," Beau said. "Which is what I'm after. A colleague suggested it, said it's been around a while."

"Only fifty-three years," Johnny said. "It's practically a landmark."

"Longer than I realized," Beau said. "What makes it a landmark?"

"It was the place to be in the sixties and seventies," Johnny said. "Live music drew everyone from bikers and hipsters to actors and movie producers."

"I guess that's why the Hendrix reference."

Johnny nodded. "The owner's dad saw him perform 'Hey Joe' here on the Strip late one night for a small crowd. Apparently it was so magical he named the bar after it. Man, I would've fucking loved to have seen that. Not that I was even born yet, but still."

Beau looked at the microphone on the empty stage. "What happened to the music?"

Johnny shrugged and leaned his hip against the counter. "The club went pay for play in the eighties when Mitch took over. Bands didn't like that, and we lost our cred. Fans followed the music elsewhere."

"How's business now?" Beau asked.

"It's all right. We get acts in here some weekends, but nothing to write home about."

Beau shrugged. "You never know. These days, it's all about the comeback."

"That would be great, but it's not pulling in half of what it used to," Johnny said, shaking his head. "Can't afford to keep the doors open."

Beau glanced up around the bar. "Well, considering its history, and if it's still got some name recognition, he should have no problem selling the place."

"That's the plan. Sell or shut it down."

"Johnny," Lola warned.

"Secret's practically out, babe." Johnny looked at Quartz and the other guys. "It's just those dummies down there who know nothing about anything."

"I take it they won't be too thrilled," Beau said.

"Some of them have been coming here since opening day," Johnny said. "No, they won't like it."

"That's a shame." Beau picked up his drink. "I should get back to work. If you'll excuse me."

He left Johnny and Lola to get a table with the other two men.

"What're you thinking?" Johnny asked, nudging Lola's shin with his shoe.

She looked from Beau's table back to Johnny. "Just that it's been a while since I heard you talk about music like that. When's the last time you and I went to a real concert?"

Johnny closed one eye as he thought. "Years. Concerts usually happen at night. We don't get a lot of nights off together."

"We should ask Mitch for one soon. They can survive one night without either of us."

Johnny kissed Lola on the forehead. "I would, but he's got a lot on his plate right now. Let's see how things work out these next few weeks."

"Oh, I remember the last time we went to a show that wasn't here," Lola said. "Beastie Boys, Hollywood Bowl." She smiled as the memory played out on Johnny's face. "And then…"

"That's right." He paused. "The night we had that huge argument."

Lola nodded and leaned toward him. "Which then became the night of the drunken angry sex." Her heart kicked up a notch. "What would you say to an encore? A bottle of tequila, a show and you getting lucky?"

"An encore? We must not be thinking of the same night," Johnny said. "We both drank way too much. I don't even remember what we fought about, just that a table lamp paid the price."

"Me neither, but I do remember one of the best orgasms I've ever had," Lola said. Her ass throbbed. It wasn't the only time Johnny had spanked her, but it was the first and last time he'd done it like he'd meant it. It'd been like sleeping with a stranger after having the same partner for years.

Johnny shook his head. "I don't understand. You want us to have another blowout fight?"

She shrugged one shoulder. "Not fight. I just think a night out could be good for us."

"That's not something I want to recreate," he said, turning away. "But I promise, once things get sorted here, we'll do something for ourselves."

Lola frowned. That night had always stuck with her in a deranged, inexplicable way. There'd been something crackling in the air. She'd assumed the same was true for Johnny, but apparently he'd experienced something else—something entirely different.

Beau was heading back toward the bar, a slight swagger in his step. He didn't look as though he'd hesitate a moment before delivering a hard slap on her rear end. Lola's breath caught.

"We'll take another round," he said, leaning his elbows on the bar. "Might as well keep them coming."

Lola grabbed a glass before Johnny could, eager for the distraction.

"You guys play?" Beau asked. He gestured to a cup of darts against the back wall.

"Yep," Johnny said. "My girl's queen of the bull's eye."

"Is she?" Beau grinned. "Up for a game, Lola?"

"Why don't you play with one of your friends?" she asked. She handed Beau his drink and pointed at the end of the bar. "Or the locals will take anyone on. When they're drunk enough, you can clean them out."

Beau lifted his glass to his mouth, shaking his head. "No challenge in that. I only go up against those who play to win."

Johnny wiped his hands on a rag and nodded over at Lola. "Then you want this one. Got a bit of a competitive streak."

Lola was wary about spending too much time around Beau. They were already hedging on dangerous territory. "Sorry, but I've got customers."

"It's all right, go ahead," Johnny said, taking the drink in Lola's hand. "I'll get these to the table."

She hesitated. "Are you sure?"

"Why not? Go. Have fun."

She shrugged. "Okay. If the boss says so."

"If you think I believe I'm really your boss, you're fooling yourself," he joked. "We both know it's just a title."

She laughed but stopped abruptly at the way Beau stared at her—as though he'd forgotten Johnny was even there.

"What should we play for?" she asked. She stuck a hand in her apron, pulled out a few dollars she'd made in tips and showed them to him. "It's all I've got on me."

"I'm thinking slightly more than that," he said.

"Like what?" she asked.

"How about a hundred bucks?"

"That's a little steep. I'm confident, but I'm not stupid."

"The higher the stakes, the better the game," Beau said. "Not worth playing if you don't have something to lose."

"It's fine, Lo," Johnny interjected. "I got you covered."

A hundred dollars wasn't chump change for Lola and Johnny, but she had a feeling it was for the man standing in front of her, waiting to play. His tie was silk, and his suit custom—nothing from the rack. Lola knew enough to tell the difference.

She came out from behind the bar, and Johnny passed her the darts. When she went to take them, though, he wouldn't let go. Their eyes met. He told her with a look that, just like Lola, he smelled the money on this man.

The dartboard was on the opposite side of the bar, against one of the dark, wood-paneled walls. She and Beau walked by the regulars, under the dated, medieval-style chandelier and by some yellowed Polaroids of rowdy patrons.

At the toe line, a strip of curling duct tape, Beau held one hand out. "Ladies first," he invited.

He didn't know much about her if he thought she was a lady—and didn't know much about darts if he thought that was how you decided who threw first—but Lola kept her mouth shut and took her place. Her dart just missed the triple twenty. She aimed the second one a little higher and landed it.

"Impressive," Beau said. "Where'd you learn to play?"

"Johnny taught me when we first started dating. Before long I was better than him." She threw the last one. "Some people just pick it up easier."

"Or maybe you're like me. I never take my eye off the target." His dart bounced off the wire. "Sometimes I miss, but I never miss twice." He threw again, this time hitting the center.

He got quiet for his last throw. She watched him, the constriction of his neck when he swallowed, the tautness of his jaw while he concentrated. If he was this self-possessed and powerful looking during a light-hearted game, she guessed he'd be a force everywhere else.

"Where'd you say you work?" she asked him.

"I didn't."

"What do you do?"

He threw his dart, but neither of them watched where it landed. "I'm a founding partner of a venture capital firm downtown."

"Those guys you're with don't look like colleagues."

"They own a tech startup I'm thinking of investing in. I like to take my time getting to know the people behind the project before I make any decisions."

"Isn't that kind of thing normally done in a conference room or over a golf game?"

He smiled. "Sometimes it's a golf game. Sometimes it's a trip to Vegas. For these guys, a local watering hole's where they're most comfortable."

"What about you, though?" she asked. "Are you comfortable here?"

"It's not my first choice." He looked at her closely. "But I don't mind a change in scenery now and then. And this is definitely a departure from my usual thing."

Lola took her spot at the duct tape and threw. "I can't tell if that's a compliment or not."

"It is. Take the women who work for me, for instance. They're all blonde. Even the ones with dark hair look blonde. I don't know how they do that."

"Well, this is L.A.," Lola said. She retrieved her darts from the board and passed them to him.

He didn't move right away, except to turn a dart over in his hand. "You don't see any with hair like yours."

"Mine?" Hers was more of a mane, black and thick as the day was long. Straight too—she got that from her dad. One of her few memories from before he'd left was a woman stopping them on the street to say Lola was her dad's spitting image. "What's that supposed to mean?"

"That color—pitch black. It reminds me of the night. Unpredictable. Smooth, but a little wild. No end, no beginning, like midnight. But then your skin," he continued, shaking his head as if in wonder, "white like the moon." He laughed abruptly and took his Scotch from the nearby high-top table where he'd set it. "Well. I've been known to get a little romantic when I drink, but this has to be a new level."

"It's nice," she said without thinking. Her palms were sweating. Come to think of it, the bar seemed warmer than usual. "This place isn't exactly known for romance."

"What's it known for, Lola?"

She blinked several times as she thought. "It used to be…electric. Regulars insist you could see this block from space, all lit up in neon lights. Hear it too."

"Still a lot of neon here," he said.

"True. It takes more than some neon signs to make a place electric, though. Lately people gawk like we're some kind of relic. Problem is, we're still here."

"Gawkers aren't good for business?"

"Not if they aren't spending. I keep telling Mitch we need to become relevant again, because we're really lacking new business. And when the tourists forget about us, we're in trouble." She took another turn. "So how come you don't know all this if you grew up in Los Angeles?"

"I know some of it. I've just never been big on nightlife."

"Why not?"

"I work a lot. In my twenties I was an employee by day and an entrepreneur by night."

"Building your firm? What's it called?"

"Bolt Ventures, but no, I'm referring to my first company," he said. "I went through a lot during those years, but it eventually paid off."

"Do you have hobbies?" she asked, arching an eyebrow. Before he could answer, she added, "Outside of work."

He blew out a laugh. "Some," he said. "Mostly it's just work, though."

"God, you must love what you do," she said and smiled. "I'm all for working hard, but it's nothing without some fun."

"Don't worry," he said evenly. "Because I work hard, I get to have fun too."

Her smile wavered wondering how a guy like Beau had fun. Johnny played guitar, but only for himself. A rock band in high school was the last time he'd performed publicly. Otherwise it was video games or tinkering with cars and bikes at the auto shop where his best friend was a mechanic.

Beau, on the other hand, wouldn't play an instrument. Not the guitar, anyway. She couldn't picture him with a gaming controller or a wrench in his hand either. He was tightly wound. If a man like him didn't loosen up once in a while, he'd snap.

Johnny didn't stress out often, but even he needed to unwind. A couple years back, Hey Joe's alcohol order had gotten mixed up right before the only bartender on duty called and quit. "At least he called," Lola had said, but Johnny wouldn't hear it. His parents had moved to Florida days before, and Lola's car—long gone, now—wouldn't start. Johnny's eyebrows had been so low on his forehead, she'd worried he'd scare off customers. With five minutes to open, Lola had taken him in the back and given him the blowjob of his life. He'd been fine after that.

Lola squinted at Beau. It'd been years since she'd thought of that. She definitely had sex on her mind tonight. Had Beau ever been blown in a seedy bar like this? Would it relax him? Turn him on? Would he find that…*fun*?

"I'm boring you," Beau said. "I never go on about myself this much. Either the Macallan's kicking in or you're too easy to talk to."

Lola was about to tell him to keep talking—she liked having a new voice in the bar. It didn't hurt that that voice was bottomless, as if it came from some untouched depths inside him. And steady, in a comforting way. She could listen to him all night. She shook the feeling off.

"So what'll you do if this place gets bought out?" he asked.

"I try not to think about it," Lola said. "It'd be hard on us. Johnny loves this place as if it were his own."

"And what about you?"

Over Beau's head were some photographs of the owner's dad with bands and customers who were long gone. "There's a lot of history here," she said, her eyes wandering over the pictures. "I'm closer to the people here than I am my own family."

"But you could see yourself doing something different," he guessed.

"Different?" It hadn't occurred to her. Johnny had been bartending for twelve years, and she'd been by his side for eight of them. They were a team. "The late-night scene can get old," she admitted. "I suppose if it were between moving to a different bar or trying something else, I'd maybe think about something else." Lola hadn't even known she'd be open to a change until she'd said it aloud. She'd assumed she and Johnny would always work together, but Johnny'd never do anything outside the nightlife industry.

"Something like…?" Beau asked.

She considered it a moment. "A restaurant would make sense, or a coffee shop. At least the hours would be better."

"So then serving food and drinks is your passion," Beau said.

She simultaneously laughed and scoffed. "I wouldn't go that far. I'm just being realistic about my options. They're limited without a college degree."

"You didn't go to school?"

"Dropped out my first semester." Lola mock-gasped with her fingers over her mouth. "Unheard of in your world, isn't it?"

"No." He frowned. "I didn't go to college either."

She cleared her throat. She hadn't expected that. Yet, he only said he'd started a business—not that it was successful. Maybe it wasn't. But there was his suit, the cut of it, the way it moved with him instead of against him. It turned his shoulders into two strong right angles with a large expanse in between.

If she pretended there were a bug, she could reach out and brush it away just to see if the fabric was smooth, scratchy or something else. And she could get an idea of what was underneath it.

"What'd you do before this?" Beau asked, oblivious to her wandering imagination.

"Before this? Nothing really. I've worked here since I was…" She almost couldn't finish the sentence. It was a lifetime ago now. In the eight years she'd been doing it, she couldn't pinpoint when she'd decided waiting tables would be her career. "Twenty-one," she finished. "That's how old I was when I started."

"So that would be, what?" Beau pretended to count to himself. "Two years ago? Three?"

"Nice try," she said as she laughed.

"I can't be that far off. You could pass for early twenties."

"Maybe compared to tonight's crowd. You and I might be the only ones under forty." She guessed at his age to see if he'd correct her, because he could very possibly *be* forty.

"Except for Johnny," Beau said.

"Obviously except for Johnny," Lola said quickly. He'd flustered her with the insinuation she'd forgotten about Johnny—because she had.

"You're a bit younger than me, though," Beau said, his voice light, teasing. "And I'm a bit older than you."

She wanted to ask by how much, but she just glanced at the floor. "Not a lot older, I don't think."

"The way you're smiling a little makes me think maybe you wouldn't mind an older man."

"Actually," Lola said, lifting her head, "I wouldn't know anything about that. Johnny's the oldest guy I've been with, and he's a few years older than me. And my guess is you're a few years older than him. And my other guess is, whether or not I'd mind an older man isn't really your business."

His eyes twinkled. "You're right. It was inappropriate to suggest you might. I'm sorry."

"I don't think you are." She turned away from the probing look on his face, more intimate now than it'd just been.

"I don't think you are, either," he said.

She paused, and against her better judgment, looked back. His cheeks were high and round, as though losing the fight against his smile. "Don't tell me you're forfeiting the game," he said.

"And give you the satisfaction? Never. I'm in it 'til the end."

"Then why are you walking away?"

"If I'm going to hang around you any longer, I'm going to need a drink for myself."

He put his hand in his pocket and stalked slowly toward her. No longer on the verge of smiling, he looked at her as though she were on display in a museum, some rare and amusing find.

She stood her ground, even when he came close enough that the tips of their feet almost touched. His eyes, their unusual oval shape and striking color—he narrowed them and frowned as if he were trying to read her but couldn't. He leaned in. He was going to kiss her right there in front of everyone. She had to move, push him—something. She looked at his mouth, his bottom lip slightly fuller, slightly pinker than the upper one.

"Are you going somewhere dangerous?" he asked.

She tried not to sound as breathless as the thought of kissing him made her feel. "What?"

He put his hand over hers, encompassing it in warmth. He turned it over. Instinctively, she opened her fingers to reveal a dart she hadn't realized she'd been gripping.

"I'll hold onto this—unless you think you'll need it for protection?" He took it and walked back a few steps. She wondered if she'd been wrong that he couldn't read her because of the way he grinned. It was as if he knew something about her she didn't.

Chapter Two

Once the OPEN sign was switched off each night and the doors locked, Hey Joe became something else. The pours went from standard to generous and the music from loud to easy. Familiar.

Lola closed down the bar with Veronica, one of Hey Joe's longest-standing waitresses, while Johnny and his leather-jacket friends surrounded the pool table like some kind of biker gang. Outsiders weren't usually allowed after hours—Johnny's rule, not the owner's—yet somehow Beau had convinced the guys to let him in on a game of pool. Lola suspected that was because they never got a chance at winning real money when they played against one another. The men Beau arrived with had left hours earlier.

Lola turned the volume up a notch for The Doors. Veronica shook her hips back and forth. Her acrylic nails clinked against drink glasses as she dried them.

"I heard a rumor," Veronica said.

"Probably the same one I heard."

"Think we'll all get the boot when Mitch sells this place?"

Lola looked at Johnny as he lined up his shot, sank the ball and swaggered around the table. "I hope not," she said.

"Word is they're looking to develop this block of the Strip into something fancy. You see that juice bar they're putting in?"

"I saw it. Can you imagine bulldozing all this history?

Vero, do you realize the fucking rock stars who've stood on that stage?"

Vero popped her gum, shaking her head. "Shit's not cool."

"They'd probably give us uniforms. You might have to wear a miniskirt."

Vero looked down at her Harley T-shirt and faded jeans. "The day I wear a miniskirt's the day I cut off my balls and serve them to my boss on a silver platter."

"You don't have balls, Vero."

"It's a saying," she said, rolling her eyes. She leaned a hand on the counter and nodded over at the pool game. "I don't know, maybe it wouldn't be such a bad thing if this place shut down. Not like Johnny can't find something else."

"But he's perfect here."

She smiled. "I know. That doesn't mean he can't do good work somewhere else, though. And maybe you could try something with computers."

"You think so?" Lola asked.

"Why not? I remember when you first started you talked about going back to school."

"Yeah, I did," Lola said. "Kept putting it off, and here I am years later."

"Happens all the time, but people do it. You've been making flyers for this place for a while. Even Mitch says they're good. Couldn't you take a, you know, flyer-making class or something?"

"I guess I could," Lola said. Mitch had even promised to let her redesign the menus he'd been hanging on to the last decade. Before he'd decided to close, of course. "I actually like the little bit of graphic design I've taught myself."

"Yep," Vero said. "But take it from me, you have to do it now. If you get another waitressing gig, you'll get stuck again. Me and Johnny? We're in this scene for good. Nothing can hide a lifetime of smoking and the pretty little scar on my lip Freddy left me with. Johnny's got his rough edges too. You can still get out, though."

Lola chewed on her bottom lip. Once in a while, she thought about going back to school. Johnny didn't like change, though. Leaving the bar would mean no more waking up late in the morning together and lounging before work—coffee, talk shows, reading the *Times* while he strummed his guitar on their tiny patio. It would mean not driving home from work in the middle of the night, sometimes with her head in his lap when she was especially tired. It would mean leaving him behind in a way, telling him this life he loved wasn't quite enough for her.

"Everyone's living in the clouds tonight," Lola said softly, thinking of the similar conversation she'd just had with Beau. "There must be something in the air."

"Nah. It's just the liquor giving me loose lips," Vero said.

"Veronica," Lola scolded. "Johnny warned you about drinking on the job."

"You know how it is. I just need a taste every now and then. Anyway, you had a drink earlier."

"That was a special circumstance."

"Playing darts is a special circumstance?"

Lola pinned her with a look. "My aim gets sharper the more I loosen up."

"Oh, okay, sure." Veronica nodded her head high.

"Keep your secret if you keep mine?"

Lola snickered. She rarely got to pull one over on Johnny. "Fine," she said. "Deal."

Vero stopped her gum smacking. "Girl, why don't you ever tell that slut to back off?"

Lola followed her nod to Amanda, one of the waitresses, as she smiled up at Johnny.

"You know why," Lola said. "She can flutter those lids until they fall off, Johnny's not dumb enough to touch that."

"Don't matter. Since she doesn't seem to have eyeballs, there're other ways to let her know he's your man."

"We have to work together," Lola said. "I don't want trouble. And Johnny puts her in her place when he needs to. Not that it does much good." Lola's gaze shifted to Beau, who stood with his pool cue planted on the ground. He was the only one not wearing something faded or leather.

"Handsome guy, isn't he?" Vero asked. "Out of the suit, that is."

Lola kept her eyes on him and shrugged one shoulder. "I don't mind the suit."

"Don't tell Johnny that. Probably never wore a suit in his life, not even to a funeral."

"I know," Lola said absentmindedly. "Maybe that's why I like it."

"Replace the suit with a cut and throw him on a bike, though? Fuck me. A face like that would put a serious dent in the pussy around here."

Beau caught them looking and raised his glass, his smile sweetly crooked.

"You didn't answer my question earlier," he said after she'd gotten herself a drink. They'd stopped playing darts and were standing close to each other at a high-top table.

"Which one?"

"I asked what you did before working here."

"Oh. Nothing really. There was high school, of course..."

"Of course." He grinned. "But you didn't work here until you were twenty-one, which leaves a few years in between. Maybe the answer to your quandary lies there."

Lola leaned toward him over the small table. The bar was busier now and the conversations more animated. She told herself it was to hear him better, but she was actually afraid of missing even one word. "And what quandary is that?"

"The one about what happens if Hey Joe goes under."

"Ah, that one." She picked at nothing on the table. "No, it won't answer that question."

"I'm pretty good at problem-solving," Beau said. "Try me."

Lola was unaware she even had a problem. A new idea to explore, sure, but not a problem. She opened her mouth, about to tell him to mind his own business. She wasn't ashamed of her past, nor was she proud of it, but something about Beau made her wish there were nothing to tell at all. Instead, she gave him a version of the truth. "I did some things, met some people. I went through a stage where I partied a lot and crashed on friends' couches."

"That's vague," Beau said. "How much is a lot?"

"Too much."

"Is that why you dropped out of school?"

She nodded. "I blew my money on alcohol and going to see bands. Sometimes drugs too. I couldn't keep up with the tuition, but I'd been missing classes anyway."

Beau studied her. "How'd you end up here?"

"Johnny," she said right away. "He's the reason I got my life

back together."

He cocked his head. "Really? Why?"

Lola picked up the darts from the table and backed away, suddenly disgusted with herself for discussing this with a stranger. Johnny never judged her, never made her feel ashamed. She was by his side every night because he'd believed in her without having any reason to. She didn't need to explain herself to Beau. "Let's finish the game," she said.

Beau lowered his drink, but held Lola's gaze a little longer than necessary as they exchanged a private moment. He turned back to the pool table.

"He seems especially interested in you," Vero said.

The memory scattered along with their moment. Maybe it hadn't been as private as Lola had thought. She wiped her forehead with the back of her hand and got back to cleaning. "Sure," she said, "if overworked barmaid is his type."

After a few minutes there was a cheer from the table, and Johnny high-fived Quartz. He set the cue in its rack and walked over to Lola. "Won back the money you lost at darts and then some," he said, leaning over the bar for a kiss.

"Good job, babe."

"I'd better quit before I do any more damage," Beau said from behind Johnny.

Johnny turned around. "You taking off?"

"Once I settle my tab. I might be a little short after that game, though. ATM?"

Johnny pointed toward the back wall and watched Beau walk away. "Lo," he said under his breath. "See if you can convince him to come back. Maybe bring some of his moneybag friends."

"What's it matter?" Lola asked warily. "The bar's closing anyway."

"Nothing's set in stone, babe. It's a long shot, but those business types love to slum it up once in a while. Go now, while he's alone."

Lola's stomach knotted just thinking about it. It didn't feel right, but Johnny rarely asked her for much. "What am I supposed to say?"

"Just be cute, flirt a little." Johnny eyed Beau then did a double take at Lola. "Not too much, though." He printed out Beau's tab and handed it to her in a black, vinyl sleeve. "Bring him his bill and ask when he's coming back."

Lola rolled her eyes but took the bill even though she doubted she could flirt with someone who always had the upper hand. If Beau wanted flirting, he'd be doing it. She approached him as he was taking his money from the ATM.

"Hey," she said with a smile. "Thanks for the game tonight. It's been a while since I lost."

He raised an eyebrow as he counted out some bills. "You're thanking me for that?"

Lola averted her eyes from the money to be polite. "It's good for my ego."

He smiled, returned his wallet to his jacket and nodded at her hands. "Then you're welcome. Is that my check?"

She handed it to him. He slid money into the fold without looking at the total and gave it back to her. "A little extra for the great service."

She took it. "Johnny says you can come back any time you want." She fidgeted with the folder. Tonight had been something different from the usual because of Beau. Most nights she and Johnny had the same dinner, talked about what the bar needed to improve, saw the same faces. She wanted Beau to come back too, but if he knew that, he might get the wrong idea. "I think he likes you," she added.

His eyes narrowed on her as if he was trying to figure something out. "Does he?" he asked. "What about you, Lola? Do you like me?"

She fumbled for an answer. "Do I like you?" she repeated, stalling. Heat crept up her neck. That was twice in one night he'd made her blush. "Sure. I enjoyed talking to you."

He threw back his head and laughed. "That's it?"

"Yes," she said. "Should there be more?"

"I thought there might be." He looked past her a moment, then his eyes shifted back. He cleared his throat. "I'm an early riser, especially when I have to work in the morning. Meaning, not much could keep me out this late."

"Well, I'm glad you had a good time," she said.

"What I'm trying to say is, you're the reason I stayed." He stepped a little closer. "Any other night I would've left with the people I came with."

"But I'm so boring." She said it with a smile because smiling and making a stupid joke seemed like the only safe response to what he was implying.

"You're the least boring person I've met in a while," Beau said, "and it goes against my nature to bite my tongue. I like you, Lola. I think you already figured that out, though."

"Let me guess. Subtlety goes against your nature too.

How many women have fallen for that?"

"Have you seen me even look in another woman's direction tonight?"

She hadn't. Once Vero'd brought up Amanda, Lola had been curious to see if Beau would talk to her. Amanda wasn't a bad-looking girl, but Lola didn't worry about her because Johnny just wasn't a cheater. He didn't have it in him.

But if Beau was looking to take home a sure thing, and he had a penchant for a bar girl he could flaunt his wealth for, Amanda was it. Yet earlier, when Amanda had smiled at him across the pool table, he hadn't even acknowledged her.

"That excuse is too convenient," Beau continued. "You're trying to cheapen our attraction by suggesting I'd take anyone home."

Attraction. To be drawn to him—to want to feel even closer to him when they were standing right next to each other. "I think it's best we end this conversation here," she said, keenly aware that her boyfriend was mere feet behind her.

"So I'm wrong then," Beau said. He stood far enough from her that their conversation wouldn't have appeared intimate. But each time he spoke, it was as if he removed another layer of her clothing, and now she was too close to being exposed. "I'm wrong that this attraction is one-sided?"

Lola glanced over her shoulder. Johnny was saying goodnight to his friends at the door. She looked back and almost told Beau he wasn't wrong, that it wasn't one-sided, just to see what he'd say. Flirting with him gave her a thrill she hadn't felt in so long. "I'm sorry if I gave you the wrong impression," she said instead. "Johnny and I have been together a long time, and we're happy."

"That's not what I asked," Beau said. "How you feel about him is one thing. Whether you're attracted to me is another."

"I'm not," Lola said firmly. She could've admitted the truth to any other man, because she was confident in her love for Johnny, but Beau wasn't any other man by a mile. Her gut told her the truth was a risk she couldn't afford to take.

Lola went to leave but stopped when she opened the bill holder. There was a stack of twenties. She counted three hundred dollars, but his total was ninety-seven.

She stuck only enough in her apron pocket to cover the bill. "This is too much," she said, turning back to Beau. "I can't accept this."

He hadn't moved. He raised his eyebrows slowly. "It's called a tip."

"No, I know, but it's too much. The tip is double the bill, and I didn't do anything out of the ordinary."

"So, let me get this straight," he said levelly. "You won't even accept a generous tip?"

He almost seemed angry. She almost *felt* angry. That much money wasn't a tip—it was suggestive. It turned their harmless, flirtatious exchange into something sordid and cheap.

She took the cash out and thrust it at him. "Please. I'm not comfortable taking this."

His mouth was closed, but his jaw worked back and forth. She didn't recognize the look in his eyes, but it cooled any warmth that'd been growing between them.

"Fine," he said, taking the money from her. "I don't believe I've ever had a tip returned to me, but I suppose there's a first time for everything."

"Thank you," she said. She walked away with her fingers gripping the empty folder.

"Well?" Johnny asked as she approached the bar. "How'd it go?"

She shot him a look. She was too annoyed to answer, but she couldn't have even if she'd wanted to because Beau was right behind her.

"This scene has been a nice change from what I'm used to," Beau said. "You've really got a good thing going here."

"Like Lola said, I hope you'll tell your friends," Johnny said. "We could use the business."

Beau looked pointedly at Lola. She hadn't mentioned telling his friends. "I will," Beau said. "Even though I kind of like having it as my secret."

Lola held his gaze, willing herself to think of anything but *attraction*. She was failing.

Nobody spoke for a few moments and Vero, who'd been busy closing out the register, chimed in. "Can I get you some water or something before you go?" she asked Beau.

"You mentioned the owner's looking to sell," he responded, glancing between the three of them.

"That's right," Johnny answered. He leaned back against the bar and crossed his arms. "Why? You know someone who might be interested? We'd really like to find an owner who wants to keep Hey Joe as it is."

"Every struggling business wants that," Beau said. "They want to keep doing what they're doing without sacrificing a single thing, but they want it to magically become profitable."

"This place has the history to back it up," Lola said defensively. "We believe in it."

"And I admire that." Beau turned to Vero. "Veronica, is it? Would you give the three of us a moment?"

Vero winked. "Sure thing, baby."

"I'll go with you," Lola said. "Give the boys a chance to talk."

"I wouldn't," Beau said. The warning in his voice kept Lola's feet glued where they were. "This concerns you."

Vero left, swaying her hips especially wide on her way to the backroom.

"Have you thought about buying this place?" Beau asked them.

"Have *I*?" Johnny set his palms on the edge behind him and sighed. "Owning a bar is the idea one day, but not this one. Even if it is on the decline—well, you're a businessman, you know. The brand has a solid reputation. It's already got the foundation for success, just needs the right owner."

"You're worried about the price."

"Nope," Johnny said. "If I were worried about it, that'd mean I had a chance in hell of getting the money."

"I have the money to buy it." Beau paused. "I can *give* you the money to buy it."

Lola's heart had already gotten a workout that night thanks to Beau, but right then it thudded once and painfully hard—as if it'd been running, come to a screeching halt and smacked into her ribcage. Everything clicked for her. This was their answer. This was why Beau had been so interested in her and the bar. He saw an opportunity, but she saw their first glimmer of hope in a while.

"You mean like an investor?" Johnny asked.

"No," he said. "I'm talking about a one-time payment to buy the business and the liquor license outright. You wouldn't owe me a dime of your profits."

Johnny pushed off the bar and stood up straight. "I'm listening."

Beau squinted at Johnny for a few seconds, but it looked to Lola as if he was somewhere else. "There's a catch, of course—"

"I think you got the wrong idea about us," Lola said suddenly. At first glimpse it'd sounded like an answer, but as Beau's eyes darkened and his tone dropped, she didn't want to hear the next thing out of his mouth. "We may not have much, but we're honest people. We do things by the book around here."

"Let the man talk, Lo," Johnny said.

She was too surprised by that to utter anything else. She and Johnny *did* do things by the book, especially Johnny—there was no reason to dismiss her.

"It's okay," Beau said. "I understand her concern. She's right to be cautious." He scratched the long, stubbled line of his jaw as he thought. "It's simple, really. I just want one thing in return for the money."

"What, our first born?" Johnny joked. "Free Macallan for life? Name it."

"Lola." Beau looked from Johnny to Lola with such intensity in his green eyes that she reached back to steady herself against a barstool. "I want Lola for one night."

Chapter Three

As if Beau's words had stopped time, Lola, Johnny and Beau stood frozen where they were. Lola didn't breathe. She might've thought Beau's proposition was a joke and even laughed if it weren't for his composure when he'd said it. As if to him, the deal were already made. He wanted Lola for one night, and that's what he'd have.

"Excuse me?" Lola asked so quietly, she wasn't entirely sure she'd spoken aloud.

Johnny stepped closer to the bar that separated him from Lola and Beau. He leaned his knuckles on the surface. "What the fuck did you just say?"

"Give me one night alone with Lola, and Hey Joe is yours."

"You're offering me money to sleep with my girlfriend?"

Lola hadn't blinked in so long, her eyes watered. When she did, her mind caught up. It raced ahead. Emotions came as fast as her heartbeat. *Thud.* Shock. *Thud.* Indignation. *Thud.* Fear.

"What I'm offering you is your dream on a silver platter." Beau looked at Lola. "Both of you."

He had some nerve putting his eyes on her. Based on the last few hours, it wasn't even that surprising he'd come on to her. But to try to put a price on her—and on their time together? Her heartbeat was pure anger now, short, quick bursts that made her ears hot. "Fuck you," she said with her hands curled into two trembling balls. She wanted to say more, but she could only think of the crudest words possible. "Right, Johnny? Fuck him."

Johnny's neck reddened from his T-shirt to his jaw. Her concern shifted from herself to him. He looked like he might lunge for Beau, but Johnny wasn't a fighter. She'd never seen him lay an angry hand on anyone. She reached out to touch him, but he ripped his arm away and pounded his fist on the bar. "Tell me this is a sick joke, man," he said through a clenched jaw. That was Beau's cue to leave.

Beau raised one eyebrow. "I still don't have my answer."

"You want an answer?" Johnny asked. "How about I jump over this bar and give it to you with my fist?"

"I'm not looking for a fight," Beau said. "As long as we both have something the other wants, this can be worked out peacefully." He paused and removed his suit jacket by the lapels. "However," he said, tossing it over a stool, "we can do it your way too."

A door slammed in the back. Beau rolled up his shirtsleeves. She needed him gone before any of the staff came back out. She jerked her hand to the exit and said, "He told you to leave," but no sooner had she looked away from Johnny than he was ducking to get out from behind the bar.

Beau didn't move except to turn and face Johnny, who was already past Lola. Johnny seized Beau's crisp, white shirt. Beau's body stiffened as he drew up to his full height and met Johnny head on. Johnny drew his arm back. In that split second, instead of raising his own fist or trying to get loose, Beau looked at Lola. There was no fear in his expression, and that scared her more than anything. Johnny wasn't a fighter. She had no idea what Beau was capable of. Somebody would end up hurt, and it could very likely be the man she loved. She jumped up and latched onto Johnny's bicep.

"Stop!" Her feet were practically off the ground from giving Johnny's arm all her weight.

"Let go," Johnny said.

"Please don't do this, Johnny," she pleaded. "You won't win."

Johnny's head snapped toward her. The tension in his muscle immediately melted under her hands. "*What?*" he asked with his mouth hanging open.

Afraid Beau might sucker punch Johnny, she forced her way between them. More specifically, she pushed Johnny back behind her since Beau was immovable. "Get out," she told Beau.

Beau held her gaze while he picked up his jacket from the stool. He blinked over her head. "Five hundred thousand," he said to Johnny. "There's a number for you. That's what this place is worth give or take."

"What about what I'm worth?" Lola asked immediately.

Beau's eyes returned to hers.

Johnny grasped Lola's shoulders. "Move and let me handle this."

But Lola could not be moved as she locked eyes with Beau. In her hasty reply, she'd missed the number. Half a million dollars. It made her flush to be associated with any dollar amount, but this dollar amount was so high that she was absurdly impressed with herself. No person would walk into a bar and offer that to just anyone. It had to be something about *her*.

Lola tried to keep her thoughts from her face, but

Beau looked as if he knew everything. She forced herself to see past the amount. It didn't matter whether this was about her specifically, because introducing money turned her from a person to a product. A service. The suggestion that she could be bought was a betrayal of her short but powerful time with Beau.

Beau raised his chin just noticeably. "What you're worth depends on whom you ask," he said to her. "If you want to know what you're worth to him, ask him his counteroffer. If you want to know what you're worth to me, bring me that counteroffer." He reached into his breast pocket and placed his card on the bar. "In case you change your minds," he said before walking away.

"We won't," she said.

He paused a moment then turned around. "Earlier, before we were interrupted, you asked me my opinion. I was going to say that you're captivating. You've held my attention from the start."

It wasn't until the door closed behind Beau that Lola lost the strength that'd been holding her together. Her legs trembled as she turned around to face Johnny. She put her face into his T-shirt. It smelled like him. She would never not know his scent. When she didn't feel his arms around her, she looked up into his face. His expressions were more familiar to her than her own, but this was one she didn't recognize.

"How could you say that?" he asked through his teeth.

She blinked at him a few times and took a step back. "What did I say?"

"'You won't win'? I was a second from pummeling him. Thanks for the vote of fucking confidence."

"Johnny, seriously? A fistfight? You're above that."

"Were we just in the same room?" he asked incredulously. "Did you not hear what he said?"

"Of course I heard. But it's not worth it. You're of more use to me here than in a jail cell. Or worse—a hospital bed."

"That's not why you stopped me," he said. "You didn't think I could take him."

Lola raked her fingers through her hair. She had too much on her mind to be stroking Johnny's ego. "Everything happened so fast. If you'd seen the look in his eyes—"

"I did. I was standing right in front of him."

She shook her head quickly. "You didn't see what I saw. I said that to protect you. One or both of you could've gotten really hurt. You don't know his background. He could be dangerous."

"Don't ever get in the middle like that again," he said. "You could've been the one hurt. I don't need *you* to protect *me*."

Vero came out from the backroom, whistling with her bag swinging over her arm. "You guys ready to lock up? The others went out the back, and I got somewhere to be."

"Yeah, let's get the fuck out of here," Johnny muttered, walking to the front to shut out the lights.

"What'd the suit want?" Vero asked. "He going to make an offer?"

"No," Lola snapped, already headed the opposite direction to get her purse from the back. When she returned, the bar was dark and empty. She heard Johnny start the car. On her way out, she remembered Beau's card on the counter. She went back to throw it away—it was the last thing she wanted to see when they came in the next day.

It was gone.

◆⊠◆⊠◆

Lola rubbed her wrist where her watch had been. Johnny brushed his teeth so hard, she heard the whole thing from where she sat on the edge of their bed.

It was always the normal-looking guys who were deranged. Given her past, she could usually spot them, but this guy, Beau—who seemed to be things she wasn't used to, like charming and refined—that level of depravity on a guy like him surprised her.

The ride home had been quiet. She'd gone over her brief conversations with Beau for any clue of what was to come. The only thing out of the ordinary was his sudden coldness toward her at the end when she wouldn't accept his tip.

She'd apologized to Johnny right before they'd gotten out of the car, but he'd sullenly ignored her. Her mind had still been playing catch up. Something in particular had nagged at her—she just couldn't figure out what.

The faucet stopped and Johnny came out of the ensuite bathroom in his boxers. He leaned in the doorway with his arms crossed. "What interrupted you?"

"What?" Lola asked.

He sighed irritably as if she'd checked out of a conversation she hadn't known they were having. "He said you guys were interrupted before he could say you were 'captivating.' What interrupted you?"

"It was early in the night," she said, swallowing. "I don't really remember."

"Try," he said.

Lola glanced at her hands. Beau had been standing across from her with his loosened tie and easy grin. Earlier. Before he'd become visibly stiff in those last moments. What had he said to her? That it was hard to get his attention, but that she had it. Such bold disregard for her relationship excited her more than it should. Nobody she knew went after anything that way—except maybe her before she'd settled down with Johnny. "I think he was trying to…to flirt with me, I guess, but you came out from the back," Lola said. "That's when I introduced you. He was being a little forward."

"Why didn't you tell me? I would've thrown him out."

"Because I can handle myself," she said. "Besides, you told me to flirt with him at the end of the night."

"Not *really* flirt," Johnny said tersely. "I meant in a way that he thinks you're flirting but you're really not. Whatever." He pushed off the doorjamb. "So did you give him a reason to make that offer?"

"Johnny," she scolded. "It's *me.* The woman you love and who loves you back." She waited, hoping his expression would clear a little. "Of course I didn't give him a reason. The whole thing was stupid."

"Come here," he said.

"What?"

"I said come over here."

She stood slowly and went to him. He took her chin and kissed her. Her upper lip pinched between their teeth, and she jerked back. "Johnny, stop. We need to talk about this."

"Later," he said. With a hand on her shoulder, he gently nudged her toward the bed.

"It's four in the morning."

"Yeah." He pulled her against him by her hips and kissed her again. He ran his hand down her backside and squeezed. "Right now, you know what I want."

She knew. Most of the time when they had sex, it was after she and Johnny had fallen into bed, or in the late morning when they woke up. Once in a while, though, Johnny got really worked up, and then he liked her on her hands and knees.

She turned around willingly. When Johnny had his rare urges, he didn't fight them, and she didn't want him to. Those were the times he went absolutely crazy for her.

She climbed onto the bed in only a long T-shirt. He lifted it up and grabbed her ass in both hands. He rubbed against her. She dropped her forehead toward the mattress as he entered her. His first few thrusts were long and slow as she warmed up to him, but they soon turned quick and hard. It normally took time for her to climax from penetration alone, but she almost always did this way. She became putty in his hands to know he was so consumed, he couldn't even bother with foreplay.

"That's it. Damn, Lo," Johnny said. "You feel good."

She gasped. "Right there. Don't stop."

"You like that?" He ran a hand up her back, then grabbed her hips and pulled her into his next thrust. "Like it hard, baby? How's that for fucking flirting?"

Her breath caught. He was thinking of Beau, which

made her think of Beau. "What?"

Johnny pulled out and slid himself up between her cheeks.

"Johnny—"

"Please, babe. Just for a minute. I need this."

"No," she said. She had no interest in anal, especially when Johnny was like this.

He breathed out some complaint she didn't catch and was inside her again as if he'd never left.

Beau had been planted in her mind, though—his flirtatious, lopsided smile.

His sexy red tie, sexy five o'clock shadow, *sexy, sexy, sexy*—and she was so sure he had a nice, big cock to back up that suggestive grin.

Oh, God. Yes.

Maybe he'd even wear his suit while fucking her from behind, too eager to bother undressing.

Yes! Just like that.

He'd pull her hair and tell her how badly he'd wanted her from the moment he'd laid eyes on her.

Lola toppled into a viscous climax as Beau's image seared into her memory. Almost as quickly, guilt flooded in. Johnny didn't last much longer.

After he'd come, he smoothed a hand over her backside and up her back. He squeezed her shoulder. "You good?"

"Yes," she said. She was breathless, not from her orgasm, but because she'd never thought about another man while she was with Johnny. Ever.

When he pulled out, she practically ran to bathroom. She locked the door behind her, turned and confronted herself in the mirror. It was a serious crime, yes. But it wasn't even her fault. Johnny had brought Beau into bed with them. There were worse things. She was only human. In the desperate moments before an orgasm, there were no rules. It was what she'd needed to cross the finish line—the thought of Beau inside her. Her sensitive clit was already throbbing again.

She forced herself to calm down so she could return to the bedroom. Johnny sat with his back against the headboard and his long legs extended in front of him. He knew. The look on his face said everything. He had to know she'd been thinking of Beau in their most intimate moment.

"So if he was flirtatious with you before I met him, that means he had his eye on you from the beginning," Johnny said. "Right?"

Lola hid her relief that he didn't suspect she'd been fantasizing. She took a tentative step toward the bed. This was a conversation best had once they'd slept on things, but Johnny didn't look like he wanted to wait. "I guess," Lola said. "Unless he was just there looking for anyone."

"What about your dart game? Did he say anything then?"

She rolled her lips together and shook her head.

"Because he made a weird comment during pool that I ignored, but now it makes more sense."

"What comment?" Lola asked, edging closer and sitting at his feet.

"He asked if I kept Amanda around to make myself feel good. Right in front of her."

Lola caught her laugh before it escaped. It reminded her of something Veronica would say if Lola'd ever let her. It became less funny, though, when she wondered what would make an outsider like Beau even ask that. "Amanda does flirt with you," Lola said.

Johnny shrugged. "It's Amanda. She's just like that. You've said it doesn't bother you enough to get rid of her."

"It doesn't, because I know you. I know us. Give me the same credit, and don't hold me to a double standard about the flirting."

He waved a dismissive hand. "Amanda's harmless. I wouldn't even notice if she stopped showing up for work, except that we'd be one person short."

"So Beau made a couple harmless comments too. I can handle myself. You were nearby if I needed you."

"You're comparing *him* to Amanda?"

Lola sighed. "Just to show that it was no big deal until it was. So what'd you say when Beau asked you that?"

"I said no, I keep her around because she's a good waitress. Then he looked at you and said I already had the best waitress around, so why the fuck would I need anyone else? He actually said *fuck*, like he was pissed or something. Amanda sulked, then it was my turn to shoot and that was the end of it."

"I don't get it," Lola said, shaking her head. "Nobody in their right mind would pay that much for one night of anything, even sex. Do you think he was being serious?"

Johnny sat forward on the bed. "He wanted to get laid. He's got money to burn. Must've figured we were hard up for cash and low on decency."

No matter how Lola looked at it, it didn't add up. A

man like that wouldn't have any problem getting women. Even if he did, there were not-so-secret secret call girl services for men with his kind of money. She'd known a girl or two who'd been through that. "Maybe he has a very specific taste," Lola murmured.

"For what?"

"I don't know. Maybe I'm his type."

Johnny had calmed down. She could sense it with him, but it never took him long to return to his easygoing self. He held out his hand and beckoned her. She moved to sit on her knees next to him.

"You know I think you're the most beautiful girl in five states. I see the way guys look at you when you're waiting tables. Great figure, nice tits."

"*Nice*?"

"Incredible, babe."

"What're you getting at?" she asked.

"Nothing. I just don't think that's enough to pay for one night what I don't even make in a decade."

Lola finally pinpointed what'd been bothering her on the ride home—Beau's insinuation that Johnny could put a dollar amount on Lola. He'd suggested a counteroffer as if one existed and they just hadn't found it yet. "How much would you say I'm worth then?" Lola asked.

Johnny took her arm and pulled her forward. She leaned in for a more intimate moment than they'd had all night. "Don't take it that way," he said, kissing her once on the lips. "I respect you too much to even answer that." He kissed her again and lay back on the bed, getting under the covers.

"It's a lot of money," she said quietly.

He fluffed his pillow. "I know you're worried about Hey Joe, but it'll all work out. I bet you Mitch gets cold feet and ends up not selling."

Lola stayed where she was, staring at the wall by the bed. He sounded so confident, but she didn't share his optimism. During the last few conversations she'd had with the owner about Hey Joe, stress had etched his face. "Johnny, did you ever think about buying the bar?"

"Guess so, here and there. Kind of feels like mine already. But never seriously or anything."

"That's the best of both worlds," Lola said. "You get the bar you love, and you don't have to start from the ground up."

"It'd be like owning a piece of history," Johnny agreed. "Rock 'n' roll history. We could get it back to what it was, you and me."

Lola glanced down at him. "What's the first thing you'd do?"

"I'd work my ass off to get good music in there again. Maybe serve some food. Open earlier in the day. People in the door, no matter what it took."

She smiled at him. She liked the times where Johnny got caught up in something bigger than their life. "You could run that place with your eyes closed."

"With you by my side, sure could." They grinned at each other, sharing the same dream. It faded from Johnny's eyes. "What're you saying, Lo?"

"I don't know. Mitch hasn't bothered with the day to day for so long that, like you said, sometimes the bar feels like ours. But I never imagined actually owning it until tonight. I didn't think it was a possibility for us."

"And what, it is now?" he asked.

"No," she said emphatically. She got under the covers too and snuggled against his side. "I told you my dad loved bikes. He used to collect Harley gear for the day he'd own one. I promised I'd buy him one when I got older. That was before he left, obviously. Sad thing is, even if I could buy him one, I wouldn't know where to find him." She paused, tracing one of the tattoos on Johnny's chest. "I've never made someone's dream come true. Or given them anything."

"You made my dream come true."

She looked up at him. "I did?"

"I have you, don't I? That's something money can't buy." He smiled and smoothed his hand over her hairline. "Don't worry, babe. We'll figure something out."

"But by then, Hey Joe might not be around anymore," Lola said. They'd been figuring things out since they'd started dating. Lola still thought about going back to school *some day*. *Some day*, Johnny would propose. They'd talked about having kids *some day* when they'd saved more and could afford things like a bigger apartment.

Starting a business didn't fit into any of that. It occurred to her that though Johnny wanted those things, he wouldn't go after them. He would wait for them to happen to him or for Lola to tell him it was time. Her role was to move them forward, a reality she'd conveniently ignored—until Beau had opened her eyes to it. If neither of them did anything, they'd be in this bed ten years from now, wondering why they didn't have the things they'd always hoped for.

Lola switched off the bedside lamp, turned back

and kissed his chest. "It's stupid, but right after my dad left, I thought if I could just get him that bike, he'd come back. Like me plus a bike would be enough for him." She looked up at him. "Is this enough for you? If we never got further than where we are right now?"

He was quiet.

"Johnny?" she asked.

No answer. He'd fallen asleep.

Chapter Four

Lola heaped potato salad onto Mark's plate. He looked at it, then back up. "That it?"

"You know the rule. Nobody gets seconds until everyone's had a helping."

"Six growing men at this picnic table, Lola."

She rolled her eyes. "If any of you are still growing, it's sideways, not up."

He pulled on his belt with his free hand and grinned. "Come on, Mama. Give your second favorite man a little extra love."

"You want more potato salad, walk your ass over to Pavilions and get it yourself. Next!"

Mark muttered as he went around Lola to sit down.

Johnny and his friends played football in the park some weekends while Lola and a few other wives and girlfriends set up food for afterward. It was a good spot, even for busy afternoons, with a playground nearby for the kids.

Johnny stood quietly with his plate between them as Lola served him.

"Everything all right?" she asked. Their morning had been normal despite their unusual night. Neither of them had brought up Beau or his offer. Johnny had even been in high spirits for football. During the game, though, Lola had looked over at a commotion and seen Johnny arguing with Mark before spiking the football hard into the grass.

"I'm fine."

"You mad because your side lost?" He wasn't a sore loser, but it was the only plausible reason for his shift in mood.

"I said I'm fine."

"Okay." She smiled and scooped him more potato salad. "A little extra for my man," she said. "Don't tell Mark."

"Thanks, babe," he said and pressed a quick kiss to the top of her head.

Lola sat across from Johnny once she'd made herself a plate. Mark gestured as he told everyone about the harrowing adventure of taking his six-year-old son to the mall. They'd gone to find his wife a birthday present, only to go home empty-handed because his credit card had been declined.

"Maybe that's because you're at a picnic in the middle of a workday," Johnny said.

"Shop's closed for renovations this weekend, asshole. You calling me out in front of my wife?"

"Now, now, boys." Brenda smiled. "Mark and Kyle ended up surprising me by setting up the Slip 'N Slide in the backyard. We played in the sprinklers all day. Couldn't have asked for a better birthday."

Mark put his arm around Brenda's shoulders.

Johnny winked at Lola. He held up a forkful of potato salad before cleaning it off in one bite.

Mark's son ran from the playground to the table. He stuck his shoe on the bench. "Tie," he demanded.

"Kyle, why don't you show everyone how you've been learning to tie your own shoes?"

"I don't want to," Kyle said.

"I'll do it, buddy," Lola said. Kyle ran over to her.

She snuck him a smile as she fixed his shoe. "You know how to do this, don't you?"

"Yeah."

"So I'll tie this one, and you can show me how you do it on your left shoe."

"But that one's not untied," he said.

Lola reached down and yanked one of the laces. "There you go."

"Lola," he cried out, raising his arms in the same exasperated way his dad often did.

"Come on," she said. "Your daddy's been bragging about this all week. But I never believe anything until I see it with my own eyes."

Kyle made a face but swapped feet on the bench and went to work. "I got it," he said, brushing her hands away when she went to help. After a few tries, he hollered "I did it" and took off back to the other kids.

"You're good with him," Brenda said to her.

"When you grow up without brothers or sisters, everything kids do is entertaining," Lola said.

"Well, you're welcome to take him any time and see all the entertaining things he does." Mark laughed. "Love that little shit, but can't say I'm not glad school starts next week."

Brenda turned to Johnny. "Wasn't she good with Kyle?"

Johnny half rolled his eyes.

"Aw, come on," she said. "Indulge me."

"Our answer's still the same," he said. "Kids cost money. Right, babe?"

She almost said they were figuring it out. The night before might not have come up again, but Lola hadn't forgotten anything. Her eyes were now widely open to their inaction. As long as they were 'figuring it out,' she and Johnny weren't doing much of anything. Her chest was tight.

"There's never a good time," Brenda said. "Mark and I were still living at my mom's when I got knocked up. You just have to go for it."

"Maybe Lola's waiting for Johnny to propose sometime this century," Mark said.

"With what, a fucking cucumber?" Johnny asked, visibly irritated.

"Why not?" Lola asked. "I don't need anything fancy."

Johnny's fork stopped halfway to his mouth as his eyes cut to her.

"We could do it here in the park," she said, sitting up a little straighter. "Maybe Mitch would donate some beer to cut down on costs. It could be a small thing, friends and family only."

Brenda clasped her hands together. "That's a great idea," she exclaimed. "We'll find you a vintage dress for next to nothing on Melrose."

Lola wasn't the type to get swept away. She'd never thought much about her wedding day like the girls she knew, but the idea of something simple brought a smile to her face. "That sounds nice, doesn't it, Johnny?"

"Sure," he said as he forked a watermelon chunk. "Tell you what. We'll pick up a lottery ticket on the way home and if I win, that cucumber'll have a big, fat diamond on it."

Someone laughed uncomfortably.

Johnny chewed, looking around the table. "What? It

was a joke. Except maybe the lottery ticket. Now *that* is a good idea."

Lola blinked at him. "The lottery?"

"Since when do you play the lottery?" Mark asked.

"Since today. Might as well. Not like my life is going anywhere." Johnny squinted into the distance, just beyond Lola. "Brenda, be a doll and pass a lemon square over here."

The table got even quieter, but Lola barely noticed. She didn't care about a wedding, but she didn't like the way he'd just dismissed her and their life together.

She ignored Johnny the rest of the meal, which wasn't hard since he kept to himself. After, she cleared off the picnic table alone so the other women could get their kids ready to go.

"Need help with that?" Johnny asked from a few feet away.

She glanced up at him. "What was that just now? Were you trying to embarrass me?"

"No, just myself." He stuck his hands in his back pockets. "Mission accomplished," he joked.

She tossed paper plates into a large garbage bag. "I don't care about a wedding. I thought the park was a nice idea, but that's all. I don't need it."

"I know you don't need it. You never need anything or anyone. But you deserve more than this crap." He gestured at the dirty table. "I want you to have a nice ring and a Hawaiian wedding."

"*Hawaii*?" She rested the bag on the bench. "What are you talking about?"

"When we were younger, you said you wanted to go to Hawaii one day because it sounded romantic.

Remember?"

"No," Lola said. "I never think about Hawaii. We could get married at the Pomona Swap Meet for all I care." She tossed some plastic silverware and resumed cleaning. "We don't have to get married at all, Johnny. We've been fine without it this long. But I'll tell you one thing—we're not doing it in Hawaii."

"Why not?" he asked.

"Why would you even want to?"

"Last night got me thinking about how we never splurge," Johnny said. "You were right yesterday when you said time off would be good for us."

Lola shook her head, grabbed a beer bottle and poured the remains onto the grass. "I think you should forget about last night."

After a beat, he asked, "Have you?"

She dropped the bottle in the bag and picked up another. She didn't like lying to Johnny and hadn't forgotten about last night. "No, but I'm trying."

"Yeah, well. I don't blame you. I'd feel pretty special if someone thought my dick was worth half a mil."

He clearly had a bone to pick with her. Lola wanted to get to the root of what bothered him, but not when he acted like that. She picked up the garbage bag. On her way past him, she said, "I don't know what your problem is, but you're being a real jerk." She walked briskly to the nearest trashcan and dumped the bag in it. When she turned around, he was behind her.

"You're right," he said. "It was a lame attempt to be funny. I'm sorry."

She crossed her arms. "Are you going to tell me

what's wrong? Otherwise I need you to take me home so I can get the laundry done before work tonight."

He looked at his feet and slowly rubbed his hands together. "The thing is, part of me hoped that whole thing last night was a joke. It wasn't. I looked Beau up this morning while you were in the shower."

Lola pursed her lips. She wasn't angry because he'd done it, but because all day, during any moment she'd had alone, she'd been fighting herself not to do the same thing. "And?"

"He could probably buy Hawaii if he wanted. He really does have that kind of money, and apparently he's got lots of women to choose from." Their eyes met, and Johnny frowned. "It's intimidating that a guy like that wants my girlfriend."

Lola's shoulders loosened. The moment either of them started to feel insecure about their relationship was the moment they opened it up to problems. "You're looking at it wrong," she said sympathetically. "You have something he wants but can't have. In fact, maybe the *only* thing a guy like that can't have. That should make you feel good."

"Except that it doesn't. He's a millionaire. I've been working since I was seventeen with nothing to show for it. I'm an asshole. And I suck at football."

One corner of Lola's mouth rose. "You're the best one out there."

"You have to say that because you're my girlfriend."

"True, but it doesn't mean shit. Those guys are terrible."

He chuckled. "Yeah. We're pretty bad."

"You should all stick to video games."

He pretended to look hurt. "Geez, you don't have to drill the point home."

She uncrossed her arms. "And you aren't an asshole. I bet in order to get to that level of success, Beau had to step on some people. You'd never do that. You're a good person, Johnny. That's what matters in the end."

He considered that a moment. Lola saw their friends heading for their cars. Thinking the conversation was over, she started to walk away, but Johnny said, "He's a venture capitalist."

Lola paused. "What?"

"Beau. He invests in tech startups, but before that, he built a website that sold for millions."

"Oh." Lola wasn't impressed. She was more concerned with why Johnny was still talking about it.

"According to the article I read online," Johnny continued, "it took him like a decade to do it. He would build a website, but either someone else would beat him to it or he couldn't get investors. He didn't give up, though, even when the market crashed. Took him seven times before something finally stuck."

Lola's throat was dry. That only reiterated one of the few things she knew for sure about Beau Olivier. "He's persistent," she said.

"The company that bought his website ended up squashing it or something, so it never saw the light of day. Now he's co-founder of Bolt Ventures." Johnny shrugged. "Did all that, and he never even went to college."

Lola knew that already, but she didn't see the point

in mentioning it. Despite her curiosity about Beau's background, the less she knew the better. She changed the subject. "Johnny, unless you're planning on going commando tomorrow, I need to do laundry today."

He furrowed his eyebrows. "I could've sworn I just did it."

"That was *two* months ago," she cried with a burst of laughter. "Where do you think your clean clothes come from, invisible fairies?"

Johnny grinned and waved her off. "Hey," he said. "Come here."

She took a few steps, put a hand on her cocked hip and narrowed her eyes playfully. "What?"

"I'll take you to Hawaii one day. Or wherever you want to go. Even if it's the goddamn Pomona Swap Meet. I promise."

Lola dropped her arm from her hip and sighed. He'd flinched when he'd said *Hawaii*. She didn't know how to make it any clearer to him that Hawaii meant nothing to her. But as she was on the verge of starting up the argument again, she stopped herself. His eyes weren't as hard as they had been the last few hours, and she didn't want to provoke him. The back and forth was beginning to drain her.

Instead, she said, "I appreciate that, but I don't need to go anywhere. I'm fine as long as I have one thing."

He spoke before she could say *you*. "Clean underwear?" he guessed.

She rolled her eyes and smiled. "Yes. As long as I have that."

◆⊠◆⊠◆

Later, at the Laundromat down the street, Lola unloaded clothing from her basket into a washer. All three of the functioning machines at her complex had been occupied, which was why she normally avoided doing laundry on the weekends. She straightened up and rubbed her lower back. She'd never owned her own washer and dryer, but that was certainly something she'd be willing to splurge on with her five hundred grand. She covered her mouth at the thought and checked to make sure no one was around, as if she'd said it aloud.

She grabbed Johnny's jeans and emptied change from the pockets into a baggie like always. Lint and a movie stub went in the trash. The last thing she pulled out was a white business card with corners rigid enough to break skin. There was a phone number and a company name. She flipped it over. It was as vague and mysterious as the man it belonged to. Across the front was only his name, printed in stiff, sharp letters.

Beau Olivier.

Chapter Five

Vero whistled low, craning her neck to see through the neon maze that was Hey Joe's front window. "Check out those wheels."

The door was propped open for the seventy-degree weather. In the early-evening dusk, a man in a suit got out of an Audi. Lola and Johnny, crowded behind the bar with Vero, looked at each other.

"Let me handle this," he said.

"What's going on?" Vero asked. "Is it the money guy?"

Lola's gaze snapped between Veronica and Johnny. "You told her?"

"Personally, I would've accepted the offer," Vero said, a teasing smile on her face. "Wonder how he feels about redheads."

"It's prostitution," Lola said.

"I prefer to think of it as a trade." Vero opened her hand toward the door. "You got something I want," she pointed at her crotch, "I got something you want."

"So you sleep with him then," Lola said.

"Honey, for that much I would. I don't care how he looks." She leaned over so Johnny couldn't hear. "But damn if that man didn't look *good*."

Lola shook her head. "He looked like trouble."

Vero laughed throatily. "You know Vero gives it up to trouble for free all the time."

Lola willed herself to look away from the door. It'd been days since Beau had been there. She hated to admit she was still thinking of him. There had to have been a reason he picked her, but she went in circles trying to figure it out. Had there been others? If so, what was the common factor between them?

She tore her eyes away to focus on Johnny. He watched the door with more intensity than he'd looked at her with in days. He hadn't really been himself since the picnic.

Lola held her breath when the man walked in. She and Johnny exhaled at the same time. "It's not him," Johnny said in a way that almost sounded disappointed. Johnny leaned over the bar. "Can I help you?"

In the light, the man was clearly not Beau. His arms were too short for his wrinkled suit jacket and his belly strained the buttons of his dress shirt. "Wow," he said. He narrowed his eyes up and around, stopping at the framed black-and-white photos of musicians on Hey Joe's stage. "This is even more authentic than it looked on the Internet. Not like the dives you see in Brooklyn where all the stuff on the walls came from a website or boutique."

Vero was refilling the bar caddies. Johnny picked up a jar of olives she'd asked him to open earlier and knocked the lid hard against the edge of the bar. Everyone jumped and turned to him. He twisted off the top and passed it to Vero without removing his eyes from the man. "What can I do for you?"

He held out his hand for Johnny, who just stared at it. "Hank Walken," he said, jovial and unaffected by the brushoff.

"Jonathan Pace."

"I'm looking for Mr. Wegley."

"Mitch isn't around right now. What's this about?"

"Heard this place is for sale. You guys worked here long?"

"About twelve years," Johnny said.

"How's business?"

The man was smarmy. Lola would set the building on fire before a guy like that got his hands on Hey Joe. "It sucks," Lola said. "In fact, the whole block sucks."

Hank nodded. "Interesting."

"Interesting?" Johnny asked.

Hank scanned the wall behind them. "Yeah," he said absentmindedly. "It's got a lot of potential. Would do well with some sprucing up."

Johnny and Lola exchanged a look. "Sprucing up how?"

"I've done my homework. This place has history. Foot traffic. Repeat business." Hank checked under the lip of the bar as if he expected to find something there. "That's not showing in the numbers, though. It needs a fresh touch. Something special. Maybe a rooftop bar or a lounge area or something."

"This is more of a local joint," Johnny said.

Hank's eyes went to a pool game happening in the corner. "I picked up on that."

"It's the complete opposite of a lounge."

"There's your problem." Hank pointed at Johnny, grinning. "You're not thinking outside the box, son. It's all about the angle. We give it a cool, hip, rock 'n' roll vibe. Get some young celebrities to make appearances at the reopening. We've already got the rep, but a new look and a little rebranding could do wonders." He nodded thoughtfully to no one in particular. "I've flipped bars before, and fives minutes in here, I'm seeing a lot of missed opportunities."

It was exactly what Lola and Johnny had been saying for years. Mitch wasn't willing to budge on a lot of things to keep the integrity of the bar, but sales suffered as a result. Not that Lola and Johnny had ever once discussed turning it into a lounge. "What opportunities?" Lola asked.

Hank looked back at her and narrowed his eyes. "Think I got this far by giving away my secrets, sweetheart?" He laughed good-naturedly but didn't answer her question.

"Business really is slow," she said. "Not sure this place can be saved."

"I disagree," Hank said. "In the right hands, Hey Joe could be at least doubling profits by this time next year." He dug his sausage-like fingers into his suit jacket. "I'll give you my card. I'm just going to take a look around. If I don't hear from Mr. Wegley, I'll try again tomorrow."

Johnny took the card. "He won't be in until Friday."

"Any way we can get him in here to take a meeting?"

"He's out of town."

"Guess I should've called before hopping on a flight from New York. That's all right. I'll wait."

Hank walked away. He swiveled his head, pausing to read flyers Lola had designed and stuck on a corkboard. He inspected the floors, touched the walls—got so close to the pool table, a man nearly twice his size asked him if he knew any surgeons who specialized in pool-cue removal.

Johnny held up the card for Lola, ripped it and dropped it in the trash behind the bar. "Are you kidding me? A rooftop bar?"

Lola shook her head. "Can you imagine if Quartz and the guys heard that?"

"Hey Joe's got history, man," Johnny said. His eyes narrowed on Hank as he made his slow way to the exit. "Seriously. You can't just flush that down the toilet."

Vero shrugged. "Something needs to change. Maybe it's time, Boss."

"And maybe you go snort some lines," he said.

"Johnny," Lola scolded. "What is with you?"

He muttered an apology, grabbed a Coors from the mini-fridge and keyed off the top. Vero muttered about checking on her tables. Lola kept her mouth shut and didn't mention Johnny's no-drinking-during-work-hours rule.

Vero hadn't put anything away. Lola picked up the jar of olives, but it slipped out of her hands and broke. "Damn it," she cried, jumping back. "Why don't you guys ever clean up your own shit?"

"You guys?" Johnny asked.

Lola glanced up at him. She saw an opening for her frustration and took it. "Yes, *you guys.* Did you not see the basket of clean laundry that's been sitting out since Saturday?"

Johnny's lips pinched. "I thought you were waiting to put it away."

"Waiting for what?" Lola asked. "There's no law that says you can't do it."

He held up a palm and the beer in his hand. "Sorry.

I didn't realize it was a test."

"It wasn't," Lola said under her breath, squatting to clean up the glass. "It would just be nice if someone else did something once in a while." She'd overreacted. It was second nature to clean up after Johnny and that transferred over to work. But the constantly taking things out and leaving them there annoyed her sometimes.

She dropped the big pieces of glass in the trash, right on top of the two halves of Hank's card. "Johnny?"

"What?" he asked. "I said I was sorry."

"No, not that." She paused. "Where's Beau's card?"

Johnny stopped staring into space and turned abruptly to her. "Why?"

"I remember him setting it on the bar, but I never threw it out. Just wondering what happened to it…"

Johnny took a long swig of his drink. He inspected the bottle. "I tossed it."

"That night?"

"Yeah."

"When?"

"Like I said, that fucking night, right after he left. Ripped it in half too. Should I have burned it?"

Lola looked at him as hard as he avoided looking at her. After finding Beau's card in Johnny's pocket, she'd hidden it in her birth control box under the sink—and it was in one piece. "Are you sure?"

"Yeah, I'm goddamn sure, Lola," he said. "What're you nagging me for?"

Vero walked up and set a ticket on the bar. Johnny snatched it to fill the order. Lola tried to convince herself she owed her boyfriend the benefit of the doubt, but that he'd kept the card meant only one thing to her. However small it was, there was a part of Johnny considering Beau's offer.

◆⊠◆⊠◆

Mitch returned to work that Friday. It'd been a long, draining week of mood swings and clipped words—offenses both Lola and Johnny were guilty of.

While Johnny was distracted up front, Lola went back to Mitch's office and leaned in the doorway.

"What is it?" he asked without removing his eyes from his computer.

"How was your trip?"

"Productive. Barb found a house she likes."

"I bet her family is happy you guys are moving there."

"They are." Mitch looked up. "Barb is too. She's wanted this for some time."

"What about you?" Lola asked.

"You know how it is. This place is a grind. Barb always said if it got to be too much, she wanted me out."

"But do you have to leave L.A.?"

He held his arms out. "This *is* L.A. Things were great when I was out there screwing around with customers all day, but now I'm back here most of the time, trying to dig myself out of this hole. Barb knows my dad's place is the only thing keeping me in California."

"Yeah." Lola picked at some peeling paint. "Have you had any offers?"

"Nothing official yet, but it won't be long."

"Oh."

"What is it, Lola? I'm kind of busy here."

"I don't know. I just...Mitch, what do you think this place needs? Why's business slow?"

He sighed. "In the eighties, when my dad handed over the reins, we were already struggling. But then grunge came on the scene and I wasn't letting that anywhere near here. Not after the rock legends we'd seen."

"So you lost the young music crowd."

"Young and some old. You know all this, Lola."

"I'm trying to see it from a business perspective."

"All right, then you want to know my first mistake? Pay for play. I let my head get too big asking new bands to cough up cash for a spot on our stage. They walked instead. I could've made up for it in the nineties, but like I said, I fucking hate grunge. Turns out a lot of people don't, though. When Fred's went belly up, the block became a carousel of crap. Except us, the only place still standing, but our knees are buckling. Barb says I either sell out or get out, so I'm washing my hands of it. I can't stick around to see what happens."

Mitch's words were hard, but she heard the regret in his voice. "That Hank guy said something about a lounge. I think he wants to turn this place high end."

"We're meeting later today, so I'll know more then, but it sounds like he wants to keep the name and image, just make it into something classier. A real scene."

"But that's not what Hey Joe is." That wasn't what Johnny was.

He shrugged. "Not really, kid. Sorry."

"Would you say this place is a good investment?"

"There'll never not be foot traffic. Just about

getting back on the map."

Lola felt her heartbeat everywhere. In the last week, she'd struggled more than ever with the pressure to take care of Johnny in a bigger way than she had been. Now it was more than that. Lola could bring herself to walk away from Hey Joe, but that didn't mean it wasn't worth saving for Johnny, for all the other people who loved it and for its history. She might be the only one who could do it. "So if someone had the opportunity to buy it, they should take it?"

"Whatever you're thinking, forget it. You don't know anybody with that kind of money."

"I might."

"I know Johnny's got his heart set on owning a bar and believe me, I'd love to make that happen for you two. Nobody knows this place like him. But there's no way in hell you can even ballpark the offers I'm hearing."

"What're the offers, Mitch?"

"Around six hundred grand," he said.

Lola looked at the floor. More than Beau's proposition—but people took out small business loans all the time, didn't they? Maybe not for that much, but the difference? She cleared her throat. "If Johnny and I could come up with the money—"

"Hey," Mitch said, shaking his head. "Come on. You and Johnny are good kids. You've always been straight. Don't tell me that's changed."

"Hypothetically."

Mitch bit the end of his pen and reclined in his seat, studying her. "If you can make me a decent offer, fine. Hypothetically? Buying this bar would be easier than Johnny starting his own, but not much considering the state of things. It's not like I want to see my dad's place destroyed, but I can't feed myself off my principles anymore. Once I get my check, it's out of my hands."

Lola returned to the front of the house. Johnny poured three shots in his bartender's rhythm, one at a time and without stopping. Lola stayed off to the side. He said something to the three girls in front of him as he patted his beer gut and laughed. That beer gut had been a valley nine years ago when she'd started dating a tall, skinny, twenty-four-year-old Johnny with darkish hair past his ears—hair that was now down to his shoulder blades and always in a ponytail. The valley was now a small hill. That beer gut had history. She liked it and what it stood for.

Johnny wouldn't survive a new owner. He'd been doing things his way for too long. And she sure as hell wouldn't stick around without him. Nobody liked change, especially not Johnny, and it was on the horizon, speeding their way.

◆⊠◆⊠◆

The ride home that night was quiet. Lola went over the numbers in her head again and again. If Walken bought Hey Joe, she figured they could be out of their jobs within weeks. She listed alternatives. They'd both have to hustle, because even though Lola had been thinking lately she might like to try something new, they couldn't survive on Johnny's wages alone. She'd have to work while she figured her shit out. Fall classes had already started, so school was out of the question for a few months at least.

She looked over at Johnny as he pulled into their

apartment complex. He'd been preoccupied, but not about losing their jobs. It was as if he expected everything to just figure itself out—the way he expected getting married, having kids and owning a business would happen on their own. He was thirty-three. They'd been driving through a tunnel for the last eight years, and they were about to come out of the darkness. She couldn't see what was on the other side, but at least *she* was trying.

"Johnny?" she asked when they'd parked and he reached for the handle.

He looked back. "Yeah?"

"You're my best friend."

"It's late, babe."

She smiled, a little resigned. "I know. But you are. When we're young, we think we're invincible. Then we get older, and it's like we realize not everything works out all the time. If you want certain things, you have to put in the effort for them. Or even make sacrifices."

Johnny put his hand over hers on the seat. "What's bringing this on?"

She squinted out the windshield. "Money was a big deal to my mom. She would say 'The toaster's broken. We got no money, so we have to live with broken toasters and ripped screen doors that won't even keep out a fly, forget about a robber.' I had no idea who'd want to rob us. We had nothing. She said that was naïve and stupid, because desperate people were everywhere.

"She told me money was the reason my dad left. There wasn't enough. So I believed money and happiness were inextricably linked until I met you and decided love was more important. I was in a dark place, but you came in and saved me. Since then, I've tried hard to convince myself money isn't important at all."

Johnny sniffed. "Now you realize it is."

"Mitch said something to me today. He said, 'I can't feed myself off my principles anymore.' It's kind of the same with love. Those things are so much, Johnny, but they aren't everything like I wish they were. Money can give us stability and freedom. It can give us choices."

Johnny released her hand and ran his palms down his pants to his knees. "Life is easier with working appliances," he said flatly.

"If someone buys the bar, we'll probably lose our jobs."

"I know."

"Do you know? You're more concerned about Hey Joe being glamorized than you are about how we'll survive."

"I don't see the point in worrying about it until we know more," he said. "Something could still happen."

"Something like what?" Lola asked. If Johnny said it out loud, she wouldn't have to. Not knowing if he wanted her to accept the offer was almost worse than if he'd just come out and tell her to do it. She was stuck, and she had no idea which door would lead to their happiness.

"I don't know," he admitted. "But there's still time."

"There isn't any more time," Lola said. "Are we stupid not to take the only exit we'll ever get? Buying the bar isn't just keeping our jobs. It's following your dream. It's building a life and having a steady income and saving a legacy. All in one night."

"So what're you saying?" Johnny asked. He wouldn't look at her. "You want my permission to sleep with another man?"

Lola turned in her seat to face him. "I don't look at it that way," she said. In fact, she had been very good about not looking at it that way. When she thought of Beau, she didn't let her mind stray too far to the man she'd thought he was before he'd tried to buy her. "All I see is what that money could do for our future. I could do this, for us, and it would never mean a thing because *you* are what's important to me."

He was quiet for a few tense seconds. Suddenly, he slammed his fist against the steering wheel.

She bit her lip. "It's not that I want to—"

"I know," he said. "It's not you I'm mad at. It's the situation. It's me."

"You?" He didn't continue. Lola looked at her hands in her lap. She assumed he was mad at himself for even considering the offer, but she was afraid to ask. "Just please tell me what you've been thinking this last week. You've been so hot and cold. I can't figure out what you want, so you have to tell me, and you have to be honest."

Johnny ran a hand over his face and blew out a breath. "You want honesty?"

"Yes."

"I keep thinking about that life," he said. "I want something of my own. We can't live paycheck to paycheck forever, but I don't know how to get out of it. I can't ever seem to catch up."

Lola took his hand again and squeezed it. "I'm relieved that you're also worried. Sometimes I feel like I have to be the one to fix it."

"I want to fix it, Lola, but I don't know how."

Suddenly she wanted to go back to ignoring the problem. She almost wished she hadn't dragged them into this conversation. "Maybe we don't have to," she said. "You'll keep on managing Hey Joe. It won't be the same, but you'll learn to love it. I'll graduate from bar wench to cocktail waitress. Or maybe we get new jobs in a different dive bar. Things would be tight while we transitioned, but they'd settle and we'd get back to where we are now." Lola's voice softened with defeat as she spoke, but she hoped Johnny wouldn't pick up on it.

"Because where we are now is the best option," he said. "You don't think I'll ever be able to give you more than this. Not without someone else's money."

"That isn't what I said."

"You might as well say it. I'll never be more than what I am in this moment."

"I'm trying to be realistic," she said. "If we want more, then I have to do this. If I don't, then this is how things will be. It was enough before Beau came along, but is it enough now? I don't know, Johnny. I don't know the answer to any of this."

He threw open the car door, jumped out and looked back at her. "You want to do this because you think it's our only chance."

Lola also got out of the car. Their doors slammed at the same time. "Don't turn this around on me because I have the guts to say what we're both thinking," she said, hurrying to keep up with him. "This *could* be our only chance. It's not like I want this."

He kept walking.

"I know you want me to do it," she said, raising her voice. "Why don't you man up and tell me the truth?"

He turned around and pointed a finger at her. "You want truth so goddamn bad? The money's all I think about. And the things I could finally do. I'm six-foot-two, two hundred pounds, but I'm half a man because I can't take care of you."

Lola reached for him. "But you do take care of me."

"No, I don't," he said, stepping back. "Five nights a week we get off work while the rest of the world sleeps. We work our asses off, and we're still struggling to get by. If I lose this job, I'll have to start all over somewhere else. I have no other skills. You think you have nothing now? It's about to get a lot worse."

"When did I say I had nothing? Would I like a washer and dryer of my own so I don't have to schlep down the street? Would I like to quit this job one day and try something else? Yes. But that doesn't mean I have nothing. If I do this, it's for the things that *can't* be bought—like our future."

"*If* this, *if* that. I'm tired of this shit. Just make a decision."

"I can't, Johnny," she said, shaking her head. "You have to do it."

"This has to be your choice. I'm not going to send you into another man's bed no matter what I want."

She put her hand to the base of her throat. "Want?" she choked. "Are you saying you *want* me to do this?"

"No," he said. In the dark, their eyes were narrowed on each other. The silence was thick. "I'm saying I won't stop you."

Chapter Six

He slept in bed next to Lola, but Johnny, who was usually unconscious as soon as the lights went out, breathed unevenly. He was awake. He flipped back and forth every few minutes. His mind was elsewhere. They each stayed on their sides of the bed.

It went on for days. When they were alone, he barely looked at her, but she often caught him staring during work. Waiting. For her to bring it up again? For her to make the decision? Did he hope she'd say yes? Or no? His silence meant she had to choose for both of them.

The more silence drew out between them, the more time Lola had alone. Beau was a strong presence in her thoughts. She couldn't forget him in his urbane suit, giving all his attention to whatever he was doing at that moment, whether it was throwing darts, savoring his Macallan—or looking at her. Being near her. Flirting with her. Everything he did, he did a hundred percent.

During a night off, while Johnny worked, Lola finally gave in to her curiosity and looked Beau up online. He hadn't always been wealthy. He'd even grown up twenty minutes from Lola. It was well known that he was a self-made millionaire and that he co-founded Bolt Ventures but had his hand in many different projects. At thirty-seven, he'd never been married, and except for stints here and there, he'd always lived in Los Angeles.

Lola looked for details about him before he'd sold his seventh try at a website, but they were hard to come by. His father had died in a car accident in France. He'd worked part-time jobs and developed his own projects in his spare time, mostly at night.

When she was about to give up, she found one of his first interviews from years earlier. The interviewer had asked what his least favorite job had been before he'd struck it rich. She had to read his answer twice—it was a six-month bartending gig at a hole-in-the-wall place in the Valley. He'd quit because with a thirty-minute commute each way, gas ate into his tips and he wouldn't get home until an unreasonable hour.

Beau had been like them. He hadn't done it for years like she and Johnny, but he'd been in their shoes. He knew struggle. And he'd done what he had to do to get out of it. The question was how far Lola would go to get out of it—and what Beau expected of her if she agreed.

◆⊠◆⊠◆

The next night, Lola was just about to open the bar when the phone rang.

"Lola, right?" asked a familiar voice.

"Who's this?"

"Hank Walken. We met last week when I came in to see the space."

"I remember," she said flatly.

"How are you?"

She hadn't expected that question. "Busy," she said. "There something I can help you with?"

"Sure. Got it. Is Mitch around?"

Lola bit her bottom lip and looked toward the backroom. "Not right now," she lied.

"How can I get in touch with him? It's important."

"Try around this time tomorrow. I can get him a message if you want."

"Just tell him to call me, and that time is money. I want this deal worked out in the next forty-eight hours if we can manage it."

"Deal?" Lola asked, her throat closing. She and Johnny had run out of time. It was now or never.

"I told you about the lounge, didn't I?" he asked cheerily. "We'll be looking for pretty, young cocktail waitresses with experience. That's a not-so-subtle hint."

She struggled to register his words. All she could think was that their moment was about to pass them by. "What about management?" she asked, even though she could barely picture herself in a lounge, much less Johnny.

"I like to bring in my own people for the higher-level stuff. Why, you tired of serving?"

"I'm the assistant manager, but I was asking for my boyfriend. The guy you met."

"Ah." He cleared his throat. "We stick with women on the floor or if we hire males, they're generally models, actors, that kind of thing." He guffawed. "If they can make a drink, even better. But maybe we can find your boyfriend something in the kitchen."

"I'll give Mitch the message," Lola said and hung up.

"Who was that?" Vero asked as Lola walked by her.

"No one." Lola went directly to Mitch's office and closed the door behind her.

He looked up from his paperwork. The radio played The Rolling Stones. "What's up?"

"We're going to make an offer," she said.

He heaved a big sigh. "Lola, I—"

"I just need a little more time."

"Hank won't like that."

She went and set her palms on his desk. Johnny could work anywhere, but he would never be as happy as he was there. She'd been lost once, and Johnny had shown her the way back. Now she'd repay him by giving him what nobody else could. "Johnny's busted his ass for you for over twelve fucking years. He doesn't ask for much. For God's sake, *I've* had to ask for all his raises. You will wait a few more days because you owe him at least that."

Mitch laced his fingers on the desk and looked down. "I just want you to be sure about taking this on. The whole thing could tank if you're not careful."

He had no idea how true that was. "We're sure," Lola said. "We're ready."

"All right," he said, eyeing her up and down. "That's what you want, I'll hold Hank off a few more days."

Lola left Mitch and went into the break room. She leaned against the counter and inhaled a shaky breath. She hoped making the decision would be the hardest part of all. Her stomach was a mix of nerves and anticipation when she thought about the phone call she had to make. She decided Johnny would do it—she already had enough responsibility.

She went back out to the bar. Johnny was mid-pour. Customers at the bar were absorbed in their own conversations.

"I've made my decision," Lola said. "I'll do it."

Johnny didn't look up. He set down the bottle of gin. Now he was the one with a choice to make. If Johnny asked her not to do it right then, she wouldn't. She'd leave Beau in his skyscraper where he belonged. Their worlds had been the same once, and now they'd be the same again. Only, Lola would be the one crossing sides this time. Beau was waiting for her there. One night on his side thrilled her as much as it terrified her, and that was why Johnny needed to tell her not to do it.

Johnny picked up the gin again and continued pouring. "Five hundred isn't enough," he said. His voice was steady but toneless. "We'll ask for more."

◆⊠◆⊠◆

Beau scrubbed his hand up his jawline and back, looking between Lola and Johnny. Lola couldn't tell in their bare surroundings if Beau was actually solemn, or if he was just reflecting what he saw across the conference table. Even the sky itself had given up the day to gray webs of clouds.

At least he hadn't made them wait. Beau'd walked into the room a couple minutes after the receptionist had shown them in. Lola had watched him round the table, wondering if he'd removed his tie to seem less intimidating or if he'd come into work that day without one. It'd caught her off guard. Suits had never been her thing, but the casual nature of his open collar and exposed neck did something to her, as if she were seeing some forbidden part of him.

Beau was exact with his attention as always. At that moment, he addressed Johnny. "Are you sure you want to be here for this?"

Although reclined in his seat, tension emanated from Johnny. Lola had refused to sit down without him, but first she'd made Johnny promise not to let things get to the level they had last time they'd all been in the same room. "Just get started," Johnny said.

Beau tapped the end of his pen once on the slim folder in front of him. "All right. Half the money will be deposited into your account by five o'clock the night of the arrangement. The other half will come once Lola has held up her end of the bargain."

Beau's formality made Lola's stomach uneasy, but she was grateful for it. She didn't think she could handle anything less tactful. "Exactly what does my end entail?"

"From sunset that night to sunrise the following morning, I own you."

Lola schooled her expression. Inside, her heart was going a mile a minute. If anyone could own a woman, it would be the man sitting in front of her. "You own me," she repeated. "Meaning what?"

Beau put his elbows on the table and played with his pen, twisting the cap. "You're mine to do with what I please, excluding physical harm," he said. "I want to be very clear—I have no intentions of making you physically uncomfortable or of hurting you in any way. This is meant to be a pleasant experience for us both."

Lola was tempted to give Johnny a reassuring look when he shifted in his seat, but she kept her eyes on Beau as if he were a snake that might strike at any time. "Everything else is fair game?" she asked with an unnaturally straight back.

"Aside from anything that puts you at risk, the arrangement ensures that you give me whatever I ask for."

"Not whatever," Johnny said. "There have to be some limits." He looked over at Lola. "There are some things she won't do."

"Johnny," she said under her breath. She refused to go into specifics in a cold, stark conference room with her boyfriend and the man she was about to sleep with sitting across from each other. Johnny was right—she had limits. But she could handle Beau once they were alone.

"We've already covered the limits," Beau said. "To everything else, there's only one answer."

"Yes," Lola said.

Beau nodded once, looking pleased. "Exactly. Just like that."

"How can we trust you won't hurt her?" Johnny asked. His voice was already raised, bordering on aggressive. "Your word doesn't mean dick."

Beau switched back to Johnny and remained calm. "You've probably figured out by now that I'm well known in the business world. I have family members, investors, employees. If anyone's taking a risk, it's me." He pulled a sheet from the folder under his hands and slid it across to Lola. "For that reason, I'll need you both to sign a non-disclosure agreement. There's a clause that if either of us strays from the agreement—including what I just said about physical harm—the NDA is null and void. That's why you can trust me. I've worked long and hard to get where I am. I can't afford to have my name attached to a scandal. My reputation is on the line."

"Then why do this at all?" Lola asked. "Aren't there

more discreet ways of buying sex?"

Beau became even more focused on her. He set down his pen. "I'm not buying sex, Lola. I'm buying you. I'd like us to be one hundred percent clear on that. Are we?"

Lola found herself unable to meet his eyes for the first time. Being referred to as an object didn't have the effect she thought it would. Instead of anger, she became acutely aware of the heat between her legs. He could have anyone. He wanted her.

"Are we?" Beau persisted. "If we're not on the same page about that, I need to know now."

She kept her eyes lowered as she looked to the side. Johnny's head was turned away from her out the window.

"I understand," Lola said.

"Eyes up," Beau said.

Lola swallowed at his curt command. Her gaze traveled over the table's surface, up Beau's crisp, white shirt and its open collar, past his smooth-shaven jaw to his eyes. They were greener than ever with the window's gray backdrop. "You're buying me," she said to him.

"Thank you." His expression relaxed. "But of course there will be sex. For that reason, I'll need you to get tested and bring the results with you the evening of our arrangement."

Johnny snapped back to attention. "Come on, man."

"That's non-negotiable. I'll do the same for you. Without that, there's no deal."

"It's fine," Lola said. "I'll get the tests."

"You have an appointment with my doctor after

this," he said. "Are you on birth control?"

Lola took her purse from the floor and set it on the table. She dug inside for her packet.

"I don't need to see it." He held up another piece of paper. "Because while I'd prefer we not have to deal with it at all, this signature absolves me of any responsibility should you get pregnant."

Lola's mouth instantly tingled. It was worse than being treated like an object. Things had happened so fast, she hadn't considered the possibility of pregnancy. Her mind flitted over the past few weeks. She'd been diligent about taking the pill. She leaned over the table and slid the paper toward her.

Johnny sat perfectly still. "I wouldn't worry about the responsibility," he said. "She gets pregnant and I'll kill you. Problem solved."

Lola stared at the paper in front of her, which was only one page, concise and to the point.

"Then we'll make sure that doesn't happen," Beau said. "But I still need Lola to sign it. My lawyers would have heart attacks if they knew I was doing this without them. I prefer not to involve anyone other than us. We can if you'd like, though."

"That won't be necessary." Lola couldn't think too hard about what she was signing or she might lose her nerve.

"If you don't deliver your end of the deal," Beau continued, "I'll be forced to come up with ways of righting the situation. I don't want to resort to that, but I haven't gotten this far in business without doing things I don't like."

"I wouldn't be here if I hadn't thought this

through," Lola said.

Beau smiled reassuringly. He looked like he wanted to say something else, but he just squinted at her. "Are you all right?"

Her body had undergone about a hundred different reactions in the last twenty minutes, from shame to arousal to indignation. Was she all right? She couldn't be sure, but she wasn't Beau's responsibility. No matter how much he paid, she would never be his to hold and comfort and reassure. She raised her chin a little. "I'm fine."

"Do you have any questions?"

Johnny moved. "We have demands," he said, rejoining the conversation.

"I thought you might," Beau invited.

"If you don't meet them, we walk right now."

Beau folded his hands on the table. "You have my attention. Proceed."

"We want our half now. Today. And Lola will only do it for eight hundred thousand."

Beau's eyebrows shot up. "Eight hundred? You realize that's sixty percent more than my initial offer?"

"You asked for a counteroffer."

"I did, but this isn't a free-for-all. As with any negotiation, I have my limits."

Johnny shook his head fast. "No. This is the only way we'll do it. Lola's worth more than what you're asking."

Lola resisted jerking her head toward Johnny only because they'd agreed to come in as a unified front. But bringing Lola's worth into the discussion was a low blow.

"Not that she has a price," Johnny backtracked. "What I meant was—"

"I know what you meant," Beau said. "Tread carefully, though. If you push me, I might pull the offer completely."

Johnny shrugged with his whole upper body. Under the table, his leg bounced up and down. "Like I said, she won't do it for a dime less anyway."

"Johnny, relax," Lola said. "You're starting to sound like my pimp."

Johnny's glare at her was brief. Before the meeting, he'd said, "When we get to the money part, let me do the talking." Sweat beaded on his temple despite the blowing air conditioning. Lola, on the other hand, had goose bumps from the cold. Even she wasn't sure if he was bluffing.

When she looked back at Beau, he was watching her, not Johnny. "That's the price you decided on for yourself, Lola?"

"It's not my price," she said. Her mouth soured. The word was as dirty as *worth*. "It's how much we need to buy the bar. The money is useless to us otherwise."

"I really prefer you didn't call my very generous offer useless," Beau said. "Do you have any concept of how much five hundred thousand dollars is?"

"Yes. It's less than eight hundred," Lola said sharply. "You two aren't the only ones who get to blather about worth. If I'm going to degrade myself, it has to be worth it to me, and that means Johnny and I end up with Hey Joe."

"Degrade yourself?" Beau repeated. His laugh was hollow. "I'd say you've already degraded yourself just by taking this meeting."

The nerve. Up until that moment, she'd actually thought he was being fairly decent considering the circumstances. Lola pinched her lips together. "That's not fair. I know you know what it's like to put a dream before everything else."

Beau's smile faded as his face smoothed. "Excuse me?"

"It's not about money or worth. At the end of the day, Johnny and I are doing this for our future. You killed yourself to make something from nothing—you know what it's like on this side."

"Exactly," Beau said. "You can never understand how hard I've worked to get here, and now I'm offering it to you in exchange for one night. Not even an entire day. You should be on your knees thanking me."

To her embarrassment, she shuddered. The sheer level of her confusion scared her. The more he talked, the angrier she got and the more she wanted to grab his shirt and pull him to her. He seemed to know exactly how to push her buttons, back her into a corner, make her sweat.

"What would you have done in my position?" she asked him.

"Me? Oh, I've sold my soul many times over," he answered. "Now it's my turn to buy."

She stood and steadied herself against the table. "You clawed your way to the top, yet you're still taking advantage of others' desperation. You're depraved. I guess it's true that you can take the person out of the trash, but you can't take the trash out of the person."

He tilted his head. "Is that what they say about

you?"

"Go to hell." She didn't have much dignity left, but she wasn't willing to give him every last piece of it. "I can't do this."

The table was silent. She didn't wait to see if Johnny would follow. With one last look at Beau, and a moment of wondering what could've been had she met him at a different time, or maybe even had he not made his offer, but had come back to the bar a second time—with that last look, she walked away.

As soon as she reached the door and her hand was closed around the handle, though, Beau spoke again.

"A million dollars."

It wasn't possible she'd heard him correctly. In her worked-up, jittery state, her mind was playing tricks on her. Beau had no reason to double the amount when he'd been so opposed to eight hundred thousand. She glanced back over her shoulder. Johnny was frozen, his eyes doubled in size.

Beau's fingers were steepled in front of him and the corner of his mouth curled into a slight smile. "One night. One million dollars. And that's my final offer."

Chapter Seven

Johnny cupped Lola's upturned face. He kissed her forehead. "You look terrible."

"That's the plan, isn't it?" With a shaky inhale, she put a smile on her face. Johnny had been surprisingly strong since they'd left Beau's office the day before—for her. She could do the same for him.

"What about the black circles under your eyes?" he asked. "Are they part of the plan?" This time he kissed the top of her head. "You look great to me, anyway. Maybe he won't think so."

Johnny hugged her face to his chest. He'd just gotten out of the shower and smelled like soap. His ratty sneakers sat by the front door next to an empty space where she always left her Converse. Usually their shoes came and went together. She tried to look away, but Johnny held her tightly. She couldn't afford to get sentimental about sneakers. It wasn't like this was the first night they'd ever spent apart.

"I love you," she said. Now that the decision had been made, there was a sense of relief between them, and with that they'd made peace. "We'll get through this."

"I'd never let you go if I thought differently," Johnny said. "It means nothing. I'll go to work like any other night. You'll come home to me in the morning. End of story."

"You forgot the part about how we're a million dollars richer afterward."

"We're already halfway there," he said.

Lola had that fight or flight feeling she always got before a big change in her life. The night she'd started at Hey Joe, she'd begged Johnny to let her go back to her old job and her old friends. At the time, that life had seemed easier than starting over. But even though it was because of Johnny's ultimatum, *she'd* made the decision to leave all that behind. Still, that hadn't meant it was easy.

She looked up at Johnny without pulling away an inch. "We could be in Vegas by midnight. We already have five hundred grand. Start over."

He smiled. "We could take that fake road trip we planned last year. With nowhere to be, it wouldn't matter how long it took. Break out the camping gear—"

A knock on the door interrupted him. Lola squeezed Johnny closer. "I don't want to leave you alone."

"I'll be fine."

"You will?"

He shook his head. "No, but it's only a night, right? Work will be kind of busy since it's Friday. It'll keep me distracted."

The knock came again.

"Will you check in with Mitch? He can't make any decisions until he hears our offer."

"He'll wait." He pushed a loose strand of her hair behind her ear and kissed her, lingering against her lips. "Lola," he whispered. "Don't kiss him like this. Promise me."

She let him clutch her another moment. She was about to step into a world where she had no jurisdiction over her own body. No matter how badly she wanted to, she couldn't make Johnny that promise. "I'll try."

He tensed when there was more rapping on the door. "Love you too," he said.

Lola was just going to slip out, but Johnny opened the door all the way. On their welcome mat stood a suited man who wasn't Beau, but who didn't look much older than him. He gestured behind him. "Good evening, Miss Winters. I'm Mr. Olivier's driver. He's waiting in the car."

Lola shielded her eyes and followed the man without looking back. At the curb, a limousine idled. As they approached it, the sun disappeared behind the apartment building across the street.

The back window rolled down. Beau's hair was styled in a wave tonight—smoother and darker from product and away from his face. It made his green eyes clearer. He was perfectly put together except for a noticeable layer of stubble. The contrast only added to his appeal.

"Last chance, Lola," he said, looking up at her. He was being playful. "You can still turn around."

She stared, unblinking, unflinching and showed him the papers clutched in her hand. "The tests you requested."

He took them through the window, read them over and smiled. "He's thorough, isn't he?"

"Very." After her tense afternoon with Beau and Johnny in the conference room, Beau's doctor had been kind and gentle with her. He'd even insisted on giving her a check-up.

"Warner, please get the door for Miss Winters."

"Certainly, sir." He stepped past Lola to let her in.

The limo had champagne and other spirits, but champagne was the only thing she could stomach. She sipped it to calm her nerves after reviewing Beau's test results.

"I admire your effort," Beau said, "but it isn't working."

She moved the glass from her mouth. "I'm sorry?"

"Are those Johnny's jeans?"

She looked down at the faded, oversized pants. "Johnny's jeans wouldn't fit me," she said, offended. "They're from Goodwill. It's this place where—"

"I'm familiar with Goodwill, thank you."

She rolled her lips together, pleased she'd hit a nerve. She covered her smile by taking another sip of her drink.

"I'm not buying the act," Beau said. "I know you're intentionally trying to make yourself unattractive."

"Do you always call your dates ugly right off the bat?"

"I'm saying the opposite, actually. Old jeans and no makeup can't detract from your beauty." He studied her. "But my guess is you already knew that."

Whether she'd known it or not, she couldn't help feeling flattered—even as she reminded herself that in the short time she'd known him, he'd never lacked the ability to charm.

"The only thing I won't let fly is your hair like that," he said.

It was a mild request. She didn't argue. She undid her ponytail, and her hair fell all at once around her shoulders.

"Better," he said.

She looked out the window since the divider had been rolled up, blocking her view of the road. "Are we going to your place?"

"No."

She turned to him. "A hotel?"

"We have a room for the night, yes."

A hotel was good—it meant there'd be people around. "Where is it?"

"Beverly Hills." He paused. "Is that all right with you?"

She'd never stayed in a hotel in Los Angeles since she had no reason to. She'd certainly never stayed anywhere as upscale as Beverly Hills. "Is your house under renovation or something?"

"We'd be more comfortable at a hotel."

Lola looked around the limo. There'd been no mention of where he lived in her research. Her heart plummeted when she realized the most obvious reason he wouldn't want her in his home. She turned back to him.

"I'm not married," he said.

"How'd you know I was going to ask that?"

"I watched it play out on your face," he said. "I like that you're expressive."

She ignored that. "Girlfriend?"

"Completely unattached. I promise."

She wondered if her relief also played out on her face. Beau had chosen *her*, had orchestrated all this for *her*, and if nothing else, Lola would allow herself to feel special about that tonight. The only thing that could take that away would be another woman. "Will we be there soon?"

Beau let her question hang in the air a moment. "Do you want to be there soon?" he asked.

It was a blunt question delivered bluntly. Her answer didn't matter—it wouldn't change the course of her night. It was almost impossible to lie to him, looking as handsome as he did in his tuxedo. He was tall and obviously well built, but was he as hard underneath as he was on the outside? Was he strong? If they had sex against a wall, how long could he hold her up? "No," she said quickly to cover up that last thought. "It all just sounds very top secret."

"It isn't," he said. "You're just asking the wrong questions. We're going to a gala."

"A *what?*" The tuxedo. She'd been so caught up in herself that she hadn't stopped to wonder why he was wearing one.

"A black-tie gala to benefit the L.A. Philharmonic. I needed a date. That's why I picked tonight for us."

She pulled on the hem of her vintage concert tee. "But I'm not dressed for that."

"Thank God you agree. You can wear that if you want, but I prefer not to spend the night looking at Stevie Nicks and her yellow hair."

Lola scrambled. "I wish you'd told me. I can find something more appropriate if you take me back."

"That won't be necessary. I didn't tell you to dress up because I planned a little extra time for shopping."

"I didn't realize…I thought we would just—"

"Fuck?"

Lola's breath caught. If Johnny ever spoke to her that way, it wasn't in broad daylight, outside the heat of the moment. "Honestly," she said, swallowing back her surprise, "it wouldn't take me long to run into my apartment. I only have one dress that would—"

"I'd be a madman to take you back now that I have you."

Lola shut her mouth. He was becoming bolder, catching her off guard more. "You will, though, won't you?" she asked quietly, not entirely sure he'd say yes. "Take me home?"

"In the morning, as promised. But not a minute sooner." He moved the test results from between them to the floor and placed his arm along the back of the seat. "First we'll go shopping. You'll wear what I select for you, and I'll pay for it."

"I'm not comfortable with that. It's not part of the deal. I can buy my own clothing."

He zapped her conviction with a look. "In case it needs to be reiterated, Lola, I always say what I mean. Nothing is open to discussion. And since you've promised yourself over to me for the next twelve or so hours, make this easy for us both and comply."

"If you were looking for a woman who'd just comply, I don't think I'd be here right now."

His eyes narrowed. "What makes you say that?"

"A man like you would have no problems finding willing women. You want someone unwilling. Someone you have to work for. You think I'm trashy, maybe a little wild, and that does something for you. I understand." For the first time since she'd met Beau, Lola felt in control. The look on his face and the quickening of his breath gave him away. He leaned into her as if he didn't even realize he was doing it. "If you tell me exactly what you're looking for," she said, "I can play that part for you. I've done it before."

"You've done what before?" he asked, hardly even blinking.

"Been someone's fantasy."

"Not their reality, though." He'd slid over in the seat, far enough that he'd have to reach to kiss her, but still close.

"No."

"I want the reality. You. Just you."

She lifted one shoulder. "You have me. My body's already yours. If it's not enough, tell me what to be."

"I made myself clear on this already. This is about you, Lola. Not just what's underneath those jeans and T-shirt. I won't accept anything less than everything from you tonight."

She shook her head coyly. "My body is one thing, the rest of me is another. What you paid for is only what's underneath these jeans and T-shirt."

The car slowed to a stop. Beau straightened up abruptly. "You're wrong. That's not what we agreed on." He looked away from her and opened the door before the driver could.

Lola took Beau's hand and unfolded out of the car. Palm trees framed the tall windows of the marble storefront, which displayed smartly dressed mannequins. "I hate to tell you this," Lola said, "but these shops are closed."

He put his hand on her upper back, trapping the ends of her hair. "Not for us," he said, guiding her forward. The brass-handled, glass doors opened with his words.

"You must be Lola," said a slick-haired blonde saleswoman, outstretching her hand. "I understand it's an important night for you."

Another woman appeared with two glasses of champagne.

"Is that what he told you?" Lola asked, taking a drink.

"Lola," Beau warned. "Don't pretend your thirtieth birthday dinner is just another night."

The saleswoman smiled. "Well, you're in good hands with us." Both women disappeared somewhere into the pristine, bone-and-black-lacquer interior.

"It's not even close to my birthday," Lola said. "Why the subterfuge?"

"It's fun to watch you squirm."

"Well, if we're playing games, could I not be thirty already? How would you like if I went around telling people you're forty when you're not for a few more years?"

How he smiled at that, crooked-lipped and dimple-deep—as if it were the best thing he'd heard in a while. "Did a little research on me, I see."

"Don't be flattered—"

"I wouldn't dream of it."

"It was only to make sure you weren't wanted for murder or something. I'm still not entirely convinced you aren't."

"Well." His smile only widened. "I'm glad you decided to put your life in my hands anyway. Funny how a little money turns the other cheek."

She followed Beau to the back of the store, frustrated at her lack of comeback.

He stopped at a clothing rack. "Here are the things I've preselected. I'd like to see them all on you."

"For one evening?" She balked at the price tag. "Some of these cost more than my month's rent." She flipped it over. "Make that two months."

"While you're with me, you'll be dressed the part—every hour, every minute." He took her champagne glass from her. "I'll refill your drink. You can change around the corner."

She picked up the first dress and took it to the fitting room, holding it away from her as though it might break. It was lovely and expensive. She hated it. The high neck and gathered fabric along one side was completely out of line with her taste.

Just as she'd stripped down to her underwear, he knocked. She glanced at the door. Beau might be proving difficult to decode, but Lola was sure about one thing—he liked power. Control. He fed on weakness—in a single bite—and it made him stronger.

Lola wasn't weak, though. She'd let Beau do the biting, but just enough to keep him satisfied and no more. It'd been a while since she'd had the attention of a man like Beau, but she had, and she hadn't forgotten this game.

Lola opened the door wide. She slid her hand up along the edge and cocked her hip just enough for him to notice. "You knocked?"

He schooled his expression in one quick second, but not before Lola caught his surprise. His slow gaze drifted down her neck, past her wide-strapped, sea-foam-green bra, over her naked stomach to her mismatched, oversized panties.

"Stubborn right down to her underwear," Beau said, more amused than annoyed.

"It's laundry day." Lola shrugged. "My less modest things are—well, probably in Johnny's hands as we speak since it's his week to do the wash."

"Good thing they carry lingerie here," he said, less amused.

"Oh, don't waste another dollar on me. I'm fine with this if you are."

He smiled thinly. "I'm not. As I said, you're to dress the part every hour, every minute. That includes our time alone." He passed her a fresh glass of champagne. "I'll take care of it, but for now, I'll be outside your door. Talk to me while you change."

She shut herself into the fitting room and went to lock it but didn't bother. If Beau wanted to come in, he would. Wouldn't he? It'd been almost an hour and he hadn't made any move to touch her yet. When he did, would she like it? Could she enjoy being touched by Beau when she loved someone else? She shivered and passed her hands over her biceps. "What do you want to talk about?"

"Have you ever been here?"

"Rodeo Drive? Sure." She removed the dress gingerly from the hanger. Despite her feelings about it, it was still a beautiful piece of clothing. "Mostly to walk around. Truth be told, it isn't really my style."

"No, I don't suppose there's a lot of leather here."

"You don't like the leather?" she asked, smiling a little to herself.

"I didn't say that. What are you doing now?"

She looked down. "Pulling on the dress."

After a moment, he asked, "How about now?"

"The dress is tight, so it's taking a minute to get on. What are you doing?"

Beau laughed. "Well, now I'm picturing you struggling with a tight dress. Something I look forward to seeing later."

"Later?" Lola had expected to be in his bed by now, but his behavior bordered on gentlemanly. Curiosity urged her closer to the door. "Not now?"

He didn't respond right away. "No," he said. "Now I'm using my imagination."

"Can I ask you why without you taking it the wrong way?"

"Which way would be the wrong way?"

Absentmindedly, she touched the doorframe with a finger. "Not that I want this or that I'm trying to provoke you." She carefully considered what she was trying to say. "But how come you haven't done anything yet? You do know we only have tonight?"

"Tonight will be over before we both know it," he said. "That may be good news for you, but I intend to unwrap you slowly so I don't miss anything." He paused. "If you were worried about me breaking into your dressing room and bending you over the bench…you can relax."

Lola's eyes went directly to the bench. If he bent her over it, she'd be face to face with herself in the mirror. She'd see everything—like Beau behind her in his tuxedo. She closed her eyes, willing away the warmth seeping through her. Things were not supposed to be this way. Her plan was only to endure his weight on top of her, not anticipate it. Not enjoy it.

"Are you all right?" he asked. "You've been quiet for some time."

She cleared her throat and moved away from the door. "I'm fine."

"What are you doing now?"

"Unfastening my bra."

"How come?" he asked.

"It's the wrong kind. Should be racerback." There was a weighty pause. "Now I'm zipping up the dress."

"What's the material?"

"Silk, I think. It must be silk."

"Why do you say that?"

"It's smooth and soft," she said. "It feels…"

"Yes?"

"Silky."

"You can't see, but I'm smiling. Can I come in now?"

She opened the door.

Beau stood from his chair. "Beautiful."

"Thanks."

"But purple doesn't suit you."

"I hate purple."

"What color do you like?" he asked.

"Black."

"I should've known."

She left the room, went around the corner and past the rack of Beau's selections. Something near the front had caught her eye when she'd walked in. She found it in her size and returned to the fitting room, where Beau remained in the same spot, watching her. Behind the door again, she was alone. "Beau?"

"Yes, Lola?"

Alone with his voice.

"Why me?" she asked.

She put the purple dress back on its hanger while he took his time responding. "I suppose I should've been prepared for this question."

"You could just be honest," she suggested.

"All right. It started with the first moment I saw you. Everything else just…ceased to exist. Time. People. Music. You stood there like a prize waiting to be claimed. It stopped me in my tracks."

Jesus. Had he claimed her yet? Or was that to come? Her face flushed as if she were back outside the bar, having just put a dent in a teenager's car with her tennis shoe. "That's who I am."

"Who are you?"

"The girl you saw that night. I'm not expensive silk dresses and Friday-night events. I'm just the scrappy kid I always was, a girl who's made some bad decisions, good ones too. Nothing special."

"That's not what I saw," Beau said. "I saw confidence, resistance, strength. Blue, bloodthirsty eyes."

The girl Beau described reminded Lola of herself when she was younger. She was still that girl, just not as vibrantly as she'd been back then. "Will you zip me?" she asked.

She opened the door and turned to face the dressing room mirror. The black floor-length gown had two straps that came around her neck and dipped in the front. Soft, pebbled leather subtly trimmed the neckline.

Beau appeared at her back. In one hand, she held up her hair. He didn't touch her once while he raised the zipper. Their eyes caught in the reflection. "This is the dress," he said. "I don't need to see any others."

"You certainly know what you like, don't you?" she asked.

They stared at each other. Slowly, he lowered his mouth to the curve of her shoulder. His stubble lit instant chills over her skin. She inhaled deeply, quietly. Her lids fell more with each careful, sensual kiss—along her neck, under her ear, on her cheek. She wet her lips and parted them for him.

"Not yet," he said in her ear.

"When?" she breathed.

"Soon. You aren't ready for me. I hope you are at some point, but either way, it will be soon." He held her gaze. "You asked me why you? I'm drawn to you in a way that can't be ignored for long. There are limits to my patience." He backed away. "Wait here," he said before disappearing.

It was a moment before she dropped her hair. His restraint surprised her more than anything else so far.

Her eyes fell to her faux-leather brown hobo-style purse slumped in the corner. It looked out of place even on the floor, which was plush, white carpet. She glanced over her shoulder then squatted and retrieved her phone to text Johnny.

Everything's fine. We're just shopping. Going to an event.

She put the phone back right before Beau entered the room with a saleswoman loaded down with shoes, jewelry and a clutch that matched the dress. She put everything on the bench above Lola's purse.

Beau also had something for her in his hands, and he was clearly anticipating her reaction.

She took the lingerie from him without flinching. "It's lovely," she said. She ran a finger over the fine lace corset and then checked the price tag. "But is it necessary? I've never spent this much on anything and certainly not to sleep in."

"It's more necessary than anything else we buy tonight," Beau said in a deeper voice than usual. "And you won't be sleeping in it."

The saleswoman visibly bumbled as she left the room.

Lola's phone chimed behind her, and Beau's eyes cut to her purse. "Perhaps I didn't make myself clear. Tonight you belong to me. And *no.* Not just your body." He went and picked up her bag, pulled out the phone and read the screen. "Your thoughts and your heart too." He slipped it into his pocket. "As long as you're with me, *he* doesn't exist."

Her mouth hung open a little. "I'm sorry if you thought any amount of money would get you my heart," she said.

He stepped close to her. Mint cooled the champagne on his breath. "When it comes to which parts of you I own, don't fucking challenge me again. Is that understood? I own them all. Period." He took a deep breath, but it didn't seem to calm him. "There's still five hundred grand on the line. Act like you want to be here with me, or I'll call everything off."

She held his glare, trying to manage her own temper. She wouldn't walk away now. Beau was regaining his hold on her, like the one he'd had the night they met. Giving all of herself over wasn't an option, though—not if she wanted anything back when this was over.

"What's it going to be?" he asked. With another step, his shirt ghosted against her nipples. "Keep the half a mil and walk right now, or give yourself to me until I say stop?"

"I asked you why me," she said. "Your answer was that you're drawn to me. I don't believe you."

"What do you believe?"

"That you have to pay women for their attention," she said. She didn't believe that at all, but his composure was unnerving, and she craved a real reaction.

"You looked me up. You saw the endless buffet of women I have to choose from."

"You're a pig," Lola said. "A buffet? You think of women as food?"

He licked his lips quickly, reached up and brushed her hair away from her neck. "Those women are a buffet. But you? You're a delicacy. I'll eat you slowly with attention to every bite. I'll drink you like fine wine, savoring your taste, inhaling your scent, letting you own me for as long as you're in my mouth."

Lola exhaled an unintentional noise.

"I'll swallow all of you, but you won't realize it until it's too late. Until you're a part of me," he said. "That's what you sold me. That's what I paid for."

It would've been enough to frighten any other woman. It should've sent her sprinting back into Johnny's arms, content with the five hundred thousand that had almost been enough. The idea of being consumed by Beau did scare Lola, but it excited her more.

She didn't know whether to kiss him or back away, but it didn't matter. He was already leaving the room. "Put the things you wore here in the shopping bag by the door," he said over his shoulder. "Everything else in this room should be on your body tonight."

Chapter Eight

It took three technicians to turn Lola inside out. She was transformed. After their visit to the boutique, Beau's next stop had been a nearby salon. Within an hour, her hair had been washed, dried and swept into a loose updo, and her makeup flawlessly applied. Her nails were the color of sweet cherries. Lola watched raptly as the makeup artist carefully glided on the final touch—vivid lipstick, also cherry, also sweet.

"Everything else will catch his attention," the woman said quietly as she worked, "but this will be his undoing."

Lola wanted to explain that she didn't care if Beau was undone or not but her lips were occupied. Beau was never far away, and now he watched her in the mirror. There was no question he liked what he saw. And she liked that he liked it.

Maybe Lola did care if he was undone. After all, no matter how hard she fought her attraction, he was still a man and she was still a woman.

A fact she was reminded of with every movement. The corset Beau had picked out was not just an undergarment—it was a promise of things to come. The stiff, black lace kept her nipples at attention. It straightened her back, bared her while concealing her. It said, *Always be delectable for whoever might look.*

Underneath, black stockings, trimmed also with lace, stopped at the tops of her legs. When she rubbed her thighs together in the chair, the sheer parts felt silky, the lace parts coarse.

She hadn't shown this much cleavage in years, and she found it ironic that even then it had been a form of survival.

When Beau approached the chair, everyone else faded instantly away.

"People have a habit of disappearing around you," she said.

"They know what I want."

Lola looked at his reflection. "And what's that?"

"Privacy." He frowned. "I told them to leave your hair down."

"I told them to put it up." She uncrossed her legs. "It suits the dress."

"I don't care about the dress. I only care what suits me."

"You don't like it?" she asked.

"I suppose." He took one of the loose strands that framed her face between his fingers. "There'll be plenty of time for me to do what I want with it later."

Seated, Lola came up to Beau's chest. The mirror framed them like a photograph. All made up, Lola finally looked as though she belonged by his side. "Beau," she said, "there are things you don't know about me."

"I imagine quite a few."

"It's not just that Rodeo Drive isn't my taste. I also don't belong here."

"Says who?"

"You think I do?" she asked, mostly to hear what he'd say.

He was no longer looking in her eyes. She followed his gaze to her mouth. "I think you should only care about one person's opinion," he said. "Mine. I don't know who belongs where, but in my eyes, you're a queen among peasants wherever you go."

Lola stammered for a response. It shouldn't have surprised her that Beau was attracted to her—he'd made himself clear on that point—but he still hadn't given her a reason she could grasp. "Thank you," she said lamely.

He looked up again. "In my office, you made a speech about how we have similar pasts, but now we're on different sides. When you grow up on one side, though, you can never really cross over to the other. If you don't belong here, neither do I."

"Don't you ever feel out of place?"

"If I do, I don't let it show. I fake it. People will believe anything if you do it with confidence." He checked his watch. "Come. It's time to go."

The limo idled out front. Her personal effects were taken from her. She didn't care. Nothing had ever felt as good on her body as the things Beau had bought her.

"The rules apply even more so in public," Beau said as they drove away from the salon. "You're with me. Only me. Act as though it were true."

"Will there be press there?"

"Yes. Let them speculate. A beautiful woman like you won't go unnoticed, and I don't want you to."

Lola had the looks to back up her swagger, but Los Angeles was a hub for beautiful people. She doubted she'd get much attention amongst its upper crust. "Why not?" she asked.

"There are people who doubt my business practices because I'm…how do I put it? Social."

"You sleep around."

He gave her a sidelong glance. "Actually, no."

She pushed his shoulder with her fingertips. "You're such a liar. You must think I'm dense or blind. Women probably trip over themselves for a shot with you."

Beau raised one eyebrow. "You didn't. If you tripped at all, it was while running in the opposite direction."

She lowered her head a little as she smiled. "That's because I have a—" She stopped herself.

"So if you didn't have a—"

"You're trying to change the subject." Beau was undoubtedly a catch, enough to make Lola wonder why he was still single. He had to have known things would be different between them without Johnny in the picture. It was one of those things better left unsaid, though. "Anyway, you were lying about how women aren't all over you."

"I didn't say that at all." He winked playfully. "But just because a woman wants me doesn't mean she gets me. I'm selective. First, I choose the woman."

"That's it?" she asked.

"Of course not. I have to get her to choose me back."

"Who wouldn't choose you back?" Lola hadn't thought before she spoke, which meant she was becoming too comfortable. She sat up straighter, leaning slightly back from him.

Beau tilted his head, studying her as if she were a science project. "In my experience, not many," he said. "In any case, I don't sleep with every woman I'm photographed with. Sometimes a photo is just a photo."

"It doesn't matter either way to me," she said quickly. She changed the subject. "I'm not one of those girls, so I don't think I understand my role tonight."

"My being unmarried doesn't make me more of a risk, but some people see it that way. I don't make a habit of kowtowing to that kind of thing unless it affects my business, which it's beginning to. It's been four months since I've been in public with anyone. There's speculation I've settled down. Might as well let them think you're the reason for that."

"So I'm the one you've 'settled down' with?" He was asking her to be herself. Instead of his sex object, now she was a person. It wasn't quite what she'd expected from the night. "How do I be that if we've only just met?"

"Only give them your first name. A little mystery is good. Don't answer anything personal. I don't want your bar, your past or your partner associated with me."

Lola's confidence took a hit. "If I embarrass you, why even bring me at all?"

"Ah," he said softly, as if comforting her. "It takes a great deal to embarrass me, Lola. I said that for your protection. The press has no regard for anyone. If they see you with me, then suddenly what I do affects you. Best if we can limit that to one night."

He wanted to protect her? More and more he was uncharacteristically gentlemanly. There was a very small possibility her assumptions about a man who offered money for sex were wrong. Maybe he wasn't completely soulless. Maybe there was more to him than money and expensive suits. Lola thawed. She couldn't think of anything to add, so she just said, "He has a name, you know."

"Who?"

"Johnny. The way you say *partner* sounds sterile."

Beau didn't respond. He seemed more interested in what was out the window.

◆⊠◆⊠◆

Beau's limo door opened, and camera flashes blinded Lola. He offered her his hand. She only took it to be polite, but the noise, the brightness, the desperation crowding in on them—they were the reasons she didn't let go.

Photographers called for him. They called for them together. They ordered her out of the picture, and Beau's grip on her hand became crushing.

She smiled in every direction. The rolled-out carpet matched her nail polish. Behind them, a vinyl wall advertised the L.A. Philharmonic and the event's sponsor, Rolex. At one point, there were A-list celebrities to her left and right. When she got her bearings navigating both the carpet and the press in towering shoes, she tried to pull her hand away. Beau kept it tightly in his. "Don't," he whispered and kissed her cheek. "I'm the one holding on to you."

Whether he'd meant it or it was for show, hearing that made her a tinge protective of him. The media was made up of too many toothy smiles to count, and in the glaring lights, they became a unit. A snarling beast, hungry for Beau.

An entertainment channel reporter had caught his kiss. "Beau? Beau!" she cried from the other side of the velvet rope. Even with her teased, platinum hair that added a couple inches, she barely came up to Lola's shoulder. In a leopard-print dress, the woman was about as opposite of Lola as it came. "Kissing in public?" She gasped. "Does this mean it's serious?"

Beau slid his arm around Lola's waist. She had to give him credit. There were practically stars in his eyes when he turned to her and said, "Very."

The reporter's gaze flickered over Lola without touching her face. "Who is she?"

Suddenly, Lola and Beau were no longer on different sides. Beau wasn't these people. He looked her in the eye when he spoke to her. He didn't talk over her or tell her to move out of the way. She craned her head to the microphone in Beau's face. "*She* is Lola."

The reporter pouted, touching Beau's forearm. "Oh, dear. Hearts are breaking around the nation. Does this mean the chance to snag the handsome Beau Olivier has passed?"

Something flared in Lola seeing the woman's long red fingernails on him. Beau had chosen Lola tonight, not whoever was under the putrid cloud of hairspray and perfume in front of them. "That's exactly what it means," Lola said. "So kindly remove your claw from my man."

The reporter finally looked at Lola with such lit-up indignation, Lola had to suck in her cheeks to keep from laughing.

"Lola," Beau said.

She swallowed her laugh. She'd had no right to say it. Beau didn't belong to her. It shouldn't bother Lola that the woman looked and acted cheap, thinking that did anything for Beau. Maybe it *did* do something for him.

Lola was appropriately sheepish as she looked up and met his glinting eyes. When he spoke, it was for her and no one else. "Patience has never been my strong suit," he said, drawing her front flush against his, "but I do take credit for resisting this long."

He caught her mouth with his. Their lips pressed together hard, the way his hand pressed the nape of her neck. Her palm went automatically to his chest. He was solid under her hand, just as his arm was solid around her. Camera flashes exploded like fireworks. When his fingers coiled into her neck and her hip, her body stirred, prickling with warmth, as if waking up from a long sleep. She was acutely aware of being so tightly against the hard length of him. She angled her head up to deepen the kiss right before he pulled back.

His expression almost seemed to ask permission, overdue though it was. People shouted at them, but it quickly became white noise.

"Your lips are red," she said.

"So are yours."

Deliriously, she laughed at the thought that they wore the same lipstick. She placed her hands on his cheeks and wiped the red away with her thumbs.

"I have a handkerchief," he said.

"We don't use handkerchiefs where I come from."

"That's okay. I think I like your way better."

She ended up smearing it over her hands and his face. "I'm making it worse."

He laughed. "Not for me. How about we clean up and get a drink?"

The reporter studiously avoided them by trying to

get someone else's attention. "You read my mind," Lola said.

Getting anywhere proved difficult. People stopped Beau every few steps. They each patted their mouths with Beau's handkerchief as a temporary fix. He held her hand. She let him. What choice did she have? Her hand, and all her other parts, belonged to him in that moment. When Beau turned away from her, Lola touched her fingertips to her lips. She doubted a single camera had missed their display. Johnny might see it.

"You okay?" Beau looked at her hand at her mouth.

"Your scruff tingles," she said. "You'd think someone going on a million-dollar date would have the decency to shave."

"I'll shave tonight if you want. Before bed."

Before bed. As if they were an old married couple who never spent a night apart. The tingling became stronger as she thought about the fact that his mouth would be on her again and soon—*before bed.* "I didn't say I minded," she said softly, her face upturned to him.

He grunted or something, a deep noise of approval as his eyes jumped between her lips and eyes. "You know just the right things to say, don't you? I have unfairly high expectations of people, yet somehow you continue to exceed them."

"And here I was trying to be less than expected," she said, but she was teasing him. The gap she'd insisted on keeping between them was closing the more comfortable she became. "You do put on a pretty good show."

He shook his head slowly. "What show?"

"Holding my hand, kissing me for the cameras?

You're sending a message all right."

"If I am, that doesn't have to mean it's a show. I believe you're mine and no one else's. I meant what I said to that reporter—tonight, it's very serious."

Lola wanted to stay skeptical. It was easier that way. Beau didn't have her completely convinced there was good somewhere underneath his suit, but she was beginning to doubt it was all bad.

"What are you having tonight?" he asked.

Well vodka with club soda was her go-to drink, but she stopped her automatic response just in time. She wasn't that girl tonight. "Dirty martini," she said. "Grey Goose, please."

Beau ordered for them. She no sooner took the drink than Beau was approached once again, this time by a sturdy, red-cheeked man just as tall as Beau but many years older. "Evening, Olivier," he said, shaking Beau's hand. "Nice to see you."

"You as well, sir." Beau turned slightly. "This is Lola, my date for the evening—"

"It's been a while, hasn't it? I haven't seen you at one of these things with anyone lately."

"I wish I could say your concern with my personal life is flattering."

"Oh, you know I'm messing with you," he said, slapping Beau on the back. "You can't expect an old, married guy like me not to want to live vicariously. You always have a beautiful woman on your arm."

Lola hadn't been ignored by any man this much since she'd grown breasts. Even Beau had turned away from her. "I prefer you don't talk about me as if I'm not standing right here," she said.

Beau smiled a little and shook his head, but the man turned to face her completely. "Well, shoot. I'm sorry, darling. Where are my manners?"

"I was wondering the same thing about everyone here," Lola said.

His laugh was more of a guffaw. "Well, aren't you a breath of fresh air from Beau's usual type?"

Beau frowned. "Excuse me?"

"She's the first—" He stopped to address Lola. "You might be the first of Beau's dates I've ever heard speak."

"Perhaps you should be thankful for that," she said.

More merry laughing—the man was quickly becoming besotted with her. "I am. I certainly am."

Beau, on the other hand, narrowed his eyes. "Come on, now. What'd those girls ever do to you two?"

"They had something that was mine," Lola practically cooed, batting her lashes with exaggeration. "In case you hadn't noticed, I'm very possessive of my things."

Beau smoothed his hand down his tuxedo shirt. "I hadn't, actually."

Lola raised one eyebrow, waiting for Beau's bantering response, but nothing came.

"Lola," the man said, calling her attention away, "are you as good at keeping Olivier in line as you are me?"

She turned away from Beau and winked. "Better."

He nodded high with his chin in the air. "I'm impressed."

"Does this mean you'll take the meeting?" Beau asked, his wits seemingly recovered.

"Let's not worry about business right now. Listen, a spot opened up at my table—why don't you two join me there tonight?"

"We'd be honored, Mayor Churchill," Beau said. "Table one, is it?"

"That's right. See you there."

"*Mayor*?" Lola asked, gaping as he walked away.

Beau smiled. "Did I not mention that?"

"Oh, God. I didn't recognize him." Lola covered her face. "I was just incredibly rude to the mayor of Los Angeles."

Beau laughed, pulling her hands away. "He was incredibly rude to you, but that's my fault. I bring it out in him."

She shook her head. "I need to learn to keep my big mouth shut."

"Please don't," he said. "I love not knowing what will come out of it next. Such as the charming way you called me a *thing* after the fit you threw over my buffet comment."

"I said what?" Lola asked.

"Just now you said you were very possessive of your *things*."

"That's hardly the same. You referred to women as something you can pick up next to a tub of fried chicken," Lola said. "I was just playing nice for your friend like you wanted. Has he ever invited you to his table before?"

Beau pursed his lips. "No."

"Then I must've done something right."

"You did something to me, at least." He scanned her face. "I like you being possessive over me."

"I'm not. I was just doing what you asked."

He sipped something dark from his glass and surveyed the room. "I'm not sure why you continue to fight this. The deal's been made, but truth be told, I think you want to be here. You just won't admit it."

She studied his profile. There was a disconnect in his eyes, as if not looking at her meant she wasn't there. It made him darker. It occurred to her just how much power he had tonight. He'd treated her like glass so far, but he could still shatter her with a flick of his wrist. "Beau? What if I decide not to go through with this?"

He blinked once and turned his head to her. When he raised his hand, she flinched. He touched his thumb to the corner of her lips. "You know what our arrangement is," he said. His voice dropped. "And on one point I've been very clear. Until sunrise, you're mine."

His thumb was still pressed against her skin, distracting her. "I know self-defense," she said.

"You won't need it." He shook his head. "Trust me."

Had she met Beau another time, a time when Johnny wasn't part of her life, she would've been attracted to him. He wasn't her type—Johnny was, with his unsmoothable edges and no-bullshit attitude. His faded hair, faded tattoos, faded black T-shirts. Beau's dark-brown hair was just enough for her to grab a handful and no more. Lola had an eye for expensive things even if she didn't own any, and nothing on Beau's body came cheap. He just beat Johnny in height, but where Johnny's T-shirts stretched across his torso, Beau's terse suits—and tuxedos—perfectly complemented his broad shoulders and muscular, lean frame.

"My eyes are up here," Beau teased.

She blinked up from his chest. "Sorry."

"Where'd you go?"

She just shook her head.

"Look," Beau said, sighing, "we have an agreement, yes, but I'm not resting on that. I'm obviously attracted to you or you wouldn't be here." He paused. "Maybe I don't need that reciprocated, but I want it. And I'm willing to work for it."

"I love my boyfriend," Lola said. "You can't expect me to enjoy sleeping with you."

"I do expect it," Beau said. "When I make love to you tonight, it'll be in a way that demands everything from you."

Lola's throat tightened. Nowhere in their arrangement had they said they'd be making love. This was just supposed to be sex—straight up sex. No romance. No fantasy. Definitely no lovemaking.

"I wouldn't pay a million *pennies* for any other woman," Beau continued. "This is about you, not me. Tonight, you're my queen." He made sure she was looking him in the eye when he added, "And that makes me your king. If you're worried about making love, don't be. I'm going to fuck you too."

Lola covered her mouth but couldn't tear her eyes away from him. "Beau," she said behind her hand.

"I don't want any misconceptions. I'm going to make you uncomfortable. I'm going to worship you. I'm going to dominate you. Any man who just has sex with a woman like you is a fool. I want to make art with you—

dirty, impossible, fucked-up, beautiful art."

Lola's mind reeled. The image he'd painted was too vivid to shut out. There were people all around them, but inside she was tightly wound and aching for him to untwist her. One hand twitched with the urge to slap him while the other wanted to fist his lapel and bring him closer.

"Now you're giving me something," Beau said, watching her with intensity. "Something I can work with."

Lola didn't even know the skin she was in. "I need to fix my lipstick. I can meet you at the table."

He straightened up. "Go ahead. I'll wait."

Lola rushed to the nearest bathroom and stood in front of the mirror. Only the slight flush of her cheeks gave her away. The reality of the situation hit her. She would be having sex with this man—this *stranger*. It was no longer about money, but about two people spending the night together. Her heart pounded from Beau's words. She could feel blood circulating through her for the first time ever.

It wasn't Beau's promise of things to come that scared her anymore. Nor was it his threat that it was too late to change her mind. What scared her was wanting this, and at the idea of being fucked by him, she had.

She took out the lipstick the makeup artist had given her. She didn't leave the bathroom until it was applied perfectly.

Beau noticed. "You look composed again," he said when she returned.

Lola hated that word. Only people with something to hide composed themselves. But he was right—she was struggling to be herself in an environment so obviously meant for someone else.

They were the last ones to the dining table. After introductions had been made, Beau put his mouth to Lola's ear and said, "Mayor Churchill is one of those who equates my inability to commit to one woman with the way I do business. An invitation to his table is an opportunity."

His warm breath pebbled her skin. She nodded to show she understood, but with him so close, her mind was back on their kiss. It'd been so convincing that even she'd believed it. There had been need and desire in the way his hands had gripped her, but something gentler and almost reverent in his lips.

Beau conversed easily with the table, but Lola wasn't listening. She watched. He had an unnerving way of focusing on whoever was speaking. It was similar to how he'd approached Lola and Johnny with his proposition. Where did business end with him? Would it carry over into the bedroom?

"So, Lola," Mayor Churchill said between dishes, "are you from Los Angeles?"

Beau took her hand under the table.

"Not too far from here, Mayor Churchill," she said. "East Hollywood."

"Same here," he said proudly. "In fact, the only thing Beau and I have in common is pulling ourselves up by the bootstraps. And call me Glenn."

"We have more in common than that," Beau said.

"Do we?" Glenn asked, smiling as he cut his chicken.

"We both love the city we grew up in and want to

do right by it." Beau nodded at Lola. "We both appreciate beautiful women."

Glenn waved his fork in their direction. "Okay, you got me there."

"Did Beau mention how we met?" Lola asked.

"Why don't you tell me," Glenn invited.

Beau went tense beside her, his hand tightening around hers.

"First you have to suspend disbelief long enough to picture Beau in a dive bar," she said.

"A dive bar?" Glenn laughed. "What, in his Prada suit and tie?"

"Exactly," Lola said. "We met under some neon signs on the Sunset Strip."

Glenn sat back in his seat. "I haven't been out on the Strip at night in years. In high school, we'd volunteer to post flyers for shows all over Hollywood so the bars would let us in to watch."

Lola grinned. Her instinct that Glenn would get the story looked right. "Have you been to Hey Joe?"

"Have I been there? I passed out in my own vomit on Hey Joe's bathroom floor before you kids were even born." He sighed heartily. "Those were the days," he muttered before glancing quickly around the table. "Don't repeat that."

"That part of the Strip might not be much these days," Lola said, "but Beau and I met there over Scotch and a show." She reasoned the night had been such a spectacle, it counted as a kind of show.

"I almost can't picture it," Glenn said. "Is it true, Olivier?"

"The place is legendary," Beau said warily.

Lola leaned over and kissed Beau's cheek. "For more reasons than one, now," she said loud enough for Glenn to hear.

"Ever see any good bands there?" someone asked the mayor.

"That was risky," Beau whispered as the conversation steered away from them.

"What, the kiss?" Lola asked, knowing perfectly well what he meant.

He shook his head slowly. "The kiss I didn't mind. It was a nice touch." He pulled her hand from her lap to his. "What are you thinking about?"

It was written all over his face—he knew she was thinking about where he'd positioned her hand. "I was remembering all the shows I've seen."

"I'll bet you've seen a lot."

She nodded. "In high school, I snuck into bars all the time for live music, usually with a bad boy whose life's mission was to get me drunk." Her eyes drifted over Beau. "That's always been my type. I never dated anyone who wore a suit."

"You're mistaken if you think only good boys wear suits."

Lola nearly lost her heart to her stomach. Bad boys had always been her thing, but since meeting Beau, she was more and more drawn to the suit. She hated to think how she'd fare faced with a combination of the two. "You're teasing me."

"Maybe." He grinned. "Maybe not."

"I don't exactly think you were an angel, but I can't picture you as rebellious."

"I was in the chess club."

Lola laughed loudly. She didn't care that people looked over at them—she was too delighted by the news. "So you were a geek."

"Chess isn't geeky. It taught me the importance of strategy, and," he paused and pulled her hand even farther into his lap, "how to manipulate the pawns in my favor."

She ignored his insinuation. "Were you any good?"

"No, thankfully."

She wrinkled her nose. "What? Why thankfully?"

"We learn far more from defeat than victory, Lola. Every loss means an opportunity to become better. Stronger. I didn't know it then, but I was preparing for the challenges that would come my way. It's made me a better businessman. And a formidable opponent."

"Opponent?" she asked.

"At chess, I mean."

She became even more convinced that for him, there was no clear distinction between business and pleasure. She narrowed her eyes. "You're too hard on yourself. Games are supposed to be fun, not life lessons."

"There's room for improvement in everything we do," he said. "Don't you think we should always try to be better?"

"No."

"You didn't even pause to think about that."

Lola looked at the tablecloth. "It's more important to me that I'm comfortable in my own skin. I'd rather look around and be happy with what I have than always wondering what's around the corner."

"You can do that and strive to be better."

That kind of thinking was for people who were in an elevator on the way up. She was fine on the ground floor, where her feet were stable. Someone like Beau had a long distance to fall. "My life may be simple, but I'm content," she said. "I have what I need."

"I don't believe you," Beau said. "Or maybe I don't want to believe you. I'm never content. And I'm happiest when I'm conquering myself."

"Spoken like a true king," she said, nodding up at his profile.

He shook his head, his eyes forward. "No. A king conquers others."

Chapter Nine

Lola ate everything put in front of her—oysters on the half shell, beef tenderloin, roasted vegetables, berry soufflé tart.

Beau looked as satisfied as she felt full. "Ready for our next stop?" he asked as she finished off her last bite.

She wiped her mouth with the napkin in her lap. She didn't answer—the question was rhetorical. Whether or not she was ready didn't matter.

Beau scooted his chair out and stood. His smile was inauthentic, but Lola doubted anyone else noticed. Except for Churchill, they seemed more interested in perfecting their own imitations at happiness. Lola was the only woman at the table who hadn't pulled out a compact at some point to check her lipstick. Maybe she should have, but she didn't own one. The men were the same with their cell phones. Beau hadn't so much as glanced at his phone once that she'd noticed, and that surprised her. A man like him had to be busy all times of the day.

"Thank you for such great company tonight," Beau told the table, "but you'll have to excuse us. Lola and I have pressing plans."

Glenn came around to shake Beau's hand. "Olivier, how come we've never had that meeting?"

"You're an important man, sir."

The mayor teased Beau by winking at Lola. "Let's get one on the books," he said to Beau. "Have your secretary call mine."

"Consider it done."

Glenn smiled and nodded over at Lola. "Word of advice? Don't screw this up. I like this one. She's good for you."

Lola thanked the mayor and let him hug her before they left.

Out front, Beau went to the valet stand while Lola waited at the curb.

"That went well with Churchill," he said, his hands in his pockets as he returned to her. "All I needed was a meeting. The rest will take care of itself."

"I don't know if anyone's ever told you, but you can be very convincing," Lola said.

"But these things aren't about business. They're about networking and relationships. Churchill liked you. That's the only reason he gave me the time of the day."

"I think that was a compliment," she said. "So thank you."

He turned all the way to her. "No, this is a compliment. You're not just beautiful, but smart too. Churchill saw that. I see it."

"You can drop the act," she said. "I don't think the valets need to hear it."

He took her chin and pulled her mouth an inch from his. "I have to be a certain person in my professional life. I try not to be that in my personal. I may not always be forthcoming or virtuous, but when it comes to you, I don't act." He kissed her softly without lingering. "Don't underestimate yourself. You may have just earned me a great deal of money."

Lola twisted her face away at the mention of money. "I'm so glad."

"You should be. Nothing puts me in a better mood than making money."

Lola stepped back a little. She couldn't fall under his spell. Once, she'd been unimpressed with Beau's past because attaining his level of success often meant screwing someone over.

"What's wrong?" he asked.

"This meeting I helped you get…it isn't anything illegal or corrupt, is it?"

"He's the mayor, Lola."

She pursed her lips. "And elected officials are always angels."

"You have nothing to worry about it. It's all legit."

"Well, what's it about?"

"You really want to know?"

Why did she care? Beau's business was just that—his business. It had nothing to do with her. She'd convinced herself coming into this that spending the night with Beau would be easiest if he were just a stranger. But to say she wasn't curious about him would've been lying to herself. She nodded. "Sure."

"The meeting's about tax breaks and incentives for angel investors—those of us putting a lot of money into early-stage startups. Los Angeles has access to so much talent with USC and UCLA, plus the arts and entertainment industry—we need to work on keeping that talent here. But it'll follow the money if it goes to a city with more benefits."

"Why wouldn't he want to do that?"

"It's not that he doesn't want to, he's just not very tech forward. I'm sure he has people telling him different things, but I want to lay it out for him from the perspective of someone who has a vested interest in this city. Unfortunately, he thinks my businessman's heart has bad intentions."

Lola lifted an eyebrow. "Does it?"

"Tax credits are good for me, no doubt. The more money I save, the more I can invest, and that's potential to earn. Local talent would also help me. If a startup is headquartered in Los Angeles or does significant business here, they're on my radar."

"How come?"

"Because it's good for our economy. Los Angeles is my home, and I want it to stay competitive with places like San Francisco and New York."

Lola could understand that—she'd never lived anywhere else, so she was particularly fond of L.A. Still, Beau would always be a man with a bottom line. "I can see why Churchill is skeptical," she said. "It's hard to believe you don't have an ulterior motive."

"I'll be upfront about how I benefit in the short and long term. I just want Los Angeles to benefit equally."

It wasn't until a silver sports car pulled up that Lola remembered Warner. "What about the limo?"

"We're finished with that portion of the night," Beau said. "I'll be driving to our next destination."

"Your hotel," Lola said.

"Not yet."

The valet hopped out of the car, beaming. "This is why I love working these events. The Lamborghini's no joke, dude. I mean *sir*. That was my first time driving the Aventador Roadster."

"How was it?" Beau asked.

"Fucking awesome. I had to restrain myself from finding out the zero-to-sixty."

"It's about three seconds," Beau said.

The valet looked Lola up and down. "Lucky bastard."

Beau laughed as he took out his wallet. "I won't argue with that."

The boy's eyes bugged wide when he accepted his tip. "And I won't argue with that! Thank you, sir."

Beau waved him off to let Lola in the car himself. The three-quarter doors rose up like wings. Inside, only the dashboard lights glowed in the dark.

Once Beau was behind the wheel, Lola found the button on the console that lowered their windows. "It's such a nice night," she said.

"I'm not really a wind-in-my-hair type of guy," he protested.

"Can't you fake it for a night?"

He shook his head at her teasing smile. "I suppose one night won't kill me."

Before he pulled into the street, he reached over and undid Lola's hair with one hand.

"It'll get messy," she said when it fell around her shoulders.

He looked at her, winked and stepped on the gas. "It already is."

Soon, they were speeding down Sunset Boulevard. "Beau," Lola called over the engine. Her hands wrapped around her neck and hair. "We're going fast."

"What other way is there?" he asked, grinning ear to ear. "Relax. Enjoy the ride."

She forced her fingers to loosen. The road seemed

to open just for them. Beau navigated swiftly through traffic, swerving between cars, racing yellow lights, leaving no room for error so her heart raced with them. Neon lights blurred together as they passed bars, souvenir shops, comedy clubs. Black palm trees silhouetted against the billboards. She released her hair, put her head back and closed her eyes.

"You're so beautiful, Lola," Beau said. "The most breathtaking thing."

It *was* beautiful. She'd never felt so unattached to everything, even her body. She opened her eyes. Nature and commercialism and Beau were all around her. She loved the car and the new way it allowed her to experience the boulevard she thought she'd seen from every angle.

But she shot up from the headrest when she noticed where they were. "Beau, you're not taking me to—"

"Hey Joe?" he interrupted. "No. Not even I'm that cruel."

They passed the bar and stopped several blocks down. She knew the building they parked in front of since she used to walk by it frequently on her way to see Johnny at Hey Joe. "What are we doing?" she asked as he rolled up the windows.

"A nightcap."

"Does it have to be here? Can't we do it at the hotel or something?"

"It has to be here." He got out of the car and then opened her door for her. He placed his large hand at the nape of her neck, guiding her down an alley until they were almost in a parking lot.

"What is this?" Lola asked. "I've never been here."

Beau knocked once on large side door. "Used to be a speakeasy."

The bouncer leaned out, then stepped aside to let them in.

"You must come here often," Lola said over her shoulder.

"I like their oysters."

"Is oyster a euphemism for something else?"

He laughed. "Would that bother you?"

"No." She looked forward again. "Euphemisms don't bother me at all."

They passed through a corridor. The fur articles in the coat check were almost too much for her—it was only the beginning of fall, and it was Los Angeles for heaven's sake. She parted heavy gold velvet curtains to enter a dimly lit room. To her right, a man in a suit clinked tulip glasses with a woman in pearls.

Despite being a few blocks from Hey Joe, Lola didn't worry about running into anyone she knew. These were Beau's people, not hers. She started to tell him she didn't like it but stopped. Underneath and behind the pretentiousness were gritty brick walls and aged-leather booths the color of whiskey. An impressive backlit wall of liquor glowed bronze. In the center of the room sat a grand piano, and the pianist played "Heart-Shaped Box."

"By the look on your face, I guess you're a Nirvana fan," Beau said.

"I don't think I could've dreamed up a stranger song for this place."

Beau ordered from the bartender while she watched the pianist play.

"The first time I heard Nirvana was on the radio the day Kurt Cobain died," she said.

"I remember that day," Beau said. "I was a teenager, so you must've been..."

"Pretty young. I fell in love, though. Johnny hates grunge. He's rock 'n' roll straight through." She took the drink Beau offered her without looking away. "How about you?"

"I'm with Johnny on this one."

"Really?" She glanced at him.

"Don't look so surprised. Pink Floyd got me through a lot of late nights at the office."

Lola stopped bobbing her head and took a sip of her drink. She looked down into the glass.

"Do you like it?" Beau asked. "It's bourbon."

"Bourbon isn't really my thing, but this isn't bad." She drank a little more. "It's smooth. Sweet."

"Fruity." He smelled his glass. "Pappy Van Winkle, barrel-aged twenty-three years. Rare, partly because it takes so long to age and there just isn't enough. Take your time—something like this should be savored."

"In other words, it's expensive."

"It depends on what you mean by expensive. Money is not the same thing as worth, and drinking a glass of this with you is worth a lot to me."

Lola made a noise of appreciation, and not just for the drink. The sweet alcohol burn, the leathery smell of the bar, the dim lights, Beau's deep voice—it was a heady combination.

"How do you feel?" he asked.

"Relaxed."

He smiled. "Me too."

"You, relaxed? I bet that's as rare as this drink." The two martinis she'd had at the gala had done nothing for her, but drinking this bourbon was like falling into a warm embrace.

"That would be a safe bet," he said.

"How much do you work? Be honest."

"Right now, I work a lot. Back when I was trying to create something from nothing, though, I barely stopped to eat."

"Your family was okay with that?"

"I did it for them as much as for myself."

"What about your friends? Girlfriends?"

Beau raised an eyebrow. "I'm something of a loner if you haven't noticed."

"Even now?"

He hesitated. "A man with money trusts his enemies more than his friends."

She tried to picture her life without Johnny and Vero and the people she saw at the bar almost nightly. While she was there, Beau was at events with eager reporters in his face and people who were often trying to get something from him. She put her hand on his arm. "That must be hard."

Beau took a moment to respond. "When you're nice to me, it makes me want to kiss you," he warned.

"What about when I'm mean?" She allowed herself a playful smile.

He palmed her lower back and drew her close to his side. "It makes me want to be mean back." He slid his hand over the curve of her backside but stopped.

"Your patience is admirable," she said, hoping he didn't notice her slight gasp between words.

"My patience is thin."

"You're the one carting me from place to place."

His eyes gleamed. "You're ready for the hotel?"

Her gaze dropped to his lips, his bowtie and jumped back up. He curled his fingers into her dress.

"I'll take your inability to answer as a yes," he said.

He took her hand and walked her out of the lounge. Coming out of the alley, she turned left, but he pulled her back. "This way."

"But the car—"

"This wasn't our stop," he said, leading her in the opposite direction. "I'd just heard about a shipment of that bourbon and I wanted you to try it."

"Then where are we going?"

He dropped her hand and didn't answer. Her heart began to pound as they walked west. He glanced over at her with that impatient look he'd gotten right before he'd kissed her on the red carpet.

"Here?" she asked when he stopped walking. "Is this supposed to be funny?"

"What's funny?" he asked, his eyebrows lowering.

"I'm not going in there. I can't."

"You can," he said, "and you will."

She looked behind Beau. On the brick wall a pink neon sign flashed the word *Girls* at her over and over. She dried her palms on her dress. After spending an evening with Los Angeles's elite, Cat Shoppe seemed like a cruel joke.

It wasn't. Any teasing, gleaming or admiration in Beau's eyes was gone. "You aren't too good for a strip club?"

They must've looked that way on the outside—she

made up in a gown, he strangled by his bowtie.

She was far from too good for it. She'd once been a part of it. A lifetime ago, Lola had spent her nights dancing at Cat Shoppe, getting caught up in the money and the partying and forming bonds with girls she no longer spoke to. When people found out she'd been a stripper, they always wanted to know why.

"Why are you doing this?" her mom asked from across the Formica table. Pleaded.

"For the money." Lola's tone was dry. "Isn't that what it's all about?"

Dina shook her head. "You're only eighteen. This isn't how I raised you."

Lola smiled thinly. "You think because I lived under your roof, you raised me? Come on, Mom. I raised myself. Nobody ever looked out for me but me."

Dina suddenly and visibly shook with anger. "How can you say that? I worked here day after day to put food in your mouth." She slammed both fists on the tabletop. "I did that for you! I sacrificed my life *for a child I didn't even want."*

Lola barely flinched. That Dina hadn't wanted her was no secret. "Think what you like," Lola said, standing. "I'm not quitting."

"Then don't come back home when it blows up in your face. I won't watch you do this to yourself."

Lola left without looking back.

She'd said she'd done it for money, but it'd been more than that. Lola had not only loved to dance, she'd loved how it'd made her feel, how men had looked at her, how the money had put her in charge of her life. It gave her control, especially over men, something her dad had taken from her by walking out one morning and never coming home.

Beau watched her intently. She wasn't willing to share that part of her life with him, and she wouldn't give him the satisfaction of a reaction. She walked right by him, by the bouncer and into the club.

The music hit Lola before anything. On the main stage of the dark club was a half-naked woman who looked in her early forties. On her palms and knees, she snaked toward an outstretched, dollar-waving hand.

Across the room, Beau talked to a bartender. Even though it'd been eight years since she'd left, Lola turned away in case anyone she knew still worked there.

A few moments later, Beau closed in on her back. "It's not top-dollar bourbon," he said, reaching around to hold the glass in front of her, "but it'll do."

She stared at the drink but didn't take it.

"What do you think of her?" he asked about the woman on the main stage. "Personally, she's not my type. She wouldn't get any of my dollars. Not like you."

Lola turned her head from the woman. "It doesn't do anything for me," Lola said. "I think we should go."

Beau took her chin with his other hand and forced her to look back at the stage. "We're not going anywhere. Does this make you hot?"

She wrestled her face away. "No."

"It will," he said. "Come with me."

Chapter Ten

Lights lasered through the dark strip club in every direction. Women danced on small podiums set apart from the main stage. The music was loud, but Lola wished it were deafening so she wouldn't have to hear her thoughts. She'd gone from a prize on Beau's arm to trailing behind him with her head down to hide her face.

She'd danced for men like Beau before, men who liked to flaunt that they had money to burn. She'd been most careful around that type. When she danced, music lived in her. It was intoxicating. Men could tell, and it was dangerous for them to believe they had that kind of effect on a woman.

Beau led her down a hallway of doors. If one was open, the lights were on, and it was chipped-paint black inside with just a pole and some scattered chairs.

He stopped at the last room. "Here we are, my queen."

"Why are we here?" She controlled the impulse to fidget by crossing her arms.

Beau gestured inside. "Go on. I warned you not everything would be comfortable."

It was the VIP room. The round stage, centered in a round room, ensured a view from every angle. One pole cut through the middle. Red velvet walls bled into Bordeaux-colored sofas that lined the space. The bass of the music from the main stage thumped through the room.

Lola looked over her shoulder. A woman in only a

shiny gold thong and pasties over her nipples came in. Numerous metallic ribbons threaded her hair. She trailed a finger down Beau's shoulder. "Good evening, sir," she said. "I'm Golden."

"And I'm Angel." Another woman stepped into the room. Her fur-lined, white baby-doll negligee matched her G-string. She placed a headband with red horns over her blonde hair. "Or Devil," she said pleasantly. "Your choice." Lola didn't recognize either of them.

Beau crossed the room and fell into a sofa. He tugged on his collar a little. Golden pushed some buttons on a keypad and the room changed to fiery pink as the music started. A spotlight shone over the stage.

Angel danced first. Beau watched her spin around the pole, her negligee billowing to reveal a flat stomach. She landed with ease on towering heels and smiled at him. He remained impassive.

The lights changed from pink to deep purple. Golden sat next to Beau and whispered in his ear. He nodded. Lola stood motionless while Golden straddled Beau, hovering her lips above his as she danced for him. The room was blue now, turning the red velvet a blood-black color. Beau looked past Golden to Angel when she bent, touched her toes and displayed her barely-there underwear for him. His eyes shifted to Lola. "Join me."

She shook her head. Watching him with another woman did nothing for her except spark some disappointment. It hadn't occurred to her that he might involve anyone else in their evening.

"It's not a request," he said.

Lola went to sit by him. Golden's breasts nearly touched his cheek with each movement.

"Are you enjoying this?" he asked.

"Why would you pay for an evening with me just to watch them?"

"I'm still with you." He leaned over and kissed her harder than he had earlier. When she jerked back, he reached up to keep her there. His lips and hand were warm. Pulling away had been instinct, but they'd be doing far more soon. Her jaw and shoulders relaxed. For now, it was just a kiss.

"It's sweet," he whispered into her mouth, "the taste of your submission." He pecked her again and looked up. "Touch her."

Lola had momentarily forgotten about the other women. Golden's fingers were soft as she combed Lola's hair away from her face.

"Have you ever been with a woman?" Beau asked.

"Once. To try."

"Did you enjoy it?"

"Not enough to do it again."

Golden ran a knuckle down Lola's cheek. She traced her way down the strap of Lola's dress to the neckline, but Beau grabbed her wrist. "Wait."

She dropped her arm to her side. Angel worked the pole, sliding over it as if it were silk against her skin, possessing it with her legs and hands. The white fabric of her top shone under the spotlight as she peeled it off. She stopped there. The topless-only rule hadn't changed since Lola's time there.

"Kiss," Beau said.

Lola snapped her head back to Beau. He was watching her, not Angel. The room became hotter. He nodded once. Golden leaned over and put her mouth to

Lola's. Gently, she ran her tongue along Lola's bottom lip.

Lola backed away a little. Beau had left the taste of liquor in her mouth. The woman's cherry lip balm would replace it. Any other night she might've preferred the cherry, but tonight she wanted Beau's bitter flavor. Golden chased her down for another kiss as she felt Lola's breast through her dress. Lola shut her eyes briefly and gave into the shameful desire that it was actually Beau touching her.

"Beau," Lola moaned, not because she enjoyed it, but because she didn't.

"Tell me what you want, sweetheart," he said.

Golden tweaked Lola's nipples into hardening.

"If you don't like it," he said, "just say so."

"I don't like it."

"Enough," Beau said. Golden pulled away, obviously confused.

"Now you, Lola," he said when the song changed. He signaled Angel to get down.

"But—"

"It's not up for discussion."

"Ask them to leave," Lola said. "If I dance, it's only for you."

Beau's lids lowered a little, but he blinked suddenly and the lusty look was gone. "How many times do I need to ask before you do what I say? Hmm? You challenge me at every turn. Get up on the stage and dance."

She stood.

"Now tell me why you're doing this," he said.

She opened her mouth, breathed softly. With the

hardness in his voice, her determination not to enjoy herself slipped. He already had all the power, but he wanted more. With each passing hour, he pushed the limits of her submission. Not even Johnny held that kind of complete control over her.

"Why?" he repeated.

"Because you told me to."

"Very good."

She climbed onto the platform. The spotlight and room had turned red.

"You get paid either way," Beau said. "So try to enjoy it."

With one hand around the pole, Lola circled the stage. The gown would inhibit her, but she got the feeling Beau wouldn't mind. The music was fast. She found a slower beat within it. She jumped, grabbed on and spun with one leg partially hooked around the pole. Angel and Golden sat on both sides of Beau. He was unblinking, unwavering in his attention. Even in the red haze, she saw the gleam in his eyes, the black shape of his bowtie. Her body rattled like a speaker with the music's bass.

Facing Beau, she raised her arms behind her. She snaked down the metal, cool through the back of her dress, and back up. Beau stood suddenly and walked to the base of the stage. He took her calf and pressed his lips to the inside of her knee. His mouth left wet spots on her dress as he kissed up her thigh to her hip. He gripped her, nuzzling the fabric between her legs.

Lola's breaths swelled from her stomach. She felt him—felt him *there*—acutely for the first time. God, it was unfair. He'd barely touched her and her will to fight him dissolved in seconds. She put one hand in his hair and pulled it with all the betrayal, shame and arousal she felt.

He looked up at her.

"Touching's not permitted in here," she said.

His smile was more than just crooked and sexy. For all her effort to hide, that smile told her he knew he had her. He turned and cleared both women from the room with a word.

He backed away to the sofa, and this time, Lola went to him. She pulled her dress up around her thighs. One knee went outside his hip and one stayed between his legs. She held on to the cushion behind his head. She was careful not to touch him as she danced over his lap, but now and then her skin would brush against the fabric of his tuxedo pants. When he looked as though he might touch her, she got up, pushed his knees apart. She let her hands wander over her body as she swayed her hips. She dipped a hand between her legs and slid the other up her neck.

Beau reached for her, but she stepped back and shook her head. "You can't—"

"Come back here." His level tone left no room for play. "Don't deny me when I'm like this."

When she was back at his knees, he took her wrist in one hand. "Kneel."

She got on the floor.

"You're all red," he said.

"It's the lighting."

"No, it isn't. You're hot." He let go of her and pressed his cold tumbler to the side of her neck. She sucked in a breath with the chill. Condensation trickled between her breasts. He lifted the glass to her lips. She tilted her head back and let the liquor run down her throat.

He set the drink aside and nodded at his lap. "Take it out," he said quietly.

This was it. This was why she was here. She had wondered several times what exactly lay under his suit, what was the source of his unshakeable confidence—now she would know for sure. Hold it in her hand.

Her fingers were slow and shaky as she undid his fly. He lifted his hips for her to pull his pants down. Through his underwear, she pressed her palm against the bulging outline of him. His head fell back. She lifted the ends of his dress shirt, dragging her fingertips up the hard crevices of his stomach. His body expanded with each breath.

"Don't tease me, Lola," he said. "I want your red lips on me."

There was new desperation in his voice that made Lola ache badly for him. And this deal—this promise—she'd already made it. Johnny, even, had made it. So she put a bullet through her guilt and gave Beau what he wanted.

She pulled him out, looking into his eyes while she took him in her mouth. He fisted her hair, then stroked it, then pulled it again. He thrust up, hitting the back of her throat. She tried to taste even more, wanting him deeper, wanting him to the last inch, but still he was too much, every bit as big and daunting as she'd suspected.

"Your mouth alone could ruin me." She paused, unsure how he'd meant that, but he kept her going with a hand on her head. "Don't stop," he said. "I want to be ruined."

With her tongue, she traced him—the ridge of his head, the veins of his thick shaft.

"You're driving me to the edge," he said. "I don't know whether to come, or bend you over and finally take you."

She became ravenous from his rumbling, suggestive words. He responded, pushing her down so he was crammed to her throat with every bob of her head. Her underwear dampened with the way he thoroughly fucked her mouth. With both his hands tight in her hair, he came. She gripped the red velvet cushion and swallowed everything.

There was calm in the eye of the chaos, in the labored breaths, the pounding music, the room, which had turned pink again sometime during it all. But while they looked at each other, anything else, including the regret she thought she should feel, faded into the background.

On impulse, Lola stretched up and kissed him on the mouth. He wouldn't lower his head to meet her or move his arms from his sides. She pressed her hands down on his thighs, her breasts into his wall of a chest. His body breathed beneath her.

"How'd you know?" she asked. "How did you know I'd react like this?"

He seemed to stiffen under her. "It's not even midnight," he said. "We aren't finished."

"I know."

He touched her cheek with his whole palm. "You're burning up."

She bit her lip. She could feel it too. "It's a good

thing."

He helped her to her feet, and they left the room while it was blue.

"You're supposed to tip them," Lola remembered once they were outside again.

"It's taken care of. They won't be millionaires after this, but they've been well compensated."

"Millionaire," she repeated to herself. She still couldn't wrap her head around it, and it'd be a while before she could. After tonight, she'd be a millionaire and all this would be over. The thought didn't give her as much comfort as it once had.

◆⊠◆⊠◆

In the car, driving down Sunset at a much easier speed, Beau asked Lola what she planned to do with the money.

"You already know," she answered. "We're buying Hey Joe."

"I know what *he* wants. But what about you? You're the one doing all the work."

Lola balked. "It makes me feel cheap when you say that."

"Believe me, sweetheart. You aren't cheap."

She shook her head and sighed up at the Lamborghini's roof. "I want us to be happy and have a shot at a real future."

"But what do you want for yourself?"

"That's what I want. Making Johnny happy makes me happy."

"Fine. Everybody's happy. Now give me something real. A new car? A trip to New York City? What're you going to do for yourself?"

"To tell you the truth, I haven't given it much thought. I'm okay with what I've got."

"Slinging drinks is what you want to do forever? Haven't you ever asked yourself what you'd do if money weren't an issue? You have some freedom now."

"Not until the sun comes up," Lola said.

Beau scoffed. "I'm glad to see one blowjob hasn't killed your spirit."

What a blowjob it'd been. Lola was incredibly turned on, and she'd barely even been touched. She made an effort to control herself, even though she squirmed in her seat a little. "What do you want me to say? That I love to paint landscapes, or I've always dreamed of backpacking through Europe? I don't and I haven't. Not everyone has hobbies or dreams. That's not the kind of life I live."

Beau slammed on the brakes. The car behind them swerved and honked. "So tell me what kind of life you live."

"What are you doing?" Lola asked. "You can't just stop in the middle of the road."

"Conventional methods aren't working," he said. "I don't want platitudes. Just give me a real answer."

"Are you drunk?" Lola asked. "You're drunk, aren't you?"

"I didn't even finish my drink. I want to know more about the girl I played darts with. Who you are when he's not around."

Lola shook her head. "You're getting sentimental on me just because I let you come in my mouth?"

Beau barked a laugh. "Can you blame me? You're so charming."

She smiled through the honking of passing cars. "You're really going to stay here?"

He nodded. "Here's an easier question. Tell me something you *don't* want out of life."

She squinted through the windshield. It was an easier question, and even though she'd never articulated it, the answer didn't come with difficultly. "I don't want Johnny to lose his sense of self-worth along with the bar. I was afraid if he didn't have Hey Joe, he'd have to start over somewhere else, and he'd feel like he'd failed."

"Failure's good for us, you know."

She looked over at him. "Are you saying I shouldn't have taken the deal?"

"I'm saying you can't be the sacrifice for the fulfillment of his dreams." He took his foot off the brake and resumed driving. "When he asked what you wanted to do with the money, what'd you say?"

Lola chewed the inside of her cheek. She wasn't sure Johnny *had* asked. There'd never been any other option. She was using the money to keep them intact. Johnny knew the ins and outs of Hey Joe. He was master of that domain. Maybe it wasn't her dream job, but she'd never had a dream job—so she wasn't losing anything. "You've made your point."

"You need to figure out what you want," he said. "Not what you want *for him*. Then you need to tell him."

"I don't know if you're right," she said, "but you might not be wrong."

He pulsed his eyebrows at her once. "That's a start. So what would it take to get you to figure it out?"

They happened to be in a familiar part of town. Giving in to Beau had loosened her up a bit, and he was working hard to shine his spotlight on her, so she decided to help him out by moving under it a little more. "How about a trip down memory lane?"

"What'd you have in mind?" he asked right away.

She pointed in front of them. "Take a right up here." After only a few minutes of driving, she told him to park at a curb. "See that place?" she asked, nodding through the window.

"The Lucky Egg," Beau read the flickering sign off the corner diner.

"When I was a kid, my mom worked there. Days *and* nights. The life of a single mom."

"Where was your dad?"

"Gone. I don't have a lot of memories of him. I remember weird things, though, like the smell of his shampoo when he'd pick me up before leaving for work, or the time he kissed my elbow after I'd fallen climbing a tree in the backyard. Then it was just me and her."

"Have you seen him since?"

"No. If he'd come back, I think my mom would've killed him. She got so angry after he left. It flipped a switch in her. They married right out of high school, so she'd never been on her own. She thought we were going to lose the house, or they were going to take our car. She'd get really rundown from working so much."

"Sounds the opposite of my mom. When my dad died, she became helpless. I kept waiting for that maternal survival instinct to kick in, but it didn't."

"I don't even think it was maternal instinct for my mom. She just saw me as this little person who drained her meager bank account. Around seventeen, I moved in with some older kids. We partied a lot. The first night I went to Hey Joe, Johnny should've kicked me out because I was underage. Guess he took pity on me, though. He gave me a tequila shot instead."

"Or he was trying to get in your pants."

Lola shook her head. "We didn't start sleeping together for a while, actually. And when we did, I didn't take it seriously until he broke up with me."

"I see. Obviously that didn't last."

Lola kept her eyes out the window. "He was sick of me screwing around. He gave me an ultimatum—grow up or get out. Quit the drugs, the partying, the—" She paused. "He saved me. Turned my life around. If not for him, I don't know where I'd be."

"You should give yourself more credit. You're a fighter. That much is obvious."

She finally looked at Beau. "If you're fighting against the wrong thing, the only person you'll hurt is yourself." The digital clock on the dashboard changed. "I'm sure this isn't how you want to spend your precious few hours," she added.

He looked at the clock too, then out the windshield. He turned the car around. "What happened to your mom?" he asked.

"Oh, she still works there." Lola turned her face away when he peered at her.

They didn't speak again until they were on Santa Monica Boulevard. "How many women have you done this with?" Lola asked.

"None."

"You expect me to believe that?"

"Why would I lie?"

"To seem like less of an asshole."

Beau chuckled. "What does it matter if you think I'm an asshole? I already got you here. If you don't like me by the time we're done, it's all the same to me."

Her eyes drifted to the clock again. She assumed they were now going to the hotel, but she didn't ask. Beau had his own agenda. "If you don't care either way, then I could be anyone."

"That's not true at all." He sighed and shifted in his seat. "I've met a lot of women over the years. All kinds—blonde, brunette, athletic, short, sweet, married, single. Something's different about you, Lola."

Lola didn't think of herself as the same as or different from anyone. But she could guess the things she was compared to Beau's usual women. For one, she didn't go for bullshit, but his world turned for it.

"Something's different about you too," she admitted. Lola wasn't proud that she'd pegged Beau as another corporate asshole during their first meeting on the sidewalk. He'd proved her wrong during their darts game, but that'd only lasted until his proposition. Then he'd been worse than an asshole in her eyes. She worried he was proving her wrong again. That would make the evening entirely different. The Beau she'd agreed to spend the night with was the repugnant one who'd offered money for her body—not the sexy one she'd known before that.

"It's always been my opinion that different is good," he said. "I hope you agree."

"You know, you aren't the first man to try and sleep with me behind Johnny's back."

"Did you?" Beau asked.

"Did I what?"

"Sleep with them."

"No," Lola said emphatically.

"Good." He hit his blinker and slowed for a light. "I don't like cheating. It's for people who don't think they can win. If you don't believe in yourself enough to play by the rules, you aren't worthy of the prize."

"Are we still talking about sex?"

"Cheating is always weak, no matter the circumstances."

"Beau, some people—lots of people—might call *this* cheating."

"I don't. And I didn't try to sleep with you behind his back like you said. It all happened in front of his face. Johnny's aware of everything. He had his chance to put a stop to it."

"Have you ever turned down a million dollars?" Lola asked wryly. Beau had been desperate before. Had he already forgotten how that felt?

"Sure I have," he said. "When the company on the table was worth more."

"I'm not talking about business, Beau. We're people. I'm talking about lives."

He didn't speak. Money, sex, worth, people—it all shaded into a gray area for them. Had anyone asked her before all this, she would've answered that a dollar amount couldn't be put on a person's life. She still believed that, but the concepts were no longer completely unrelated in her mind.

"Let's not argue about it," Beau said, sighing again. Ahead, they were entering Beverly Hills. "I don't want you wasting any more energy. You're going to need it soon."

Chapter Eleven

On the sixteenth floor of the Four Seasons Los Angeles at Beverly Hills, Beau and Lola exited a gold elevator. They'd been quiet since the car. To their left, a large window showcased the dark sky and the faint silhouette of mountains on the horizon. She followed him the opposite direction past the elevator bank to a hallway. At the end of it was a single black-lacquer door with a knob in the center. The corridor was long and carpeted, muting their steps. As they approached the door, her heart beat faster. It'd been nine years since she'd been with a man other than Johnny. And about that long since she'd wanted to.

When they reached the door, Beau pulled out his key and unlocked it with a *click*.

Lola's stomach was beyond butterflies—she was sure an entire zoo had been released inside her. She stared at the doorway, which was a threshold, a point of no return, a choice plain and simple. Sweat beaded on her upper lip.

"It's too late to turn back now," Beau said.

She didn't look away. "Not if I give back the money."

Beau let the door close. "I know what you're doing." He walked to her, his steps deliberate. "If I force you into that room, then it isn't your choice."

"Nobody forced me here," she said. "I made every decision. I had to. That doesn't make my choices right."

"Lola," he said softly. "You don't have to put on a

show. Tonight is about you and me only. Take control of what you want."

She glanced up at him. "You think you know what I want?"

He moved forward until the wall was at her back. He pushed a hand in the neckline of her dress. "You're right," he said. "I have no idea what you want. Since your nipple isn't hard between my fingers. And you weren't wet earlier as you sucked me off."

"Just because you manipulate my body's reaction," her voice wavered, "doesn't mean I want this. You can't control my mind or my heart no matter what you say."

His hand stilled. The muscles in his jaw flexed. "You're so fucking concerned about your heart? Keep it. I'll use your body. I won't be gentle. And when I'm finished, you can have it back."

He could take what he wanted. It wouldn't mean anything to her. It shouldn't. But his words were even more erotic than his touch. Her legs trembled from them, threatening to give out.

Lola tried to push him off, but he grabbed her wrist with his free hand and pinned it above her head. "This is what you want, isn't it?" he asked. "For me to take your choice away? Then no one will have to know that you want this just as badly as I do. That you wanted it the night we met."

She shook her head rapidly. His nearness smothered whatever sense she had left. She was becoming the puddle of desire she'd been at the strip club.

"Let me help you out," he said when she didn't speak. "You say, 'Yes, Beau.' Then I open the hotel room door. And every time I tell you what to do, you say…"

She fixated on his bowtie, breathing hard.

"I'm sorry, I didn't catch that. Can you speak up?" he asked.

She looked up at the sharpness of his tone. "Yes. Yes, Beau."

"Good." He released her and backed away. He opened the door again. The ghost of his grip pulsed around her wrist. "Ask yourself this," he said. "Do you have to want this to do it? Or are you going to do it anyway?"

She looked between him and the door. She was going to do it anyway. The decision shed a layer of resistance she'd been hiding behind. She entered the suite, where the only light came from the distant cityscape.

"Wait here until I call for you," Beau said.

She didn't move. Her nerves melted away. She was in Beau's hands now and if the past few hours were any indication, it would be an experience she'd never forget.

Glass clinked. The faucet ran. After minutes had passed, Beau spoke from somewhere in the suite. "Come to the bedroom."

"I don't know which way," she said. Directly in front of her was a piano and windowed door that led out to the balcony.

"You'll find me," he said. "And you'll do it on your hands and knees."

Her dry throat protested when she swallowed.

That a tyrant in everything else would also be a tyrant in the bedroom didn't surprise her—that there would be a show of strength, a struggle of wills, an expected submission—she might have guessed. But knowing and doing were two different things. She'd never lived it. She knew girls from the club who had. Some liked it, some didn't. For most, it wasn't that simple.

Lola sank to her hands and knees faster than she would've thought. The tile was hard underneath her, but she was on the carpet soon. The dress caught between her legs while she crawled, slowing her down. Beau didn't rush her. She went the opposite direction of a flat screen TV, past a round dining table with several chairs. As she got closer, warmer, her breath came faster and her legs seemed heavier—the tender place between them, specifically.

She found Beau on the edge of the bed, still fully dressed except for his jacket.

"Don't stop now," he said. "You're almost here."

She didn't remember ever crawling one day of her adult life. Inside she screamed at herself to get off the floor, but she closed her eyes, inhaled and quieted it. This wasn't about her.

Or was it? Beau had unusual power over her. She'd never been put in this position while someone else watched, nor did she think she'd allow it from anyone else, even with the money. She was still dressed, but she felt stripped and exposed. Crawling for him was a form of intimacy. She opened her eyes.

"Your struggle is a thing to watch," Beau said just loud enough for her to hear. "If I thought you'd respond honestly, I'd ask you how it feels to submit."

"It hurts my knees."

A corner of his mouth lifted. "Maybe you can give me something less tactile."

"I feel…helpless." Vulnerability was rare for her. She'd learned young that it didn't pay to be vulnerable. But with her helplessness came a relief that left her confused. She had no responsibility other than giving Beau what he asked for. No other choice. And it wasn't a bad thing. "That's what you want, isn't it?" she asked. "Me, helpless?"

"Don't tell me what you think I want to hear. You can tell me if you hate being on your hands and knees. Maybe I'll let you stand."

She stared at him, unmoving. He was going to make her say that she liked this out loud or he would take it away. She should've been thankful, but letting her stand felt like a punishment.

"Lola," he said. "Everything between us lives and dies in this room. It's safe."

Her fingers curled into the carpet, but not with frustration. The slow throb between her legs was stronger. Could Beau see it? Smell it? He looked as if he knew. "I don't."

"Don't what?"

"Hate it." She couldn't say much more without giving herself away. However gone she was, there was still a shred of Johnny in her she couldn't bring herself to betray. "You make it not repulsive."

"Well, not repulsive is something." There was such approval in his smile that she flushed. "But it'll be hard to do anything to you when you're so far away."

She finished crossing the room until she was at his feet.

He removed one cufflink, set it on the nightstand, then the other. Lola's heart beat between her breasts. Beau rolled up one sleeve, stood and leaned over her. He gathered up her dress and pulled it over her hips. He hiked up the panties he'd bought her, wedging them between her ass cheeks. His firm hand ran soothingly over her backside as if she were a treasured plaything. She bit her lip to keep any sounds inside.

"I'm going to take you apart," he said. "Find out what makes you feel so good it almost kills you."

"Don't."

He stroked her skin until he brushed a spot that made her jolt. He made a deep, rumbling noise from his chest. "Then I'll bring you back to life. Put you back together."

"Don't do it like this," she said. "Just use me and throw me out. I'm begging you."

"Let's see how deep your protest goes." He slid a fingertip under the elastic of her panties. "Mmm. Just as I suspected."

"What?" she breathed.

"You waxed. There's a chink in her armor."

"I didn't do it for you."

"Of course not." His hand grazed down one thigh to the top of her stocking and up again. "And your legs are shaved. I suppose that's not for me either."

She began to tremble lightly, alive with him so close to giving her what she'd been needing since the strip club—or longer. He circled her with two fingers and eased them in.

Her head bowed to meet the floor. She gasped when he went deeper. He murmured her name, moving in and out. Searching. At least the tile would've been cool against her face.

"Look at me."

She lifted her head.

"Make yourself wet," he said as he removed his hand and put two fingers to her lips. She opened, sucking him into her mouth and tasting herself on someone else's fingers for the first time.

He replaced them between her legs and leaned in to kiss her while rubbing her slippery clit from behind. When she convulsed and moaned, he took his hand away.

"Why are you stopping?" she demanded through the ringing in her ears.

"There's someone at the door. Would you mind?"

"What?" she asked.

"Answer the door."

She got up from her aching knees and wrists. Her dress fell around her legs. The heat in her chest and face pulsed with every punch of her heart.

It was room service. A young man wheeled a food cart into the living room, glancing at Lola from the corner of his eye. He positioned the cart and waited.

"One minute," she said.

She went to the bedroom. Beau was standing in the same spot, one sleeve rolled up and his hand splayed. "Yes?" he asked.

"It's room service. He brought food."

"And?"

"And…he needs his tip."

"So give it to him."

"You took my purse." She crossed her arms. "I

have no money."

"Ah." He smiled and pulled his wallet from his pants. "Have him bring it in here."

"Bring it in here," she called without uncrossing her arms or looking away from Beau.

Beau blew out a laugh, shaking his head. "I suppose I could've done that."

When the cart was where Beau wanted it, the attendant took his tip, ducked his head and left.

Beau picked up a bowl. Before he could ask, she went to him. "Strawberries," she said. "Not very original."

"I'm not very original."

She picked one out of the bowl. He caught her wrist on the way to her mouth. She raised her eyes to him.

"Aren't you going to share?" he asked.

She lifted it to him. His teeth bit down just before her fingertips. He had a sexy mouth made for eating strawberries—and other things. She also took a bite and dropped the stem in the bowl. They had two more this way—him holding her, feeding him, feeding her.

He let go of her arm to pour them each some champagne.

"We're around the halfway point," Lola said, her mouth fizzing as she took a sip. "You're running out of time."

"We'll get to that." He took the champagne glass from her and set it down. "Hold your hands behind you."

She laced her fingers at the small of her back, jutting her breasts forward. Beau scooped whipped cream from the bowl with two fingers. He touched them to her closed lips. "How's it taste?"

She tested it with her tongue. "Light. Sweet."

"Have more," he suggested throatily.

She closed her mouth around his fingers and sucked him clean. "It's good," she said. There was grit in both their voices. "You should try it."

"I think I will." He smeared some whipped cream on the skin above her neckline. He took his time cleaning it off with his tongue, no matter how fast her breasts rose and fell.

He slipped one strap off her shoulder. "Keep your hands there," he said when she moved. He released the dress to her waist, trapping her arms with the straps. He took both breasts in his hands through her corset. She gasped up at the ceiling when he squeezed them.

"You like it a little rough," he said.

"I don't know."

"You'll know after tonight."

She swallowed, still looking up. "You said you wouldn't hurt me."

"I'll fuck you within an inch of your life, but it won't hurt. It will calm you. Your only job is to do what I say. And, of course, enjoy yourself."

He still had her breasts in a firm grip. It wasn't enough without his skin on hers, and she arched into his hands. "What if I don't like it rough?"

He let go. "Tell me now. I can do it in a way that you think we're making love."

Her face fell. "I don't want to make love."

"How does Johnny do it?"

For a second, she thought she'd misheard him. "I'm

not talking to you about—"

"Don't protect him," Beau said. "He didn't protect you."

Her heart panged sharply. With her body in Beau's control and her mind out of focus, she was in no shape to dig in to that statement. "He's never been anything but Johnny with me," she said. "It's nice."

"Then I don't want to be nice." He pinched her nipple unexpectedly, and she inhaled sharply. He massaged it. "But I won't be mean, either."

"Thank you," she said.

He trussed one breast up and bent his head. "You are welcome, *ma chatte*." He sucked her nipple into his mouth, soaking the fabric around it.

"What does that mean?" she asked breathlessly.

He tugged her nipple between his teeth, and the pinch traveled down her body, ending between her legs. She released her hands when he yanked the dress over her hips. It puddled at her feet.

"It means," he said, and touched her boldly through her lace underwear, "this is mine."

"Only for a few more hours." As the inevitable loomed, her arousal was finally overtaking her determination not to give in. "Tick tock."

He raised an eyebrow at her. "Brave girl. Touch yourself with me." She reached into her underwear. He closed his warm hand around hers, guiding it along her.

He put his other hand to the front of his pants, massaging himself. "Tomorrow," he said, "you'll be home, and you'll think of this. How I feel against you. How we feel together."

She raised her chin. "Maybe."

His eyebrows rose even higher. "Maybe?"

"So far you haven't given me much to think about. Frankly, I'm not sure you have the guts."

"Excuse me?"

"You talk and talk, but here I am. You've barely touched me."

One corner of his mouth lifted. It was somehow both menacing and suggestive, and it dried her throat. He grabbed her shoulders in a flash, spun her to face the bed and pulled her back to his front. "Feel that, pussycat?" he asked, thrusting his erection into her lower back. He pushed her and she caught herself on the mattress. "Bend over," he said. "Put your arms out to your sides."

With her cheek against the bed, she stretched out and took two fistfuls of comforter. Her shoes propped her ass in the air at an uncomfortable angle, so she moved to take them off.

"Leave them," he said. "Lines you right up for my cock."

Her fists tightened. She wanted to turn around and watch him undress. Was his suit the source of his power? In her imagination, it wasn't—he was just as commanding with nothing between them except his hard-on.

He stripped her underwear down to her ankles. "You have no idea how hot you are in your black stockings." His zipper hissed. "Tell me you want it, Lola."

"I can't."

"Why not?"

"It's one thing to do it. It's another to want it."

"You'd walk away right now if I let you?"

She squeezed her eyes closed. She couldn't picture Johnny no matter how hard she tried, through the haze, through her heartbeat pounding in her brain. Beau's skin was warm against the backs of her thighs. He nudged himself between her legs.

"Answer me," he said. "Your secret stays here."

She was unraveling on the inside. Her nerves were surfacing—exposed and sensitive. Her mouth and her pussy were already slick. "I want it," she whispered.

"What do you want?"

"You. I want to feel you inside me."

He slid his crown up and down her slit. "Stay very still." He worked his way in, slow with every inch. It made him feel impossibly big. The comforter sucked into her open mouth when she gasped. She bit down on it. He placed his hands on the bed around her and his mouth at her ear. "You're so fucking beautiful in this position," he said. His chest pinned her down. "No escape, feeling every single movement between us." His voice vibrated against her back. He was still sinking himself in with extraordinary patience. He kissed her cheek and the corner of her mouth. "I want to hear you."

She moaned when she said, "Yes, Beau."

"Louder." He thrust in to the base, and she cried out. "Like that," he muttered into her hair, littering kisses there. "Just like that, Lola." He said her name with such affection that she momentarily forgot how he was overcoming her. He undid the hooks of her corset, one at a time down her spine. He opened it, smoothing his wide, rough hands over her skin.

"I want it, Beau," she said. "Don't make me wait anymore."

He cleared the hair from her back and buried his face into the crook of her neck. He moved in and out of her slowly. "This is for you," he said.

Everything in her was building, rioting, begging for it. His rhythm never broke, and each stroke of his cock inside her was deliberate. It had such certain purpose—break her piece by piece.

His breath stuttered against her while whispering how soft, hot, pliant she was. Each word from his mouth was sharper than the last until finally he said, "Now it's for me."

He pounded into her, pulling her head back by her hair until her roots screamed. His lips stubbornly attached to hers from the side as he took her mouth. His other arm wrapped around her shoulders and he became even more merciless until—

"Don't stop," she almost sobbed when he pulled out.

"Turn over."

She flipped onto her back. He towered over her, a force of strength and power. There was no vulnerability in his nakedness. Her shoes were tossed aside. He rounded the bed to the other side as she watched with her head tilted back. He slid her across the mattress by her armpits until her head hung over the edge.

"Is your mouth as hot as your pussy?" he asked, cupping his hands under her head.

She opened immediately for him. He fed her firmly but gently, his forearms flexing as he maintained control, then tightening as he lost it and thrust all the way in. She could only leave her mouth open for his use and hang onto the bedspread as she writhed with the need to come. He pulled out and pushed her breasts together, squeezing his cock between them and fucking her that way.

"Is there any part of you that isn't perfect?" He slipped against her skin easily, wet from her saliva. "You fit right into my hands." He pressed her into the bed as he went harder. "If I'm not careful, I'll come all over you. Would you like that?"

"Yes, Beau," she said.

"Christ, you're sweet." He released her. "Get up. Tell me what you want."

She climbed off the bed and stood in nothing but her stockings. Her clit radiated heat, burning her up from the inside out. "I just want to come," she said shakily.

"There are lots of ways to get there, though," he said, stroking himself as he looked at her. "If you want me to decide, I will."

She nodded hard. "I'm yours."

"Hmm." He circled around her, stopping at her back. He wedged his fingers against her asshole. "I could finish you this way. Have you ever come with a dick in your ass?"

"No," she rasped.

If ever there were a moment she would agree to it, it would be that one, but he let go and said, "I'm far too impatient to break you in right now."

"I want to see your face when you come," she said.

He wrapped his arms around her from behind and kissed her neck. "Then ride me," he said into her ear.

She turned in his arms and pushed his chest. He sat back on the bed. She put her knees on both sides of his hips and held him with one hand as she sank down. "How's that?" she asked coyly.

"You're too far," he groaned.

"I'm as close as I can get."

"No, you aren't."

She bent forward and put her lips to his, creating a curtain around them with her hair. He angled up to kiss her. She circled her hips over him. Their mouths became hungrier, and he sat up to bury both his hands in her hair.

"Not a day's gone by these past two weeks that I didn't imagine your legs around me," he said.

She lifted herself up to free her legs and wrap them around his back. With her arms circling his neck, she was as close as she could get.

"Dance for me," he said.

"I already did. Now I'm fucking you."

He released her head to clutch her hips and slow her rhythm. "Like this," he muttered. "Dance for me, with me, around me. But do it slow. Savor what you devour."

He slid his hands to the center of her back and pushed her breast into his mouth. He moved from one nipple to the other, sucking on her as she danced herself into a fiery orgasm that consumed everything in its path.

He flipped her onto her back and took what he needed as she tried to keep up with every overwhelming sensation. His muscular arms propped him up, the tendons in his neck strained, his eyes stayed on her bouncing tits until finally he slammed one, two, three times and came deep inside her.

Lola was slick everywhere. She couldn't take her eyes off him as their bodies heaved. A sweat rivulet trickled down his temple onto her stomach. He held himself up with one hand and put the other just above her mound. He circled his thumb once over her pulsating clit. "I want to feel you clench around me again, nice and slow this time."

Her back arched from the mattress. "Ah," she breathed. She was sensitive, but he was gentle—until she was so hungry for her orgasm that she needed it a little harder. She raised her hips, and he increased his pressure, using only his thumb as the rest of his fingers splayed and pressed down on her lower stomach.

He slid in and out of her only a little. "Just to feel my cum inside you," he said lustily. His heavy-lidded eyes didn't leave her face. She tried to tell him it was the most erotic moment of her life, but her words came out as gasps. His arm began to shake from holding himself up, but he didn't stop. Her orgasm seemed to return rather than start again. It roiled through her, slower, deeper, with her hanging onto his cock in a way that made him moan along with her.

His arm gave out, and he collapsed over her. He nuzzled into her neck, kissed her hairline. "Salty," he murmured. "I can't wait to find out how you taste everywhere else."

Lola was ravaged. She welcomed his weight on her already sinking body. She descended limb by limb into the mattress while her mind floated into darkness. Her entire body jerked as she gasped and opened her eyes. "Oh my God," she said. "Did I fall asleep?"

He lifted his head and chuckled. "Just for a second."

"I'm sorry."

"Sorry?"

"I assumed it…wasn't allowed. Sleeping. I thought you wouldn't want to."

He kissed her forehead, her temple. "I don't," he said into her ear.

Her stomach growled.

His body shook on top of her in a silent laugh. "Hungry?"

"Any chance there's actual food on that cart?"

"I can order up something."

"It has to be two in the morning by now."

"For what I'm paying a night, they'll bring us food at any time."

"Mind if I shower while we wait?" she asked.

"I mind."

She wrinkled her nose. "But I'm—"

"Exactly how I want you," he finished. He pulled out from between her legs and fell back on the bed. She turned onto her side. He wrapped one arm around her shoulders and kept her close as he reached for the phone and pulled it to his ear.

"I'd like to order breakfast," he said and paused. "I don't care what time it starts. Send up whatever you have. Omelets, bacon, croissants, orange juice."

"French toast," Lola whispered.

He pulled the phone away. "What?"

"French toast," she said, looking back at him.

"And two orders of French toast." A beat passed before he said, "Well, perhaps tomorrow night I should find a hotel that *can*." He winked at her as he listened. "Ah, I'm so glad you'll make it work."

"Coffee," she added.

"Most importantly, I'll need some coffee too. Yes, that's fine." He hung up and hugged her from behind with both arms. "So she likes French toast."

"As a rule, anything breakfast food."

"Well. I'm glad we get to eat breakfast together." He looked down at her. "But apparently you aren't. You're frowning."

"Sorry," she said quietly.

He rubbed his stubbled chin against her neck, and she smiled. "Good thing you tickle easily."

"I do not," she said, but when he went to do it again, she wriggled in his arms and cried, "Okay, okay, I do."

"So, why the frown?" he asked.

She sighed. "Eating breakfast together almost seems…"

"Worse?" he asked.

"Sounds stupid, doesn't it?"

He leaned in and whispered, "Just think of it as fuel."

"Beau," she chastised, but she was smiling.

"All I can think of when I'm near you is how to get closer."

"You're practically on top of me. You just fucked my tits for God's sake."

He nipped her earlobe. "And you just turned me to stone again with one sentence."

"Already?" Lola asked.

"I've wasted enough time, don't you think?"

"Room service will be here any minute."

"Then we'd better be quick."

He rolled her over and lay on top of her. He swept his hands over her hairline and his lips over her nose and mouth.

"This isn't quick," Lola said, but her sentence ended in a sharp gasp.

He'd reached down and slid his fingers into her. "Just let me appreciate you. That sound you make." He kissed her neck. "The way you feel in my hand," he said against her skin. "That birthmark above your hipbone."

It seemed her mind had turned to mush—she could only answer him in moans. *But you barely know me*, she meant to say. She put her arms around his back.

"Could you see yourself with me?" he whispered, as if someone might hear. He kept stroking her.

"Don't." She closed her eyes. Her voice sounded far away. "Not right now."

"Right now," he countered. "You can't lie when I'm inside you."

When she swallowed, she did it quietly, even though Beau could see her throat. "I don't even know what you're like."

"I'll tell you. Morning is my favorite time of day because it's quiet and no one needs anything from me. So I wake up early and either use the gym or run in the Hills where I live. At work I mostly meet with investors or founders or wherever my secretary sends me. Some nights, more than I'd like, I attend events or parties. Other nights I come home and work more, which I prefer. I don't get a lot of time alone at the office."

Lola had been looking between his and his mouth

as he spoke, but her mind was spending the day with Beau. In a way, the complicated life she'd imagined he'd have was even simpler than hers. There was no emotion in his routine, and that made it too easy to stay detached.

"I could ease up on the work," he added as an afterthought. "I've just never had a reason to."

Lola dropped her gaze to his neck. That life didn't appeal to her, but Beau did. Those early-morning or late-night moments when they could intertwine like they were now. He needed that. She didn't. She already had it. Johnny and Beau were miles apart, but even so, one person's taste couldn't be so divided. *Lola* and Beau were miles apart.

"Maybe if things were different," she said. "But they're not."

"Like what? Give me one reason aside from the obvious one."

"The obvious one is a pretty big one," she said. "But okay. I sleep until around noon, so…"

He chuckled. "That's easy. Get a job with regular hours. I'd help you find the right thing. Next?"

"Next?" she asked. "That big reason. Johnny."

He tilted his head at her. "You really think he's the one you're meant to be with?"

She bit her lip when he crooked his fingers inside her and massaged. "I don't believe there's only one person out there for each of us."

"You'll change your mind when I go down on you."

She laughed breathily. "I don't even know what that means."

"It means…I'm confident we'll find that my mouth

is made for your pussy." He flashed her a smile. "You'll see. They're meant to be."

"Don't be ridiculous," she said, also grinning.

"Ah, Lola. I don't know what's better, your eyes or your smile."

"You don't have to seduce me," she said. "I'm already in your bed."

"I have to say," he pulled his fingers out and slid them all over her, "I like having you in my bed."

"It's not, though…" The ache in her built again, spurred on by his fingers. "Not your bed. Why would you stay here again tomorrow night?"

"What makes you think I am?"

"You said on the phone."

"Ah," he said. "I just like to get out of my house sometimes."

Her bullshit radar went off. It wasn't even a decent lie. "You're bringing someone else here," she guessed. The words came out sour. Not all of what they'd just done was pretty. Some of it was crude, but those were the moments Lola had submitted completely. Because nobody else could do those things to her that way and make them so good she could've screamed. Her mind flitted between the bedspread underneath her, the mouth above her, the warmth surrounding her. Could he so easily turn around and share that with someone else? She couldn't. "I don't want you to," she said abruptly and unprompted. "I don't want you to do these same things to someone else right after I was here."

"I'm not bringing anyone else here," he said, but it felt as if he was placating her. "Hey."

She'd been staring down again, avoiding him.

"Don't look like that," he said. "It's the truth."

She lifted her eyes again. She was ridiculous for letting her mind go there. It wasn't like her to act jealous. "Okay. Sorry."

"You know what I liked tonight?" he asked. "You on that stage. Asking me to send those women away. I lost it after that. God, you were sexy on that pole. Where'd you learn to dance?"

He was still coaxing her, not enough to get her off, but enough to charm words out of her. She was tempted to tell him the truth—*I used to take off my clothes for money*. There was the risk he might see her differently, though. She didn't want that for the little time they had left. "Ballet," she said.

"Ballet?"

"Classes." She moaned. "In middle school, I took a year of ballet, and we had this…this…," she swallowed, "teacher…"

"Yes?"

She breathed in and out. "I can't think when you're touching me like this."

He stopped but didn't remove his hand. "Your ballet teacher," he prompted.

"She thought I had potential. She took me under her wing. For years after, she let me attend lessons for free. Since I couldn't—Beau, this is worse. Either do it or don't."

He smiled and narrowed his eyes on her. He traced his finger along the outside of her and slipped it inside again.

"She gave me free lessons because I couldn't," her voice pitched, "afford them."

"A ballerina," he said reverentially. "So she loves to dance."

"She loves to dance." Lola nodded and cocked her head. "I think I heard something."

"Impossible," Beau said. "I just called downstairs."

There was a knock at the door. "Guess they don't have a lot of orders this time of night," she said.

"Ignore it. They'll wait."

She laughed lightly. "You practically threatened their lives if they didn't bring you your breakfast."

He sighed. "Then I guess we'll have to pick this up later." He got up and pulled on his boxer briefs. Lola unpeeled her stockings, found a robe in the bathroom, slipped into it and went out just as Beau was signing the receipt.

He shut the door and turned. "My robe on you," he said, shaking his head slowly, "an image that'll soothe me on my deathbed."

"I was indecent."

He wrapped his arms around her waist. "You were very indecent. But seeing you dressed just makes me want to undress you." He backed her up against the wall and nibbled her neck.

"The food," she said breathily but laughing.

"I'm not hungry."

"Beau," she whined.

"Ah, fuck. Fine." He released her but not before kissing her once on the lips. "First, we refuel."

Chapter Twelve

Beau moved breakfast plates from the food cart to the hotel room's dining table while Lola watched. He distributed silverware and poured them each orange juice. Seated with a napkin on his lap, he drizzled syrup onto his French toast. He cut four bite-sized squares with his fork and knife before looking up at Lola. "Lose your appetite?"

"No."

Earlier, on her way to the bathroom to change into a robe, she'd paused at the closet. Beau's suit had been hung. It'd been done haphazardly, but it was on a hanger nonetheless. There'd barely even been a moment to do it. She'd been faced away from him when he'd taken it off—had he hung it then? It was turning out that the bedroom was the only place Beau could get dirty.

Lola tended toward tidy, but not at that level. She hadn't forgotten Beau's description of his daily routine and as he took a bite of his portioned food, she envisioned him eating that way every morning, alone in a spotless kitchen.

She picked up her French toast, loaded the plate with bacon and fruit and stuck a fork between her teeth. With her other hand, she put the syrup under her arm, picked up a bowl of powdered sugar, turned and walked away.

"Where are you going?" he called after her.

"Eating in bed," she said between her teeth.

He followed her. "You'll make a mess."

She put everything down on the white comforter.

"You already got syrup on my robe," he said, pointing at the sleeve.

"So what? Don't you get maid service?"

"Well, yes. We aren't finished with the bed, though."

She forked an entire half of toast and tore off a bite with her teeth. "So we get a little sticky," she said, chewing. "A little sugary. That so bad?"

He raised both eyebrows at her.

"You ever heard of breakfast in bed?" she asked.

"I don't think this is what's meant by it."

She waved her hand. "Sure it is."

Lola didn't eat breakfast anywhere other than her kitchen, but Beau needed his boundaries pushed a little. She'd crawled on the floor for him—he could handle some unscheduled fun. She took another bite as they stared each other down. When he still hadn't moved, she hopped up on the mattress.

"Lola, what—? Watch the syrup."

"Does this bother you?" she asked, jumping once. The syrup tipped over.

He lunged forward and caught it before more than a few drops escaped. "I just don't understand why—"

She grabbed the syrup from his hands and stuck a finger in it. She glossed some over her lips. "Ready for me?" she asked.

"What—"

She threw her arms around his neck. He caught her just as her legs went around his waist. She kissed him hard on the mouth, spreading syrup all over him.

"What's gotten into you?" he asked.

He'd gotten into her. She wasn't just testing him—she was actually giddy, experiencing a second wind for the night. She licked the sauce from his upper lip. "Hmm. Interesting. There's syrup all over your face, my face, your robe, the bed. And yet, we're still standing."

"Well, *I'm* standing," he said, grinning. "You're just wrapped around me being silly."

She nodded. "Is silly okay?"

"Silly is okay."

"So then come have breakfast in bed with me."

"If you insist, though I don't really see the point."

"There's no point. This isn't a negotiation or a board meeting where there needs to be an explanation for everything. There's absolutely no fucking point at all, and that is the point."

He shook his head. "Fine. We'll eat in bed, but you'll have to get down."

"Take me with you." She twisted to set the syrup back on the bed. "You might need extra hands."

He laughed but adjusted her ass and walked them to the table. She took both glasses of orange juice while he supported her with one hand and carried his plate in the other.

When he lowered her onto the bed with one arm, the powdered sugar teetered. They looked at each other and smiled.

"I feel like a child," Beau said once they were seated and eating. "Even more like a child than when I was a child."

She smiled with her mouth shut as she chewed. "Me too," she said when she'd swallowed.

He took a bite and glanced up. "Why are you

looking at me that way?" His legs were crossed in front of him. His forehead wrinkled.

"I'm trying to picture you as a kid," she said. "It's hard. You have a very serious way about you."

"Is serious okay?"

"Well…" She pretended to think. He tore off a piece of bacon and threw it at her. It felt like progress. "Serious is okay," she relented, smiling. "But kids shouldn't be too serious."

"I was responsible," he said. "My dad was not reliable, and he'd leave for periods of time. I kind of became the man of the house."

"You said he was French? Did you ever live there?"

"For a summer when I was seventeen. He went there on one of his stints and God knows why, but I asked to go with him."

Lola put down her fork. "I had the impression you grew up without much—like me."

"I did. He was an artist, and he insisted he couldn't work in America, so he'd go back to France when he could. My mom didn't travel. She'd get on his case so he'd pick up a job for a few months, but he could never keep it. Basically we lived on her secretary's salary."

"He must've really loved you guys to keep coming back when he didn't want to be here."

Beau looked up from his plate. "I ask myself that a lot. Why he even bothered coming back." He cleared his throat.

"He probably missed you," Lola said, chewing. "It's nice to be missed." Her heart sank as she said it. She was probably being missed that very moment. She had to look away from Beau, who was the reason she hadn't been missing Johnny as much as she'd thought she would.

"Have you been to Paris?" he asked, calling her back.

"No," she said. "Vegas is the farthest I've been from here."

"Perhaps a trip is in order." He drank his orange juice, looking at her over the rim of the glass.

She shrugged. "Not right now. This is a chance for us to turn things around."

"Us?" he asked, furrowing his brow. "Me?"

"No, me and Johnny. Owning our own business is a lot of responsibility, and I don't want to mess it up. I—" She paused at the shadowy look in his eyes. "What?"

"I've already told you," he said. "Tonight is about you and me only. If I were your boyfriend, would you keep bringing up your ex?"

"I just thought since we were—"

"The rules haven't changed just because we screwed."

Lola's mouth fell open. It was as if a switch had been flipped from a few minutes earlier when they'd been as playful as two new lovers. "Do you realize how you sound?"

"Inform me," he invited with a gesture of his fork. "Please."

"Like I'm your puppet or something. I don't think I've ever met anyone so controlling."

He shrugged. "You didn't seem to mind my control earlier. In fact…I think you said it was *not repulsive*."

Lola stood from the bed and crossed her arms.

He looked up. "What?"

"Don't throw my honesty in my face like that. Do you think that was easy for me to say? That I enjoy being with someone other than—"

"Don't you dare say his name," he said, setting down his silverware.

"I'm sorry, Master," she said. She was pushing him, and from the look on his face, he didn't like it. She was too worked up to care. "Why don't you just go ahead and tell me what I should say."

"Is it too much to ask that you don't talk about your boyfriend when you're here with me?" His body locked up as his spine straightened.

"Fine. I won't talk about him." She instinctively took a step back. "Doesn't mean I won't be thinking about him."

"Now you're deliberately testing me. I don't want you talking about him, and I *certainly* don't want you thinking about him while you're in *my* bed."

She pointed a finger at him. "You think money gives you the right to do anything. You pay me, and I'll do whatever you say. You know what, though? You can't control my thoughts."

His face closed, just as she'd expected would happen if she threatened his control.

"How does that make you feel?" she prodded.

He got up from the bed. "Lola, I'm trying to be patient—"

"Muzzle me all you want," she muttered, moving to walk around him, "but there's nothing you can do to stop me from thinking about him when I'm with you."

"Where are you going?"

"I need a minute."

He blocked her with his entire body. "You don't get minutes unless I give them to you. Understand?"

She bolted to the right, but he caught her waist from behind and lifted her. They struggled against each other until Beau had her front pinned up against the window. He grabbed at the lapels of her robe, pulling it open and pressing her bare breasts up to the shockingly cold glass. One hand went over her mouth. He pushed his pelvis into her so her hipbones met the window.

"Take it back," he said in her ear.

Cityscape lights poked holes in the night. Her back was warm with Beau's heat, but her nipples hardened with a chill. She whimpered, unable to speak.

"If I take my hand away, not another fucking mention of him unless *I* bring it up."

She nodded. He released just her face.

"People might see us," she said, ashamed by the obvious thrill in her voice.

"I don't give a fuck." He pushed up the fabric of her robe and entered her from behind.

She moaned, so completely filled with him.

He stilled. "Tell me the truth. Were you thinking of him earlier?"

She gritted her teeth. As if she could think of anything else when Beau had her where he wanted her.

He thrust once. She braced herself against the window with her palms. He grabbed her wrists and held them there as he slid in and out quickly, impatiently. "I'm going to bend you over and spank you so fucking hard if you don't answer." It was not an empty threat. Before she could even begin to formulate a response, he let go of one of her arms and slapped her ass.

"What are you doing?" she cried. It was a slap intended to punish her, and that made her thighs quiver outside her control. She was going to come already.

"Answer me, or I'll turn that sweet, white ass flaming red, Lola. Tell me the truth."

She sucked in a breath. The threat did nothing but make her wildly hot. "What do you want me to—? I-I love him—"

He smacked her again, harder this time, with a swift, delicious sting, right on the outside curve of her behind.

"I didn't think of him," she confessed in one heated gasp. "I couldn't. When you're inside me, there's nothing else."

"Good girl." He seized her wrists again to brace both him and her. The glass rattled under her body as he took her. "You think that was controlling?" he asked between thrusts. "You don't know the half of it. I want to lock you up in this room, feed you and fuck you on my schedule. Then you'd really be mine." He wrapped his hand around her throat to keep her from looking anywhere but outside. "Give them a show, ma chatte. Don't be shy." He released her face to massage her clit.

She pressed her cheek against the window, fogging the glass. "Right there," she said. Her fingers curled into fists. "I'm going to come."

He pulled out and stepped back. "Not yet."

"Please." She dropped to her knees and put her hand between her legs.

"Don't," he said, looming over her. "Do not make yourself come."

"I'm not," she said. "I'm trying to stop it."

"*Stop it?*" He looked incredulous.

"I want you to do it."

"Ah." He smiled and backed away. "You're good. Very good." He took a strawberry from the cart. "Will you come to me?"

She crawled along the floor, hobbling because of the persistent ache between her legs. She let him feed her the strawberry. He bent over and sucked the sweetness from her lips.

"Now lie on your back and bend your knees," he whispered into her mouth.

It was a command that she obeyed without hesitation.

"Wider," he said.

She bared herself to him.

"Reach up…"

She felt behind her head and grabbed the bedpost with both hands.

"That's it," he said. "Hold on to that."

"You treat me like a dog," she said, but even she heard her own panting.

"And your obedience deserves a reward. Don't you want to know what it is?"

She salivated. There was nothing in her world except him, large and naked, hovering over her. "Yes, Beau."

He squatted and trailed a finger down her stomach and over her pubic bone. His knuckles brushed the inside of her thigh as he traced the outline of her. "You're trembling," he said. "Ask for what you want."

"Touch me," she said softly.

"I already am."

"Lower."

He put his hand on her knee. "Here?"

"Higher."

He slid his hand to the crease of her ass. "You mean here."

"No," she whispered. "Higher."

"You'll have to be more specific."

"My pussy," she said.

He smiled. "I would love to touch your pussy."

Lola's chest rose with exaggerated breaths.

"What should I touch it with?" he asked.

Her eyelids fluttered. "What do you mean?"

He wet his finger and circled it around her opening while she strained to see. "This?" He waited until she looked up at him again. "Or something else?"

"That," she said. "Your mouth."

He ran his hands up her thighs to hold her knees, pushing them apart as wide as they'd go. He returned his hands between her legs, parting her lips with this thumbs. Her back arched, sending her breasts toward the ceiling.

"Perfect," he said. "Just stay that way."

He got on the floor with her. His arms curled around her hips to secure her to his face right as he sucked her into his mouth, thrusting his tongue inside her. Her spine felt as if it would snap in half if she bowed it any more.

"Now I know," he said. "This is what I've been hungry for all along."

She reached down to touch his hair, but he caught her wrist and pushed it back toward her. "Use your words, ma chatte. It makes me hard just hearing your voice."

She gripped the bedpost again. "That," she said when the tip of his tongue massaged her clit. "Keep doing that."

He kept doing that, and when she was close, he moaned with his mouth buried in her. It felt like a crack in his shell, that sound, as it sent vibrations up her body.

"You're right," he spoke without moving away, "mouth is so much better."

She came. His voice was always deep and solid, and it made the words themselves unexpectedly sensual. They had ways of destroying her control. He continued kissing between her legs until she'd finished.

"How's that?" he asked, his lips running a gentle course along the inside of her thigh.

"Do you have to ask? I'm consumed."

"So am I." He took her waist in his wandering hands and squeezed her. "I could enjoy you for hours. Days. I think maybe we should get some rest, though."

She released the post and got up on her elbows. "Rest?"

"We have a couple hours or so left. Don't worry, I won't oversleep."

"It's not that," she said. As fast as he'd taken her against the window, he hadn't finished. "Don't you…?"

"Don't I what?"

She looked away. What did she care if he was satisfied? It wasn't a requirement of their deal. "Nothing," she said. "Sleep is fine."

"Good." He got to his feet and helped her up. He piled all the dishes from their breakfast onto the food cart and tossed oversized pillows aside. They hadn't even gotten to the sheets yet.

"Are you sure this is what you want?" she asked tentatively. For a savvy businessman, he hadn't used his hours very wisely. It was hard to believe after all the stress she'd endured making the decision that the night was almost over.

"The only thing I want more," he said, getting into the bed without looking at her, "is to smash the alarm clock with my fist. But I can't. Just let me have this."

There was an empty ache where her heart should be. Should be, because only a heartless person could resist Beau in that moment. Should be, because her heart didn't belong in this bed. She climbed right into his arms and curled up to his warmth.

He turned out the bedside lamp. "If I hadn't worn you out, we could've used this time to talk some more," he said. "I would've liked that."

Her eyes were already closed and he said nothing else, so she gave in to the heady feeling of his arms around her and slept.

Chapter Thirteen

Her name and a kiss. And again, her name, clearer, a kiss, firmer. Their bedroom was colder than usual, but it made the bed a haven of warmth. It was dead-of-night quiet. She was being squeezed from behind with a strength and intensity she wasn't used to. All at once she remembered where she was and opened her eyes.

"Lola," Beau whispered. He moved her hair from her forehead. "It's time."

The room was dark except for the boxed, green numbers on the digital clock. Through the large window, black was seeping from the sky, leaving rich sapphire in its place.

"I need to shower," she said. Beau was present everywhere on her body.

He stroked her jaw. She raised her chin to kiss him. She was exhausted and made no effort to hide the fact that she wanted that kiss. He rolled on top of her in one motion and her legs opened for him. He didn't enter her right away, but kissed everywhere above her neck his lips could reach. He pressed himself against her thigh, close enough she could almost feel him inside her.

"I'm ready," she whispered.

He thrust into her and groaned as if he'd been waiting to do it all night. They got slow and quiet, waking up together.

It was good. Too good. She felt him—*him*, not fast and hard and mind-blowing, but satisfying and warm. This slow, sleepy fuck was no less passionate than it'd been against the window. His groans came from somewhere deep inside. It was good—but it was dangerous. When she caught herself clutching him, digging her nails into his back, she stopped and squeezed her eyes shut. "I can't," she said.

"Okay." He kissed her cheek, her nose. "It's okay."

He held her head. It was too dark to see his expression. It meant she could imagine he was Johnny and remove some of the guilt she struggled with. She didn't. Even this way, in the pre-dawn, with his lovemaking, Beau demanded all of her.

As he came, he dropped his face into the crook of her shoulder and gripped her scalp. Then he exhaled what sounded like everything in his lungs. His body loosened on top of her. She stared up at the ceiling. Her limbs, depressed in the mattress, tingled. "I can't feel anything."

"I'm crushing you," he said but didn't move.

"It's not that," she said. Dread had seeped through her in seconds, numbing everything it touched. Her body was in survival mode. Facing Johnny would be as impossible as pretending the night had never happened. Neither thing could be avoided, though. She had to face him. Then they'd have to move on with their lives.

Beau raised his head and opened his mouth. If he asked her not to leave, she didn't know what she'd say. Of course she'd say no. It didn't matter that she wasn't ready to go, or that she was leaving with more questions than she came with.

He spoke. "We should go. You can't be late."

There was an important detail she'd forgotten for a moment, but when it returned, it overpowered everything else. "I need to shower."

He pulled out of her and pushed the covers back as he got out of the bed. "There's no time."

Her body coiled. She could not walk into Johnny's home this way. "I have to shower," she repeated.

"You can't." He put on his boxer briefs and disappeared into the walk-in closet. "I'm already worried about traffic," he called. "If we don't leave now—"

"Johnny will understand if we're a few minutes late if it means I get to shower."

"No," Beau said firmly. He tossed a shopping bag onto the bed. "This isn't up for discussion. I've never broken the terms of a contract in my life."

Lola sat up, grasping the sheet to her chest. Any numbness dissipated in her panic. "You can't be serious." She dumped out the contents of the bag—the jeans, T-shirt and underwear she'd left her apartment in. "But I'm—I can't go home like this. I'm disgusting."

"Then you should've thought of that earlier. I'm not kidding, Lola. Get up. *Now.*"

He was already dressed in a hoodie and jeans, standing with his back straight and his hands on his hips. His hair was messy from sleep, something she would've found cute if anger wasn't rising up her chest. She choked on her words. "C-can't I at least—"

"What aren't you understanding? The sky is already light. Get dressed, or I'll do it for you."

She clamped her mouth shut. What a fool she'd been to want to stay. Beau had been fire and ice all night, his moods swinging higher and further apart each time. "Then turn around," she snapped. "I don't want you to watch."

He shook his head. "Time's almost up, but not quite. You still belong to me."

She swallowed thickly and let the sheet drop. She hooked herself into her bra and tugged her shirt over her head. He looked at his watch. She got out of the bed.

"I have to say," he said thoughtfully as she pulled on her underwear, "this went even better than I imagined."

There was something in Beau's voice Lola didn't recognize. The hair on the back of her neck bristled. "What did?"

"Buying a person."

She stopped moving and looked at him. The shift from who he'd been in bed to the stranger standing in front of her had required less effort than a deep breath. "You didn't buy 'a person.' You bought a body." She didn't want to be either to him—she wanted to be the girl he'd seduced over darts, the image that would soothe him on his deathbed. "There's a difference."

"I'm not debating this with you again. There's no difference."

He was so smug, without any trace of the Beau she'd gotten to know. He should've used her like he'd said he would. No talk of family, of possibility. Of her in his life. Anything more than using her body was a kind of cruel that went beyond the boundaries of normalcy. "I hate you," she said. It had come out slippery and unintentional, but she didn't take it back. In that moment, it was true.

"Fine," he said. "But I bought you fair and square. Say it."

"You did *not*," she said. "I am not my body. I am

feelings, a brain, a heart. There's so much more to me than what you got."

Beau was gripping his hips so hard, his knuckles were white. She looked away and buttoned her jeans, trying to hide the fact that he'd hurt her.

"You can't just change the terms of an agreement, Lola. Business doesn't work that way."

"This isn't business," she said. "I'm a human being. I didn't sign over my heart to you. You have no right to say you owned anything other than my body."

"Are you saying none of it was real? That your heart wasn't in it?"

"It was real for me, Beau. But it takes a lot goddamn more to earn someone's heart. You can't expect that in one night, and you damn well can't demand it."

"Enough," he snapped. "Now would be a good time to shut your mouth."

She didn't. It fell wide open. "Beau—"

"Just—" He held up both his hands. "Stop. Stop talking."

She grabbed her purse from the bed. "I'm ready," she said, flipping him off as she stormed by him.

They rode the elevator down in silence. When the doors opened, she practically ran outside. It didn't matter. Beau and his long strides were never far behind. She went straight to where Warner waited against a town car.

"I can go alone," she said over her shoulder, knowing Beau would be there.

"I'm coming."

"I don't see why you have to."

He ignored her. "Warner," he said. "Don't waste any time."

"Yes, sir."

Lola opened the car door herself even though Beau reached for it. She ducked inside and slid as far away as she could get from him.

"Lola."

"Don't talk to me." Her voice threatened to quiver, but she forced it steady. "You're a fucking bastard."

He sighed. "You're right. I'm a bastard and an asshole. Such an asshole. I didn't mean what I said up there. I'm sorry."

She jerked her head to him. The words, in their apologetic, defeated tone, sounded wrong coming out of his mouth.

His eyebrows were drawn. "I mean it. I don't know what came over me." He made a face when he swallowed that made him look as if he was in pain. "Lola, you have to understand. This isn't easy for me. We shouldn't have to say goodbye like this. We shouldn't have to say goodbye at all."

Lola's fists uncurled a little. It was all so confusing, except for the fact that she wasn't ready to say goodbye either. Not even when he was an asshole. "Walking away is easier if we're angry. You were pushing me away."

"If you were smart," he said quietly, "you'd let me."

She looked back out the window. "It doesn't matter. This is the end, anyway."

"Not yet. Come back to me, even just for our last few minutes."

It truly was the end. The horizon was orange. She could be what Beau so obviously needed for a few more minutes. At least she had someone waiting at home for her. She turned back and moved across the seat as he angled to face her. "I never expected it to be this good." He stroked her cheek with his thumb, cupping her jaw. "For you to be so beautiful. For this to feel so right." He paused. "For it to be so hard to say goodbye."

Her breath hitched. She took his wrist with both her hands, overcome with need to give him the truth. "If we'd met earlier, Beau, or if our circumstances were different, I know I could've—"

"Stay another night."

She blinked. "What?"

"Don't go."

"I can't," she said, shaking her head. She removed her hands and held them to her chest. Fantasizing that he'd ask her to stay and experiencing it were two different things. Even if she wanted to with every fiber of her being, which she didn't, because she loved Johnny—she couldn't. It was ridiculous. "You're not serious. No. I can't."

"Would you do it if I didn't pay you?" he asked.

"No."

"Then I'll pay. He gets his money, and I get you. One more night."

"Absolutely not." She turned forward in the seat and looked away. "I need my phone back."

Fabric rustled. The car slowed. She made the mistake of glancing back at him. His hair, still in disarray, alerted her to a new fracture in her heart, because it became a little deeper in that moment.

He held out the phone for her. "Thank you. Even though it wasn't, it still felt like luck having you at all."

She scanned his face, still incredibly handsome despite his lack of sleep, and took her phone. Out the tinted window, the familiar gates of her apartment complex came into view. When the car stopped, she gripped the door handle painfully hard.

"Lola."

Don't look back. Don't look back. She looked back.

"Come here," he said.

She hesitated, then leaned and met him halfway. He put a hand on her cheek to hold her there. "I have my flaws. I don't deserve a yes from you," he said. "There's more to you than one night, though, and there's more to me. He can have the money. We can have the rest of each other." He kissed her. "I won't change my mind. You know how to reach me." He let her go and turned back to his window.

She stepped out onto the sidewalk. The car pulled away from the curb. Her feet had walked this path thousands of times—they knew the way home on their own. She willed them to move. Going home was the right thing to do. She and Johnny were forever altered, but he was waiting for her.

The car braked at a stop sign a second too long, and her breath caught.

The price of a million dollars was not her body. It was glimpsing what could've been and wondering for the rest of her life if she should've been in that car. It was the seed of doubt planted in her mind that could potentially grow many different branches.

The car turned and drove away. She glanced over her shoulder. She was out of time. The sun was just beginning to rise over the city.

Domination

EXPLICITLY YOURS • BOOK TWO

JESSICA HAWKINS

Chapter One

Lola had not had time to think ahead to this moment. She'd never been much of a planner—a fact she'd even prided herself on. Lately she'd been wondering if she'd been wrong, though. She could've set aside some money to start a class or two at the local community college. Or tried harder to find a better job than waitressing at Hey Joe. Maybe then she wouldn't be standing here, about to face her boyfriend of nine years after sleeping with another man for money. All so they'd have a shot at a decent future.

Not just another man. A man who'd seen her on a sidewalk and specifically picked her. He was drawn to her, he'd said—she was a prize, waiting to be claimed by him. At the time, she hadn't known what he'd meant by that. Now she did. It hadn't taken long for her to give in to her attraction to him, but it had to go away now. As if it were a mask she'd slipped on for one night. Or was it that she was putting one back on?

She'd been seduced. She'd been claimed. And then she'd been returned to her doorstep. He wasn't just another man—that was Beau Olivier.

Behind the eggshell-colored door with a brass number six nailed to it, Johnny waited. Johnny and her new life with him. Lola sucked in cool, early-morning air and flushed hot, tainted breath out with her exhale. Apartment six was on the ground floor, just through the gate and within steps of a mold-rimmed pool. All she had to do was turn the key and go home. That, and forget Beau.

The normally finicky lock gave her little resistance. It was dark in the apartment. Thick. Suffocating. Had it always been that way? She opened the shades. Johnny lay lengthwise on the couch, clutching a pillow to his chest. She went and stood over him.

She hadn't thought of Johnny as much as she should've while she was with Beau, but when she had, she'd envisioned him anxiously waiting for her, driving himself slightly insane. Apparently she'd been wrong. If she'd been any later than sunrise, which was when Beau had promised to return her, Johnny might not've even known. She didn't think it was much to ask that after what she'd done for him, Johnny make sure she arrived home safely and on time.

She dropped her purse near his head, and he woke with a start. "Shit—Lola?" He blinked up at her rapidly as if she were an apparition. "Is it over?"

She offered her palms. "I'm here, aren't I?"

He rubbed his eyes and got up on an elbow, tossing the pillow aside. "I'm—I must've fallen asleep. Sorry."

She picked up an empty bottle of Jack Daniels from the floor. "You drank the rest of this by yourself?"

"When I got home from Mark's."

"Mark's?" she repeated, unsure she'd understood him. There'd been no discussion of him doing anything other than coming straight home from work. She hadn't even thought it was necessary. "You went out last night?"

"As opposed to sitting here and thinking about what you were doing? Yeah. I didn't want to be alone."

"When did you get home?" Lola shook her head. She didn't have the energy to argue at the moment. "Never mind. I don't even care."

"Are you mad?" he asked. "What was I supposed to do? I'm sorry if—wait, how am I the one apologizing?"

"Why would either of us apologize?" Her tone dropped to a warning level. "Surely you don't expect me to."

Johnny shut his eyes, leaned back against the couch and ran both hands over his face. "No," he said, sighing. "That's not what I meant. I'm still buzzed. Just give me a minute to wake up."

"Take a few. I'll be in the shower."

He peeked at her through his fingers. "You haven't showered?"

Beau had been so adamant about getting her back by sunrise, it was almost as if he hadn't wanted her to shower. And now she had to stand in front of Johnny, thoroughly worked over by Beau. Even from a distance, Beau exercised his control over them. Her throat was suddenly thick. "There wasn't time."

She had to walk away. It would hurt Johnny to see her get upset since she so rarely did. They both had enough to deal with as it was. "If you want to talk, get coffee ready. Otherwise I won't be able to keep my eyes open."

She went directly for the bathroom and turned the shower on hot. The night had been a flash of lightning. Intense, blinding, crackling—and over before she could even blink. One moment the life-changing decision to sleep with Beau weighed heavily on their shoulders.

Now, it was done. Had it changed her life? How could it not have?

She and Johnny knew each other better than anyone. Years ago, he'd taken a chance on her. Burly, gruff, but kind-hearted Johnny. He didn't have to put up with the lost girl Lola used to be, because women liked him. He could've had his pick. Lola partied too hard and had little regard for anyone—even herself. Even Johnny. But he'd believed she could be better. Johnny didn't deserve for Lola to be standing in the shower, her mind drifting away from him.

Drifting to Beau, to his hands, cock and mouth between her legs. His forbidden words in her ear. He liked her tight. He liked her helpless on her hands and knees. He liked her with a red ass. And he was everywhere on her.

She shouldn't have been thinking of any of that. Johnny was in the next room. She was being torn in different directions. The last twelve hours came down on her at once. Big, hot tears mingled with the stream of water. She'd betrayed Johnny with more than just her body—in ways she would've never expected possible in just a night. And despite herself, she missed Beau already.

He wanted a second night, but that was greedy. He'd taken too much already and without apology. How much more could she open herself up to?

The bathroom door creaked. She turned to face the wall, wiping her cheeks. "I won't be long."

There was no response. After a shuffle, Johnny turned her by her shoulders and hugged her to his naked chest. It was all she needed for the tears to flow.

"Did he hurt you?" he asked.

"No. I'm just tired."

"Promise me."

She looked up at his tone. In his face was a shadow of how worried he'd been. "He didn't," she said. "Promise."

He ran a hand up and down her back. "I'm sorry, babe. It was a lot to ask of you."

She returned her cheek to his chest and nodded. "It's done, though. Over." She almost told him it was okay to feel angry. Selfishly, that would make it easier for her to be angry. But she felt very much like a house of cards that couldn't take any more weight without collapsing. Later would be a better time for them to get angry.

"Thank you," she said.

"For what?"

"Not being afraid to touch me."

"How could I be? You're my girl." He kissed the top of her head. "I love you."

She almost rose up to kiss him but was afraid he'd pull away. "Please go make coffee," she said, separating from him.

He left the shower. She didn't cry again. She soaped her breasts, behind her ears, under her feet. All the parts Beau had touched. Everywhere. She was owned, just like he'd promised. She rubbed between her legs a little longer than necessary—one second comforting that unfulfilled ache, the next trying to make it stop. Only an hour earlier, Beau had been inside her. She couldn't come, not so in between Beau and Johnny. Her mind and body had been there with Beau, but her heart knew

Johnny was minutes away. She wished she'd just been able to fucking come, because now Beau's ache might never go away. She turned off the water.

Johnny returned to wrap her in a towel. He dried her off and patted her hair. "There's coffee in the living room."

She kept the towel around her, and they went to the couch. Johnny sat at one end while she curled her knees to her chest at the other. He was patient while she sipped from the mug.

"I think maybe it's best I don't go into details," she said.

"That bad?" he asked.

"It's just, I've heard some couples do that. After affairs or whatever. Seems stupid to me. Like asking for trouble."

He nodded, looking into his coffee, thinking. "All right. Last thing I want is to make things harder on either of us." He looked up. "But you were safe? Were you scared?"

"In the beginning a little. He took me to Rodeo Drive—"

"Seriously?"

"Only because I couldn't go in jeans. To the fundraiser, I mean—the event I texted you about. But being around all those people actually made things better. It didn't feel like such a dirty secret."

He coughed. "About that last text. I'm sorry. It was selfish of me. I'd already had a drink—"

She glanced up from her coffee. "Text?"

"You didn't read my response?"

She shook her head. "He took my phone away."

"What do you mean he took it away?"

"He had a very particular way of doing things. He didn't like me mentioning your name. When he found out I'd texted you, he took my phone."

"So basically he's a complete dick."

She looked at her handbag. Johnny's last request the night before had been that she not kiss Beau. Had the text been about that? Or had it been something even bigger—maybe an apology that they'd decided to go through with this at all?

"What'd it say?" she asked.

"Nothing. Just continue. Where'd you go after the event?"

His face was red, as if he were embarrassed by the text. She hesitated, but decided not to pursue it. She would read it later. "After? We went for a nightcap. There's this insane, secret speakeasy on Sunset—"

"Heard of it," he said. "Don't know anyone who's been, though."

"It wasn't anything," she said, shrugging too hard in an attempt to seem convincing.

"Right. After that?"

"I think we should stop there."

"Oh." He bobbed his head slowly. "All right. If that's what you want."

Lola did want to tell him, because only he would understand why their next stop had been so strange. That Beau had taken her to a strip club at all was unusual—but that it'd been the same one she'd worked at? If she mentioned it, Johnny would ask why they went there. He'd want to know if she'd danced for him. Cat

Shoppe was a sore topic for Johnny, who'd risked their relationship to get her out of there.

"It's what I want," she said, returning her time with Beau into the vault where it belonged.

He looked around the room. She drank more coffee.

"I checked while you were in the shower. The other half of the money still isn't deposited."

"It's the weekend," she said.

"Right, but it would still show as pending. What if he doesn't pay?"

"He will. I trust—"

Johnny looked at the floor. He didn't blink for so long, she thought she should explain. Not that she trusted Beau himself, but that she trusted him to pay. She hadn't meant anything by it.

He put his hand around her ankle and smiled a little. "I'm glad you're home."

"So am I," she said. "But I'm exhausted. I didn't get much…I just think I should lie down."

"I get it," he said, releasing her foot.

She crawled over the couch and kissed his cheek. "Good morning," she said.

"Good night," he said back.

◆⊠◆⊠◆

Lola had shut the bedroom windows. The California sun could be too much at times. Regardless, when she opened her eyes, daylight sliced straight lines through the shutters.

Beau would be—what? Working? Sleeping her off? She had no idea, because she didn't know him. That was something she'd have to learn to live with, just like the ache between her legs he'd given her. It throbbed for attention, but she refused to take care of it. She couldn't do it without thinking of Beau, and thinking of Beau now when the entire experience was supposed to be over was unfair to Johnny. The idea of Johnny doing it for her made her stomach cramp.

She reached over the side of the bed and took her phone from her purse. Beau had turned it off. She waited for it to start up, then read the text message Johnny had written barely an hour after she'd left the apartment.

This doesn't feel right. Ask him what happens if we change our minds.

A lump formed in her throat. She put the phone back, took it out again and erased the message. She never wanted to read it again.

She stood from the bed and called out for Johnny, surprised he hadn't woken her since they should've left for work already. There was a note on the kitchen table that he'd given her the night off. Underneath, next to a large, scribbled dollar sign was *We're millionaires.*

It was something to celebrate, but she was in too strange of a mood, stuck somewhere between elation and devastation, asleep and awake, Beau and Johnny. It was her first moment completely alone since before Beau had picked her up.

They had their money. Their dream future would soon be a reality. It'd been fun to consider her options, like doing something other than Hey Joe, but now it was final. Why else would she have sold herself if not because she wanted this too? It was hard to stomach the idea that she'd done it all for Johnny like Beau had suggested. *Sacrifice* was the word he'd used—she couldn't *sacrifice* herself for someone else's happiness.

Lola found leftovers in the fridge, ate them with her beer and went back to bed. If Beau was right, she'd been sacrificing herself for a long time. Some part of her had always felt she'd owed Johnny that for taking a chance on her years ago. Now she wondered if that debt would ever feel paid.

Chapter Two

Lola and Johnny's one-bedroom apartment didn't have much space, so the kitchen became their office. Because Johnny had given Lola the night off work to sleep, she woke up earlier than normal on Sunday. She ran out for donuts, made fresh coffee and got to work.

On their dining table, Lola's laptop screen was crowded with information about buying an existing business. When Johnny walked in, she looked up from the notepad she'd been taking notes on.

"Morning," he said, tossing a football in his hand. "You were up early."

She glanced at the football. "What's that for?"

"Game today."

Lola set down her pen. "We're not going to the picnic. We have too much to do."

"I thought we were doing all this tomorrow."

"We are. Today and tomorrow." She gestured at the donuts. "Look, I got all your favorites. They even have the custard filling I never let you get. I'm not above bribery."

He picked one up and bit into it. Multi-colored sprinkles fell onto the table. "But we don't have the details yet," he said, chewing. "We won't until we sit down with Mitch."

"I know, but I want to be prepared *before* we sit down with Mitch. I think we should go in with a plan. Did you know it can take months to transfer a liquor license? We should get started on that now."

"Now—as in right now? Can't it wait until after the game?"

"Six hundred thousand is a little high for a bar on Sunset Boulevard," she continued, ignoring him, "especially one that's struggling like we are. But that's the number Mitch gave me. I think he's factoring in the worth of the brand. We'll have a lot of expenses off the bat too, including the food and liquor licenses. I figure that leaves us with around three hundred grand."

"That's a good cushion," he said, leaning his hands on the back of a chair.

She shook her head. "It's not a cushion, Johnny. If we're doing this, we have to do it right—like renovations to the kitchen that's been out of use for decades. You said you wanted to serve food, so we'll have to go through a health inspection."

Johnny brushed off his hands on his pants. "Sounds like you got this covered."

"I don't," she said. "You know more about running a bar because you love it. I'd rather focus on advertising and marketing, and I'd like a decent budget for that since we're trying to generate new foot traffic."

Johnny set the football on the table. "All right. I see where you're coming from. But I won't be any good to you now. My head's already in the game. So I'll tell you what—why don't we go down to the park, play some football, eat some lunch and chill a little bit. Then tonight I'll tell Mitch neither of us are coming in. That gives us tonight and all day tomorrow."

"We can't just take the night off like that."

"Why not? Not like we're desperate for the money anymore."

"Johnny, you're not hearing me. We need every last cent. I don't want to nag you, but you've got to take this seriously. Running a business is not about doing what you want. It's about buckling down and doing whatever it takes, even on the weekends. It's late hours and waking up earlier." She looked over at the clock. "You can't be sleeping until eleven anymore."

He held up his palms. "I understand this is serious, I promise, but we haven't even sat down with Mitch yet. Let's take a little time to get adjusted."

He ate another donut. She'd already lost him for the morning. Johnny wouldn't be any good to her if she forced him to stay home—as if this had been *her* dream. As if she'd always wanted a bar of her own. She'd have to feed off Johnny's passion to make this work, but he wasn't showing her any.

"Go ahead to the game," she said. "I'm staying here. You really think Mitch'll give us both the night off?"

"It's a Sunday," he said. "They can handle things without us. But, um…"

The look on his face told Lola she was about to hear something she wouldn't like. If he asked her to make potato salad, when the reason she was skipping the picnic was because there was so much to do, she'd really let him have it. "What?" she asked, already irritated.

"Well, I've been thinking about this the last few days. Everybody knows we don't have the money to come in and buy Hey Joe, especially in cash. So the money's got to come from somewhere."

"Okay," she prompted.

"So I got this idea. After the game, I'll call in and tell Mitch there was a death in your family. You didn't hear about it until now because you never knew him, but the guy—let's say your great uncle—left you a huge inheritance."

"No way," Lola said, turning back to her notepad. "That's too fucked up."

"I tell Mitch I have to stay home with you, so it gives us the next couple days off to work on the plan, and it also explains the money. They already know you don't got much family, so it wouldn't be weird that you find out about this long-lost cousin."

"Uncle," Lola corrected.

"Whatever. Lo, how else are we going to explain it?"

Normally Lola's answer would've been the truth—that was a pretty good explanation for most things. But not in this case. She looked up at him again.

He shrugged. "What else? The lottery? A death in the family invites no questions, and it kills two birds with one stone."

"We can't do that," she said. "Mitch, Vero, Quartz—they're like family. What about Mark and Brenda? Are you willing to lie to your best friend about this?"

Johnny looked out the tiny window over the kitchen sink a minute. "Well, then I guess we tell them the truth. You slept with a wealthy guy. Makes me look like a chump, but I'm more worried about you."

Lola had been scribbling absentmindedly on her notepad. They wouldn't get away without an explanation. It was the first she'd thought of it, though. She stopped doodling and gripped the pen. "We can't tell them the truth. So I guess we have no other choice."

"All right, that's settled then. Don't worry about them. I'll take care of it." He came over and squeezed her shoulders. "You seem tense."

"I thought the hard part was over," she said. "But we still have a lot of work ahead of us."

"It'll all come together, babe. Don't stress." He massaged her, and she relaxed back in her seat. "Sure you don't want to come? Just for a few hours?"

"No, it's okay. I'll get everything in order, and we can sit down when you get home."

"Cool. They'll be pissed about the potato salad," he teased.

She smiled a little. Potato salad didn't seem like such a big deal anymore, now that she was lying about a death in her family. "Swing by Pavilions on your way. Nobody'll even know the difference."

He kissed the top of her head and lingered there a moment. "Of course they will. You make it the best." He straightened up, ruffled her hair and left the kitchen.

Lola glanced at her computer screen. When she'd researched Beau before their night together, she'd come across a feature a few years back naming him as one of Los Angeles's top investors in startup companies. Lola searched for the article. Each featured investor had been quoted alongside their stats. At the time, she hadn't given Beau's piece much thought. But now it seemed worth revisiting.

"I'm looking at the people just as much as the project. Without those who are willing to work hard and sacrifice, a company won't make it. There's no lack of good ideas or passion

out there, but building something with your own two hands takes endurance."

Beau had passion for his work. She hadn't realized it until they'd talked about it at the gala. He'd also toiled, stayed dedicated, overcome defeat. Regardless of how he flaunted his money or that he'd treated her like a commodity, he'd earned all of his dollars, and there was something to be said for that.

Having passion was the easy part. If she and Johnny didn't even have that, how would they make this work?

◆⊠◆⊠◆

They went to Mitch that Tuesday afternoon. He listened to their offer, his face more saggy than normal while he stared at them across his desk. When Johnny finished, it was a few moments before anyone spoke.

"I'm just a little…" Mitch seemed to struggle for words. "I didn't really expect you to pull this off. Where's this money coming from?"

"I told you Lola's relative passed away," Johnny said. "He also left her some money."

"I thought you said you found out about him this weekend. You came to me last week and asked me to wait for your offer."

"Well, we found out last week," Johnny said. "We just weren't sure if the money would come through, but it will. It didn't really hit Lola until Sunday, which is why she needed me there."

"Right. Sorry to bring it up. Lola, this is what you want to do with your money?"

"Yes. And it's our money," she said. "This is Johnny's dream. I don't want there to be any question about who's in charge."

"What about you?" Mitch asked.

The night before, Johnny had caught Lola on the Santa Monica College website, browsing through the degree programs. "I'm thinking of going back to school," she'd said.

"But Hey Joe will require all of our time and money now," he'd said. "Your words."

It was true—she'd said that. And school would always be there. But they could end up in trouble if they weren't careful, and neither of them had any business experience. She'd agreed and let it go. She'd already missed registration anyway.

"I'm completely on board," Lola said to Mitch. With or without the education, she was dedicated to making this work. "But Johnny's the one sailing this ship."

"Six hundred K," Johnny said. "That's a pretty sweet offer, Mitch."

"It is, but—"

Lola curled her hands in her lap. "But what? You said that would be enough."

"I did say that, yes. When Walken found out I needed more time because I was hearing another proposal, he upped his offer."

"To how much?" Johnny asked. Lola closed her eyes.

"Eight hundred," Mitch said.

The room was quiet. Lola shook her head and looked at Mitch again. "That's ridiculously high."

Mitch shrugged. "I know."

"I researched the value of nearby businesses," Lola said. "Six hundred was too high. Eight hundred is just…"

"Too much," Mitch said.

"Hank can't possibly think he's getting a deal."

Mitch nodded. "I'm agreeing with you. But I'm going to turn down an extra two hundred because the guy's an idiot?"

"We can do eight hundred," Johnny said.

Lola turned to him. "Johnny—"

"Mitch, listen to me," Johnny said, putting his hands on the edge of the desk. "We'll take it for eight hundred. We've got our hearts set on it. But please don't let Walken drive it any higher. Promise me here, now, as my friend of over twelve years—this is everything I've got."

Mitch sighed. "I can't promise—"

"Mitch." Johnny leaned forward. His fingers pressed down until they were white. "Do you really want to see your dad's place ruined for a little more money? Don't get greedy, man. Don't sell out. You know Lola and I will keep your dad's vision alive."

Johnny was at the edge of his seat, practically falling forward onto his knees. The last time she'd seen him so impassioned was when he was asking her nineteen-year-old self to quit her self-destructive lifestyle so they could be together. This big-picture excitement was what she needed from him, but it had to trickle down to the routine parts of running a business too.

"Son of a bitch," Mitch said. "You'd better not let me down."

"So we have a deal?" Johnny asked, standing.

"Just don't mention that last part to Barb, all right?" Mitch said. "She finds out I could've gotten more money and she'll have my neck."

Lola wasn't sure what to feel. It was what they'd wanted, but that money would cut into their already limited budget.

"I have to tell you, though," Mitch continued, "the landlord's wary of the whole thing. His dad dealt with my dad, and our families have done business since opening day. He wants six months' rent upfront plus a security deposit."

"What's that look like?" Lola asked.

"Deposit is thirty grand, and with half a year's rent you're looking at over a hundred K."

Lola and Johnny exchanged glances. That would mean they'd be going forward with less than a hundred thousand to fall back on. It didn't seem like enough.

"It's not a problem," Johnny said.

Lola touched his forearm. "Maybe we should take a minute and think about this."

"We'll still have enough," he said quietly. "It's not as much as we set aside for renovations, but it's enough to get started."

"What about advertising?"

"We'll worry about that later, once we get some profit coming in." Lola was about to explain there might not be any profits if they couldn't get customers in the door, but Johnny cut her off by reaching out to shake Mitch's hand. "Thanks, man. Really, I mean it."

"Can't wait to see what you do with the place. Why don't you two take the night off? Go do something fun."

"You're giving us *another* night?" Lola asked, raising her eyebrows.

"Just one. As a congratulations." He sat back at his desk. "It could be a while before you both get another night off together."

They thanked Mitch and headed out to the parking lot together. Time alone was just what they needed. It was what they deserved after everything they'd been through.

Johnny surprised Lola by picking her up and spinning her around. "Can you fucking believe it?" he said, grinning. "We're doing it. Buying a goddamn bar."

Lola smiled despite the pit in her stomach. "I think I'm still in shock."

"Not me. I've been ready for years."

"We should change the name to Hey Johnny," she joked.

He chuckled, squeezing her. "I wish. Where should we celebrate? And don't say a bar."

She also laughed.

"God, I love your laugh," he said. "Always have."

"Johnny," she said, burying her face in his neck. He could still catch her off guard and make her blush. He was happy, and even though she worried, she was happy too. That eased the pit in her stomach a little.

◆⊠◆⊠◆

Lola owned one dress for such a special occasion—fitted but not flashy, sheer from her neck to her cleavage, including the sleeves to her elbows. Black, of course. She'd worn it once for Johnny's kid sister's college graduation party.

She came out of the bathroom, all fixed up. Johnny pushed hangers around the closet, still in his underwear.

"Babe?" she asked. Normally he was ready in half the time it took her.

"Don't have anything to wear," he muttered. "I'll have to get some new things."

"What you've got is fine, Johnny. You don't have to dress up."

He looked over his shoulder at her, up and down. "I've never seen that dress before."

"Yes, you have. I wore it to Natasha's graduation."

"Oh." He turned back to the closet. "Well, I'd call that pretty dressed up. I can't exactly show up in jeans when you're wearing that."

"I can change," she said. It made no difference to her. She wasn't even the one who'd chosen the restaurant, an expensive steakhouse in Beverly Hills they'd read about in the paper a few weeks earlier.

"No, don't. You look too pretty." He pulled out a checkered, long-sleeved button down. "How's this? Also what I wore to her graduation."

"It's—" She turned toward the kitchen when her phone rang. "That shirt's great, honey," she called as she left the room. "You look good in red."

She found her cell in her purse, and her heart leapt at the unknown number. It couldn't be him, though. Beau was not allowed to just sneak up on her that way—not when it was so important that she put him behind her. With a quick glance back toward the bedroom, she answered it and held her breath.

"Lola," there was a pause on the line, "are you there, *ma chatte*?"

She placed the phone over her chest, then pulled it away, worried he'd hear her nervous heartbeat. She went out the front door, closed it quietly behind her and put her cell to her ear again. "What do you want?"

"You haven't given me an answer," Beau said.

"I told you no in the car that morning."

"You discussed it with Johnny?"

She hesitated. Before her first night with Beau, she'd been stronger. She was able to see clearer. She hadn't told Johnny about Beau's second offer. If Johnny made her decide again, she had a feeling she knew what her answer would be. It was better not to ask the question at all. "You shouldn't be calling me."

He made a low, humming noise that reminded her of his mouth between her legs. "Don't change the subject."

"It doesn't matter what Johnny says. The answer is no."

"Have you bought the bar yet?"

The change of topic took her a moment to register. "Yes. Well, no. We gave our offer, and now it's just a matter of paperwork."

"Do you have a lawyer?"

"Johnny's cousin is one."

"Johnny's cousin," Beau repeated to himself. "Who will represent you?"

"What? There is no me. There's only me and Johnny."

"You need representation too."

"No, I don't. And even if I did, it's none of your business."

They were quiet a moment. She pictured Beau in his office at the end of the day. He could've been at home, but he sounded tense. Maybe Lola brought that out in him, though. It seemed they were frequently on the verge of arguing.

"I'll have my lawyer contact you," he said finally. "He'd keep only your best interests in mind. My treat."

"I can't go to Johnny with my own lawyer. That's absurd."

"Are you buying the place together?"

"Yes."

"So your name will go on everything?"

"Yes, but it's Johnny's baby."

"How will you share the profits? Fifty-fifty? What if you break up?"

"Break up?"

"That's why you need someone looking out for you."

"I have someone," Lola said softly. "Johnny. We aren't breaking up."

"I just want you to be careful. Smart. You've never had money like this to complicate things."

She'd only had the money a few days, but that was turning out to be true. Before Beau had walked into their lives, things had been simple. Now, every day came with a new problem that was above her and Johnny's heads and new tension between them.

"Money's supposed to make life easier," she said.

"It doesn't. People think that, but they don't realize there are downsides to wealth."

"Are you calling to talk me out of taking the deal?"

"So you're considering it then?"

"No. I didn't mean it like that." Or had she? Was she considering it? A night like the one they'd had could never be duplicated. It also couldn't be forgotten. It was tempting enough to wonder what would even happen during a second night, much less actually consider it.

"I should go," she said.

"Don't sign anything without having someone read it over first."

Lola suppressed a smile. "So that's why you called. To hound me about a lawyer?"

"Yes." He sighed. "No. Not really. Your voice—I missed it. Has anyone ever told you how comforting it can be?"

He'd spoken it softly, as if it were their private secret. They had enough secrets, though. Having breakfast in bed—it felt like a secret. Her willingly opening her legs to him? Secret. They were things that couldn't leave the presidential suite. And this conversation needed to end before it went any further. "Beau—"

"I wish you were here now to whisper to me."

Lola looked over her shoulder again. She remembered him whispering to her, not the other way around. Telling her how it felt to be inside her, how tight and hot and wet she was. Her heart clenched longingly. With Beau, it didn't take much to draw her in.

"What…what would you have me say?" she asked.

"I wouldn't have you say anything. What fun is that? I'd want you to say whatever comes to you."

That ache returned between her legs—or maybe it'd never left. It still hadn't been taken care of. "'Goodbye, Beau.' That's what comes to me."

"I won't stop until I get the answer I want," he warned. "Talk to him."

She shook her head, ended the call and looked around the courtyard. The complex was muted by dusk. Beau's voice was more intense on the phone. Bolder. Huskier. He'd said "whisper to me" suggestively, with promise, as if he knew she would be doing it soon.

"Beau," she whispered aloud to the silence. She felt his weight on her again, his chest to her back, slick with a sheen of their sweat. His mouth at her ear, his hot breath, his even hotter words.

The apartment door opened behind her, and she whirled around so fast she almost lost her footing.

Johnny held his arms wide open. "How do I look?" he asked, showing off his shirt.

Her heart raced as though she'd been caught doing something wrong. "You look," she cringed, but the words were already falling out of her mouth, "like a million bucks."

Chapter Three

Lola stepped out of the car as the door opened for her. She was greeted by the valet's smile. Johnny came around the hood to meet her.

"Sorry about the car," Johnny said to the young man. "It's old. Probably a lot shittier than you're used to."

The valet shrugged. "It's fine. You should see my ride."

Johnny nodded ardently at that. "Yeah. Cool."

Lola waited until they were out of earshot, just before they entered the steakhouse. "Don't apologize for something as stupid as our car," she said. Their car had seen better days, and it was a stick shift, but it didn't merit an apology. "Like the valet really gives a crap about anything other than his tip."

"Oh, I'll give him one hell of a tip. Just don't want anyone thinking we're going to dine and dash or something."

"Nobody thinks that. Do I really look that out of place?"

He rolled his eyes. "You know I didn't mean it like that."

"You make it sound like I shouldn't eat here because I'm not wearing a designer dress."

"All right, all right," he said with exasperation. He took her hand. "You made your point."

Lola was beginning to see how a sudden influx of cash could go to someone's head—except that in her mind, there was no cash. It was almost all promised away. "Sometimes it's good to let people underestimate you," she said.

The hostess greeted them warmly, smiling as she complimented Lola's dress. Lola tried not to look smug as they were led to their table. "We're so honored you've chosen to dine here this evening," the woman said. "We hope it exceeds your expectations. If you need anything at all, please let your server or me know."

"We should hire her," Johnny said when she excused herself. "It's nice to make your guests feel special."

"We can start calling Quartz 'Mr. Quartz.'"

"And we'll replace all the glasses with crystal ware."

"And we'll finally put in a new toilet so it doesn't make that gurgling noise anymore."

"Let's not get carried away," Johnny said, laughing.

The waiter was just as friendly, making small talk as he laid black napkins in their laps.

"We'll take the most expensive champagne you've got," Johnny said without even opening the menu.

"Johnny," Lola said. "That's not necessary."

He glanced from the waiter to her. "We can afford to splurge for once in our lives, Lola."

"But it's champagne. Really. It'll be gone by the end of the night. Let's get a nice, reasonable bottle of red wine."

"Shall I come back?" the man asked.

"No," Johnny said. "Bring the champagne."

Lola looked up at the server. "Can you give us a minute?"

"Certainly."

"No champagne," Lola said firmly while he walked away. "It's excessive."

"Listen to me." Johnny leaned forward on his elbows, twining his fingers. "One *million* dollars. You comprehend that, right?"

She blinked slowly. "Are you seriously asking me that?"

"Okay, but—"

"And it's not a million anymore," Lola continued. "Once this deal goes through and we have to pay that rent, we've got barely anything left."

"It's still a ton of money, Lo. More than we've ever had. I'll talk to the landlord and get us out of paying upfront."

"It's not a ton of money. I told you we needed all the extra help we could get. Aside from the big things, there's maintenance, and wages and all the other expenses that come with owning a business." Lola's breath wasn't coming as fast as she needed. The reality of their commitment came crashing through the dream, right down onto her shoulders. "Honestly, a million's not even enough for what we just agreed to."

"Lola, honey. Calm down. I'm not asking to take a vacation, all I'm saying is for this one night, we can afford to—"

"Do you think I fucked a stranger for a bottle of champagne?"

The tables around them got quiet, but Lola kept her eyes on Johnny as her words hung in the air.

"Christ," he said. "You really believe that's what I think? That might be the shittiest thing you've ever said to me."

She covered her mouth. "Oh, God. You're right."

"You can quit staring," Johnny said to someone behind her. "Nothing to see here."

Lola's phone chimed with a text message. She pulled it out to see the same unknown number that she'd answered earlier.

You're still here with me. Say yes.

"Who is it?" Johnny asked.

"No one." She put the cell away. "Brenda about this weekend." Lola stood. "I just need a minute alone."

"No. Sit."

She looked at the table and sat back in her chair.

"The last few days, you've left the room in the middle of our conversations more times than I can count. What's going on?"

Sometimes it was all just too much to take in. Johnny was so happy about the bar. She was happy for him. She couldn't seem to get further than that.

While they'd been seated at the kitchen table Sunday night, working on their plan, she'd glanced up once to find Johnny staring at her. She knew what was on his mind, but she was too afraid to bring it up. What did he think happened that night? Was the truth better or worse than his imagination?

"Hey," Johnny said, calling her back from the memory. "Forget about the champagne. What're you thinking right now?"

"I feel guilty," she said quietly. "You're hurting. And it's my fault."

"No. We went into this together." He craned his neck to catch her eye. "Didn't we, Lo? Start to finish, you and me. Have I given you any reason to think I'm hurt?"

"You've been so supportive." He had been, in his own way. He didn't judge her or put the blame on her. He was quiet, but that didn't mean he wasn't there for whatever she needed. "Somewhere inside, though, you must be angry."

He sighed, working his jaw back and forth. "I try not to think about it. I think about the money and us. As long as I focus on you and me and what's ahead of us, I'm okay."

She tried not to think of it either, but Beau's grip on her—his large, enveloping hands physically on her body but also the unwavering way he demanded her attention—would flash over her without warning. Sometimes that was the real reason she had to leave the room. Johnny had been so calm about it all, but his lack of reaction was beginning to worry her. "If you thought about it," she said, "how would it make you feel?"

"Crazy. Hurt." He looked away for one quick second. "And yes, angry. But none of that is directed at you."

"Are you sure?"

"Yeah. Those feelings will go away, I just need a little time."

"If you had a second chance at the money, would you take it?"

"You mean would I have said yes, knowing what I know now?" He spun his water glass on the table. "I can't really answer that, babe. I don't know what you went through. I mean, look at what we did today. I never thought handing over that much money would be one of the best moments of my life, but there it is. Even though we didn't yet—I already feel like I finally own something. And that something will mean a better life for my girl."

She pressed her palms together in her lap. "That's not what I was asking."

"What then?"

The damp spot on the tablecloth grew while Johnny absentmindedly played with his water glass. She'd decided not to bring it up for a reason. The plan was that she'd never see Beau again, but his voice was still in her ear. He expected her to say yes. To submit to him another night. "Never mind," she said. "I shouldn't have said anything."

"Said anything about what? Look at me."

She met his puzzled eyes. "He made me another offer, Johnny."

"Who?"

"You know who." She chewed her bottom lip. "I told him no."

"He made you another *offer*?" He rubbed his forehead, shaking his head. "I don't understand. When?"

"The morning after, when I was getting out of the car."

He dropped both forearms on the table and fixed his attention on her. "That was days ago. Why am I only hearing about this now?"

"I didn't want to make things worse."

"Worse?" he asked, raising his voice. "That's not fair. Have I been anything other than completely understanding through all of this?"

"You've been amazing," she said, her head lowered.

"If anyone has secrets, it should be you and me. Not you and him."

"It wasn't a secret, I just—"

"Don't. Stop."

She lifted her eyes again.

He leaned in. "I don't think you *understand* how *understanding* I've been. I didn't go crazy. I haven't treated you differently since then." He pointed to his chest. "I don't deserve to be shut out."

"You haven't said no yet," Lola pointed out.

He sat back against his chair and crossed his arms. "I mean, what the fuck am I supposed to say to that? What exactly went on that he'd pay another million for you?"

"Johnny," she exclaimed. His words sent a stabbing pain through her stomach. Apparently, he was just as capable as Beau of making her feel cheap.

"No," he said. "I want to know. If this is on the table, I need to know what happened that night. What exactly he got for his money. Where he took you."

Her mouth fell open. "We agreed—"

"I did that for you. You don't think I want to know the truth? It drives me insane wondering what a million dollars bought that prick."

"Stop." Lola's throat was so thick, she couldn't catch a breath. "I feel sick."

"Yeah?" He banged his fist on the table. "Well, so do I."

"Sir," the waiter said, hurrying over. "I have to ask you—"

"I knew it," Johnny said. He threw his napkin on the table and stood. "I'm sorry we're not good enough for your fifty-dollar steak. We'll go."

"I didn't say that, sir. Absolutely not—we value your business. I was just going to ask you to keep it down."

"Johnny, just sit," Lola pleaded.

"I have to get out of here." He walked away.

"I'm so sorry," Lola said to the waiter, grasping for her purse from the floor. "I can pay."

"For what?" he asked. "Bread and water?"

"I don't know. I'm just so sorry."

"Don't be." He smiled. "You aren't the first couple to fight before appetizers."

She thanked him. His graciousness reinforced her idea that people from all walks of life had money, and she and Johnny had as much right to be there as anyone. It was an effort, but she kept her eyes up as she made her way through the tables to the exit.

The valet stood from his station when he saw her.

"Did my boyfriend just come out here?" she asked.

"Guy with the ponytail? He just left."

"With the car?"

"Yes, ma'am."

Lola looked down at her dress and heels. Johnny wasn't the type to abandon her, which meant he just hadn't thought of her at all. She wasn't sure which was worse. No matter how you looked at it, she had no way of getting home, and she wasn't even wearing clothes she felt comfortable in. That was Johnny's fault.

"Asshole," she muttered. She took out her phone to call him. Beau's text was still on the screen.

You're still here with me. Say yes.

She read it again. *Here with me.* Their night had gone so fast, it was almost as if it hadn't happened at all. Except that once in a while, she *was* still there with Beau, reliving their moments together. She'd seen Mayor Churchill on TV that morning and remembered holding Beau's hand in the crowd at the benefit. On the way to the restaurant earlier, Nirvana had been on the radio, and Lola had hummed along, back at the speakeasy.

She moved her finger to hover over his phone number. It wasn't long ago they'd talked. With a tap, she could call Beau to come get her. Maybe he still had the hotel room. It shouldn't have even been an option, but it was—and a luxurious one at that. She knew with certainty that Beau would come, just like she knew he wouldn't have left her behind in the first place.

She cleared the text and called Johnny instead.

◆⊠◆⊠◆

It was after two in the morning when Lola heard noises outside their apartment. She stood from the couch. "I've been trying to get ahold of you," she said before the door was even open. "Where have you been?"

Johnny toed off his shoes and left them by the door. "Thinking."

"Drinking?" she asked.

"No. Just thinking."

"I was worried."

"I know," he said. "I was also worried. About you."

"Serves you right for leaving me there," she said.

"I had to get away before I said something I regretted."

She fell back onto the couch. "I know." She'd been angry for the first few hours. The whole cab ride home, she'd been tempted to give the driver the address to Beau's hotel. If he'd been there, Beau would've made sure she was comfortable, and that sounded appealing after the week she'd had. But her anger had turned to concern around midnight. Now she was just glad Johnny was home safely.

He came to her and bent to take her cheeks in his hands. He kissed her. "You're always so good. So understanding. What did I do to deserve you?"

"Sit, Johnny. We should talk."

He sat close to her and held her hand. "I know what we agreed on, but if I'm going to consider this, I need to know what happened that night. I can't send you back in there if I don't."

So he *would* send her in to do their dirty work again. Lola rested her elbow on the arm of the couch as she leaned away a little. Johnny was fine enough with the first night that he'd let her do a second.. If she were a spiteful person, she'd tell him all about her night and see if he still felt that way. Johnny wasn't built for details.

"What makes you think I'd do it again?" she asked.

"You brought it up. I figured if you weren't considering it…you would've kept it to yourself."

"I brought it up because I thought you should know."

"Yes, right after you brought up money. I hate to admit it, but maybe we are in over our heads."

"We can still call the whole thing off," she said. "We don't have to buy Hey Joe. We could do something else."

"I can't." He shook his head. "You didn't endure what you did so I could give up before we even got started."

She swallowed at the word *endure*. It wasn't the word she would've chosen, which was why a second night of it could be dangerous. "I don't want you to give up. We'll just have to get creative and take on as many tasks as we can so we don't have to pay other people."

He released her hand and put his arm along the back of the sofa. "Can't believe I'm saying this, but a million dollars is a hell of a lot less money than I thought."

"But it's not nothing," she said. "Maybe we could even take out a loan in the beginning."

"True."

She waited. "That's it? 'True'?"

"You keep saying how we need every last dollar. How it's not enough. And you—you already did it once. We can never take that back. Once the line is crossed, it's crossed."

She watched him closely. To her, a second night was not the same as a first night. It meant sinking deeper into Beau and the way she felt when she was with him, but there was no way of explaining that to Johnny. "What are you saying?"

"I guess that if you look at it from a strictly business point of view—this kind of money for a few hours is unheard of. You'd already know what you were in for. We sort of already broke the seal off this deal."

"Looking at it from a strictly business point of view makes me feel like a prostitute," she said flatly. He still hadn't said no. She couldn't tell if that was a yes. "Is that how you see me?"

A red splotch appeared on Johnny's neck. "A *prostitute*? God, no." He kneeled in front of her to take her stiff, tense hands in his warm ones. "If that's how you feel, of course we won't do it. What we have now will be enough. How did we even get in this mess?"

"I have no idea," she said.

Johnny looked at her earnestly. She put a hand on his face.

"Feel better?" he asked, smiling up at her.

She averted her eyes. Beau's offer had only been on the table a few hours, but she'd already begun to think about how it would be to see him again. Yes, she had an idea of what a second night would entail, but Beau also had ways of surprising her.

No, the possibilities *would've* been endless.

Johnny stood up. They held each other's gaze a minute. "So it's decided," he said, turning.

"Wait, Johnny." She grabbed his hand.

He looked back at her.

She put her lips to his knuckles. "Johnny," she whispered. Her hand fit perfectly in his. *Remember this?* A gentle touch to love her. Fingers that had been everywhere on her body, over and over.

His eyes traveled from her face to their hands. "You think this is a good idea?"

"I don't know." She pulled him back down to the couch and let go of him to lift her tank top over her head. It left her bare from the waist up. He looked. She leaned over to undo his slacks before climbing onto his lap.

"You…" He kept his eyes on her breasts.

"What, Johnny?" she asked. What did he need? Reassurance of her love? To know if he'd been a better lover than Beau? She grew hungrier by the second. She'd had sex on her mind since she'd left Beau, but she hadn't wanted to make the first move. "Ask me anything, and I'll answer."

He cleared his throat. "He showed you his test results, right?"

Lola stilled. It wasn't what she'd expected. It was something a man should never have to ask his girlfriend, even if it was a perfectly reasonable—almost necessary—question for their situation. "Yes. He's clean."

"Okay." He looked up finally. "What?"

"Nothing." Right before they made love was not the time to anguish over the heartbreak of a question like that. She forgot it and set her palms against his shirt. "Put your arms around me."

He did, pulling her closer by her backside.

"Stop thinking," she said.

He kissed her. She settled her hips to get closer to him as she unbuttoned his shirt. She reached between them, felt for him, rubbed him. And rubbed him harder, until he also reached down to move her hand away.

"I think I need more time," he said. "My mind keeps going somewhere it shouldn't."

"I'm still me, Johnny."

"I know." He kissed her, and he was present. His forehead rested against hers. "I know. Can you just say it out loud? Maybe it will help."

"Say what out loud?"

"That you did it. You never even said you did it."

"How would that help?"

"I don't know. Can you…?"

Her eyes fell to the exposed skin at the base of his neck. She hadn't said it. Maybe it'd been intentional, because she was having trouble getting the words out. "I slept with him. That was the deal."

His chest rose and fell. He nodded. "I know. I don't know why I wanted to hear it."

"It's all right." She dipped her head to get him to look at her. "We're in uncharted waters here. You can always tell me what you need."

"So good," he whispered. "So understanding."

"I'm trying," she whispered back. "I know you are too." The resignation in his eyes was too much to handle. She'd forgotten that for her, all of this was real from the moment she'd gotten into that limo—but Johnny had never had that moment. He was in limbo somewhere between making the deal and getting her back. "You must be hungry," she said, the only fix she could offer at that moment.

"Not really."

"I can make you a sandwich."

He shook his head. "It's okay. I'm sorry I ruined dinner."

"I heard fifty-dollar steak sucks anyway." They both laughed a little. "However, I happen to make a mean peanut butter and jelly sandwich." She winked. "And all it'll cost you is one kiss."

Chapter Four

Vero poured two shots and slid one down the bar. Lola caught it and drank it down in a gulp. "What was that for?" she asked, sending back an empty glass.

"Think you need it. Should I get Johnny one?"

"Why?"

"Think he needs it too."

Lola turned to lean her hip against the bar. "What do you mean?"

"He's been staring at you the way I see the regulars stare at a new woman in this bar. Like he wants to meet you but doesn't know what to say."

"Need a pitcher of Fat Tire," Amanda called over the bar.

"Got it." Vero got started on the order as Amanda walked away. "You and Johnny all right?"

"We're fine," Lola said. Since their steak dinner the night before was a bust, they'd splurged on gourmet hamburgers for lunch that day. It was a fraction of the cost of the steak, but it was them, and that was the most important thing. They'd had a little too much beer and sun followed by a nap. Beau and his offer hadn't come up. She'd thought it was nearly the perfect afternoon, but when she woke up, Johnny had left for work without her.

"You roleplaying something kinky?" Vero pressed on. "Like the whole stranger in a bar thing? If so, I'm cool with it. Maybe I can help."

Lola laughed, shaking her head. "Well, we're not really supposed to talk about it, but you're impossible to shut up."

Vero set the pitcher on the bar and turned to face Lola. "This sounds real kinky. Lay it on me."

"No, it's not that." Lola lowered her voice. "Johnny and I are buying Hey Joe." Lola grinned at Vero's expression. She wasn't sure she'd ever seen Vero's mouth open with nothing coming out.

"Are you messing with me?" Veronica asked.

"Nope. We're doing it. Soon it'll be ours."

Vero slapped the bar with one hand. "Holy shit, girl—are you kidding me?"

"Not messing, not kidding. You happy?"

"Happy? Haven't been this excited since nasty cousin Herb fell face first into a pile of mud at the family reunion. This is cause for celebration."

Lola smiled harder. "Thanks, V."

"How'd you pull it off? This got something to do with that cousin of yours who died?"

"Great uncle," Lola corrected.

"Uncle? I could've sworn Johnny said…" She narrowed her eyes. A couple seconds passed. Lola's hands went clammy as Vero's expression morphed and she tilted her head back, shaking it. "No. Something's off here."

"Nothing is off. Seriously."

"Lola. Oh, fuck. What did you do?"

"Nothing—"

"You slept with that man." She tiptoed closer. "You *slept* with…? Oh, honey, I wasn't serious when I said—I didn't think you'd go through with it."

The room was too hot. Vero was too close. Lola hopelessly fanned herself with her hand. She'd never been a good liar. "It-it's complicated. Even if I thought I could explain, it wouldn't make any sense."

Vero looked across the room. "Johnny let you do this?"

"He didn't 'let' me do anything," Lola said. "We made a decision. Together."

"Hell, no." She shook her head like her mass of frizzy curls was on fire. "No, no, no. My man ever asked me to have sex with someone else, he'd see the business end of my fist before he got the words out. Don't matter how much money's involved."

"Vero," Lola said. "There's so much more to the situation than you think. Just let it be."

"Let it be? I can't. This is not cool."

"Johnny and I have been through hell these past few weeks," Lola said. "There's no way you could understand."

"What I understand is that you just took a very wrong turn down a dangerous path."

"Veronica," Lola said, shocked. "You're judging me? Have I ever *once* judged your choices? Didn't I support your decision to stay with Freddy after the way he treated you? Didn't Johnny and I take you in for weeks when you finally cut him loose?"

"That's different. That was between me and Freddy. But this isn't between you and Johnny because you brought a third person into your relationship, and now he'll never go away. Promise you that."

Lola frowned. It wasn't that Vero was necessarily wrong, but Lola couldn't handle her on top of Johnny on top of Hey Joe. She didn't need anyone to tell her what they'd done was wrong.

"What I need right now is a friend, Vero," Lola said.

Vero abruptly reached out and hugged Lola. Hard. It took Lola a moment to reciprocate. "You and I go back," Vero said softly. "When you came here, I thought you were just another chick. But knowing you has changed my life. You need me, I'm here."

"You're the one who changed mine," Lola said. "You and Johnny straightened me out."

Vero drew back a little to look Lola in the face. "Because it didn't take me long to see that you're better than this shit. And now I hear this." She shook her head sadly. "It's Johnny I'm pissed at, babe. Not you. But I'll keep it to myself because you asked me to. I'm just sorry you felt the need to do it. I-I hope it was, you know, worth it."

"It will be when we all get Hey Joe back to what it should be."

"If anyone can, it's you two. You'll survive this. Strong as an ox, girl."

Was she? Was Lola strong enough? She wasn't so sure. Now that they'd decided not to take Beau's offer, the weight of reality was growing heavier. Every hour she was in the bar, she thought of how soon it would all be theirs. It was more responsibility than she'd ever had in her life.

Vero finally let go of her. "What was it like?"

"With Beau?" Lola bit her bottom lip. "Like a wild dream stuck on fast forward. I think I went to another world for a few hours—like it wasn't even *real*."

Vero looked around the bar and held her palms face up toward the ceiling. "And now you guys get everything you wanted."

"Mostly," Lola said. "Turns out running a bar's expensive."

"I could've told you that. But we'll make this work. Even if I got to show up on time, I'm with you guys."

Lola half smiled. "Thanks. Means a lot."

Vero was suddenly even closer. "So, all right. We know it was fucked up, but sometimes that's the best kind. I bet that tall drink of water stripped off his designer suit to reveal all kinds of kinky. Tell me about the sex."

Lola blushed furiously, waving her off with a rag. "Stop it."

"That good?" Vero's eyes got big. "You *enjoyed* it?"

"Quiet," Lola said. "That's the last thing Johnny needs to hear."

"So you did," she stated as if that proved anything.

Lola looked at her hands. It hadn't been kinky to Lola. It'd been more natural, just—right. He'd done new things to her, like commanding her to her hands and knees, and she'd liked them. He'd done normal things and made them worthy of fireworks. The sixteenth floor of the Four Seasons was a private space for her to be completely herself and to experience Beau without guilt. "It was different," she said carefully. "Completely and utterly different than anything I've ever experienced." Lola looked up. "Just different."

"Lola. It's sex. It's okay if you enjoyed it. That's kind of what's supposed to happen."

"Let me put it this way. He's everything you'd think by looking at him and more."

"More?"

Lola thought immediately of his cock, how large it'd been in her hand, how it'd dominated her mouth. It wasn't what she'd meant, but she had a feeling Vero was thinking the same thing. "More. Sometimes it was like he knew me better than I knew myself. Like he'd memorized a map beforehand or something. And not just of my body. It—I can't really put it into words."

"I can. Basically he fucked your brains out."

Lola was done blushing. This time she tutted at Vero, but she said, "Right out of my head."

"Damn." Vero shrugged. "That's all I got, just—*damn*. He must've been something else."

"He was. Just don't mention any of this to Johnny."

"How's he taking it?"

"I'm not sure." Lola glanced over at her boyfriend. He was laughing with a table of customers she didn't recognize. He always made people feel at home. "He's been pretty quiet about it. I'm just glad he's getting all this."

"He'll do great, the bastard," Vero said. "Give it some time, though. Guess that's all you can do now. Don't overthink things."

Don't overthink things. Lola had tried to erase Beau's text message and his number. Each time, she hesitated until the screen went black. His number within reach—that felt like thinking about him. Like he was right there. Once she erased it, he would be gone. Officially.

When the bar was at its busiest a few hours later, Lola snuck out back for a cigarette. She'd assumed no one would notice, but Johnny opened the door a minute later. He looked around until he spotted her leaning against the building's brick wall.

"You all right?" he asked, coming over. "Been a while since you had one of those."

She nodded. "Are you?"

"I'm fine."

She offered him the cigarette, and he took a drag. "I've missed that," he said with his exhale.

"Tell me about it."

"Look at us," he said. "We're buying a business. We quit smoking. We're adults."

"When did that happen?"

"Fuck if I know. We had fun, though. Think we're still fun?"

"Fun adults? I think the two are mutually exclusive."

He smiled. "Yeah. Last week I told Tom if he opened the bar late one more time, I'd beat his ass. I'm my dad."

Lola laughed. "You even sound like him when you say it."

Johnny put the cigarette to his lips. He had that far off look in his eyes she'd been seeing too much of lately.

"What's going on, Johnny?" she asked. "Are you pissed at me?"

He looked down at her. "Pissed?"

"You're distant. You've barely talked to me all night."

"You were right the other day. I have to get serious about the bar now. I can't be screwing around anymore."

"That's not what I meant. This is a lot of work, but it's supposed to be fun too. This is a dream come true."

"Yeah. Just need a little time to get adjusted."

"You left home without me today," Lola said. "I had to hitch a ride with Vero."

"I had a meeting with Mitch."

Lola felt as if she'd been slapped. It had never once occurred to her that either of them would need to meet with Mitch alone. She leaned toward him. "You don't think maybe I ought to be there for that?"

"That's what you want, babe, sure. I thought I was supposed to handle the business stuff."

She proceeded with caution for both their sakes. Johnny's voice had an edge to it that she'd heard during their arguments, usually when he was too frustrated to remain rational. "I want this to be your baby," Lola said. "It's your dream. But I'm part of this too—a big part. You're in charge, but that doesn't mean I'm not at all in charge. I'm here to make decisions *and* to support you however I can."

He laughed just under his breath. "However you can. I'd say so."

"You know what? I don't like this snarky side of you." She'd probably said things she shouldn't have at some point too, but it wasn't in either of their natures to be deliberately mean.

He shrugged and looked up at the sky.

"Are you mad because I won't do it again?" she asked. "Or because I would?"

"Well, which is it?" he asked, his head still tilted back.

"Whatever you want it to be," Lola said.

"I just want the truth."

"And that's all I've ever wanted from you."

"All right, so give it to me straight." He glanced back down at her. "You want to or you don't? Did you enjoy yourself?"

"We agreed not to get into details."

"Jesus Christ." He laughed in disbelief. "No wonder you don't want me asking questions. You *did* enjoy it."

"Would you prefer I hated it? On my back, silently crying, pleading at the ceiling for it to be over?" She turned her face away as her cheeks got hot. It was almost as if he'd heard her conversation with Vero, but he'd been across the room.

The cigarette burned down in his hand, and he didn't respond.

She knew the answer to her own question. Things could've gone much worse with Beau, and she was grateful they hadn't. She'd do a lot for Johnny, but she wasn't going to wish it'd been terrible for her just so he would feel better. "I'd do it again," she said. "If you thought it was for the best."

"For the best," Johnny murmured. "The best being money."

"The best being our future."

"But here's the clincher, folks," he said. "The kind of future they want costs money."

"If you feel that strongly, just tell me not to do it."

"Thought we already decided you wouldn't." He tossed the cigarette on the ground and stamped it out. "You want to do it, then do it. Don't try to make it look like I'm asking you for it. You did it once, so it's not even like it's that big of a deal."

Lola set her jaw. "How can you say that?"

He walked away. "You got his number," he said, pulling open the back door. "You don't need me to make the arrangements."

Lola stared after him. She had the strange but satisfying sense that she'd gotten away with something. Like she'd get as a young girl when her mom would occasionally let her pick one thing from the candy aisle. But it was more than that. Johnny wouldn't make a firm decision, so she had to, and if he came to regret the outcome, he'd only have himself to blame for not speaking up. She was free to make the mistake that—she was slowly figuring out—she wanted to make.

She hadn't stopped thinking about the way Beau had owned her, as if it were a craving she couldn't kick. Beau's unwavering attention—the only kind he knew—could easily become addicting.

She took out another cigarette to calm herself—her hand shook as she lit it. Money? What money? It was becoming less important the greater her need grew. Not just any kind of need, but the kind Beau incited in her, that built and built to an unbearable level. The kind only he could fulfill. She was feeling that way more and more lately, whenever she thought of him like she did now.

And now she'd get her fix again. The decision was made for her. Johnny had cemented it when he'd walked away. She took her cell from her pocket and pulled up Beau's phone number.

"Lola, ma chatte," Beau answered. His voice was low and raw.

"You were sleeping," she said.

"It's one in the morning."

"I'm sorry."

"Don't be," he said. "Unless this is a dream. Then you should be very sorry."

She smiled. Except for a yellow streetlamp nearby, it was dark. They were alone.

"How are you?" he asked.

She blew out a breath and flicked ash from her cigarette. "I'm okay."

"Most women who call me in the middle of the night are not okay."

"I don't want to be most women," Lola said quietly.

"You aren't. Not to me."

She closed her eyes. "I wish you wouldn't say things like that."

"So this call isn't personal, then. That would make it business."

Lola waited. Her mind was even more made up hearing his voice, but she couldn't sound too eager. Just like Johnny, Beau had to know with certainty that money anchored their arrangement. That there were boundaries. "What are the terms of your new offer?"

After rustling on the other end and a short silence, he said, "The same. Including the test if you've slept with Johnny again."

"Why would that matter?"

"If you've had a partner after the test, then it matters."

There was that sterile word again—*partner*. "Beau, he's my boyfriend."

"You weren't with him the night you were with me. Who knows how he kept himself occupied?"

She stared daggers at the back door. She knew Johnny better than she knew anyone, and he wasn't a cheater. "Johnny would never. You don't know him."

"I don't have to. I know people. Resentment is ugly. It makes people do ugly things."

She shook her head. "He wouldn't."

"So have you slept with him?"

She took a drag of her cigarette. She imagined Beau sitting forward in his bed, the sheet around his lap. The corner of his hungry mouth twitching as he waited. His mouth was so goddamn hungry when it was on her. "No. Have you?"

"He's not my type."

"Be serious. You know what I mean."

"I haven't seen anyone. The impression you left is…unshakeable."

"How romantic," she said dryly to hide the fact that she wanted it to be true.

"You asked me to be serious. I am. Housekeeping has replaced the sheets but I smell your perfume here. It's impossible, I know." His voice dropped even lower. "The window is still smudged from your tits."

Her pulse stuttered. From the start, he'd been catching her off guard, startling her with his brashness. She bit her lip, knowing any noise she made would come out sounding like a moan. "I—I don't wear perfume."

He chuckled. "So, Lola. Do we have a deal?"

"Five hundred the night before. Five hundred the next morning."

"Sunset to sunrise."

"When?" she asked.

"If I hadn't already lost the hours, I'd say right now. God knows I want you here. Can it be tomorrow?"

"It's a weekday."

"But you work nights," he said. "You can sleep the next day."

"I meant for you."

"Don't worry about me. My impatience reaches disconcerting levels where you're involved."

"I'm flattered. I think." She hesitated, not ready to get off the phone. Talking to him was smoothing out the rollercoaster week she'd had, a temporary cure for her distress. "Tomorrow."

"Tomorrow," he repeated.

She hung up before she said something she shouldn't—like "I can't wait" or "I look forward to having you inside me again." The stab of guilt in her gut was drowned by the quick beats of her heart. Vero and Johnny were both right. Lola liked this. She enjoyed it. Not only that—she fucking *wanted* it.

Chapter Five

Lola couldn't come up with the words to tell him. She and Johnny had been driving home from the bar for ten minutes, but she'd been pretending to sleep with her head back against the passenger seat headrest. In fact, she'd been awake, searching for those impossible words to say she'd promised herself to another man tomorrow night. It was hard enough without wondering if Johnny would be relieved or angry. Was *she* relieved? Was she angry? Johnny wasn't acting like the man she knew he was. It made her wonder if he'd ever been, or if it was possible she'd built him up to something else over the years.

Johnny pulled into their parking spot and shut off the car. "When we own the bar, does that mean we can hire other people to work this late?"

She looked over at him. It was the first attempt at conversation he'd made since their argument.

"We're getting too old for this shit," he continued. There was something in his voice—nerves? Guilt? When she didn't respond, he said, "I'm sorry about earlier. I acted like a jerk."

Lola glanced at her hands. "I'm not admitting to that. To the thing about being too old." One thing she appreciated about Johnny was his ability to admit his faults. When they fought, he almost always apologized first. And when he didn't, it was because he didn't think he'd done anything wrong. "I promised my early-twenties self that I'd never get old," she said. "But my late-twenties self is having a tough time holding up her end of the bargain."

Johnny grinned—she knew without even looking. Things were right with him again, but not for long. As they got out of the car and walked to their apartment, the air around Lola seemed thick, as if a storm were brewing.

Johnny fought with the lock on the front door. "Every damn time," he muttered. He flipped on the lights once they were inside. "We should think about getting a new place."

"I'd like that," Lola said.

He tossed his keys on the coffee table. "How much would you love not paying rent?"

"So much," she said on the way to the kitchen. "Adults pay mortgages, after all."

"Yep." He came up behind her, curling his arms around her middle as she poured herself water from the tap. "You know what else adults do?"

"I can think of a thing or two," she said.

He nuzzled her neck, squeezing her to him. "How about a shower to wash the night off? We both stink like cigarettes." He slid his hands up to her breasts. "Good thing I like you anyway."

"A shower at three in the morning?"

"I don't care. Horny, babe."

Water flooded the glass in the sink. She was unaffected by his advances. His cruelty and abrupt dismissal earlier still left her chilly. But even if she responded to Johnny's touch, she couldn't sleep with him. Not after she'd told Beau she hadn't.

"Johnny," she said.

"Yeah."

"I called him."

He stopped moving. His breath warmed her cheek. Her anxious heart was trying to burst out of her chest.

"What?" He released her. "You're going back?"

She turned around and steeled herself against the sink. "Yes."

"But you—I thought we'd discuss it more."

"You said what you had to say outside the bar. I didn't like it, but you said it. So I made the call."

"Well, fuck." He ran his hands over his scalp and held them up. "You just made the call, that's it?"

"He agreed to another million," she said. "Same terms as before."

He dropped his arms at his sides. "You should've discussed this with me. What if I didn't want you to do it again? Or what if we could've gotten more? We hold the cards here."

She gripped the counter, narrowing her eyes. The money was becoming too important a factor for him. "Don't be ridiculous. Another million is more than enough. And you're the one who told me to call."

"Come on, Lola. You know how I am. I was mouthing off because I was pissed."

She'd known exactly that, but she'd made the call anyway. Did that mean she was to blame? "So, what? You don't want me to do it?"

He blew his cheeks out with his exhale. "I…"

They both looked away from each other, he into the next room and she at the stove. Her heartbeat had slowed. There was no point in pretending he didn't want that money enough to let her do this again. She wasn't the only bad guy. Her desire to see Beau became less of a weight on her shoulders.

"I saw a video online. You and him at that benefit or whatever." Johnny's eyes darted over the floor.

"When?"

"A couple days ago."

She'd forgotten he might see that. Johnny'd wanted details—how was that for one? Her red lips glued to Beau's mouth, turning his lips red too? "Why didn't you tell me?"

He shrugged in his lumbering way, looking up again. "Brenda found it on one of those entertainment news sites. Mark showed me it on his phone."

"What'd you say?"

"It caught me totally off guard," he said. "I had nothing."

Her stomach heaved. She covered it with one arm. Mark and Brenda weren't judgmental people, but that didn't matter. A situation like this was nearly impossible to justify. "You told them the truth? Please tell me you're joking."

"What was I supposed to say, it was your long lost twin out for a night on the town with one of the richest men in Los Angeles? Mark and I played pool with the guy the night he came into the bar."

"Too many people know."

"You should've thought of that. Did you not notice the cameras? I asked you not to kiss him, so you went and did it in front of thousands of people."

"But, Johnny, he—"

"Yeah, yeah, he made you do it. They called you 'Beau Olivier's Sassy Mystery Woman.' *Sassy*? In what universe do people use that word? And to describe *my* girlfriend?"

"You don't understand. I was playing a part."

"You were damn convincing too. Especially when you told that reporter to take her hands off your man. Real *sassy*. You think I liked having to watch that in front of my best friend? Trying not to react?"

Lola rubbed under her eyes with her knuckles. "I'm sorry you had to see that, but you know what I was dealing with."

"Whatever." He started to leave, but turned back to her. His stance relaxed, and he put his hands out, as if asking her for help with something. It reminded her of the first time he'd come with her to the Laundromat, and she'd explained the concept of delicates. "So tell me how this goes," he said. "He picks you up. Takes you—where, his place? A motel? Does he push you onto your knees or do you go willingly?"

She flinched. "Stop it."

"In your stupid dress and red lipstick—yeah, I saw that on the video too. Why don't you wear lipstick like that for me?"

"Like what?" she asked. "You want me to wear red lipstick while I wait tables at a dive bar?"

"Did it ever occur to you that I might like to see you in such a fancy dress?"

"No, because it's not us. That was some girl Beau dressed up like a doll."

"Oh, drop the act. What girl wouldn't love to be fussed over like that?"

So what if she had? The hair on the back of her neck rose. "You want me to dress up for you, then maybe you could make a fucking fuss over me once in a while."

His eyebrows shot up. "You think I don't? I brag about you to anyone who'll listen. My hot-as-shit girlfriend Lola—have you seen her in leather pants? Do you know how smart she is, how many ideas she has? Have you seen those eyes? I love those fucking blue eyes, man." Johnny leaned his hands against the tiled counter and took a deep breath. "I'm the luckiest son of a *fucking* bitch."

Johnny had his moments, but hearing how highly he thought of her was harrowing. It was almost enough for her to confess her attraction to Beau so it would stop feeling like such a secret between them. But she couldn't bring herself to. She'd already imagined Beau at the curb several times, waiting for her to come to him. It *was* a secret, and it was dirty.

If she didn't go now, her mind would fill in the blanks of their night together. Driving somewhere exciting to start the night. Beau, unable to keep his hands off her in public knowing how good it could be.

"We can't do this," Johnny said.

Lola jerked her head to him. But she'd made the decision for them both. He'd had his chance. He didn't get to say no now. Did he? She couldn't cancel. She didn't want to.

"We can't fight," he continued. "If we don't go into this together, then you're going in alone, and that puts us on opposite sides. With him in middle. We can't let him get between us."

Divided they were weaker. Beau knew that too, though. Her connection with Johnny stretched thinner the more it was pulled in opposite directions.

"We've done this once already, so how do we do it better this time?" He pushed off the counter and paced in front of her. He pulled on his chin. "It's like this. B— no, not business. Logical. This plus this equals that. Remove the emotional side and look at it logically. I'm not so good at that, babe, but you are. And I can try."

"Logical?" she asked. There was nothing logical about her and Beau in the same room, but there could be between her and Johnny. She followed him with her eyes.

"You already know what to expect," he said. "It was, what, less than twelve hours? For a million bucks." He paused. "He didn't hurt you. He didn't force you."

She shook her head.

"Say something."

It couldn't be done. Beau couldn't be managed. But Lola already felt him. She already tasted him. He was too close for her to walk away now. So she said, "I think you might be right."

"Two million gets us everything we wanted for the bar plus a new place and a car for you. Wouldn't that be enough?" he asked.

"Yes. It'll leave us a decent amount."

"Good." He nodded.

"But this is where we draw the line," she said. "I don't care if it's ten million for a week. This is far enough for me." No matter how tempted she was to spend more time with Beau, he'd bought enough of her. This had to be the last night for them.

Johnny stopped walking and came to stand in front of her. He cupped her face. "It is. This will be enough." His hands twitched like he was going to let go, but he didn't. "You know what else this gets us?"

"What?"

"A wedding fund."

Lola bit her lip. "Johnny."

"And a college fund."

It was the worst moment to bring up marriage and kids. It blended her budding desire for those things, her guilt over wanting Beau and her disappointment in Johnny—and herself—into the same pot. She pressed her hand to her chest. "Are you…you're serious?"

"Thought I was a piece of shit for wanting to bring a kid into the world when I had nothing to give him. But now? Everything's different. Send him to fucking Harvard if I want."

Lola hadn't even known where Harvard was until a few years ago. She couldn't keep up with what Johnny was saying. While she was selling her body for their future, there was no space in her mind for what that bought her. The picture wouldn't form.

Everything teetered dangerously close to the edge. She wasn't sure if the right decision was to reach out and pull it back—or to let it fall.

Chapter Six

When Lola was fourteen, she'd stolen makeup from a nearby drugstore. Some crimes were small. Some were big. Some were never found out—like the makeup—and then, were they really crimes at all? Lola paced in front of the window, pausing every few minutes to see the sun a little lower. She didn't even need what she'd taken. For years, she'd walked an extra four blocks to a different drugstore.

Lola stopped her march to watch the building across the street eat the last sliver of sun. Almost right away, a black limo appeared through the complex gate.

By the way her palms sweat and her heart pounded like they had fifteen years ago, Lola knew instinctively—she shouldn't get in that limo. There was more at stake than Johnny realized. Maybe enough to change them permanently. What kind of crime was it to do it anyway? If nobody knew but her, did it matter?

Beau had sent over a large box earlier that day with a red bow around it. The gift was lavish—a gold, beaded dress that crisscrossed in the back and had one slit all the way to her upper right thigh. Johnny had played it off—Beau had to pay for Lola's attention, and Johnny got that for free. But Lola had ignored him, running her fingers over the intricate beadwork. She didn't need to be pampered or spoiled, but that didn't mean it wasn't nice once in a while.

Lola had waited to change until Johnny'd left for work. She'd done her makeup, attempting to recreate her look from her first evening with Beau so he'd look at her again the way he had in the reflection of the salon's mirror. This time, though, she left her hair down.

Lola opened the door before Warner had a chance to knock. "Good evening, Miss Winters. Mr. Olivier is ready for you."

She locked the apartment behind her. "How long have you worked for Beau?" she asked as they curved around the pool and crossed the courtyard.

Warner kept his eyes forward. "Almost ten years."

"You must've been young when you started."

"Only a few years older than Mr. Olivier."

"Have you always wanted to—drive? Do you do other things?"

"I also drive Miss Leroux."

"Who?"

He leaned forward and opened the limo door. Beau had a pile of papers on his lap and a phone to his ear. He nodded at her and covered the mouthpiece. "Wait there a moment." He returned to his conversation as Lola stood on the sidewalk. Warner had disappeared.

Beau hung up without even a goodbye. He made a note on the paperwork in his lap, then tossed it on the car floor. He smiled up at her—like he was a king who'd just returned from a long day ruling his kingdom and had found her waiting for him. He got out of the car.

"What are you doing?" she asked.

He stood up to his full height and looked down on her. He lifted her chin with his knuckle, and just that one point of contact covered her in goose bumps. She'd selected her highest heels for the evening, but her head still tilted back for Beau.

"Thank you for dressing the part tonight," he said. "Though you were stunning in old jeans, something this beautiful finally does you justice."

He was sincere. The compliments he paid her never seemed to serve as a means to get something, even a reaction. It made her uncharacteristically weak in the knees.

"Any credit goes to the dress," she said. "Thank you for sending it."

Neither of them looked away. There were memories in the way they took from each other's eyes. For Lola, it was the way she fit into his arms as they fell asleep. It was the way he fucked her like he owned her.

"Let's go inside."

She took an automatic step back, blinking everything between them away. "Inside?" she asked, touching her chin where he'd just touched her. "What?"

"I'd like to see your place."

"No."

"No?" His tone was reminder enough that no matter what moments they'd had, he was in charge.

She panicked and blurted the first thing that came to her. "We can't. Johnny's home."

"I don't believe you. Last time he watched from the window."

She hadn't known that. She glanced over her shoulder. "Well, okay, you're right—he's…he's at work, but—"

"He didn't stay to see you off?" Beau asked, tilting his head.

"We decided it was better this way. The whole emotional goodbye thing was hard last time."

"So then it shouldn't be a problem. If you don't want him to know, don't tell him." He took a step, but she moved into his path.

"Why?" she asked.

He shrugged. "I want a glimpse into your life. It will help complete the picture in my head."

Her apartment was the last piece of her and Johnny Beau hadn't infiltrated. It was Johnny's kingdom, but she worried Beau would make it his the moment he walked in. "I'm not comfortable with that."

Beau made a point of turning and squinting at the sky behind him. It was still light out, but the sun was gone. He looked back at Lola. "Should we review the terms of our agreement?"

Sweat coated her upper lip. She licked it away. "No. That won't be necessary."

He inclined forward as if to kiss her and stopped. He'd taken his time the first night to make sure she was comfortable, but they were past that now. Did he need an invitation? She resisted the urge to lick her lips a second time.

He turned away to take something from the car and close the door. "Go ahead, ma chatte. Lead the way."

She went back the way she'd just come, Beau close behind her. Despite her wariness of his request, her body thrummed being with him again. She jiggled the key a few times until the lock gave and cleared her throat. "It's stubborn."

Beau walked into the apartment with one hand in his pocket. Under his arm was a medium-sized package wrapped in brown craft paper. Another present? It was uncomfortable, him spending money on her when he'd paid so much for one evening. He'd already given her the dress, and whatever plans they had tonight that warranted such a gown wouldn't come cheap.

He glanced up at the ceiling, then at a pillow on the couch. Johnny'd slept there the night before since he'd been unusually restless and hadn't wanted to keep Lola awake. Beau wandered across the room and looked down the hallway toward their bedroom.

"I wasn't expecting company," Lola said, picking up Johnny's dishes from the coffee table. She carried them to the sink.

Beau found her in the kitchen. "I like seeing people in their natural states. Don't clean on my account." He walked to the fridge and pulled a photo from under a magnet. "Camping?"

"In Yosemite."

He studied Johnny and Lola's smiling faces. "You have freckles."

"They're more noticeable when I get sun."

"You look young," he said. "And happy."

"We were."

He looked up at her with one eyebrow arched.

"Young, I mean," she said. "We *were* young. We're still happy."

His thumb pressed into the corner, sending a wrinkle through the center. He dumped the package heavily on the kitchen counter. "That's the first half of the money. I brought it in cash this time to avoid unwanted attention."

"Oh." She stared at the parcel, feeling foolish. It'd been presumptuous to assume it was a gift. "Maybe I should put it in a closet or something."

"That would be wise."

Before she could move, he dropped the photo on top of the money and walked over to her. She held up her hands to stop him, but he took her face and kissed her, backing her against the counter.

She shoved him off. "Stop," she said, panting. "This is his home."

He looked into her eyes. "That's the last time tonight I'll allow you to push me away. I've been as patient as I can." He was also breathing hard. "Since we said goodbye, you're all I've thought of."

"You wanted to see my place, fine. As long as we're here, though, I'm off limits. Completely. I don't give a damn about our agreement."

He continued to stare at her. She braced herself, knowing how touchy he could be when it came to Johnny. Instead, he took a step back. "Then we'd better go. I'm having a hard time getting ahold of myself."

They made their way outside, and she locked up. Had he said he'd been thinking of her since they'd said goodbye?

On the way to the car, he took her hand and brought it to his lips. "I'm glad you called. What we discussed on the phone—it still stands, doesn't it?"

"I haven't been with Johnny."

"I can't say I'm surprised."

He was baiting her, but she didn't even want to know what he'd meant by that. She looked at the ground. Did Beau think Johnny would be repulsed by her? Or that Lola was the one who didn't want it? She took the bait. "Why aren't you surprised?"

"I challenge any man to be okay with knowing the woman he loves was just with someone else. Not just the act of it, but the intimacy. The closeness. The touching, whispering." He glanced over at her, narrowing his eyes a fraction. "I'm not okay with it. Far from it."

His voice was almost accusatory, as if he were in Johnny's shoes. "Are you talking about him or yourself? Does it bother you, Johnny and me?"

He returned his eyes forward as they approached the car, and it was a moment before he answered. He leaned over to open the door for her. "Yes."

She didn't move. "But I'm not the woman you love."

He remained passive except that the angles of his jaw sharpened. "Just imagine if you were."

Chapter Seven

Within seconds of pulling away from the curb of Lola's apartment complex, Beau placed his hand just inside the slit of her dress and squeezed gently. She didn't expect his touch to overwhelm her like it did, as if it were the eye of a hurricane, the spot the rest of her body revolved around. She grabbed his wrist and pulled him off.

"What's wrong?" His cheek dimpled at one corner of his mouth.

"It's too much," she said.

"But it's nothing."

"It should be."

He replaced his hand but this time slid it under the dress. "You say you're doing this for the money. Maybe that's what he needs to hear. Your body tells a different story, though." His fingers edged along the inside of her thigh. "I know the other night's played a loop in your thoughts, just like it has in mine."

She shored up her resolve. Beau no doubt expected her to give in completely, but it was early. It was his nature to push, and it was hers to push back. She was having a hard time remembering why she should, though, with his hand burning against her skin. "Where are you taking me tonight?" she asked to change the subject.

"Care to take a guess?"

"In this gown, somewhere fancier than I've ever been. Right?"

"I don't know where you've been." He was teasing her, mischief in his twinkling eyes.

She pressed her lips together to suppress a smile. "There's a movie premiere in Hollywood."

"Not that unusual."

She shifted in her seat. "And the L.A. Opera season opened this week. *La Traviata* is playing."

"You've given this some thought."

"I looked online." Lola didn't want to sound overeager, but she'd been wondering all afternoon what was in store. "Of course, it's L.A.—there're tons of things happening. But those both sounded exciting."

He smiled. "Our first stop is to see my sister in the Hollywood Hills. It won't take five minutes."

Lola's brows furrowed. While researching Beau, she hadn't read anything about siblings. "You never mentioned a sister. Is she younger or older?"

"Younger by a couple years. You can wait in the car if you'd like."

She feigned interest in her fingernails. "Yes, that's probably best."

After a brief silence, he said, "Or, you can meet her. I'd like that."

She glanced up. "Wouldn't that be weird?"

"Not for me. Brigitte and I often attend the same events, so she's met some of my dates."

"Were they also paid to stand by your side, though?"

Beau looked as though he'd bitten into a lemon. "Of course not. You don't have to give her all the details."

"Right," she said. "I guess that would be fine."

"Good." He rubbed her leg. "I like that you wore the dress," he said softly. "I like that you shaved your legs again. Even if it wasn't for me."

His hand moved over her skin as though they'd never parted. Their connection hadn't weakened with time apart. She was just as hungry for his hand to move higher—to give her what only he could. She was supposed to be pushing back, but his pull was strong.

"It was," she said.

She was there, somewhere she both did and did not want to be. She could fight—he would win. She could give everything over—he would demand more. There was a war in and outside of her. Her against herself. Her against him. His weapons were growing, even as she inched over to his side.

He moved a little closer. His stiff hair smelled of men's product. She reached up and took a piece that had separated and fallen over his forehead. She slid her fingers along it to put it in place, but it just swung back. He had touched her—her chin, her leg, his lips to hers, his hand around hers, but she had not yet touched him except for that strand of hair. She wanted more. Wasn't it okay to take it? Isn't that what all three parties involved had agreed to?

This was her life for the next however many hours, and in that moment, she didn't feel like pretending she hated it. "Beau."

"Lola."

"Roll up the partition."

He swallowed audibly. "We're almost there."

She leaned over and hit the button herself. "This won't take long," she whispered. She thought her advance would've surprised him, but no sooner had she lifted a knee than he was pulling her onto his lap. He released her to unbutton his slacks, but she stopped him.

"Let me," she said.

She moved his hands to her breasts. He felt her impatiently, his fingers so hard she winced. She took him out. He went to put his mouth on her nipple, but she caught his face and lifted it to hers. "There's no time for that," she said. Her mouth pulled to his like a magnet to steel. They kissed with the same fury of urgency. She pushed aside her underwear and helped him inside her, taking a few agonizingly long moments to adjust to his girth when all she wanted was to screw him fast.

They began to move. She took his earlobe in her mouth as they found their rhythm. His fingers dug into her scalp, skin—anywhere he could get.

He took over, securing her hips to him and thrusting up into her. Her head fell back. The car ceiling blurred with bright spots. He guided her with one hand and circled her clit with the other. The ache from the last few days balled low in her stomach, growing and growing until she gasped in a silent scream with the crest of her orgasm. Beau pulled her off of him. He took himself in one hand, held her hip with the other and came all over the insides of her thighs.

"Beau," she panted. "God, Beau. How? How are we so…?"

His breaths were also labored. "Fast?"

She was going to say "good together," but even in her state, she knew she shouldn't. He looked at her as if he knew anyway.

They were no longer driving. Beau searched the space around them and scratched the back of his head. He frowned. "I didn't plan for sex in the car."

"I apologize for the disruption to tonight's program," she said, her mouth tingling with the urge to smile.

"It's all right," he said distractedly. "I just—aha." He picked her up and moved her from his lap to the seat. He reached for a beverage napkin from the limo's built-in bar, pulled her leg open and wiped the inside of one thigh.

"What are you doing?" she asked.

"Cleaning you."

It was unnecessary, but she didn't stop him. Being felt that way only added to the warm satisfaction her orgasm had left her with. "Why'd you pull out?" she asked.

His eyes traveled up. They glinted to match his smirk. "My sister can be intense. Your concentration should be on her at all times. I didn't want to leave anything behind that might—distract you."

"Oh. Always one step ahead," she murmured.

He dropped the napkin but didn't stop touching her.

Lola's head fell back against the window. "Your hands feel good."

"You mean when they aren't trying to get in your underwear?"

"That too." She smiled. "But this is also nice."

He pressed his thumbs to the insides of her thighs and massaged. "You keep tensing. Are you nervous?"

"No," she said, her eyes closed. "You have strong hands. And I'm not used to this."

"To what?"

"A massage. I haven't had many in my life."

He stopped. "You haven't?"

She lifted her head to look at him. "Our definitions of luxury are probably a little different. For instance, a car wash is something I only allow when we're flush."

"Oh, no." He crawled over her body and kissed her. "Tonight." He pecked her again. "You're getting the massage of your life."

"From you?" she asked.

"As if I want anyone else touching you."

The window rattled suddenly, and they jumped away from each other like teenagers caught making out.

"Beau?" came a woman's voice. She peered through the glass.

"Don't worry," he said as he tucked himself back into his pants. "They're tinted."

Lola fixed her underwear and dress. Instinctively, she leaned over and straightened Beau's tie. It was red, like the one he'd been wearing the night they'd met.

Before she could move away, he put his hand around her wrist and pulled her back. "Thanks," he said, kissing her once. "If I haven't said it yet, thank you for saying yes. I love—having you by my side."

He unlocked the door and got out while Lola stayed frozen where she was. He'd stumbled over the word *love* as if he were going to say something else. Something like "I love *you*." Her—*Lola*, which was ridiculous. True, from the moment they'd met, their relationship had been intense. Their first night had been a series of dates in the span of a few hours. They had a connection—an *attraction*—but it didn't matter.

"You've been sitting at the curb for ten minutes," she heard from outside in a woman's noticeable French accent. "What the hell were you doing?"

Beau cleared his throat. "Business call."

"Business?" She eyed Lola as she exited the car behind him. "Of course. Yes."

Lola found herself face to face with a woman who looked nothing like Beau. Her raven-colored hair was wrapped into a chignon. She just came up to Lola's chin, and she seemed to know it, turning her thin, pointed nose up in the air for added height.

Lola extended her hand and introduced herself.

His sister waved at the air around them. "I'm sure I'm coming down with something," she said. "I'd hate to get you sick."

Beau took Lola's hand instead and brought it to his side. "Lola, this is Brigitte. Who apparently has plans tonight."

Brigitte sighed and smoothed her hands over her tight, red sleeveless dress. "I don't, but my mother loved to say 'always dress for company.'"

"We're hardly company," Beau said.

"Good evening, Miss Leroux," Warner said from over the top of the limo.

"Ah," Brigitte said, "but Warner is here. Is he not worthy of such a beautiful dress?"

She trotted in her heels around the car to throw herself in Warner's open arms.

"Ignore her," Beau said to Lola, rolling his eyes. "She's that way with anyone who gives her attention.

Warner took her to an event last week, yet she acts like he's just returned home from war." Brigitte stroked Warner's suited arm. He looked stunned by her—and Lola had to admit, she was stunning.

"We don't have much time," Beau interrupted their moment. "No time at all, actually."

"You're always rushing me," Brigitte said, turning her back on Warner without so much as a glance. She led the way up the sidewalk. "Is this the girl?"

"Brigitte," Beau warned.

"What girl?" Lola asked. She followed Beau into the house through a front door twice as tall as them.

"Don't be shy, brother." Brigitte looked over her shoulder at Lola. The ordinary brown of her eyes should've been comforting, yet they were far too sharp for that. "It's just that Beau rarely mentions anyone, except that he's been talking about this one girl…"

Beau inhaled a deep breath and closed his eyes a moment. "*Brigitte, sois sage.* Is Louis in the study?" He looked at Lola. "Our lawyer."

Lola's attention was drawn up to the entryway's chandelier. "Wow."

"Ah, yes. It's called a *Montgolfier*—after the brothers," Brigitte said. "Do you know them? They're French."

Lola shook her head.

"They only invented the hot air balloon. That's why it's shaped like one but upside down."

"It's lovely," Lola said, "just like your home." Her heels, shorter than Brigitte's, clicked on the foyer's marble floor.

"Technically it's Beau's," Brigitte said. "He lets me stay here."

"It's *our* home," Beau said to her. "I think after nearly a decade here, it's okay to say."

"I just hate for you to think I'm taking advantage." She looked at Lola. "Beau must be careful about that sort of thing."

Lola didn't want to go down that road. She slid her hand from Beau's. "I don't understand. You live here?"

"Yes," Brigitte answered.

Just moments ago, Lola had been thinking how well they knew each other for such a short time. She must not have known much if she didn't even know where he lived. It hit her that maybe he wanted it that way. Why else would he bring her to a hotel when he had a home nearby?

Lola turned away to avoid Beau's inquisitive look. The pearl-colored living room had matching drapes that framed long, French doors. Gold molding trimmed the room, complementing the gold accents in the lamps, vases and side tables. The walls were lined with simple, elegant artwork that continued into the hallways and up the spiral staircase. A large vase of white and purple Calla lilies sat center on the entryway table.

She'd done a complete turn and now found Brigitte with her arms surrounding Beau's neck. Her eyes were large with admiration for him, and there was lip-gloss grease on his cheek. "Did you miss your baby sister?" she asked.

"Come on, Brigitte," he said. "I saw you two days ago. Let me go check with Louis."

She dropped her arms with a huff. "Yes, he's in the study. I'll keep Lily company."

"Lola," he corrected.

"Right."

Beau leaned over and kissed Lola's cheek. "Will you be all right?"

She nodded. "Go ahead."

"A few minutes, ma chatte."

Brigitte scoffed just loud enough to be heard.

He ignored her, winking at Lola before disappearing behind double doors.

Brigitte turned to her. "So, have you known my brother long?"

"A couple weeks."

"Oh. That *is* long."

Lola smiled thinly. "Not for most people."

"Beau isn't most people. But I'm sure you've figured that out."

"I have," Lola said. "He's certainly unlike anyone I've ever met."

"Don't worry if you're flustered by him. That's normal. My brother isn't easy to read unless you know him like I do." She arched one thin, black eyebrow and looked from Lola's feet to her face. "You, on the other hand, I'm not so sure."

"Sorry?"

"My brother's money gets many admirers. He has a good nose for bullshit, except when it comes to particularly studied actresses. That's where he needs my help."

Lola crossed her arms. "That isn't me."

"No?"

"No. And my relationship with Beau isn't anyone's business but ours. He knows exactly what I want from him."

Brigitte circled Lola, watching her the entire time. "You aren't Beau's usual type."

"If you're trying to intimidate me, it won't work."

Brigitte came to a stop in front of her. "My, my. You truly aren't his type." Her knuckles brushed along Lola's arm. "I can see why he's attracted to you."

Lola glanced at Brigitte's hand and smiled faintly. "Are you coming on to me, Brigitte?"

"If it's money you're after, I'm no pauper myself."

"As if you have the slightest clue what I'm after."

Brigitte cooed and fluttered like a little bird. "I see you're not worried about making a good impression on me."

"I have no delusions about my relationship with Beau. It's temporary, and he knows that. Therefore I have no reason to impress you."

"Temporary," Brigitte repeated. "You flinched at the word."

Lola had hoped Brigitte wouldn't catch that. She narrowed her eyes. "And *you* have a vivid imagination."

"Do you love him?" she asked.

The question flustered Lola, but this time she was ready for it. Her face remained smooth. "If I do or don't, it isn't your business. You aren't your brother's keeper—or are you?"

Brigitte's eye twitched noticeably. "What was that he called you? Ma chatte?" She said the endearment so sharply, venom might've sprayed off her tongue. "Do you even know what it means?"

"His cat," Lola answered.

"Close. More like *his pussy*," Brigitte said.

Lola leaned in. "Well, it is."

"I can smell him on you."

"That's because we fucked on the way over."

Brigitte's lips paled with a tight smile. "Beau," she called loudly over Lola's shoulder. "We're finished here."

The door opened. "So are we," Beau said from behind Lola. "We'll be on our way then."

"See you tomorrow night," Brigitte said to him. "And goodbye, Lola." She didn't walk them out.

"Was she hard on you?" Beau asked on the way to the limo.

"I can handle her."

"I wouldn't have left you alone if I didn't believe that."

Warner already had the door open for them.

"She seems oddly protective," Lola noted.

"She's not actually my sister," Beau said.

Warner sniffed. He shut the door once they were inside.

"I shouldn't be surprised," Lola said. "You neither look nor sound anything alike."

Beau tugged on the end of his sleeve. "Would you like a drink?"

"No."

Lola waited as he fiddled with his cufflink. His brows got heavy, as if it required great concentration. Finally he said, "I don't talk about my family often. I prefer to keep my personal affairs—well, private."

It'd taken Lola a few months to introduce Johnny to her mother. She loved them both, but they represented two different things for her—her past and her future. Johnny and Dina now got along better than Lola and Dina. "I understand," Lola said. "We can talk about something else."

"No, I…" He looked up and cleared his throat. "I want to tell you. It's part of who I am, and I want you to know me."

It was a step in a different direction for them—forward or backward, Lola wasn't sure, but she'd always been curious about this side of Beau, especially right after his proposition.

"I told you when I was seventeen I went to Paris with my dad for the summer. The trip was cut short because of his car accident. That's how he died."

Lola covered her mouth. "While you were there?"

"Yes. And he wasn't alone. He was with a woman he'd introduced me to as a friend earlier that summer—but as it turned out, they'd been having an affair for years. She was also killed."

"You didn't know about her?"

Beau shook his head slowly. "I had no idea. When I met her, she offered for her daughter, Brigitte, to show me around Paris since I didn't know anyone my own age. Brigitte and I became friends." The leather seat creaked as he shifted. "I found out later she knew the truth about our parents but didn't tell me. If I'd known, I would've stood up to him. For my mom."

There was irony in this information, considering how Beau was coming between Lola and Johnny. But maybe the two events were somehow related. Lola didn't mention it. Beau was clearly outside his comfort zone, and she didn't want him to clam up. "How'd Brigitte end up here?"

"She was born here, so she had dual citizenship even though she grew up there. She begged me to bring her back to America with me."

"But you'd only just met. Why would she want that?"

"She just felt…alone. Nowhere to turn." He pulled a little at his collar. "Imagine explaining to my mom about the fifteen-year-old girl I got off the plane with."

"She took in her husband's lover's kid?"

"Yes, and she didn't deal well with it. His death and finding out about the affair sent her into a deep depression that lasted almost two years. I had just finished high school, but I couldn't leave her like that so I lived with them. Then one day she was fine again."

"Just like that? What changed?"

"She was better for about six months. She lost weight, bought new clothes, cooked us lavish meals. She even took a trip. I moved out and Brigitte was getting ready to graduate. Everything was great."

"Until?"

"Until…we realized why she'd been so happy. As Brigitte's guardian, my mom was in charge of her inheritance—and in those six months, she'd spent all of it."

Lola's mouth fell open. "You're kidding."

"She tried to tell me we deserved that money more than Brigitte. And she's convinced Brigitte uses me for my money as revenge against her."

"Does she?"

"No. My mother has an active imagination."

"What makes you so sure?"

Beau frowned. "Brigitte and I lived together for a long time before I made even a dime. Brigitte was there through all of it, for every late night. When I couldn't see straight anymore, she pushed me forward. She believed in me, even when I was no one."

Lola had a sinking feeling. It didn't matter what his life was before—for Beau, money defined people. He actually believed he was nobody before it. "Where's your mom now?"

"With her sister in Florida. We aren't very close, but I support her how I can."

"With money," Lola said.

Beau pulsed his eyebrows once. "Not that she deserves it, but she's my mother after all."

"That's why you said money complicates things."

"One of the reasons."

"I'm sorry," Lola said.

"Everyone has things in their past to be sorry for. We can't let it shape who we are. Right?"

She glanced at her hands on the leather seat. She supposed everyone had things to be sorry for, but she'd made peace with her past. If that were true, there wasn't any reason why she shouldn't be honest with Beau about the fact that she used to strip. But was there any point in telling him now and risking that he'd see her differently?

"So," she said, "where are we headed next?"

"Let Warner worry about that. Tell me something, Lola. What've you got to be sorry for?"

"Not much," she said. "I'm not exactly a model citizen, but I have no regrets. My past *does* shape me. It's made me who I am. I don't believe in hiding from it."

"You've hidden things."

"Hidden? No. Not volunteered…yes."

"Why?" he asked. "Are you ashamed?"

As one of the few people she knew who'd actually learned from her past instead of buried it, she was almost offended. "You haven't earned the right to ask me that," she said.

"I'll earn it then."

He didn't have to. She was his for the rest of the night, and he could make all the demands he wanted.

"You might take it," she said, "but you won't earn it."

"I will. Trust me."

The way his voice had dropped when he'd said *trust me* made her want to do the opposite. It was becoming clear Beau had a weakness for a challenge. "That kind of thing can't be earned in one night," she said. "And I promise, Beau—this is the last night we will ever spend together."

"Why? Your bank account's hit its limit?"

It was like being back at Hey Joe, when she'd been transfixed by Beau, and he'd nearly knocked her off her feet with his proposal. "I don't get you. One minute you're tender and the next you've reduced me to nothing more than—"

"A whore?"

She was unable to keep the shock from her face. *He'd* put her in this position. "Excuse me?"

"I'm being honest," he said. "A person who takes money in exchange for sex—what would you call her?"

Lola dug her fingernails into her palms with the urge to clock him.

"Maybe courtesan is better?" he asked. "It's more romantic."

Beau had a weakness for a challenge, but Lola's weakness, it turned out, was Beau. There was no other explanation for why she kept letting him in. He had a way of getting her to lower her shield so he could stick her with a knife. She didn't seem to learn her lesson. She leaned away from him. "Fuck you. I'm only doing all this because of you."

"You entered into this agreement willfully." He tried to take her hands, but she smacked him away and vaulted backward. He grabbed her wrists to pin her arms to her chest and her back against the seat. When she stopped resisting, he said, "I don't think you're a whore."

Her chest heaved. He was so close, she breathed on his face.

"But I'm going to fuck you like one tonight."

She wanted to fight back, protest, but she was melting at his touch, craving more of him despite his words. "You're awful. You treat me awful."

He kissed her. His grip never loosened, and she never stopped pushing back.

"Which one of us are you fighting, Lola?" he asked against her mouth. "Me or you?"

"I don't know," she moaned, trying to catch her breath. She was hot, and some of it was anger. She'd empathized with him. It meant a lot that he'd opened up to her. She hadn't been that vulnerable since he'd made her dance for him at Cat Shoppe. "You're doing it again."

"Doing what?"

"What you did to me last time."

"Can you be more specific?"

"First you make me comfortable. Loose. Then you try to humiliate me."

He released her and sat back. "I don't know what you're talking about."

"I'm right, aren't I? Last time you took me to a star-studded fundraiser so I'd be awed and see you at your best. Then suddenly you put me on stage and command me to strip. Tonight you take me to meet your sister, open up to me, then call me a whore?"

"My, my." The corner of his mouth crooked. "What an imagination you have." His smile vanished. "Remind me to punish you later for being so impertinent tonight."

"Nowhere in the terms did it say I couldn't fight back."

"But it did say I'd always win."

The threat in his tone resonated everywhere—in her heart, in her stomach, between her legs. Beau would always win, because whenever he decided tonight, he'd have her. As much as he wanted.

"Don't look so frightened, ma chatte." He took her chin in his hand and lifted her head. He trailed his fingers under her jaw and behind her neck. "I am going to love you in the way I fuck you. I'll make everything better," his voice dropped, "and worse."

He took his hand away, but his touch remained—a reminder that her body wasn't in her control. His words were just as unshakeable, and she quickly forgot about her body. Now she worried about his hold over the rest of her.

Chapter Eight

Lola hadn't noticed they were heading toward the Four Seasons until the limo turned into the hotel's half-moon drive. She looked at Beau. "Did you forget something?"

"No."

Her door opened. Fleetingly she'd wondered why she was even more dressed up than the week before while he was in a suit instead of a tuxedo. Now she had her answer—he just hadn't changed yet.

They unfolded from the car. Beau placed his hand at the center of her back. In the lobby, he guided her right, away from the elevators. "First, a drink."

He directed her to the hotel lounge. The few people seated around the room were as cool and modern as the bar's interior. They spoke and sipped their drinks privately. The bartender placed two napkins in front of them. "The usual, sir?"

"And the Colony Cocktail for her."

Beau had a "usual." Was it a girl and a Scotch, only his choice of drink the same night after night? What were the other girls like—and did they all have Colony Cocktails? Lola's dress was elegant—she was not. She wondered if anyone at the bar could tell, and moved closer to Beau.

He looked down and smoothed a hand over her hair. "All right?" he asked in her ear.

She was bothered thinking of him with another woman, but it hardly seemed fair to bring it up, not that she wanted to. It would only invite questions. She nodded that she was fine.

When their drinks were served, Beau picked a corner booth and they sank against the pillows. He clinked his Scotch against her glass. "To the night," he said. "Underneath its faithful cover, we can be who we want. Or in some cases, who we truly are."

"Or, *I* can be who *you* want," Lola said. She took a sip.

"Meaning?"

"This dress. The limo. The cocktail—too expensive, I might add. I'm simply a product of your fashioning."

"Or," he said, grinning, "a masterpiece sculpted from clay."

"Whatever you want to call it."

"I like to think the masterpiece is already there, underneath. I'm just chiseling the clay away."

"I was nothing until you came along. Is that what you mean?" In case her sarcasm was lost on him, she smirked. "Your money's made me worthy?"

He touched her knee. Her smirk faltered. "No. I like you just as you are. You don't pretend to be something you're not like most people I know." He slid his hand up her thigh, and it left a tingling sensation in its wake. She exhaled louder than she meant to. "You don't hide who you are, do you?" he asked.

Her focus was shifting from their conversation to his touch. She wasn't sure she grasped what he was getting at. "No."

"You wouldn't pretend with me."

She understood. Fighting their connection, keeping her feelings to herself—it was the same as hiding parts of herself from him. It went against who she claimed to be.

"It's not that black and white," she said. "Everyone has some darkness inside to hide what they need to." She paused. "Even you. Maybe you most of all."

He looked as surprised by her statement as she was. But it was true. She'd glimpsed his dark side here and there. It didn't scare her. The opposite, actually. It made her want to know more.

"Do you?" she asked.

"Like you said, everyone has some darkness."

"What's yours?" Even as the question came out, she knew he wouldn't answer. Beau seemed to have levels. He'd let her beneath the surface—somewhere she didn't think many people got—but then there were layers over his heart and his trust that not just anyone could peel away.

His hand on her thigh tightened. He glanced over at the bartender, absentmindedly watching him make a drink.

She regretted her question. It was her job to make sure her feelings stayed physical, but they were edging on dangerous territory. She *was* just anyone to him. She couldn't be the one to remove his layers. "Never mind," she said. "It's too much for just one night."

He quickly turned back to her. "No. It's okay. I'm just not used to talking about these things. That doesn't mean I don't…want to." He cleared his throat. "During the two years my mom was depressed, she stopped leaving the house and I took on all the responsibility.

She'd say I was nothing like my dad. My dad would've run away, but I didn't. I took care of her. I spent time with her every day. I bought all the groceries and Brigitte and I would cook each night. I made sure the bills were paid and that Brigitte kept up with her schoolwork."

Lola had a familiar feeling in her gut. She'd also been forced to take care of herself, but at least she hadn't had other people depending on her too.

Beau rubbed the bridge of his nose. "It's just that none of that did anything. None of it was enough. The only thing that made her happy again was that money—Brigitte's inheritance. And once it was gone, she picked up and went to Florida." He looked up at her. "I couldn't take care of her—or anyone for that matter. My dad needed a whole other family, because I wasn't enough."

"I understand, Beau. My dad left too."

"I know." He studied her a moment. "Do you ever feel like you aren't enough?"

A lump formed in her throat. As a kid, it'd been straightforward, like an equation—if she could get her dad a bike, he'd come home. She thought she knew better now, but maybe she didn't. Beau didn't seem to. "Is that what drove you to work as hard as you did? Not being enough?"

"Is that why you're here tonight?" he countered.

They stared at each other. For once, Lola didn't try to shut him out. She held his gaze—let him strip her down for a few moments.

"You're afraid if Johnny loses Hey Joe, all he'll have left is you. You want to give him something else—his own bar, money, a family—because you think you alone aren't enough."

It sounded so simple when he put it that way, as if it hadn't been years building. It wasn't that she hadn't thought of the effect her dad leaving had on her relationship with Johnny, but when she did, it was in an abstract way. It wasn't the way Beau dealt with his insecurity, where money equaled love and there wasn't much more to it than that.

"And as long as you have money, you have something people want," she said. "Somebody can always be there if you need them. But it also means you don't have to let anyone get close."

"*You're* getting close."

"Why?" she asked. "Why are you telling me all this?"

He picked up his drink and swirled it. "I guess it's because I know nothing will continue past sunrise. It's almost like…"

"It doesn't count," she finished.

She and Beau weren't so different, but it wasn't just that they had something in common. Having the same fear over their heads and recognizing it in each other connected them deeper—in a way many people never did.

She covered his hand with hers. "You're enough without it." She swallowed. He winced. "Maybe the money is what got me here, but it was never what I wanted. It was a means to an end. I want you to know—in my eyes, you are enough without it."

He got closer, leaned into her. "Give me that too, Lola. Something no one else has. When I'm inside you tonight, when I take you, I want to know something about you he doesn't."

She shook her head.

He stroked some of her hair behind her ear. "I told you things I've never told anyone."

"Johnny knows everything," she whispered.

"There must be something. Close your eyes. Say it in the dark."

His clean, natural scent invaded. There was, in fact, something Johnny didn't know—something she didn't even want to admit to herself. Something that could only be said in the dark. She let her lids fall shut. "I'm here tonight because I want to be," Lola said. "Not because of the money or so I can buy him his dreams." She took a deep breath, fighting herself. Giving this to Beau was like taking it from Johnny. "I'm here because every way you touched me last time was the right way and because it meant something to me."

"Lola," he murmured. He was so close that he swallowed her words before the world heard them. He kissed her softly. "*I* am exactly where I want to be—for the first time in a long while."

"I think you might be right that I didn't know what I wanted until you showed me."

His took her face in his hands firmly. "Yes. You need a man who can be that for you. A man worthy of your love."

"Love?" Her eyes flew open. "Wait—what?" She removed Beau's hands by his wrists with great effort. "That's not what I was saying. Love has nothing to do with any of this."

"It has everything to do with this. Is Johnny enough?" he asked. "Maybe I had it wrong before. Maybe you're more afraid *he* isn't enough, and without Hey Joe, it'll all fall apart."

Throughout their relationship, she'd catch herself feeling that way and snap out of it. The guilt of thinking he wasn't enough—when *her* fear was not being enough for him or anyone—could be suffocating. She'd buried it deeper any time it threatened to emerge. "He's enough," she said, but her voice was shaky. Unconvincing even to her own ears.

"I don't believe you. You need more. You deserve more. Did he do everything in his power to stop you from coming here tonight?"

"No, but—"

"Did he throw himself at your feet and beg you not to go through with it? Did he tell you if you did, you'd never see him again because he couldn't live with himself? Did he say he didn't care about the money—that without you, it would mean nothing?" He put one hand on the table, trapping her in the corner. "I would buy you over and over again, Lola, but I would never sell you. Not to see every dollar bill in the world stacked at my feet."

Lola's eyes darted between his. It couldn't be true. Beau hadn't known her long enough to make a declaration like that. But for some reason, she believed him. "Beau, I…I don't—"

"You should know what you're worth." He ran his hand through his hair. "It's his job to make sure you know."

She just shook her head. "I don't know how you expect me to respond to that."

"I don't." He smoothed the hair he'd just disturbed. "I'm not asking you for anything. I'm not saying I deserve you either. But be here with me tonight—just me. You might be surprised to learn that love comes in different packages, even ones tied in a black ribbon."

He stood and left the table.

Love? Was that what he wanted? Was he her doomed gift that should remain wrapped? Or was she the one topped with a black ribbon, left out to tempt him?

She found him waiting for the elevator and went to stand silently next to him.

He gathered her hair in his hand and let it fall down her back. "I got carried away," he said. "I think about all the late nights, all the things I missed out on for work. Fueled by just the smallest hope that one day I might have it all."

She looked up at his profile. He stared somewhere above the elevator. He seemed to have relaxed, but the hard angles of his jaw naturally made him appear tense.

"My youth. Family. Happy hour with co-workers. Women. Why did I do it? So I'd never want anything I couldn't have. So my family wouldn't want for anything, and so I could give another person everything she wanted when that time came. She'd have no reason to ever walk away from me." He glanced down at her. The elevator dinged. "That's what you're worth." He walked inside and turned to look at her. "Not a dollar amount. All those nights for these two nights with you."

"Me?" she asked. How was it she could have that much power over this man, who stood tall in his suit, looking capable of taking on the world in a moment's notice?

"Ironically," he said, "for a moment just now at that table, I thought I would give it all up for you. My kingdom for my queen."

Her footsteps echoed in the elevator bank as she followed him. She wrapped her arms around his middle. His body was stiff. She pressed her cheek against his chest. The elevator was like this moment between them, warm and private. The walls were wood paneled, except for the doors, which reflected their embrace as distorted and brassy. "If it weren't for him…if we'd met a different way. If things weren't how they are."

"You could love me?"

She wanted to give herself over completely, just for the space of one night, but she knew she wouldn't come out the other side the same. And at some point in her life, keeping things the same had become important to her. It was the threat of change that had gotten her to this place—that's how far she and Johnny had gone to keep things the same.

Could she love him? There were moments she and Beau were impossibly close for the short amount of time they'd spent together. He picked and picked at scabs that had formed over the wounds time had healed. She was most connected to him when he was also vulnerable, like just now in the lounge. When he took her there, they went together.

"Maybe. That's all I can give you." She couldn't risk her life with Johnny to love and be loved by Beau for one night. "Maybe I could love you."

"If at any hour of this night you think you do, tell me. Promise me that."

She should've laughed at the absurdity of it. Or come back with some witty response meant to deflect. But it wasn't funny. She'd lied to him. There was no "maybe." Her answer was yes—she could love him. Maybe part of her already did.

Chapter Nine

The presidential suite transported Lola to her first night with Beau when the air had been thick with sex and excess. Now the room seemed spotless. The door was already closed behind them. Lola looked to Beau, waiting.

He watched her too, his eyes suddenly and rudely penetrating as he loosened the knot of his tie. He slid it from around his neck and unbuttoned his collar. He moved behind her and lifted it over her head. "Have you been blindfolded before?" he asked, hovering it in front of her eyes.

"Once. Not seriously." At the beginning of their relationship, she and Johnny had spontaneously stopped in an adult toy store after a night out. They hadn't bought anything, but unexpected moments like that sometimes inspired Johnny to be more adventurous. "It didn't last long after I hit my shin on the bedpost."

"Not with me. I won't let anything hurt you," Beau said as her world went black. The tie was cool and smooth on her lids, but rough where he knotted it against the back of her head. His hand slid up the nape of her neck. He grabbed her hair and kissed her under her ear. "Walk."

She took one step.

"Until I say stop."

She instinctively put her hands in front of her. He guided her by her hair until just her thighs were up against something smooth and cool, like wood. He never told her to stop. "What are we doing, Beau?" she asked. "Why are we here?"

He touched the skin on her lower back where her dress dipped. He slid his hands up to her exposed shoulder blades, under the beaded, crossed straps and yanked hard.

"Beau," she gasped when they snapped.

With another jerk, he split the dress down the back. Beads scattered, and the heavy dress slumped to the floor. "This was always the only destination," he said softly behind her.

He kissed her between the shoulder blades and guided the upper half of her body down with a firm hand. She folded into a mattress and realized she was bent over the footboard. "But the dress—"

"Is ruined." He separated her feet with the toe of his shoe and something silky brushed her bare calf. He dragged it up the inside of one thigh and slid it back and forth between her legs, rubbing it over her underwear. He wrapped it around her upper thigh.

"What are you doing?" she breathed.

"Don't force me to become a cliché by asking you to trust me."

She bit her lip when he pulled the fabric tight.

"I'm tying you to the bed," he said.

He moved to her other thigh.

"Are you comfortable?" he asked.

"Physically, yes. But I don't think I am with being tied down."

"That's fine." He ran his hand up the back of her leg and slapped the crease of her ass.

She winced. The sting resonated through her just as

deliciously as it had the first night when he'd spanked her.

"Beautiful," he said. "I do appreciate the change in attitude where your undergarments are concerned."

She breathed from her mouth. "They aren't anything expensive, but—"

"They're perfect."

He pulled her thong down so it stretched over her thighs. She could picture it, the siren-red, lacy thing that molded to her hipbones, now bunched and cutting into her skin. Beau's fingers had barely grazed her legs.

Glass chimed against glass. The pungent smell of hard liquor hit her. "Beau…"

"Are you saying my name because you know what it does to me?"

Her unease at being blinded and bound had dissolved as she'd anticipated his touch again, but it returned now. "I'm trying to trust you."

"But you want to know what I'm doing."

"Yes."

"I'm appreciating," he said with a resigned sigh. "If I were a less decent man, I'd take a picture right now to remember you by."

Lola's hands dashed to the blindfold. "You—"

"Don't take that off." His command came so strong, she froze. "I'm not going to take your picture. I told you to trust me. A camera wouldn't do you justice anyway."

She replaced her hands on the comforter. "You dress me up, bring me here, then make me spread my legs for your viewing pleasure while you have a Scotch?"

"Whiskey," he corrected.

"Scotch *is* whisky."

"Touché. Except this is the American sort."

"A technicality."

"Technicalities are not to be overlooked."

"Here's a technicality—you could not *be* a less decent man."

He laughed. "If you could see how beautiful you look right now, you'd understand how much I'm enjoying this."

"I doubt it."

He hummed. "Lose the attitude for a minute, Lola. Listen to what I see—possibly the most entrancing woman I've ever encountered, folded over my bed with her sweet pussy displayed. Just for me."

Her body thrilled with his words. Even blindfolded, Lola had to shut her eyes. Her heels propped her ass in the air, and her black hair would be messy from Beau's tie. Without stockings, her legs would be long and white. Her body rose and fell faster on the mattress with each breath.

"The burn of quality alcohol in my throat," he continued, "while I think of what I want to do to you next. I didn't plan this part. If I'd let myself think of having you in this room again, I would've shown up at your front door and dragged you back here."

Beau's deep voice pushed its way into her. She gyrated her hips a little against the lip of the bed, trying to hit the right spot. He had that kind of control over her, even without touching her.

"I'm hard for you. I want to be inside you. But right now I need a moment to memorize the way your hands are clenching the sheets. Your red lips parting with each gasp. So fucking sue me. If this is my last night with you, I'm going to appreciate it."

She practically writhed on the mattress. "You're screwing with me, and it's working," she said. "I don't care. Am I supposed to admit I want you? I do. I'm ready."

His footsteps made little noise on the carpet, but she knew he was coming. There was a sudden, wet heaviness on her lower back. "Do not spill my drink," he said. "I'm taking off my belt."

She forced herself to keep from squirming.

"Now the rest of my clothes," he said. "My cock's reaching for you like you're food and it's been starving for months."

She turned her head so her other cheek pressed into the mattress. She was getting uncomfortably warm. She squeezed her eyes shut behind the blindfold.

He thumbed her cheeks apart, then her lips, opening her for him. Without her vision, she never knew where his fingers would probe her next, heightening her anticipation.

"You weren't lying about being ready." His crown collected her wetness, sliding up and down. "God, Lola. I must've sold my soul at some point for something this good."

Unable to take what she wanted, she was stunted but growing feisty. All she had were her words. "You think even the devil would have you?"

"He already does. He's got me."

"And you have me," Lola said. "You're my devil."

He thrust inside her all at once. She made a noise between a yelp and a moan as whiskey sloshed onto her back. Beau removed the glass and lapped up the liquid, his tongue slick and slippery, leaving goose bumps along her spine. "Whiskey and Lola," he said against her skin. "My new favorite flavor."

"You're going too slow," she said.

He dropped all of his weight on her back, sinking her body into the mattress. "How do you want me? Faster?" he whispered in her ear, picking up his pace. "Harder?"

"Yes," she said. "Yes to everything."

He slid his hand under her neck and lifted her head backward as he gave her what she wanted. "Waiting for you to come back was torture," he said while he fucked her. "Does that make you happy? Knowing how hard it's been for me?"

"No."

"Liar. You like to watch me suffer. Tell me I've owned you too."

He would never stop. He wanted more and more. She'd known this about him from the start—he was driven. Ambitious. Strong. She hadn't realized how it might be to have him go after her with all of that. She hadn't realized how much she'd want to give in. She bit her lip. "I'm the one who suffers."

"How?"

"I can't have what I want."

"What do—"

"You."

"I'm here, Lola. Right here."

She grit her teeth. Nothing mattered outside that moment. She could take what she wanted, and nobody would ever know but them. "You've owned me. Not just my body."

"How else?"

She was barely able to focus, but she still knew the things she could never say. *I could love you. If you don't stop, you'll own my heart too.* "I don't want to leave you," she said, her voice pitching.

"If I never untie you, you'll have no choice." He stopped moving. "Is that what you want? Me to take away your choice so you feel no guilt?"

"No," she said. "I don't know. Don't stop. Please."

"Tell me how you belong to me."

"You know what's true. Don't make me say it."

With one hard thrust, he was pounding into her again. "Then tell me what's mine."

"My pussy is yours."

"*Bon petit chatte,*" he groaned. "Keep talking."

"I don't want to say goodbye. I don't want to leave."

He pulled on her hair as she buried her head in the bed. The comforter muted her cries when her orgasm broke her apart from the inside, leaving her a shivering mess beneath him.

He didn't slow his rhythm. He took what he needed, hard, unrelenting, still pulling her hair, sucking on her earlobe, whispering almost inaudibly in her ear until he came too.

He didn't move off her for some time. Her breaths were soft whimpers. He removed the blindfold, but Lola's eyes were closed anyway. She sighed, only lifting her head when Beau pulled out. The white bedspread was smeared red from her lipstick.

Chapter Ten

Lola lay comfortably on her stomach while Beau propped himself up on one elbow next to her. He caressed her everywhere, from the marks on her thighs the ties had left behind up to her neck and shoulders.

She focused on Beau's touch on her skin to avoid feeling him anywhere else. It was as if he was inside her now—for good. He'd been fighting his way in, prying her open with words and caresses. She had no defenses when his only goal was her submission.

"You feel good," she whispered.

"You keep saying that. I'm afraid I'll get used to it."

She smiled and turned her head on the bed so she faced him. They looked at each other a moment. "About what I said—"

"Don't."

She closed her eyes. "Obviously I can't stay. I didn't mean it."

He cleared the hair from her face and then resumed stroking her back. "I know. Just don't leave me yet."

She shook her head. "I'm here. But if you don't keep talking, I might fall asleep."

"What do you want to talk about?"

"Anything. Whatever's on your mind."

"All right. Do you worry about getting pregnant?"

She made a startled noise. "Do you worry about killing the mood? Jesus. *That's* what's on your mind?"

"I'm curious," he said with a deep chuckle. "You don't seem worried."

"We already discussed birth control."

"It isn't a hundred percent effective."

She sighed. "I'd be worried if I thought of it, but I can't. I just can't. So I don't. It would be devastating."

"Would it?"

"To have the child of a man who bought me for a night? Yes."

"Funny how much tighter the knots in your back just got."

She couldn't even picture Beau as a dad—terse, uptight, suit-wearing Beau, picking up his toddler daughter on his way out the door to work as Lola watched, her hip against the counter, coffee in one hand, clutching her robe closed with the other. All of them smiling.

Or maybe she could.

She chewed the inside of her cheek. "Do you make all your partners sign a pregnancy waiver?"

"No, and it's not called a 'pregnancy waiver.'"

"You should be careful who you sleep with, you know. A lot of women would see an opportunity there and take advantage."

"I think you think I sleep around more than I do. And I use condoms always. It's not like those encounters are…"

"Prearranged?"

"Precisely."

There was certainly more to think about when you had money. Lola figured she might have to start looking over her shoulder as well. "Do you trust me?" she asked.

"I do, but I have to protect myself."

"Do you really trust me, or are you just saying that?"

He kneaded her shoulder hard. "That's a big one," he said after a few seconds.

"Happens when you work on your feet."

He kept working the knot. "Have you ever considered doing anything else?"

She didn't mind the topic change. He didn't have any reason to trust her, but she didn't want to know how it'd feel to hear him say it. "Once I applied as an office manager for a place in Century City."

"Did you get the job?" he asked.

"Yes. I turned it down. I couldn't bring myself to wear a suit to work."

"It's hard to pretend to be something else day after day."

"Most people just become what they're pretending to be."

"I suppose," he said. "Is it still your dream to become an office manager or did the wardrobe kill it for you?"

Her laugh sounded as contented as she was. "I told you, I don't dream. I didn't grow up with choices. Just options. Waitress. Cashier. That kind of thing."

"Says who?"

"It's just the truth about the life Johnny and I lead. Neither of us went to school or had opportunities. Johnny's parents get by, but not enough to help us out."

"You're a smart girl. Seems like you could've figured it out if you wanted."

"I guess it's possible that," she hesitated, "I got a little too comfortable at Hey Joe. But things will be different now."

"How?"

"I'll be on the business end of things. Making decisions, coming up with ideas."

"You won't continue bartending?" he asked in a way that sounded as if he already knew the answer.

"Well, I will in the beginning." She inhaled when he hit a sore spot in her lower back. "I'll keep doing that until things are running smoothly. Hopefully not more than a few years."

"Do you think things will change because of the money?" he asked.

"What do you mean?"

"If I were Johnny, things wouldn't be fine for me. I couldn't live with myself after this. Then again, I wouldn't have allowed it in the first place."

"You keep saying that," Lola said, "but you don't know. You made it nearly impossible for us to turn it down."

"That's true. I wouldn't have offered it if I hadn't known you'd accept."

"There's no way you could've known," she said. "I almost said no."

He was quiet a moment. "But you didn't."

No, she hadn't. And apparently he'd known all along what her answer would be. She pursed her lips. "You have issues, Beau. Anyone ever told you that?"

"Maybe an ex-girlfriend here or there."

If she could've rolled her eyes without opening them, she would have. "Is that why you don't have a girlfriend? Nobody can handle you?"

"No." He sounded offended, like a small boy. It made Lola smile, picturing him that way. "It's because nobody interests me at the moment."

"Not even me?" There was definite flirtatiousness in her question, but it was natural to be flirting in bed with the man who'd just done what he had to her.

"People or things that defy my expectations get my attention," Beau said. "So, to answer your question, yes, you do."

"Oh, I see. I get it," she said. "The trashy girl from the slums who doesn't put up with your shit. The one who tells you 'no' when you're constantly surrounded by yes men."

He grunted. "You've been watching too many movies."

"It's the truth, isn't it?"

"I'd be lying if I said I wasn't attracted to that side of you, but it isn't all you are, is it? You really should stop referring to yourself as trash."

"I was being facetious."

"But you believe it, even if you pretend not to be bothered by it."

She grew up in a poor neighborhood without a father. She'd been a teenage stripper. Lola had no disillusions about what people probably thought of her. If that was their conclusion, better that she beat them to it. That didn't mean she believed it. "Admit it. You must've thought that, even a little, when you first met me."

"I didn't. And I don't want to hear it again. It's beginning to irk me."

"Well," she said, sighing, "I wouldn't want to irk you."

"Not sure I believe that."

He continued to rub her back, occasionally massaging her shoulders or ass. "Are you sleeping?" he asked after a while.

"Yes."

"So you never pretended to be a singer or a teacher or President like other kids?"

"We're still discussing this?"

"I'm just trying to understand you better."

"I didn't play like that," she said. "I had my one Barbie, and we were just fine."

"What a shame."

She agreed—it was a shame. She didn't remember where she'd even gotten a Barbie. Her mom hadn't been much for typically girly things like dolls or Disney princess movies. Lola blinked out of her haze a little as the memory came to her. "Wait. Actually, she wasn't even a real Barbie. She was a knock-off Barbie I found at a daycare and named Nadia after the babysitter. My neighbor made her have simulated sex with her authentic Ken doll, and then she threw Nadia on the ground after."

"That's," Beau blew out a short laugh, "the most depressing thing I've ever heard."

"Then I'll stop there."

"Why, what happened next? Skipper kicked her into the street and she was run over by a semi?"

"Probably something like that." She couldn't help laughing but then got quiet. She was awake again, Beau touching her, make her warm. What time was it? How long had they been talking? "Why are we talking about this? Really, you're not very good at paying for sex."

"For what it's worth, Nadia sounds like a hell of a lot more fun than Barbie."

"She can certainly take more."

"I like a woman who doesn't break when you bend her."

"Nadia wouldn't," Lola said.

"What really happened to her?"

"No idea," Lola said. "One day I went to look for her, and she was just gone."

"I'm sorry to hear that."

"Just as well. I was looking for her to throw her out."

"Why?" he asked.

"Someone at school said dolls were for babies. I hadn't played with her in years, but I still wanted to get rid of her. I didn't want anyone thinking I was a baby."

"I can't imagine anyone accusing you of that."

"They didn't. I may not have had much growing up, but I had the respect of my peers." Respect had never been a problem for her, no matter her age, even with those who'd known how she was making her money. "If only they could see me now."

Beau kissed her hair above her ear. "Don't be so hard on yourself."

"Right. That's your job."

"A job any other man would envy."

She pressed her lips together, smiling a little. "What about you, Beau? Do you have any regrets about what do you for a living?"

"None."

"Why? What specifically about it makes you happy?"

"It's the perfect setup. I use my money to make more money. That's something I can see and understand. Of course, there are no guarantees when it comes to these things, but we're very thorough in our research and projections. Generally the companies we choose are poised for success. So far, thanks to that and a little luck, the returns have been incomparable."

"Not buying it," Lola said immediately. "What is it that drives you every day? What makes you smile?"

Beau was silent as if deciding how to respond. Finally, he said, "I guess it would be giving someone a chance at his dream. Not many people in this world have that gift to give. Some of these people are kids still—twenty-two, twenty-three—they work so fucking hard just on the belief they have what it takes. Like I did."

"You like helping them," she said. "You give them more than just money."

"Before I make any decisions, I have to get to know the founders. Really know them, their values and how they do business. That's why I brought those two guys to your bar with me. If I'd taken them to an expensive restaurant, they would've clammed right up. They needed a place like Hey Joe, where they were comfortable and could be themselves so I could see what I was investing in."

"You do that with all your potential ventures?" It was clear to Lola she wasn't just a deal Beau had made, but an actual person he took interest in. Beau had led those guys down a path of his design in order to understand them. The way he'd mapped out his dates with Lola. Did that make her like them, though? If so, she wasn't much of an investment at all. She produced no returns.

"I do," he said. "Intuition is a driving factor in many of my decisions."

"So if Mayor Churchill meets with you one on one, he'll understand your intentions. And then tax breaks for you and your friends means more investment money and more opportunities to give."

He laughed. "I don't know about calling all the rich people in Los Angeles my friends, but otherwise yes. And that's just the start. I'd love to get more incentives for startups here so they'll consider L.A."

"What else?" Lola asked. Ideas excited her. Acting on them. It was what Hey Joe needed to turn around. Passion, ambition, motivation. Someone to take the lead and bump them past the level of talking about what they should do next. For a fleeting, shameful moment, feeding off Beau's enthusiasm, Lola wished Johnny were more like Beau in that sense.

"Coding needs to be mandatory in high schools," Beau said, "but offered as early as elementary level. If I'd taken it in school, I'd be light years ahead of where I am, and I'm already pretty advanced. Girls need to be educated that technology's not just for boys. I put on this yearly conference free for aspiring or existing entrepreneurs, and there are a few sessions for those under eighteen who're interested."

"Back up. A conference for entrepreneurs?" she asked. "You put it on?"

"My company, Bolt Ventures, does. But it's really a personal project for me. It's one weekend in Los Angeles with workshops, panels, free legal advice, things like that. And entrepreneurs with a business plan get to pitch their ideas to investors with five-minute, rapid-fire presentations. There's also opportunities for one-on-one time with people who've been in their shoes and succeeded."

"Wow," Lola said. "I admit—I'm a little shocked. What do you get out of it?"

"Nothing, really."

"That can't be. Exposure maybe?"

"I got screwed over with my first company, and I didn't even realize it at first."

"Didn't you make millions off that deal?"

"Yes, but once they had my company, they didn't value the work I'd put into it. I guess this conference is a way of providing the tools I didn't have so others don't have to make decisions they shouldn't be making without all the information."

Lola struggled to envision a world where a ravenous, bulldozing businessman like Beau Olivier did something so selfless.

"There's some exposure for Bolt. People in the industry know I'm behind it. They have to. I need my contacts to make it successful. But it's maybe the one business venture I do that's not for financial gain. It's for them."

"I don't think I've ever heard you this passionate," Lola said, her eyes still shut.

Beau snorted. "Do I have to tell you you're wrong about that?"

Her cheeks warmed. "You might be right."

He moved hair off her face. "You must've been a cute little Lola."

"That's what you got from the picture I painted earlier?"

"No. I got that from the way you just scrunched up your nose when you smiled." He fell quiet again, raking his fingers through her hair. "I want to know what that girl thought her future looked like. Maybe it's something I could give you."

He'd already afforded her one future. With two million dollars, she and Johnny could do anything. She parted her lips to ask him what more he could possibly give her, but she closed her mouth. It was a question that could lead them down many dangerous paths—what could he offer her that she didn't already have with Johnny?

She opened her eyes, blinking several times to adjust to the light. In the dark, it'd almost been as if she'd dreamed the past few hours. "We're just supposed to be having sex," she said. "All these questions about my past—my future? I hope you aren't falling in love with me."

"I can't tell if you're joking. But what if I were?"

Her heart pulsed, even though she knew that was impossible—impossible for anyone, but even more so for people like them, who'd had to grow an extra layer around their hearts. "You can't fall in love with someone in a night."

"Just like you can't buy a person?"

"What?"

"Nothing. Never mind."

Lola stared at his naked pecs. Whenever he worked out a kink in her back, there was obvious strength in his hands. Now she watched the muscles in his arm and chest tighten.

She'd told Johnny she loved him on a weekday. It wasn't anything worth remembering, like during an expensive dinner or an especially gripping orgasm. She'd just worked a shift at Cat Shoppe, and it'd been late. Her body had dragged like it was made of lead. He'd been in the parking lot, waiting to give her a ride. She'd been so grateful for not having to take the bus home that it just came out. She'd had no idea back then whether she really loved him, only that it felt right to say it.

"It's not possible," Lola murmured out loud. "Not in one night."

Beau bent to peck her cheek. She tilted her head up and met him with her mouth. He pulled her closer by her nape. Their tongues were slow, gradual, tasting. Probing. Then consuming.

Lola thrummed, partly from listening to Beau talk about his work. It added a dimension to him she hadn't known much about. His drive was sexy, the way he commanded all of her in the bedroom was.

Just as she was about to climb on top of him, he pulled away and put a hand on her back to keep her on her stomach. The mattress sank as he straddled her. He grabbed lotion she hadn't noticed before from the bedside table. Next to it was a bottle of lube. He squeezed the lotion onto her back and tossed the bottle aside. His hands became even more powerful over her skin.

She tried to tell him how good it was, but she could barely make noise. He kneaded his fingers up her neck, into her hair, then down to her shoulders, her lower back. He dipped them between her legs. He squeezed and separated her ass cheeks, letting his thumbs run along the insides.

"Beau," she murmured. With a shock of cold on her lower back, she opened her eyes. The lube was also gone from the nightstand.

"Relax," he said. He dropped his hand lower, spread the lube around and added more.

"I can't," she said.

His throat sounded raw. "Can't what?"

She bit her lip when he circled around her clit. "I know where you're going with this." She swallowed and exhaled against the bed. He took his hand away. He hovered over her back as he kissed his way from one shoulder blade to the other. Her attention struggled between following his lips and the insistent hardness against her thigh.

"The way you melt into the mattress like this," he said quietly, brushing his mouth down her spine to the center of her back, "it gets me insane. Turns me on like crazy."

His hand returned between her lubed cheeks, and he pressed a finger against the one place it couldn't be. Her reflex was to blush furiously. She considered herself adventurous in the bedroom except when it came to this.

She hadn't let Johnny anywhere near her ass until years after they'd started dating. Everything in her body coiled into a tight spring with a mixture of fear and anticipation.

"Don't brace yourself." His other hand rubbed her lower back firmly, coaxing her. When he was demanding, she was powerless to him—when he was gentle, like he was now, she lost all control over herself.

He worked a finger inside her, and her awareness of anything other than its snug fit vanished. He slid it out slowly then back in, massaging her at an easy, relaxed pace. Her embarrassment waned, but her face burned hotter with a mix of emotions. She liked what he was doing, but she worried anything more would hurt.

She'd only let Johnny get as far as this, but he hadn't been as calm as Beau about it. She hadn't enjoyed it. It was almost as if Beau were touching a different spot than Johnny had. Beau did this for her, not for himself. She was no longer bracing herself.

"Good," he said, grit in his voice. "You're doing good."

Pride swelled in her. She wanted to prove to him she could enjoy it, elicit more praise. As he added a second finger, she focused on her breathing through the initial bite of pain. Soon, as his probing became deeper, quicker, she not only accepted him inside her but wanted him there.

"God," she exhaled, "damn."

His only response was a low grunt and to stretch her even more with another finger. She'd warmed to him and deep in her belly, gradually, a knot of pleasure began to form. She curled her hands in and out of balls around the comforter. He withdrew his fingers without warning and in their place came a much heavier pressure.

"Wait," she said.

He rubbed the head of his dick against her puckered opening. "I'll stay gentle," Beau said, coating them both in more lube. Though the pain worried her, it wasn't enough to stop her. She was too turned on to tell him no for that reason alone. It was that this was something she'd never given Johnny—something he wouldn't forgive if he found out.

"I can't let you have this," she said.

He slid the length of his shaft between her cheeks. "Why not?"

"I've never..." Sharing her and Johnny's sex life with Beau seemed wrong. Everything was wrong—him pressing against such an intimate place, her not only allowing it, but wanting it, when she never had before. But those things were also spurring on her arousal. "I just can't...shouldn't."

"It's part of the deal." He sounded frayed, edgy with impatience as one of his hands kneaded her ass cheek. "When and how I want." He blew out an exhale. "Where."

"Johnny's tried, and I've told him no every time. He's begged me, Beau. You don't understand what this means."

He put one elbow by her head and closed his body over her back. "Yes, I do," he said into her hair, "and it only makes me want it more." The tip of his cock intruded on her, begging to enter. "Remember how good it felt to submit to me?" His hot breath warmed her ear. "That's all this is. Yielding. Taking everything I give you, because that is our arrangement. Because you like it that way."

She'd been determined not to let Beau have this. He had the power to turn her body against her, though—her mind too. He would never be satisfied. This was her last defense against him, but he'd reduced her to a quivering mess and set her on a fragile, tenuous edge that might give any moment and plunge her into absolute vulnerability.

"I want this part as mine." His insistent pressing gave way to short, slick strokes as he entered her. It stung and throbbed, and her instinct was to reject the invasion, to recoil, to push him out, but whenever she tensed, he released a *shh* into her hair then kissed her in the same spot, waiting until she calmed. Her blood seemed to simultaneously rush and drain through and from her body. He was *big*, unfairly *big* it seemed in that moment, so much that she almost wished Johnny, not quite as *big*, had broken her in first.

"You're so tight. Let me fuck your ass, Lola, your tight virgin ass—not because I want it. Do it because you want me to have it."

He inched in. Didn't he know he could have whatever he wanted? Not because they'd agreed to it, but because she was utterly *consumed* with him, irrevocably *owned* by him? The pain was nothing to give him this—one more thing to link them together long after they'd said goodbye. He'd always be the first to feel her this way, to break down her every last barrier.

He pulled out and edged in deeper. She felt a little more of him and hurt a little less with each push. "That's it," he said. "Just relax. Let me do all the work."

She swallowed and swallowed, her throat impossibly dry. He moved off her body, and she realized she was sweating—or he was, or they both were. He put both hands on her ass and leaned into her, spreading her, thrusting, splitting her apart, holding her together. All she could do was groan, unable to process so much happening at once.

"All right?" he asked. He was gritting his teeth.

Every part of her that touched the bed was sweating now. "Yes," she exhaled.

"I won't last long. Just watching you is enough." When she'd think he was all the way in, he'd pull out a little and go deeper still. "Give me your hand," he said.

She bent her arm around to her lower back, and he laced his fingers with hers. He picked up speed, became less gentle. She couldn't tell who was grasping whose hand.

Any shame she'd been clinging to dissolved as he fucked her most intimate spot. He filled her, all of her, discovering her, claiming her—from the inside. She had to know he was feeling this too. "What's it like for you?" she asked.

"I just feel you, baby, like fucking heaven." He panted over her, squeezing the life out of her ass and her hand. He stopped moving, still squeezing, still panting. "I want you to feel me back," he said. "Move on me. Make yourself come."

She was hesitant at first, even though she would've done anything he asked at that moment. It was counterintuitive, but she pushed back onto him, then forward into the mattress. She did it again—back and forth, her hips up and down, riding him slowly, taking every inch. When her need surpassed her timidity, she gyrated harder, faster, grinding against the bed, feeling his cock so fat inside her that there wasn't room for anything else in her body. She became fueled by an insane need to get off, by Beau's primal grunts she'd never heard before—not even the times he'd fucked her to the hilt, every muscle in his body strained. Her backing onto him was doing something to them both. Her fist was a vise around the comforter as she pulled and pushed. She opened her mouth, but her screams were silent, that was how hard she came—so intense and blinding, so unlike anything she'd felt before.

"I'm going to come already," he said, cutting right through her haze. "I can't watch you come apart like that. I need to go fast. Relax everything except your grip around my hand."

She held him tightly, biting her lip as he pulled out of her slowly. She was immediately empty without him.

He took her arm. "Come. Up. Hurry."

He couldn't get her off the bed and into the bathroom fast enough. He ran one hand over his cock as he flipped on the shower and tested the water with his hand.

"In," he commanded.

She got under the water before him. He hugged her from behind, grasping her breasts and sucking a spot under her ear. Her hair slickened. He was insistently hard against her backside. "Thank you," he murmured. "Thank you, Lola."

She fumbled with the hotel soap and threw the plastic wrapper on the ground. After lathering it, she turned around and took him in her hand.

"Ah," he gasped up at the ceiling. "Lola."

She cleaned him, rubbed him, worked him with two hands and still couldn't feel all of him at once. When she looked up, he was also watching. Water dripped from his hair, down his nose.

"You're sexy," she whispered.

His eyes jumped to hers.

"I don't think I ever told you because I'm supposed to hate you," she said, "but you're so handsome it hurts. And so sexy."

His Adam's apple bobbed when he swallowed. "You—"

"No," she said. "This is about you."

She climbed his cock with both her hands, one after the other, faster and faster. He made an expression she'd never seen on a person, something almost pained. But neither of them looked away. He leaned in, took her mouth with his and lifted her by her ass. He pressed her back up against the shower wall with the force of his kiss.

"*Ma lumiére*," he said hotly in her ear as he searched for her with his hand. He found her slick and teased her opening with his cock before entering her. "It means my light. So sweet, so soft, you are the light in my world tonight."

Her fingertips did everything but consume his textured jaw, his pliant hair, his wide, hard back and tensed shoulder blades. She was forced to stop touching to hang around his neck when his thrusts came too fast and out of control. The shower steamed over as hot water rained against his back and her limbs around him.

She was warm everywhere except for her back, which slipped and slid over the cold marble.

"I'm going to come," he said, a hint of a growl in his voice. "Kiss me."

She drew back and let herself be devoured as he took her in every way. He thrust deep and came with his mouth on hers and his fingers denting her ass cheeks.

He removed one hand and ran it between them, gliding it over her wet skin and taking her breast in his hand. He released her to touch her clit.

"I can't, not again," she whimpered. She was raw, sore, used, but his deft fingers relentlessly rubbed her. She put her head back against the wall and gasped up at the ceiling.

He kissed along her neck and the underside of her jaw, running a course up to her ear and finding his way back to her mouth.

She could, and she did—she constricted her arms around him with all her strength as her orgasm roiled through her.

They breathed hard, he into her shoulder, she into his damp hair. Even when she became aware she was still clinging to him, she didn't loosen her grip. From start to finish, it had been too good to be true. She was afraid if she let go, he'd disappear.

"Lola," he whispered eventually. "Are you all right? Did I hurt you?"

She shook her head against his neck.

"Say something. Anything."

"I can't," she said. "I just gave you everything."

He stroked her hair with his hand, pressed his lips to the same spot, to her temple then her cheek until they were mouth to mouth again. He let the wall take her weight and kissed her like he did everything else—unforgiving, firm, but with attention to every detail.

She'd thought he couldn't possibly possess her any more after their first night, but each time he was inside her, they became even closer. Her chest stuttered, and her eyes welled. She didn't want to stop the kiss—she wouldn't let him see her cry. She was overwhelmed, and it clouded her mind. Whatever was making her feel this way wouldn't be fought off. Was it love? It wasn't the same thing she had with Johnny, so she couldn't be sure.

She pulled back anyway, needing to see his eyes.

"What is it?" he asked, blinking his wet lashes.

She hated to lose his green even for that second. "I don't know," she admitted. "How do you do it?" She ran her thumb over the corner of his eye. "Are you like this with everyone?"

"No," he said, all his severity in that one word.

"Why me?"

"Why you, Lola? When I see inside you, it always feels like the first time."

"You can see inside me?" she asked.

"Can't you feel me there?"

She knew she should look away. Immediately. When had they crossed into this territory? He was gaining traction where he never should've been in the first place. If she didn't stop him now, he'd only sink his claws in deeper. She had to give in or fight back. Beau wouldn't allow anything in between. She could no longer stand anything in between.

Her heart pounded as if magnetized to the thumping organ directly across from it. Her teeth fretted against her bottom lip.

Could she feel him there? Like a thunderstorm.

She pulled him back into the kiss and gave him anything she had left. She told him with her kiss what she couldn't with her words—Beau had her. Body, heart and soul.

Chapter Eleven

The city still stood, even though Lola's world had shifted. She was thankful for the bedroom balcony that gave her what she needed in that moment—fresh air. Fresh perspective. Whatever was in that room, it was getting to her.

How could she have let herself get so wrapped up in Beau? Johnny had said since she'd already done this once, a second time wouldn't be a big deal. How foolish they had been. This time was an even bigger deal—this time, Beau demanded more from her and she was hardly putting up a fight. Because she no longer had the desire to. What had she bitingly told Beau in the beginning?

"I'm sorry if you thought any amount of money would get you my heart."

She should've known if Beau decided that was what he wanted, that was what he'd get. The money no longer even registered for Lola—it was something else entirely. She and Johnny now had bigger problems.

Beau enfolded her from behind with his arms and rested his chin on her robed shoulder. "So you didn't run out on me," he said.

"I just needed a minute."

"I want to give you lots of things," he said, "but minutes aren't one of them."

"There's still half the night left." With her own words, she brightened. She and Johnny needed to have a conversation when she got home, but for now, she wanted to forget anything but being with Beau. "You should've taken me to dinner or something. What are we supposed to do until sunrise?"

"I don't know. I'm all fucked out for the moment."

She laughed and relaxed into his arms. "Me too."

"We could sleep," he suggested.

"Does that mean I have to give you a discount?"

He tsked in her ear. "Since when are we joking about this?"

She shrugged. "Since I've finally accepted this is how things are—this is our situation."

"Really. After all this, with only half a night left, you've finally accepted it?"

"Better late than never." It hit her then. There wasn't "still" half a night left—there was "only" half. Lola couldn't deny her feelings for Beau, but she and Johnny had history, and a lot of love between them. Aside from that, Beau hadn't signed on for anything more than a night. So after sunrise, she and Beau were finished. "You know something?"

"Tell me, beautiful."

"I don't think I want to sleep, because—" She hadn't thought through what she was about to say. It was a huge admission. She wavered, swallowing as if she could keep the words down.

Beau nuzzled into her hair. "Hmm?"

"Because this isn't just your last night with me," she said. "It's mine with you."

He kissed her cheek. "This is our space," he said softly. "You can always say what's on your mind, and nobody will know but us."

His arms were surrounding her. She was protected, but it was more than that. She was safe. While she was with him in their space, nothing could harm them. Nothing but themselves, she thought, right before pushing it out of her head.

"We can do whatever your heart desires with the time we have left," he said. "We can go to goddamn Paris if you want."

"I don't think our agreement holds across international lines."

"Yes, it does."

She shook her head. "I don't think so. There was no mention of that in anything I signed. I mean, for God's sake, what if I got pregnant in Paris?"

"Well—"

"That wasn't covered in the pregnancy waiver," she continued. "How would we proceed? And then there's the fact that we'd never make it back in time for sunrise—unless," she put a finger to her lips, "we adjusted for time change—"

He nipped the shell of her ear. "You're teasing me."

She giggled and covered his arms at her middle. "You're the only one who gets to have fun?"

"You're having fun. I know you are."

"You seem determined that I do. Why?" she asked, looking up at the sky. "Why do I matter to you?"

"Why does anyone matter to anyone? You're asking me to explain something impossible."

It still bothered her, though, that he'd never given her a reason. To pay that much just because he was drawn to her? Was that enough? She sighed. "Try."

"If you think any of this would be happening if you weren't you, you'd be wrong. It's not that I paid for a night with a woman. It's not that you're so beautiful, it almost hurts me."

The same was tragically true for Lola. She was there because of Beau, and she suspected that'd been the case all along. Johnny's happiness and Hey Joe's preservation were the reasons she'd convinced herself she could do it. She would've denied it until her last breath, but now she knew without a doubt—she would've refused anyone else's offer.

"What was the reason then?" she asked.

"That I simply had to have *you*. Can't you understand that? And maybe, can't you admit you understand because you feel the same for me?"

She was quiet. To know that herself was scary enough, but to say it out loud was traitorous—and it was terrifying. It could set something in motion, and she wasn't ready for that. There was nothing to be gained by a confession like that except more damage.

"Don't feel guilty, Lola. Johnny knew this was a possibility. There's no rule we can't fall for each other."

She looked over the balcony railing. "Maybe not. But I can't jump, Beau."

"There's more than one way to fall," he said. "Say, if you were pushed."

"If you push me," she said to the ground sixteen floors below, "it will be messy."

"It already is messy," he said. "Just trust in this—my hands on you."

His protection. A safe place in his arms. Nothing about him was trustworthy. Anyone who made as much money as him had to have put his needs ahead of everyone else's at some point. And he used that money to get anything he wanted, including her. When he was interested in a company, he designed their meetings around what made them most comfortable. Was that because he cared, or was it manipulation?

A thought struck her for the first time. Had his proposition at Hey Joe been spur of the moment like she'd thought, or had he done it there because that was where *she* was most comfortable?

"When was the first time?" she asked.

"The first time for what?"

"You said in the shower when you look inside me, it's always like the first time. When? What moment?"

He was silent for so long, she began to worry.

"Beau?"

"It was at the beginning," he said.

"The beginning of what? At Hey Joe? Or you mean the first night we spent together?"

"No," he said. He squeezed her so hard that she gasped a little.

"Beau?" she asked again.

"Remember at Hey Joe, before I left, I tried to tip you."

"Yes, I remember." Of all the moments and silences they'd had between them, that one was fairly insignificant in Lola's mind. "It was then?"

"No," he said. "Why didn't you take it?"

She mostly remembered it because it was right before he'd shifted from a mysterious, attractive man to a man who'd thought she could be bought. A lifetime had happened since then. "We'd been flirting," she said. "You asked me if I was attracted to you, and I was, but I couldn't say it. When you tried to give me that much money, it seemed somehow connected to that. Like you were cheapening our time together."

"I wasn't. I genuinely meant it to be nice."

"'Nice' isn't giving people money. It's giving them things money can't buy, like how you took me to that speakeasy because you thought I'd like it. Or letting me get syrup on your bed because it made me happy." She paused. "I don't care about your money."

His entire body tensed around her.

"But I know you worked hard for it. That's what I—" She caught herself before she could say it was what she loved about him. "It's what I care about. Your passion and drive, and that you love to help people create."

"You're reading too much into what I do."

"No, I'm not. I see you, Beau." She saw him, but she couldn't have him. Not when she and Johnny had given each other nine years of their lives, and not when she owed him more. "Why'd you ask about the tip?"

He shook his head on her shoulder. "Never mind."

"Beau—"

"Stop looking over the balcony. You're making me nervous." There was an edge to his voice, even though he held her tightly enough that she wasn't going anywhere. He hadn't answered her question, but she didn't want to spend what little time they had left arguing.

She blinked her eyes to the sky again. "All right. Is up okay?"

"Up is okay."

"You asked what I wanted to do tonight," she said. "I'd like to see the stars with you."

Beau's chin remained on her shoulder, and *he* was still looking over the balcony. "Can't see them now?"

"Not enough of them. I want to see them all."

He kissed the side of her head over her hair. "Go get dressed."

"Really?"

"I can do spontaneous. I know a place. I have to make a call, but I'll only be a moment."

"In the middle of the night?"

"Business overseas."

"Oh." She nodded. "Wait, what about—"

"In the closet," he said. "I have some things in there you can wear."

Things she could wear? Her jaw set. "If you think I'm wearing another woman's clothes—"

"They've never been worn," he said. "They're yours. I can be spontaneous—rarely—but I am also always prepared if I can help it."

That certainly sounded like him. She extricated herself from his grasp, went inside and found a couple plain, jersey women's T-shirts hanging in the closet. She chose one the muted color of raw clay. The jeans were almost equally as soft, and on the floor sat a pair of brilliant-white Chucks in her size.

She was dressed and combing her damp hair when Beau came into the bathroom. He also wore a T-shirt and jeans.

"We almost look like a normal couple," Lola said to his reflection in the mirror.

He frowned, watching her.

"Is everything okay?"

"Fine," he said. "Everything's fine. You ready?"

The look on his face matched his cross voice on the balcony. She'd seen him that way before—and since it was on her mind, she realized one of those times was right after she'd refused his tip. Before she could think anything of it, his face relaxed with a smile.

"Yes," she said. "I'm ready."

Downstairs, the valet ran for Beau's car, seeming eager for something to do in the middle of the night.

Beau took her hand as if it were the most natural thing. "I've been riding without the top lately," he said when the valet pulled the car up. "You've liberated me."

She smiled. "That's a nice thing to do to someone."

The roads were relatively quiet at that hour, and Beau took advantage of it. He turned up the music. The drive was all at once fast and slow, the speedometer needle climbing to sixty, seventy, eighty before Beau would let up on the gas. The wind had a way of soothing her conscience and wiping her clean, as if she were moving into a new state of awareness. She could no longer hide the truth about her feelings for Beau from herself. It was past midnight—the end of one day, the start of another.

They climbed the Santa Monica Mountains. Beau hugged each curve and took the sharp ones without flinching, anticipating them like he'd laid the pavement himself.

Neither of them spoke, but once in a while, Beau would look over at her and she couldn't help looking back. Then he'd return his eyes to the precarious, winding road, and she'd allow herself a few more seconds of Beau's hair, disheveled by the wind, and the stubble that had tickled her earlier. To feel that kind of thing over her lips, along her jaw, between her legs—it was ownership.

Beau eventually slowed the car to a stop, pulling over to a lookout point.

"Mulholland Drive?" she asked. "I thought you knew a place."

"I do. This is it."

"Every Angeleno worth his salt knows about Mulholland."

He laughed loudly and looked up past the open roof. "So much for trying to impress you."

"If you're trying to impress me, you're going to have to do better than a stunning view and some orgasms."

He made a noise and raised an eyebrow at her. "Careful or you'll wake the beast again."

"By saying 'orgasm'?"

"He's easily aroused."

She rolled her eyes.

"I saw that," he said.

"How?" she exclaimed. "It's nighttime."

"Not all of night is dark. There's the moon, the stars."

"Just like even dark people have light, right? Is that what you're getting at?"

"You think everything I say has another meaning."

She turned in her seat to face him. "I thought to make an offer like you did that you must be a monster. Now I don't know what to think."

"I appreciate your candor," he said dryly.

"I'm just trying to figure this out. Figure you out. How can someone be anything other than morally bankrupt and vile to pay another man's girlfriend for sex?"

He dropped his hands along the curves of the steering wheel. "You're looking at it from the wrong angle, Lola. I'm a man who doesn't let anything get in the way of what I want. If my bank account had a zero balance and I wanted you badly enough…I wouldn't let that stop me. I'd find a way to get you."

"You make it sound so simple—like people are commodities." She paused, waiting for a response. She supposed maybe he had thought of her that way once. "By your own logic, there's nothing you can't have."

"I like to believe that." He looked over at her. "Why?"

Deep inside her not hours ago, he'd said he wouldn't let her go. Lola had made her own heated promises—why? To get to the finish line? Or because they were true and nothing counted in those lust-fogged moments? Beau had said if he wanted something badly enough, he'd go after it. It knotted her stomach to think of a Johnny-Beau showdown in which she'd have to choose between them. "Never mind."

Beau glanced over his shoulder and back at her. "I've never been here at night, but I should've guessed it would be closed."

Just behind him was a lookout point with a view of downtown Los Angeles. Lola had been going there since she was a teenager, often at night. Sometimes to drink with her friends, which seemed reckless now.

"There are ways around the gate," she said.

He arched an eyebrow at her. "You want to sneak in?"

"Would you?"

"We drove all the way up here." He went to open his door, but Lola put her hand on his forearm. He turned back.

"I don't need it," she said. "I've seen it. Let's just sit together."

He settled back into his seat. "Describe it to me."

"The sky is black, but the lights glow. Orange, green, yellow." She wiggled her pointer finger in the air. "Little dots. The buildings are like music bars of light and dark." She glanced up. "More often than you'd think, you can catch a shooting star. But right now, everything is mostly…still."

"Sounds almost perfect. But we're missing something." He shifted in his seat to dig in his pocket. "Vodka and Cheez-Its."

She half smiled. "What?"

"From the minibar." He held up a tiny bottle between two fingers and a bag in his palm. "I also brought tequila—if you're feeling adventurous."

"A surprise picnic under the stars? You're really clueless when it comes to wooing women, aren't you?"

"Take that back or you get no tequila." He twisted off the cap, took a sip and quickly shook his head. His thick hair, relaxed for once because of their shower, took a moment to settle. He blew out a breath. "Jesus. Now I remember why I don't drink tequila straight anymore."

Lola grinned. "Suck it up, pretty boy."

"Pretty boy? I take offense to that."

"It was intended to offend."

He laughed and passed the bottle. She finished it off as Beau watched her.

"And that's how it's done," she declared right before turning her face away to cringe.

"Busted," he said.

"I was just clearing my throat."

"Seriously? I know what I saw."

"I'll prove it," she said. "Pass the vodka."

He surrendered it to her with one palm in the air. "Yes, ma'am."

She opened it, downed half of it easily and offered him the rest.

He shook his head. "No more while I'm driving precious cargo."

Her eyebrows furrowed. "Precious—?"

There was that laugh again, deeper this time from the bottom of his throat. She wanted to bottle that sound and save it for later. For when they'd parted ways. She had to push the thought away quickly to stay in their moment.

"God, you're cute," he said. "*You*, Lola. You're the precious cargo."

"Oh," she said, warm in the face. "Got it."

"Just don't get sick in my car, all right?"

"It'd take a lot more than a mini-bottle to make me sick. Vodka's like water for me." She drained the bottle. "Been drinking it since I was thirteen."

He opened the Cheez-Its and ate some. "I want to hear more about this rebel-teenager Lola."

"She's still around, so don't provoke her," she said.

"I know you meant that as a threat, but I'm only more intrigued."

She turned her head toward the windshield. Everywhere she looked, there was something to see—a distant view of Los Angeles, the Big Dipper, the small one, the sandpaper mountains behind her. Beau.

"Maybe intrigued was too casual of a word," Beau teased. "Don't make me beg for more."

"I'm the same person I was then, just older. And maybe a little wiser."

"I may be older, but I don't feel any wiser," Beau said.

"Me neither," she said. "That was a lie." At the time, no matter how lost she'd been, she'd always thought she'd had it figured out. "What about you? Were you rebellious?"

"Nah. I was consumed by other things, like work, family and survival. Growing up poor really lights a fire under your ass. At least it did for me."

"I think everyone handles it differently. Your way of dealing was to take on all the responsibility. My mom was like that too, saddling the load on her back. Being poor was tough, but it made me stronger. I didn't let it rule my life."

"I bet you, Lola, were already strong to begin with."

"I was by myself a lot." She glanced over at him. Maybe it was the vodka, though she doubted it, but she was okay going places with him she hadn't been in a while. It was their space, like he'd said. "My mom wouldn't even take my birthdays off. Her reasoning was I'd only get a present if she had a job and she wouldn't have a job if she gave away shifts. When I said presents didn't matter, she asked me how I felt about food. For weeks I ate one meal a day because I was worried we'd run out."

Beau looked at the steering wheel. His hands balled and flexed against his thighs. "I wish you hadn't told me that. Things weren't that bad for us."

"They weren't for us either." They truly hadn't been, but she also had the urge to comfort him. "Looking back, it was never as dire as she made it seem. She hustled for her tips, and she never spent a dime on anything frivolous. The manager worshipped her, so she was never in jeopardy of losing her job. Our situation and our relationship fluctuated, but the one thing that stayed the same was that *she* thought there was never enough money. I couldn't do anything because there was no money. My father left because we—meaning I—cost him too much money."

"Is that true?" Beau asked.

"It's what she told me."

"He didn't explain to you why he left?"

"He went on a work trip and never came back. I don't think he was planning it because he left a lot of his stuff. I was too young to remember much anyway."

"Haven't seen him since?"

"No. So, like I said, alone a lot. Except at school. I didn't participate in a lot of stuff, but I had friends whether I wanted them or not. Then when I got home, it was silent. Nobody around. Except for Barbie fucker across the street."

"I'm not sure I like you hanging around with that girl."

Lola shook her head, smiling. "She was all right. Sometimes I wished I'd had a brother or sister, though. At least you had that."

"You wouldn't say that if you'd had Brigitte."

"Why not?"

"She was only fifteen when she moved here and had just lost her only family. She was so insecure about not belonging to anyone. She called me her brother from day one, and my mom 'Mom.' Unless she was angry, and then it was Pam. Looking back, it was something of a self-fulfilling prophecy. She didn't believe she deserved our love on top of our hospitality, and my mom already thought she was doing Brigitte this enormous favor by taking her in when we didn't have much to spare."

"No wonder she's a handful," Lola said.

He rested his head against the seat and looked up. "She was even before the accident. I didn't have to know her long to get that. Everything is extreme for Brigitte. Life. Love. Hate. She doesn't know who she is without that, and she thrives on the attention it gets her."

Lola frowned. "You're very close, aren't you?"

"She only has me. That's all she wants, though. Sometimes I give her projects at the office, and she usually does fine. I could never hire her fulltime, though—she's too volatile. I'm afraid others won't either. That's part of why I continue to help her. It's not a financial burden for me to take care of her when she has no one else. And after what my mom did, she has trust issues on top of that."

Lola peered at him in the dark. It was becoming clear that Beau had one sure way of showing he cared—his money. Earlier he'd said he'd given up years of his life to work, hoping one day he could provide for his family. The price didn't seem worth it, but she didn't think he felt the same.

"Your relationship doesn't sound healthy," Lola said. "For either of you."

"It's exhausting sometimes. She knows it is."

"Is she why you took me to a hotel rather than your house?"

He was silent a moment. "I've tried to get her a place of her own, but she cries and begs me not to. She says she'd rather one of us leave the house when she gets to be too much. As long as I don't go far. She gets more put out than I do, so I go through periods where I stay at the hotel."

Lola was instantly alarmed. If she hadn't known better, she would've thought Beau was describing a possessive girlfriend. "*That's* why you have the room? Jesus."

"I know. She just has two levels—low or high."

"Tonight was high?"

"Yes. She sniffed you out like a dog. Put her in a crowd, especially where men are involved, and she shines. One-on-one is more difficult. In case it's not obvious, she gets jealous of my attention."

Lola looked up at the stars. "I can understand that."

"Can you? You don't seem like the jealous type."

When Beau's attention was on her, Lola wasn't just the only girl in the room—she was the only girl in the world. It was intense—unnerving—but in an addictive way. She was warm when his eyes were on her, cold when they weren't. She shuddered.

He glanced at her. "Would you be jealous of my attention?"

Beau could most likely make any girl feel that way if he wanted. She squinted at nothing. "That would require thinking past tonight, and I don't want to."

"I'll be out there with other women, Lola. You'll be with Johnny. Everything will be normal again."

Things would never be normal again. Even if Johnny thought they were, or if she faked it until things were as close to normal as they'd get—no, they'd never truly be normal again. The question was whether Lola could live with that. "I don't know," she said. "All this has given me a lot to think about."

"Will I be there in those thoughts?"

He already was. She blinked a few times. "How could you not be? You started all of this."

"So what're you saying, Lola? You're going to go home and still be thinking about me?"

"Johnny and I…we're supposed to get through this on our love alone. On nine years' history. I think I knew we might not, but I called you anyway. When your limo pulled up tonight, it was as if Johnny and I had made some fatal mistake." She paused. "But I still went through with it."

Beau cleared his throat.

Lola noticed a symphony of crickets she hadn't before. She looked at him. "I mean, don't get the wrong idea," she said, flustered by his silence. This from the man who'd been so vocal, she'd wondered if he was considering going to battle with Johnny over her. "I'm not suggesting I leave him for you. It's just, the fact that Johnny and I even went through with this means something. Somebody owes somebody an explanation, I just don't know which one of us is at fault."

"I don't think it's anyone's fault," Beau said. "Not even mine."

She shook her head. "It isn't your fault." She couldn't pinpoint when she'd changed over the years, but she had. She'd thought putting her sordid past behind her meant she'd matured. Now she was beginning to question what part of the life she had now she'd chosen. Johnny had become her priority, and his hobbies, friends and work had become her hobbies, friends and work. She wanted more from herself and *for* herself, except that Johnny, with the greatest opportunity of his life ahead of him, still wasn't stepping up to the plate. "If things were right between Johnny and me, I wouldn't be here right now."

"I thought you were happy with him," Beau said. "At least it seemed that way from afar."

"I was," she said. "God, I *am*—I thought so. I had no idea anything was wrong. But you shook us up like a snow globe."

"If you're expecting an apology—"

"I'm not." She glanced at him and away.

"Lola," he called her attention back. "Come here."

She leaned across the console. He put an arm around her, pulling her close so their mouths nearly touched.

"Was I a fatal mistake?" he whispered.

"No." She shook her head slowly, holding his gaze. "Maybe."

He chuckled quietly.

"But don't think I'm going all psycho and dumping my boyfriend because of a couple nights of good sex."

Beau jerked his head back. "*Good?* Fuck. That hurts."

She rolled her eyes but smiled. "You know what I mean. Amazing."

"You can do better than that."

"You'll hold it against me."

"Probably."

Her smile widened. "Fine. Sex so good I think I went blind for a few seconds. Unparalleled sex."

"Unparalleled," he mused. "Meaning unmatched. Nobody can match it. Meaning…the best sex you've ever had."

She wriggled in his arms. "Don't get cocky on me."

"Hmm. I'd like to get cocky all over you," he muttered, brushing hair from her forehead. "Should we go back? Have you had your fill of stars?"

"Never," she said. "But it's not like we have eternity."

She went to pull away, but Beau's arm tightened as he kept her there.

"What?" she asked.

"I just wanted to say…I don't know what'll happen when the sun comes up—"

"I go home," she said, "is what happens."

He searched her face. "You should know how real this is for me." He took her cheek with his other hand. "If ever there were a prize worth winning, you are it. Just know that these stars, this moment—it's real. Everything I'm experiencing is real."

She looked back and forth between his eyes, trying to read him. There was truth there, but it wasn't the only thing. Something else brewed deeper. Something she didn't recognize. What did he want to tell her? To leave Johnny for him? He couldn't ask her to do it, but it was written on his face, woven in his touch.

"You don't have to say anything," Beau said. "We both knew what we were getting into. I just hope we each find what we need come sunrise."

What we need. Foolishly, she rarely considered what Beau needed, because he was always a pillar of strength. Maybe that was how Johnny saw her. Someone strong who didn't need much, and who was better at taking care of herself than anyone else would ever be.

She pushed Beau gently back against the driver's seat, keeping her eyes on his face. She felt under his T-shirt and up his flat stomach. He was warm and hard under her hand. His head fell back, and his eyes closed. His Adam's apple bobbed when he swallowed. "When's the last time someone touched you like this?"

He didn't answer.

"Not to get anything," she said. "Just to feel."

"A while," he said. The gravel in his voice made his answer almost unintelligible. "Maybe never."

She caressed his chest. To hear him say never made her heart sink, made her feel lucky for the years of tenderness Johnny had given her. "Let's go back to the hotel, Beau."

He blinked his eyes open, looking up for a minute. "We have a few hours. Maybe we can get some sleep."

"That'd be nice," she said.

He started the car.

She didn't tell him that she had no plans to sleep. That all she wanted to do was lie in his arms and try to stay awake.

Chapter Twelve

The drive back to Beau's hotel went quickly with the absence of traffic. On their way to Mulholland, there had been promise in the wind—now, just finality.

They took the exit for the hotel, and Beau pulled into a gas station and up to a pump. "I didn't feed you tonight," he said through her window once the tank was filling. "I'd planned on room service again."

Lola shrugged. "We had the Cheez-Its."

"Which is not all that bad of a dinner, but hardly fit for a queen." He winked. "Since I doubt there's French toast inside, how would you feel about gas station hotdogs?"

"Best with relish," she said.

"Then relish you will get. I'll be back in a minute."

Lola watched him walk away, enjoying every second of his firm behind in blue jeans. She caught herself grinning—over hotdogs. It lit her up from the inside that eating hotdogs was such a normal thing to do, as if they had all the time in the world. She didn't even particularly care for hotdogs, especially not ones that'd most likely been sitting on a rotisserie for the better part of a day. It was that she'd be having them with Beau.

But then she did start to think about the hotdogs themselves and how she actually was hungry, having eaten very little all night. Whenever she and Johnny took a trip, they'd stop for gas and sweets on their way out of town, even if they didn't particularly need gas. Johnny would get M&Ms but her cravings came in waves. She never knew what she was in the mood for until she saw it all in front of her. That was why she'd be the one to go get the candy while Johnny filled up the tank.

Now she couldn't stop thinking about chocolate, and Beau would have no idea what to get her. She didn't even know herself. She unbuckled her seatbelt and climbed out of the car. He'd paid for so much so far—dessert would be her treat. Beau probably had an old favorite, like Johnny. Men were like that. They found something that worked and stuck with it.

She pulled open the gas station door, walked in and stopped cold. Beau stood frozen at the counter, and a large, bearded man held a gun to his head. Beau's hands were clenched at his sides. The gas station attendant transferred cash from the register into a garbage bag.

"I told you, there isn't a single thing in my car," Beau was saying, his head slightly tilted as the barrel pressed into his temple. His eyes flickered to Lola and back. Slowly, he signaled with his hand for her to leave. "Everything's on me. I have plenty of cash. I just need to reach in my pocket and get it."

"Which pocket?"

"Back right," Beau said.

Every beat of Lola's heart was acute. Rabid. She ached. He wouldn't hold her as she lay awake tonight. There wouldn't be a heartbreaking decision to make in the morning. They had fought each other, themselves, those around them—why? For it to end this way? She would've run to him if she could move. Her mouth was open, but she hadn't even been breathing.

"There's nothing here," the man said.

"Must be the left pocket." Beau widened his eyes at her, nodded once and mouthed, "Go." She barely registered that he was trying to distract the man from turning around.

"You're fucking with me." He reared back to hit Beau with the gun.

"I have it," Lola cried out. She couldn't even remember what she was supposed to have, her mind spun so fast. He wanted something. She would give it to him. Anything to change the picture in front of her—Beau, her strong, solid Beau, with a gun to his head.

The man whirled to her. "On the ground," he said.

He waved the gun back and forth, and when it stopped on her, her scalp went cold. His matted gray beard matched his leaden eyes, matched the pistol aimed at her face. His oversized army-green jacket had holes.

"Down," Beau ordered through his teeth. He gestured again, this time for her to lie on the floor. His dark eyes bore into her, willing her to submit.

She had to be brave. If she lay down, Beau would remain the target. She couldn't have that. Her breath came short as she looked between them.

"Listen, bitch." He put the barrel to Beau's head again. "This will be you if you don't get the fuck down."

Beau thrust his hand into his front pocket. "She's lying. My wallet's in—"

The man cocked the gun and shoved it harder into Beau's skull. "I told you not to move, motherfucker. Put it in the bag and do it slow."

Beau slid it out and dropped it in with the rest of the money.

"Now you," he said, nodding at Lola. "Throw your purse over here."

As long as the gun was on Beau, she saw nothing else. All it would take was a slip of the finger, a burst of anger. "Not until you put the gun down."

"Who the fuck you think's in charge?" the man asked.

She held up her purse, waving it as if he were a bear and she had his dinner. The man was off—he could snap at any moment, but if he did, she'd make sure that gun was pointed anywhere but at Beau. Even if it was aimed at her instead. "If you want it, come take it from me."

"Throw the fucking purse," Beau said sharply.

Purse. Wallet. Money. Her brain began to thaw. "I have cash." Her legs wobbled. She took a step back and raised her chin. "I just came from the ATM."

He looked from Beau to Lola and back before walking toward her.

Beau lunged, but the man was fast. He spun around and trained the weapon on Beau again. He backed his way to Lola, feeling for her with the same hand he clutched the garbage bag in. She couldn't tell how lucid he was. She didn't want to test him, so she stayed where she was. He grabbed her shirt and pulled her in front of him, wrapping an arm around her shoulders and jamming the cold muzzle under her chin, forcing her head up. He slid his hand down her stomach. "Give it to me."

The barrel pressed into her throat when she swallowed. She tried not to cough and instead inhaled a wilting blend of urine, body odor and hard alcohol.

Without moving more than she had to or looking down, she surrendered the purse.

"She and I are going to walk out," he said to Beau. "If you want to keep her alive, don't make any moves until I'm gone. Got it?"

"I lied," Beau said hastily. He was below her line of vision, on her peripheral, but there was clear desperation in his voice. "About the car. And what's in it. I can get you anything you want. I have more money than you can dream of."

The man released the gun just enough for Lola's head to drop. Beau flexed his hands in and out of balls, imploring her with his eyes. She couldn't read him, and that made her stomach churn. She had no idea what he might do.

"How much we talking here?" the man smacked in her ear.

"Millions. All yours if you just let her go. I'll go out to the car with you instead."

Lola held her breath, sucking in her nostrils to prevent smelling anything.

He laughed. "Now I *know* you're fucking with me." He pulled Lola backward with him.

Beau, as if connected by a string, walked forward also. "Look outside," Beau pressed. "That's my Lamborghini. You can have it too. Outrun the cops, no problem."

Lola didn't dare check to see if the man looked.

The man whistled in Lola's ear. "You weren't kidding. Keys in the car?"

Beau patted his pockets. "Yes."

"You stay here while we check," he said, dragging Lola backward with him. "Everything's good, I'll let her go."

"Leave her," Beau said levelly.

"Nope. She's my collateral."

"The car is nothing." Beau's jaw clenched and unclenched, causing his face to contort. The gun was still on her, between her and Beau, putting them on opposites sides of danger. "I can get you so much more. We don't have to get the cops involved. Just let go of her."

Lola couldn't hold her breath anymore, and she gagged.

"What's wrong, little lady?" the man asked tauntingly. "You know, there's one thing you've got that he can't give me." He squeezed her more tightly against him.

She'd die before she let that happen. Before she could gag again, she grabbed his forearm. "Let go of me."

"Shut up," he said with a hard shake.

Beau's hands had stopped moving. His expression smoothed as any emotion drained away, leaving his eyes colder than she'd ever seen them. His back became unnaturally straight. "You might want to rethink who you're pointing that gun at," he said. "I don't think you realize how much you've just pissed me off."

A wave of panic crashed through Lola. He had the same indifferent look he'd had the night Johnny had gone after him at Hey Joe. It was the complete inability to predict his next move that terrified her—not that he'd do anything to jeopardize her, but that he wasn't thinking of his own safety at all.

Beau strode forward, each step longer than the last. The man pushed the gun into Lola's throat then pulled it away. It wavered in the air a split second as he seemed to hesitate. He pointed it at Beau and shot. Lola screamed. Shoved back into a display stand, she lost her footing and fell as it crashed around her. Beau was at her side in an instant, yelling at her, but all she heard was the reverberation of the gunshot.

Frantically, she reached up and felt his chest. "He shot you?"

He grabbed her arm, checked her over and left her on the ground. He ran back to the counter and lunged over it, reaching for the attendant.

"Beau," she said lamely, unsure he could even hear her. "What are you doing?"

Beau grabbed the kid by his shirt and pulled him forward. He was tearing something from the guy's hand—a gun. He was going after the man. Dread rose up her throat.

He bolted for the door. She scrambled to her feet, hurtling into his path. "It's just money. It's not worth it," she cried.

He went to move around her, but she grabbed his shirt in two tight fists. Now that she had him back, she couldn't risk losing him again. "Please, I'm begging you. Don't do this."

"It's not about the money," he said, his face bright red, his chest heaving. "I won't let him get away with this."

"I need you here," she said. "Don't abandon me."

He glanced anxiously behind her. "I can't just do nothing. I'll come right back."

She couldn't shake the thought that he'd been shot. Her chin wobbled. "You might not come back." Her strength seeped away, leaving her knees weak. His arms automatically went around her waist, and the gun pressed through the back of her T-shirt, cold even through the fabric. "Let the police handle it. Stay."

"He deserves to pay," Beau said through clenched teeth. "You're asking me to let it go? People don't just get away with this. He could've killed you, Lola. He deserves to run for his life—from *me*."

He was like a wolf separated from fresh meat with only Lola in between. His heartbeat was strong under his chest, and all his muscles were tensed as if he might break into a sprint at any instant.

He wanted payback. Why couldn't he see the gift they'd been given? A second chance? He would risk his life to make an insane man pay—for what? They were both unharmed. She shook him by his shirt. "*I* don't deserve to lose *you*. Not after all this. I need you here where I can see you and touch you. If you go, I go with you."

He opened his mouth, trying to speak but nothing came out at first.

"If you go, I go," she repeated.

"But he…and you…" His face closed. "What the hell were you thinking?" he demanded. "Why didn't you leave when you had the chance? Why didn't you just do what he said?"

She would take all of Beau's anger if it meant keeping him there in that building. Her fingers loosened with her relief. "Why didn't you let him take me outside?"

He looked up at the ceiling. "You know why."

"Then you know why I couldn't leave you here."

There was a word for that, but Lola couldn't let it form in her mind. If she did, she'd never see clearly again. They stared at each other, both breathing deeply.

He detangled from her finally and went to turn away, but reached back and took her arm. "Do not leave my side." He walked them up to the counter where he placed the gun down but didn't release it. He kept his other hand on Lola. The attendant was on the phone with the police.

"Tell them we can still catch the guy," Beau said, glancing at the door. "And to hurry the fuck up."

"Beau?" Lola asked.

"Not now. I have to do this." He let her go and took the phone right out of the kid's hand. "Is someone on the way?" he asked and waited. "Every second that passes, he gets farther away. I don't even know—"

Sirens sounded out front.

"Never mind," Beau said, dropping the receiver.

He took two steps before the attendant called after him. "Dude, my gun. You go out there with that and they'll turn you into Swiss cheese."

Beau rubbed his forehead tensely and looked at his hand.

"Put it down," Lola said. "He's not coming back."

He slid it across the counter to the attendant. "Stay here," he said to Lola. He didn't move a moment, then took her shoulders firmly. "Do you hear me, Lola? Don't try and be brave. Just stay put until I come get you."

He was afraid. Now that her sense had returned, she was too. She nodded quickly, breathlessly. "I won't move."

His fingers loosened, but he wouldn't stop looking at her. "You really fucking scared me, you know that? This is why I never stray from the plan—not ever."

She searched his face. "What plan?"

"There's always a plan, Lola. Tonight was about you and me, and that's why I wanted to stay in the hotel room. Just be with you. This is all my fault for not sticking to the plan."

"But it was my idea," she said.

He pulled her against him hard and hugged her. He buried his face in her hair. "Goddamn it," he whispered.

He released her all at once and strode out of the convenience store. The attendant was already in front. She stood frozen to the spot. Her breathing hadn't calmed. Her heart felt like it was bottoming out.

She'd almost lost everything in minutes. Her life. Her future. Their future. Beau. She shook her head. He wasn't everything. He was just a man she'd spent two nights with. A man she'd already been planning to say goodbye to in a few hours.

She'd risked her life for that man. For a man she'd never see again after tonight. And he—he had done the same by not letting her out of his sight, even to save himself.

She'd almost lost him in minutes. He was everything.

There was a word for that—it was *love.*

◆⊠◆⊠◆

The car dipped as they entered the hotel's underground garage. The gun's cold metal was still under Lola's chin. She wanted Beau's touch to replace it. To replace the last hour of being separated from him as policemen questioned each of them. Lola rubbed her hands up and down her thighs. She'd stopped shaking, but she was jittery.

Beau pulled into a parking spot and shut off the car. "In the morning, we'll—" He stopped.

What, go get a bite to eat? Give the credit card companies a call? Pick her up a replacement cell phone? That wasn't their life. Their life followed the sun's schedule, and it would be waking up soon. "In the morning, we'll nothing," she said. "Nothing."

They were silent. The police had asked if Beau was her boyfriend. Where they'd been. Where they were going. Why they needed a hotel if they lived in Los Angeles. The dashboard in front of Lola blurred and doubled. She breathed in and out.

What would they have said if she'd told them the truth?

"We're not what you think, Officer. He's paying me to be here right now. In this gas station. I'm being paid for this."

She didn't want Beau's money. She could give it back and not leave in the morning, but then there was Johnny. Johnny, who hadn't protected her. He hadn't known if Beau would hurt her, or if she'd come home in one piece. He'd sent her off into a potentially dangerous situation—twice. *He* would've let the man with the gun take her outside to save his ass.

She undid her seatbelt.

"Lola?" Beau asked.

She put a knee over the console and climbed onto him. He didn't protest, just took her hips as she settled into his lap. She put her hands on both sides of his face and kissed him. He was solid. Real. Immovable. He tasted salty. One of them was crying.

"It's okay to be scared," Beau whispered. "You don't have to be strong all hours of the day."

"For you." She was trembling again, but this time it wasn't because of the gun. She couldn't say goodbye to him. She wouldn't. She'd walked into the gas station. He'd had a gun to his head. It was branded into her heart. His stubble scraped against her fingertips and her palms. She might've never felt that again.

"I was scared for you," she said, her tears sliding down both their cheeks. "Scared something would happen to you."

His arms tightened around her. "We're both safe now," he said in a humming, soothing voice. "I'll keep you safe."

He had needs too. She kissed his lips, his cheek. "What about you? Who will keep you safe?"

"You did, Lola."

She shuddered. If she had saved him, it was to protect herself. She couldn't live without knowing if all of her life had been leading up to this moment. She stayed in his lap, dug her fingers into his face and released. She fought herself.

"What is it?" he asked, his eyebrows heavy. "We're running out of time."

She reached for his fly to undo it, but stopped. Sobs racked her body. She fisted his shirt, stretching it. There was everything, and there was everything else. Beau had remained solid through it all. Beau had been strong and unwavering. Beau was hers. Nobody was going to take him away from her.

She clung to him. "I'm falling in love with you."

He stilled completely. It was dark, but his eyes were green as they looked up into hers. She felt his chest again, as if checking for a bullet wound. He slid his hands down her back and into the seat of her pants, pulling her against him. Their lips met fast and hot like flames licking at their faces, every touch gasoline on the fire. He opened her jeans, yanking them down over and over, trying to get to her. She had to lift her knee to get one pant leg off so he could angle upward, his own pants barely undone, to find his way inside her. He took control of her hips, pushing her down on him. There wasn't even time to moan, to think, to do anything but feel him hard and filling her.

"Look at me and say it," Beau said.

She found his eyes with hers. They weren't words, just breaths. "I love you."

He pulled on the neckline of her T-shirt, grabbed her breasts. She arched into his hands, throwing her back against the steering wheel. The horn honked and her jeans ripped somewhere and she was coming as hard as he was thrusting up into her. He groaned louder and louder until he also came.

She reached out to grab onto anything. Her palm connected with the cold window, her other hand landing on his heaving chest. They were real things, unlike love, unlike fear, which she couldn't hold.

The car was closing in on her. She opened the door and would've tumbled out if Beau hadn't caught her waist. She slapped his hands away and stood. It took her three fumbling tries to get back into her jeans. She ran both hands through her hair. "Fuck," she screamed. It bounced off the gray, concrete walls. She loved two men, but she loved them differently. With Johnny, it was in a way that she'd let him go before she returned with only part of the heart that had belonged to him. With Beau, her love wasn't that selfless. It was an annihilation of her senses. A conquest, a theft of her entire self. She squatted between two painted white lines and pulled hard on her hair. "I'm so fucked," she said.

A car door slammed, echoing around the garage. Beau walked up next to her.

This had to be her moment alone. She deserved to do this on her own for the way she'd led everyone into this mess. She could've ended it all with a firm, simple *no*. "Go away. I can't do this right now."

"I'm not going anywhere."

"I mean it," she said.

"You're in the middle of a parking spot." He leaned down to help her up, but she jumped to her feet. He had tricked her. Pulled the wool over her eyes. It was the only explanation. She hadn't even tried to keep love out of it, because love hadn't been an option. It had blindsided her completely. She shoved him backward. "I said go. I hate you."

He took two large steps and grabbed her wrists before she could push him again.

"I hate you for this," she said. "You ruined everything. We were fine before you. We were happy."

"You said it yourself—you wouldn't be here if that were true." He forced her against his chest where she broke down and bawled. He wrapped his arms around her, rubbing her back with his large hand.

"Nobody has ever made me feel so alone," she said.

He pulled away slightly. "I make you feel *alone*?"

She'd learned her lesson as a kid when her dad had walked out on her and her mom—the only person she could rely on was herself. Not even Johnny or her mom. But she couldn't see beyond tomorrow, beyond Beau, when she'd have to go back to a life that had been fine before him. "I could always take care of myself. I've never needed anyone." She wouldn't look at him. "I haven't even left yet, and I already feel alone."

Even she didn't trust herself. Just yesterday, it'd been Johnny she'd loved. Nothing could erase that, but their love had stopped growing somewhere along the way—not because it hadn't been nourished or tended to, but because from the start, it could only get so big.

What she felt for Beau was new, but already it seemed as though it could reach a terrifying size. It couldn't be trimmed, monitored or kept. It was a vine that had the potential to overtake everything in its path. Lola didn't know which of the two was the right kind, only that after glimpsing the possibility of her and Beau, a stunted love with Johnny wouldn't be enough anymore.

Beau covered her hair with both hands. His grip was firm, but his words were soft. "I don't want you to feel alone."

She looked up finally. "What do you want me to feel?"

"Loved."

"Johnny loves me."

His eyes darted between hers. The garage was silent except for the one rapid heartbeat between them. He opened his mouth and shut it. He put a hand on her cheek. "Lola."

He said her name so thickly, she could almost reach out and touch it. Her fingertips tingled. She was back in the drugstore as a teenager about to commit a crime. She wouldn't stand in the way anymore. She wanted him. She'd chained it up inside early on, but it was coming loose. If Johnny had fought for her at all, Beau had fought harder.

His eyebrows gathered as he frowned down at her. "Sometimes I think you can see through things other people can't. You see me. You make me powerful, but more," he paused, swallowing, as if the words were fighting within him, "you make me powerless."

Powerless. That was what she'd seen in his eyes when she couldn't read him. It wasn't that he'd been asking anything of her, but that he'd been unable to do anything for her, and Beau thrived on his power.

"And I don't want to put you in that car at sunrise," he said.

"You don't?"

"No, but I have to. It's our agreement."

"I don't care about the money," she said. "I love you. I love him. Tell me what to do, Beau. I'll do it."

"Okay." He was dependable. He made decisions in her best interest, not his. Even when he commanded her, he did it to give her things she hadn't known she wanted. He smoothed his hand lovingly over her hair until he was cupping the back of her head. "Here's what you're going to do, Lola. You're going to go home. You're going to tell Johnny it's over."

Involuntarily, she curled her hands harder into his T-shirt. They were two distinct concepts in her mind. There was loving Beau, and there was ending it with Johnny. They'd been two mutually exclusive ideas, one she was submitting to and one she hadn't seriously entertained. Beau wanted to merge them. "Just like that? Over?"

"Isn't it?" he asked. "How can you be with him after this?"

She shook her head. "How can I do that to him?"

"I told you once, you can't sacrifice yourself to make him happy. You know what you want, but somewhere along the way, he helped you bury your instinct. Go there again. What does it tell you?"

Her heart swelled. Johnny liked Lola's edge, but it was true. He preferred her a little dulled. Beau, on the other hand, wanted what he'd been asking for all along—her. He hadn't even put one day between meeting her and making his proposition. Within an hour of their sidewalk encounter, he'd told her she had his attention. His assurance was in his actions. Maybe he'd known all along. Maybe this had always been his plan. It was the reason she'd been pressing him for. He'd chosen her because he was a man who knew what he wanted.

"My instinct tells me that Johnny and I have history," she said, "but that he's not my future."

"And why not?" he prompted.

"Because you are."

Chapter Thirteen

Back on the sixteenth floor, Lola and Beau went about their tasks. She showered again to rid herself of the man with the gun and gathered her things while Beau changed. When she was ready, she sat on the edge of the bed.

Beau set his cell on the nightstand. "Warner'll be here in a few minutes. I'm not coming with you."

"How come?"

"I want you back here tonight." He rubbed his forehead with tense fingers. "Warner will sit out front until you're ready while I take care of things here. I have the suite as long as we need it. Leave whatever you don't need there. We can figure the rest out once this is done."

"I don't think I can just walk in there, get my things and walk back out," she said.

"That's why I can't go. Warner will wait as long as it takes, though. I don't want you staying overnight there, Lola."

He was shifting back into business mode as the night dissolved into dawn. Lola bit her bottom lip. "Are you sure about this?"

He didn't answer right away. He reached out, fingered a piece of her hair and tucked it behind her ear. With his thumb and forefinger, he lifted her chin. "I'm not Johnny. I don't waver in my decisions. I don't backtrack. I don't put anything on your shoulders if I can help it. If I could do this part for you, I would. Yes, I'm sure."

She drew on his strength, lengthening her spine and holding his gaze. "I can do this part myself. It won't be easy, but I can do it if you're waiting for me."

He smiled. "There's the girl on the sidewalk I had to have. The one who kicks cars and doesn't apologize."

She nodded, but hard as she fought it, her mind was creeping ahead of the moment. It was in her apartment, waking Johnny up from a dream to plunge him into a nightmare. "I think it's best I call Johnny to let him know I'm on my way."

"Why?"

"He should be completely awake for this conversation. I'll tell him to have coffee ready."

Beau raised his eyebrows at her. "You're telling me he's asleep right now? While you're here with me, he's *asleep*?"

If things went like they had her first night with Beau, Johnny would be sleeping off his drunkenness. She shook her head. "It's a good thing. He'd drive himself crazy otherwise."

Beau sighed and pointed at the nightstand. "Your cell phone was in your purse?"

"Yes."

"Use mine. Also—" He paused, hedging. "The other half of your money's in the closet. I was also going to give it to you in cash."

"Was?" she asked.

"Like I said, I've never broken the terms of an agreement, but I'm making an exception on this point. Understand me when I say—I don't have many regrets in my life, but making you feel worthless is one of them. This money does not belong to you because you did not earn it. You are not this money. Understand me?"

It was all she'd wanted to hear since this thing had started, she just hadn't realized it until then. That she, her love, was worth more than any dollar amount. Lola's chest ached. "I don't want it."

"Good." He put his hands on his hips and dropped his forehead toward the floor. After a deep breath, he opened his mouth. "There's something else—" He shook his head. Paused. Cleared his throat.

"What else?"

"Nothing. Never mind. We can talk later."

It was a rare thing to see him nervous. It could've been because of what they were about to do, but it almost seemed like something else. "Talk about what?" she asked warily.

"Everything. There's a lot to figure out, but now you'd better go." He walked away. "I'll grab shoes and walk you down."

She had to make the call. Lola's body was a tornado of emotion. Her heart beat so hard, it practically reached for Beau as he disappeared into the closet. Her stomach, on the other hand, was in knots. It was not a conversation she'd ever pictured herself having with Johnny, but now she couldn't imagine not doing it. She'd made the decision to leave him so quickly that she wondered if it'd been waiting just below the surface, and if so, for how long.

She picked up Beau's phone. As she dialed Johnny's cell phone, a text message from Brigitte popped up.

Good luck this morning. Remember what I said last night. Stick to the plan. The bitch is just getting what she deserves. Can't wait to hear all about it tonight. See you downstairs. xo

Lola read it one more time before the screen went black. Her throat closed. Her hand shook. It was possible the text wasn't about her at all, yet it was even more possible that it was. Just moments ago she'd told herself to trust Beau, but that was already crumbling. She stood.

Beau emerged from the closet. "Ready?" he asked, patting his pockets. "Oh, I left my phone—" He glanced up at Lola, who'd raised the phone in front of her with the screen toward him.

"What is this?" she asked.

Beau's expression cleared as if he knew instantly. "Lola." He held out his hands, either to placate or reach for her. "What did you see? What does it say?"

"A text message from Brigitte."

He looked up at the ceiling. "You've got to be fucking kidding me."

She couldn't breathe. Any doubt she'd had that the text wasn't about her was gone. Lola gripped the phone until her knuckles were white. "What plan?"

He looked at her again. "Listen to me. If I tell you the truth like this, you won't understand." He put his hands palm to palm in front of him. "Trust me on this. Go home. Talk to Johnny. When you come back, I'll explain everything."

That was the reverse of how she wanted to do things. She had everything on the line as she was about to throw nine years down the drain. "Do you honestly think I'm that stupid? Don't tell me you'll explain this *after* I uproot my life for you."

"You don't want to hear the truth," Beau said with warning. "You have to trust me here, Lola."

"I can't."

"You *can't?*" he asked. "You put yourself in front of that gun for me tonight, and now you can't trust me?"

Her eyes darted over the floor. She'd done it without hesitation, and he'd protected her too. At least, she'd thought he had.

But there was a plan.

And it involved her.

"There's always a plan, Lola."

The text message was casual, as if it were nothing for Brigitte to call Lola a bitch to Beau—the man who was asking her to trust him. Her decision maker. The man who'd demanded her surrender and who'd received it. Brigitte had a reason to believe Beau wasn't on Lola's side.

"No," she said. "Before I walk into my home with the intention to walk right back out, I need you to tell me exactly what Brigitte meant by that."

He took a threatening step toward her. "You aren't the only one uprooting your life. You think this has been easy for me? Letting someone in who's in love with another man?"

"You shouldn't have," she said, her voice rising. "I didn't ask you for that. I didn't want any of this."

"And *I* wasn't the one who was supposed to—" He stopped.

"Supposed to what?" she asked after a silence, but he only stared at her. "Come on, Beau. Tell me what the plan was. Tell me what I was supposed to do that I didn't." She grit her teeth. "I did *everything* you asked. I fought you tooth and nail but I gave you what you wanted."

"Yes," he said. "You did everything right."

"So what is it then?" She cocked her head. The longer he clung to the truth, the more Lola had to know. Whatever it was, he wasn't going to give it up easily, which meant she needed to go deeper. "Maybe it's not what I *didn't* do, but what I did."

His jaw set. "What do you mean?"

"Power is a funny thing, isn't it? Sometimes the one who thinks he holds it…doesn't hold it at all."

He shook his head in warning, narrowing his darkened eyes on her. "Don't."

"That's it, isn't it? You want to love me more than you want to control me, and it scares you. You'd let me have that power to keep me."

"Nobody has that over me," he clipped.

"Someone did tonight," she said, raising an eyebrow. "That man could've taken everything from you with one bullet."

He stepped closer to her. "He didn't, because we protected each other. We were in control. I'm still in control."

"That's fine, Beau. Control isn't what I want. I want truth. You can keep your ridiculous obsession with having it all."

"Ridiculous?" he asked, his nostrils flaring. "You think power comes over night? You think I decide? No. I fucking earned it. I've worked my ass off so people would respect me. So I could buy you expensive dresses and drive you around in a car people would literally kill to have. That man tonight—he could've killed you if he'd taken you out there, all for what I have."

"Who says I want any of that?" she countered, pushing back against his anger. "I could give a crap about your car or your empty lifestyle. Without it, you're just you, and that scares you. I make you powerless."

"Are you fucking kidding me?" He charged forward, and she retreated until her legs hit the bed. He snatched the phone away, launching it against a wall as she flinched. His large shoulders moved up and down as he breathed hard. "I can't *believe* I let you get to me like this again."

"Again—?"

"You're so righteous, aren't you, Lola?" He towered over her. "You don't need or want anything like the rest of us. You can't be bought. Your pussy's not for sale."

She flushed. He made her sound high and mighty for that, as if any other woman would've rolled over and given him what he wanted. She had nowhere to put her hands, so she covered her stomach.

He laughed, and it was as hollow as his eyes. That emptiness was even more frightening than his indifference had been. "You were wrong. You said it couldn't be done, but *I* did it. Me."

"What did you do?" she asked, dread softening her voice. Suddenly she didn't want to challenge or push him—she just wanted him to be himself again.

"Imagine this, Lola. Ten years ago, it's the biggest moment of my life—what everything else has led up to. I've just signed a contract to sell one of the companies I practically killed myself to build. For years, I've denied myself everything for work—women, fun, sleep, life. It doesn't matter, though, because it's finally paid off. I'm going to be a multi-millionaire.

"I want to celebrate," he continued. "But I have no one. I'm alone. So I walk into a strip club looking for anybody, but I see this girl on stage with long, black hair and kitten ears on her head—furry black triangles. She looks over her shoulder and directly at me with the bluest eyes. She's got this body men *kill* for and is wearing a fucking—are you still with me?" He gestured up and down at her. "It looks like a bikini made of goddamn diamonds. It's so bright, it almost blinds me when the spotlight is on her. She's the most stunning thing I've ever seen. I have to have her. *Her.*" He pointed into the distance. "*That one.* I pay for Cat Shoppe's most expensive room. I pay to see her dance, for her attention. She gets so close to me that our legs touch, even though that isn't allowed. She's flirting. I tell her I need her—I'll do anything, *pay* anything for her. I offer her a grand, but she shakes her head. Five grand. She just smiles. Ten thousand dollars. She looks me right in my eyes, bats her lashes like a little cunt and says—"

"I'm not for sale," Lola whispered.

"That's right," he said. "But you were wrong, weren't you?"

Lola wavered on her legs, reaching back to steady herself on the mattress. She narrowed her eyes on him, recalling the young, handsome man from that night. "That was you at Cat Shoppe." Her entire body shook. "You knew who I was on the sidewalk at Hey Joe?"

"Yes."

"Why? Why are you doing this?"

"You thought you were too good for money I broke my back to earn. Because you couldn't give me that one fucking thing on the most important night of my life. Because—" He faltered, leveling his eyes on her.

For a brief second, he looked as pained as she felt. The whole thing was made even more shocking by the fact that there were depths to him she hadn't even scratched.

He'd earned that money so he would be enough. So nobody could turn him down or walk away from him, because in his eyes, everybody had a price. Perhaps he was right. She'd once thought she could never be bought, no matter the amount.

"I hurt you," she said, hating the break in her voice.

The pained look vanished. "I promised myself nobody would ever make me feel that way again. There would be nothing my money couldn't buy. And then there you were again out front of Hey Joe, just as beautiful as that night ten years ago. It was like no time had passed. And when you returned my tip and insisted there was no connection between us, I was just as weak." He splayed his hands over his chest. "You're the only person who does this to me, Lola. You're a threat to everything I've worked for."

She shook her head. "I'm not a threat. I didn't hurt you on purpose. You...you can't do this."

"It's done. I've proven anything can be bought. Today, I get back the power you took from me."

"I am not a thing to be overcome. I'm a person." She clutched her throat. Her skin was burning. "If this were true, you would've told me after the first night."

"I tried, believe me." He crossed his arms. "But you, so stubborn, had to go and say that buying someone's body didn't count. It had to be their heart." He hesitated only a moment, but he'd gone too far down whatever path he was on. He couldn't seem to stop himself, even as Lola's heart broke right in front of him. "I was going to end it there, but you wanted to play. And as you know, I'm not one to turn down a challenge. She thinks her heart isn't for sale? I'll buy that too, I thought. You only have yourself to blame for loving me."

A challenge. That's what this had been about. Conquering her, teaching her a lesson, winning a game. He'd been dropping hints along the way, most likely for his own amusement. "Fuck you," she uttered. "You think my life is a game?"

He uncrossed his arms and ran both hands along the bridge of his nose. "It was until it wasn't. I realized tonight, with you in my arms, telling me you love me, how wrong I've been. But I promise you, from the first minute, I meant everything I said, Lola. I never lied about how I felt. I want you—"

She scrambled back so fast when he reached for her that she landed on the bed. "Don't you dare fucking touch me."

He grabbed the comforter on both sides of her and pulled it, sliding her back toward him. He jerked her to her feet by her biceps. "You want to test me? You'll lose. Want to fucking run away from me? You can't. Fight me all you want." He kissed her hard. "Hurt me. I can take it. But you can't outrun me. You're strong, but you're not strong enough to take me on. You might as well give in."

Her knees threatened to buckle. There was undiluted pain and frustration in his voice. He loved her, even if he couldn't say it. She loved him. And she'd never wanted to hurt anyone worse in her life. She looked him in the eye and said, "I want my money."

It took a moment for anything to register on his face. His mouth parted. "Your *money*?"

She had to fight not to look away from him. He'd hurt her, and words were all she had. She struggled to push him off. "That's all you're good for. All I am is my pussy and all you are is your money. So give it to me so I can go."

He tightened his grip. "That's not true, and you know it. That isn't what we are."

She dug deeper. Sank her claws into her pain. What he'd done deserved her worst. "Go buy some more people, and get the fuck out of my life. Build your empire and run it all by yourself. Alone. No matter how much money you spend, you will never have me, and you and I will never have what Johnny and I do."

He tilted his head with a jerk as if his lid were about to fly off. "Liar. Earlier you said—"

"Earlier I was hysterical," she spat. "I thought I was going to die. I don't even know what I was saying. I love Johnny, and I just want to go home to him."

He raised his chin, looking down at her. His jaw worked back and forth as he breathed through his nose. He pushed her backward hard and stormed to the closet. Her chest stuttered viciously as if collapsing in on itself. She wanted to run away from him and to him in equal parts. She needed to believe in his arms around her, but every time he'd touched her, it was a lie. It was to get something from her—not just something, but the most valuable thing she had to give. Her heart.

He reappeared with a brown package like the one he'd brought to her apartment the night before. "Here's the other five hundred grand," he said, tossing it. It landed with a heavy thump at her feet. "Now get the fuck out."

She only needed to be strong long enough to leave that presidential suite in one piece. The money was heavier than she expected, and she had to heave it from the floor into her arms. She walked right up to him, standing under his nose. "Coward. There's a reason you had to have *me* that night and a reason you're still thinking about *me* ten years later, and it wasn't to win some stupid game."

"You're probably right. And it's the same reason you're still standing here when I told you to leave."

She gripped the package until her fingers hurt. "You could've had me without the money," she said. "You could've come back for me, but you were too scared to even try. Now you've lost me. I took your power, and that means you've lost your game."

He didn't shy away from her anger. His green eyes fixed on her, the thick of the forest, the dark, inconceivable pit. He was a monster, but a beautiful one with his sharp, dimpled chin and mussed coffee-bean hair. If only, with his confession, he'd also been forced to shed the mask he'd used to lure her in.

"You're wrong. I haven't lost anything," he said. "Because I'm not the one who fell in love."

"Yes, you did. I want to hear you say it. You made me say it, you fucking coward. Now you say it."

"You will never hear me say it," he said. "Get out."

He might as well have slapped her. She almost wished he had, because at least then she'd be able to feel her pain in a physical way, instead of as a gaping hole in her chest. "You can thank Brigitte for me. She saved me from making the biggest mistake of my life."

Lola left the room. She had somewhere to be and not long now to get there.

But she wasn't finished with Beau. He'd committed the greatest crime there was—he'd played with love. And nobody should ever be able to get away with that.

He'd made mistakes, thinking she hadn't been paying attention, but she had. He'd exposed his weakness to her and handed her the weapon she needed.

He survived on power—she would take it from him.

He was in love with her—she would use that to do it.

As she rode the elevator down to the ground floor, she made a decision. Somehow, some way, Beau would get what he deserved. She would break him too, and she'd do it without the mercy he'd tried to afford her. He'd hidden behind his money so long, he'd never let anyone close enough to hurt him. Except for her. She was there. She was certain that he loved her—and that he'd come to regret it.

She wasn't sure how.

She wasn't sure when.

She only knew one thing.

Beau Olivier would be sorry he'd ever laid eyes on her.

Provocation

EXPLICITLY YOURS ◆ BOOK THREE

JESSICA HAWKINS

Chapter One

Present day

Lola's heels clicked against the hallway's hardwood floors like the countdown of a ticking time bomb. Windows lined one side, and the rising sun striped the opposite wall with sharp-cornered shadows. The house, square between the curves of the Hollywood Hills, was renowned for its modern design. But Lola didn't see the appeal in a home that echoed her every move. To her, it was a shell—beautiful on the outside, hollow on the inside. Just like its owner.

She crossed the foyer on her way to the kitchen. At the entryway table, under the garish *Montgolfier* chandelier, she stopped to center a vase of Calla lilies—amongst such perfection, the slightest flaw glared. She slid a flower out of the arrangement and dragged her fingertip up its stem, bending it nearly to the point of snapping. Even the house's feminine touches were stiff. Lola had once loved Calla lilies, especially the purple-hearted ones like this that were edged in white. But she'd learned to be wary of anything that thrived in such barren surroundings.

"You're up early," she heard from behind her.

Lola replaced the flower, slipping it back into its spot, and turned around. Beau leaned in the doorway, his suit straight and sharp, a newspaper folded under his arm.

She went to him. “I wanted to say good morning before you left.”

He checked his watch. “By the skin of your teeth.”

She smiled thinly. Beau was punctual. That was no surprise. But when she’d fantasized about spending a morning with him, it hadn’t been anything like this—scrounging for extra minutes. Not that it really mattered.

She put slinky arms around his neck, drew his head down to hers. “Are you hungry? I can make you something quick.”

“What do you think?” His voice deepened as he rested a hand on her lower back, at the base of her zipper. “I’m a man who hasn’t eaten in almost three weeks.”

Lola lingered a moment, their mouths close, prolonging a kiss that wasn’t just a kiss. It was a sneak preview. A tease. A warning. She pressed her lips to his like a woman who didn’t want her boyfriend to walk out the door. Like a woman in love.

When she pulled away, one corner of Beau’s mouth curved into a smile. “Wow. Careful, or I won’t be held responsible for breaking your rules.”

She shrugged and fixed his tie, even though it was perfectly straight. “I’ve been thinking—about us.” She glanced up at him from under her lashes. “About the rules.”

He took a handful of her backside. “Probably not as much as I have.”

“I’m ready, Beau. Tonight.”

His expression didn’t change, but she caught the slight twitch of his eye. “Don’t tease me,” he said. “It wouldn't be wise to put chocolate cake in front of a starving man."

Lola removed her arms to take his cheeks in her hands. "I know it's been difficult these past three weeks—"

"Two and a half."

This time, Lola flinched. As if she needed a reminder of how dangerous it could be to let her guard down for even a second. She ignored the comment. "You've been patient," she continued. "I haven't forgotten anything, but I'm ready to start moving forward."

With his hand on her ass, Beau pulled her against him, forcing her feet to shuffle forward the last few inches. "Why wait until tonight? I can be a couple minutes late."

Lola's heart hammered once, the way it always did when Beau got like this—impatient. He could be convincing in a way that was hard for her to resist, but she had to. Giving in to him now could unravel everything. "I want it to be special—not in the doorway on your way to work. You can survive until tonight."

"I'm not so sure about that," he said. "I've never slept next to the same woman this many nights in a row without so much as a handjob. It's miraculous I'm still upright."

Lola shook her head but smiled. "You are a true romantic, Mr. Olivier. I'm a lucky woman."

He put his knuckle under her chin to keep her eyes on him. "I'm the lucky one."

"Are you?" The words came out of her mouth too fast. Now, around him, she filtered everything. But today was a day she'd been anticipating for a while, and that alone was a reason to be even more careful.

Along with excitement came a tiny crack of doubt inside her, though. It was silly. She knew how Beau felt. He was happy she was there, even if he wasn't around all the time. He loved her, despite the fact that he hadn't told her. He didn't always show it, but she was his priority. She had to believe those things were true, because if not, then all this had been for nothing.

"Am I lucky?" he asked. "I've been given a second chance I didn't deserve. I thought I had it all, Lola, but I was coming home to an empty house. I just didn't realize that was a bad thing until I started coming home to you. I'm a lucky son of a bitch. And I'm the happiest I've ever been."

She glanced away, but only for a second—it was a telling habit she'd been trying to kick. Beau didn't consider himself romantic. Lola disagreed. The rest of the world could keep their flowers and candy. For her, Beau was taking a dull hammer to his brick walls, a slow process, but one that meant more to her than anything money could buy. It still wasn't enough.

Despite fighting herself every waking moment, she loved him. She couldn't have faked all the things she had without that. When he'd broken her heart, though, she'd buried that love—and she threw more dirt on it every day. Because Lola *wasn't* happy. And if Beau thought she was, then he didn't know her at all.

"I should get to the office," he said when she didn't respond. "The sooner this day is over, the sooner I'll be home with you."

Beau was sweeter in the morning, before the day had gotten to him. She didn't doubt he meant what he said, but during the week, he only came home at a decent time when they had an event to attend. Those nights, he was always standing too close, touching her somewhere, as if assuring himself she was real.

"Be home by seven o'clock." She didn't smile. She crossed her arms, tapping her index finger on her bicep. "And I don't mean *leave* work at seven. We have a reservation at seven-thirty."

"We do?"

"I told you last week I was making dinner plans and not to schedule anything."

"If I did, I'll cancel it. Now that I know what's in store for tonight." He tucked some of her hair behind her ear. She knew the low-lidded look he was giving her well—she got it several times a day. She'd asked him once what he was thinking about when he made that expression, and he'd just said, *"Us."*

"Listen—why don't you let my assistant handle tonight?" he asked. "Pick any restaurant, I don't care how exclusive. She'll make it happen. I want the best for…"

Lola stopped listening, pressing her lips together, her jaw tingling. She wanted to ask him what the hell made him think she'd prefer an expensive restaurant to anything else. Hell, an In-N-Out burger and a chocolate shake was enough to make her mouth water. Despite the staggering amount of cash she had stashed in a locker downtown, she was still the same Lola who wore beat-up Converse and regularly chose beer over wine.

"You surprised me with balcony seats to the ballet last week," Lola said, interrupting whatever he was saying. "I want to return the favor."

Beau arched an eyebrow. "It's a surprise?"

She smoothed her hand over his tie. "You're always in charge. Just relax. Let me do this for you."

"I like being in charge."

With the drop in his tone, an unexpected thrill ran up her spine. If Beau did one thing well, it was taking charge. That was how she'd ended up on her stomach on his hotel bed their second night together, letting him have her in ways Johnny hadn't in their nine years together. It was also the reason she had to be on alert at all times.

"At least let me send you a new dress," he said.

"If you keep buying me dresses, we'll have to add on another wing just to store them."

Beau smiled. "That can be arranged."

Lola had never owned so much in her life. But what was actually hers? Beau didn't like her to spend her own money. He thought she'd deposited it into a savings account where it was earning interest, and he'd made her promise she wouldn't use it. "Save it for something nice here and there," he'd said. As if 'something nice' was the *real* reason she'd accepted a million dollars to fuck him.

"I already have an outfit planned," Lola said slowly, "and I think you'll like it very much."

Beau ran his hand up over her backside, lingering, slow. There were some things she never had to fake, like swooning at his touch, or the gradual but electric creep of warmth it sent through her.

He liked the dress she'd chosen that morning. She could tell by the way he absentmindedly touched it while they talked—rubbing the soft wool, playing with the tail of the zipper. It was short, which was fine, because she had great legs, and the neckline was high. Conservative but sexy, the kind of woman Beau should have on his arm. Her leather pants were still stuffed at the bottom of her duffel bag, though to his credit, Beau had asked about them. He liked those too.

"What're your plans today?"

Lola lifted one shoulder. "Shopping. I have some small things to get for tonight."

"Good. Put everything on my card, all right? I don't want you spending money on me."

Had this been the special evening Beau thought it was, Lola would've given it more thought. She would've taken him up to Mulholland Drive, brought some hotdogs since they'd never gotten to eat theirs, played Pink Floyd on the car stereo and made love to him under the stars. Money wouldn't've even crossed her mind, but that was where Beau always went, and that was one of the reasons he and Lola were very, very different.

That was the life he'd chosen not to have with her. Lola agreed to charge her shopping to him—not because she felt good about spending his money, but because she'd cut up all except one of her credit cards the night before.

Beau leaned in, kissed her once on the lips and walked away. "Warner can take you today. I'll drive myself."

"Beau?"

He turned partway around and nodded at her. "Yeah?"

Lola's throat constricted, as if she physically couldn't speak. She had tried many times to tell him she loved him for the sake of making this work, but each time, she'd choked on the words. It was the truth, but it felt like a lie.

"Can I take the Range Rover?" she asked instead. She needed to be alone today, and while Beau's driver was good at blending into the background, he wasn't much for disappearing completely.

"Of course. You know you don't have to ask. But I don't mind driving—"

"I hate it." Lola sucked in a tiny breath. She was getting sloppy. She couldn't go around blurting things without thinking first.

"You hate what?" He faced her completely, his attention snagged.

Being treated like a doll. Lavished with expensive things I don't care about. Sitting around all day, waiting for you to come home. "Warner driving me around," she said. "It feels extravagant."

He shrugged, his hands in his pockets. "Warner drives me all the time. It's more normal than you think."

"Maybe for people like you."

"People like me?" Beau tilted his head with interest. She would've preferred to drop it, though, this conversation they would've had if things had been different. If she cared about making this work. "You *are* people like me. Now."

Lola kept a poker face, even as her blood simmered a little. Letting her emotions get the best of her was the kind of thing that got her into trouble, but *that* pissed her off. She wasn't like him. She hadn't even wanted the money—she'd just been a pawn in a transaction between Johnny and Beau.

"I didn't mean it like that," Lola said, regaining her silky smoothness. "But it makes sense for you because you work in the car. I don't. I just sit and stare out the window, so I might as well drive myself."

"Fine," he said. "Take the Range Rover."

Lola walked over to him and touched his forearm. "Why don't you give Warner the day off? I'm sure he'd appreciate that."

"Why don't you just let me buy you a car?"

She smiled up at him. "Because there are two in the garage, and two people in this house. Again, extravagant."

"Better get used to it, *ma chatte*." He kissed her one more time. "I really have to run. See you tonight. Seven o'clock."

Beau walked out of the room, and she listened for the conclusion of the morning show—the rumbling garage door, the roar of the Lamborghini's engine. No matter where in the house she was—eating toast in the breakfast nook, staring at Beau's pillow in his bed—that was when everything in her body unclenched. Being around him was constant mental warfare.

Lola went into the kitchen to locate the keys to the Range Rover. This would be the one day she'd enjoy spending Beau's money. Her to-do list wasn't very long, but each thing was an important cog in her plan.

Not long ago, Beau's kitchen was the last place she thought she'd be standing. As she'd fled his hotel room, doing her best to hold her broken heart together, she'd never wanted to see Beau's face again—much less be living in his home. But this morning, knowing what was to come later that night, there was nowhere else she'd rather be. As it turned out, a hell of a lot could change in three weeks.

Chapter Two

Three weeks earlier

There was a reason Beau never thought about that night at Cat Shoppe. He'd pushed Lola—and the memory of her on stage—down into his depths years ago. She was never meant to surface. It should've been the best day of his life—selling his first company for millions after a decade of struggle. It would've been, had he just gone home after his last celebratory drink.

But he hadn't, and now he stood in the Presidential Suite at the Four Seasons, staring at the door Lola had just left through. Their words echoed through the hotel room—cold, hard confessions and accusations. His normally steady heartbeat raced as if he'd just run a sprint. It unnerved him. Remaining calm was something he'd trained himself to do, a survival tactic for situations like leading a boardroom full of megalomaniacs.

He couldn't—*wouldn't*—allow anyone that power over him. She'd done him a favor by walking out before he could explain, opening his eyes when he'd been blind for her. What had he thought—that Lola was anything more to him than another challenge? The thing that'd made her special, that'd set her apart from other women, ceased to exist. She no longer had his power. It'd been a struggle, but he'd taken it back. Now, she was just another defeated opponent, a discarded chess pawn.

Beau returned to the suite's master bedroom. It was

hot in the room, as if the heat had been on all night. As if it'd all been some sort of fever dream—intense, vivid, colorful. Over with the new day's dawn.

Except that Lola was everywhere in that hotel room. Her red lipstick, smeared into the comforter. His white robe that she'd worn, strewn across a chair. His tie, still knotted, on the floor where he'd discarded it after blindfolding her. She'd really gotten to him, burrowing deep, making him think the ending he'd planned wasn't what he wanted after all. It wasn't the first time she'd drawn him under her spell.

Ten years earlier, Beau had become the man he'd always wanted to be. Now, he and his money were respected in the business world. Sought after. The definition of power. And underneath it all had always been his weakness—the girl in the black kitten ears.

Beau crouched at the footboard and picked up the gold dress he'd ripped off her body. Beads bit into his palms when he squeezed it. No—none of it'd been a dream. Thrusting inside her, wondering how it was possible, with all the fucking he'd done in his life, that he'd never felt anyone that way—that was real.

It was real, the way she'd approached the gas station the night before, a small smile on her face, her eyes turned up slightly as if lost in a daydream. With a gun to his head, he couldn't move, couldn't scream at her to run, couldn't do anything but watch her pull open the door and step into a nightmare. He would've done anything to stop it, would've handed over everything he'd worked for, but he could only stand there.

Beau tossed the dress aside and stood, running his hands over his hair. He needed to get ready for his day.

He and Lola were done—there was nothing more to say. Warner had her now, and she'd be home soon—getting her things, breaking Johnny's heart. Beau hoped she'd be brutal. No man should get off easy for selling the woman he claimed to love.

He thought about calling Warner and telling him to stay with Lola. When she was finished, she'd need to leave quickly, shed that sorry excuse for a boyfriend. Warner could drop her off—where? It occurred to him she might not have anywhere to go. That she'd get in Warner's car and feel like she had no one. That she might not get in Warner's car at all. That without a reason to leave, she might—stay. With Johnny.

Across the room, Beau's cell was in pieces on the floor from when he'd hurled it at the wall. He went for the hotel phone. He was unreachable, having instructed the front desk to hold his calls so his time with Lola wouldn't be interrupted.

He began to dial Warner. Just because he didn't want Lola didn't mean he wanted her staying with Johnny. This part was easy for Beau, anyway. With one phone call and a little cash, Warner would handle it. Whatever Lola needed—a ride, a hotel room for a few days, a new job—Beau could give it to her without even a word between them.

He paused, his finger hovering over the last number. His heart beat hard enough for him to notice. Lola wasn't his problem to fix. And like Beau had told her—he wasn't Johnny. He didn't waver in his decisions. He didn't backtrack. The game was over, and Warner was returning Lola to the past where she belonged. There'd be other women to fuck after an expensive dinner, new challenges to hold his interest, more ways to buy what he wanted. She had the money if she got into trouble. She didn't need Beau. And he—he had an empire to run.

Beau set the receiver back on its cradle and glanced out the door of the balcony. The sun was cresting over the mountains. From the start, Beau had always known there'd be a moment when it would all come to an end. This was that moment.

Chapter Three

It'd all started with a look.

Lola had stepped out from behind Cat Shoppe's curtains, center stage, the night's main feature. Nineteen, lithe and limber, but what'd set her apart most was that she'd loved to dance—the owner's words. Then again, the other girls had been at it much longer, and they'd seen a lot more than her. If they'd ever loved to dance, maybe they'd found more reasons not to.

Seconds into her number, she'd glanced over her shoulder and met eyes with a strikingly handsome man who looked sorely out of place and with no clue about it. That man would change the course of her life. He'd buy her body for a night, and then he'd buy her heart, and that would bring her to this moment—arms full of money, legs stretching wider with each step. Unable to get away fast enough.

The doorman just barely pulled the handle in time to let her out. She fled the Four Seasons hotel. The Beverly Hills concrete was smooth under her Converse, the opposite of the sidewalks around her apartment.

"Wait!" a male voice cried behind her. She stopped. The sun was still behind the mountain, but it would be up soon. She turned around, squinting at the figure jogging toward her in the semi-dark, waving his arms.

Lola would've reveled in the pitiful display if the man was Beau, but he wasn't. Beau would never run after anything—or anyone. Not that it mattered. If Beau wanted something badly enough, he'd catch it anyway.

She recognized Beau's driver as he slowed to a stop in front of her, his breathing labored. "I'm supposed to take you home, Miss Winters." He straightened his tie and left it even more crooked. With a nod back toward the hotel, he said, "I have the car waiting. I'm to take you home and stay out front until you're ready to come back here."

Lola's broken heart ached a quick second, a longing sigh. That'd been their plan, made only minutes ago, and it'd seemed solid. She and Beau were upside down, inside out, backward—and, somehow, they were just right. Until the truth had dropped into the room, diffusing their fantasy future like it'd been nothing more than a cloud.

Lola narrowed her eyes at Warner. Her disgust for Beau branched out, disfigured fingers on a dying tree, looking to take anything down with it. "Is that what you're *to do*?"

He looked from side to side without moving his head a millimeter. "Um—Mr. Olivier called about fifteen minutes ago and specifically instructed—"

"Mr. Olivier can instruct his foot up his ass. Take another step toward me, and I'll scream."

Warner swayed back as if she'd swung at him. "Excuse me?"

"I'll find my own way." Lola turned back around. She and Beau no longer owed each other anything, not even a lift home. She started the two-something mile walk back to her apartment.

Innumerable customers had passed through during the two years she'd stripped at Cat Shoppe. It was a wonder she remembered that particular night at all, but she did. That man across the club had worn a suit, not unusual for their clientele. Cat Shoppe had been more exclusive in those days. He'd been older to her then, but now she just recalled him as smooth and spotless. Not the hard, angular man he was now. How she could've forgotten Beau's bottomless green eyes, she wasn't sure, but she'd tried not to look too hard into anyone's eyes when she'd worked there.

He'd stayed near the entrance, watching her. She'd been stared at before, but this was different. It was the same feeling she'd gotten on the sidewalk at Hey Joe—as if he'd been passing by and something had stopped him in his tracks.

Backstage, the owner, Kincaid, had pulled her aside and sent her to the VIP room. At first, Beau hadn't demanded anything or tried to grope her. He'd seemed more interested in talking. He'd looked into her eyes when speaking to her, not at her tits. Although, he'd looked at those too. Beau was right that she'd brushed against him when she'd danced for him, even though that wasn't allowed.

And then, out of nowhere, he'd offered her money to go home with him—and doused any interest she'd had. It was presumptuous, and in a way, disappointing. Up until then, she'd been a girl intrigued, wanting to know more about this man who wasn't like the others who paid for time alone with her. As if it'd been some warped version of a first date.

He'd left abruptly after she'd turned him down, and she'd forgotten it by the next day.

Beau hadn't. Her rejection had struck something deep inside him—something that'd compelled him to lead her right into the mouth of a fire just to watch her burn. It didn't matter that he'd changed his mind at the end. It only took one ember to send everything up in flames.

She'd had this sick fullness in her gut before—an unruly customer pulling down her thong during a lap dance. She'd knocked the scrawny guy on his ass with a lucky punch. When one of her mom's boyfriends had struck her, she'd launched toward him, claws out. She would've lost if her mom hadn't stepped in, but that didn't matter. Both times, she'd fought back.

Lola readjusted the package of cash in her arms. The sun's fiery-orange arch peeked on the horizon, silhouetting palm trees. Even though she had the money—the money was *all* she had—she refused to get a cab. In her eyes, it was no different than accepting a ride from Beau.

Besides, the sooner she got home, the sooner she'd have to face Johnny. It wouldn't be difficult to hide what she'd done—declaring her love for the enemy. She doubted Johnny'd even think to ask. The problem was that she'd meant it. No matter how badly Beau had hurt her, love didn't come with an off switch. She couldn't go home to Johnny and pretend none of it'd ever happened. And after what she'd been through with Beau, she wasn't sure she wanted to anyway.

She and Beau were fire and ice. They were never meant to be together. They clashed. They exploded. He heated her when she was cold and soothed her when she was burning up. That couldn't be faked. In the convenience store, with a gun under her chin, Beau wouldn't let the man take her outside where Beau couldn't see her.

Johnny wasn't a protector. The moment Beau's business card had gone missing from Hey Joe's countertop, her trust in Johnny had begun to chip away—a gradual process she hadn't even been completely aware of.

She'd had no idea the two men would each tear out half her heart, leaving a gaping wound in its place. She'd had no idea that as much as Johnny had loved her, and as much as Beau would worship her, it would end this way.

Lola picked up her pace, flexed her weighed-down muscles. Half a million dollars was fucking heavy. Hadn't she been good to both of them? For Beau, she'd risked everything. For Johnny, she'd given him whatever he'd wanted the last nine years. She hadn't asked for much in return. Just to be safe, loved—to be enough.

She wasn't safe. She wasn't enough. And now, she didn't have anyone. Beau had taken all that away from her. But as sure as that money in her arms, she was still standing. They'd landed their punches, but neither of them had knocked her off her feet.

It wasn't over yet, though. Lola and Johnny still had to face the truth. They'd made a deal with the devil, and the devil was cashing in. From Lola, he would take her heart. From Johnny, he would take Lola.

Chapter Four

Beau strained his hands against the fabric of his trouser pockets as the elevator leveled with the hotel's ground floor. He hadn't slept a wink, but when the doors opened, he straightened his shoulders and strode out like he would any other day. Because it was any other day. There was nothing particularly special about this one, except for his early-morning meeting with Mayor Churchill—a meeting he'd been trying to get for some time, and one he wouldn't have without Lola's help. At least she'd been good for that.

"Good morning, Mr. Olivier."

He smiled at the familiar face behind the front desk. "Morning, Heather."

"New tie?"

Beau touched the knot at the base of his neck. "Thank you for noticing."

"I always do. How'd you sleep?"

As he passed, Beau rapped his knuckles against the counter and winked. "Like a baby. Cab's out front?"

"Yes, sir."

Living in a hotel had its perks. Being greeted in the mornings by the Four Seasons' model-actress concierge, Heather, should've been one of the best. But the quickest way to turn Beau off was to make it easy for him. Girls like Heather had become a dime a dozen the day he'd put on a bespoke Prada suit and stepped onto the sidewalk of Rodeo Drive.

The attention had been fun at first, but the appeal had worn off quickly. It'd been some time since Beau'd picked up a random girl for a night, but he figured after what he'd been through the last twenty-four hours, maybe it was just what he needed. A nap, a strong drink and a good, meaningless fuck. Not necessarily in that order.

Out front, Warner waited at the passenger's side of his town car, his expression typically stoic. Beau'd worked with the man ten years, though, and he sensed something was off when Warner didn't jump to get the car door for Beau.

"I already arranged a ride," Beau said, checking his watch—6:56 A.M. Approximately thirty minutes since Lola had bolted from his room. "I thought you'd be longer."

"I tried calling. Miss Winters refused a ride home."

Beau slowed to a stop. "Did she?"

"Yes, sir."

Beau blew out a heavy sigh. Of course she had. Lola could be stubborn and proud—a potentially self-destructive mix. "I take it you put her in a cab?"

"She walked."

Beau's body locked up. The hotel's sidewalk curved along the driveway and disappeared behind a wall of greenery. When she'd left, the sky had still been dim. Beverly Hills or not, she shouldn't have been walking alone at that hour. Especially not with all that cash. He didn't like it.

"What the hell were you thinking letting her walk?" Beau asked.

"Sir, with all due respect, I've never given any of your dates a ride home. I didn't think you'd mind." Warner's mouth twitched at the corner. "And she can be very convincing."

Beau raised his chin. It was true. When Beau spent the night with a woman, he'd usually send her off with more than enough cash for a cab and didn't think of it again. He flexed his fingers, which he didn't remember curling into fists. "Of course. You're right. She'll be fine."

Warner moved to get the car door for Beau. "We could probably still catch her."

Beau unbuttoned his blazer. Lola was a smart girl. She wouldn't put herself in danger. And if she did, that was Johnny's problem, not Beau's. He got into the backseat. "I can't be late for this meeting. Miss Winters will have to handle herself from here on out."

"Very well, sir." Before Warner closed the door, he cleared his throat. "If you'd like, I can drop you off and go look myself. I didn't mean to imply she's just another—"

"I said no." Beau sniffed. "Don't bring it up again."

Warner nodded and shut the door.

Beau'd had enough of thinking and talking about Lola. She'd made the choice to walk out when he'd asked her to stay and trust him. Maybe that was a lot to expect, but he'd deserved that little bit of faith after what they'd been through. Beau looked out the window and tried to focus on his upcoming meeting. He wanted to be done with Lola, wanted her out from under his skin. All the more reason to find himself a Heather for a night—and soon.

What Beau didn't expect to find was someone better than the attention-hungry Heathers he normally met. Upon entering Mayor Churchill's City Hall office, he was *not* greeted by a pretty, young brunette. She didn't even look up from her computer when he approached her desk.

"Appointment?" she asked, clicking her mouse furiously.

"Yes, I have an appointment," Beau said deliberately. "Beau Olivier."

She glanced up for a brief moment and then away. "I'll let the mayor know. You can take a seat."

She had long, dark hair and fair skin. There was skepticism in her blue eyes—of him, of everything around her. She resembled Lola enough that he didn't want to stop talking to her.

"Mind if I stand?" he asked. "I'm not very good at sitting still."

"Makes no difference to me."

"I could use a coffee," Beau said. "Didn't have time to stop."

She sighed, finished whatever she was typing and left the room.

She was clearly annoyed with him, and Beau loved every moment. He glanced at her computer clock. He had four minutes before the meeting began. It could be done. He'd turned a girl from cold to hot in less time.

She returned and handed him a paper cup. "I hope you like it black. We're out of creamer."

"It's perfect—" He stooped to read the nameplate on her desk and chuckled. "Heather. Is that your real name?"

"What kind of a question is that?" she shot back.

"Never mind. Have you worked here long?"

"Yes." She scratched her neck, leaving a bright red mark on her skin. Just like Lola, her throat was long, slender and pale.

"You must really love your work," Beau said. "You've barely taken a second to breathe."

"I do."

When she didn't continue, Beau asked, "Why? What do you love about it?"

She blinked a few times at the screen and stopped typing. "Well, Mayor Churchill's so—I really like working for him."

"How come?" He craned his neck to the side to catch her eye. "A lot of people actually hate working for politicians."

"That's just it," she said quickly, turning to him finally, her expression brightening. "He's not your typical politician. The mayor's very dedicated to this city. It's an honor to be on his team. When I was young, I wanted to be an elementary school teacher, but then I took this poly-sci class in school, and it's so weird, because…"

Beau was sure it was weird, but he didn't care. He stopped listening. It turned out that almost-black hair, blue eyes and a white throat didn't mean anything. But that was the point, wasn't it?

He smiled at her, nodded.

Heather was still talking when he looked up to find Churchill standing in the doorway of his office, watching them. He straightened up. "Good morning, Mayor."

"Glenn is fine." He stepped aside. "Come on in, Olivier. About time we did this."

"I agree." Beau crossed through reception and shook his hand.

"Thank you, Heather," the mayor said, inviting Beau into his office with an open arm. He shut the door behind them and rounded his desk to sit behind it.

"Mayor—Glenn, thanks again for clearing time in your schedule to see me," Beau started. "This meeting isn't about you or me. It's about Los Angeles. Together, we can—"

Churchill held up a hand. "Slow down, Olivier. It's not even eight in the morning yet." He picked up a mug with a large, black mustache printed on the side. Before taking a drink, he held it out and nodded. "Isn't that something? Got it for Christmas last year from my nieces. Makes me look like I've got facial hair when I drink out of it. Watch."

Beau shifted in his chair as Churchill took a sip, the mustache lining up right under his nose.

Churchill swallowed, raised the mug and laughed as he reclined back against his seat. "Isn't that something," he repeated. "Got any plans for the weekend?"

"No, sir. Just work."

"Work? You're not serious."

"The way I see it, Saturday's just another day to get things done," Beau said. "Every day might as well be Monday to me."

"Huh." Churchill nodded slowly, studying his coffee a moment. He raised his eyebrows at Beau. "That's a shame. Saturday mornings, Lois and I like to take a walk through the neighborhood, get some fresh air while it's quiet out. Then we meet friends at a Santa Monica-based coffee shop and roaster. If we aren't careful, we'll sit there all day talking about absolutely nothing."

Beau smiled. It was a nice picture, but it wasn't him. And it had nothing to do with why he was there. "I'm glad to hear you support small businesses in the area. I try to do the same. Just like the talent coming out of our universities that I'd like to keep here in Los Angeles." He sipped his coffee.

"How's Lola?"

Beau coughed, nearly spitting out his drink. *Lola?* Gone, that's what she was. Out of his life for good. And she needed to stay gone. Beau'd watched Churchill fall in love with Lola the night of the gala—her spunk, her fire had worked on him. He didn't blame the poor man. If she could sucker Beau into falling for her, then Churchill had no chance.

Beau opened his mouth to answer and quickly decided to use this to his benefit. He cleared his throat. "She's doing well. Keeping busy."

"I imagine she'd have to if you're working weekends."

Beau pursed his lips at the thought of having an entire weekend with Lola. Even though he'd spent nearly every morning the last few years working, it wasn't that difficult to picture it—driving to Venice Beach with the top down, enjoying the sun and breeze, eating ice cream cones on the boardwalk. Things he hadn't done in years and years. He ran his hand along the arm of his chair. "I make time for her too."

"I don't know what it is," Churchill said. "There's just something about her that's stuck with me. Think it's that she reminds me a little of my wife when we were younger. I asked Lois out probably ten times before she finally gave in just to shut me up."

"I'm sure she's thankful you were so persistent."

"My wife is the most amazing woman I know," he continued. "You probably think I'm an old fool to say this, but I believe it—the caliber of woman a man chooses to have by his side says a great deal about how he does business."

Beau looked down into his coffee. That was one of the many differences between Lola and the Heathers of the world. Lola was even more than what she gave herself credit for. Beau'd seen that even from across the room when he'd entered that strip club. No matter how much he tried to forget her, he couldn't take that from her. She'd always be that caliber of woman.

Beau shook his head a little. "I don't think I need to tell you that it's rarely a man who chooses a woman. It's the other way around."

The mayor laughed. "How right you are. Especially a woman like that. I said it once, but I'll say it again—don't let go of that one."

A memory hit him hard, flooding into the tiny cracks in his resolve. Lola in his arms as they'd stood on his hotel room balcony the night before. He'd held her tightly, afraid he wouldn't be ready to let her go when the sun rose. He shut the thought down, refocusing on Churchill. "You're a busy man, Mayor. I am too. Should we get started?"

"I've been paying attention to you since our dinner," Glenn said. "You have an impressive track record, Olivier. When you choose a company, it almost always succeeds. What's your secret?"

Finally, a topic Beau was happy to distract himself with. "It's the other way around, actually. I choose them because they're poised for success. It's all about meticulous research. At the firm, I make sure we cover all our bases. We pore over numbers, we do case studies, we submerge ourselves in the markets."

"Sure, sure," Churchill said, waving a hand. "But it's more than that for you, isn't it?"

Beau set his coffee on the desk. "I'm sorry. I don't think I understand the question."

"You have an unorthodox way of dealing with the founders of the companies you invest in. Instead of sending your employees in your place or just gathering research online, you spend weeks courting them, getting to know them firsthand."

"That's all true."

"You're not investing in these companies. You're investing in the people."

"Well, businesses don't run without people. I vet them thoroughly, which is why I'm so confident in my portfolio." Beau slid the end of his tie through his hand. "As a result, the returns have been staggering."

"Beau," Glenn said, dropping his smile. "Be straight with me. I looked into your background. It took some digging, but I found that yearly conference thing you do. You never mentioned it before."

"It's no secret that Bolt Ventures sponsors *Entrepreneurs in Tech*."

"Not just sponsors. You and your company put it on, every last detail."

Beau nodded slightly. In fact, he'd even helped design the conference's lunch menu, since he'd been the one paying for it. "It's important. To us. And me."

"What I don't understand is why your name wasn't front and center on the project. What do you get out of it if not publicity? What's your concern with young, struggling entrepreneurs like the ones behind these companies you endow?"

Beau released his tie. He had answers prepared for everything. He liked having the right response, one he'd perfected over the years based on people's reactions. He never lied, but how you said things was sometimes more important than what you said. People picked up on keywords, tone, delivery.

Churchill wasn't responding to that. He valued truth and authenticity. Those were things Glenn'd seen in Lola, and they were the reasons she'd 'stuck with him.' Beau knew how that went. She'd stuck to Beau like glue, and he was beginning to think he wouldn't get to just shrug her off like he'd hoped.

"I know what it's like to struggle for something that might never happen." Beau spoke carefully. Weakness wasn't something he talked about if he could help it. "I also know what it's like to have someone take a chance on me only to have them turn around and virtually incinerate all my work."

"You're talking about VenTech?"

"Yes. When they bought my website ten years ago, they assured me they'd take it to the next level. Since they offered me more than it was worth, and I was eager to start another venture, I was hasty to accept. They didn't volunteer the fact that one of their private subsidiaries was an up-and-coming competitor of mine. They picked my work apart until it was a carcass."

"You came out on top, though. I read all about it. You got more out of that deal than you should've."

"If I hadn't sold it, my website would've destroyed the competition. George Wright, the founder, looked me in the eye and told me I could trust him, though." Beau paused. He couldn't remember a time in the last ten years when he hadn't been tracking VenTech's stock, waiting for the company to stumble. "I guess back then, it wasn't all about the money." It felt more like an admission to himself than to the mayor. It'd been a while since his fortune hadn't sat in the number one spot on his list of priorities.

"So that's why you put on the conference?" Glenn asked. "To prevent others from making the same mistakes?"

Beau had his go-to response ready—he funded the convention because the young entrepreneurs of Los Angeles were America's tomorrow. But instead, he gave Churchill the real reason. "I never forgot how it felt when those bastards trashed years of blood, sweat and tears. Yes, I do it to provide entrepreneurs with the resources I didn't have, either because they don't know about them or can't afford them. Even though I came out on top in my deal, perhaps with proper legal help, I could've put that company on a better course."

Glenn nodded knowingly. "I understand. A man never gets the taste of his first real failure out of his mouth. Not with money, not with revenge." He frowned. "I'll be honest, I was reluctant to take this meeting. People are always coming to me with what I can do for them. Not what they can do for Los Angeles."

"I've always been upfront with you about the fact that I'm a businessman first, but entrepreneurial growth in Los Angeles benefits us all in the long term. And that starts with a conversation about tax reform."

"When you cut the bullshit, Olivier, you're all right. People like me, we see a lot of crap. Men putting me on, getting me a drink here and there, trying to shake my hand, hungry smiles, wives slobbering on men who aren't their husbands. It's a breath of fresh air to see this side of you. And I know where it's coming from."

"I'm sorry?"

"We've talked here and there at events. Seen you in the tabloids with women too. You're different with Lola."

Was he different? Or was Churchill under Lola's spell, the way Beau had been? Who was he kidding—Beau was still under her spell. He fought himself not to look at his watch. He hadn't forgotten that Lola might still be walking home.

Beau opened his mouth to tell Churchill he was right—Beau was a changed man, and it was all because of the amazing woman at his side. It wasn't exactly a lie. Beau *had* been different with her. "She's…"

Glenn tilted his head. "Yes?"

Beau could easily ignore everything they'd just discussed and take the easy route. But Churchill was a good guy who deserved the truth. "She's not too happy with me at the moment," Beau admitted. "We had an argument, and it's—well, things between us are—over."

"I see." Glenn took his mug by the handle but didn't drink. He just squinted at Beau. "I'm not all that surprised, actually. I don't mean this as an insult to you but a compliment to her—it would take a certain kind of man to hang on to a woman like that. Do you think you're that man?"

Beau had no doubt he was. If he wanted Lola as his own, for good, he could have her. There was no question about that—he'd done it once, and no matter how much work it would be, he could do it again. Beau was a better man than Johnny—and fuck, he was certainly a better man *for Lola* than Johnny.

"Yes," Beau said. "Lola and I are—" What did he want to say? Not that they were a perfect fit. Maybe that they were *both* hard to handle, *both* impossible to hang on to, but that if anyone could, it would be each other.

"Look," Churchill said. "Can I give you some advice? Don't be an idiot. Whatever you did, make it right. If Lola truly is like my wife, which I suspect she is, she needs someone who won't be deterred by anything."

Beau hadn't been deterred by anything yet. Not Johnny, not Lola's resistance to his offer, not the fact that in order to win her love and win his game, he'd had to open up to her in a way he never had to anyone—not even Brigitte, who was like family.

Beau only focused on challenges that held a prize worthy of everything he had. He'd wanted his pride back. He'd wanted to redeem himself of the one failure he'd never overcome. But now it began to dawn on Beau—maybe he'd made the mistake of ignoring what was truly at stake. And maybe he'd been fighting for the wrong prize all along.

Chapter Five

The front door of Lola's apartment was unlocked, and she walked right in.

Johnny sprang instantly from the couch. "The sun's been up over an hour." He met her at the door, clasping her shoulders. "Are you all right?"

She looked into his earnest face. His concern was clear, but it was also overdue. Any number of things could've happened to Lola overnight. She could've been kidnapped by a crazy gunman and whisked away in a pricey sports car. She could've encountered a stilted admirer from ten years ago who'd never let go of his grudge. Considering whom she and Johnny were dealing with, being late at all was actually a perfectly valid cause for alarm.

"I'm fine," she said.

"I was worried. I thought about calling the cops."

"Did you?"

"Well…no." His eyebrows lowered. "What would I have told them?"

Maybe that she'd spent the night with the devil himself?

"I don't know," she said, wriggling out of his grip. The glass coffee table shook when she set the package of money on it. She stretched her aching arms and rolled her wrists. "We got into an argument. I refused a ride, so I walked."

"From where?"

"The hotel."

Johnny cocked his head. "He took you to a hotel? Doesn't he live in L.A.?"

Lola stared at him a moment. Johnny was a pretty big guy. He wasn't quite as tall as Beau, but he was meatier. *He* should've been the one to keep her safe in the gas station, but he hadn't even been there. She would've been there for Johnny. *She* never would've let him go off with a stranger. All so he could buy a fucking bar.

She was already heated from her walk. The more she'd thought about all the wrongs done to her by both men, the faster she'd strode and the higher her temper had risen. She knew what she had to do—what she *wanted* to do—but in all her anger, she hadn't stopped to figure this part out yet.

She turned away from Johnny, and her eyes landed on several days' worth of mail scattered on the counter. She'd start there. She walked over and sorted quickly through it, grabbing anything addressed to her.

"Was the hotel nearby at least?" Johnny asked.

"Beverly Hills."

"That's miles away."

She was well aware. She returned to the coffee table and dropped some envelopes next to the cash.

"I would've picked you up," Johnny said, following her from room to room. "You should've called."

She faced him, and her heart clenched. He could be so clueless. His simplicity was one of the things she loved about him except when she needed him to not be that. Like now, when what she was about to do would be that much harder because he had no idea it was coming.

She wrung her hands. "Johnny—"

He waited. "Yeah?"

Her heartbeat ping-ponged at the same rate as her thoughts. There was no right way to say *I care about you, but you screwed me over, but I don't want to hurt you, but I can't stay here anymore.* Was it fair that maybe some small part of her might *want* to hurt him for this? Did she even owe him an explanation? Had he just sat here on his ass all night, staring at a wall as she'd been bound, fucked, wooed, robbed, loved and then broken? Her chest stuttered with a deep breath, her fear ebbing slightly as anger took over again.

"I couldn't call you," she said. "My purse was stolen last night, and my phone was in it."

"Stolen? What the hell happened?" He let her pass to the bedroom. "Lola, for God's sake, stop moving around and talk to me."

She turned around. It was a plea, not an order, but she was tired of being told what to do. Just because Johnny didn't do things the same way as Beau didn't mean he hadn't also treated her like a pawn. Not giving her a straight answer, forcing her to make the decision for both of them—that was how he'd manipulated her. She hadn't seen it clearly at the time, but now it was all she saw.

"Don't tell me what to do," she said, her eyes narrowed.

He pulled back a little. "What? I'm not. I just want you to slow down, and tell me what's going on."

"Why should I? Do you honestly care how my night went?"

He raised his eyebrows and scoffed in a way that sounded like a laugh—as though she'd made a joke. "Of course I care. What kind of a question is that? You're acting like—" He stopped. His neck reddened around the collar of his T-shirt. "Holy shit. Did you…did he give you something?"

Beau had given her lots of things. Almost as many as he'd taken. But she didn't think that was what Johnny meant. "Like what?"

"You're not yourself. You can't stand still, and you look at me like you don't recognize me. No matter how long it's been, I haven't forgotten how you get when you're high."

Her mouth fell open. *High?* She wasn't high. She was pissed. Johnny *would* jump to that conclusion at the first sign of her old self. Spending two nights with Beau had reminded her of the girl she used to be. As Beau had embraced that about her, it became clearer that Johnny never had. He didn't like her wild.

The accusation was so offensive, she couldn't even deny it. The man she loved acted as though he didn't even know her. If she'd changed over the years, maybe he had too. Or maybe it was that she'd cared so fiercely about him, was so grateful to him, that she hadn't seen the truth. He wasn't etched into her heart, woven into her soul. She didn't feel him in her every movement—it wasn't *his* love that coursed through her veins like blood.

She went to the hallway closet and slid a cardboard box from the top shelf.

"What're you doing?" he asked.

She crouched, lifted the lid and fingered through some folders until she found one labeled *Important Papers—Lola.* She took it, along with her passport and a credit card she'd filed away earlier that year when she and Johnny had opened a joint account.

"Did you hear me?" he persisted. "I asked what the fuck you're on."

She stood up. The papers rustled as she clutched them. "I'm not high, and you have no right to ask me that."

"I have every right. It's the only explanation. It's just like those nights you used to come into Hey Joe after an especially rough shift."

Her mouth tingled, bitterness on her tongue. She'd barely been an adult back then—she'd fucked up just like every other teenager. Why was she paying for those mistakes now? Everything in her body was tight, and if he kept plucking at her, she would snap.

"Look at you—you're shaking," Johnny said. "Your eyes are watering, your hair's a mess—"

"My eyes are watering from lack of sleep and because cars have been kicking dirt into my face for the last hour. I'm shaking because I just carried five hundred thousand dollars over two miles."

"If I'd known, I would've picked you up. I told you that. Don't take it out on me."

As if he hadn't played a role in any of this. As if her anger was completely out of left field. "Fuck you, Johnny. Just fuck you."

His eyes doubled in size. "Fuck *me*? Why?"

"You know why." She continued to their room and grabbed a duffel bag from the closet.

"You come in here like a tornado, get me all worked up and say fuck *me*?"

"You used me. Both of you." She was practically shuddering now. "Everybody got what they wanted, even me, but at what price?"

Johnny threw both hands in the air. "Seriously, what the fuck? That's completely unfair. We made every decision together."

"*I* made every decision. By myself. *I* had to decide how much money I was worth."

"Bullshit. We both knew it was just an exchange. It was never about what you were worth. I didn't ask you to do this."

"You didn't ask me not to." She ripped articles of clothing off their hangers and stuffed them into the bag. "What choice did I have? If I'd said no, you would've always resented me for the life we could've had. I did this for us."

"And you didn't enjoy it at all, did you?" His lips compressed into a line. "You practically jumped at the chance do it again."

Her throat closed. He wasn't wrong—she'd been clinging to the lie that she hadn't wanted to go back to Beau. What did that make her? What did that make Johnny? If he'd even suspected she'd wanted this and he still hadn't stopped her, then he'd gambled with her.

"Just admit that you liked it," he said. "A million-dollar price tag made you feel pretty damn special."

"*Special?*" She could barely get the word out, her head burning like her entire body was on fire. She slammed her fists on the bed. "You think having two men use me to boost their egos is *special?* I have a stranger's cum on my pants and more money than I know what to do with. Does that make me *special?*"

"Jesus Christ." Johnny staggered back. "Like I need that fucking mental image."

"Yeah?" She grabbed a stack of his jeans from a shelf and threw them on the ground. "Well, at least you didn't live through it!"

"I did live through it," he said. "Except I had to use my imagination. All the things he was getting for his money. Tell me what they were, Lola. Why you? What did you give him that someone else couldn't?"

She shook her head. He had no idea the mental images she could give him—like the one where Beau had *seduced* her in to fucking him every which way while he plotted how to hurt her the most. "You don't know what you're asking for. You can't handle details."

"Try me."

"I know you, Johnny. Just let it go. It's not worth—"

"I can handle it," he said, raising his voice. "What was he like? Was it better? What did you let him do?"

Lola's body tightened at just the threat of a memory. As if she'd had any control over what Beau did to her. Once the sun went down, her body had become his. It'd breathed for him, thrummed for him, come for him. And he'd been thorough with each inch of her, leaving no part untouched.

"Everything," she said levelly.

He shook his head hard. "I don't believe you."

"Everything one man can do to one woman, he did to me. My mouth, my pussy, my ass. He had it all."

"You let him—?" Johnny reached back, grasping at nothing. "But you never…you wouldn't—for years I've asked you for that. He got it in two nights?"

"That's what you *sold* him. Don't act like you didn't know. You were there for the negotiation."

"And you promised me you were safe—that he didn't force you into anything."

She'd protected Johnny too long. No matter what he thought, he hadn't lived through what she had. He had to accept his share of the blame for everything that'd happened the last few weeks. "He didn't take a thing, Johnny. He waited for me to come to him, and I did. I gave him what he wanted."

"Liar," he said. "You can enjoy it, but you can't want it. That's not fair."

"It wasn't just sex for me. It was more."

Johnny pointed at the duffel bag. "Is that what this is about? You're going to see him again?"

"No. This is about you and me." While Beau might've been the catalyst behind their breakup, he wasn't the reason. He had his own sins to pay for, but she couldn't blame him for this. "I'm not the girl you want. I tried so hard, I honestly thought I was all these years. But I need more. I don't want to spend my life doing something mediocre, like working at Hey Joe. It doesn't make me happy."

"Mediocre?" he repeated. "Oh. I see. One night with a millionaire and suddenly you're too good for me. That's just bullshit." He picked her bag up off the bed and held it to his side. "I know you're angry. So am I. But stop and think about what you're saying."

Lola tried to take the bag. "We're finished—"

"No." He pulled the duffel back and went to block the doorway. "You don't just fall out of love overnight because you slept with someone else."

"I already told you, this isn't about him. You fucked up, and because of that, I see the truth. What we have is easy. I love and care about you, Johnny, but I'm not in love with you." She tried to get by him, but he stayed where he was. "Give me my bag. I'm leaving."

He visibly tried to speak, but nothing came. He opened and closed his free hand as if grasping for something.

"Johnny. *Move.*" She shoved him aside, and he dropped the bag to grab her wrists. They struggled for a second and then both stopped, their breathing labored. Neither of them moved as they stared at each other.

He released her. "Don't do this."

She hoisted the bag off the ground and walked down the hallway.

"Amanda blew me in the stockroom," he yelled. "I guess that means I fell out of love with you too. Is that how it works?"

Lola's heart dropped. Her hand went automatically to her stomach as she turned around. "Amanda?"

He ran a hand over his hair, also looking like he might be sick. "Doesn't feel so good, does it?"

Lola could've smacked the pathetic, somehow smug, look off his paling face. She hadn't thought him capable of cheating, but the last few weeks, he'd been a different person. A weaker one. It didn't surprise her as much as it should've.

"When?"

"Last night."

"You piece of shit."

He shrugged, but he looked anything but casual. "I needed someone, and she was there."

Lola's eyebrows weighed heavy. She was too livid to feel hurt. "And where was I?" she asked. "Screwing another man to give you *your* dream."

"Oh, don't fucking kid yourself. You're the only one who gets to have a little fun on the side?" His face fell. He walked toward her, but she backed away. "I drank a handle trying to forget what you were doing. It didn't even put a dent in me, Lo. I tried to stop her. I pushed her away. It meant nothing."

It meant everything—a permanent nail in their coffin. "It's not nothing to me. You gave me away twice, and now you sealed your fate. What if I'd come home, and we'd moved on with our lives? Did you think I could forgive this?"

"Yes, because it was all I had. I was desperate. I've never been as miserable as I was last night."

"Poor fucking baby." She scoffed. "I can't believe Beau was right about you."

"About me?" He touched his chest. "What did he tell you?"

"He said resentment makes people do ugly things—like cheat on their loved ones. He said you'd do that."

"That's rich coming from him of all people," Johnny said. "You let him talk about me that way?"

"You don't seem to understand," Lola said evenly. "I don't let him do or not do anything. He *does* and *says* what he wants. Did I think he was completely crazy for saying that? Yes. But apparently I was the crazy one for thinking I could trust you."

"This is such bullshit. And I was supposed to trust you after finding out you actually enjoyed sleeping with someone else? By my count, I'd say we're about even."

Her jaw tingled. She was disgusted with the whole thing—Johnny and that desperate slut. "Asshole. Did you stick your dick anywhere other than her mouth last night?"

"No."

"Did you finish? Come all over her? I bet she just gobbled it up. How many times have you done this behind my back?"

"Never. You know me better than that."

"I don't know anything or anyone anymore." She turned and left the hallway. "You can all go to hell."

"Where are you going?"

She had no idea. She just had to get out of there as soon as possible. She transferred everything from the coffee table into her bag. "I'm taking my half of the money."

"Lola, come on. Don't do this. I'll go to Mark's and give you some space to cool off. We'll figure this out when we both calm down."

She looked over her shoulder at him. "You know it's over. Don't act like I'm the only reason we're through. You had to have known at some point this could happen."

"I didn't. I swear. Did you?"

She bit the inside of her cheek. He could only be that oblivious if he was shrouded in denial. "Yes," she admitted.

"When? Did you know this could end us before you left the apartment last night?"

She turned to face him completely. For nine years, she'd believed Johnny was the one. She would've married him if he'd asked. She'd wanted his children.

She'd convinced herself that what she'd done for him—maturing, settling down—was something everyone did at some point. It was hard to believe that not only had she not questioned that, but that it'd only taken her two nights with Beau to wake up.

She'd been blind to her needs and feelings too long, but she was paying attention now. That part of her life was over, and in this next part, she'd be putting one person first—herself. She wasn't sure where she was going or what she wanted, but it would be on her terms.

When had she known it was over with Johnny? Perhaps it was when she'd sat in Beau's lap and told him she loved him, the words falling out of her mouth, slippery and dangerous. Maybe it'd been even earlier than that, when she'd made that phone call to Beau in the middle of the night, or when she'd gotten into his limo the second time. But when had it all started?

"I knew we were in trouble when I realized you were considering Beau's offer. I trusted you a little less. I need to know I'm more important to the man I'm with than anything else."

"But you are the most important thing," he said. "I love you."

Lola went to the kitchen. She found the package of cash Beau'd left on the counter the night before. It was unopened with her and Johnny's camping picture still sitting on top. She dumped it into her bag with the rest of the million dollars. She left the photo. She left the apartment. She didn't stop to check if Johnny was all right—because she left that part of herself behind too.

Chapter Six

Beau rolled his neck until he got a satisfying crack. The elevator beeped with each floor it passed, the digital numbers ticking down. It'd been a long day of slicing through the usual bullshit red tape that came with his line of work. He counted his meeting with Churchill a success, and he'd put out a fire at work while simultaneously closing a deal, but his duties weren't over yet. His assistant had sent him back to the hotel at four to change for some event tonight, one he didn't even remember committing to. He'd lost track of how many hours had passed since he'd slept. Over twenty-four. Lola had been gone around twelve. He was lucky to be standing.

The doors split apart. He exited, turned the corner on his way to meet Brigitte and ran right into Heather the concierge. She dropped a folder of papers that scattered on the lobby floor.

"Oh, shit," she said, crouching. "I'm so sorry."

Beau also squatted to help her as people passed around them. "My fault. I wasn't watching. Where are you off to in such a rush?"

She smiled at the floor. "As soon as I get these to the back office, I'm done for the night. I worked a double shift. I need a drink."

"I see." Beau glanced up and handed her the papers he'd gathered. He could guess what was coming.

"I was just going to grab one here if you're interested," she said, pointing in the direction of the lounge.

Blowing off whatever event he was going to didn't sound like such a bad idea, but Brigitte and Warner were waiting out front. "I have somewhere to be, and I won't be back until after ten." He stood, brushing off his pants. "I should get going, actually."

"Well," Heather said as she also rose, running a hand through her hair, "that's only a few hours. I don't mind waiting—"

Beau did a double take at the mirror over Heather's shoulder. In the reflection, just as the elevator behind him closed, he caught a flash of dark hair, a stark-white dress. His gut lurched—*Lola.* He jerked around a second too late. The doors had shut.

He blinked. It couldn't have been her. It didn't make sense. Lola had no reason to be at that hotel unless it was to see Beau, and in order to get to the elevator, she would've walked right by him.

Beau blinked and looked back at Heather. "You said you've been at the front desk all day?"

She nodded earnestly.

"Did a woman named Lola check in? Black hair, blue eyes."

Heather grinned and swatted his arm. "Do you have any idea how many people come through this lobby a day? I couldn't possibly remember—"

"Try," he said. "Lola Winters. It's important."

Her smile fell. "Um. Doesn't sound familiar?"

Beau looked behind him and stared at the elevator, willing the doors to reopen. The numbers above it rose until stopping at eleven. He waited. After a brief pause, they began counting down again. If she were there to see him, she would've gone to Beau's room, which was on the sixteenth floor.

Beau rubbed his eyes. All day, they'd been burning with fatigue. He needed sleep, and that was the only explanation for his confusion. He hadn't even napped, not that he would've if he had the time. The last time he'd taken a nap was between shifts when he was in his twenties—and he was no longer that kid. He'd made damn well sure of it.

"Mr. Olivier?"

He looked at Heather. "What?"

"I asked if you'd like me to go see about your friend."

"Oh. No." He checked his watch. "I don't know what I was thinking. I've got to run."

"What about the drink?"

"Can't." Beau stepped around her. "Night, Heather."

Out front, Brigitte leaned against Warner's town car in a short, red dress. Through the dusk, a tiny orange light buzzed around her like a fly. For all intents and purposes, Brigitte was his sister, more family to him than his own mother. For that reason, her risqué attire had no effect on him, but Beau wasn't sure the same could be said for Warner. He didn't even notice Beau walking in their direction.

As soon as she spotted Beau, her back straightened. "There you are." Her French accent made it sound less accusatory. "I've been trying to reach you all day."

Beau silently thanked his assistant for keeping Brigitte at bay all day. "My phone is in pieces. I had to get a new one."

"Oh. Sounds positively sordid. I want all the details from last night."

"I'm not in the mood, Brigitte."

She arched a thin, manicured—and angry—eyebrow. "Not in the mood?" she repeated. "Ten years you've been sulking over this woman who fucked you over. And now that you've gotten your revenge, you're not in the mood to share? I thought you'd be bursting at the seams."

"I'm not." He eyed Warner. "Thanks for keeping her company."

"My pleasure, sir. Good evening."

"We're headed to the Los Angeles Athletic Club for an event."

"Yes, sir." Warner leaned over Brigitte to get the door for her.

She touched his cheek, smiling. "*Merci, mon chéri.*"

Warner simply nodded, but there was no mistaking the red tint of his face.

Beau waited until Warner'd returned to the front of the car to look back at Brigitte. "I don't care that you're a merciless flirt, but does it have to be with my employee?"

She took a deep drag of her cigarette and waved him off. "You're grumpy."

Beau took it out of her hand and tossed it on the ground. "You'll smell like smoke all night," he said, mashing it with his shoe.

"Everyone smokes in Europe."

Beau got into the car, grumbling, "We aren't in Europe."

She followed him into the backseat. "I looked up the guest list for tonight's event, and it's primarily Europeans. There're potential investors around every corner. You know that."

"I see. And the smoking is so you'll fit in?"

"I don't need to tell you people's wallets loosen when they're more comfortable."

"All right. Do what you like." Beau turned to the window. The woman on the elevator had jolted him. It was a split-second glimpse, but he'd been sure. He didn't trust his gut with Lola, though, not after the last few weeks, not when he was this tired. She had no reason to come back to him and no business on the eleventh floor.

He'd been trying not to think of her, but her name had been phantom-like on his mind all day, like a number he was trying to remember for later. She'd disappeared, clean and quick. There one second, gone the next. According to plan. There'd be no stuff of breakups—late night calls, pleas to reconsider, checking in on someone you cared about.

Beau sat forward, the leather creaking. Even if he wanted to, he couldn't drop by Hey Joe or her apartment or even call her. She wouldn't be there. Her purse had been stolen—credit cards, phone and all.

"Beau."

Startled by Brigitte's sharp tone, he turned back to her. "What?"

"What happened last night? You're completely out of it."

Fatigue was setting in. Beau wasn't in his twenties anymore, and while he wouldn't have taken back any of his time with Lola, pulling two all-nighters in the same month was taking its toll. "I could give a shit about these parties. We went to a fundraiser on Monday. I have a gala to attend tomorrow night. Why?"

She put her hand over his. "You know this comes with the territory. It's never bothered you before."

He set an elbow on the armrest, massaged the bridge of his nose. "Maybe it has, and I just never told you."

"Nonsense. We're a team. We've been at this for years, networking. Don't tell me it doesn't pay off."

Beau wanted his hand back to check his phone. He normally took time in the backseat to catch up on work, but if Brigitte lost any of his attention, she would only work harder to get it back.

"Sometimes it's too much," he said.

She sucked in her cheeks just a little, tightening her grip on his hand. "What's too much?"

People were always trying to get to Beau. With wealth, things fell in his lap—opportunities for him to get in at the ground level, to make a killing, to fuck up. The carousel never ended. It was supposed to be a good thing, but Beau was rarely cavalier with anything, and everything required research. It could get exhausting. Brigitte wasn't the only one vying for his attention. There was no way to put it into words without sounding ungrateful, so he shook his head. "Never mind."

Brigitte was quiet a moment, and he was thankful for the reprieve. Her fingers were still curled tightly around his hand. "You didn't go through with it."

He stared out the window. "Yes, I did."

"I don't believe you. You didn't break things off, and that's why you don't want to go tonight. You're just waiting to get back to her. Where is she? In the room?"

"I told you, it's done."

"Then why are you acting like this? We're supposed to be celebrating our victory, not sulking."

He looked back at her. "*Our* victory?"

Brigitte reeled away. "I've been there every step of the way, haven't I? You were my rock when our parents died, and you make it so hard for me to repay you for that."

"Nobody's keeping score. You don't owe me anything."

"I do it because I *want* to. I never would've gotten through my mom's death alone. When someone hurts you, they hurt me too. I lived your pain when she undid all your hard work and ruined everything. Last night was redemption for both of us."

"You didn't do any of the dirty work, though. You didn't see her face." Beau could. He could see it right then—her mouth, normally hard, had finally become delicate with him. She'd hated him that first night, and he'd gotten her to love him by the end. Her hard-won delicate mouth, mangled with disgust when he'd told her the truth. The immediate reversal of everything he'd worked for. The way she'd flinched, recoiled, when he'd tried to touch her. He'd thought, if he could just get her in his arms, he could make her see.

"Describe it to me," Brigitte said. "I want to know it all."

He blinked at her. "Did you mean for her to see that text?"

Brigitte loosened her fingers, tapped them giddily over his knuckles. "You mean this morning? Why? Did she?"

"It doesn't matter. It's all over—me and her, her and Johnny."

"Really?" Brigitte asked, her tone pitchy. "Here I was worried you'd chickened out,. but I should've known—you never do anything halfway."

He angled his head at her, knowing he should let it go. "Excuse me?"

"She and Johnny are over—why?" She paused only a second. "Because she chose you, right? You're the center of her world. She loves you. But she also hates you. You did more than break her heart—you grabbed her by it, pulled her inside out. You put her life on a completely different course. That's power, Beau."

It was a cold truth, one that would sicken anyone else. Not Beau, though. Lola's world revolving around him made him feel good. Wherever she was, she was thinking of him, and her thoughts weren't casual. They weren't nothing.

"Or maybe I'm wrong," Brigitte said, throwing the words out like a fishing line in a pond.

He bit. "Why?"

She studied him. "You're on her mind, there's no question, but she's also on yours. It would appear after all you've done to overcome it, she still has some power over you."

The car stopped at a light, turning the backseat tomato-red. The engine hummed. "Nobody has power over me," Beau said evenly. "Not even you."

Brigitte leaned over to stroke the back of Beau's hair. Her arm reeked of cigarettes. "You're frustrated, and I know why. It has nothing to do with her."

Beau sighed deeply, pointedly not asking why. He considered telling Warner to turn the car around so he could end this day already.

"You miss the thrill of conquest," Brigitte continued. "For weeks, you had this singular goal to focus on. Now that it's over, you don't know what to do with all this nervous energy. Trust me, it isn't Lola you want."

"I suppose you know what I want."

"Of course I do." She smiled. "We need a new challenge."

"There's no *we*, Brigitte. Any mistakes I've made are mine alone. This was my game."

Brigitte returned to her side of the car. "Mistakes?"

The glasses of the built-in bar rattled as they turned a corner. He'd meant to say conquests, not mistakes, but maybe that's what this had all been. One big mistake. "Yes."

"Don't you dare insult me by saying that whore means anything to you," Brigitte said. "I'm the one who *saved* you from making a mistake—twice."

"Calm down. You're getting hysterical."

"You called and woke me up last night to tell me you didn't think you could go through with it. I talked you off the ledge. Obviously, I didn't know if she'd see my text this morning, but I knew you would—and I knew you'd regret it if at any point in the night, you got off course."

"You don't know shit. You weren't there. You didn't see what I did."

"Jesus, the woman makes a fool of you over and over. It's disgusting."

Beau pitied his sister. She wanted so desperately to be a part of something, to belong, that she resorted to grasping at straws. Anything to get under Beau's skin. He wondered if there would ever come a time she didn't want to be there.

"That's enough."

"It's sad to see you think you're in charge when she is. Even I have more control—"

"Enough," he snapped.

"What are you going to do? Spank me? Is that what you did to her when she said something you didn't like?"

Beau's nostrils flared with a sharp inhalation. He could still picture the red curve of Lola's ass after he'd smacked it. He hadn't held back in the least, but she'd taken everything without complaint. If he wanted to do it again, why shouldn't he? There was no woman out there who'd walk away from him if he put his mind to getting her in his bed—including Lola.

Brigitte rolled her eyes. "Just like every other pathetic idiot who's charmed by a decent pair of tits."

He grabbed her bicep and pulled her across the backseat. "I'd watch my mouth if I were you. Nobody talks to me that way."

The car jolted as Warner hit the brakes. "Sir," he said, glancing at them in the rearview mirror.

"Stay out of this, Warner. Brigitte knows exactly what she's doing."

"What am I doing?" she asked, blinking at him. "You're my brother, and I love you. All I want is for you to be happy. Believe me, she won't make you happy."

"You only want me to be happy if it means I'm alone. You're worried if I find someone else, you'll lose me."

"Someone else?" Brigitte's eyes twinkled. "Surely you don't mean Lola? Come on. Deep down you know the truth."

Beau restrained from flinging her away. She would say anything to needle him, and she couldn't possibly know what the truth was. She hadn't spent more than ten minutes in the same room as Lola and Beau. But he spat the words, unable to help himself. "What's the truth?"

"You'll never have her. Do you honestly believe after what you've done, you could get her back?" Brigitte sniffed. "Your money didn't matter to her then, and it means even less now. You can't buy her, and that's the only way you know how to get anything."

"Bullshit. I went twenty-seven years before I ever made a dime."

"Exactly, and not even Warner would've looked in your direction before your money. You had nothing and no one."

"Brigitte," Warner cautioned from the front seat.

She ignored him. "No one except me."

Beau's temper was getting the best of him. "Brigitte, I'm about as patient with you as can be most of the time, but you're pressing the wrong buttons."

"You have no way of winning Lola back. You'll never be what she needs."

Beau pushed her off. "You don't know what you're talking about."

"She's better off without you."

Beau set his jaw and stared forward at nothing. He didn't have to look at her to know she wore a smug expression. "Put some perfume on. You fucking stink."

What pissed Beau off the most was that Brigitte was right. Lola was better off without the man she'd met in front of Hey Joe, but Beau didn't feel like that man anymore. If Lola hadn't left that morning, if she hadn't seen that text, Beau would've taken care of her in ways Johnny never could've. That had to count for something. And if he wanted her back, nothing would get in his way.

Chapter Seven

They'd circled her neighborhood twice already, Lola biting her nails, the cab driver growing impatient. "Come on, lady, where you want to go?" he kept asking.

Walking out on Johnny had sounded easier when she'd known Warner would be out front, waiting to drive her back to Beau at the Four Seasons. For a little while, she'd had two homes, and now, she didn't even have one.

They hadn't had a real relationship in a while, but Lola could've shown up at her mom's house without an explanation. The place she'd grown up had stopped being home a long time ago, though, and she hadn't gone crawling back yet. Her mom might not say "I told you so," but she'd be thinking it, the words close to the surface even eleven years after Lola'd moved out to strip.

She put her hand on the black duffel bag and felt the money just underneath the fabric. She had little of her own, but what she did have was hers without a doubt. An inordinate amount of cash. A freedom most people couldn't dream of. The chance to leave her troubles behind. There were things at the apartment she might've liked to keep—mostly photos or mementos—but everything she needed was there on the seat next to her. She no longer had anything tying her to Los Angeles.

Beau had cut deep, though. In two nights, he'd seen inside her, and like she'd told him in the shower—she'd felt him there like a thunderstorm. On her stomach, on his hotel bed, he'd had her at her most vulnerable, but it was more than physical. She'd trusted him. And in return, he'd treated her like one of his companies, an investment, a challenge, leading her down a path painstakingly designed to get her where he wanted.

How many people had fallen prey to his charms, been the subject of his fascination, been manipulated by him? She had no idea, but she knew this—Beau had never paid the price for his sins. Nobody'd ever had the weapons to use against him, and he'd made sure of that. Every careful step Beau made in his life was toward wealth, but Lola knew it wasn't the money he cared about. It was the power it afforded him. While his bank account was fat, nobody could ever deny him anything.

Lola felt it like a knot in her chest, the indignity of it. Beau couldn't be allowed to play with people's lives anymore. He deserved to feel her pain as if it were his own. He'd once said to her that a man of his wealth trusted his enemies more than his friends. Lola was an enemy now, but she'd been a friend to him once, and she could be that again.

Lola looked at the driver in the rearview mirror. "Take me to Rodeo Drive."

If she was going to play Beau's game, she had to look the part—and that meant buying herself a wardrobe fit for the queen Beau had once believed her to be.

◆⊠◆⊠◆

Lola stepped out of the cab and looked up at the towering Four Seasons. With a garment bag draped across her arm and a million dollars slung over her shoulder, she entered the hotel. She wore her new white dress, a form-fitting, short little thing she never would've looked twice at before. She was greeted by three different men before she reached the front desk.

"Good evening." The male concierge smiled. "How can I help you?"

Lola handed him her passport, currently her only form of identification. "I need a room."

He dropped his eyes to the computer. After a few clicks of his mouse, he nodded. "You're in luck. We have a couple left. How many nights?"

Lola traced her finger over the marble counter. She had to act fast. Beau was a man of resolve, but she meant something to him. He'd be confused by that, his memories and wounds fresh, his need for revenge less pressing than he'd thought. She needed to worm her way back in before he'd hardened into something unbreakable again. "One night. And I'm paying in cash."

"That's fine," he said. "I'll need a card for incidentals, though."

Lola hesitated. She had no plan yet, and she preferred to stay off the grid until she knew more. "You won't charge it?"

"Not unless you give us a reason to. There will be a pending charge, but it'll fall off after a day or two."

She gave it over reluctantly, leaving her hand open for the few seconds it took the concierge to swipe it. He handed it back to her and slid a keycard across the counter. "How's the eleventh floor?"

"Fine."

"Do you need assistance to your room?"

She shrugged a shoulder and showed him her bags. "This is everything I own."

He glanced over the counter and raised his eyebrows. "Not much, is it?"

A voice behind her stopped Lola's response in her throat. She would've recognized it anywhere, from the gates of heaven to the depths of hell and everywhere in between.

Her heart pounded. The concierge spoke, but she couldn't hear him. Five minutes in the lobby, and she was already going to see Beau again. She hadn't planned for it, but she hadn't planned for anything yet. Her only goal was to reconcile with him as quickly as she could.

She inhaled a deep breath to calm herself. Beau would sense any fear and trepidation in an instant. She picked up the key from the counter and turned around. Beau was squatted on the floor next to a pretty blonde.

She didn't wait to find out why. She seized the chance to pass him while his head was down. This wasn't the right time to see him. She needed time to figure out some kind of strategy.

"There's always a plan, Lola."

Lola punched the "Up" button, thankful the elevator was already there. Inside, she selected the eleventh floor and tried to turn away. She couldn't. She watched in a nearby mirror as he stood. It was almost reassuring to see him again. It was clear as day to her now, how she'd associated being near him with safety. The feeling passed quickly, and she concentrated instead on grasping tidbits of his conversation with the girl.

"…somewhere to be…after ten."

"…only a few hours. I don't mind waiting…"

The doors began to close, and as they met in the middle, Beau's eyes shifted over. Her breath caught. A second passed, and the elevator rose with a jolt. Even if he'd seen her, she didn't think it'd been enough time to recognize her. Still, with every floor she passed, tension gripped her, and it didn't let go until she was safe in her room.

She dumped her things on the cloudlike comforter and went directly to change the temperature. Johnny had always kept the thermostat low, complaining about the heat even on the mildest Los Angeles nights. The men in Lola's life were oversized children who'd chosen themselves over her time and time again. And yet they always seemed to come out on top—Johnny had half her money and a new plaything. Beau had blonde girls at his feet. Her dad was off somewhere, not taking care of anyone, the way he liked it.

Lola got to her knees and opened the minibar. She downed three bottles of liquor, one right after another, making a mental note to pay for them later in cash. Who did *she* have? Herself. She wasn't an abandoned daughter. She wasn't Johnny's girlfriend or Beau's conquest. Nobody would tell her where she was going or how to get there anymore. She wouldn't give them that control. She drank three more bottles and crawled over to the hotel phone. She picked up the receiver and angrily punched in the number for Hey Joe.

Johnny answered. "Hello?"

"You weren't supposed to cheat. Ever. But why her? She wasn't even a blip on my radar."

"I—"

"I don't even care," Lola said. "That's bad, isn't it? He hurt me more. I'm sorry if that makes you sad. I saw him with a woman today, a fucking blonde."

"I think you have the wrong number."

"I thought he liked brunettes." She frowned, her mind playing catch up. "What? Is this Hey Joe?"

"No. You called a home number."

Lola hung up and lay on the carpet. Life hadn't been that fair to her, but she didn't remember ever feeling like this. To still be so deeply in love with someone who'd gone out of his way to hurt her was more than one person should have to handle. She thought she should cry—it seemed like a healthy reaction. Nothing came. She stared up at the ceiling, forcing her eyes to stay open until they watered, until one salty drop slid from the corner of her eye to the edge of her lip. She wondered how much she'd have to drink for her tears to taste like vodka.

The sun set, painting the room orange. It was vivid and majestic, different from any sunset she'd ever seen. Or maybe it just seemed that way from upside down, drunk, eleven stories above the city.

She groaned. It wasn't enough, but she couldn't seem to move from that spot to get more alcohol. She closed her eyes, and the sunset streaked neon against the backs of her lids. Her hands and armpits were clammy, the hair at her temples damp with sweat.

Who was she to be angry with Johnny, though? He didn't even know the depth of her sins. *Her sins*—fucking the enemy and enjoying it. Letting the enemy close enough to break her heart. Loving the enemy.

Beau had a soft side. She already missed that. She even missed his hardness. Despite all the reasons not to, she'd come to trust him. Only a monster could invent a scheme to hurt someone so thoroughly. Only the devil himself would actually go through with it, though.

Beau's room was only five floors up from Lola's. She would've requested a room above his, but it seemed he was always at the top. The devil shouldn't get to live at the top, hiding in plain sight, moving people like pawns. The devil should have to suffer—just as his victims had.

Chapter Eight

Beau shut his eyes in the backseat of Warner's town car and pulled his necktie loose. The dinner conversation at tonight's event had dragged more than usual. Bids for his attention had been pushier too. In those situations, he was grateful to have Brigitte by his side. Unfazed by their earlier argument, she'd been her charming self all night.

"How'd it go?" Warner asked from the driver's seat.

Beau opened his eyes and blinked off sleep. It wasn't like Warner to chat, so it took him a minute to figure out if he'd dreamed it. He sat up a little. "What?"

"The event. Was Brigitte okay? I was afraid you might snap earlier."

"Oh." Beau nodded a little. "She's fine. She was great, actually. Nothing puts her in a better mood than getting me riled up."

"It's because she cares."

"All right." Beau didn't know what else to say. It wasn't really Warner's business, except that it was, because he was always there, observing. Beau just wanted to sleep, but Warner was glancing at him in the rearview mirror like the conversation wasn't over. "It's good for business anyway," he added.

"What is?"

"Brigitte, when she's happy. She's my secret weapon."

Warner grinned, a rare sight. He seemed satisfied with that and looked back out the windshield.

These events were prime hunting grounds. Old, rich men were weak for Brigitte's candid, often crude remarks—always delivered in a French accent. When Beau needed capital for one of his companies, he and Brigitte were a team that was hard to refuse. Usually.

Tonight, she'd dropped off buttered-up men at Beau's feet and strutted around like a lion after a fresh kill. Beau, on the other hand, had been distracted. He'd mixed up two of his companies and called an important man by the wrong name. There were things on his mind, though—like the woman he'd glimpsed in the reflection earlier.

Once, before they'd sat down to dinner, Beau had caught himself looking around the room for Lola, ridiculous as it was. She could be anywhere, though, including right there in that room. He still had no idea what'd happened to her once she'd walked off hotel property, and it was making him more and more agitated.

Warner turned the car into the Four Seasons' circular driveway and stopped to let him out. Beau reached for the door handle.

"I know you doubt yourself, but you're good to her," Warner said.

Beau looked to the front of the car. "Lola?"

"Brigitte." Warner frowned, his forehead wrinkling. "You're more patient than you think. She just loves having your attention."

Beau hesitated, somewhat embarrassed he'd thought Warner was talking about Lola. "Right. Well. It's been a long day—"

"Goodnight, sir."

"Yes. Goodnight." Beau shut the car door behind him and looked up. The hotel glowed, the lobby and the rooms, like it was filled with gold. Was Lola up there? Or was she just—gone? Walking inside was like trudging through mud. He was shutting down, his body crashing without enough sleep. He was almost to the elevator when he heard, "Mr. Olivier?"

Beau stopped, turning to the man at the front desk. "Yes?"

"Your visitor's in the lounge."

Beau was already removing his cufflinks, sticking them in his pockets. "You're mistaken. I'm not expecting anyone."

"She's been in there half an hour. She was very clear that you'd be expecting her and that she'd wait as long as necessary."

Beau squinted in the direction of the hotel bar, then glanced at his watch. It was 10:32 P.M., half an hour after he'd told Heather he'd be back. She'd be an easy fuck, requiring little to no effort on his part—just what he'd thought he needed. Sleep sounded more appealing.

"Do me a favor? Tell her I'm not interested and that I've gone to bed."

"I understand, sir." He cleared his throat. "She'll find someone who is. Half the staff is enamored by her."

Beau had turned toward the elevator again, but he stopped. There was no reason someone shouldn't be enamored by Heather—after all, she had tits for days, perky too, always a plus. But it made him think of Lola, sitting at a bar, single for the first time in almost a decade. No man in his right mind wouldn't be enamored by her, that was for certain.

It could only be Heather waiting for him. It had to be. Yet Beau found himself turning back and heading for the lounge. He wasn't one to ignore his instinct, and it told him it wasn't Heather he'd find in there—but the woman who'd been firmly entrenched in his thoughts since she'd walked out of his life that morning.

Chapter Nine

Present day

It wasn't even noon, and Lola had already charged seventeen hundred dollars to Beau's credit card. She hadn't lied to him in his foyer earlier that morning—each task on her to-do list was important, including shopping. In only weeks, she was becoming a reluctant regular on Rodeo Drive.

Beau worked long hours. Most days she met him for lunch, keeping herself fresh in his mind, but he rarely had more than a half hour to spare. So she would go to the park or to a museum or a matinee, and when she'd exhausted all those venues, Rodeo Drive welcomed her like an old friend—as long as she was carrying Beau's black American Express.

The Burberry trench coat in her shopping bag fit her like a second skin. All designer clothing was smooth that way. Easy to wear, easy to move in. If it wasn't, though, Beau's tailor would come to the house, take it away and return it to her better. But this particular coat wasn't for her. She wouldn't wear it to feel good or to exhibit wealth. She'd wear it for Beau—to make *him* feel good. That was the power of a well-made piece of clothing. Even though she only needed it for one night, if she bought herself anything less than the best, it would raise questions from him—and she didn't need questions she couldn't answer. She was playing a role in Beau's life, and that role was expensive.

Only three blocks constituted the main part of one the world's most expensive shopping streets. She walked over plaques honoring fashion icons and under California's signature palm trees, stopping in front of a high-end lingerie shop she'd been eyeing for a while.

She pulled open the glass door and descended black marble steps. Her heartbeat picked up a little. She might've been a woman just looking for something to please her man—or she might've been a woman experiencing her fantasy, three weeks in the making, coming to life.

A lady with a pinched smile approached her. "Good afternoon. What are you shopping for today?"

"Lingerie."

"What kind?"

Lola touched a white silk negligee and let it slide over her palms. "The kind that does the most damage."

The saleswoman made a noise. "I think that depends on the person wearing it."

Lola turned around to see her smile had turned genuine. Before Lola could answer, a flash of light near the window caught her eye. She crossed the small store and picked up a black, lace corset that sparkled when the sun hit it.

The garment was embedded with hundreds of tiny, glistening gemstones. "They're Swarovski crystals," the saleswoman said.

Of course they were. In Beau's hotel room, the night she'd learned the truth, Beau had said, almost accusingly, that Lola'd been covered in diamonds when he'd seen her on Cat Shoppe's stage. He must've thought very highly of her as a stripper if he'd believed that. They were actually rhinestones. She'd purchased the two-piece bikini in November during a Halloween clearance sale. It'd come in a plastic zip bag. At the register, she'd grabbed a pair of cat ears to top off the outfit. Every other girl at Cat Shoppe had had a thing, and she'd needed a thing. There'd already been a couple of feline-themed strippers, but none of them had sparkled like her.

But that was then, and this was now. Now, Lola had Beau—the kind of man who appreciated extravagance. The kind who expected his stripper to wear diamonds when he put her up on his pedestal.

"I'll take it," Lola said, "as well as black underwear and thigh-high stockings."

The saleswoman nodded. "Shoes?"

"I have them. Four-inch Louboutins."

"You must be looking to deliver quite a blow."

"Something like that." Lola opened her purse and pulled out Beau's weighty credit card. Before she handed it over, she paused as she was hit with an idea. "By any chance, do you carry cat ears here?"

"I'm sorry?" The woman's hand twitched, as if resisting reaching for the credit card. "I'm not sure what you mean."

Lola held her hands on both sides of her head and pointed upward. She wiggled her fingers. "You know, like the ones you wear on Halloween?"

"Oh. No. Of course we don't."

"Hmm." Lola tapped the card against her bottom lip, thinking. "That could really pose a problem for my outfit."

"I'll take care of it." The saleswoman watched the card, her eyes fixed on the rhythmic back and forth. She held her hand out. "I'll find some and have them delivered wherever you like along with your purchase."

Lola smiled and handed over the credit card. "That would be fantastic. They don't need to be anything fancy. I'll take the lingerie with me, but I'd like those sent somewhere else."

"That won't be a problem, Miss…" She checked the card. "Olivier."

Lola paid for everything and returned to the Range Rover, which she'd parked at a meter. She slipped into the front seat and rested her hands on the steering wheel, but she didn't turn the engine on. She glanced at herself in the rearview mirror. What a funny thing money was—it bought not only things, but people's time. Lola had discovered how true that was since she'd been by Beau's side. Just now, in the store, she'd used her newfound wealth as leverage to get what she wanted. Was it too much time around Beau that had Lola acting like someone she didn't recognize? Or was that just how money worked, no matter who you were? It was addicting to have it that easy, and part of her understood, for the first time, how complicated Beau's relationship with his fortune must be.

Lola shook her head quickly. She couldn't think too hard about Beau this late in the game. It was as simple as this—Beau wasn't the man she'd thought he was, and for that he deserved whatever was coming to him. Three weeks had seemed like a lifetime to fake all the things she had—forgiveness, affection, submission. Now that it was ending, she worried she wasn't prepared. Beau was used to getting his way, which meant a number of things could go wrong. Lola needed to keep her head in the game and a sway in her hips. It was a delicate operation, pulling the string that unraveled him without yanking it. He'd been salivating over Lola for long enough now that he was right where she needed him. That was what she had to distract him with—his own crippling need. It was the art of misdirection, and the key to pulling off her magic trick.

◆⊠◆⊠◆

Cat Shoppe's music thumped so loudly, Lola felt it in her bones before she even reached the entrance. The bouncer took one look at her plum-colored vinyl miniskirt and opened the red velvet rope for her. Even in the middle of the day, several men and a couple women sat around the stages, drinks and dollar bills in their hands. The place stunk, as if the furniture was soaked nightly in vats of beer, and the men bathed in cheap cologne.

She'd changed in the Range Rover, sinking down in the backseat to swap her Alexander McQueen dress for a vintage concert tee. She'd smeared her perfectly-applied lipstick onto a tissue before caking on glitter eye shadow.

At the bar, she ordered a shot of tequila as reinforcement from a girl in a platinum-blonde wig. At least, Lola thought it was a wig, the way it poofed around her chipmunk cheeks and met under her chin like a heart. This time, the tequila didn't make Lola wince the way it had in Beau's car up on Mulholland Drive. It was courage. She'd never grimace after a shot again if she could help it.

The bartender took the glass back. "Another?"

"No, thanks." Lola dug a twenty out of her pocket and put it on the bar. "I'm here to see Kincaid."

"You looking for a job?"

"Not really."

"Good, because there's not enough to go around as it is. As you can see, I've got to work the bar just to make some extra cash." She took Lola's bill off the bar and went to the register.

"Keep the change," Lola said.

She turned back. "Really? It was three dollars."

Lola waved a hand. "It's fine."

"Cool." She stuffed the money in her white bikini top, not even cashing out the shot. She fixed the string of her bottoms, then looked up and caught Lola watching her. "Marilyn," she said, pointing at the drawn-in birthmark on her upper lip. "Monroe?"

"Oh." Lola nodded.

"Also known as Susan, but that's not really my gig."

"Nice to meet you."

Marilyn-Susan refilled Lola's glass with tequila and set it in front of her. "On the house. You dance?"

Lola picked up the shot. "Not anymore. I worked here a while back, though."

The girl's breasts bounced when she clapped her hands together. "Really? So you know Glinda the Good Bitch?"

Lola smiled hearing her old friend's name. Glinda'd been stripping as long as she'd had something to show. She'd taken Lola under her wing just like she always did with the new girls, kind of like a mentor. They'd grown apart when Johnny'd come along, though. He'd forbidden her from going on a girls' trip to Vegas, and after that, she'd begun to lose touch with the group. "I used to, yeah. Best dancer this side of Hollywood."

"Not lately. Been hitting the blow too hard. She's in a bad state."

Lola glanced down at the bar. The news didn't surprise her, considering how easy it was to get sucked into that life. She almost had. A lot of girls, some she knew, many she didn't, had gone too far down the path Johnny had pulled Lola back from. She was indebted to him in a way she could never repay, and no matter their history, she'd never forget that.

"I'll go grab Kincaid," Marilyn said, walking away.

While Lola waited, she looked over her shoulder at the girl writhing on stage. Her hard nipples grazed the floor as she danced for the dollar bills fanned around her.

"She's got nothing on you," said a man behind her.

Lola turned to see Cat Shoppe's owner. "Kincaid."

"Lola." He put his hand on the back of her stool and kissed her cheek. "Or do you go by Melody now?"

"Still Lola."

Marilyn was back behind the bar. "Was Melody your stage name?"

"No. It's my full name, but I don't use it."

"Melody," Marilyn repeated. "Like a song. That's sweet."

Sometimes, she thought her given name was the only thing her mom liked about her since she'd picked it out. Lola had once cried as a kid about not having a middle name, though, so her dad had told her it could be Lola, short for Melody. The nickname'd stuck, and Lola had a theory Dina had taken it personally.

Back in the day, Lola was the only one at the club who'd danced under her real name, the rest of the girls making up something sugary and anonymous.

Lola turned to face Kincaid completely as he pulled up a seat next to her. "So, how are you, Kincaid?"

"It's been a while."

"Not as long as you think," she said.

"Aha. So that *was* you I saw on the security camera a few weeks ago."

Lola hadn't seen Kincaid when she'd come to Cat Shoppe with Beau, but she remembered his diligence when it came to security. He almost always had someone on the cameras, making sure his customers stayed in line. "Yep. Kind of an unexpected trip down memory lane."

"With someone who's got money to burn." Kincaid gave her a once over. "That guy you were with? You wouldn't believe what he paid for a room, two of our girls and some privacy."

"Actually, I would believe it." When she swallowed, she tasted tequila. Tequila and Beau, that first night she'd put her lips on him. "I hope you didn't watch the whole show."

He smiled cautiously. "Seen enough couples come through here to know when to look away. What I did see, though, was good. Can't fake that kind of love for the dance."

"Actually, that's why I'm here." Lola cleared her throat. The backs of her thighs had begun to sweat, turning the stool's leather tacky against her skin. She needed Kincaid tonight, or her entire plan could go to shit. "The man I came with last time loved the show so much, I want to give him another."

Kincaid shrugged. "Not a problem. Same girls, or—?"

"Just me," Lola said. "He has a kind of fascination with watching me dance."

"Right. Angel and Golden said it was the easiest money they ever made. The guy barely looked at them the whole time they were in VIP."

Lola nodded and tucked her hair behind her ear. She'd definitely had his attention that night. "I want him to have a real, true-life, gritty experience, though. As if I worked here, and he wandered in off the street."

"You want a room for a few hours, you got it. I have to charge you, but—"

"Money isn't the issue. What I'm asking for is—I want to be…one of your girls again. Just for tonight."

Kincaid narrowed his eyes, searching her face. "I'm not sure what you're getting at. Can't be good, though. You look like the cat that swallowed the canary."

"It's good," Lola said, reassuring, nodding. "There's a lot of money in it for you if you play along."

Kincaid made an inviting gesture with his hand. "I'm listening."

"This is how it'll go. Tonight, I work for you. I belong to you—no one else. I want him to have the full experience."

"You said that already."

She leaned forward, conspiring with him, looking into his eyes. "I want your protection."

"My protection?" He absentmindedly picked at some peeling plastic on the countertop. "Sounds serious. What about your bartender a few blocks down? As I recall, you two were pretty tight."

"We're not together anymore."

"That so? Completely done? Because he was the reason you left all this behind."

Lola ran her tongue along her upper teeth. "Yeah, well. Things change."

"What things?"

"You ask a lot of questions." She flipped her hair over her shoulder. "Do we have a deal?"

"You know how I am about my girls and my business. It's all I got. I don't need any jealous boyfriends coming through that door."

"He won't. Trust me—Johnny and I are through. So, can you do this for me? I told you, there's good money in it for you."

"I'll do anything for you, Lola, soon's I understand what you're asking me."

Lola shifted in her seat. Some people were not as easily bought as others, and that would've given her some comfort if she didn't need this last piece of the puzzle. "Customers don't come here expecting to take one of us home," she said. "It's like a fantasy, right? They watch us. They let us tease them. I could sit Beau in a kitchen chair and dance in his lap, but it wouldn't be the same. There, I'm his girlfriend who he gets to fuck after. But here? It's a game, and I'm a prize he can't have."

Kincaid nodded. He was no idiot—he understood her. He'd made a living off keeping women just outside of men's reach. "What do you need me to do?"

Lola opened her purse. "I'll pay you now. Cash. I'll explain the rules to Beau over dinner. But as soon as we walk in the door, he's a customer, and I'm an employee. I'll take him to the VIP room. Just watch him, and make sure he behaves."

"You know we got the big rules here. For the employees, bottoms stay on, no sexual activity. For customers, it's no touching unless the dancer initiates it, and even then, it's all over the clothing."

"Exactly. I'm not agreeing to allow any of that."

"All right. So what if he doesn't behave?"

"Same as if any customer were to touch one of your girls." Lola handed over enough cash to rent the VIP room for an entire night, though she didn't think she'd need even an hour. "You don't let him get away with it."

Chapter Ten

Beau stared at the buildings just outside his office window, a whiskey in his hand. All day, he'd been wondering about tonight, what this secret was Lola had planned, how long she'd make him wait for the main course. He was eager to get his last meeting over with so he could go home to her.

He was becoming someone he didn't recognize. Work had always been his constant, but the only thing that calmed him now was her—specifically, the security of having her in his arms where he could see and feel her. He'd thought paying for her had been the way to own her, but he'd been so off base, it almost made him laugh. Knowing she loved him enough to let him earn her trust again—that was how he owned her, how she owned him.

Except that today, just knowing that wasn't enough. He was restless, and he needed more. He'd always been able to read Lola, but that morning in the foyer, it was as if he'd been looking into someone else's eyes. Since their reunion, she hadn't kissed him with that much enthusiasm. Something was off.

Beau sipped his drink. She was nervous about tonight. As she should be. Beau wiped a bead of sweat from his forehead. He hadn't had to wait this long for something he wanted in a decade. Almost three impossible weeks of watching Lola, touching her, kissing her, sleeping next to her—all of it with restraint. He was ravenous, and only she would satisfy him. The thought of another woman did nothing for him, not that it really ever had. Until Lola, he hadn't known what it'd meant to truly bury himself inside someone and be willing trade the world just to have her come. Giving her that kind of pleasure was as addicting as having any part of her around his cock.

It was a sweet kind of torture, coming home from work and watching her get ready for his events. That was why he took her so many places. He loved to sit on their bed as she picked out a dress, hiding in the closet while she changed.

She would come over to the bed and turn her head over her shoulder. "Zip me?"

He would stand and obey. Fabric would swallow the lacey edges of her undergarments as he zipped her dress, the only morsels she'd throw him. He wasn't even sure she knew how those small slices tempted him. He'd let his knuckle brush along her spine, thinking, *"Soon, I will get to touch all of you again. Soon."*

Lola wore perfume on those nights, and it would stick to his suits, linger in her hair. Before it could fade completely, there'd be some other occasion to dress up for. He wondered if she'd always applied her makeup so carefully, coating mascara on her lashes with long strokes and gliding eyeliner on with the kind of concentration she didn't even give him. It bothered him that he couldn't remember the exact details of the night he'd met her at Hey Joe, like whether or not she'd been wearing that much makeup. He would never forget how blue her eyes were or the noisy leather of her pants, but that wasn't enough. He wanted to remember everything.

He'd been skeptical that anything could give him as much satisfaction as his work, but Lola did, even without the sex. That was why he devoted his days to making sure she'd never want for anything—to be able to give her anything upon request. He'd worked hard before, but now, he *labored* for her. Late nights would always belong to them, though. After events and long hours at the office, that was when he'd get as close to her as she'd let him, and then he'd always try for a little closer.

Beau walked through the quiet house to the bedroom, his fingers pulling impatiently at his bowtie. Lola had been living there four days, and everything had changed. Just having her on his arm at tonight's gala had turned a chore into a chance to show her off to anyone who'd look. And even though it'd been a form of torture to stand by her all night and keep his hands to himself, it'd been worth it to see her at her most exquisite. The only other times he'd been this high were his first two nights with her, undressing her, touching her skin as slowly and as quickly as he could. He wasn't ready to let that feeling go.

He entered his bedroom. Through a sliver of doorway, Lola moved around the bathroom in her robe, removing makeup from her face, jewelry from her body. He pushed open the door and went to where she stood at the sink. He'd promised to behave, but after tonight, he wasn't sure he could. God knew he didn't want to. He slipped his arms around her waist and buried his face in the sweet scent of her hair. "You already changed?" he whispered. "I wanted to watch."

Since she'd come back a few days earlier, he'd been careful about touching her. When he did, she'd tense up. This time, though, she remained calm. Maybe it was the wine from the gala or maybe, he hoped, she was feeling the same thing he was tonight.

"I never let you watch," she said.

"That doesn't mean I don't."

There it was—the delicate but noticeable stiffening of her body. But at the same time, her breathing sped. He'd missed that—the way she would fight her arousal with him.

"You watched me?" she asked huskily.

"Mmm." He moved her hair aside and kissed a spot under her ear. To watch her undress would most certainly mean losing control. She'd been fluid in the long gown she'd worn tonight, and he wanted to see what was underneath. Desperately. To reach his hand into the tight neckline and take one of her perfect tits. "No," he said. "But it's been very tempting."

Beau started at a knock on his office door. He rubbed the corners of his eyes, trying to dissipate the haze brought on by thoughts of fucking Lola. Just a few more hours until he'd get back there again, and he could barely see straight from anticipation.

"What is it?" he called out.

"Your four o'clock is here."

He was hard. Fuck. Still staring out the window at downtown Los Angeles, he wondered who out there had worked for him at some point or another. That was a game he played to calm himself sometimes—how many people depended on him to stay afloat?

God, he was a sick bastard.

"Five minutes," he told his assistant, swigging the last of his drink. He willed his cock to relax as he tried to think of anything but Lola's soft, naked body, warm everywhere from weeks of wanting him.

Waiting for him.

He didn't deserve her, but that made him even more grateful. He planned to spend all his nights reversing the pain he'd caused her. And to think—he'd almost lost her.

No, Beau didn't recognize the person he'd become, but he didn't mind. He was forever changed that night he'd thought he'd lost her for good, only to walk into the lounge of the Four Seasons hotel and find her.

Waiting for him.

Chapter Eleven

Three weeks earlier

At exactly 9:51 P.M. on the same day she'd fled Beau's presidential suite, Lola slipped into a high-backed seat at the hotel's lounge. She'd passed out on the floor of her eleventh-floor room for a few hours, but after a cold shower, she'd slipped back into her white dress. She was reborn—and ready to enter the arena.

Revenge went against her nature, but Lola's motive ran as deep as Beau's betrayal had cut. This wasn't eye for eye or tooth for tooth—it was the most valuable thing you could give another person. Hope for a future, raw vulnerability. This was heart for heart.

"Evening." The bartender slid a napkin in front of her. "What're you having?"

Lola's back was unnaturally straight, her body tense. Tonight, she was both predator and prey, target and huntsman. It was an entirely normal inquiry from a bartender—what drink did she want—but she'd come to learn that friendly strangers were strangers nonetheless, and strangers could be dangerous. She repositioned herself in the chair, trying to get more comfortable. "What do you recommend?"

He grabbed a menu from the bar and held it open in front of her. He tapped it with his finger. "I'm new here, but I'm told the Colony Cocktail is our most popular drink."

Lola's mouth soured. The last man who'd picked her drink had also chosen that one, and it hadn't exactly turned out well. "I'll have anything but that."

He laughed, clapped the menu closed and tossed it aside. "How about I make you my off-menu specialty?"

She tried to smile, but it felt more like a grimace. The bartender was a poor distraction. Beau could be back any minute, she had no idea. "Sounds great. I also need a Macallan, neat."

"You got it." He picked out a couple liquor bottles and moved down the bar.

Lola released a breath. She was tempted to turn and check the entrance, but she kept her eyes forward and her back to the door. To put him at ease, he had to believe he was in charge, that he could sneak up on her.

The bartender set down both drinks, and Lola moved the Scotch to the side. She unsnapped her clutch.

"It's on the house."

Lola looked up from her lap. She'd worked in a bar a long time, and drinks never came free. "But the Macallan. It's expensive."

He shrugged. "It's my second night here, and my manager left me alone. Why not?"

Lola closed her purse. "You won't get in trouble, will you?"

"Maybe, but it'd be worth it. If I could get a smile."

There it was, the price of her drink. A little bit of herself. And surely, he expected her to be flattered by his manipulation. It occurred to Lola, she'd agreed to a game of darts with Beau knowing little more about him than she did about this bartender. It'd led to a more dangerous game.

He stood there, waiting, not reading her skepticism.

She smiled. At least she knew better now. "Thank you. What is it?"

"Blood orange juice and gin." He glanced between her eyes and the red drink. "Strawberries on top. It's called an *Amore Vietato*."

"Amore." Lola picked up the martini glass and took a sip. "That's Italian for love, isn't it?"

"Yes."

"What's vietato mean?"

"Forbidden."

She shifted her eyes to meet his. A love that shouldn't exist, that survived despite the odds. Or because of them?

"Excuse me," he said when another customer sat a few seats down.

Lola checked her watch and glanced around. It was after ten o'clock. The bar was right off the lobby, but the hushed conversations and low lights made it feel secluded. It was made for seduction, but that was only half the reason she'd chosen it. She wanted to remind Beau of the hour they'd spent there on their second night, their drinks barely touched, her mouth closer to his than necessary.

Like any woman worth her salt, Lola could fake intimacy, but men weren't wired that way. Beau's adoration had been in his touch, his eyes, his whispered words. Even if it was only an ember, something burned in him for her.

Lola sipped her Amore Vietato and took comfort in the fact that even roaring, rampant fires had started as embers.

Minutes passed. When Lola's posture began to slouch, she corrected it.

The bartender returned and leaned his hip against the counter. "So, what is it? Blind date?"

Lola shook her head. "Just a friendly drink with a…friend."

"Right." He raised an eyebrow. "That dress is about as opposite of friendly as it gets."

Lola cocked her head. "You think?"

He dropped his gaze for the briefest moment. "If he's male, your friend might get the wrong idea."

"And I guess that would be my fault."

"Of course. You know what you're doing. Nothing is ever as it seems with you ladies."

Lola stuck her elbows on the counter like she and the bartender were old friends. "That's a lot to put on an article of clothing."

"My ex wore white when she'd done something especially devilish. It was a subconscious way of seeming innocent so I'd take pity on her."

She squinted at him. There was no ring on his hand. Not even a tan line where a ring would be. That didn't mean anything, though. A ring could change a person's entire identity, and it could also be slipped on and off. Like her, he was black-haired and blue-eyed, but his face was round and inviting. Her face was not round, it was heart-shaped, and she doubted it was particularly inviting tonight. That would have to change once Beau got there.

She lifted one shoulder. "What if a dress is just a dress?"

The saleswomen of Rodeo Drive had shown Lola many outfits earlier that day. Red was aggressive. Black was too *her*—she didn't want to be herself tonight. She only wanted to play herself. White'd been the least threatening. Perhaps the bartender had something there.

"It's just a theory," he said, another shrug. "I never asked her. Then she'd know I was onto her."

Lola was leaning a little farther over the bar now, envisioning what Beau would see if he'd walk in right then. "Sounds like you two had some trust issues."

"Show me a relationship without trust issues, and I'll show you bullshit." He laughed, genuinely amused, then scanned her face. "I'm Sean, by the way."

She shook his outstretched hand. "Lola."

"Beautiful name for a beautiful woman."

Lola rolled her eyes. He wouldn't have said that if she'd been herself, normal clothing, just a girl having a beer. This dress, this hotel in this part of town, it was like a parallel universe. "Surely you can do better than that."

He shook his head, shamefaced but grinning. "You're right. How about—an angelic name for an angelic dress. As for the woman in it…"

"Not angelic?" she suggested, crooking the corner of her mouth.

"That's to be determined." He winked, then looked over her shoulder, his expression souring like he'd just eaten something questionable.

Lola didn't have to ask what'd caused that look. Something ghosted against her ear, causing the hair on the back of her neck to stand on end.

The familiar voice was deep, warm and unequivocally male, but Lola sensed the edge in his words. "What are you doing here?"

She turned to face him, the man she loved and loathed, her expression soft and her hands balled into quiet fists—fragile as a vase hiding igneous rock.

Chapter Twelve

Beau loved Lola's hair—to feel it between his fingers, to pull it in a fist as he took her from behind. She responded to that as much as he did, arching and moaning toward the ceiling. Even with her back to him in the hotel lounge, there was no mistaking her shiny hair, obsidian-black against her white dress.

Lola turned her head over her shoulder, hesitating a moment before she looked up at him. After the way they'd parted in the early hours that morning, he would've expected anger. Their time together had been short, but he'd learned to read her mood through her eyes—she was calm.

"I'm sorry." She sighed as if she'd been holding her breath a long time. "To just show up this way. I didn't know where else to go."

Beau stood up straighter. He was more than a part of her world—he was all of it. She had nowhere to go—because of him. Yet she'd returned. Why? She wasn't the type to come slinking back.

He reluctantly shifted his gaze from Lola to the bartender, who needed to be dealt with before either of them said another word. Beau'd walked in on an unpleasant scene—Lola, in an uncharacteristically sexy dress, getting winked at by a bartender. Hadn't Beau taught her about the dangers of unfamiliar men? As the day had passed, he'd been less convinced she'd broken things off with Johnny. *Johnny*, who deserved his balls in a vise, might still have Lola, and that brought Beau's blood to a boil. Now he had to worry about the entire male species?

"You must be new here," Beau said.

The man crossed his arms. "And you are?"

"A man with a very helpful tip." Beau picked up the amber drink next to Lola and studied it, his upper lip curling. "The staff is here to serve, not to enjoy my things."

Lola glanced up at Beau.

"I don't understand," the bartender said.

"The valet doesn't take my car out for a joyride. The housekeeper doesn't wear my Rolex while she cleans." Beau put his other hand on the back of Lola's chair. "You look at her like that one more time, I'll have you fired."

The man's jaw dropped into a disbelieving, open-mouth smile. "Dude, I was keeping her company. Bugs me to see such a beautiful woman waiting on anyone." He unfolded his arms and set his palms on the edge of the bar, leveling a glare at Beau. "Especially someone who just referred to her as one of his possessions."

"Don't, Sean," Lola said in warning. "It's not your problem."

For Lola's sake, Beau refrained from explaining that up until recently, she had been his possession. The way she'd referred to Beau as a problem, though, he was tempted. Instead, he slid his glass across the bar. "This isn't Macallan."

"It'll have to do." Sean pushed the glass back. "We're fresh out."

"We can go somewhere else." Lola tried to stand, but Beau put a heavy hand on her shoulder, keeping her in her seat.

"If you'd like to keep your job past the end of this conversation," Beau said, ignoring her, "you should check again."

"My job?" Sean raised his eyebrows. "I'm sorry—I wasn't aware I had a new boss."

"I'm worse than your boss—I'm a guest here. An important one. Make my drink, and put both mine and hers on my tab."

Lola shifted in her seat. "Mine was on the house."

"No, it's not." Beau didn't take his eyes off the guy, who wouldn't have felt like a threat any other time, but Lola being suddenly there was throwing him off. "Charge it to my room. Beau Olivier."

Sean blinked once and pushed off the bar, taking a step away. "You're Mr. Olivier?"

"That's right."

"Of course. I'm so sorry." Sean picked up Beau's drink and set it down again. "I didn't realize—I just started here. I thought you'd be…different. Like an old guy."

"How about that drink?" Beau was eager to get back to Lola. From the corner of his eye, he could see her staring up at him, her eyes wide, like he was God. It was making his pants tight.

"Yes, sir," Sean said, turning in almost a complete circle as he mumbled to himself, "Beau Olivier, Macallan, neat. I knew that."

Not until the bartender was out of earshot did Beau look back at Lola. "When I talk to the manager, that poor kid'll be fired. Because of you. Doesn't that make you feel bad?" Beau slid his hand down her shoulder, tracing a finger along the low-cut neckline of her dress. Less than five minutes, and he had the overwhelming need to touch her again. "Or does that kind of power over another person turn you on?"

Lola closed her hand around his, stopping it in its tracks. "I didn't come here to screw you."

"What makes you think I want to?"

She glanced down at his pants and licked her lips, forcing Beau's eyes directly to her now-glistening pink mouth. He'd done unspeakable things to that mouth, and to her round tits, her flat, quivering tummy. And the first time he'd touched the petal-soft skin of her inner thighs, parted them like the sea, it'd been with ten years' worth of anticipation.

"My mistake," she said smoothly, drawing his attention back up. She glanced over at Sean, who was pouring Beau's drink.

Beau took her chin and turned her face to his. "Don't look away from me."

She just blinked at him. "I'm not."

"You're alone?"

She swallowed.

"Is it over?"

"Do you want it to be?"

Beau didn't answer right away. He was having trouble reading her for the first time. Without knowing why she was there or what exactly she wanted, he wasn't about to admit anything she could use against him. "It makes no difference to me."

Her expression stayed clean, but her cheek twitched. "You were right about him."

Beau's hand tightened a little around her jaw. He was on edge, and he didn't want to hear about Johnny, but that statement wasn't something he could ignore. "What was I right about?"

"A lot of things." Her voice had softened—because of his hand? Or because she was hurting? "He was with Amanda last night while I was here."

His mouth was closed, but he ground his teeth hard. It didn't surprise him. Beau had seen Johnny for the coward he was the night he'd met him in Hey Joe. For one, Johnny hadn't beaten Beau to a pulp for propositioning Lola. He was weak, selfish. Beau considered himself above physical altercations, but right then, he wished he'd taken a swing at Johnny when he'd had the chance.

Beau loosened his grip a little. "I warned you that would happen."

"It's not the reason we broke up," she said, her voice hedging but her intent clear, like she wanted him to know that. "By the time I found out, we were already done. There's so much more to it than that."

Beau didn't need to hear the reasons. He nodded. "I know."

"You asked why I'm here—that's why. My mom and I don't speak. I don't really have anyone else. If I go back to my apartment—"

"You're not going back there."

She shied away as much as she could while in his grip, which wasn't much. "Then where am I going?"

Beau didn't have an answer for that. He wasn't sure why he'd even said it. The idea that he wasn't ready to let Lola go had been growing on him all day, but now it was a fact. He wasn't finished with her, and she was there, but that didn't mean he understood why he was happy about it. "You could go to the eleventh floor."

Her lips parted, a small gasp. "You knew I was staying here?"

He almost laughed at her shock. Had she learned nothing about him and what he was capable of the past few weeks? "I saw you in the lobby earlier."

Her eyebrows gathered. "When I checked in? Have you been—following me or something?"

"You walked right by me." Beau ran the pad of his thumb under her chin and tsked. "Didn't even notice. You really should be more careful, ma chatte."

"How do you know my room number?"

Beau didn't know which room she was in, but he could find out before she'd even finished her drink—the one turning her mouth an affected shade of red. "It's my business to know these things."

She scoffed. "What I do is none of your business. You made sure of that."

Beau cocked his head. Finally, a reaction—the fire that excited him as much now as it had the first night they'd spent together. "You should know by now—if I want to, I make it my business." She tried to look away, but Beau wasn't about to let that fire go out now that he'd sparked it. "What're you really here for?" he asked. "An apology?"

She shook her head. "Words could never make it right, what you did."

It didn't matter. Beau's plan had never had a second part. Once he'd dropped the axe on their connection, it was supposed to have severed any hope of redemption, of reconciliation. Like any deal worth making, he'd been ruthless, anticipating Lola's every move, manipulating her to his own end. He'd proven he could buy things that couldn't be bought. He was a master at something that couldn't be mastered.

So why did he feel as if he'd lost something? After he'd gone through so much to own her for those two nights, she didn't belong to him now. When they parted ways tonight, she wouldn't be where he could see her. She wouldn't come when he called.

Beau released her face. "What could?"

Lola raised her chin, her eyes narrowing almost imperceptibly. "You're asking me how to make this right?"

She was as proud as he was, yet she'd come back. Her feelings for him were even stronger than he'd thought. Was love that overpowering, that healing? Was Lola finding the strength to move past the pain, to accept Beau's flaws—in the name of love? It was as if some softer, calmer version of her sat in front of him instead of the real thing. The problem was, Beau had fallen for the real thing—the girl who'd stopped him in his tracks when she'd put a dent in a car with her Converse.

"I'm asking if it can even be made right."

Lola glanced down at her hands, laced in her lap. Her knuckles were white from pressing her palms together. With a deep breath, she relaxed her fingers and looked up at him. Not a single muscle on her face moved until finally, she blinked. "Yes. If you want that."

"I'm missing something here," Beau said. "You were irate this morning. You should be broken."

"*Should* be?" Lola asked, raising an eyebrow. "If I'm not, does that mean you failed?"

He opened his mouth. Did it? Did Beau have his power back if he hadn't actually hurt her as much as he'd thought? There was no outcome to this where they both won. "No, I didn't fail. You're hurt, angry, confused. You want to know why I did this."

"Yes, all of that's true. That doesn't mean I don't still l—," she hesitated but continued to look him in the eye, "care about you."

Beau was suddenly warm in his suit. It'd been so long since he'd slept, he could almost convince himself he'd misheard what she'd been about to say. He didn't doubt she loved him still—that didn't change overnight. But love was anger and hurt and demanding the truth. He didn't want this person, who was turning a blind eye. He wanted more, because when she loved him—*that* was power.

"Do you remember Hank Walken?" Beau asked.

Lola's jaw shifted left then right. "How do you know Hank Walken?"

"He works for me."

"He's slime."

"That's why I keep him around." Walken had done things for Beau he couldn't have done for himself. Reaching for a dream was nice, but those who got there had to grab it by the throat, kill or be killed. Sometimes, it wasn't pretty, what had to be done. "He'll do anything for a buck. Like make a fake offer on Hey Joe."

"It wasn't fake. He was going to turn it into a rooftop bar. A lounge with—with celebrities, and…" They stared at each other, Beau watching the realization hit. "That was never going to happen?"

"Not on my watch. Hey Joe is a dump. Wasn't worth my time." Beau brushed Lola's hair over her shoulder. "My time, my money—they were better spent on other things."

"Were they? You're such a savvy businessman? By my calculation, you lost big time on this deal. If you pit Walken against me and Johnny, then you knew Johnny and I would have to come back to you with a higher counteroffer for the first night. That would put you in a bidding war with yourself."

Beau nodded. It was, by far, the most careless he'd ever been with his money, and that hadn't been easy. But it'd almost been unavoidable, the seed of the idea planted early, maybe even on the sidewalk before they'd spoken.

"Walken put pressure on you to make a decision," Beau said. "Johnny could justify anything because he'd never survive without Hey Joe. I knew that. More importantly, though, you knew it."

"So instead of five hundred thousand, which was already more than what Hey Joe was worth, you drove the price up to a million."

"No, actually. My offer was always a million."

Her nostrils flared, but he could see she still didn't understand. "It was five hundred. Trust me, a girl doesn't forget the first time someone assigns her a dollar amount."

"It was always a million." Beau sniffed. He'd wanted to protect her in the hotel room that morning with Brigitte's text, but instead she'd wanted the truth. That's what he'd give her.

"I don't understand."

"I've dealt with many Johnnys in my life, and I knew he'd come back with a counteroffer. If I could get you to consider five hundred, there was no way you'd turn down twice that."

Lola jutted her chin out, the cogs turning in her mind as she pieced the puzzle together. "You lowballed us. I knew I was being manipulated, but this is something else."

"It's basic negotiation," Beau said. "Getting you into my bed was no different than any other business transaction. It should bring you some comfort to know it wasn't all personal."

"Comfort?" Lola snapped, jumping up from her stool. "You can't treat people that way—commodities to be traded and moved around however suits you." Her white cheeks were tinted pink, and the spark in her eyes had returned.

It reminded Beau of the first night when they'd argued, moments before he'd turned her around and fucked her against the hotel room window. Beau's blood also rushed a little quicker. "I treat people how they allow me to treat them," he said slowly. "You seem to forget I never forced you into a single thing."

"Exactly. You made me ask for these things, beg for them. Fuck you." She snatched her purse and turned away. "This isn't worth it."

Beau refrained from grabbing her arm like he wanted. They weren't finished until he said they were, and he wasn't ready to walk away yet. Especially after a comment he didn't understand. "What isn't worth it?"

Lola turned back and came right up under his chin. "After the first night, Johnny and I thought we had the bar, but we were in over our heads. What about that?"

"You agreed to buy something you couldn't afford. At the end of the day, that's why you took the second offer."

"But you knew all along that would happen. You made it so I'd have no choice but to accept your second offer." She smirked. "It's a shame you weren't confident enough in your abilities alone."

"Oh, I was," Beau said. "Nobody comes as hard as you did and doesn't crawl back for seconds. Or thirds…"

Lola raised her hand to slap him, but he caught her wrist before she could. "You're heartless," she spat, breathing hard. Her hair fell over one eye as she struggled to get her arm back. "There's nothing there, where your heart should be—just a big, fat dollar sign."

He loved the way she tried to take him on, every time she did it. Too much. He was getting hard, and he had a weakness for her—the combination of the two was like poison to his control. "Keep pushing my buttons. See what it gets you."

"I couldn't be any worse off than I am right now." She jerked her entire body, and he released her so she stumbled backward.

"No?" he asked. "Let's go, then. What you need is a good, hard spanking for your behavior tonight and an even better orgasm to ease the sting."

She gaped, her mouth opening wider, presumably to tell him off, but nothing came. She snapped her jaw shut. "That's all it ever was to you."

He couldn't tell if it was a statement or a question.

The lines around her eyes faded as she unwrinkled her nose. Her tone evened out. "Sex. Revenge. Fuck me, because I fucked you first."

He'd seen this look on her face before—losing her struggle to submit. It'd been the first time he'd brought her to his hotel and made her crawl to him. Lola had become so much more than a conquest that night—she'd fulfilled Beau's need for the impossible challenge he'd been looking for ever since he'd sold his first company. Beau was just as turned on now as he had been then.

"I have one last question," Lola said. "After that, if you want me to leave, I will."

Beau raised his eyebrows. If *he* wanted *her* to leave? She'd been in the middle of storming off, but she hadn't yet. And the longer she stayed, the less he wanted her to leave. More and more, he needed to take her upstairs and have the night they were never supposed to have.

"Was any of it real?" she asked.

Beau stared at her, almost angered by the question. He had told her *repeatedly* that it was real, both while it was happening and after the fact. How many times could he say it? Despite manipulating her, he'd never once lied to get her there. Lying would've been cheating to win, and Beau never cheated. He played ugly, but he played fair.

"Everything was real, every detail I shared with you. I never lied about my past or my family. Not about my feelings. If you hadn't read that text this morning, you would've gone home, broken up with Johnny, and I would've been here waiting for you when you got back." Beau was breathing hard, but the admission came easily. His time with Lola had been so limited, he'd had to learn how to open up fast. Without that, he never would've had a shot at getting her to love him. Now, his honesty felt natural.

She searched his eyes. "The stars?" she asked quietly. "Why did you drive me up Mulholland Drive? Where did that fit into your plan?"

Beau's shoulders tensed. As they'd climbed the Santa Monica Mountains in his convertible, he'd glanced over at Lola. Her head had been tilted back to see the stars better, her hands cupped over her hair, loose strands flying around her face. She'd looked back at him right before he'd returned his eyes to the road.

Having her look at him that way—it'd been part of the plan. But the way it'd made him feel hadn't. Could he have possibly stopped that feeling, though? Earlier that night, he'd been inside her where nobody else had been. Her body had melted like butter underneath him, the last of her walls coming down. She'd trusted him, and she was his. He'd known it then. They'd always had an expiration date, but sudden and deep panic had hit him in the chest. He couldn't discard her, and he couldn't keep her.

"Mulholland was a moment of weakness on my part," Beau said carefully. "I thought it would make you happy."

"You didn't answer my question. Was it planned?" Her eyes dropped to his chest, and she closed them. "And the gas station?"

"What do you mean, the gas station?"

Lola was quiet as the question hung between them. Her insinuation became clear, and Beau would've laughed at the absurdity of it if it didn't feel like such a punch in the gut. "You're asking if I *planned* that?"

She opened her eyes. "You could've."

Beau rubbed his forehead hard. "You think I hired a man to rob us at gunpoint," he said evenly. The memory alone made his heart pound as if he were standing there again, completely helpless.

"I—"

"Hired him to scare the shit out of you. To put his hands on you."

"You've done worse."

She angled away from him a little, but he grabbed her shoulders, brought her close to look her straight in the eye. "I have never done worse than that. If you'd've let me, I would've gone after him. I would've hunted that motherfucker down and killed him for putting you in that position."

"I don't understand you," she said suddenly, her voice cracking. She bit her lip when her chin wobbled. "How do you do it?"

He released her immediately, stunned. Just the threat of her crying struck him, reminded him of how she'd broken down in his lap after the mugging and told him she loved him. She rarely showed vulnerability, that'd been clear to him within moments of meeting her. How many times had she cried since that morning? On her way home from the hotel? When she'd found out about Johnny and Amanda?

"How do I do what?" he asked.

"Turn everything off. Teach me how. If you can't love me, teach me how not to love you."

Beau's chest tightened. Lola was strong and stubborn. She wasn't this girl standing in front of him, submitting to her pain. Fighters, like Beau and Lola, turned sorrow into strength. He didn't know how to handle her as a girl whose heart he'd broken.

"I don't turn anything off." Beau's hands flexed in and out of balls. It took so little for her to turn him in a circle. His instincts about her were always changing, and that felt like losing control. "Do you think I liked watching you leave this morning? You never even gave me a chance to explain."

"Leaving was a mistake," she said bluntly but backed away.

Beau automatically stepped forward. He hadn't realized how much he'd wanted her to admit that.

"Or was coming here a mistake?" she continued. "I don't know, Beau. Should I not have come? Do you want me to leave? Tell me what to do."

Beau looked down at her. Her face was open, just like it'd been the night before when she'd trusted him with the biggest decision of her life. *"I love you. I love him. Tell me what to do, Beau. I'll do it."*

Glenn Churchill had painted a picture of love for Beau—taking precious hours from his work to do absolutely nothing with Lola. Nothing but enjoy her company. Maybe they went to a coffee shop with friends, maybe they stayed in bed half the day. Not just a few times, but every weekend. Could he and Lola ever be that couple? The hurdle before them was massive.

"We aren't supposed to be together," Beau said.

Lola chewed her bottom lip. She stared at him, but she seemed lost in thought. "Okay. All right." After a brief hesitation, she turned around.

"Lola. Hang on." Beau rubbed the bridge of his nose. He closed his eyes, but he knew she was walking out. It was always going to end. It'd already gone on longer than it should've. Beau had never been good at ignoring his gut, though, and against all odds, it was telling him to go after her.

He crossed the room, strode through the lobby and caught up with her in the elevator bank, where she was waiting with her arms crossed.

"You didn't let me finish," Beau said.

She didn't even blink as she stared down the elevator doors.

"We're not supposed to be together. I don't see how it could ever work."

"Then let me go back to my room. I'll find a new hotel in the morning—or maybe I'll just go home. Either way, you won't see me again."

"I don't want that." Beau didn't like talking to her profile, but she avoided his eyes. "Come upstairs with me."

She exhaled a short laugh. "Upstairs? To your room? You must think I was born yesterday."

Beau raised his palms as if not to spook her. He might, if he didn't tread carefully. He regretted that he'd made a pass at her earlier. She suffered, because of him, and he was no longer sure he wanted that. "I don't think that, but it feels wrong for you to be here in my hotel and not with me."

She opened her mouth, but he continued before she could interrupt.

"I have a guest room. You can sleep there tonight, and after we've both gotten some rest, we can continue this talk."

The elevator arrived. Lola boarded it before the doors were even all the way open and hit a button.

He followed. "Lola."

She looked at him. "What?"

The doors closed. They were alone now—him, with Lola. He knew her, knew how to handle her, how to get her to respond. It was instinctual. "You're not going back to your room tonight."

"I see. Suddenly, you've decided you want me, and I'm just supposed to obey?"

"Neither of us knows what we want," he said. "But we both know you're not ready to walk away forever. Neither am I."

She readjusted her arms and tapped one gentle finger in sync with each *ding* of a passing floor.

"What do you need?" he asked. "Just to agree to come for tonight?"

She turned to face him without hesitating. "I need you to make me a promise. No matter what happens, no matter how good or bad it feels between us, no sex. I can't sleep with you right now. I'm too confused. I need to feel—safe…again."

"I understand."

"I don't just mean tonight. No, we don't know what's going to happen, but if it lasts a minute past tomorrow morning," she paused, "you can't touch me until I come to you and tell you I'm ready."

Beau sighed. He was exhausted—he'd have to be to agree to that. He would've said anything to get her up there so he could go to bed, though. Because he wouldn't be able to sleep without knowing she was in the next room.

It wouldn't be easy. Lola's power over him wouldn't go away just because he wished it would. That was becoming obvious.

"You have my word."

Lola looked at him a second longer and turned back toward the elevator doors. "Okay," she said. "I'll come."

It wasn't until they were walking to his room that he realized they'd never even stopped at the eleventh floor. When she'd gotten on the elevator before him, she'd pushed the button to go to the sixteenth.

Chapter Thirteen

Lying on her back, with her hands folded over her naked stomach, Lola stared up at the dark ceiling of Beau's guestroom. Beau'd kept his promise and shown her to the opposite side of the suite without so much as a handshake. From the dark circles under his eyes, she guessed he hadn't slept since well before she'd left him that morning.

She was tired too, but her thoughts were coming fast. Lola was far from the master Beau was. She hadn't had as much time to plot as he had, and she'd stumbled and faltered her way through their interaction tonight. He'd riled her. She'd almost walked away. It'd been risky, threatening to leave, but she was still here. And she wasn't ready to give in yet—she could learn this game.

She reviewed the evening with careful attention to detail—like his anger when she'd questioned his authenticity. It was most uncomfortable to turn the magnifying glass inward, though, to figure out what about Beau derailed her. She'd almost broken down learning the nuances of his layered plan.

She shouldn't have been surprised about Hank Walken's involvement—she might've figured it out if she'd given it enough thought. But the extent and depth of Beau's reach scared her. When Sean, the doting bartender, had turned from confident to cowering, Lola had realized how alone she was in this. Nobody could take Beau on, because there was nobody Beau's money couldn't buy.

Lola took a deep, meditative breath and closed her eyes, but not because she was going to sleep. She assumed somewhere out there, a star was shooting across the night sky. She made a wish—that Beau should suffer from his love the way she had. That she would be the first to bring him to his knees for what he'd done.

She had no choice but to return to a place she didn't want to. She had to be the Lola he'd fallen for in the middle of the night. The girl he'd touched as if she'd belonged to him rather than someone else. The girl who'd looked up at the stars and wondered how long ago her feelings for Johnny had begun to change. Who'd stepped in front of a gun for a man she hardly knew but one she knew she wasn't prepared to live without.

Beau had given her a picnic under the stars, but he'd also given her a pair of brand new Converse in her size when any old tennis shoes would've been fine. He paid attention when it counted and when it didn't. Lola's love for Beau was as fresh as the wound he'd left her with. That was good. She needed to feel the sting of both in order to pull this off.

She checked the clock by the bed. 2:17 A.M.

Lola folded back the comforter, swung her legs over the side of the mattress and stood. Beau had given her a robe, so she slipped into it. She easily knew her way to his room in the dark.

She stopped in his doorway. Her life had changed in that room. In that bed, she'd given him everything that'd meant anything to her. She had crawled across the floor to him, opened her legs to his mouth, bit the comforter as he'd broken down her last barrier. In that moment, Lola's love might've been hard to find, but her attraction to Beau was as loud as the beating of her heart. It was dangerous, and it'd require all of her strength to control it.

Lola tiptoed to the edge of his bed. His heavy, steady breaths told her he was sleeping peacefully. How could he not be when he'd gone so long without rest? She bent at the waist and peered at him in the dark. It would take nothing to hurt him. It would also be just as easy to fuck him. Was he naked? Did he dream of their two nights and what a third would be like?

His breathing stopped instantly. Before Lola could react, Beau's arm shot out and grabbed her robe by the belt. "What are you doing?"

She touched his hand at her waist, his skin radiating warmth. When he didn't object, she wrapped her fingers around his wrist. "I couldn't sleep."

"What do you want, a lullaby?" His tone was harsh, but his hand slipped inside the robe. Her breath stuttered as her body reacted to his touch in an alarming way—thawing as if it'd been frozen and waiting for heat. It disgusted her, the way Beau aroused her. He didn't deserve her, and he wouldn't have her—but he had to believe he could. She knew from experience, hope was one of the most painful things a person could lose.

Beau's palm flattened over her stomach and slid up around her waist. "Take this off," he said. "Come here."

She tightened the robe around herself but pulled back the covers and got in.

Beau sat up on an elbow and looked down at her. With his other hand, he touched the lapel of the robe. Lola's heart nearly stopped. He'd promised to respect her wishes, but did it matter? Wasn't it his way, to take what he wanted while making her think she wanted it too?

He moved his hand to her face, leaned in and kissed her. Every part of him was warm from sleep—his lips, the inside of his mouth, his breath. His thigh pressed against hers. She couldn't ignore the dull throb between her legs. No matter how much he'd hurt her, she'd always want this. But Beau had taken it away from her. This was his fault.

She didn't stop him right away. Men needed to touch and feel, to know she physically existed. It had to be done, and it had to be convincing, so she melted into the mattress, gripped his face and ran her fingertips down his scratchy cheeks. He opened his mouth wider, kissed her harder.

She pushed him back by his chest. They stared at each other, panting. "You promised," she said.

"*You* crawled into *my* bed."

"To be close to you."

"Let me get this straight." He placed his palm right below her throat, on the only skin the robe exposed. "You're asking me to sleep next to you and not touch you?"

If Beau moved his hand any lower, if he commanded her, Lola wasn't sure how she'd resist, but she had to. Her dignity was in shreds, but sleeping with him would destroy everything.

Lola rolled her lips together and glanced out toward the balcony, lit up from the moon. "I need time, Beau. You hurt me, and the worst part is, you did it on purpose. You can't expect me to—"

Beau sat up and switched on the bedside lamp.

Lola shielded her eyes. "What're you doing?"

"What do you think's going to happen when you come in here in the middle of the night? After everything we've been through in this exact spot?"

Lola reached over him and turned out the light. It was too harsh. Maybe she'd come to him too soon, but they needed to mend the bond they'd broken, and it had to be fast. Too fast for him to realize it was happening. "Do you want me to leave?"

He lay on his back again, looked up at the ceiling and sighed as if he carried the weight of the world on his chest. "No."

Lola put her hand on his bicep, softly stroking the hard muscle with her thumb. Touch was good—a weapon, even—as long as she could control it. "I'm not talking about your bed. Should I go?"

"I already told you. When I make a decision, it's done. I invited you here tonight. You aren't leaving." He rolled his head toward her, removed her hand from his bicep and pulled her down next to him. "Not this room. Not this spot."

Lola's body thrilled, but it was with a different kind of adrenaline. This feeling—this kind of *power* over someone—it wasn't like she'd never experienced it before, even with Beau. When her mouth was on his cock, or the moments right before she undressed, he'd get this look in his eyes like there was nothing he wouldn't do for her. This was something else, though. She was doing this to him with her words, using him against himself.

"Will you still feel that way tomorrow?" Lola asked. "What if—"

"I don't do 'what if,' Lola." Beau turned onto his side, put his arms around her and pulled her against his chest. He yawned in her ear. It was a moment before he spoke again, and his voice sounded far off. "Tomorrow is tomorrow. We'll deal with it then. If you're worried I'll wake up and…"

"And what?"

"Change my mind…"

Lola waited, willing herself to stay perfectly still. If she tensed even one muscle, Beau would notice. That was the kind of attention she was dealing with. After a few seconds of silence, she realized he'd fallen asleep. "Beau?"

"Hmm?" He inhaled deeply and sighed. "What?"

"You said if I'm worried you'll wake up and change your mind…?"

He tightened his arms around her and whispered into her hair, "I won't."

He fell back asleep. She bit her lip to keep her relief inside and the smile from her face. It seemed to Lola that within only a few hours, she already had the bastard exactly where she wanted him.

Chapter Fourteen

Beau opened his eyes at 5:58 A.M. on the dot, just like every other morning. It didn't matter that he hadn't gotten enough sleep—routine was one of the secrets to his success. It kept him on track. It was the framework by which he measured his output.

This wasn't every other morning, though. Lola was in his arms. It didn't surprise him, but the memory of how she'd gotten there was foggy. Beau didn't like being woken up by anyone. It put him at a disadvantage. But if she hadn't, she wouldn't have been there in his bed that morning. And he liked her there.

He slid his arms out from under her and got up on an elbow. Her heart-shaped lips were parted for small, even breaths. He brushed a lock of hair from her cheek. Based on the previous morning, this was the last thing he would've expected to wake up to. Even knowing Lola loved him, he wouldn't have thought her pride would allow her to fight for him. She had a weakness for him the way he did for her.

Beau got out of the bed and pulled on his boxer briefs. Before leaving the room, he turned back and took his cell phone from the nightstand. God knew what kinds of incriminating things Brigitte might text him.

In the suite's kitchenette, he took two mugs from a cabinet. If Lola had slept as little as he did, she'd need caffeine when she woke. He rarely made his own coffee, but he didn't want to leave her alone to go get some. He got a pot started and checked on Lola to see if she was still asleep. She'd flipped over, her black hair strewn on the pillow like a sinister Sleeping Beauty.

He went to the foot of the bed, let his eyes travel the sheeted curves and bends of her body. He could take what he wanted from her. Waking her with a kiss would lead him between her legs in no time. He knew her body better than she did, how to touch it, read it, manipulate it. He traced the arch of her foot underneath the sheet, and she stirred.

His respect had to be earned. That was a tall order for the women he'd slept with. But he and Lola had been through enough that he felt he owed her at least that. It wasn't a stretch, not at all, to think he might love her. That was why he left the bed despite wanting to climb in next to her. He wouldn't keep his hands off her if he did.

He went out to the balcony and let the morning air cool his urges. The sky had shaded from black to cobalt, silhouetting the mountains against a blue as rich as Lola's eyes. He closed the door to the room and called Brigitte.

"Beau?" she answered and cleared her throat. "What time is it? Is everything all right?"

"Sorry to wake you." He looked back at Lola through the windowed door. Her chest rose and fell rhythmically. This was what he'd missed those mornings she'd left at dawn. Anticipating the moment she'd wake up. Planning what they'd do with their day. "I'm coming home."

After a moment of silence, she spoke, the smile clear in her voice. "Well, that's news worth waking up for. I've missed having you around the house these past few weeks."

Beau kept watching Lola. He went out of his way to avoid fights with Brigitte, but this was one he needed to have. He wanted to do right by Lola from now on, and that wasn't stashing her away in a hotel room. "I'm not coming alone."

"Meaning?" She waited. "You're bringing someone over? Who?"

"We've been talking about getting you your own place for a while—"

"You've been talking about it," she said, sounding more awake now. "I haven't."

"I wouldn't ask you to go if I didn't think you'd like it. Being on your own." Over time, Brigitte had grown less independent and more reliant on Beau. He didn't mind taking care of her, but he planned on having Lola around a lot. And for her sake, he wanted his home back. "You have to trust me."

"Trust you?" she asked, her voice rising. "You're throwing me out on the street. How am I supposed to trust you?"

Beau closed his eyes and took a deep breath. He pinched the bridge of his nose. "Don't blow this out of proportion. I'll talk to my real estate agent today, and in the meantime, Warner and I will find you something temporary. You'll be more than comfortable."

"Pass me off to Warner like always. Did he know about this?"

"*I* didn't even know until just now. And I do not pass you off to Warner. Remember our conversation about wild exaggerations?"

"It's not an exaggeration. When was the last time you did anything for me that required more than making a phone call or writing a check? When I had that kidney infection last year, *Warner* took me to the hospital."

"And I paid your medical bills without flinching," Beau said evenly. "I'm your brother, not your employer."

"That's not the point. You wanted new furniture for the guestroom last month, so I got it. But you couldn't even come by the store to give me a second opinion on what I'd picked out. 'Just put it on the card, and have it delivered.' Whenever I need help or a ride or anything that doesn't absolutely require your presence, you send something else in your place. If it's not Warner, it's your credit card."

"Damn it, Brigitte, we've been through this before. I'm fucking busy. How do you expect me to take care of you if I'm not working my ass off?"

"Maybe I need to be taken care of in other ways," she snapped.

"I do as much for you as I'm capable of. I'm not your goddamn boyfriend. If you want someone to go shopping with you, find someone who has the time and inclination." Beau ended the call, gripping the phone. All people ever wanted from him was money, and he was fine with that. Why couldn't that be enough for Brigitte too? He didn't need to be constantly reminded of his shortcomings as a brother and a son. He gave his family what he could, and that was more than what ninety-nine percent of the world had. He held up his phone again, but this time he sent Brigitte a text.

Start packing. Will have arrangements for you by tomorrow.

He turned off his phone and went back inside.

Chapter Fifteen

Twenty-four hours after she'd stormed out of his hotel room vowing never to touch him again, Lola woke up in Beau's empty bed. She stood and tightened the belt of the robe she'd slept in. The balcony doors sat open, inviting a chill into the room. Lola stretched her arms toward the ceiling and refrained from patting herself on the back. She'd snuck into Beau's room in the middle of the night and had come out the other side in one piece. It was a small miracle she hadn't caved to his advances, but now she knew just what she was capable of.

"You're still here."

Lola looked over her shoulder. Beau stood on the other side of the bed with a towel around his waist and shaving cream all over his jaw.

"Why wouldn't I be?" she asked.

He pointed behind her. "Old habits."

Lola turned forward again. The rising sun sent pink and orange streaks across the sky—the moment Lola would be climbing out of Beau's limo back to Johnny. "I'm not leaving."

"I don't want you to," he called from the bathroom.

She followed his voice. Beau leaned over the sink. It was unfamiliar territory for them, the fresh scent of his shaving cream and the scrape of the blade over his stubble.

"I was worried you might change your mind this morning," she said.

He glanced briefly at her in the mirror's reflection. "I didn't."

"How do we do this?"

He dragged the razor up his cheek, mowing down each of the bristles Lola loved to feel against her face. Beau had enough money to buy a human, but apparently not an electric razor. That was him in a nutshell—rewards meant nothing if he hadn't worked for them.

He rinsed the blade under running water. "It's early. Why don't we eat before we start in on this?"

Lola's jaw tingled. The thought of eating breakfast food with him withered her insides. During their French toast meal the first night, her walls had begun to crumble—she'd even found herself *happy* despite how she'd gotten there. Reliving that would be more intimate than sleeping by his side. "I'm not hungry."

Beau splashed water on his jaw and, without warning, pulled the towel from around his waist. Lola swallowed her gasp before it escaped. She kept her eyes up, but it was nearly impossible not to peek.

He held her gaze as he patted his face dry, walked over and kissed her head. "Just coffee then," he said on his way out of the bathroom. "I already have some brewing."

When she was alone, she released her breath. She had to keep it together. This was the equivalent of entering his conference room to negotiate, and that'd been his first power play. Knowing him, there was more coming.

Lola returned to the bedroom, glancing around. Any trace she'd been there before then was gone. There was no lipstick on the comforter, and her beaded dress had been cleaned up. Beau'd probably thought removing her from his life was as easy as calling for maid service.

She went to the balcony and snuggled into her robe. It'd been out there, in the middle of their second night, that it'd hit her how much she'd already given Beau. It turned out, though, she hadn't given him anything. He'd taken it.

She rubbed her hands over her biceps. In that spot, Beau had held her so tightly, as if he'd thought she might disappear right before his eyes.

What if she had? What if one moment she'd been there, and the next she was gone, leaving him holding on to nothing but air?

"What're you thinking about?" Beau asked from behind her.

Lola looked back at him. He had two mugs in his hands and, thankfully, pajama pants on his body. "Why?"

"You're tense."

Lola forced her shoulders down from around her ears. Beau was a man who took great care when dealing with his adversaries, but she didn't have the resources or the practice he did. Honesty was one of her only weapons. "I was thinking about the last time we were out here. I was scared."

"Scared?" he repeated.

"Things were happening so fast. I was falling for you, and suddenly I realized that I didn't *have* to stop it. That I could fall, because—"

She stopped to let Beau's imagination fill in the blanks. At the same time, she pushed herself to relive those moments and tap into the pain that would fuel her.

He came up behind her. She sucked in a breath. Out of instinct, her muscles locked up. His touch could threaten her focus, and she could never forget that.

He set their coffee on the railing and wrapped her in his arms. "You're shivering."

"Am I?" She hadn't realized it.

"What were you going to say?" he prompted. "You could let yourself fall, because…"

Lola wanted to steady herself on the railing, but she couldn't move while he held her that hard. She closed her eyes and returned to Beau's arms that night, under the stars where an unexpected love bloomed inside her. She didn't fight the memory. She used it. "I was going to change my entire life for you. It was terrifying and risky, but you made me feel safe. For a few hours, at least."

He rubbed his smooth cheek against hers. She missed the scruff. "I told you if you left Johnny, I'd be here," he said. "And here I am. I think I had to lose you in order to learn the truth."

"What's the truth?"

"This isn't over. I can't take back what I did, but I should've told you everything before you found out that way. When you wouldn't listen, I got angry. I can't seem to figure out how to give up some control without losing it entirely."

Lola opened her eyes. The mountains were indigo shadows that seemed impossibly far away. In the time she'd known Beau, he'd always been very aware—of himself, of her. How could he not have seen the pettiness of what he'd done, the sheer egoism of it? He'd stood to gain real love and a life that centered around something other than work. Instead, he'd thrown it away in the name of pride. That was something she couldn't explain to him, though. It would have to be a lesson learned.

"I can't just pretend nothing happened," Lola said.

"I don't expect you to. I know I have a lot to make up for."

She narrowed her eyes. "So you're willing to try?"

Beau took a mug of coffee and handed it to her. Instead of picking his up, he returned his arm around her. "If you're willing to take it day by day. This is new territory for me, but I'm a fast learner. You know I'll do what it takes to fix it."

Lola did know. If her forgiveness was his prize, then he would make it his. It was an impossible feat, she knew. But he didn't. It would drive Beau even more, sink him in deeper. "When do we start?"

"We already have." It sounded like he was smiling. "I work on Saturdays, but I'll leave it for Monday. You're my queen this weekend."

"And after this weekend?"

"We go home."

"Home?" she asked. "As in…?"

Beau took an arm off her to drink some coffee. "As in you, where I am, when I wake up, when I go to sleep. When I leave for work, when I get back."

Lola felt like she'd eaten cotton. So little time had passed, it was hard not to still want that with Beau—*home.* A life, a future. For him to forgo his work to spend time with her was his highest compliment. But with her wounds so fresh, she was a slave to her pain, and it ran deep. This wasn't a new life with him. It was a chance to be by Beau's side every morning and every night. To get so deep under his skin, he couldn't rid himself of her. To bring down the walls around his heart so she could hold it in her palm, exposed and unprotected. It wouldn't be easy to love the devil, but she could do it if it meant sending him to hell where he belonged.

"I want that too," she said.

"Good. You know I'd get my way even if you didn't."

He was teasing her, so she laughed lightly.

"Now that that's settled," he continued, his voice hardening, "how about enlightening me to your thought process when you left my room yesterday morning."

"Yesterday morning?" Lola took a sip from her mug, stalling. Abrupt, probing inquiries like that needed consideration before answering.

"Warner said you walked home from the hotel."

"That's right. Yes, I did."

"It was still dark." He waited a moment, as if that warranted a response. "Well? What in the hell made you think that was a good idea?"

She squinted out at the skyline. "I had to blow off some steam."

"You couldn't have done that in the back of a car?"

"No." Lola shifted on her feet. There was an edge to both their voices. This was too familiar to them, and they slipped into their battles easily. He'd been putty in her hands for a moment, but she should've known he wouldn't allow that very long. "Why do you ask?"

"I don't know," he said in a tone that conveyed he definitely did know. "Maybe because we were robbed at gunpoint a few hours before that. Correct me if I'm wrong, but it seems like safety would've been pretty high on your list of priorities."

"Does it matter? I made it in one piece." She sniffed. As if he had any right to worry about her after he'd cast her aside so carelessly. "Anyway, I didn't have a choice. I needed to be alone."

"With no cell phone and no credit cards. In the dark." The air around them thickened. "It gets me worked up again just thinking about it."

"Does it?" Lola continued to look forward, carefully tucking it all away for later. His cares, concerns, triggers. "Well, then, it's a good thing I had plenty of cash, thanks to you."

"Are you fucking kidding? People have killed over far less money than what you had in your hands." He removed his arm from her. "Where's that money now?"

Lola turned around and leaned back against the banister. "Downstairs in my room. I fit as much as I could in the safe, but—"

"Jesus Christ, Lola." He jerked his thumb over his shoulder. "That money needs to go in the bank yesterday. You're asking for trouble carrying that kind of cash around."

"You're right." Lola set down her mug and put her arms around his neck. There was no way in hell she was loosening her grip on the one thing keeping her afloat. That money was all she had left. "I'll do it soon."

"Not *soon*. You'll do it Monday. And today, we're getting you a new phone. You can't be without one."

"I don't mind being out of touch, actually." Lola had to stop herself from grinning. Toying with Beau had always been fun, no matter how she'd felt about him.

"It's so refreshing to be free from the chains of society for once—"

"I'll stop you right there," Beau said, removing her hands from him by her wrists. "You're getting a phone today. It'll be our first errand. Then we'll see about getting you a temporary credit card until we can get you a real one. I'll give you one of mine too, but you should have a couple in your name just in case—"

"Beau, don't you think you're overreacting a bit—?"

"No. Look at me." Lola lifted her eyes to his and waited. He pulled her hands back to his chest, right over his heart. "Yesterday, even though I thought I'd never see you again, it still drove me insane knowing you were out there with nothing. Don't fight me on this. Without a cell phone or credit card, anything could happen to you, and I wouldn't even know."

Lola's heart jumped into her throat.

"It drove me insane…out there with nothing…I wouldn't even know…"

Beau had reassured her that he never backtracked on his decisions. Never changed his mind. When he wanted something, he took it. Always. But what would happen if the thing he wanted most slipped right through his fingers—and not even his fortune could get it back?

Lola had the motive to bring Beau to his knees, and she had the means to make it happen. All she needed now to complete the puzzle was Beau's heart in her palm.

She stepped even closer to him and looked into his fiery, green eyes. Gently, she twisted her hands out of his grip to reach up and cup his face. And what a face it was—the kind a girl could get lost in if she didn't know any better. "If that's what you want, Beau, then I'll do it. I trust you."

Beau kissed the insides of her hands. Any bitterness left his expression as his features softened.

Beau loved to play—to hunt his prey. That must've been because he'd never lost.

Maybe someone ought to beat him at his own game. Maybe then he wouldn't think it was so fun.

Chapter Sixteen

Present day

Beau wasn't home at seven o'clock for his big surprise date with Lola—he was home earlier. His last meeting had been a homerun despite being distracted and had put him on track to close a lucrative deal. As if he hadn't already been riled thinking of all the things he'd finally get to do to Lola, making money always gave him a buzz. He'd waited her out—not patiently, but he'd waited—and he didn't want to miss a minute of their evening together.

Now, he was perched on their bed while Lola finished getting ready. She came out of the bathroom with a towel wrapped securely under her armpits.

"Come on," Beau said, practically falling off the edge of the mattress. "Just give me a sneak peek."

She smiled. "You only have a few hours left. Your reward will be that much sweeter if you wait."

She'd been stubborn from the start, but Christ did it frustrate him in the best way possible. Night after night, sleeping next to her, sharing a bathroom and a bedroom with her, and she'd only slipped once. He'd been clinging to that memory like a castaway to a raft.

"You're a tough negotiator," Beau said, following her with his eyes until she disappeared into the closet.

"It isn't a negotiation," she called. "You broke the terms of our agreement once. Do it again, and it'll be the last time."

"If you're trying to torture me, it's working. Hearing you talk business gets me even harder."

She leaned out of the closet, giving him a glimpse of her naked shoulder and the outer curve of her breast. "Why? It reminds you of that morning Johnny and I came to your conference room?"

Beau licked his lips. He was as close to having her now as he had been that day. She'd sat across the table from him, statue-like, but once in a while, her face would flicker with hurt or embarrassment when Johnny spoke—or when he was decidedly quiet. All Beau had gotten from her was anger. "Would it upset you if it did?"

"No." She ran her finger along the edge of the doorway. "Maybe one day you can fuck me on that table."

Beau had been teasing about getting hard, but her dirty talk was an alarm to his sleeping cock. Beau resisted standing up. He wasn't sure he could keep himself in check. "Let's skip dinner."

She shook her head. "I've been planning tonight for a while. Besides, I'm *hungry*."

"Give me sixty seconds, and you'll forget the meaning of the word."

"Sixty seconds?" She grinned and returned into the closet. "Is that what I have to look forward to?"

"It would serve you right after keeping me on edge for so long."

A dresser drawer rolled open, then closed with a wooden thump. He was more tempted than ever to sneak in and steal a look at her white breasts and long, tight tummy. He'd showered after work, but already he could use another cold one.

Beau was in love with her, at least he was pretty sure of it, and that feeling was strongest in moments like this one. For a woman who'd worn as many jeans-and-shirt combos in her life as Beau had suits, she was completely at ease in the things he picked out for her. He could just sit and watch, and he never had the urge to walk away. If any other woman had told him 'look don't touch' night after night, Beau would've laughed at her on his way out the door.

Lola came out in a structured black trench coat. "Do you like it?" she asked with a twirl, her high heels' red soles flashing.

She could've been wearing a nun's habit, and he would've said yes. The coat cinched at her waist, all hips and breasts. She'd pulled the collar up around her neck. It was buttoned all the way, but her long, bare legs invited him to look.

"Can I see the dress?" he asked.

"Not yet." She walked over to the bed, bent over and pressed a light kiss to the corner of his mouth. "Soon."

She straightened up to walk away. He grabbed her wrist, and her head jerked in his direction, her lips splitting apart as if he'd startled her. It took a second, but her mouth spread into some mutation of a smile. She slid her hand through his and walked into the bathroom, promising, "Five more minutes, then we can go."

Five minutes sounded like a lifetime. Anything longer felt impossible. He'd waited long enough for her. From where he sat, he could see her bent over the sink putting in her earrings. Seeing her in that position again made his brain foggy. He could easily fuck her over the bathroom counter before dinner. He wouldn't last long anyway. An appetizer. Then, later, the main course—taking his time unwrapping her, tracing the lines of her curves with his hands and lips.

Beau blew out a sigh. He'd thought he'd been patient their first two nights together by not taking her the moment the sun had set. He'd had no idea what was in store for him.

Lola came out of the bathroom and held her hand out, rescuing both of them from him. "Ready?"

◆⊠◆⊠◆

Beau raised his wineglass over the table. "To you," he said to Lola.

She made no move to pick up her drink. "Why me?"

"Because there's nothing more worthy of toasting. Unless you have a better idea?"

"Us." She spun the wineglass between her fingers on the tablecloth. "And the end of a very difficult journey."

"That's not how I see it. In a few minutes, my patience over the last few weeks will earn me a great reward."

She grinned. "We are not having sex in a few minutes. We haven't even eaten yet."

Beau sighed. "Fine. A few hours. Whatever. Regardless, tonight isn't an ending. It's the start of a life we've both deserved for a long time."

"To that—exactly." She clinked her wine with his, and they each took a sip. "Thank you for giving Warner the night off like I asked."

"I told you I'd let you plan your night. Brigitte needs the company anyway."

Lola raised her eyebrows. "He's been spending a lot of time at her apartment."

"Someone has to, and it's not going to be me. All my free time goes to someone else."

"Who?" Lola asked. "Because it isn't me."

Beau cleared his throat. He couldn't tell if she was joking. He understood that his schedule bothered her, but what he couldn't comprehend was why. Every day he'd worked the past ten years—and every hour he worked now—was for her, even if he hadn't known it. He went in early and he stayed late to give her more and more and more. "I do my best."

"Do you? She has a point about Warner, you know. If you'd ever sent him home to eat dinner with me because you couldn't make it, I can tell you right now, it would not have gone over well."

Beau put his glass down. "What neither you nor Brigitte seems to get is that if I don't give my job one-hundred-and-ten percent, there'd be no Warner. There'd be no five-thousand square foot house to come home to. No extra bedrooms for a family, no cinema or pool—"

Lola shifted backward in her seat, her eyebrows needling together. "A family?"

Beau maintained eye contact the way he would if he'd slipped up in a meeting. It wasn't like children were at all prevalent in his day-to-day thoughts, but some abstract idea of a family had crossed his mind since Lola had moved in. He leaned his elbows on the table. "I'm making a point."

She looked at her lap. "Have I made you feel like I wouldn't be happy without those things?"

"Which things?"

"A big house and a chauffeur. A closet full of expensive clothing."

He didn't mean to glance at her new coat, but he did. She noticed. "I love the coat on you. I want to give you beautiful things." He was uncomfortable, but she looked at ease. He never knew how to take it when she got angry with him for spending money on her. "Why don't you take it off, show me your new dress? You don't need a coat in here."

"There is no dress."

He looked at her a second longer, then back at the coat. No dress? *One* layer of fabric sat between him and heaven? "You mean…?"

"Has anyone ever told you you're good at changing the subject?"

He pressed his lips together, jolted from the fantasy of what he'd find when he untied her belt, slipped each button open. He backtracked into the argument from the coat to beautiful things to her being possibly—unhappy?

"Lola, it makes me feel good to give you that life. It's a labor of love. Otherwise, what've I worked for all this time?"

After another delicate sip of wine, she said, "You were fine before I came along."

"I was fine." Beau nodded. He reached out, pulled her hand across the table, held it tightly in his. He'd mostly only seen her with nerves of steel, so her clammy palm felt foreign. She still wasn't acting like herself. Perhaps he hadn't given her the comfort she'd needed to do what she was about to do—open up to him again. "Now, I'm not fine. I'm so much more. I'm happy, Lola. Because of you. Because I—"

Lola jerked her hand back and coughed into it. She cleared her throat a couple times and drank water, droplets falling onto the tablecloth. "I'm sorry. It's the wine. It makes my throat dry." She glanced over his shoulder. "Oh, look—our food."

The waiter set down Lola's steak. Beau didn't take his eyes off her, but she examined her plate so hard, he wondered if she was avoiding him.

"Looks delicious," she said. "This place had great reviews."

Beau opened his mouth to finish what he'd been about to say, but she took a bite. He'd be damned if he told her he loved her for the first time while she had a mouthful of tenderloin. He picked up his fork and knife and cut into his T-bone, deciding to wait until later when they were home in bed. He figured there was no better time to tell her than right before she made herself most vulnerable to him.

He continued to watch her as he chewed. He did love her. It wasn't easy for him to say, never really had been, which was why he'd been trying to tell her in other ways. He'd gotten her tickets to the ballet because she'd told him how she'd taken lessons all through her childhood. That, and it was another excuse to take her out, show her off.

They ate silently. Beau didn't mind. The less talking they did, the faster they'd finish and get home. It was all he could do not to rip the fork out of her hand and hurry her to the car.

As soon as Beau had wiped his mouth with his napkin and dropped it on his plate, the waiter appeared. He must've sensed Beau's animal need to get the fuck out of there.

"Can I interest you in any dessert?"

"We're in a hurry."

"I'll bring the check, and…?"

Lola nodded up at him. He inclined his head and walked away. She took a compact mirror from her purse and reapplied her lipstick.

"What was that with the waiter?" Beau asked.

She ran the tip of her index finger along the corner of her mouth, wiped excess gloss on her napkin and shut the compact. "I have something for you."

"Give it to me at home." Beau slid out his chair, stood and buttoned his suit jacket.

She looked up, and a smile spread across her face. Now, she seemed the complete opposite of nervous. "What's the rush?"

"Weeks, Lola. It's been weeks." The waiter headed back toward them with something in his hand. "I'm dying here."

"Sit down, Beau. I promise you'll like your gift."

He unbuttoned his jacket again, ran a hand through his hair and sat. Unless his gift was Lola spread eagle on the restaurant table, he doubted it was worth another few minutes of him not having sex. "All right. Where is it?"

Lola's cheeks turned pink. "It's already here. I wanted it to be a surprise."

The waiter returned to the table and set the check in front of Beau. Next to it, he placed a flat, white box tied with a red ribbon.

Beau tilted his head. "What's this?"

"Your gift."

"I thought it would be—" He stopped. He didn't know what he'd thought, but he hadn't expected it to come in a box. He looked up at her. "I can't believe I didn't think to get you anything."

"There's no better gift you could give me than what will happen tonight. Please, open it."

Beau pulled one end of the bow, and the ribbon fell away. What could it be? He already had plenty of cologne, and an enviable collection of Montblanc pens. The box was the wrong shape for those things anyway. He listed in his head the things Brigitte or ex-girlfriends had bought him over the years—cufflinks, courtside basketball seats, a sterling silver money clip. He lifted the lid.

It took a moment to register what he was looking at. He picked up a headband topped with a pair of jet-black, furry cat ears. Each one had a smaller pink triangle in the center. "What is this?"

"It's what I'm going to wear when I dance for you tonight."

Beau's eyes jumped to hers. "Dance for me? Tonight?"

She nodded. "We've been through a lot. I want to go back to where it all started."

"The only place we're going is home." Beau tossed the ears on the table and scribbled his signature on the check. He leaned across the table toward her but didn't bother lowering his voice. "You think I'll last two minutes watching you dance for me? You'll be lucky if I don't jump across this table and give this entire restaurant a show they'll never forget. My patience is gone, Lola."

"Beau—"

"Tomorrow, I'll lounge on the couch all day long while you twirl around wearing whatever you want on your head. And I'll love every minute of it. But right now, I'm going to fuck the living daylights out of you faster than you can say pussycat."

Lola leveled her eyes on him with a playfulness that hadn't been there before. She ran her tongue along her bottom lip. "Pussycat."

Beau rose from his chair so quickly, it almost toppled over. "We're leaving."

Lola also stood, quietly placing the cat ears back in the box and covering them with the lid. "Our date isn't over. Like I said this morning, I've planned it all out."

"And I appreciate that." Beau took Lola's hand and walked away from the table, pulling her along. "You can tell me all about it on the way home."

He opened the door to the restaurant, ushered her out. One nod, and the valet took off down the sidewalk, remembering Beau and his car without prompting.

Lola yanked her hand from his. He looked back at her as she clutched the box to her chest, her breasts rising and falling. "I didn't wait this long just to have you ruin everything because you can't wait a couple more hours," she said, her face flushed, her words clipped. "Do you have any idea what tonight means to me?"

"Yes. Of course I do." Beau sighed and ran his hands over his face. "I'm going to take my time and appreciate you like I did before. I promise. But I've thought of nothing else since you told me tonight is the night, and I'm at the end of my rope here."

She approached him slowly, as if he truly might pounce. He opened his arms to show her he wasn't angry. He wasn't—just really goddamn horny.

She walked into his embrace, looking down as she played with a button on his shirt. "You've been so patient, but I want to do this one, very special thing for you first. Just one more stop. Can you give me that?"

He rubbed his hands up her back between her shoulder blades. The Lamborghini's engine rumbled as it rounded the corner. "All right, pussycat. You have me in the palm of your hand, you know that? Where are you taking me for our last stop?"

She blinked her almond-shaped blue eyes up to his, and her nose twitched. She looked remarkably feline in that moment. "I already told you. We're going back to where it all began. We're going to Cat Shoppe."

Chapter Seventeen

Beau wasn't easy to catch off guard. The incredulous expression on his face excited Lola—she would've been disappointed by anything else. The Lamborghini's growl, quiet but distinct, was the only sound. It idled at the curb where the restaurant's valet had parked it.

"We're going where?" Beau asked finally, his arms loosening around her.

"Cat Shoppe."

"You're going to wear those," he nodded at the box in her hand with the cat ears, "and dance for me?"

Lola grinned. "Surprised?"

"A little. Yes. That night you want to recreate wasn't exactly our best moment."

"I don't know," Lola said softly, fixated on his shirt button, circling her fingertip over it. "You and I remember it different."

"We do?" His chest rose with his inhalation. "You never mentioned that."

She blinked her lashes up to him again. God, those green eyes, when he focused them on her—a tornado could hit, and she wouldn't even notice. She stopped her fluttering and blinked hard, getting back on track.

She wasn't a liar at heart. With Beau, she'd been dealing words like cards from a deck, checking them close to her chest before setting them down. But this story? She didn't need to edit or tweak it. It was all true.

"A handsome stranger comes in to my shit job and demands to have me all to himself. We flirt. I brush against his leg on purpose, even though we could both get in trouble for that kind of thing." Lola leaned in and nuzzled his Sandalwood-aftershave-scented neck. "While we talk, I think to myself—this is the first time in here I've ever wished a man was just a man. Not a customer. I wonder how I can even bring up the idea of leaving with him without it sounding bad."

He looked down at her. "Is any of that true, or are you just trying to get me to agree to go?"

"Are you agreeing?"

"I had no idea you felt that way."

He would've if he'd asked, but he hadn't. She dropped her hand from his chest. "I did. I liked you. But I know that night was awful for you, and that's why I want to replace it with this one. That's your gift."

"I don't want to replace that night. I loved everything about it right up until you turned me down." Beau put his knuckle under her chin and ghosted his thumb across her bottom lip. "And we wouldn't be here right now if it hadn't happened."

Lola almost moved away from him—it never got easier, hearing him say the things she deserved to hear. But Beau was nothing if not observant when it came to her. One misstep, and he'd suspect something was wrong.

He turned first, opening the Lamborghini's passenger-side door for her. "Coming?"

She stood in place a moment, collecting herself. His spell was strong tonight—or maybe she was getting nostalgic. She could call everything off, and he'd be none the wiser. Go home, give in to the love she'd been fighting, let him take from her what he wanted. And take, take, take, always without consequence.

She got in the car. On their way to Cat Shoppe, he took her hand in his as he sometimes did when he drove. She doubted he even realized it. Like the time he'd found her in the Four Seasons lounge and wrapped her jaw in his hand. By his firm grip and unforgiving tone, he'd meant to be threatening, but he'd gently rubbed his thumb against her skin. As Beau's guard lowered, his body language became easier to read every day.

Lola glanced over at him. And every day he somehow got more handsome. Once or twice, at night, when he'd assumed she was asleep, she'd peeked at him poring over his laptop, sheets of paper all over the comforter. He'd said bringing his work to bed was a new thing for him, but either he did it there next to her or alone in his study. It was a sweet threesome—her, him and his mistress, the Bolt Ventures quarterly report.

Then, in the morning, they'd wake up together, even if she wasn't getting out of bed. Without fail, he'd lean over and whisper hotly in her ear, "Shower with me." Lola knew better than that, though. She'd been strong so far, but she wasn't made of steel.

"What's wrong?" Beau asked.

Lola blinked several times, clearing the haze of her thoughts. "What?"

He looked at her from the driver's side. "You've been staring at me."

"Oh." She sat back in her seat. "I was just thinking about how this is our last night like this."

"Like what?"

Out the windshield, Hollywood's bright lights blurred, stars pinholed the dark sky. She'd given so much thought to the details of their date that she hadn't had time to consider the next morning. What would he do?

"Never mind," she said. "In case I forget, I did laundry today, but I didn't get a chance to fold it. It's in the dryer." She picked at her fingernail. "And I moved the glasses and bowls back into their own cabinet."

"But you like them with their matching dishes."

"No, you were right. It makes more sense to sort them by type. It's your kitchen, after all."

Beau laughed harmoniously, squeezed her hand and brought it to his lips. "Relax." He pressed a quick kiss to her knuckles. "Don't be nervous. You already know how this goes."

She tilted her head in his direction. "Do I?"

"I'll do the work. I already know every single thing I'm going to do to you tonight. You just get to enjoy the ride."

He looked back at the road, but she studied his profile. Once in a while, it took all her strength to remember how she'd gotten here. It'd been a dewy Friday morning before most of the city had been awake. He'd crushed her without mercy. He'd ripped away something she'd finally let herself have—hopes and dreams for an extraordinary future with him. He was beautiful, and she loved him, but the only thing that would ease the constant throb of her broken heart was his suffering.

Lola was closing in on him. At the dinner table, she'd sensed he'd been about to tell her he loved her. It was the validation she'd been hoping for, but she'd interrupted him, suddenly terrified that if he said it, she wouldn't be able to go through with tonight.

She didn't need to hear it anyway. She already knew he loved her—she just wanted him to know it too. If he didn't, he would soon.

"Enjoy the ride?" she whispered to herself. "I think I will."

◆⊠◆⊠◆

Typical for a Friday night, Sunset Boulevard was clogged with traffic. It was a small detail that hadn't crossed Lola's mind, but as they crept down the street toward Cat Shoppe, then passed it, her spine lengthened.

"What're you doing?" she asked Beau.

He flipped on his blinker, waiting for the cars in front of them to move. "Parking around back. There weren't any spots on the street, and I don't have the patience to wait for one."

Her throat went dry. The first time he'd brought her here, he'd slid into a front spot. That was how she'd envisioned this going, and it could pose a problem later. She craned her neck, praying for an open spot. "You don't want to leave your car in back."

"Why not?"

She adjusted her buttoned-up collar, already dampening with sweat. The air was cool, but it suddenly seemed fucking stupid to have worn a coat she couldn't take off until they were alone. "Shady characters. There's, like, no lights in the parking lot. A car like this won't last five minutes."

He laughed as traffic opened up, allowing him to turn onto a side street that led to the back. "There're lots of people out tonight. It'll be fine."

She rubbed her hairline. If she pushed it, he'd ask her why it mattered to her. She'd just have to work around it.

Beau pulled into a spot and shut off the car. They sat there for an unusually still moment, a dreamlike state, Lola still not sure she could pull this off. Maybe if she didn't move, she wouldn't have to. She shook her head quickly to shoo the ridiculous thought. This was what she'd wanted for weeks, and she wasn't turning back now.

Beau looked at her in the dark. "Thank you."

"For what?" she asked, keeping her eyes forward.

He reached over and turned her head to him. He leaned in, pulling her closer by her chin, and kissed her once on the lips. "Sometimes I forget how it feels to receive a gift without a price tag. I know you put a lot of thought into this."

"I did." Lola forced herself not to look away. Was he just figuring out that what made something special was the thought behind it, not the dollar amount? Sporadic comments like those made her think Beau was changing in little ways, that maybe he wouldn't always put money and work first. She hoped he'd keep going down that path. "There's something else."

"More?"

Lola removed the lid from the box in her lap and held up the cat ears. "As soon as I put these on my head, I'm no longer your girlfriend. I'm a stranger. A—sex worker."

The corner of his mouth crooked into a smile. He dropped his hand to one of her thighs, squeezing it right under the hem of her coat. "Is it bad if that excites me?"

Lola removed his hand by his wrist and placed it back on his side of the car. "That means absolutely no touching tonight. You're getting an authentic experience. You're my customer, and you've hired me to dance for you, just like you did that first night. Which means keeping your hands to yourself."

Beau sighed up at the roof. "I've come this far—what's a little longer?" He looked back over at her. "Anything else, my queen?"

No—there was nothing else. Except that she couldn't seem to move from that spot and get out of the car. He was being so good tonight. Attentive. A real boyfriend—better than Johnny, even better than Beau at his best. "Yes," she said softly. "Kiss me."

Beau put his hand to her cheek without hesitation. He inclined over the console and brushed the tip of his nose against hers. He pecked her once, but she put her arms around his neck before he could pull away. They opened their mouths to each other at the same time, their warm tongues meeting in the middle. It wasn't in her plan. It wasn't even her parting gift to him. This one was just for her.

He inhaled and separated from her but kept his forehead pressed against hers. "You sure you don't want to just go home?"

She hesitated to seem genuine, but she was ready. She was picturing ahead to being inside, dancing close to him, turning him raw and defenseless. She lifted the cat ears on her index finger and dangled them in front of him. "Want to do the honors?"

He took the headband and placed it over her hair. "Perfect."

Beau got out and rounded the car to get her door. He held out a hand to help her, but she shook her head at him.

"Right," he said, dropping it back to his side. "No touching."

She unfolded out of the Lamborghini, and they walked around to the front, shoulder to shoulder.

The bouncer took one look at Lola and opened the velvet rope for them. "Evening, Miss Winters."

"You really went all out, didn't you?" Beau asked behind her.

She ignored him and passed through the entryway into the club. The music hit her like a fist to the gut, uglier than usual, all hard bass without any detectable rhythm. Or maybe her brain was jumbling things that didn't matter, unable to afford the extra attention. Kincaid was at the bar, watching over things like he sometimes did. Neon streaks cut through the dark like they were trying to dismember him. They exchanged a nod.

"Follow me," she said to Beau over her shoulder. She was in charge for once. That was how she knew she had Beau. He was letting her get away with more than he would anyone else, especially tonight.

She walked him down a long hallway until they reached the last door. There, Lola took a moment to herself. With a deep breath, she adjusted her headband

and smoothed her hand over her trench coat. What had Kincaid called her earlier that day?

"The cat that swallowed the canary."

She liked that. She'd have to remember it.

Lola opened the door and led Beau into their final moments together.

Chapter Eighteen

Cat Shoppe's VIP room was more than familiar to Lola and Beau. After all, this would be their third time renting it.

"VIP?" Beau asked from behind her as they entered.

"It was either here or out there," Lola teased, nodding toward the main stage.

Beau stepped so close to her, she felt his heat on her back. "You don't think I'd let you dance out there, where anyone could see. Do you?"

Lola walked deeper into the room to get away from him. Just being back there, remembering how she'd gotten to her knees and sucked him off, was enough to make her heart beat a little faster. She gestured toward the red-velvet couch, which curved around the circular room. "Sit."

He obeyed, easing into the seat, looking amused as he crossed an ankle over his knee. "If I'm the customer, aren't I in charge?"

"If it makes you feel better to think so." Lola took her time unknotting the belt of her trench coat. "Sometimes I'm not sure which one of us is in charge—but I guess that's just the dynamic of our relationship, isn't it?"

He wasn't listening. His eyes were fixed on her hands as she slid each button through its slit. Appreciating her, that was what he liked. Owning her body, even from a distance. The poor man hadn't even seen her tits since the night she'd fled his hotel room.

She removed the seventeen-hundred dollar trench coat and let it fall on the ground.

His foot slipped, and he planted it on the floor, leaning his elbows onto his legs. "Fuck. Lola."

"I'm not Lola in here." This wasn't just about revenge. Beau wasn't the only one who could have fun. Her real name would be a clue, but he was so distracted, he would miss it. "I go by Melody."

She stared at him, staring at her. He didn't move or even blink, but he didn't look particularly happy either. For the first time, she noticed how quiet the room was except for the bass thumping from the main stage.

She glanced down quickly, checking her outfit—could she have forgotten an important part? The Swarovski-studded corset pushed her breasts up, plump and smooth. Where the hem stopped, a black, lacey thong started and attached to matching, thigh-high stockings. The ears had come with a black cattail she'd haphazardly pinned to her underwear in the restaurant's bathroom.

He still hadn't reacted. She tried not to fidget. "Do you like it?"

He cocked his head, stabbing his tongue into his cheek. "It's the same thing you wore that night."

"Is that a yes?"

He rubbed his hands over his face without removing his eyes from her. "I don't know. It makes me think of how you used to dance here. And the other men who came before me."

Lola shifted from one foot to the other. The point was to trigger his memory, to make him crazy for her. Jealousy was an unexpected reaction. "It was a long time ago."

"So? Those men looked at something they had no right to." His eyes were dark and narrowed when he finally looked up at her face. "They sat here. They thought about you when they got home. They're animals. They're—"

"They're *you*." Lola took a breath. There was too much bitterness in her voice, and *he* wasn't supposed to get to *her*. "You were one of them."

"I was not." He shook his head and blinked a few times, hard.

Lola tried to keep her limbs loose when all she wanted to do was tense up. This was not going as she'd hoped. "What are you saying?"

They stared at each other. If he got up to leave, she might not be able to stop him. It took a great deal to distract a man like Beau—she'd hoped two-and-a-half weeks of keeping his hands to himself would be enough.

He glanced behind her briefly and back. "I don't know. I can't think straight when you're standing there in that." His eyebrows lowered. "Take it off."

Her body thrilled. He was giving her the green light. This was the Beau she'd been anticipating. She traced her finger along the corset's sweetheart neckline. "And if I don't?"

"Then I'll do it for you. I wanted tonight to be special, but you want to get bent over in a filthy strip club? I'm game, baby. It'll be just as sweet for me anywhere I fuck you."

Lola flushed all at once, as if she'd swallowed a ball of fire. She was back in his hotel room, crawling to him across the floor, the opposite of mad about it. Staying apart had been hard for her too. There were times she'd wanted nothing more than to give in to his advances, let him pleasure her the way she already knew he could.

"Remember what I said outside. I'm serious." Lola turned away from him. She had to be careful. Nothing made her knees quiver faster than Beau at the end of his patience, nothing on his mind but how to get inside her.

She crouched to slip an iPod from the pocket of her trench coat, then plugged it into the stereo. Jazz started slow, sensual. *Fever* was something you wanted when Shirley Horn sang about it in her smoky, hypnotic voice.

Lola got on the round stage, a pole down the center, the same one she'd danced on for him before. Tonight, the room didn't turn colors—there was just a single, white spotlight from the ceiling that illuminated her and shaded him.

Lola looked down at her feet and took a couple deep breaths, exhaling each one slowly. She glanced up at him. Her lashes were heavy with mascara, a black shadow over Beau. She hadn't even begun, and her chest already rose and fell rapidly. She did love to dance, especially for Beau, because she felt him in her every move. He could direct her without a word or touch.

She took the pole, cold and solid, and started in a slow circle. Her resolve strengthened each time her heels hit the compact floor. She slid her palm high up the smooth surface, grabbed the pole with both hands. She jumped it like a boyfriend she hadn't seen in years, swinging with her legs locked around it. The furry cattail belted her thigh.

Beau flexed his large hands over his knees. "Come here."

Still suspended from the pole, with both hands gripping the metal, Lola arched her back. Her hair cascaded behind her. She lowered herself to her feet and turned away from him, zigzagging her hips as she danced into a squat. Watching him, she zigzagged back up.

His eyes followed her every movement. He looked like he'd forgotten how to swallow. "I surrender. You've got me. Just come down here."

"Patience," she said, turning to face him. With a hint of a smile, she unhooked her corset just enough to free everything above her nipples. "This isn't about satisfaction. It's about torment."

"It's about me climbing on that stage in two seconds and nailing you to that pole."

Lola practically purred her assent, her insides turning to jelly with his tone. This was working even faster than she'd expected. She descended the steps steadily, keeping her eyes down, and went to stand between his parted knees. She turned slowly. Lola liked to feel free when she danced, but she forced her hips to stay with the tempo. Beau would pick up her cues, staying slow along with her.

He grabbed her tail. She turned her head over her shoulder and tsked at him.

He smiled a little and let go. "You have no idea, do you?"

"What?"

"How it's been for me." His face fell. "How fucking badly I've needed you."

"It's been like that for me too," Lola said, still twisted to see his eyes, still dancing.

"Has it? Sometimes I don't know."

Lola faltered but didn't stop. These moments of clarity he kept having weren't helping. She hadn't anticipated anything from him other than consuming, dumb lust. "I don't know what you mean."

"You still have a wall up, and I can't blame you for that. But I'll break it down with every last tool I have. I'm doing the work, Lola. Even if you can't see it all the time."

She swallowed. The finality of it all began to sink in. Once upon a time, Lola and Beau had made a plan to spend all their nights together. Now, they didn't even have one left. It was another thing Beau had taken away—this was *his* fault, not hers. He had ruined this.

"Don't call me that," she said, angry. "I told you. It's Melody."

Beau raked a hand through his hair, disheveling its perfection. "Would you stop moving a minute?"

"You ordered me to dance."

"Well, now I'm ordering you to stop."

Lola stilled her hips and looked at the floor. She'd spent the last three weeks studying him. Learning him inside out. Handling him. She could do this. She turned to face him.

"I—" He paused and took a breath.

Lola's heart began to race. There was no way he'd tell her he loved her *here* of all places. In the middle of a striptease. Part of her wanted to hear it, but the part that wanted to leave was stronger.

She climbed onto the cushion and straddled him with her knees, careful not to touch him.

"I should've stopped this already," he said. "I don't want to do this here."

Lola lowered her voice to a sultry whisper. "Then where do you want to do it?"

"At home. In our bed."

She couldn't resist getting a little closer. He smelled like the man who'd uttered nothings in her ear—who'd made love to her while he'd fucked her. But her love for him had torn through her like a hurricane too many times, trying to bring her down. She gripped the cushion behind his shoulders and steeled herself against the urge to give in to him.

She glanced at his lap. "You're hard, Beau. Do you want me?"

He groaned. "On your knees, on your stomach, on your back. Every way. Any way."

She almost sucked in a breath, wanting that too, but she only needed to be strong a little longer. She opened her mouth and finally said what she'd been thinking for weeks. "Your hands are the only ones that ever lit a fire under my skin. God, Beau. I dream about you touching me at night, and I fantasize about it during the day."

"I want to," he said. "I need to."

"I'm right here."

"You made me promise…"

She inhaled his scent, committing it to memory along with the things that were already there—his foggy-green eyes, his razorblade jawline and sexy cleft chin. His thawing embrace. "It's too much. You told me once, when you fucked me, it would calm me. I can't even see straight."

He grabbed her by the waist, making her gasp, and pulled her onto him. He yanked her thong out of the way and sank a finger in her.

Lola threw her head back, bit her lip to keep quiet and looked directly into the surveillance camera. She didn't expect the second finger, and she moaned gutturally.

"There's my girl," Beau said.

There was an eruption, and Lola looked back just as the door bounced off the wall. Beau was still gawking, knuckles deep inside her when she was hauled backward off his lap.

Beau's hands were suspended, open and empty. "What—"

A security guard seized his bicep, pulling Beau to his feet. "You're out, pal."

"Get your hands—" Beau jerked his arm away. "Don't touch me."

The man's muscles, as big as Lola's head, stretched the sleeves of a faded-black T-shirt. His face reddened. "Exactly. Did you miss the huge fucking sign out there that says '*no touching*'?"

"She's my *girlfriend*," Beau said, his voice as sharp-cornered as his back was rigid.

Another security guard entered the room and got between Lola and Beau. "You good, Havermann?"

Beau laughed like a shotgun, short, aggressive barks. "Is this some kind of joke?"

"No joke," the man called Havermann said. He reached up but stopped as Beau raised his hands, a warning to back off. "You don't touch the girls. Everyone knows that. Automatic removal. Let's go. Now."

Beau looked between Lola and the man too quickly to even register her. "She's not one of your girls. She's mine, and I don't like how you're blocking her from me," he said to Havermann. "Get the fuck out of my way. Lola, tell them."

Lola opened her mouth. *I have to settle the bill. I'll meet you out front.* She froze, unable to get the words out.

Havermann moved, obstructing Beau almost completely from Lola's sight. "Don't worry about her. You got another concern right now—me. Get out, or I put you out."

"Beau, go," Lola said suddenly, trying to shuffle around Havermann. She didn't want it to get physical. "I'll meet you out front."

"And leave you here alone?" Beau lurched from side to side to see her better. "Are you out of your mind?"

The other security guard crossed his arms. "You got three seconds."

Lola bit her thumbnail. "Go ahead. I know these guys. I just have to settle the bill, and get my things—"

"I'll buy you new things."

One of the men grunted. "Three."

Her heart pounded as she hesitated. "I'll only be a minute—"

"Two."

"Did you not hear what I said?" Beau snapped. "So help me God, Lola. Leave your shit, and let's fucking go. *Now.*"

Havermann's chest swelled. "I'm not letting her leave with you. Not when you talk to her like that." He lunged for Beau's arm. "Come—"

Havermann stumbled when Beau stepped back. "Put your hand on me again, I'll break every bone in it."

"You got a fucking death wish?" Havermann grabbed Beau's lapel and yanked, but Beau was faster. He already had two fistfuls of Havermann's SECURITY shirt as he threw him backward into a wall. Beau pulled Havermann forward and slammed his body a second time. "I don't think you understand."

Lola covered her open mouth. She was as afraid of his expression as she was of him taking on two security guards. "Beau—"

"I've been this way for weeks," Beau said through gritted teeth. "I'm on the edge, and in two seconds, you're going to know exactly what that means. I'm holding back because jail is the only place I'll be worse off."

The other security guard pulled Beau off by the back of his suit. "All right, ladies, enough."

Beau was breathing hard. He stared Havermann down as he was dragged away, then looked pointedly at Lola. "Let's go."

Havermann regained his footing, pinching at his shirt like it was a fine suit. "Just get the fuck out. She said she'll meet you in front. You got to cool off before we leave her alone with you."

"Jesus Christ. She's my goddamn girlfriend."

"Yeah, we heard you." Each of the men took an arm, forcing Beau out of the room.

Lola stood frozen to the spot, her blood rushing, her head spinning like she'd spent the last two minutes running in circles. She held her hands out for balance, worried she'd have to sit, and she didn't have time to sit. It could've gotten violent. But it hadn't. It hadn't, it wouldn't, and it wasn't her problem anyway. She didn't deserve to be the one coming to Beau's defense when the pain he'd inflicted on her was worse than any fist to the stomach.

She flinched with her entire body and snatched her trench coat off the floor. She got it on, throwing the belt into a knot, and stopped at the door. Her plan had worked. Not as smoothly as she'd hoped, but it had—and this? This was the easy part. Walk away. Let go, so everything else could take course. Her dignity, her power—they were there for the taking. She just had to walk away.

She looked down the hall, the way they'd come. It was quiet. Her steps were brisk but her strides long as her memory guided her to Cat Shoppe's backdoor. When Lola had worked there, she and the other girls would slip outside between numbers, leaving a heel in the doorway so they wouldn't get locked out. Lola yanked on the handle, but it didn't budge. Her heart, already racing, began to hammer.

"Damn it," she whispered, pulling it with all her weight. Stuck like a mouse in a cage. There was only one other way out, and Beau was waiting there. She could picture him, a fuming bull, eyes squinted and nostrils flared, his urges pinballing between mowing the place down with his car, breaking Havermann's arms and fucking through his rage.

"Sometimes it sticks," Lola heard from behind her.

Lola whirled around. Marilyn, the bartender-stripper she'd met earlier that day, stood three feet away in her white, vinyl bikini and blonde wig. Lola cleared her throat. "I, um—need a cigarette."

"You don't got to explain. I heard some of what you said to Kincaid today. He hurt you, that guy you came in with?"

"Not like you think."

Marilyn nodded as though she'd heard it a hundred times. "I've been there." She reached over and jerked the handle upward, throwing herself into the door. "There you go," she said as it opened. "We've got to help each other out, right? Some of us really got nobody."

Lola exhaled an unsteady but relieved breath. Something about Marilyn struck her as trustworthy. Maybe it was that no matter how Lola dressed or did her makeup, she'd always have some of the Cat Shoppe girl in her.

Lola reached out and hugged her. They each went completely stiff. For the first time, Lola realized how far she'd gone to sterilize her heart for Beau—it was extending outside of their relationship now.

"Please, don't mention this to anyone," Lola said.

Marilyn shouldered her way out of the embrace, a tight-lipped but sincere smile on her face. She pinched her fingertips together and slid them across her closed mouth. "Our secret."

Lola leaned outside, peering into the dark. It took her eyes a moment to adjust. The backdoor closed and latched, swallowing the club's music. There wasn't time to spare, she knew that. Beau's car sat at the edge of the lot, and she tried to make out the driver's seat. It looked empty.

She took off the cat ears and walked toward his Lamborghini, passing her thumb back and forth over the fur band. Something scurried across her path, and she stopped short, clamping a hand over her mouth to keep herself from screaming. She inhaled a breath and continued to the driver's side.

Beau was smart. Cunning. He would figure out why she'd left, but not at first. She needed to leave something behind so he'd understand she'd made this choice. Otherwise, he might involve the cops. And she didn't need that. She twisted the Lamborghini's side mirror up, kissed the glass and hung the cat ears on it.

She pulled her coat tighter around her body and strode toward an alley, glancing over her shoulder before she entered. The only light came from a Thai restaurant's illuminated sign at the other end. She'd been eating there for years. When she exited the alley, she waved through the window.

The owner met her out front with a plastic bag of hot food and a single key. Lola handed him a fifty, waving off the change. "Thanks for keeping an eye on it."

Directly in front of the building was a car, but not just any car. It was a brand new, violently-red Lotus Evora she'd purchased that afternoon—in cash. She slipped into the driver's seat—the fresh, unbroken leather giving her a noisy welcome—and put the key in the ignition. It was easy—all she had to do was turn it, and she was home free.

Lola had been dealing with men since she was a teenager. They weren't difficult creatures. Beau was in love with Lola. And Lola knew as early as six years old, when her father had left, that your first broken heart was also your most painful. That was what she wanted for Beau. It was simple but effective—moving something he loved just outside his grasp was enough to drive him to the edge. Because one thing was for sure about a man who already owned anything money could buy—the only things left to want were the ones he couldn't have.

They were both getting what they deserved. Her, a chance to start over and find peace, and him—nothing. They couldn't both win the game. She had to choose herself over Beau.

Lola started the car. She didn't have to go by Cat Shoppe on her way, but it would be her only glimpse of victory, even if it was through her black-tinted windows. She looped around and waited for a lull in traffic, then drove by the flashing, neon *Girls* sign. Beau paced the sidewalk, his eyes glued to Cat Shoppe's front door. Had he understood, while being escorted out against his will, how little control he really had? Had he started to realize yet just how much he'd lost?

Lola turned her eyes back to the road, pressed her high heel to the gas pedal and gunned it.

She was out of town within half an hour.

Chapter Nineteen

Tick.
Tick.
Tick.

Beau didn't remove his eyes from Cat Shoppe's front door except to check his Rolex. Seconds slid by in a steady rhythm until almost ten minutes had passed. The bouncer sat on a stool, watching Beau pace like a caged tiger. He'd been instructed to remain twenty feet from the entrance.

"I just want my girlfriend so I can get the fuck out of here," Beau said across the sidewalk.

"Any closer, and you're leaving here in cuffs. Like I said, security didn't take too kindly to your attitude."

Beau pulled his wallet from his suit jacket. "A hundred bucks if you get her out here for me."

The bouncer remained slumped on his seat, chewing gum like it was his job. After a few seconds, he shifted to unclip a radio from his belt. "What's she look like?"

"We arrived together. Black hair, tall."

He globed a hand in front of his chest. "I mean the titties—big? Small?"

Beau glared. "Fuck you. That's my girlfriend."

"Hey, I don't mind the small ones. More of an ass man myself." He chuckled, held the receiver to his mouth. "You got a read on the chick in the kitten ears?" He winked at Beau.

Of course the doorman had noticed Lola, her black Burberry trench and red pout. He had a heartbeat, didn't he? Beau tugged at the ends of his shirtsleeves, though what he really wanted to do was push them up, knock the fucker out along with the rest of the men in that place. They stood between Beau and something that was his. He would've barged back in to get to her, but that'd either land him in a hospital or a jail cell, and then he'd be leaving Lola alone with brutes. He wiped sweat from his hairline, an all too familiar feeling settling in him as the image of Lola with a gun under her chin flashed by.

The radio shrieked with static. "It's Kincaid. That was Lola Winters, worked here back in the day. We checked everywhere. She's gone."

They looked at each other. Beau took a step closer. "Gone?"

"You sure, boss?" the man asked. "She didn't come out this way."

The LED *Girls* sign by the door burned into Beau's retinas. He rubbed his eyes with stiff fingers, searched the sidewalk. The street was busy with cars. A group of people passed by, looking at him, none of them even remotely familiar—as if he'd exited the strip club onto another planet.

Beau took out his phone, his adrenaline spiking when he saw that neither of his last two text messages to Lola had gone through.

"She ain't in here," Kincaid said. "Must've gone out the back."

"There's a backdoor?" Beau started toward the corner.

"Yo—what about my money?" the doorman called after him.

Beau broke into a jog, shouldering through a human cluster. Lola'd definitely promised to meet him out front. Had she needed a quick exit from security? Coming here had been a bad idea. Parking in back, where she was probably waiting in the dark, was a bad idea.

His Lamborghini was in an end spot, close to the street. The only light was a distant sidewalk lamp. Not a person in sight. He looked in the passenger's side window. He got onto his hands and knees to check underneath. She wasn't there, or behind a nearby dumpster, or in the next building's parking lot. He went to the backdoor and pulled on the handle, banged on the metal slab.

He called her. A black shadow near the driver's side door caught his eye—something hanging from the side mirror. He got closer, bending to see it better.

After three melodic beeps over the line, he heard, *"We're sorry, you have reached a number that has been disconnected or is no longer in service. If you feel you have reached this recording in error—"*

Beau ended the call and picked up Lola's black kitten ears. On the glass was a red lipstick mark in the shape of a kiss. He looked between the headband and the mirror. The ears had been on her head. She'd been wearing red lipstick. Had Lola been outside at some point in the last fifteen minutes?

He looked up suddenly. "Lola?" he called, her name fading instantly. "This isn't funny. It's not safe out here."

He turned in a circle. It *wasn't* funny, but no part of him thought this was a joke. The strip club had been busy, but he hadn't noticed a single person. Not one except her. That didn't mean someone hadn't noticed them. He tried to picture a face, anyone's face, or something out of the ordinary. The only thing he saw was Lola's back as she'd led him to the VIP room.

He clutched the cat ears. He'd let security separate them. He shouldn't've left her side, not without a fight. Someone might've hurt her, drugged her, taken her somewhere.

He turned and kicked the dumpster. A metallic thud echoed around the lot, reminding him how empty it was. He paced the sidewalk, rubbing his temples. *Think, think, think.* He was used to remaining calm during a crisis, but his thoughts jumbled. His palms sweat. Her phone was disconnected—how long did that take? Could it be done in—? He checked his watch. Eighteen minutes?

He beat the door with his fist until his palm began to throb, and finally, it cracked open with a heavy click. An older man peered at him. "What?"

"Where is she?"

"I told you already." The man spit chewing tobacco on the sidewalk next to Beau's feet. "She ain't in here."

"She has to be. She's not out here." Beau took a threatening step closer. "You know her?"

The man just looked him over. "Yeah. I'm the owner, Kincaid."

"So what the fuck happened tonight?"

"Not my business. You take that up with her." He went to shut the door, but Beau grabbed it, stopping it cold. Kincaid was short and squat, not nearly as meaty as the security guards.

"Tell me, or I'll get LAPD here within five minutes. I know the chief. You don't want them sniffing around."

He shrugged. "Call them. I got nothing to hide. Maybe you ought to get the police on the phone anyway, because like I said ten times already, your girl isn't in here. And I tell you, I got a real thing about possessive boyfriends. Don't like them, don't want them hanging around. Kind of a pet peeve I got."

Beau didn't remove his hand from the door. He didn't know the police chief personally, but he had a solid link to him. He wasn't going to involve him, though, not yet anyway. He'd had a neighbor call the police on him once, when he and Brigitte had lived in a dump with thin walls, and she'd gotten hysterical over something. The officer'd arrived to find her calm and charming, and by the time he'd left, it was with her phone number. The police had done nothing for Beau that day or since, and they certainly wouldn't give a fuck about a woman who'd gone missing from a strip club twenty minutes ago.

"All right," Beau said, lining up his options. "Okay. What do you want? Money?"

Kincaid reeled slowly back, as if Beau'd offered him a bag of shit. "I want you to get the fuck off my property. That's all we been telling you since the moment you touched her."

"Just tell me why. Why'd you kick me out?"

Kincaid sighed, looked around the lot. "Something fishy here, but if it'll get you to leave, I'll tell you. Lola was here this afternoon, said she was bringing you by, said if you touched her, I should remove you. Treat you like any other customer, but I'll be honest, the guys went easy on you. Weren't really sure what we were dealing with."

Beau breathed through his nose, trying, failing, to put the pieces together. She'd arranged it beforehand, that he'd known, but why go through everything she did, from warning him not to touch her to begging him to? "If I find out she's in there—"

"She ain't. She got a key to your place?"

"Of course."

"Probably at home then. Good luck." Kincaid pulled on the door, and Beau released it. He fumbled with his keys, got into his car and sat with his hands gripping the wheel. He shut his eyes and envisioned himself at the head of his boardroom faced with a problem. Everyone around the table, looking to him for the solution. Because there was an answer. He just needed to find it.

Beau was no angel—he had enemies. Powerful ones. Business was their battlefield. It'd never crossed into personal territory for him—but perhaps he'd pissed off the wrong person.

Beau opened his eyes and looked into the side mirror again, the lip mark plastered on his reflection. It seemed like a message that had nothing to do with business. It was a stretch, thinking someone had targeted Lola to get back at him. Those weren't the kind of enemies he'd made, and Lola wasn't a damsel in distress.

Beau tried her cell again and got the same recording. He turned his phone over in his hand, checked the screen and battery. He dialed Warner as it occurred to him Lola might've contacted him for a ride.

Beau spoke as soon as the line clicked. "Warner, have you heard from—"

"—reached the voicemail of—"

He hung up. Of all the days he could've given Warner off. He called the house, reasoning if Lola had left right after he'd seen her, she could be back there by now, but nobody answered.

There was only one other place she could be, and the last place he wanted to go. He started the car, the engine waking up like a hungry lion. As he pulled out of the parking lot, he made another call.

"Hey Joe." It was a man, not difficult to figure out which one.

Beau cursed silently. He wasn't about to ask Lola's ex-boyfriend if he'd seen her. Lola had talked about two other people she'd worked with, Amanda, who'd blown Johnny, and Veronica, a friend.

"Hello?" Johnny asked.

"I'm calling for Veronica."

"One sec. Vero!"

Beau waited through some shuffling until a woman came on the line. "Yeah?" she asked, already wary.

"Is this Veronica?"

"Who is this?"

"I'm looking for Lola Winters. Have you seen her tonight?"

Veronica grunted. "She doesn't work here anymore."

"Have you seen her, though? Tonight? Is she there now?"

"Now? I haven't seen her since—"

"Who is that?" Beau heard in the background, Johnny again.

"Nobody," Vero said. There was more rustling on the line. "Johnny, what—mind your own fucking business."

"Sounds like my business," he said.

"It's not. Go pour a drink or something."

Beau was halfway between Hey Joe and Cat Shoppe now. He didn't want to go in if he didn't have to. No good would come from being in the same room with Johnny.

"You still there?" Veronica asked after a few silent seconds.

"You haven't seen her since when?" Beau asked.

"Since before she and Johnny broke up. I heard she was with you."

Beau glanced out his window. "You know who I am?"

"You have a way of sticking out. How come you're calling here asking for her when you know she don't work here?"

"You're sure she's not there? If she is, I need to talk to her. It's important."

"I'd tell you if she were. I love her to death, that's why I never want to see her in here again. She don't belong."

Beau frowned. He wouldn't like that either, Lola going to Hey Joe if she were in trouble. "If you see her, tell her to call me. It's important."

"You said that already." She sighed into the phone. "Look, I have to go. Johnny's giving me the death stare."

"Don't mention this to him."

"I won't. My loyalty left the building with Lola once I found about Amanda."

Lola must not've talked to her about Beau, then. Veronica would've certainly shared her opinion of him if she had. Beau stopped mid-Boulevard and flipped the car around. "Thanks for your help," he said and hung up.

Lola was out there, alone, in the dark. He couldn't remember if she'd taken her purse inside. He leaned over to the passenger's side as he drove, feeling around, then did the same in the backseat. No purse. At least she had that, unlike the morning she'd walked home from the Four Seasons. His heart palpitated the same way it had that day, when he'd realized he had no way of getting ahold of her.

Beau was driving in the direction of his house, but he had no idea if it was the right place to be. His phone rang, and he grabbed it without even checking the screen. "Lola?"

"Sorry I missed your call, sir."

"Warner." Beau shut his eyes briefly, a current of dread running through him. "Is Lola with you?"

Warner hesitated. "Is she supposed to be?"

"I can't find her. She disappeared in the middle of our date. I was hoping she'd called you to pick her up."

"No, sir. I haven't heard from her. Have you tried the house?"

Three weeks earlier, when she'd walked out of his life, *she'd* found *him*. Maybe she was already at home. He'd heard when it came to a missing person, it was best to stay in one place so they could find you "Not yet."

"Maybe she took a—one minute." His voice went distant. "Yes, it is. Something about Lola going missing. Just let me—"

"If that's Brigitte," Beau said, "I don't have time. Just let me know if you hear from Lola." Beau hung up, more confident that he'd walk in the front door and find Lola in the kitchen, eating spoonfuls of Rocky Road from the carton the way she sometimes did.

He made it home in record time, parking in the driveway and jogging up to the front. He dropped his keys, cursed as he picked them up, and finally got the door open. The house was dark.

"Lola?" he called out, flipping the switch for the chandelier. He tossed his keys on the table and headed through the house, turning on a light in every room. As he entered the kitchen, he prayed for the glow of the refrigerator, the sound of silverware, anything. There was nothing. He went to stand in the middle of the room. "Hello?"

He heard footsteps behind him, the click of high heels. Relief spread through him.

"Beau."

He turned around as a light came on above him. Brigitte and Warner stood in the kitchen doorway, as far as they could get from him. "What're you doing here?"

"We were concerned," Brigitte said. "What the hell happened?"

Beau shook his head, checked his phone and set it on the counter. "Honestly, I don't even know."

"Warner, get him water." Brigitte crossed the kitchen toward him. "You don't look good."

"I'm fine. I mean—I'm not. I'm fucking worried. But not about myself."

Warner opened and closed cabinets.

Brigitte leaned a hip on the counter. "Start from the beginning."

"We went out to dinner. It was a special occasion, and she wanted to plan the evening. She said it was a surprise."

"What was the occasion?"

Beau opened his mouth. The occasion was private, that's what it was—him, finally getting to show her what love meant to him. Upstairs, in their bedroom, removing her trench coat. Crawling over her body as she breathed heavily on the bed, anticipating his first touch.

"That's not important," Beau said.

"I don't understand. What happened at the restaurant?"

"It wasn't there." Beau would've rather kept the details to himself, but this whole thing was getting bigger, and he was willing to sacrifice some privacy for answers. Several times over the years, he'd come to Brigitte with a business problem, and she would point out the piece of the puzzle he'd been missing. She had a surprising knack for empathy when she tried, unlike Beau. "We were at Cat Shoppe."

"You're kidding," Brigitte said, deadpan.

"I wish I were. Some way of replacing our past, I guess."

Brigitte looked at Warner. "What's taking you so long?"

"The cups moved again."

"I can get my own water." Beau remembered that Lola'd rearranged things. He wasn't even thirsty, but he went and got a glass, needing something to do with his hands. "So she had a special dance planned. She warned me not to touch her, but I thought we were playing some kind of game. Because as soon as I put my hands on her—"

She had begged him with her eyes. Tempted him with each sultry movement. He would've done anything for her in those moments, crazy for her.

"What?" Brigitte prompted. "What happened when you touched her?"

"She just…disappeared."

Chapter Twenty

Brigitte and Warner stood side by side in Beau's kitchen, quieted by the details of Beau's night. Beau drank the last of his water, set it on the counter, looked at it. Nobody spoke.

"…I moved the glasses and bowls back into their own cabinet...it's your kitchen, after all."

Lola had come into his home and disrupted his system. During the ten years Brigitte had lived there, she'd tried to do the same, but Beau'd always put up a fight. Not with Lola. He was happy she could make those little changes that made her feel at home.

Beau'd found her unprompted comments earlier about laundry and dishes adorably amusing, her nerves obviously strung tight. Her behavior had been mildly strange all day, though, up until she'd sat him down in the VIP room. She'd been collected then, as if she'd done that dance a hundred times. She *had*, but he didn't want to get that same dance. It should've made all the difference that it was him sitting in that seat.

A pit of doubt formed in his stomach. Perhaps her comments hadn't been so offhanded. Maybe they were meant to serve as a hint, something more significant than he'd thought.

He looked up from the glass. "I'm out of options. I have to call the police."

"Not yet. Just wait a minute." Brigitte played with her bottom lip. She'd been staring out the window behind him for a good two minutes, since he'd finished telling them exactly what'd happened. Brigitte went and got the cat ears from the foyer table. Beau didn't even realize he'd brought them in. "You said these were just hanging on your driver's side mirror? And her phone's disconnected?"

"Yes."

Brigitte's expression changed, her eyebrows angling inward. Beau didn't get looks of pity often. "Beau…"

"Never mind." He picked up his phone again. He had more phone calls to make, starting with the LAPD. If Brigitte was going to tell him this wasn't an accident, he didn't want to hear it.

"I think—"

"I don't care what you think." He focused on scrolling through his contact list. "You don't know the whole situation."

"Warner, give us a minute." Brigitte waited until Warner had left the room to come over and touch Beau's forearm. "Come upstairs with me before you call anyone. I want to see one thing."

Beau hovered his thumb over the call button.

"If I'm wrong, we'll call the police."

Beau returned his phone to his pocket. "What's upstairs?"

She left the kitchen, and he followed. Before reaching the second floor, she glanced back, as if to make sure he was still there. In his bedroom, she opened the closet's double doors. She ignored Beau's side and went to Lola's dresser. The top drawer was full of lacy undergarments.

"Is it all there?" Brigitte asked.

"How should I know? I don't keep track of her fucking panties." Beau went deeper into the closet as Brigitte shut the drawer and checked the one underneath it. "What are you looking for?"

She didn't answer. Beau sifted through Lola's dresses and touched the peach-colored one he'd bought her for their evening at the ballet. For once, he'd gotten her out of black—her go-to, safety color. She'd looked stunning. Good enough to eat—and he would've, had he had the chance. He slid the smooth silk through his hand. Any excuse he could think of to touch her that night, he'd used. She'd let him, up until a certain point, and then she'd politely moved his hand away and said, "Beau, you promised." He couldn't count the number of times she'd said that to him. Yes, he'd promised, but he was only a man, not a fucking saint.

Brigitte was at the bottom drawer now. She slammed it shut, squatted on the floor.

"Brigitte, I'm wasting time."

"I don't know. Maybe I'm wrong. It looks like all her stuff is here."

"Why wouldn't it be?"

She didn't look up at Beau, and that made him nervous. Normally, she delivered any news with a tremor of excitement. "I mean—the cat ears, the lipstick mark, choosing Cat Shoppe for a special occasion…it's almost like a message. A 'fuck you.'"

Beau's ears static-crackled when he swallowed. It sounded like Brigitte was suggesting Lola'd gone out of her way to hurt him, but that wasn't possible. He had no doubt Lola loved him. "You think she set me up?"

Brigitte picked at nothing on the carpet. "I think nobody gets over being hurt that bad as quickly as she did."

"She wasn't over it. We were working on it."

"Still." She looked up. "She moved in here two days later."

Beau took a step back. It didn't sound like Lola. She didn't lie or manipulate. She wasn't malicious. She would never do to him what he'd done to her.

Would she?

He wiped his temple with his sleeve. "Maybe she's still angry, and maybe she wants to hurt me. That I can wrap my head around. But not planning it ahead of time to the point you think she would've packed a bag." He shoved a finger toward the dresser. "All her shit's here."

"I don't see her personal things."

"She only came here with one bag," Beau said. "She left everything else at Johnny's."

Brigitte shook her head slowly. "I'm talking about irreplaceable stuff. Passport, license, social security card, birth certificate. She wouldn't've left those things behind."

"She didn't. I have them. I filed all that in the study when she got here."

"Is it locked up?"

"No. I wanted her to have access to…" Beau narrowed his eyes. His chest was burning, most likely from the steak. That, or his body knew something his mind refused to register.

"You hate Cat Shoppe. She knows it's a night you'd prefer to forget, and she made you relive it. That woman—you hurt her. Bad. You didn't break her heart, Beau—you put it in a goddamn blender."

"I'm not denying—"

"Have you slept with her since then?"

He paused. Were they clues, her rabid efforts to keep him at arm's length, the kisses that sometimes felt off? His face heated. Was it possible, after making him wait like a fool, that she'd never planned to sleep with him?

"Not your business," Beau said.

"Fine." Brigitte stood. "Check the study."

"I will. Only to show you you're wrong." Beau left the room, went downstairs. Lola wouldn't do this to him. Not after the progress he'd made the last few weeks. Not after he'd promised her he would do better. *Be* better. He had a lot of work to do, but it was early. What were a few rocky weeks when they had their whole lives to figure this out? Leaving him when he'd just let her closer than anyone'd ever been—it was unfathomable.

He opened the door of his study too quickly, accidentally knocking it against a wall. One drawer of the file cabinet sat ajar. He went directly to it, opening it all the way.

His heart hammered up against his chest. Lola's folder of paperwork was empty. He pulled it out, dumped it upside down. Nothing. He dropped it. The other files belonged to him, but he proceeded to check each one for something of hers, also tossing them when he found nothing. Anything important to Lola was gone.

"Gone," he said.

"That's what I thought," Brigitte said behind him.

He shoved his hands in his hair, grabbing it in two fists. There were papers everywhere. Lola was gone. She'd pulled the rug out from under him, and this was all she'd left behind—a mess at his feet. Why? To punish him for loving her?

He yanked the drawer all the way out, scanned it one last time for any stray papers, then threw it on the wood-paneled floor with a deafening *clang*. "What the fuck?"

He'd made the grave mistake of underestimating her. He'd thought the game was over. He'd waved his white flag too soon.

He was losing control. He didn't care. He wanted to lose it. He was the master—and she'd played him. She'd turned predator into prey. Without thinking, he slammed his fist into the steel cabinet. Satisfied by the throb in his hand, he did it again and again.

"Beau," Brigitte cried over the noise, "you have to calm down."

He turned on her. She had her palms over her ears. "Calm down? You want me to *calm down*?" He'd let himself *love* her. She'd pretended to *want* that from him. She'd made a fool of him *twice*, and nobody got away with that. He overturned the entire file cabinet, smashing it on the floor. "Do you have any idea what she's put me through?"

Brigitte held her hands out. "It'll be okay. I'll get Detective Bragg on the line. He'll find her—"

Beau laughed hollowly. "You think I want to *find* her?" He picked up a *Young Entrepreneurs* award from his desk and launched it against the wall, shattering it into a million little pieces. "I hope I never see that fucking bitch again."

Brigitte covered her mouth. She was trembling. "Beau. Brother. Go upstairs and rest. I'll bring you ice for your hand. None of this will seem as bad in the morning."

Rest? That was the last thing he needed. Maybe an all-night bender, or a grueling session on his treadmill. But it wasn't his body he wanted to punish.

"What's going on?" Warner asked, entering the study.

Beau went to his bar cart. "Get out. Both of you."

"Sir—"

"We aren't leaving you," Brigitte said. "You're not in the right state to be alone."

"*Don't tell me* what I am or am not. I'm not your goddamn puppet." He poured himself a generous helping of Scotch and turned his back to them, wired with adrenaline. "Do me a favor, Brigitte. Get her shit the fuck out of here. By the time I come out of this room, I want Lola completely erased from this house."

"Beau—"

"If I see anything of hers," he continued, "I will go into a rage like you've never seen." He looked over his shoulder at her. "Is that what you want?"

Warner moved in front of her, but she stopped him with a hand on his bicep. "No."

"Then *get rid of her.*"

"I will." She nodded slowly. "I'll handle it. The housekeeper will come first thing tomorrow and scrub this place until it's shining. Just promise me you'll calm down."

"Get out."

Beau returned to his alcohol once they'd gone and the door was shut. He finished his drink off in one large gulp and poured another. Lola would've needed nerves of steel to pull a stunt like this with someone like him. He'd told Brigitte he never wanted to see Lola again—that wasn't true. Not by a long shot. Just like anyone who screwed him over, Lola had to pay for this. And he wanted to be there when she did.

Chapter Twenty-One

Beau wasn't any calmer by his fourth drink. Slumped in a desk chair in his study, he'd replayed the entire evening twice already, more and more certain he'd been set up.

Lola had been quiet since they'd left the restaurant, and he could feel her eyes on him as he drove, even though his were focused out the windshield. "What's wrong?" he asked.

"What?"

Beau looked over at her. She was fidgeting with the cat ears in her lap. He still wasn't sure how he felt about this whole thing, but she seemed more excited than he'd seen her in a while. "You've been staring at me."

"Oh." She paused. "I was just thinking about how this is our last night like this."

"Like what?"

Beau drank more. She'd never answered him. Or if she had, he couldn't remember what she'd said. The alcohol was making his brain mercifully fuzzy.

He'd centered his phone on the desk, staring at it. It never rang. He'd been toying with an idea, one he hadn't been sure about, but with each drink it sounded better. He couldn't sit there anymore and do nothing. He wanted to know where Lola was, where exactly she was going to undress, shower, lay her head tonight. It was unclear to him still what he'd do with that information, but at the very least, it would give him some of his power back.

He dialed a number he hadn't used in a while. He'd already wasted enough time doing nothing.

A man answered. "I told you before—"

"I know what you told me," Beau said, "but this time it's personal. I need someone I can trust." The line was silent. "Are you there?"

Detective Bragg hacked into the phone. "I'm here. All sixty-eight years of me."

"I'll make it worth your time."

He grumbled. "My rate doubles during retirement."

"Fine."

"Triples when I'm woken up in the middle of the night."

"Don't push it, Bragg. It's only eleven."

"Middle of the night for me. I went to bed hours ago."

Beau waited through another coughing spell.

"That's what happens when you disturb an old man's sleep, Olivier. So what's this personal business? Brigitte? Your mom?"

Beau stared down into his drink. The policeman-turned-private-detective was the only person he trusted with important matters. "Why do you assume that?"

"You got nothing else personal. You don't got a wife, so she ain't cheating. No kids, so it isn't a runaway teen. There a cat in your life I don't know about? Check the trees—I hear they like to climb."

"Jeff," Beau warned.

"All right." He heaved a sigh. "Go."

Beau picked up his Scotch, stood and paced his study. His shoulders were already loosening. "You're going to find someone for me, and it has to be tonight. She won't be very far yet."

"She?"

"Yes. A woman."

"What woman?"

"Do you need to know?"

Bragg cleared his throat. "Guess not."

"One minute I was talking to her, and the next she was gone."

"When was this?"

"About an hour ago."

"As in sixty minutes? Hang on while I grab a pen. I haven't even shit out what I had for dinner yet. An hour's nothing, kid."

Beau massaged the bridge of his nose. It *was* nothing. An hour was a long time in his and Lola's story, though. He'd only actually known her two or so months. Lola was beginning to seem like a wild dream, a hallucination brought on by a night fever. Something untouchable.

"Got my pen," Bragg said. "Shoot."

"Her only family in the area is her mom. She works at The Lucky Egg diner in East Hollywood."

"What about the girl? Where's she work?"

"She left her job at Hey Joe on Sunset Boulevard a few weeks ago."

"Think the folks there'll know anything?"

Beau spun his drink on his desk. It wasn't impossible that Johnny knew something. Veronica too. Maybe Lola *had* mentioned something to her, and they were all in on it. They weren't friends to him. Fuck, Lola might've stopped there to say goodbye. Maybe she was there now. Beau could be there in twenty minutes, and with money as leverage, he could have Johnny talking in twenty-five.

Johnny responded to threats, but Beau didn't. He wasn't going to play Lola's game and track her down himself. He was an important man. He hired people like Bragg for that.

"They might know something," Beau decided. "Her ex-boyfriend works there. Start with him."

"Going to tell me how to do my job? You want to do this yourself, be my guest."

"I've got better things to do," Beau said. "That's why I'm paying you."

Bragg muttered something into the phone. "All right. Tonight—what's the last place you saw her?"

Beau's mind went to the strip club, Lola's hips swaying within his reach. She was in her element there, sexy as hell. Just like the night her sweet, red mouth had lovingly eaten his cock the first time. "Cat Shoppe. It's a strip joint, also on Sunset Boulevard. You know the place?"

"What do you think?"

"I'm not allowed in there, so don't mention my name until you know what you're dealing with." Beau rubbed the skin above his eyebrows. "On second thought, maybe you should start there."

"Sounds like you got ideas on how to do this, which is fine since the clock's ticking. You go talk to the boyfriend, and I'll hit the strip club."

"No. Like I said, this isn't worth my time."

"And like *I* said, don't tell me how to do my fucking job. So what else you got?"

"That's everything. She's got black hair, blue eyes." And she'd leave you with an impression that stayed no matter how many times you tried blinking it away. Like glimpsing the sun. Beau grit his teeth against the thoughts he wanted to shut out. "Don't worry, Bragg. You can't miss her."

"I'll start with the titty bar after I get something going on her license plate number and credit cards."

Beau took another long gulp of his drink, welcoming the burn of alcohol down his throat. He set the tumbler on his desk. "She doesn't have a car."

"Don't tell me that."

"No license plate. She could be on the goddamn city bus for all I know."

"The bus? She's a slippery one, eh?"

"Apparently."

"How about a name? She got one of those?"

"Right. It's Lola. Lola Winters."

"Lola…Winters," he repeated slowly as if writing it down. "Middle name?"

A middle name? At times, he'd thought he'd known Lola inside out. He'd anticipated her every move, directed her, surprised her. Once in a while, though, he was reminded how little he knew. Like the girl she'd been before Johnny, how many kids she wanted or even if she was a dog or cat person. He'd never thought to ask her middle name.

"I don't know."

"How about a cell number?"

Beau rubbed the back of his neck. "She doesn't have one of those either."

"Let me get this straight. You want me to find some chick who's got no job, no car, no cell. And she disappeared into thin air?"

"I called you because you're the best."

"Yeah, well—the best is going to cost you, Olivier."

"Bill me." Beau hit 'End' and put his phone away. It was only a matter of time now before he had her back.

The question was what he'd do with her.

EXPLICITLY YOURS • BOOK FOUR

JESSICA HAWKINS

Chapter One

Lola drove straight through the heart of night, her only company the stars and the Lotus Evora's hum, which she preferred to the radio. Not even the moon showed its scarred face. She straddled her past and her future, unstuck but not quite free. She refused to think too hard of *him* until she was far enough away that she couldn't turn back.

Her plan had played out even better than she'd thought, except that she'd expected to feel more vindicated by now. It was still early, though. Not even the sun had risen since she'd left Beau at Cat Shoppe, pacing out front, waiting for her to emerge. How long had it taken him to realize she never would?

When her fuel tank neared empty, she finally loosened her grip on the steering wheel and pulled off the freeway. She found a gas station and, once inside, did a quick scan of the building—a side effect from the time she'd walked in on Beau with a gun to his head.

The clerk stared openly at her chest. "Nice car."

Lola closed the top button of her coat. She slapped cash on the counter, making him jump. "Pump five, a pack of Marlboros, a lighter and coffee."

"Sure thing, babe." He took the money.

Night fringed and frayed into dawn. She set the tank to fill and leaned against a wall to smoke. Her shiny, spotless new Lotus held two duffel bags—one had her personal things, and the other, stashed in the trunk, held what was left of her million dollars. All that money, right there, made her head swim. She tapped ash from her cigarette and glanced over her shoulder. The clerk was watching her through the window.

She was on her own now. With Johnny and Beau, she'd always had someone behind her. Tonight, her back was up against the wall, and everything she owned in the world was right in front of her. One twist of fate, one slip up, and she could lose it all. An accident. A thief.

Beau Olivier.

He would come after her, at least at first. She had to watch her every move—not even a footprint in the sand he could track. Because if he caught her, there was no telling what he'd do to her for this. For tricking him into loving her and making him a fool ten times greater than she had the first time.

Lola didn't want to think about that. It was a happy night. She stubbed out her cigarette and got back in the car. She'd already scarfed her beef Pad Thai and steamed vegetables somewhere around Bakersfield. Gas and coffee would buy her a few more hours until she needed to crash. She debated going back in for a candy bar, but she wasn't as far as she wanted to be yet, so she started the car instead.

She drove straight to the next biggest city. Night and day wrestled as the sun woke up over California. Lola put on her oversized, designer sunglasses, one of the few things left from her life with Beau, and relaxed back into her seat. As San Francisco's skyline came into view, she thought—*so this is it. This is my freedom, my revenge.*

She watched out the windshield as she passed the St. Regis hotel, glimpsing its swank interior through tall windows. Lola was flush now, but she was heading into an uncertain future. She had to be careful with what she had, and she'd already spent a good chunk on the Lotus, a gift to herself.

Motel 6 was more her speed anyway, and she'd already made a reservation. She'd be comfortable there. She paid for the room in cash and drove around back. After shutting off the car, she sat a minute, checking the parking lot and then all her mirrors.

Far as she could tell, no one was around. She got her things, popped the trunk for the bag of money and carried everything to the room. Inside, she went directly to the closet. Every Motel 6 was supposed to have a safe—but she slid open the door and found nothing.

The cash weighed heavily on her shoulder. Lola dropped it on the bed, picked up the phone and hit a button.

"Front desk," a man answered.

"I need a new room. I'm in 103."

"Is there an issue?"

"This one faces the parking lot." Lola sniffed. She wasn't about to advertise how badly she needed a safe. "I want to be near the pool."

"Hang on." The line went quiet a moment, and then he said, "Nothing open by the pool."

"Maybe I should go somewhere else then."

"Um…" His voice trailed off jaggedly, a froggy sound. "Want me to suggest another hotel in the area?"

Lola sighed. Threatening to take her business elsewhere didn't quite have the same effect as when Beau did it. "No. Is there anything else available?"

"Yes, ma'am. Just not by the pool."

"Whatever. Any other room is fine."

Lola picked up the duffel again, put it back in her trunk and drove around to the front desk. She locked the car, exchanged the key and parked where she'd be able to see the Lotus from her window. This room had a safe, but it wasn't big enough for her bag. She took out stacks of cash, fitting as much in as she possibly could and put the rest under the mattress. She'd also stuffed a small amount into the spare tire compartment of the car. Diversifying your wealth was important. Or so she'd heard.

When she'd gotten the rest of her things, she closed the blinds, bolted the door and crawled under the covers. Thanks to Beau, she'd developed quite the habit of going to bed *after* the sun came up.

Lola closed her eyes, exhausted from the last twenty-four hours. So much had gone down, but she didn't want to think about any of it. She just wanted to sleep. Her immediate plan had been to get as far as she could in a small amount of time. Now, the whole country was open to her. She had no obligations—no other reservations or arrangements. She'd worry about that when she woke up, though.

Lola turned onto her side and pulled a pillow between her arms. Sleeping next to Beau had never been hard. He usually was out a few seconds after he closed his eyes, and then she could relax in his presence and enjoy the way he held her—protectively, like someone might try to take her in the middle of the night.

His waking moments, though—they'd given her some trouble. The past three weeks, Lola had tried not to think too hard about abandoning her plan and staying with Beau. The temptation had been too dangerous then. But what was the harm in it now?

Things had been far from perfect between them. Beau'd claimed to know her inside out, but he hadn't even realized how empty her days had been. He'd bungled little things, like buying her a peach dress for the ballet when it was the last color she would've picked for herself. He'd fucked up the big things too, though, like thinking she could be content just to be by his side—no job, no life of her own. Just her, at his beck and call.

Lola sighed, hugging the pillow more tightly. The night they'd discussed her getting a job was one she remembered well. It'd almost been a turning point for them. If Beau had done and said all the right things, would she still be here now, sleeping without him?

Alone, in the darkened room, without a steel cage around her heart for the first time in weeks, she let herself go there.

Chapter Two

One week earlier

Lola didn't look up from her plate when Beau entered the kitchen. He was late. She didn't actually care—presuming he might miss dinner again, she'd eaten without him—but that wasn't how a woman in love acted. So she'd made herself a new plate of food and read a magazine until the garage door rumbled open.

"I left work as soon as I could." Beau loosened his tie and opened the refrigerator to grab a beer. In Beau's world, that was as close to an apology as she was going to get.

"You said you'd be home three hours ago." Lola stood, picked up his plate and walked over to him. She shoved it between them, steamed carrots rolling off onto the floor. "Is this how it's going to be? After everything we went through, work's always going to come before me?"

"No." He took the plate from her and set it on the counter. "Of course not."

"This isn't what I signed up for."

"And it's not what you're getting. You have no idea the day I've had. I'm not even hungry. All day, I just wanted to come home and," he put his knuckle under her jaw, "and…kiss you."

Lola parted her lips but turned her head away when he leaned in. The argument wasn't over. Night after night, she sat by herself, waiting for him to come home. She hadn't given up her comfortable life to live unhappily in second place. "You're supposed to be making some changes."

He guided her face back to his. "I know what I said, and I'm trying. There's going to be an adjustment period, Lola. I can't suddenly start leaving the office at five when I normally work twelve-hour days." He touched his thumb to the corner of her mouth. "As much as I want to get home to you, I have to ease into this."

"I know," she said. He looked like he was going to kiss her. She salivated. Not every part of her could be schooled. "I just thought we'd get more time with each other. I'm used to having someone around. Johnny and I were together morning, noon and—"

"Don't." Beau pinned her with a look and dropped his hand. He inhaled through his nose. "Get mad at me if you want, but don't bring him up. That's the last fucking thing I want to hear after a long day."

"You're right. I'm sorry." Johnny was a weapon that never lost its potency. It had as much effect on Beau now as it had their first night together when he'd lost his cool and fucked her up against the hotel window. Lola shivered at the memory and slid her arms up around his neck. "Ready for that kiss?"

He hummed a noise of approval. She rose onto the balls of her feet, threading her fingers in his hair, bringing his lips down to hers.

"This right here," he said, "may be the greatest threat to my work. How am I supposed to focus knowing you're here waiting for me each night?"

"That's all I want," she whispered. She rested her forehead against his and opened a vein. It was necessary, sometimes, to tell the truth in order to draw him in. To feel the things she tried not to. "To be enough for you to leave work early."

"You are. I'm not the kind of man who leaves work early, though, and you knew that. I love what I do, even more so now, because it enables me to give you what you want."

"But…you're what I want. Not clothing or parties or cars. I want time, and I want it with you."

He pulled her closer by the small of her back so they were flush against each other. "You make an excellent case," he whispered in her ear, as if someone might hear. "Let me make it up to you."

She shook her head. "Not yet."

"That's not what I'm getting at. Tonight, I'm all yours. I'll shut off my phone, and we can talk and catch up. All night long, if that's what it takes."

Lola pulled back a little. "But you have to work in the morning."

"Don't worry about that. I've done it before, if you recall."

Lola narrowed her eyes. The corner of her lip twitched. "Aren't you getting a little old to pull so many all-nighters?"

He laughed, slapping her rear end lightly. "Sounds like you don't think I can do it. Is that a challenge, Miss Winters?" He released her and walked away, disappearing into the pantry.

She gave in to her smile. "Does that always work on you?"

"What?" he called.

"Well, for example—if I were to tell you I don't believe you can do laundry, would you do it just to prove me wrong?"

"I do laundry just fine." Beau came out with a bag of ground beans. "I'm going to put a pot on. Let's move this to the couch."

Lola took the coffee from him. "I'll make this. I'm sure you're dying to get out of your suit."

He kissed her quickly on the lips and brushed a lock of her hair from her forehead. "Have I said how much I love having you around to take care of me?"

Lola caught herself grinning after he'd left the kitchen and quickly wiped the smile from her face. She had an entire, uninterrupted night to worm her way into his heart. And he wasn't going to lay a hand on her. For as obstinate as he could be, Beau wasn't as difficult to move around the playing board as she would've thought.

Once the coffee was ready, she poured two mugs and met Beau in his den. It was the only room besides his that was remotely comfortable, and while he rarely spent any time in there, she frequently did.

Lola sat beside him on the couch and handed him his drink. He clinked his mug with hers. "To keeping my dick in my pants another night—Lord knows it isn't easy."

She laughed and pushed his shoulder. "I'm not drinking to that."

"All right." He winked. "To quality time."

They both took a sip, and she set her cup on the coffee table. She scooted closer to him and ran her fingers over his hairline, just above his ear. "So, why was it such a long day?"

"I don't want to talk about work." He readjusted to face her better. "What'd you do today?"

"Slept in."

He raised his eyebrows at her. "You don't say. Then what?"

"I read the newspaper. Looked up some stuff online. Before I knew it, it was almost time to start dinner, so I went grocery shopping."

"Sounds nice." He cleared his throat and rubbed her knee. "It makes me happy that you don't have to work. But have you thought about doing something more…um—doing something else with your free time?"

Lola rolled her lips together. Of course she'd thought about it. She was bored all the fucking time wandering around this shell he called a home or going shopping for things she knew she'd have to leave behind. She wanted a job, and not just because she knew a million dollars wouldn't last forever. But there was no point in getting one when she was leaving soon.

"I've thought about it a little," Lola said. "It's just so nice not to have to bust my ass cleaning up after drunk idiots anymore."

"You were wasting your potential at Hey Joe. I knew it the minute I walked into that dump."

She cocked her head. "But I have no other skills."

"Go back to school." His eyes lit up, and he shifted his body even more toward her. "I have connections at UCLA and USC. It wouldn't be a problem to set you up there."

Lola felt a little like moving away from him, but she stayed where she was. It was Beau's kneejerk response to any problem—how could his money and status solve it so he didn't have to?

"I suppose you'd also be willing to pay my way," she said.

"Why wouldn't I?" He shrugged. "Look, I'd have absolutely no problem with you staying home every day and doing nothing if I thought it'd make you happy. Plenty of guys I know have wives who do that and go to expensive luncheons every month so they can call themselves philanthropists." He sipped his coffee. "That's not you, though. You can do whatever you want now. You never let yourself have dreams and aspirations before, but there's nothing holding you back anymore."

Lola also picked up her mug and took a drink, hiding her face for a moment. If he kept pushing her, everything she'd been thinking lately might come pouring out. There were lots of things she wanted to do, and going back to school was one of them. She'd been debating between majoring in graphic design or business. Maybe both. She wasn't limited—she could be a goddamn mechanic if she wanted. But she wasn't focusing on herself yet. It was Beau's time in the spotlight.

She changed the subject. "What if there're other things I want to do first?"

Beau settled back, crossing his arms. "Such as?"

"I want to travel. I've never been past Vegas."

Beau nodded approvingly. "Where should we go? Paris? Bali? New York City?"

She hadn't lied earlier—she really had spent a good portion of her day kicking back, researching things to do around the country. "That's a little ambitious. Did you know the world's largest ball of twine is right here in the United States?"

"It's nothing to write home about."

She smirked. "You haven't seen it."

"You're right, I haven't. Big balls don't do anything for me. But if they impress you, I can show you a couple—"

"Don't even." Lola rolled her eyes, grinning.

"You have the whole world to choose from, and you pick—where'd you say this ball was?"

"Kansas. Where would you go if you were me?"

"I've been a lot of places. For me, it's less about what I'm seeing than how it makes me feel."

"So what's made you feel?"

"Hard to say. There's so much to choose from." Beau blinked away, drank a little coffee. He looked into his mug.

Lola studied him. He seemed to forget she was there for a moment. "What are you thinking about?" she asked.

He glanced up. "The last trip we took as a family before my dad died was the Grand Canyon. Standing there, the world seemed so big. So many possibilities. It was the first time I started to think I could do something with my life. If there were things out there like the Grand Canyon I still didn't know existed, then there must be a way for me to find them."

"Always so serious," Lola murmured. She laced her fingers with his. If she ever came across a little boy like the one Beau had been, she vowed to buy him an ice cream or tell him a dirty joke. There were consequences to taking oneself so seriously. "Have you been back?"

"Yes." He glanced down at their hands. "After I sold my first company, the same night I met you, I doubted myself. I wasn't sure which way to turn. I drove to Arizona and looked out at the Grand Canyon, waiting for answers. A place like that really makes you realize how little control you have. But it also puts things in perspective."

"I get the feeling keeping perspective hasn't really been an issue for you."

"Not usually. It helps to separate emotion from most things." Beau took Lola's mug from her, set their drinks on the coffee table and looked at her. "Don't think I don't realize how lucky I am. I almost lost you because of pride, but you gave me a second chance and saved me from a lifetime of regret."

Lola let herself get lost in the comforting green of his eyes. Tonight, she was one half of a normal couple. How could Beau not see right through her? Hear the undercurrent of her distrust in everything she said? *She* was the one left with regret—regret that he'd made her do this. And that she'd never get to witness his suffering.

He leaned in to touch his lips to the bow of hers and made his way around her mouth with light, gentle kisses. She could've told him right then that she loved him, and it wouldn't be a lie. But the closer they got to the end, and to each other, the more afraid she became that saying it aloud would feel too good.

His hands were on her cheeks now. His patience unnerved her. "I'm hungry, Lola," he said so softly, she almost missed it.

"I'll heat up your dinner." She went to pull away, but he kept her there.

"Not for food." He ran the pad of his thumb along her bottom lip. "I want to know you inside out. And for you to want the same from me."

"I do."

"Do you?"

"It's not a race, Beau. Be patient."

"I am. We have all night."

That was almost true. Lola wasn't sure who fell asleep first, just that it happened sometime before the sun came up, after they'd talked and talked about everything and nothing in particular.

Around dawn, Beau stirred. Lola squeezed him closer with her arm, not ready to lose his warmth. "Stay," she murmured.

"It's almost six."

"Take the day off."

He kissed the top of her head and raked his fingers through her hair. "I can't. Not right now."

Lola sighed deeply. She was already drifting back to sleep when he moved her arms and shifted her aside so he could stand.

"Want me to take you upstairs?" he asked.

"I'm fine here." Her eyes were still closed. She felt around for a pillow to take Beau's place, yawned and burrowed into it. "Have a good day, honey."

The room was quiet a moment, and she assumed he'd left. Then he said, "You've never called me by anything other than my name."

It took her a moment to realize she wasn't dreaming. Lola blinked her eyes open. She got up on an elbow and squinted at him. "What? What'd I call you?"

"Honey."

Beau's hair stuck up on one side from sleeping against the arm of the couch, and his eyelids were heavy. Light was just beginning to filter through the blinds. Lola couldn't remember how she'd gotten there and what she was supposed to be doing.

Beau came back to the couch and squatted to kiss her on the forehead. "It's nice waking up with you. My day can only go downhill from here."

He stood, but Lola grabbed his arm. "Then stay with me."

He brought her hand to his mouth and kissed it. "Call me when you get up. We can get lunch."

He let go and left the den. Lola rubbed her eyes and watched through the door as he climbed the stairs toward his bedroom. It'd been a nice moment, but it was cut short by Beau's devotion to the only thing that had his loyalty—his work. Business. The empire he looked down upon from his office in the sky.

And then Lola remembered where she was and how she'd gotten there.

Chapter Three

Present day

Twelve hours, thirty-one minutes, eleven seconds. That was how much time had passed since Beau'd hung up the phone with Detective Bragg. Lola had been missing even longer. She wasn't missing, though. She was just gone. Beau couldn't wrap his head around how easily she'd erased herself from his life. Between disappearing without a trace and Brigitte cleaning out Lola's things, it was as if she'd never even been there. She had, though, and once he found her, this uneasy feeling she'd left him with would finally go away.

Beau rubbed his eyes with tense fingers, the air in his office stale. She'd told him once she'd never been past Vegas. There was a whole fuck-of-a-lot beyond that. Every minute that went by, she got farther away from him. He wouldn't even entertain the notion that her first stop might've been LAX airport—he couldn't take on the rest of the world right then.

Beau finally got some relief when his cell vibrated on his desk, Bragg's name popping up. He answered it. "How far did she get?"

"I got nothing."

Beau's grip tightened. He didn't have the brain capacity to accept that Bragg might fail him. Bragg was a go-to man, someone who'd made a decent living making things happen. "I'm sorry, can you repeat that? I thought you said you have nothing."

"It's what I said. Went to Cat Shoppe last night and talked to Kincaid, the owner. After a chunk of cash that I'm tacking onto your bill, I finally got him to show me the surveillance tape. That's some show your girl put on for you."

Beau's gut smarted as though he'd been punched. "You watched?"

"Don't get shy on me, Olivier." Bragg chuckled into the phone. "That's what you wanted, isn't it? Leave no stone unturned? I see what the fuss is about, though."

"Get to the point." It'd been his last intimate moment with Lola, her dancing on stage just for him, but now two greasy old men had shared in it too. That was the fucking goodbye gift Lola had given him.

"After security removed you, Lola talked to a girl, but she swears up and down Lola didn't tell her nothing. Just needed help getting the backdoor open."

"So she walked out the back. Then what?"

"Some brief indistinguishable activity by your car and then poof. Gone."

"What, in a car? Bicycle? Come on, Bragg—this is rookie shit."

"It look to you like I got a crystal fucking ball? I only see as far as the camera does, and it stops in the parking lot."

"What about the owner? What's he know?"

"Said she used to work for him, and she stopped by earlier that day to arrange the VIP room. Paid him a lot in cash. That was all he'd give me. Not sure if he knows more—bouncer said he's protective of his girls."

Beau leaned his knuckles on his desk. "I got the same thing from him."

"Only reason he showed me the tapes was because I threatened to get the police involved. Didn't seem too bothered about it until I flashed my old badge."

Lola was too good. She must've considered Beau might go after her, and she hadn't left him any obvious clues except the ones on his car. He pushed off his desk and turned to look out the window. "What about Hey Joe?"

"Yeah. Bit of a confrontation there. You spoke to Veronica?"

"Lola's friend."

"Says she hasn't spoken to Lola since she left Hey Joe, and I believe her. But the ex-boyfriend and his new girlfriend really don't like me there—he starts pushing my buttons."

Beau cocked his head. "His girlfriend?"

"Skanky thing."

"Amanda?"

"Yeah, that's her. Her lip curls just hearing Lola's name. Anyway, I had to rough Johnny up a little."

Beau had been picturing Lola's reaction to hearing Johnny and Amanda were still together, but that got his attention. "You *what*?"

"I may be getting up there, but I got almost fifty years of training behind me," he said defensively. "The kid tested my reflexes and got a surprise. He'll be all right—nothing a towel of ice and a blowie from the skank won't take care of." Bragg coughed into the phone. "Next stop is the diner to see the mom."

Beau didn't have any sympathy for Johnny. He had it coming. But he had no idea what they were in for with Lola's mom since he knew little about her. Suddenly, it didn't feel right sending a stranger to her workplace. "Forget the mom," Beau said. "What about the airport? Her credit cards?"

"Nothing and nothing."

Beau paused. "Nothing—as in, you haven't gotten to it yet?"

"No activity on the card you gave her. I assumed you canceled it."

"No." It hadn't occurred to him that he should, and he wouldn't now that she didn't have a cell phone or credit card he knew of. It was stupid of her, and she wasn't stupid. You didn't grow up how they did and not look out for yourself. She was her own responsibility, she'd made that clear, but Beau couldn't help thinking of the trouble she might run into.

"You ought to think about it," Bragg said.

"What?"

"You know, canceling any other cards she might've stolen. Checking to see if you're missing anything of value—jewelry, cash, art…"

Beau shook his head. "This isn't about money. You tried seeing if she opened a new card?"

"Can't find nothing under her name."

"Try Jonathan Pace."

"Already did. She had a card with him, but it was canceled a few weeks ago too. You said it was stolen, right?"

Beau tapped a finger on his desk. Lola'd told him she'd ordered herself a backup credit card in addition to what he'd given her. He should've insisted on seeing it, but he'd been happy enough that she'd agreed to stop spending her own money.

"Don't worry," Bragg said. "She's got to be paying for stuff somehow."

Beau's heart thudded once. He didn't know if Lola had a cell phone or credit cards. He didn't know how she was traveling or where. The only thing he knew for sure was that she had cash. Cash *he'd* given her. "She has money," Beau said quietly.

"She'd need a hell of a lot to stay off the grid much longer, though."

Beau closed his eyes. There it was, the cherry on top of this shit sundae. The final nail in his coffin—and he'd hammered it in. "She has more than a lot."

"Yeah? Well, cash is a different beast, Olivier. How'm I supposed to find someone who's gone out of her way not to leave a trail?"

"I don't know. I hired you to figure that stuff out." Beau's mouth was as dry as a cotton ball. Pieces of the puzzle were falling into place, and the blame was coming down on his shoulders. "Don't tell me this is impossible, Bragg. I need you on this."

Bragg sighed. "Someone's got to talk to the mom. Clock's ticking."

The line went dead. Beau had always known exactly where to find Lola if he needed her—Hey Joe, her apartment, the Four Seasons, and then, his own home. It was a luxury he hadn't realized he'd been afforded. Now, it'd been yanked away.

Lola had disappeared without a trace and left no sign she was coming back. That was what his money had bought her.

•⊠•⊠•

Beau boarded the elevator. After Bragg's useless phone call, he only had more questions. When he'd sold his first company and found himself unsure of which way to turn next, he'd gone to the Grand Canyon, but he had a meeting in forty-five minutes, so he'd have to find another way to get perspective.

He stopped at the coffee stand in the lobby. Bolt Ventures had moved into the top two floors of this downtown Los Angeles skyscraper nearly ten years ago, yet he couldn't recall ever having ordered anything from the little shop near the building's entrance. His assistant always had a pot waiting when he arrived for the day.

"Black coffee," he told the girl behind the counter.

She entered his order into the register. "Two seventy-five."

"For a small?"

"There's only one size."

Beau raised both eyebrows at her before peeling some ones from his wallet. Three dollars for coffee was painful. He took no issue with splurging on certain things—a glass of Glenlivet or a bespoke suit—but those tastes had taken time to cultivate. He'd been raised frugal. A three-hundred-something-percent markup didn't sit right with him.

Beau took his drink outside to walk around the block—another thing he'd only done a handful of times.

He didn't recognize half the shops. The sidewalk seemed more crowded than the last time he'd been out there in the middle of the day without a car.

He'd spared no expense for Lola. She was the smooth and supple whisky, the Merino wool with price tags he hadn't batted an eyelash at. His bank account was considerably lighter for having known her—mostly from what he'd spent for two nights with her—but there was the extended hotel stay, gifts, room service, shopping that'd come with it. He didn't mind. He'd rather have spent his money on her than himself. Though there were days he'd wanted to leave work early to be with her, he'd reminded himself that his success was dependent on the time he put in each day. It belonged to her too, his success. Or, it had. Now, he questioned all those hours he'd been at the office instead of home with her. Would it have changed anything?

Beau'd been walking blindly, ignoring his surroundings, until a dark-haired woman twenty feet in front of him caught his eye. Despite it being a weekday, and a cool one at that, she wore a gold, floor-length gown that elongated a tan, smooth back. Just like the tan, smooth back he'd recently worshipped. Just like the gold, shimmering dress he'd ruined their second night together.

Beau tossed his coffee in the nearest trash and picked up his pace. Lola was playing a game with him. She could show up just as suddenly as she'd disappeared. Was she so brave to come to his office? Nobody just picked up and left the way she had—without a plan, without anything but a bunch of cash.

He flexed his hand with the urge to grab her elbow, yank her through the nearest door and take her up against a wall before she could even explain herself. She'd wreaked havoc on his life. She'd used sex as a weapon to keep him distracted. Anger and need surged through him.

She turned a corner. He broke into a jog, weaving through the crowd of tourists and businesspeople. He rounded the block and stopped short to avoid stumbling over a large orange cone.

A short man in a headset stepped into his path. "You have to go around. Street's closed for a photo shoot."

The woman stood in the center of an empty, blocked-off road, surrounded by a team of people dressed in black. She turned and caught Beau staring at her. Her midnight-colored hair shone in the sun, and she shimmered in liquid gold. She wasn't Lola.

"Hello?" The man waved his clipboard. "You can't get through here."

Beau backed away, keeping his eyes on her. A man in a tuxedo joined her in the street.

"Put your arms around her," a photographer said, his camera aimed at them.

The male model took her by the waist, and she lifted her face to his.

"Don't let him kiss you. Make him work for it."

She put her palm on his chest, and he leaned in, but she stayed just outside his reach. The camera snapped over and over. Right before Beau turned away, the woman glanced over at him and, he could've sworn—smirked.

Chapter Four

Lola strained to see out the passenger's side window. Nothing could've prepared her for the grandeur of the Golden Gate Bridge or the view it gave her of San Francisco. She'd spent the evening before walking around the city without seeing the same thing twice—and now, for these few seconds, she could see the entire place all at once.

She took her camera from her purse, snapped a one-handed picture out the window and put it away. She put *San Francisco* away—it was time to move on after only one night. Beau would be looking for her by now, and she couldn't stay anywhere too long.

Once she was on the freeway, she checked her rearview mirror and then the speedometer. The needle hovered at seventy miles per hour. It was a crime to finally be in possession of a car like the Lotus and not be able to take flight. But Beau didn't know how she was traveling, and she wanted to keep it that way. Information was just one of the things his money bought him, and she couldn't afford a ticket on her record.

Lola left California behind and crossed the border to Nevada, the only other state she'd been. She stopped at a motel in Salt Lake City in the late evening. There were few other people around. Just like she had in San Francisco, she paid the clerk in cash, bolted the door and shoved as much cash as would fit into the safe. With a bag of Doritos and a Coke from the vending machine,

Lola sat on the bed and turned on the TV. She scarfed chips and flipped through every channel twice before shutting it off. The digital clock read 9:58 P.M.

On a whim, she changed into a bathing suit, took a threadbare towel and went to the pool. Having closed at ten, it was quiet and dark, so she hopped the short fence and got in the hot tub.

The door to her room was within her view. Always in the back of her mind was the cash. In the safe. In the car. Under the mattress. Stuffed into her jean pockets.

The night was cool, but the water was warm. She didn't turn on the bubbles, afraid they'd draw attention. For the second day in a row, she'd only spoken to motel clerks and gas station attendants. Even with them, she was cautious.

She set her head back against the edge, letting the heat soothe the stiffness in her neck. The drive from San Francisco had been long, but the road ahead of her was open, proof she was free. If she decided to go south instead of north, west instead of east, right instead of left—it didn't matter as long as she kept moving. She'd never believed in fate or destiny. There was always a master. Every choice, every decision she made put her on a new path. She wouldn't give anyone else power over her again.

Lola couldn't shake the feeling of a chain around her ankle, though. As if Beau would only let her get as far as he wanted, and when he decided he was ready, he'd start reeling her back in. She couldn't lose focus. The more distance she put between them, the stronger she became—but the opposite was also true.

She wiped beads of sweat from her hairline. She'd been away from him forty-eight hours, and he was hundreds of miles away. Was it far enough to save her from him? From herself? She sank deeper into the warm water—into the torture of another memory she knew she should forget.

Lola removed her new diamond earrings and set them on the bathroom counter. She glanced up at her reflection. Beau was in the doorway, his bowtie hanging around his neck, a shadow of stubble on his jaw. He came up behind her and slid his arms around her waist. "When did you change?" he whispered. "I wanted to watch."

"I never let you watch."

"That doesn't mean I don't."

Lola's heart skipped as he nuzzled her neck. The idea that he'd seen her undress without her permission made her flush. He was a dog—she knew that. He'd treated her like a dog. What made him think he could get away with that—standing just out of sight as she unzipped the long zippers of the dresses he'd bought her, unclipped the stockings of her wasted lingerie, unclasped her heavy, expensive necklaces. "You watched me?" she asked, her breath coming faster.

"Mmm." He moved her hair aside and kissed a spot under her ear. "No. But it's been very tempting."

Lola inhaled a slinky breath and opened her eyes. She was hot everywhere, her body's memory of Beau much more favorable than her mind's. She got out of the spa, curled her toes over the edge of the dark pool and dove in. A November night in Salt Lake City wasn't the optimal time for a swim, but the biting water shocked her system. It jarred her in a necessary way, that sudden switch from hot to cold.

Chapter Five

Beau waited at the host's stand as a young girl wound through the diner's empty tables. She grabbed a laminated menu from its slot and popped her gum. "One?"

"Is Dina Winters working?" Beau asked.

"Yep."

"Seat me in her section."

"We don't have sections tonight," she said. "Just one waitress on duty."

Beau sat in a plastic booth and took the menu. Lola's love for breakfast food made sense if this was what her mom had fed her regularly. Everything at The Lucky Egg seemed to have eggs as an ingredient.

"I know you?" came a voice.

Beau looked up at a woman with burgundy hair and gray roots. Her apron folded between the rolls of her stomach. "Are you Dina?"

"Depends who's asking."

"I'm a friend of Lola's."

"Oh." She tapped the end of her pen against her order pad. "Then, yeah. That's my daughter."

"Do you have a minute?"

She looked around the restaurant. "I got lots of minutes, but what's this about? Is Lola all right?"

Beau gestured to the seat across from him. "I just want to talk. I'll pay for your time." It came out like a bad habit. Money solved his problems all the time, but he wondered when it'd become second nature—especially outside of work.

Dina snorted but didn't object. The booth whooshed when she sat. "You got ten seconds to tell me what you're after."

"Lola."

"Nine seconds."

"Have you seen her?"

"Since when?"

He rubbed his chin. "Forty-eight hours?"

The woman laughed. "You got the wrong person. I think I've talked to her two or three times in as many years. Johnny calls now and then, good boy that he is. If not for him, I wouldn't know nothing about her."

Beau looked at the table. He'd doubted she'd know much, but this was worse. His palms began to sweat.

"She owe you money or something?"

"No," Beau said emphatically, looking up again. "I'm just trying to get in touch with her."

"Oh. Well, she works at a bar not too far from here on Sunset Strip. Hey Joe—you know it?"

Beau scrubbed his palm over his stubbled jawline and nodded. "I know the place."

"She's got a boyfriend, though—Johnny. And he's good to her. So whatever you're after, might be best you just walk away."

"Thanks for the tip," he said dryly.

"Sure. Now, what can I get you?"

Beau cocked his head. "What?"

She pointed her pen at the menu. "To eat, honey."

"I don't care." He slid it away. "Whatever you recommend. Breakfast food."

"Coming right up."

He considered leaving. If Dina thought Lola was still with Johnny, she was worse off than him. She waddled over to the counter, ripped off his ticket and refilled a water glass at the only other table with a customer. Beau didn't want breakfast food. He wanted to find Lola.

His cell vibrated in his pocket, and he answered it immediately. "Bragg?"

"More dead ends. I can't find anyone named Lola Winters staying in the area. I can go national, but can you give me some kind of direction? Maybe a favorite spot?"

Beau had nothing. He could probably rule out Las Vegas since she'd been there. Apparently, that was how well he knew the woman he'd fallen in love with. "Motels?" Beau asked.

"Nope."

"Airports? Car rentals? Fucking train stations?"

Bragg was silent.

"Damn it," Beau said.

"There's one thing I haven't tried. Hospital and jail records."

Beau looked down at the table. For a shameful moment, he preferred that to the alternative. In jail, in a hospital, she would need him. There'd be no pretense. He could handle those situations better than anyone he knew, whether it was getting her the best care or paying off whomever he needed to if she were in trouble. Anything was better than not knowing why. Or where. Or if. If she'd really left on purpose, or if this was all some big misunderstanding.

"Search them," Beau said. "Every few hours until we know more."

He hung up as Dina set an oversized dish of French toast in front of him. It must've been a joke. Lola had to be watching from the kitchen, laughing at him in her carefree way. Like the time she'd thrown her body into his arms and wrapped her legs around his waist.

"...come have breakfast in bed with me," she said.

"If you insist, though I don't really see the point."

"There's no point. This isn't a negotiation or a board meeting where there needs to be an explanation for everything. There's absolutely no fucking point at all, and that is the point."

Beau understood that conversation better now, after having spent more time with her. He was the one who'd set parameters around his life, and he was the one who could tear them down. Breakfast for dinner. Eating where he slept. They were childish things, but they weren't illegal—he'd gawked at her as if they were.

"Come on. Eat up," Dina said. "It was Lola's favorite. Mine too."

Beau took a reluctant, painful, memory-filled bite. His mouthful of syrup tasted like Lola.

"Can I get you anything else?" Dina asked.

Beau needed her to keep talking so he could survive that French toast. For the first time in two days, he didn't feel an ounce of anger. "Did she grow up near here?"

Dina glanced around the diner. Her other customer had his eyes glued to the overhead TV set. "Five or so minutes away," she said. "How'd you say you know her?"

Beau wiped his mouth with a napkin and cleared his throat. "I guess you could say we worked together once."

"Oh." Her mom nodded high, keeping her eyes on Beau. "I see. Well, Lola only worked at two places in her life, so I got a pretty good idea what you're getting at."

Beau didn't look away, though he wanted to. When had he ever faced the family of someone he'd screwed over? Beyond Johnny, he'd never considered how hurting Lola might extend to those who loved her.

"Hang on," Dina said. "There was that 7-Eleven she worked at for a while as a cover up for what she was really doing. She must've thought I was dumb to believe money like that came from selling bubblegum and cigarettes." Her smile fell. "Completely slipped my mind. But no, I'm not about to believe that's where you know her from."

Beau smiled thinly. "It's not." Walking into a 7-Eleven years ago and coming face to face with a young Lola might've changed his life. Before his money, he'd been like any other boy trying to get a girl's attention. For the most part, he was too distracted by work to care, but he couldn't imagine walking away from Lola back then, before he'd ever tasted power—or rejection.

"She never worked here?" he asked.

"This place? You mean the diner with quicksand floors?" She laughed at her joke. "People get stuck here. Mario in the kitchen came in to use the restroom twenty years ago. I didn't want that for her. She can do better than her old lady."

"Lola's very smart," Beau agreed.

"Pity she got stuck on the Strip," she said.

"At Cat Shoppe, you mean?"

Dina eyed him. "No. I'm talking about Hey Joe, where I said she works now. Not that I did any better for myself, but I wanted her to become something. She was a proud little girl, though."

"Pride's not always a bad thing."

"You don't watch out, pride'll get you. Lola didn't want nobody telling her what to do, especially me. Thought she knew better. She had a fighting spirit. Too much. Then she hooked up with Johnny, and he calmed her down lots, but while she's with him, she won't go much of anywhere." Dina was barely looking at him anymore. "Johnny's a good man, but sometimes I wonder where she'd be now if she hadn't met him. Maybe this whole side of town's quicksand."

A hint of thickness in her voice made Beau wonder if she missed her daughter. "Why don't you two speak?"

Dina shook her head slowly and looked up at the ceiling a moment. "I wasn't a good mom. I know that. She knew it too since she was little. Like you said—she's smart. Smarter than anyone in my family."

Beau'd heard enough of Lola's childhood to know Dina could've done better. The fact that she kept Lola out of the diner said something, though. She saw the same potential in Lola Beau had. "I'm sure you weren't as bad as you think."

She snorted. "When I got pregnant with her, I quit smoking. Not because I was worried about the baby, but because it made me sick. Nausea, heartburn, all that. I was pissed about it, thought it was unfair. I loved my cigarettes. What's that say about me?"

One of her bushy eyebrows crinkled. He wanted to tell her that everybody made mistakes and that most people never copped to them. They went on thinking they'd been good people. Beau had seen it in business time and time again—those who owned their mistakes, like Beau, were successful because they didn't make them a second time.

"Anyway, when I found out about the stripping," she continued, "I told her to stop. Said I hadn't done much for her in my life, but I was putting my foot down. I think that made her want to do it more."

So Lola had been stubborn from the start. It didn't surprise him, and he understood why someone like Johnny had tried to tame her. Wild horses were as easy to lose as they were to love. "Were you ever close?"

"No. I never planned for her. It was her dad who wanted a kid until he had one. He bolted when he realized it wasn't all fun and games. Took me a lifetime to get over it, but that doesn't mean I didn't want good things for her."

It'd been a while since Beau had taken an interest in anyone's life when it didn't benefit him. Even Brigitte. He set down his fork and got comfortable in his seat. "Tell me more."

"Not much to tell. She was young when he left, and I got all the responsibility I never wanted. And no money, either. He took what little we had, the low-life scum. Anyway, I'm not trying to dump the past on you—not like I even think about this anymore. You asked why we don't speak—answer's that we just don't got anything to say to each other. She lets Johnny do the talking."

"Sounds like the same bull-headed Lola I know." Syrup dripped over the sides of his toast, pooling on Beau's plate. "Knew, I mean."

"You work downtown?"

Beau looked up again. Dina's eyes were narrowed on him. "Am I that obvious?" he muttered.

"You don't look like you belong in these parts."

"These parts? This is Hollywood, for God's sake. It's not like we're on Skid Row."

"You just don't look like it."

"I grew up not far from here," Beau said defensively. He was beginning to think it was more than just his suit that gave him away. It shouldn't have bothered him that he'd risen so high above his social beginnings, he was unrecognizable to his peers—he'd worked hard for that kind of esteem—but it did. He'd been one of them once. And his success hadn't come without struggle or sacrifice. "For twenty-seven years, I barely had enough to get by. I didn't grow up spoiled or privileged. Why is that so hard for everyone to believe?"

Dina's face was harder now. "Tell me what you're really doing here."

"I already did. Looking for a girl I used to know who told me once her mother worked at The Lucky Egg."

"Sounds suspicious as get out to me. Not sure what you're after, but if it's good for Melody, I hope you find it. If it's not, you'll have Johnny to answer to."

"What did you just say?" Beau asked.

"You heard me, young man. You're not exactly someone I'd want to mess with, but neither's Johnny, and he—"

"No, not that. Melody?" The name was vaguely familiar, something he'd heard recently.

"Oh. Lola's a nickname her daddy gave her, but I call her by her given name when I get worked up. Doctor doesn't like me to get worked up. I got high cholesterol, which you can probably guess—"

Beau stood, digging his wallet out of his jacket pocket. He remembered where he'd heard that name. He'd thought it was a stage name, and Lola had been teasing him in the strip club when she'd insisted he call her that. Maybe it'd been a clue—right in front of him the whole time.

"Hey, you barely touched your breakfast," Dina said. "Don't you like French toast?"

"I like it fine." Beau set a hundred-dollar bill on the table.

"Honey, I don't got change for that."

"Said I'd pay you for your time." Beau was nearly one foot out the door. He stopped himself from saying she'd earned it. Maybe it wasn't his suit that gave him away, but comments like that. "Thanks for your help," he said instead.

Chapter Six

In the past week, Lola had seen more of the world than she had in all twenty-nine years of her life. It was exhilarating, liberating, exciting. She covered her mouth for a yawn. Well, not all of it. Beau had been right about at least one thing—the world's largest ball of twine underwhelmed.

Lola stared at the popular roadside attraction, trying to warm her hands in the pockets of her denim jacket. She'd only been there five minutes, and she was ready to leave, but she'd driven through far stretches of countryside to get there. It really was just a big, stinky ball, though.

Lola giggled as Beau's comment came back to her.

"Big balls don't do anything for me. But if they impress you, I can show you a couple—"

A grown man was now hugging the ball as a woman photographed him. Lola looked around to see if anyone else was having the same immature reaction she was, the one Beau would've had too if he were there.

Beau took himself too seriously, but he had his moments. In a way, because his silly side was infrequent, it made him more endearing. She couldn't envision him letting his guard down that way with many other people.

Lola sighed and took a picture of the twine ball with a digital camera she'd purchased. If she'd had someone to text it to, she would've sent it along with some witty comment. Of course, she would've needed a phone for that.

"Want me to take one with you in it?" asked the woman with the ball-hugging man.

"No, thank you."

"You sure? Take it from me—when you get home, the pictures with no one in them get old real fast."

Lola suppressed a smile. Everyone else was doing it, but she couldn't help feeling a little ridiculous. "Okay," she said. "Why not."

"Anyone you want in it?"

Lola shook her head. "I'm alone." She handed the woman her camera. When it was her turn, she stood just in front of the ball and smiled. She refused to hug it.

"Good one." The woman returned Lola's camera. "You'll be glad when you get back. That's definitely going in the scrapbook."

Lola thanked her and left. During her trip, whenever she'd remembered, she'd taken at least one photo at each stop. At a rodeo in Wyoming, she'd sat in the stands with her cotton candy and watched a roping competition. Afterward, she'd won a goldfish at the state fair and given it to a little girl, making her hold it up for the camera. Lola had never been much of a moviegoer, but in Denver, she'd spent two days in the dark, gorging on foreign films during a festival. She'd photographed the sun rising between two gray mountains. A group of oddly-shaped pine cones. Tree trunks floating in the fog. Those were all from an early-morning hike she'd taken. She wasn't in any of the pictures, though, and she wasn't sure why she had them. They weren't for a scrapbook—or for anything, really.

Lola stretched her arms and legs before getting

back behind the wheel. Driving an entire country could be hard on the body, and she was achy a lot of the time. She unfolded her map panel by panel, revealing America in seconds. Without a phone or GPS, navigation was a new skill for her. The options were many—Botanical Gardens in Des Moines, the St. Louis Arch, Chicago—but she'd already decided on the Ozark Mountains. After days of cities and crowds, solitude in nature sounded luxurious.

Lola put the car in drive and hit the freeway. Hours crept by, as endless as the yellow, rolling wheat all around her. Clouds skidded across the blue sky and as she drove into the afternoon, they began to gather, low and gray on the horizon.

Everything had darkened by the time she reached the Ozarks, even though it was only late afternoon. She scanned her way through radio static, searching for a weather report. Thunder rumbled in the distance. The map got fuzzy around the mountains, and she didn't want to get caught in the rain looking for lodging.

She pulled off the road at the first place she saw, her tires chomping as she found a place to park. In her Hey Joe hoodie and a jacket, the warmest things she'd brought from California besides her trench coat, she walked up to a tiny, hole-in-the-wall bar with a lit Fat Tire sign in the window.

Inside, Lola blinked a few times to adjust her eyes to the dark. It was empty—nobody drinking his dinner yet. The interior wasn't an exact replica of Hey Joe, but they were cut from the same cigarette-burned cloth. She walked up to the bar. Johnny's third favorite Led Zeppelin song, "Babe I'm Gonna Leave You," played in the background as if someone'd forgotten to turn the music back up after a conversation. Some postcards of Midwest attractions were tacked on the walls. The retouched photographs were more vivid than what Lola'd seen with her own eyes. The real thing had been good, but it could always be better.

Lola hadn't contacted anyone, though she'd often thought about it. A message that she was fine. Better than fine. Amazing. She was seeing things that were good enough for postcards, learning about the country she'd grown up in—and herself too.

Above a wall of hard alcohol was a photo of bikini-clad women in snow boots and furry hats.

It may be freezing outside, but Missouri is still the hottest state in the U.S.A.!

She smiled. In Denver, she'd almost bought that same postcard with *Colorado* instead of *Missouri.* It would've made Beau laugh. She looked forward to a time when her tinges of nostalgia would die off, and she could fully enjoy Beau's suffering.

The bar served food, only three items—hamburger, hotdog or cheese fries. And then a list of beer sorted by draft or bottle. Lola hadn't eaten since Kansas. Sometimes, during long stretches in the car, she'd wonder what would've happened if she'd walked into that gas station weeks earlier and Beau hadn't had a gun to his head. If they'd bought a couple pieces of candy and scarfed hotdogs on the way back to the hotel.

She slid a hand along the pitted lip of the bar. The wood wasn't as smooth as Hey Joe's. Or maybe that was just how she remembered it. It wouldn't have mattered—the hotdogs. Beau would've gotten what he'd wanted from her one way or another. If not that night, then the next. Or the next. Beau never gave up. Did he?

Lola hadn't seen the look on Beau's face when she'd disappeared. With his control issues, it would be the not knowing that'd quickly drive him insane—where had she gone? How? Would she be back? When? Those questions, over and over, until he didn't know what was stronger—the hurt or the anger. Until he was teetering between never wanting to see her again and questioning how he could go on without her.

Lola turned to leave the bar but stopped. A tall, burly man dressed in black blocked the doorway. He stomped his leather boots on the ground, shaking out his long, brown-and-gray-streaked hair. "Help you?" he asked.

She checked over her shoulder, absentmindedly patting her wallet in her pocket. The alarming amount of cash she had in her car and on her person was never far from her mind. Nor were strange, oversized men who might be on the lookout for women traveling alone. "No. I was just on my way into town."

"Better get a move on then."

She edged around him, glancing sidelong at the patches on his motorcycle cut before deciding to keep her eyes on his face. This guy looked meaner than the diluted versions of him she'd served in Hollywood. He shifted to let her by.

With her first step outside, something dripped on the crown of her head. The sky slumped, resting on the mountains. A white spec floated down and landed on her face. "What the…?"

"First snow of the season."

She glanced back at the man, who leaned in the doorway. "*Snow*?"

"Yep."

She'd only seen machine-made snow once—on the ground in Big Bear. This was something else completely. More flakes drifted down on her, glitter in a snow globe, dampening the top of her hair. She put her tongue out to catch some. It was natural that something other than rain fell from the sapphire-gray sky, but it was foreign to her—like reading about music and then hearing it for the first time.

"It's beautiful." Lola blinked crystals off her lashes. "I've never seen anything like it. It's—"

"Goddamn obnoxious. You ever shoveled this shit? Plus, it brings on the insomnia, the cold." He paused. "But you know how that is."

She squinted at him over her shoulder. "No. I sleep fine."

"Dark circles don't lie." He disappeared back into the bar.

She touched her cheek—she'd noticed them too. All that driving left her restless at night.

The parking lot was empty. Her car glowed red against the muted gravel, the buzz in the air tainted by the smell of petroleum. For eight days, she'd convinced herself staying under the radar was necessary. She'd barely spoken to anyone. She wanted to tell someone how amazing it was that she'd never seen this before. Lola pulled her jacket closer around her and shivered.

The magic of the moment was short-lived for the

same reason her one-handed picture while crossing the Golden Gate Bridge had come out blurry. She was alone. Beau could've been standing by her side for her first snowfall if he hadn't been so proud and childish. He was a grown man behaving like a boy who'd had his feelings hurt. Was that what he thought of Lola, that she'd taken her toys and disappeared in the middle of the night?

They hurt themselves to hurt each other. It was almost as if Lola could look past the pain when she saw it that way—she just wasn't sure she was ready to.

Chapter Seven

Lola stood in front of the roadside bar in the Ozarks, snow falling a little faster now, dampening her denim jacket and hoodie.

"Not much of a coat you got there."

Lola turned quickly at the gruff voice. The man in the leather boots was back. "I'm from California," she said.

He held out a paper cup. "Here."

She shuffled toward him a little, the soles of her sneakers scraping against the dusty-brush sidewalk. The drink instantly warmed her hand.

"So, you lost, California?" he asked.

She inhaled fresh coffee and took a sip. "No."

"Liar."

She almost spit out her drink, raising her eyebrows at him. "What?"

He nodded at her pocket, where she'd stuffed the guidebook. She'd folded the corner of a page that had information about a nearby lodge.

"What brings you around?" he asked. "Business? Pleasure?"

She took another drink, too quickly this time, and burnt her tongue. She ran the tip of it over the roof of her mouth, her eyes watering. He didn't strike her as anything other than curious, but she'd thought the same of Beau when she'd met him. "Mostly sightseeing."

"Anything good so far?"

"Sure." She angled her body a little more in his direction. "I stood in the geographic center of the continental United States."

He laughed. "Well, that's something, isn't it?"

Lola nodded. It'd been more exciting than the twine, at least.

"Where you headed?" he asked.

She glanced upward. Information was precious. "I…"

"Give me that." He held out his hand for the guidebook, so she passed it to him. He flipped to the dog-eared page and grumbled, "Moose Lodge. It's for tourists, you know."

She shrugged. "Aren't all hotels?"

"Got a point. Not much to see around here, though."

Lola frowned. She didn't mind that. The open road and countryside had been good for her. The snow was magical. Kind of like Los Angeles from a distance when it was all lit up at night. Her heart thumped once when she thought of home.

"This lodge isn't far," he said. "You by yourself?"

Lola glanced at the lid of her coffee. She palmed the cup, welcoming its warmth. Yes, she was by herself. No, Beau was not waiting in the car for her. He was where she'd left him, where she'd spent twenty-nine years of her life—minus eight days.

"Ah," the man said. "I see what you got now, and it ain't insomnia."

"What is it?" Lola asked, still looking down.

"Lonely. I got that too, plus the insomnia, ever since my wife passed. Not a nice combo."

Lola nodded, swallowing. Things were rarely as bad as they seemed when she looked outside herself. "How long were you married?"

"Almost twenty years."

"Long time," Lola murmured. A long time to screw things up, to break each other's hearts. A long time to put them back together.

"She had cancer," he continued. "But you know how she died? Hit by a car. Believe that?"

"I'm sorry," Lola said lamely.

"So was I, until I realized all the ways Maxie makes me better, even from the grave. Just this morning, I drive a few towns over to Costco and someone's pulling out of a front spot. Never happens, right? I wait a good couple minutes. Then this guy comes from the other direction, swipes it at the last second. You know what I did?"

Lola hesitated, almost afraid to ask. "What?"

"Before Maxie passed, I would've taught the scrawny shit some manners. Instead, I rolled down the window and said, 'You know what? Take the goddamn spot. I'll park in back, get myself some exercise.'"

Lola chewed her bottom lip, trying to connect that back to their conversation. She'd never been much of a religious person, so she wasn't sure of the polite way to proceed. "So, you're saying…that was Maxie's way of keeping you fit?"

He chuckled, shaking his head. "I'm saying since she left me, I don't sweat the small stuff. Actually, I don't let the big stuff get to me anymore either. Because it's really not that important if you think about it. I'm going to go to Costco lots more times before I die, God willing, but never again with her. I'd park in the back every day if it meant she were walking by my side."

Lola's nose tingled. What Beau had done wasn't small stuff by any means. Not to her. It wasn't like he'd stolen her parking spot. This man would agree if he heard her story. Wouldn't he? He'd lost the love of his life—well, so had she, and it wasn't either of their faults. To forgive Beau would be a betrayal to herself—she'd always believed that. But maybe this man was telling her the opposite was true. Forgiveness was the path back to herself, to the woman who'd never gone out of her way to hurt someone else the way she had Beau.

"Life is short," Lola said in summary.

"That's right. We'd better try to have a good time while we're here." He rubbed his hands together, warming them. "So, what're you running from, California?"

"What makes you think I'm running at all?"

He raised his brows at her. "My family's owned this bar since before I could walk. Seen a lot of people pass through this town because it's quiet. Hidden. Sometimes women trying to escape with their lives."

"It's not like that." Lola shook her head. Running away was weak. She was taking back her life, fortifying herself after years of living for others. "I'm starting over."

"That's what a lot of these women say. Sometimes they get caught. Most of the time they go back on their own. But they're almost always hiding." The man raised his coffee cup at her. "Somebody were going after my wife, I'd want to know about it."

Lola slid her wallet out of her back pocket. Suddenly, she wanted to be alone the way she had been her whole trip. It felt as if she were on the verge of understanding what all this had been about. She didn't want to lose that. "How much do I owe you for the coffee?"

"On the house. As for Moose Lodge, you're going to take this road down another mile and turn right. It'll be on your left." He returned her guidebook. "Get home safe, wherever home is."

Lola didn't have a home anymore. Johnny had come close, but that feeling of safety had vanished quicker than she thought possible. Now, only one idea came to mind—but an empty shell was no place for anyone to call home.

◆⊠◆⊠◆

Lola found the lodge easily, and it was a good thing, because the storm was picking up. Her Converse crunched snow as she walked up to the lobby. Inside, she removed her hood, plucking her sweater to rid it of flakes.

"Early this year, isn't it?"

Lola looked up at a young girl, whose eager smile gave her chipmunk cheeks. "What?"

She nodded behind Lola. "The snow. I thought we'd have a few more weeks."

"Oh. I wouldn't know. This is my first time in Missouri." She approached the front desk. "First snowfall too."

The girl clapped her hands and wiggled her pink-tipped fingers. "How exciting. I don't even remember my first. I was a baby."

Lola laughed a little at that. Enthusiasm was infectious in this friendly town. "I would've called ahead if I'd realized there was a storm coming. Do you have a room for tonight?"

"We sure do." She grabbed the computer mouse and began clicking. "King bed all right? All the rooms are one-fifty plus tax."

It was the most Lola'd paid for a room yet, but she wasn't about to go hunting for something else in this weather. It wasn't like she didn't have the money. "I'll take it."

"Great. Just give me a sec while I set you up."

A wailing noise came from outside. Lola left a couple hundred-dollar bills on the counter with her license and went to the window, drawing the curtain aside.

It was dusk now, but the pine trees surrounding the Moose Lodge glowed white with powdered branches. A little boy in a puffy jacket and knit cap cried noisily, gulping air. His mom stood by their car, hunched over her phone to protect it from the snow. Lola had the urge to go pick him up, comfort him, anything to stop his bawling.

After a minute, the mom snatched a toy airplane from her purse and handed it to him. His face smoothed immediately, and he took off running, his arms planed at his sides as he weaved through the tree trunks. She'd done the same with her doll, Nadia, as a little girl. She'd dressed it up for imaginary tea parties. At home alone, that was her friend, and that was enough to content her. Children played games for themselves, not their opponents.

Lola crinkled her nose with an unexpected wave of tears. Either she was hormonal or homesick, because thinking of her past wasn't the kind of thing that usually moved her.

The boy jumped into fresh snow with both feet. If Lola'd brought proper boots, she would've joined him. She decided when she had a kid, she'd make sure he or she got a chance to play in the snow. And she'd be right by his side.

His mother stayed in the parking lot, tapping at her cellphone. Lola's cash-filled car was ten feet away.

Johnny'd had a mantra—no kids until they had the money. Well, Lola was sitting on hundreds of thousands of dollars now. That kind of money was a new home, a college fund, clean clothes and never missing a meal. Lola had put all that and more on the line just to spite Beau. She'd not only lost touch with the future she'd once wanted, but every day that money wasn't in a bank, she'd also risked it. For what? To hide out in motels in hopes of making Beau suffer? Who was actually suffering?

Lola'd been avoiding thinking of where and when her trip would end, but she had to start making decisions. She'd hoped to get some answers from the road, and in that moment, one came to her—Los Angeles was her home. Before Beau, before Johnny, it'd been her first true love, and it was where she one day wanted to watch her own son or daughter run around in her backyard.

She'd been looking for the wrong thing. True freedom would never come with revenge. Lola had spent a decade angry with her mother for reasons she couldn't even pinpoint—she didn't need that shadow at her back looming larger. She wanted herself and those she loved to live in light.

"Oh, shoot," she heard from behind her. "We don't accept cash."

Lola turned back to the front desk. The lodge was a step up from the motels she'd been crashing at, but not a huge one. "You don't? My credit card is…" Lola hesitated as she returned to the counter. "Is there any way you can make an exception? I've been traveling for over a week and haven't had a problem paying cash anywhere else."

"My dad, he's strict about it." The girl shook her head. "We need to swipe a card at check-in and have it for incidentals and stuff. We had some problems before."

Lola took the money back and nodded. Finding another place at this time of night and in these snowy mountains wouldn't be easy, but it wasn't impossible, but Lola was beginning to question the fact that she'd taken so many chances already. She took out an emergency credit card hidden in her wallet and handed it over. The girl grinned again and swiped it.

Lola decided in the morning, she'd deposit her money in a bank. Driving around with as much cash as she had in her trunk had been reckless. One day, she'd have a family, and she had put them at risk. The price for revenge suddenly seemed much too high.

Chapter Eight

Melody. Lola. Had he even fucking known her? Beau entered all his interactions with at least a small amount of cynicism and distrust. It'd served him well in affairs both business and personal. But Lola represented a time before he'd had to be that man. When she'd kicked a car outside of Hey Joe, he'd been just as attracted to her as he had seeing her on stage at Cat Shoppe. He should've walked away based on the fact that he hadn't wanted to. Something in her blue eyes had kept him planted on that sidewalk, though. She'd inched closer and closer, peering at him in the dark, neon lights reflecting off her shiny black hair. Some predators stalked their prey. Others waited for their prey to come to them. In those few seconds as she'd approached him, he hadn't been sure which one of them was predator and which was prey. Even before his money, he'd never had that feeling before. But he'd recovered quickly. He was Beau Olivier—and he was nobody's dinner.

"Olivier."

Beau looked up from the presentation binder in front of him. His business partner stood at the head of the conference table. Lawrence Thorne was the other half of Bolt Ventures, and one of the only people Beau trusted. But that was all their relationship'd ever been. Larry had a wife Beau knew from myriad events and two kids Beau'd only met once.

"Think you might want to wake the fuck up?" Lawrence asked. "It's four in the afternoon."

Their lawyer, Louis, rapped his pen on the table. "You've been silent the entire meeting. Since when do you have no comment on the fact that VenTech's stock closed at a record low?"

Beau furrowed his eyebrows and turned the page to a graph labeled *Potential Holdings Research Report—VenTech*. The squiggly line had dipped far into the red. That always caught his attention, but he hadn't noticed it in the twenty minutes they'd been sitting there. Instead, he'd been thinking about the former holding who'd taken a nosedive into disastrous territory.

"This was today?" Beau asked.

Louis nodded. "Word is, they're done for."

Beau looked at both of them. "Then let's move."

"We have people looking into it," Larry said.

"I'm tired of waiting." Beau'd been patient as always, and as always, it'd paid off. But he had his limits, and he was ready to pounce on VenTech, the company that'd bought his payment services website ten years ago and picked it apart until it was nothing more than a carcass. Now, Beau was in a position to save VenTech from bankruptcy. He wanted to look the founder, George Wright, in the eye, and tell him he owned him. He leaned forward on his elbows. "Draw up the offer."

"You're sure?" Larry asked. "Established companies aren't really our thing."

"VenTech is desperate. You know I've been tracking them for a long time. You promised me the day we partnered, Larry—you'd back me up on this."

Larry nodded. "I did. And if this is what you need, I'm on board."

"Good. Get the paperwork started."

"Consider it done." Louis reclined back in his seat, steepling his fingers. "So, you going to tell us whose call you're expecting?"

Beau slid the binder away. "I don't know what you're talking about."

"Last time you were like this," Louis said, "you were wooing a new company but wouldn't tell us which one. You've been checking your phone like an addict waiting to hear about a fix. So who is it?"

Beau glanced in the direction of his office. If he moved now, he could have a drink in his hand in under sixty seconds. "It's personal."

Larry snorted. "Bullshit. What's more important to you than this?"

"I don't know," Beau said, "maybe an ear infection?"

"You're mad because I left in the middle of the day last week to take my kid to the ER?" Larry asked. "The fuck's wrong with you, man?"

"I'm not mad." Beau ran his hands through his hair. "I'm saying maybe I've got my own shit to deal with too, yet I'm here more than anyone else."

"So take an afternoon off. You're the one who wants to be here all the time."

Louis nodded. "You don't need anyone to tell you when you can go home for the day. You got plenty of underlings around here who live to pick up the slack."

None of this was news to Beau. Larry had started going home at five a couple years ago, and the office had survived. Thrived, even, without one more opinion in the mix.

"I'll be honest, Beau." Larry shut his laptop and sat. "You look like shit. Even more than when we're going through a rough acquisition. I think productivity might pick up if you take your gloomy ass out to a matinee or something. Treat yourself to a haircut while you're at it."

"Fuck you, Thorne," Beau said, but his heart wasn't in it.

Larry just smiled.

Beau reached in his jacket for his phone but stopped when Larry and Louis exchanged a glance. He didn't need to check it anyway. He tested his ringer several times a day, and it was working fine. He'd ignored two calls from Brigitte that morning just out of sheer anger that it hadn't been Detective Bragg calling.

It'd been eight goddamn days since Lola had left. If this was a game for Lola, she hadn't left him a single clue. The leather pants and T-shirt she'd worn the night he'd met her were gone, but other than that, he didn't know what else she'd taken with her. Nothing he'd bought her, except what she'd been wearing that night. Bragg was also frustrated. He'd had better luck tracking down criminals with actual reasons to hide. Criminals who preyed on young, beautiful women traveling alone with lots of cash.

Beau was always hot lately, but with that thought, warmth traveled to his feet and scalp. Waking up with Lola, coming home to her—it'd been a new, irregular world, but she'd centered him. Now, a week later, he didn't even know if she was dead or alive. That seemed unfair. If anyone should get to decide her fate, it should be him. He at least wanted that choice again.

More and more, he worried she hadn't been real, just a dream. They shared none of the same friends or daily routines. There wasn't anywhere on his way to work where he'd stop and remember a moment they'd had. Had she been an illusion, a sleek magic trick? His last moments with her, he'd been dumb with lust, two fingers inside her sweet pussy silk.

Beau laced his hands in his hair, suddenly aware of how long it was, and that he'd forgotten to style it that morning. He stood. "I need some fresh air."

"Yeah, fine, just don't come back today," Larry said dismissively. "Go home or something."

Beau didn't go home, and he didn't get air. He went to his office and looked out his window with a drink in his hand.

Orange skyscrapers reflected the late afternoon. Where was she, his beautiful kitten, that sly minx? All by herself, no trail left behind? Was she wearing her skintight leather pants and asking for trouble? Was she flirting with men who could hurt her far worse than Beau had?

Beau unbuttoned his collar. He couldn't get his breathing under control. Work was supposed to be where he found balance. He would've slammed his fist into the window except that he'd hit a few things over the last few days, and it never seemed to do any good. The leather pants bothered him. He couldn't stop picturing her in them.

He'd lost track of how many times he'd listed in his head all the things he knew about Lola. The food she ate. The drinks she drank. Any mentions she'd made of places she'd wanted to see or things she'd wanted to buy. He didn't think it'd be as easy as showing up at the world's largest ball of twine and finding her there, but he'd called the box office anyway. They didn't attach names to cash transactions, and why would they?

Lola had more money now than she must've ever dreamed. When Beau had sold his company, he'd signed on the dotted line and gone from thousands in debt to a multi-millionaire. Sex had been suddenly and oppressively on his mind. He'd wanted to fuck with all the power he'd finally had. Lola had taken that away from him—that little cat, with big blue eyes and black, furry triangle ears, had captivated him from the moment he'd walked into Cat Shoppe. It was as if she'd called his eyes right to her. He'd just been handed the key to his kingdom, and he could've had anything he'd wanted—and what he'd wanted stood underneath a white spotlight, dressed in nothing but a diamond bikini and cat ears. She became the one thing he needed that night and the one thing he couldn't have. With four words—*"I'm not for sale"*—he wasn't enough again, not even as a man with something to offer.

Lola would know that same power now—because of him. Because of him, she was out there in her leather pants—fucking, drinking, spending cash, laughing at him. Beau'd thought he was the one in charge, but just the sway of her hips had disarmed him long enough to steal his power a second time. He was halfway between wanting to worship her and wring her neck for pulling this off. His heart pounded at the thought of holding that slender column under his fingers as she begged his forgiveness.

His phone beeped, and he jumped. His hands were curled into two tight fists.

"Mr. Olivier?" came his assistant's voice.

"What?" he snapped. "What the fuck is it?"

It was a moment before she continued. "I-I'm sorry. You said—you were very clear that I should interrupt you any time Detective Bragg called."

Beau turned from the window. He leaned his knuckles on his desk and spoke directly into the phone, as if that would get him answers faster. "He called?"

"Just now."

"Why didn't he try my cell?"

"He said he did."

Beau took out his phone to see he had a missed call. "Piece of shit," he muttered, tossing it aside. "Get Bragg for me. Now."

"He's already on the line," she said. "And he says he's got something for you."

Chapter Nine

Beau came home to a light on in the kitchen. His heart in his throat, he hung his coat on the hook by the door. Nobody'd been home to greet him since Lola'd left eight days ago. The housekeeper had been there that day, but she didn't leave lights on. Beau'd explained to her how that was a waste of money. And she didn't cook him dinner. He followed the smell of food and the clinking of dishware.

The weight that already sat on his shoulders grew heavier with each step. A few nights before Lola had left, she'd made pulled pork tacos in a "Kiss the Cook" apron she'd bought herself. She'd kept his food at the perfect temperature until he'd walked through the door, and it was the sexiest thing he'd ever seen—Lola, in a red-and-white gingham apron, making him dinner with barbeque sauce on her cheek. He'd kissed her, cleaning her face with a restrained lick of his tongue.

Beau held as breath as he entered the kitchen. Despite his conversation with Bragg an hour earlier, he half expected to find the same thing in the kitchen he had two weeks ago.

And that was exactly what he found—except that it was Brigitte wearing the apron, and she had something in the oven instead of the slow cooker.

Her face lit up as she raised a glass of red wine. "Welcome home. I thought you could use a homemade meal."

Beau clamped his mouth shut as his stomach turned, his eyes glued to that kitschy fucking apron and the barbeque sauce stain near the hem. "Where'd you find that?"

"What?" Brigitte followed his gaze down. "The apron? Hanging in the pantry. Honestly, I was surprised you even owned—"

"It was Lola's." Sweat formed on his hairline. Of course he wasn't going to find Lola in his kitchen. If she had any sense, she'd be terrified to ever face him again. He unknotted his tie and slid it off. "I told you to get rid of her shit."

Brigitte shrugged and grinned blue, her mouth tinted from the wine. "It's just an apron. Don't erupt, Mt. Olivier." She walked over and gave him her glass. "Drink this. It'll calm you."

Beau took the wine and set it on the counter. "I don't need to calm down. Your car isn't in the driveway."

"Warner brought me. He's the only person who ever checks on me." She blew out a heavy sigh, heaving her chest and shoulders. "I hadn't seen a soul in two whole days, and I couldn't get you on the phone. What, did you smash it again? Anyway, I absolutely couldn't take another minute. I had to come over."

"You'll have to learn to deal with being alone, Brigitte. I don't want company right now."

She plumped her lower lip. "I'll try not to take that personally. What's the matter?"

Beau removed everything from his pockets into a dish on the counter. He didn't need Brigitte in his business, adding her two cents at every juncture. "Long day. That's all."

"You've been so distant since you kicked me out. You know I don't do well on my own, Beau."

He picked up the clean pile of mail his housekeeper had organized and sorted. "I've had a lot on my plate. And I didn't kick you out. There just wasn't enough room here for both you and her."

"Does that mean I can come back?"

Beau glanced up. Her eyebrows were raised. So that was why she was there—to scope things out and see if he might be distracted enough to let her back in. He didn't have the energy to argue, and it made no difference to him if she was there. His house had turned from sanctuary to hell now that he'd glimpsed a life he couldn't have. And Brigitte there, cooking for him, was a thorny reminder. "I don't care. Just take off that fucking apron."

Beau's phone rang. He checked the screen, saw it was Bragg, and cleared it. He'd call him as soon as he went upstairs to change. If he rushed off to his study, Brigitte would pick at him until he spilled everything to her.

"Who was that?"

"Nobody." Beau opened a bill and tossed it aside, having already paid it online. He made a note to switch it over to e-mail and picked up another envelope, avoiding Brigitte's penetrating stare, her loud silence. Finally, he sighed and looked up. "What?"

"It's about her, isn't it?"

"Who?"

"Come on, Beau. You know who. There's something going on with Lola."

"I hardly think of her."

"You must think I'm blind. Tell me."

Beau slid his mail away and set his elbows on the counter, rubbing his face. He wasn't as annoyed with Brigitte as he tried to be. Bragg had been his only confidante in over a week, and all the detective cared about was facts. Those sporadic, nonsensical facts were insignificant compared to how Lola's void actually made him feel.

"I found her," he said.

Brigitte's back straightened. "I didn't even know you were looking for her."

"I wasn't. Detective Bragg was. I hired him when she left." He shut his eyes and shook his head. "Says she's in Missouri."

"Missouri?" Brigitte asked. "What the hell is she doing there?"

"I have no idea. Other than one hotel charge, there's no other activity on her credit card."

Slowly, Brigitte's eyes widened as she inclined her head toward him. "You tracked her credit card?"

Beau nodded. That was minor in comparison to interrogating Lola's closest friends and family, but he decided to keep that to himself—Brigitte's eyebrows were already halfway up her forehead. "Yes, but there were no charges over the last eight days. Now there's one pending."

"Oh." She crossed her arms, curling her nails into her biceps. "So you're going to go find her?"

"No," Beau said immediately. "I sent Bragg."

Brigitte tilted her head fractionally. "How come?"

Beau didn't know how to answer that. He knew he should just leave her alone, for both their sakes. He didn't want to, though. He was hurt. He still loved her. But above all, he was angry with her. He couldn't walk away, and he couldn't go after her himself. That would tell her she was worth something to him. She was, but Beau wanted to smother that feeling, not nurture it.

Money gave Beau the gift to waste someone else's time instead of his. Bragg would handle everything. He'd bring Lola back kicking and screaming if Beau asked him to. Throw her at his feet. And Beau would get his answers.

"I have to stay close to the office," he said. "I don't have time to chase her down. I just want to know where she is before I decide…"

Their eyes met. Brigitte turned her back to him and put on her oven mitts, but she didn't move beyond that. "What'll you do if you find her?"

"I don't know. But I can't let her get away with this."

Brigitte looked over her shoulder at him. "Then why not go yourself?"

"I told you—I have a company to run. That's why I have people like Bragg."

She faced him again, her mitted hands at her sides. "Why waste Bragg's time if Lola isn't worth enough for you to go yourself? Time is your most valuable resource, but your money and energy are equally precious. She's bleeding you out, Beau. Jesus. Warner says he's never seen you this distracted. Just let this thing go."

Lola had been a strain on him one way or another since he'd found her again—yet knowing her had been rewarding in ways he hadn't anticipated. After his proposition to her to spend the night with him, he'd returned home to Brigitte, who hadn't thought it was a waste of anything then.

"You were always on board with my plan," he said. "You even said a million was a small price to pay for what I wanted in return."

"Because it was a game, and you needed that win. Her rejection had been a weak spot for you all those years, and you're the strongest person I know. It was never about getting laid." She shook her head. "This isn't a game anymore, Beau. Part of your success has come from your ability to cut deadweight loose the way most people can't. The moment hesitation or indecision creeps in, you're letting emotion get in the way of your sense. She's offered you an exit, and you need to take it."

Beau asked himself if he could go upstairs, go to bed and never think of Lola again. Bragg wouldn't care either way. He'd walk out of the airport right now, so long as he got paid. Lola and Beau had both hurt each other, but the score would never feel even. How long could it go on? He didn't know, but he couldn't forget her. He hadn't in ten years, and he wouldn't ten years from now. He had to confront her. A small part of him wondered if she wanted him to find her. If she'd made that one credit card charge hoping he'd follow it.

"Can we drop this already and eat some lasagna?" Brigitte asked, sighing as she pulled the oven open.

"Why?"

She slid the dish out and set it on the stove. "Because I'm hungry, and this discussion isn't—"

"No," he interrupted. "Why do I need to take this exit she's given me?"

Brigitte rolled her eyes, removing the oven mitts. "I don't want to see you get hurt yet again. She's put you through enough, and she isn't worth it. Clearly, she doesn't even want to be around you."

Beau folded his arms against his chest and leaned back on the counter. Brigitte never wanted to see him get hurt, and that was why she'd hated Lola from day one. Brigitte and Beau had always decided who got close enough to find their well-hidden weak spots. They'd only been teenagers when the car accident had killed their parents. With his dad's death came the news of his affair with Brigitte's mom. It'd been a day—a lifetime—of struggling with hurt and anger, loss and betrayal. Beau didn't think of it much anymore, but it affected how he dealt with others. Until Lola, he hadn't had a good enough reason to let anyone close.

"Maybe it's time we start living in the real world again, Brigitte. Where people get hurt and they fuck up. Then they come out stronger. Didn't we come out stronger after what we went through?"

"Yes, you and I—"

"I mean as individuals," Beau clarified. "Not as a unit. Maybe it made us too strong."

"That's ridiculous." She waved a spatula in his direction. "Who are you right now? You sound like a therapist."

Beau didn't have to be a therapist to see she was deflecting. He wasn't ready to change the topic, though, and that was unlike him when it came to Brigitte and serious issues. Ever since his breakfast-dinner with Dina Winters, he'd been wondering when he'd become so disconnected from people.

"Let me ask you something," he said. "When's the last time you went on a date?"

She looked over at him, her eyes huge. "What?"

"You heard me."

"Since when do you care?"

"Answer the question. Or are you afraid to?"

"I got out with men all the time."

"I mean someone who actually interests you. Not a potential investor or a business contact."

She twisted her lips. "Don't turn this conversation on me. This is about you and your control issues. Letting go of Lola is the best thing—"

"I see." Beau was annoyed with her as usual, but he couldn't help a small smile. "So everything's about you except what you don't feel like talking about?"

"Everything is not about me. You're frustrated with yourself, and you're taking it out on me so you don't have to deal with it." She dug the spatula into the lasagna. "Let's just have a nice dinner and forget the rest until tomorrow morning. After some good food and rest, you'll see I'm right as usual."

Beau's smiled eased. He'd been supporting Brigitte financially for a long time, but she was the one who took care of him. He'd never asked for it—he didn't even need it. Because it wasn't for him. She did it for herself. "I'm not enough for you, Brigitte. This, us—it's not enough."

She cut squares into the lasagna, the utensil methodically hitting the bottom of the glass dish. "I don't know what you're talking about. You just want me to leave you alone."

"You could be happy, but you choose not to be. You're afraid if you lose me, you won't have anything at all."

She stopped moving, kept her profile to him. "And you're an expert on what I need? You wouldn't even know me if I didn't force you to all the time. You think money is the answer to everything, including me. I'd bet you were the same with Lola. If a problem can't be fixed with a check, all of us are shit out of luck where you're concerned."

Anger surged through Beau, but it died out just as quickly, as if it'd been a conditioned response. He didn't like Brigitte's assumption he valued his money more than Lola, but that didn't mean it had no merit. "I'm not claiming I've been good at any of this. Boyfriend, brother or even friend. Yes, sometimes I send Warner in my place—because I trust him to give you what I can't."

She shook her head. "I don't even know why you're bringing him into this."

"Yes, you do. You're only blind or stupid when you want to be." Beau looked hard at her, the only person he'd ever felt really close to before Lola. Brigitte was more family to him than his own mother. Even with her avoiding his eyes, he could sense her terror. Any time Beau had to leave, whether it was for a business trip or when he moved to the hotel to get some space from her, she got this way. She didn't think she could do it on her own, but once she stopped clinging to Beau, she'd see that wasn't true. "If you knew what would make me happy, wouldn't you want me to have it?" he asked.

After a moment of silence, she said, "Yes."

"I want the same for you. Look who's standing right in front of you, who's there for you whenever you or I call. It isn't me."

"That's what he gets paid to do. I'm just a nuisance to his boss. He gets stuck dealing with me."

"Maybe in the beginning, but much of the time he spends with you isn't because I send him. He wants to do it."

Brigitte stayed quiet. He didn't believe it'd never occurred to her that Warner loved her or that she could have him if she let herself. But Beau obviously knew less about the women in his life than he realized, especially when it came to love.

When it was clear she had nothing to add, Beau went to leave the room.

"Lola," she said suddenly.

He turned around. "What?"

She looked at him finally. "You said if I know what would make you happy, I should tell you. That's what love is, right? Your happiness over my own?"

"Neither of us is happy, Brigitte. Can you honestly tell me this is the life you want? You living here, keeping house, while I work myself to death?"

She shuddered, but her expression didn't change. "You're the only person I have." Her voice was soft. "I don't know how to be without you."

"Warner could be the best thing that's ever happened to you, but you'll never know if I'm in the way."

"And what about Lola? You're going to send a complete stranger after her when she's alone in the middle of the country? I don't understand your fascination with her, but I don't need to. I see you're going crazy without her." She took a deep breath as if it'd required effort to speak that much.

Beau's eyes were dry. He blinked, the first time since she'd started talking. It was the last thing he'd expected to hear from her, but if one thing had always remained true, it was that she loved him even more than she did herself. She just rarely showed it in a non-destructive way.

"You think I should go after her," Beau stated.

"I don't want you to." She held his gaze, also unblinking. "That's how I know you have to."

Chapter Ten

Beau pulled into a parking spot and rubbed his eyes with tense fingers. After a sleepless night at LAX and hours of flying and driving, he still didn't know what the fuck he was going to say to get the information he needed. He got out and shut the door behind him. It'd been daylight when he'd left Los Angeles, but it was almost evening now. The parking lot was dark with storm clouds. The Moose Lodge's exterior could almost pass for a cozy hotel, except that the buzzy glare of its neon sign gave it away as something seedier. The word *Vacancy* was lit underneath it. He hated to think of Lola here by herself, in this slow-life Missouri town, where there was an unwelcome chill in the air.

Across the street, a man in hunter-green camo pants leaned against the wall of a liquor store, watching Beau. A cigarette dangled from his lips. He could've easily been one of Hey Joe's beer guzzlers, the ones Beau'd seen leering at Lola as she'd wound through two-top tables, her effortless confidence drawing eyes.

Men like that and places like this had gone round and round in Beau's mind the last nine days, a haunted carousel with Lola trapped in the center. The homeless man from the gas station was always on it, and the guy across the street looked eerily similar to him. Him, with his hands on Lola while Beau had stood there, helpless.

Through the gas station's glass door, Beau watched Lola approach, her purse swinging in her hand. The corners of her pressed-together lips curved slightly upward, as if it was a real effort not to smile. In the split second before she pulled open the door, her movements were airy and light, like a woman—he hoped—in love.

Beau would've shouted at her to run if he hadn't thought startling the cagey man who held a gun to Beau's head would earn one of them a bullet.

She breezed in and stopped dead.

"I told you, there isn't a single thing in my car." Beau had been trying to convince the man to stay inside with him instead of going out there, where Lola was. She'd come to them anyway. Beau attempted a discrete but firm jerk of his hand in her direction.

He pleaded with her however he could—with a quick glance, with a stiffening of his body. She should've been far away from there. Leave. Go.

She didn't move an inch. Beau sent the man on a hunt for his wallet as a distraction.

Leave. Get the fuck out of here.

She didn't budge, but cried out, "I have it," and the gun was no longer on Beau.

Beau'd barely slept on his one-way flight out of LAX. After talking to Brigitte, he'd called Bragg to stop him from getting on a plane, but the Midwest storm had done it for him. The detective'd been at the airport for two hours trying to get to Missouri. Beau took his place, waiting out the snow, every passing hour another chance for Lola to slip back into the night. When he couldn't take another minute of that, he demanded a flight that would get him closest to this little lodge in the Missouri mountains. He'd flown into Dallas and driven his rental car eight hours. In the meantime, the storm had mostly passed.

Beau walked up to the front office's glass door and stood just outside of view. That memory of the gas station was always too ready, too easy to call up. Beau still hadn't figured out why he was there. He'd know when he saw her. He just needed to lay his eyes on her again—that was step one.

A potbellied, balding man sat at the check-in desk, a phone lodged between his ruddy cheek and his shoulder while he pounded on a computer keyboard. He said something into the receiver and slammed it down.

Almost immediately, a girl came out of the back, her blonde ponytail swinging. She furrowed her eyebrows, put a slender hand on his shoulder and pointed to something on the screen. The lines in his forehead eased as the splotches on his cheeks became less angry. They smiled at each other, and he stood and left the room.

Enter Beau. He straightened his suit jacket and smoothed his palm over his styled hair. He still needed a haircut, but at least he looked presentable today. Bells chirped against the glass door when he walked in, a jingle to announce him. The girl, no older than eighteen or nineteen, looked up and froze.

"Hi." Beau forced a smile and leaned an elbow on the counter. "How are you?"

"Fine." The word barely disturbed her parted lips.

Neither of them spoke a moment. He didn't get this kind of thing much anymore—the curious, innocent-lust look she was giving him. The women he spent time with had already had their rose-colored glasses removed by someone. He glanced at the monitor and back at her.

"Oh." She jumped into action, clasping the computer mouse in her hand. "You need a room?"

"Actually, no," Beau said, still smiling, still leaning.

She looked up. "No?"

"Well, sort of. I'm hoping you can help me out—what's your name?"

"Uh." She checked over her shoulder. "Matilda?"

"Nice to meet you, Matilda. I'm Beau." He should've been an actor. Or a detective. A story was already brewing inside him, a warm stew to go down easy. "My wife is staying here on business." He declared it—no question about it. Men in bespoke suits did not just wander into motel lobbies and tell lies. "Tonight's our anniversary. She thought she'd have to spend it alone."

"That's strange," the girl said. "We don't get a lot of business types out here, not like Springfield or Harrison. Even then, companies usually book at the Best Western in town." She pointed behind Beau as if he could see from where he stood.

Beau glanced over her head at the backdoor and absentmindedly straightened his tie. "Well, the point is—I drove a long way to see her. To surprise her."

Matilda beat her palm once against her chest. "Really?" she crooned. "That is so romantic."

"I know." Beau kept a smirk from his face. "Here's the thing, Matilda. I don't know which room she's in."

Her face fell except for one blonde eyebrow, which rose. "Oh?"

Beau could almost taste his anticipation. Within moments, he'd be standing in front of Lola's door, and she wouldn't even know it. He'd worried, as he'd driven, that she wouldn't be there anymore, that she'd only stayed one night. But his doubts were gone now. He could sense her there, nearby, unprotected, unsuspecting. Caught in her own trap. "If you could just get me a key to her room—"

"I can't give you that." Terseness clipped Matilda's words, made her back rod straight. "That's illegal."

Illegal? Did this girl think she was in an episode of *CSI: Missouri*? Beau blinked slowly at her. "Not if she's my wife."

"Um, yes, even if she's your wife. Why can't you call her cell phone?"

"I told you, it's a surprise." Beau sounded almost sulky. He envisioned Lola slipping out the backdoor again, right through his fingers just as he closed them around her. So he was no detective. But a starry-eyed teenage girl was no seasoned negotiator. "All right, the key is a lot to ask. I'll just take her room number."

She shook her head.

"What's your objection?" Beau asked.

"It's wrong. How do I know she's actually your wife, and you're not some stalker?"

"I'll leave my wallet and ID here with you. I can get it on my way out."

"You're leaving tonight?"

"That's the plan."

She wrinkled her nose. "Why, if your wife is here?"

"I'm taking her with me."

"But…she has her work thing—"

Beau's nostrils flared. His negotiation skills were better suited to businessmen than stubborn, inquisitive teenagers. He'd once had a good laugh with a subordinate whose fifteen-year-old daughter had seen a picture of daddy's boss and called Beau a 'total hottie.' He plastered on a smile and inclined a little further over the counter. "Matilda, let me ask you something—do you have a boyfriend?"

Her mouth opened and closed. "Not anymore."

"He dumped you."

"How'd you know?"

"Because I've met enough women like you to know how it works. Pretty girls come and go, but it's the ones who're smart *and* pretty who catch shmucks like me off guard." Beau shrugged. "We're intimidated by girls like you, so we screw it up."

She blushed, looking down at the desk. "My dad says that too."

"He sounds like a smart man. My wife—she's one of you." Beau didn't have to reach far there. Lola stunned men, and she was sharp in a way most people weren't, even without logging much time on a college campus or facing a boardroom of Harvard MBAs daily.

But that kind of smart could get you into trouble too. After Beau, Lola should've run home and cried onto Johnny's shoulder like most girls would've. Her life with Johnny never would've been the same, but it would've been safe. Stable.

That wasn't Lola, though. She'd picked a dangerous path instead, willingly entering the ring with a man who had the means—and now an ironclad motive—to bring her down for good if he chose to.

"I've been to hell and back for her," Beau told the girl. "But every time I see her face, I'm reminded why I do it. Help me out, Matilda. I just want to see the expression on her face when I walk into her room. She'll light up with pure *shock*."

Matilda's eyes had grown big and watery, her shoulders slumped with longing. Done deal. He held out his palm for the keycard.

She straightened up, though, pressed her lips together. "I'm sorry, sir," she said, not sounding the least bit sorry. "I legally can*not* give you that information."

Beau dropped his hand on the counter with a slap. This was bullshit. Bragg could've hacked her computer two times over by now. Beau had one negotiation tool she didn't, though, and it was bulletproof. "How much?"

She tilted her head, looking utterly confused. "How much what?"

He hadn't noticed how quick he was to resort to money until he'd done it to Lola's mom in exchange for information. It was beginning to bother him a little, like a dull cramp in his side. It had upset Lola too. He knew, even when she didn't mention it.

The portly man came through the backdoor and waddled over to them. "What's going on, Matty?"

"Dad, this man is asking for a guest's *room key*."

Beau cleared his throat. What was happening to him that he couldn't crack a teenage girl? But at least going up against another man put him back in his comfort zone—because man to man, fortune favored the alpha. "Not a guest," Beau said. "My *wife*. And I don't like being kept from her like this. Do yourself a favor and give me her room number. It'll save you a lot of hassle."

"Calm down, sir," he said. "No need to overreact."

"Overreact?" Beau curled a hand into a fist. "I drove all the way from Dallas to surprise her. That's eight goddamn hours. If I call her, it'll ruin everything."

"She's your wife?" the man asked. "Let me see your license. The names match, we won't have an issue."

Beau refrained from rolling his eyes. His wallet burned a hole in his suit jacket, but showing them his ID with a name that didn't match hers could mean the end of the conversation. "Well, actually, I don't have my license on me—"

"Didn't you say you drove here?"

"Right. Yes. Sometimes I forget it, though." Beau slid his wallet out. He'd be needing it anyway. He made a show of looking through it, keeping it close to his chest. "That's what I thought. I left it at home. All I have in here is cash." Beau looked up. "Plenty of it."

Both of them shook their righteous heads. "Not going to help you here," the man said.

Beau put his wallet away and leaned his elbows on the counter. "Look. Her name is Lola Winters. Just look her up."

Matilda typed with agonizing slowness. She cocked her head at the computer screen. "What'd you say the first name was?"

"Lola." The look on Matilda's face told Beau something was amiss. It occurred to him that Lola had a reason to stay hidden—him. And he wasn't supposed to know her real name. He added, "It could also be under Melody."

"Here she is."

"Seriously?" Beau asked, taken aback. Confident as he'd been, the news still hit him right in the chest and sent his heart racing with excitement.

"Yeah." The man had been watching over Matilda's shoulder, and he looked up from the computer screen. "You sound surprised."

Beau covered his ass with the biggest smile he had—and it was genuine too. In no time at all, he'd lay his eyes on that black, shiny hair, those big, lying blue eyes. "I'm just eager to see her. Very, very eager."

"I remember her," Matilda quipped. "Checked in last night because of the storm. She didn't mention anything about work."

"That's great," Beau dismissed with a deep inhalation. "Which room? I have flowers in the car, and they need—"

"Oh, no." She shook her head at the computer, her eyebrows triangled in the center of her forehead. "She already checked out."

His heart stabbed him right in the chest, that fickle motherfucker. Bragg had warned him about this—people on the run rarely spent two nights in one spot. But Beau had convinced himself that on some level, Lola wanted him to find her. That maybe, somehow, she wasn't really on the run. She was just drifting. "When?"

"This afternoon, right after the storm let up. Not too long ago. That's weird she didn't mention it to you, especially since she had to work today. What'd you say she does, anyway?"

Beau closed his eyes. He pictured her running away from him through Middle-American wheat fields, her head over her shoulder as she smiled, waved at him. *Ha. Gotcha.* Not knowing where she was had been torture, but just missing her by a few hours was almost worse. If he'd flown to Dallas right when he'd arrived at the airport. If he'd driven twice as fast.

"Did she leave a note?" he asked evenly. "Anything behind?"

"I didn't check her out, but I haven't seen—"

"How about lost and found?"

The girl looked up at her dad.

"Why don't you just call her?" he suggested, watching Beau carefully. "Maybe she went back home or moved to another hotel in the area."

Beau opened his mouth to make his demands. He wanted to speak to whoever'd checked her out. To see surveillance footage. To check the room she'd stayed in for clues. He took a deep breath and walked outside, leaving behind two suspicious expressions. With the time difference, he'd lost two hours between California and there, and it was almost six o'clock at night.

Beau extracted his cell phone from his suit pocket, cringing as if it were painful. He called Bragg and spoke first. "She's gone. Are there any new charges?"

"Not since last night."

"Check again." Beau ignored the detective's sigh and waited on the line. He could still catch her, no matter where she was. If she was driving, he would fly. If she moved fast, he would move faster.

"Nothing, boss," Bragg said into the phone. "You going to stay out there or come back?"

Beau hung up the phone and stared at the black screen. He didn't know where to go from here or if he could go through this again another night. How the fuck could she do this to him? Toy with him this way? He purposely chose not to see the irony in the situation.

He needed to think—to be in a clean, uncluttered place, alone with his thoughts—and to sleep. He'd stayed at The Ritz-Carlton in St. Louis before. He wasn't sure how far it was. There had to be a nearby city with something upscale. But Lola had stayed at the Moose Lodge last night, and suddenly, feeling close to her seemed more important.

He returned to the front office. "I'm sorry if I seemed angry," he said and, to his surprise, he meant it. By not giving Beau information, the young girl had been protecting Lola. No matter how mad he was, Beau could only hope everyone else Lola had encountered so far had done the same. "It's just, my wife—" He practically choked on it. *My wife.*

"Poor thing. You can't even spend a night without her," the girl said—alone again, a hopeless romantic again. "Are you going to be all right?"

Beau nodded. He took his wallet out once more. "Can I get a room for the night?" he asked, holding out his credit card.

She withdrew as though he'd just sneezed on it. "I don't know."

"Please," he said, too exhausted for anything other than begging.

She sighed and took it. "Oh, all right."

"Any room is fine."

She shrugged. "They're all the same, unless you want to be by the icemaker or something."

"Any room is fine," he repeated.

He took his key, then crossed the street to the liquor store. The man in camo was gone. Beau bought the most expensive Scotch they had, a brand he'd never heard of and didn't plan on remembering.

He returned to his room at the Moose Lodge, where there was no minibar, no luxury showerhead, not even a robe. He sat on the edge of the bed with a drink in his hand and stared at a crack in the wall that ran out from behind the midsized TV. There'd been many cracks throughout his life, but very few the last ten years. Money had a way of smoothing them over.

When would she stop? How far would he go? There was a finish line. An edge. There had to be. He couldn't follow her to the ends of the earth and keep his sanity. Selfishly, he hoped at some point she'd run herself into a corner. When she did, he'd be there—right behind her, right in front of her.

The pillows were lumpy, the bathroom lacking in toiletries, the vending machine broken. And except for the fact that almost having her and losing her again felt as if he'd dropped his heart a short distance and fractured it—he was fine at that motel that was not The Ritz-Carlton.

Chapter Eleven

Lola was engrossed in her fifth conversation of the last hour, except that she hadn't said a word. She sat on the terrace of Café Du Monde surrounded by people who'd unknowingly let her into their lives for a few minutes here and there. The family of four to her right had stopped in New Orleans for *beignets* on their drive home from Disneyworld. The little girl wore a Minnie Mouse hat with an oversized red bow that matched her sunburnt nose. The boy's T-shirt, with *Florida* written in Disney lettering across the chest, was also colorfully decorated with food stains.

Lola sipped her second *café au lait*. She'd also heard a French couple's flowering and heated conversation behind her. She couldn't understand or even see them, but she'd imagined their quarrel would catapult them into each other's arms before the night's end.

Her table was like the center of the world that hour, with tourists from all different places to her left and right, in front of and behind her—sitting, drinking, eating, conversing and then leaving to give their table to the next group.

Being as caught up as she was in what was happening around her, she'd almost forgotten she herself was one of them until someone spoke to her.

"I was beginning to think being alone around here was a crime."

Lola glanced over at the nice-looking man at the

next table. "It might be," she said. "But I wouldn't know since it makes quick getaways easy."

His answering chuckle was deep and throaty. A piece of his black hair flapped as a breeze passed over them. He held open a hand. "This is risky sixty seconds in, but I'll take the chance. Join me for a pastry?"

His brown eyes matched her milky coffee. The lines around them crinkled with an inviting smile. The last two days had been the regular driving, eating, sleeping and sightseeing. She'd spent more time alone on this trip than she ever had in L.A., but she was only lonely when she thought of Beau. She smiled back at the man. "Thank you, but I'm happy here."

"All right." He dropped his elbow onto the table. "Are you a local too?"

"No." Lola turned in her chair slightly to see him better. "I thought only tourists came here."

"Myth. I've been eating beignets for years, and unfortunately for my figure," he patted his stomach, "I never grow tired of them."

Lola grinned, understanding all too well. Between driving five to ten hours a day and rarely cooking for herself, her pants were getting tight. "It's my only night in New Orleans. As a local—anything I shouldn't miss?"

"Done the French Quarter, I assume?"

Lola nodded. "And a walking tour."

He shrugged. "The best part of this city is…the way it is. I don't know how to describe it. Walk along the Mississippi River or through the streets. To experience New Orleans, just pay attention to what's around you."

"That sounds too easy," Lola joked.

"Existing in the moment? It's harder than you

think."

Lola glanced at her hands. The parents returning from Disneyworld had been talking about the workweek ahead of them. A group of girls who'd been sitting near Lola earlier had been reminiscing about New Orleans before Hurricane Katrina. Like most people, Lola was often looking forward or backward while life happened around her.

"What would you say to some exploring?" The man waved at her, bringing her back from her thoughts. "Let me take you around the city, buy you a drink at my favorite spot. New Orleans has a lot of secrets, ones only the locals know. I'll show you how to forget tomorrow and enjoy the present."

Then again, existing in the moment could be overrated. Lola signaled for a waitress, shaking her head at the self-important pick-up line. "No, thanks."

"Are you taken?"

"No."

"Then why not?"

"I'm just not interested." What she didn't say was that even though she was alone, she didn't feel single. A large chunk of her heart still belonged to Beau, and mere weeks wouldn't change that. Lola took out her wallet.

The man held up a hand. "I've got your bill. Go on and enjoy the rest of your night here."

"But—"

"I insist." He leaned over and took the receipt from her table. "If you want to thank me, pay it forward."

Lola wasn't sure what to do other than leave the restaurant. She stopped at a corner market for a new pack of cigarettes, having finished the last one somewhere around the Missouri-Arkansas border. Once her trip ended, so would the bad habit she'd started up again. Cigarettes had become a form of comfort, reminding her of her early days at Hey Joe, when she was off drugs and alcohol completely. Lola knocked the pack against her palm, walking along the Mississippi River.

She eventually stopped and rested her elbows on a railing to watch the day fade over the river. She took a drag of the first cigarette from her last pack. She'd decided in the Ozark Mountains that it was time go home to Los Angeles. Tomorrow, she'd start the trip back. She didn't want to be anywhere else.

Ending the trip felt like closing the door on Beau for good, though. Letting go of her anger meant severing any remaining link to him. That was for the best, but the idea made her stomach turn and her eyes water. It was unexpectedly physical, the process of saying goodbye. Even her jaw tingled. It got stronger, prickling down her throat. Without warning, she gagged.

Lola pulled the cigarette away from her face and looked it over. The river water rippled below her. She put a hand over her mouth, the ground suddenly unsteady, as if she were out at sea.

She realized it wasn't thinking of Beau that'd turned her cheeks warm and her palms clammy. But a cigarette hadn't made her this nauseous since she'd sucked down her first one at fourteen. Lola stuck the butt between her lips and pulled out the pack to check for an expiration date. And then it hit her, the reason her mom had been forced to quit smoking twenty-nine years ago. Lola's mouth fell open. The cigarette dropped onto the concrete, scattering ashes at her feet.

Chapter Twelve

Four weeks earlier

Lola removed her new diamond earrings and set them on the bathroom counter. She glanced up at her reflection. Beau was in the doorway, his bowtie hanging around his neck, a shadow of stubble on his jaw. He came up behind her and slid his arms around her waist. "When did you change?" he whispered. "I wanted to watch."

"I never let you watch."

"That doesn't mean I don't."

Lola's heart skipped as he nuzzled her neck. The idea that he'd seen her undress without her permission made her flush. He was a dog—she knew that. He'd treated her like a dog. What made him think he could get away with that—standing just out of sight as she unzipped the long zippers of the dresses he'd bought her, unclipped the stockings of her wasted lingerie, unclasped her heavy, expensive necklaces. "You watched me?" she asked, her breath coming faster.

"Mmm." He moved her hair aside and kissed a spot under her ear. "No. But it's been very tempting."

The thin silk of her robe did nothing to hide the fact that Beau wanted her. It was a blunt reminder of their knee-quivering chemistry, of being owned by him.

He slid his hand down the smooth fabric and cupped her backside. "All night, I couldn't keep my eyes off you." When he spoke, it was into her neck and hair, breath so hot, him so close, she struggled to maintain focus.

She tried to swallow, but her mouth dried, and her pussy got greedy-wet. She put her palms on the counter, bracing herself as she began to slip under his spell. "Stop," she murmured.

"I'm not doing anything." His fingers curled around the meat of her ass, brushing the private underside of her.

She saw herself—breathing through her nose, reddening from the neck up. Beau was also watching, and their eyes met. He moved both hands around to her tummy and pushed his pelvis into her, sending her gasping toward the mirror.

"You hide it well," he said. "Until you don't. You want to fuck as badly as I do."

She would've denied it, but her vocal chords wouldn't cooperate. He roamed his hands down her body, then up the backs of her thighs, and up and up until he was cupping her tits through the silk. He squeezed them, rubbed them, released them to slip his hands inside her robe and put his skin on hers.

"Oh, God," she said, bending over the lip.

"That's it," he said, keeping her breast in one hand as he undid his pants with the other.

Her protest was a moan. She'd been there less than a week, but her body was rubber-band tight, so tight, and she wanted that release. Needed it. She hadn't even touched herself since the last time he'd been inside her—had just slept chastely by his side the last few nights she'd been living there.

It fascinated Lola to see them together that way. Beau's jaw set as he glanced down and back at her. She'd seen that reckless look in his eyes before—the first night, in Beau's lap at the strip club, and many times after that. He always wanted to get inside her with a determination neither of them could fight.

He slid a finger along her slit, then pressed the tip of his cock to it. Neither of them moved. The bathroom lights glared, suddenly blinding. The longer he rested just his head between her folds, waiting, the harder she throbbed around it.

She knew what he wanted. It wasn't enough to give herself over—she had to beg for it, for him to finish her off for good.

"I can feel you getting wet," he said.

Lola shook her head hard, avoiding her own eyes in the mirror. Her knuckles whitened from making fists.

"No?" he asked. "You think I don't know when your pussy's hungry? Feed it. Push back onto me."

"I can't."

"It wasn't a request."

"You can't tell me what to do," she said. "You don't own me that way anymore."

"I was hoping you'd talk back," he slapped her ass, and she inhaled loudly, "just so I could do that."

She dropped her forehead down as sweat beaded on her upper lip. Her skin smarted where he'd spanked her, radiating to her pussy. It was as if her nerve endings only existed in the places Beau touched her.

"You don't know the satisfaction I get from watching you fight yourself," he said. "Do yourself a favor. Give in." He stepped back, removing the pressure from between her legs.

"What're you doing?" she breathed. She didn't want to ask for it, but she sure as hell didn't want him to stop.

"Hold yourself open for me."

Lola hesitated. Beau was as stubborn as her, and he would walk away to teach her a lesson, even if it meant he wouldn't get to fuck her. Lola reached back, still bent at the hip. She bared her soft, slippery lips, gingerly at first, and then wider as her need took over.

"It is perfection, *ma petite chatte*," he said. "When you behave, all I want is to reward you." He returned behind her, lining his cock up again. "Fuck me."

Lola breathed in and out, her head swimming. She readjusted her grip, spread her pussy and pushed back onto him slowly. He had to help her, to work his head in to loosen her up. When her body gave way, Lola slid back, filling herself with him, her mouth becoming impossibly dry.

"Keep going," he said. "And don't look away from me."

All she wanted to *do* was look away. He was playing dirty, making her break her own rules. Lola watched him as she urged her body forward, gliding up his cock, and then back down, slow and awkward. Beau's expression remained smooth as he watched her face, mild amusement in his eyes.

Her bottom lip was between her teeth, her fingers digging into her skin. She was right where she'd wanted to be the last few days and right where she knew she should never have been again.

"You can let go now," he said.

She released herself just as Beau put a hand on her upper back and pushed her down, her nipples hardening against the cool granite. He grabbed her by the hips and thrust all the way in. They both exhaled a sharp, "*Fuck*."

He didn't waste another second, suddenly insatiable. He took her fast, pushing her farther over the sink with each drive until she was on the balls of her feet. She held onto the faucet.

"I told you to look at me," he said.

She raised her head, and they found each other in the reflection again. This was something she'd never seen—herself, getting fucked by him from behind. It was better than she'd fantasized. His bowtie was still around his neck. Except for his pants, pushed down around his ass, he was fully dressed. He held her hard, went at her hard, his eyes were hard—but none of it in a bad way.

He practically had her off her feet by the time she came, her climax so ready, it was both effortless and raw. He talked her through it—she was so beautiful, he'd needed this so much, had been dying for it.

With her last spasm, she loosened her grip on the faucet. His neck strained, her breasts swayed, his fingers dented her hips as he pulled her into each thrust. Her eyes darted between everything like she'd walked into the middle of a crime scene and couldn't decide where to look first.

Beau smacked her ass, groaned her name like a prayer and touched her everywhere as he came.

Her hand flew to her mouth, reality slapping her across the face. She'd fucked up—with the worst person possible. The enemy. In a matter of seconds, he'd shattered her carefully-constructed walls like they'd been made of porcelain.

"Christ, Lola." Beau ran his hand up and down the silk of her back, admiring her. His Adam's apple bobbed when he swallowed. "You have no idea, the plans I have—"

"Get off me."

His eyes jumped to hers. "What?"

They held each other's stare, still except for the frantic, synced rise-and-fall of their chests.

"You promised," she said, hating that her voice cracked. "Get *off* me."

"Hey—come on." He smiled a little, the smug fucking bastard. "You're going to tell me that was one-sided?"

She looked up at the ceiling. She'd been stupid to think she could actually do this—be this close to him and not ever *once* let her guard down. She'd known if she did, he'd see that weakness and pounce. She'd been right.

"Fuck you," she said. "You couldn't even do this one simple thing you promised me."

He slid out of her, stepping back. "This has been anything but simple," he said, pulling his pants up quickly, tucking himself into them. "It's goddamn torture following your rules. There's nobody else I'd let get away with that bullshit."

She turned to face him, her robe whispering around her hips. She pulled it closed around her with trembling fists. "Bullshit? It's *bullshit* for me to ask for a little time to recover after what you put me through?"

He ran both hands over his hair. His smile was completely gone, at least, replaced with a solemn frown.

"Jesus. I didn't realize this was such a big deal. I thought you were—I don't know. Playing around. Teasing me."

Lola clenched her jaw against a wave of tears. She had to make a choice—break him or leave. Otherwise, she'd never be anything but a pawn to him, and their relationship would never be anything but a game. "I thought I could do this. I thought I could play, but I'm out of my league here."

He shook his head, his drawn eyebrows wrinkling his forehead. "What are you talking about?"

"This isn't working." She took a step forward. "I'm leaving."

He blocked her path. "Like fuck you are."

"Give me one reason why I shouldn't." She looked up at him. "Why would I stay?"

He scoffed and held his arms open. "All of this. The last few days. I make one mistake, and you're going to walk away? Like we didn't fight like hell to get here?"

"I have to. If you don't respect me by now, you never will. I came back for you. I swallowed my pride. Every day I stay despite my better judgment. I asked one thing of you—keep your hands to yourself. Just for a little while."

"You're right. I'm sorry."

Lola flinched. It was unexpected—the sweet kind of desperation on his face she wasn't used to seeing. Her plan might actually have been working the last few days, small and subtle changes right before her eyes.

"I didn't understand why this meant so much to you," he continued, "but I do now."

She shifted on her bare feet. "How do I know you aren't just saying that?"

He reached up and hesitated, his hands hovering over her cheeks. When she realized he was waiting for permission, she nodded slightly. He touched her face with his palms, as if committing it to memory, then took hold of her shoulders. "Don't go." He pulled her closer to him, and she went. He kissed her forehead and the bridge of her nose. "Be mad. Scream at me. Make me pay. But don't go—that would be the worst. All right, Lola? I want you here. I really want you here."

Her posture eased a little. He did love her, she knew it, clung to it. She'd screwed up huge, but it would have to be a lesson learned. Staying alert wasn't enough. She had to be vigilant around him. She had to monitor every touch, every look, from somewhere outside herself.

"Let's just go to bed," she said quietly, looking to the side.

He released his grip a little. "Thank you."

He walked out of the bathroom, but she stood there a second longer. Her anger drained with the blood from her face. She hadn't taken birth control in days. That month's pack had been in her purse when it was stolen, and she hadn't thought to bring the rest from her apartment.

Lola straightened her robe and combed her fingers through her hair before leaving the bathroom. She was fairly certain birth control didn't leave your system for a while. Either way, nothing would happen—because it couldn't. It just couldn't. She had enough to worry about as it was, and anything more would surely be the last straw for her. It was hard to imagine anything beautiful could come from this ugliness anyway.

Chapter Thirteen

Present day

Beau left the Moose Lodge behind in the backwoods of Missouri to be closer to an international airport. He didn't know where Lola would go next, but this time he'd be ready. Beau found sitting still one of his greater challenges, but he worried if he went up, she'd go down, left or right.

Two days he waited, during which his assistant arranged for him to meet with a couple startups, both of which impressed him. They were green but viable, and more surprisingly, unaffected. The big-city entrepreneurs he normally met with were eerily familiar to him—they were versions of Beau before he'd hit it big. They had dark circles under their eyes all the time and consumed caffeine like water. They were always trying to stay ahead of the game, but sometimes that cost them.

When Bragg called, Beau was visiting a major hotel in Memphis. He held his Entrepreneurs in Tech conference in Los Angeles every year, but it'd occurred to him sometime over the last couple days that he and his partner had been focused on California too long. There was talent everywhere—even Tennessee. An entire nation waited to be discovered.

That didn't mean, for even a moment, Lola was far from his mind. Beau kept his eyes up all the time, wondering if he might turn the corner and run right into her.

Beau held up a finger to the hotel's sales manager when he saw Detective Bragg's name on the screen of his cell phone. "Excuse me, I have to take this."

"Louisiana," Bragg said into the phone before Beau'd even spoken.

Beau put his hand on his hip. "She's there?"

"I woke up to a pending charge at a gas station in New Orleans. Called around the immediate area and found a motel with a Lola Winters staying there—you might have to write a check for that info."

"I might or I will?"

"What's a few hundred more bucks?"

Nothing to him. But he'd developed this strange habit, this rapid reach for his wallet. Beau valued his fortune, having been without it most of his life, but the look people got when they had a chance at easy money—it was seductive.

The lights in the conference center got brighter, or so it felt. He blinked a few times, already moving in the direction of the exit. He pulled the phone away briefly to tell the woman showing him the space, "My assistant will be in touch."

Bragg coughed into the phone. "I'll e-mail the details right now."

"How far is New Orleans from me?"

"Six hours in the car, four in the air, minus boarding."

"I'm getting on the road now."

"I got a feeling today's the day, want to know why?"

Satisfaction tinged Bragg's voice, something Beau'd been waiting on for a while. "Why?"

"Every day since we got her real name, I've been hunting car salesmen, trying to find one who worked with a Melody Winters. Those guys love their cash upfront. Well, goddamn if I didn't put a bullet in one's ass this morning. She's driving a red Lotus Evora. Got the plates too. How's that for you? She may be flying under the radar, but in a car like that, doesn't exactly seem like she wants to stay hidden."

For the third time in two days, Beau tasted victory. It was even sweeter now that he knew how she was traveling and what to look for. He would've guessed black for her, but he liked the red. A lot. "Good work, Bragg." Beau hesitated. "But you didn't really shoot anyone, did you?"

The detective guffawed into the phone. Beau was afraid it'd devolve into another coughing fit, but Bragg just said, "Not today, kid," and hung up.

Beau decided to drive to Louisiana. Behind the wheel, at least he'd have some control. Airports were too sluggish, even when they were fast-paced, the stale air like sludge for hurried travelers.

Why had she chosen to go south now? It was an unusual move, and to keep going across country, she'd have to come up again eventually. Unless she went west, and that would put her back toward Los Angeles. Home. He wanted to get to her before then. He fantasized about catching Lola in the act, making eye contact with her amidst the Bourbon Street crowd, sending a Sazerac to her table as he watched from the bar, standing inches behind her as she took in a sunset behind the three-steepled St. Louis Cathedral. As if her reaching L.A. before he'd caught her meant she'd be able to deny this'd ever happened.

In the car, his assistant called. "They're ready to finalize the VenTech acquisition," she said. "I can arrange a meeting first thing in the morning."

They'd had to move quickly to prepare an offer for VenTech's founder while its future was bleak, and before anyone else could. Beau had known this was coming, and even though he was the only one who really cared about the buyout, he couldn't help cursing the timing. "Make sure Larry's there," Beau said. "I'm not sure I'll make it in time."

"I already looked at flights," she said. "Getting you into LAX by tomorrow morning shouldn't be an issue."

Beau looked up from the road. Small, white-bellied birds flapped across the sky in formation. Once Bolt Ventures had put the finishing touches on the paperwork, it would only be days before Beau could go to George Wright with an offer—a laughable one, but one Wright couldn't afford to turn down. But that would mean getting on a plane tonight and missing another chance to find Lola.

"I'm the one who wanted this," Beau said. "I should be there."

"Probably, but…"

"But what?"

His assistant didn't respond. He knew where she was headed, but he'd bitten her head off enough times when she'd suggested unloading his work to others.

Beau uncurled his fingers from the steering wheel, splaying them, an invitation. "You think they can manage without me."

"You can't be everywhere all the time, Mr. Olivier."

"Sure I can, thanks to modern technology."

"You can videoconference. Although, that doesn't mean you should. It sounds like you have more important things going on."

"All right." Giving in to others was physical for him, a tightening and loosening of his shoulders, an anxious nod of his head. "Fine. If I'm free, I'll video in. If not, they'll have to proceed without me."

"Okay—"

"But make sure Larry calls me before they make any—"

"I'll take care of it, Mr. Olivier. Just enjoy your vacation."

"I'm not on—"

The line went dead, the first time she'd ever cut him off that way. He set his phone down, envisioning everyone in the office break room, celebrating his absence. He doubted that, though. Beau could be hard, but he was a good boss and a good man to work for—he knew that. Maybe that was why they all seemed to think he needed time away.

He shifted in his seat, the road out his windshield narrowing into the horizon. He thought about e-mailing his assistant and asking her to send detailed minutes of the meeting directly after, but he let it go.

Lola had mentioned more than once his frustrating devotion to work. She'd wanted more of his attention than she got. Well, she had it all now.

◆⊠◆⊠◆

Beau spotted the New Orleans motel a second too late, and his tires shotgun-shrieked against the pavement when he slammed on his brakes. He veered across oncoming traffic into the parking lot. Lola wasn't far now. She might not be in her room, but he had all evening to find her. They'd been playing this game for too long—it had to end. They would argue, that was unavoidable—he was angry. Seeing her again would test his control. But then what?

Beau entered the front office chest first, his authority unmistakable. "I'm looking for a woman who checked in here earlier."

The long-nosed, pimple-faced clerk was unimpressed. "We get a lot of those—women."

Beau flattened his hand on the counter. "My associate called and spoke to someone. Was it you?"

"Your associate?" He looked over Beau's shoulder, then his own. "Uh, it wasn't me."

"Is there anyone else working?"

"Yeah, but he's on his break for another twenty minutes."

"Fine. Her name is Melody Winters. Check your system."

The man blinked once slowly before turning to the computer. His mouse clicked, his fingers tapped the keyboard. He shook his head. "I don't see her…"

"But I was told that she's here."

The clerk raised his eyebrows. "Hmm. Uh…"

"What?"

"What'd you say the first name was?"

"Melody."

"Oh." He shook his head. "Nope."

Beau rolled his eyes. He inched his hands closer to the computer, tempted to jerk the screen in his direction. "How about Lola?"

"Oh." The man nodded. "Yep."

"She's here?" Beau's frustration yielded to relief. "Which room?"

"I can't—"

"Money. I have it. You can have it. For your cooperation." Beau almost cringed, barely able to form a full sentence. He wanted to be better, to do this the right way, but he couldn't help himself. He'd come too far, was too close, to start following some ambiguous set of rules. He fumbled in his jacket pocket for his wallet, pulled out three crisp one-hundred-dollar bills. "You can come with me if you don't trust me. Keep my wallet as collateral. Whatever. Just give me the room number."

The man looked from the money to Beau to the door behind him. He slid the cash toward himself on the counter and pocketed it. He wrote something on a slip of paper and held it out.

Before Beau could take it, the clerk pulled it back and whispered, "I never gave this to you."

"Fine."

"Destroy it when you're done."

"Give me the fucking paper."

The man's eyes widened. He handed it over.

118.

Beau went to room 118 and knocked. He sniffed, stuck his hands in his pockets. So much for a thought-out, specially-tailored plan. He banged on the door until it opened to reveal a short, gray-haired woman.

"Who are you?" he demanded.

She scowled. "You knocked on *my* door."

"I'm looking for my—my girlfriend…my wife…"

"Well, which is it?" the lady asked.

"She told me she was in room 118."

"Harold," the woman called behind her without removing her eyes from Beau.

"I'm not here to bother you," Beau said, holding up his palms. After a nostril-full of air, he said, "I'm just looking for my wife—have you seen her by any chance? Dark hair, slim, tall, blue eyes, shiny hair—"

"Oh—shiny hair," the woman exclaimed. "How on earth does she get it so shiny?"

"What?"

"I know exactly who you're talking about. Lola."

"Right," Beau said so loudly, the woman jumped. "That's her. Is she in there?"

"In *here*?" The woman shook her head. "What a doll. What an angel. You are a lucky man."

"I'm a desperate man," Beau said. "Where is she?"

She tapped a finger on her chin. "Gone, I think." Her eyebrows knit. "She didn't mention anything about a husband."

His heart dropped. It was impossible. He wasn't even in the room, and the walls seemed to be closing in around him. Somebody had to be responsible for putting him through this shit hour after fucking hour. He would wring that person's neck for it—the clerk, this woman, Bragg. Lola. He steadied himself against the doorframe. "Gone? When did you see her?"

"Well, earlier this afternoon, Harold and I were checking in at the front office right over there," she pointed to where Beau had just been, "when this girl comes in behind us. See, Harold and I had some trouble with our trailer this morning, so we had nowhere to sleep and not much cash on us."

Beau's face was getting hot. He rolled his lips together to keep from hurrying her along.

"We were trying to work out a deal when Lola taps me on the shoulder and says she paid for two nights—"

"Word for word," Beau interrupted. "What'd she say?"

"Ah. Um, let's see. She introduces herself and goes, 'I was thinking of canceling my second night, so why don't you take it instead?' I ask if she's sure, and she says something like, 'I'm sure. I just got some news, and it's time for me to move on.' The darling girl, she didn't charge us a thing and was out of the room in ten minutes."

Beau was shaking his head. "No. That's bullshit."

"You're a bit pale," she said. "You want to sit down? My husband's right inside, so don't get any ideas—"

He walked away, got in his car and stared forward. Now, it was the roof that was falling on him. Lola had to have known he was coming somehow—to have done this on purpose. Revenge. Wasn't it? She couldn't know, though—it wasn't like she'd violated his privacy like he had hers, scouring his credit card statements, tracing his phone calls, hunting for clues. He slammed his palms into the steering wheel. He did it another time, honking the horn.

"What the fuck, Lola? What are you doing to me?" He took a deep breath. "Enough is enough. I'm done with this. I'm done looking for you in the corners of the earth. I've had enough."

But he took out his phone and dialed the number he'd already been abusing almost two weeks.

"Let me guess," Bragg answered. "You're so grateful for my help, you're calling to see where you should send my bonus. I appreciate that, I really do—you got a pen?"

"Have there been any other charges?" Beau asked. "Anything at all."

Bragg sighed heavily. "No, kid. I'm sorry."

"Are you sure there isn't any way she has another card or a cell phone? How'd she get this far without charging more?"

"We've been over this. It's the cash."

Beau looked at his lap. She had run because of him, and she stayed hidden because of him. He'd thought buying her would give him the last laugh, but he sat in his car, unable to even remember the happiness he'd had just a short time ago. And to think there was a time he'd thought he could slice her right out of his life like a bruise from a peach. He'd done this to himself—and it'd been *deliberate*.

Bragg cleared his throat. "Look, Beau…"

Beau lifted his eyes a little. "What?"

"Maybe it's time to take a break. You've been looking for this girl for a couple weeks now, and you got nothing to hang your hat on." He hesitated. "Thing is, you haven't even told me the reason."

"You want to know why?"

"Guess I should've asked this earlier, but you didn't strike me as the vengeful type—it's not because you want to hurt her, is it? Just that you seem a little strung out."

"No," Beau said flatly. "I don't *want* to hurt her. There are a lot of things I don't want to do, though, like keep chasing her or go home without her."

Bragg grunted. "Could it be that you're in love with her?"

It was such an odd question, even odder coming from Bragg, who never asked why—who rarely strayed from business. Beau didn't answer.

"Don't you have someone you can talk to about this?" Bragg asked. "Brigitte?"

"Brigitte hates any woman who has my attention."

"I don't know anything about that," the detective said, "but I do know this ain't healthy. You've got to let Lola go. I think she wants to be let go."

"I know, it's just that we had these two nights…" Beau said.

Bragg was silent. Beau didn't blame him. It was a weird thing to say. He'd had no one to talk to about this. He wasn't even sure he could count his time with Lola after those two nights—not if she'd been plotting against him the whole time. His heart sank. Maybe that was how she'd felt about *all* of their time together.

"You fell in love with someone in two nights?" Bragg asked. "That's—"

"What, impossible?" Beau laughed grimly and hung up the phone. Bragg had no idea just how possible it was.

He jumped at a noise. The woman from 118 was tapping on his window, motioning for him to roll it down. He opened the door and got out.

"Are you all right?" she asked. "I'm sorry if I was rude about you knocking on my door, but you were in a fit. Still are. You don't look like you should be driving."

"Did she say anything else?" Beau asked. "Anything at all? What was she wearing?"

The woman shook her head. "Jeans, I think. Nothing out of the ordinary."

"Was she in a red car?"

She frowned and reached toward him. After a brief hesitation, she rubbed his shoulder. "I'm real sorry, honey. I wish I knew more. She's a lovely girl. I'd hate to lose her too. Maybe there's some way Howard and I can help you find her."

He searched her eyes, finding warmth that hadn't been there before. He'd barged into that hotel like he'd owned it, demanding things and banging on doors. What the fuck was happening to him? What he had wasn't enough—he had to make people feel small too?

"Why would you help me?" he asked.

She smiled a little. "You seem like a good man who got caught in a nasty web. You have that look about you like you might take off running any second." She shrugged. "You know, Lola did say one more thing on her way out the door that makes me think she might like me to help out."

His ears rang. "What was it?"

"I asked if there was any way we could thank her. She says, 'All I did was pay it forward. If you want to thank me, do the same.'"

Chapter Fourteen

Lola stepped out of the motel shower onto a frayed floor mat and wrapped a towel under her arms. After seven hours of traveling, her shoulders ached. The fluorescent light flickered angrily. She wiped steam from the mirror, her face developing in parts. She looked older. A couple vertical wrinkles between her eyebrows remained even after she'd stopped frowning. Smaller ones were forming at the corners of her eyes. Her hair was longer than she'd ever worn it, the wet ends stuck to her breasts, right above her nipples. She couldn't remember when she'd last had it cut.

Even after a shower, her skin showed indents from the waistband of her pants. She turned sideways and ran her hand over her naked tummy. It was too early to see any change, but she thought she could. On the counter next to her was a stick that looked like a headless toothbrush.

After check-in, she'd made herself watch TV for an hour while drinking water and patiently waiting for her bladder to fill. She didn't want to do it wrong—it was the first pregnancy test she'd ever taken, anyway. She'd peed on it and chanted—*two lines pregnant, one line not.* As if she might forget and have to check the instructions a second time.

They had faded in, two lines, distinct and solid. She'd already known what the verdict would be, so she'd gotten in the shower without making a big thing of it.

One night of tossing and turning plus a drive from New Orleans to Houston had been a good amount of time to let the news sink in.

Lola dried her hair with the towel and caught herself smiling in the reflection. She was going to be a mom.

She dropped the pregnancy test in the trash behind the toilet, then reflexively tried to catch it at the last second. Was she supposed to keep it as some sort of souvenir? The thought made her wrinkle her nose. She left it and washed her hands for a third time.

She changed into her pajamas, sat on the bed against the headboard and aimed the remote at the TV, but didn't turn it on. Suddenly, she covered her mouth and giggled into her hand. So the news hadn't actually sunken in—not completely. She kept having giddy, heart-soaring moments where she wanted to run outside and tell someone, anyone, how drastically her life had changed in mere months. That kind of news was hard to keep inside.

Lola stuck her thumbnail between her teeth, checking the clock from the corner of her eye. Her suitcase was by the bed, sleeves, pant legs and bra straps sprouting from all sides. Pregnancy would mean the death of her leather pants, at least for a while. She couldn't imagine chasing a juice-sticky toddler around in them. The pants' last night out had been when she'd met Beau, their stiff creak the only sound as she'd cautiously approached him, both of them lit up by the neon signs in Hey Joe's window.

She and Beau were forever linked now. She wouldn't be able to keep the secret long, nor did she want to. The time would come to tell Beau he was going to be a father. Maybe he didn't want that. Maybe he would be angry. She looked at her fingers, bit at a hangnail. He'd made her sign that contract in the beginning, absolving him of any responsibility should she get pregnant. The thought of having his child had disgusted her then, but now she couldn't drum up a negative feeling about it. If he wanted nothing to do with them, she'd deal with it. She wasn't sure what role she wanted him to play anyway.

It was 7:32 at night on the West Coast, two hours behind Houston. That meant in California time, she was still waiting for her bladder to fill, the pregnancy test placed conspicuously at the edge of the bedside stand.

Lola could only think of one person to share her news with. She wasn't sure how her mother, who hadn't even been happy about her own pregnancy, would take it, but Lola had gone too long without talking to anyone familiar. Any reaction seemed better than none. Lola picked up the phone by the bed and dialed a number she'd never forgotten, even though she rarely used it.

"Hel-*lo*?" Dina asked. Just answering the phone had already annoyed her.

Lola opened her mouth. She'd half expected to get the answering machine since her mom often worked nights at the diner.

"Yeah?" Dina said. "Why you people always calling me a minute after I sit down to dinner? Hello?"

"Mom? It's me, Mom."

"Lola?" There was quick screech in the background. "Hang on, I'm sitting down."

Whenever Lola pictured her mom, it was usually in her uniform—dumping a Styrofoam container on the kitchen counter after a shift, or at the diner, swishing by the booth where Lola sat, her legs hanging over the edge as she colored or did homework. Lola rarely thought of her at home, eating a solo dinner. She wondered if she ate at the kitchen table or on the living room sofa. She used to fall asleep there watching PBS specials like *Andy Williams: Greatest Hits!*

"You there, Lola? I thought you were a telemarketer."

Lola nodded, looking down at her lap. It was comfortingly familiar, that gravelly voice built for hollering out breakfast orders. "How are you?"

"I'm fine. Been worried about you, though."

Lola raised her eyebrows. "Really?"

"Tried to reach you, but that girl at the bar, Veronica, she told me nobody's seen you. Said Johnny didn't phone because he's scared of me. Hasn't returned my call."

"That's because we—did she mention—?"

"You and Johnny are done, yeah. Wouldn't say why, though, not her business."

"Okay. Well, that's not why I'm calling."

"But you know how I feel about Johnny. I been trying to figure out what could've gone wrong. I spoke to him a few months ago, and everything seemed fine."

"It's a long story. We both got sort of…off track."

"Off track? Both of you? Him too?"

"He's not the angel you think he is, Mom."

She grunted. "Maybe not. What about you, though? You getting off track got something to do with the man who came by the diner?"

Her ear tingled, as if Dina's words had physically tickled her. Even though Lola'd gone through so much to get away from him, she hoped that man was Beau. And not because going as far as to track down Dina definitely meant he was unraveling. "Who?"

"Come to think of it, I don't think I got his name." She made a noise like she was thinking, coming up short with ways to describe him. "He was wearing a suit."

"When? What did he say?"

"Almost a week ago. He was looking for you."

Lola only realized her hand was flattened on her chest when she felt her heart beating against her palm. "Did you tell him anything?"

Dina laughed in one loud bark. "What would I say? I know less than anyone. He'd have had better luck with Johnny and them."

Lola's blood froze. *Johnny and them.* She hadn't thought, in very much detail at least, of Beau going down to Hey Joe and turning the place upside down looking for her. "Have you heard from anyone since?"

"Just when I talked to Veronica. Already told you my whole conversation with her. What's all this about, Lola?"

"Johnny and I—yes, that man has a lot to do with it," Lola said carefully. "He's why I left."

"Where are you?"

"Texas."

"Well, shit, Lola. I know we don't speak, but I'd like to know when you're leaving the damn state. You been gone this whole time?"

"About two weeks." She smiled a little. "I'm seeing so many things, and I've barely scratched the surface. This country is…big."

"So I've heard."

Always with Dina, what she didn't say was louder than what she did. She'd never had the chance to see the country. Too much of her time and money had gone to raising Lola. "Do you ever think about retiring from the diner?"

"Nah. I never had that itch to go anywhere." Dina cleared her throat. "I know you did, though. Before you met Johnny, I didn't think you could stay in one spot for so long."

"I'm coming home, though. I want to."

"Vacation's got to end at some point, right? Couldn't've saved up much bartending. Where you going to live?"

"I don't know yet. But…there's more. The real reason I'm calling—" Lola's stomach churned, her nerves suddenly popping like firecrackers. Lola hadn't been a happy surprise for Dina. This baby couldn't be worse timing for Lola, and she wasn't sure she wanted a child right now. But even if he was the man who'd hurt her, even with the damage he'd caused, there was something intrinsically comforting about it being Beau's. She would carry his baby with pride.

"You know," Dina said when Lola didn't continue, "I love Johnny lots. Think he was good for you. But I think it's for the best, you moving on. At first, I thought you needed to calm down, and he was good at that. Now, though…ah, I don't know what I'm trying to say, just that—maybe I took his side sometimes, and I'm real sorry for that. You're my family, not him." She rushed out the last few words, as if she might lose her nerve before she could say them.

Lola's throat got thick, her mouth full of marbles. It was hard for both of them to come out and say how they felt, admit when they were wrong. "Thanks," Lola said, her eyes watering a little. "You're going to be a grandma."

"You what? Hang on. Damn TV's too loud." The chair scratched against the tile floor again. The TV got louder, then went quiet. "What'd you say?"

"I'm pregnant," Lola said, pronouncing each syllable.

"What I thought you said," Dina muttered.

The line went static-still for a few seconds. In the silence, over and over, Lola thought—*I can do this by myself.* She might have to. She was strong enough. Her mom's disappointment would only steel her for Beau's reaction.

"Who's the daddy?" Dina asked.

"The man in the suit."

"You sure? He made it sound like he hadn't seen you in a while."

"I'm sure." Lola had been over this already. Her last period had ended the same day Beau'd fucked her over the bathroom sink.

Lola thought about explaining it further, but how could she? She wouldn't lie to her mom, but she couldn't tell her the truth—not at this point in time anyway.

There were too many intimate, complicated details to her story with Beau, details only she and Beau could ever know or understand. Beau was the only person who'd never judged her for taking that money, and the only one who never would.

"Motherhood's not cut out for everyone, Lola. Look, not saying I regret it, but I wasn't right for the job back then. You sure you want to go through with it?"

Lola's swallowed. She couldn't bring herself to seriously consider abortion, the same way she'd never thought to take a morning-after pill. She'd convinced herself one unprotected night with Beau, whom she'd considered the devil himself, couldn't result in anything positive.

"Yes," Lola said. "I'm on my own, but I can do it. I had a good example."

Dina made a noise like she was trying to get something out of her throat. "That's sweet, but we both know I was no good at the mom thing."

"Yeah, you are." She'd left her mom's house over ten years ago, bitter and determined to do her own thing. A mom who hadn't given Lola much didn't get to tell her how to live her life or shame her for how she chose to make a living. But Dina had been consistent. She'd always had some kind of dinner on the table and had never spent even one night away from the house when Lola was home.

"We fought a lot over my choices," Lola said. "I used to think it was because you were trying to ruin my life. But you were just being a mom."

"I wanted to be around more, believe it or not. When you told me about the stripping, I blamed myself. Thought it was because I did wrong."

"I know." Lola picked at nothing on the comforter. "You did the best you could, and I see that now."

"How far along?" Dina never made apologies for changing the subject when it suited her. "You know the sex?"

"Only five weeks." Every day since Lola'd seen the boy playing in the snow outside the motel, she'd thought of him. He'd made some kind of unshakable impression on her. The strange thing was, she'd been inexplicably drawn to him but hadn't even known she was pregnant at the time. "It'll be a boy. I'm pretty sure."

"Lucky. They're lots easier than little girls." Dina laughed good-naturedly, and Lola giggled along with her.

"Come and see me when you get back? If you need a place to stay…" Dina hesitated. "You know. We'll figure this out. You're not alone, baby."

Lola needed to get off the phone. She wouldn't be able to keep the tears from spilling much longer. Her mom hadn't called her "baby" since she was a teenager, since before she'd announced she was taking a job at Cat Shoppe and it wasn't open for discussion. "I will. Night, Mom."

Lola hung up and dried the corners of her eyes with her sleeves. Her burden was a little lighter knowing her mom would be there for her again.

Her relief was short-lived, though. Now, Lola had her confirmation—Beau was looking for her. She didn't believe he was capable of hurting her, but Lola had purposely tried to drive him to the edge. And if he was there, he'd want her there with him. Lola glanced down at her hands, instinctively spread over her stomach.

Chapter Fifteen

Beau emptied his pockets into a small, circular tray and added his Rolex to the top of the pile.

A stocky security woman by the metal detector waved in the direction of his feet. "Shoes too."

He slid off his Italian loafers and placed them on the conveyor belt. She nodded for him to pass.

On the other side, he put himself back together, tucking his wallet into his jacket, delicately twisting his feet into his shoes. He normally had a shoehorn in his carryon, but it only occurred to him now that he'd packed it away. He'd already held up the line at check-in, unable to find the airline confirmation in his e-mail. It took a phone call to his assistant to remember he hadn't asked her to book anything.

The first flight out of New Orleans to Los Angeles was a redeye. Beau didn't have to wait at the gate long before priority members were invited to board. He sat, his window rain-splattered, the runway misty. He looked away and checked his e-mail. There wasn't enough to keep him occupied.

People filed by him. He actually hoped to get stuck next to someone chatty. Bonus if it was a beautiful woman. Nobody stopped, though, and eventually the cabin doors shut, the engines vibrated to life. A glassy-eyed flight attendant recited her safety speech.

When they were in the air, she made her way down the aisle. "Get you anything, Miss? Sir, would you like a drink? Do you need anything?"

She parked her cart next to his seat. He looked up at her. "Scotch, neat."

"Right away, sir."

She left it on the seatback tray in front of him. The cabin dimmed and went dark, leaving him alone with his drink. He punched on the light above his head and opened the inflight magazine to a random page.

"Ten Midwest Destinations You Can't Miss."

He'd been to three. What about Lola? Had she driven to the St. Louis Arch in her red sports car and tight leather pants? Where did she keep all that cash? Beau looked up at the low ceiling, stretching his legs out under the seat in front of him. If first class was this cramped, he didn't think he'd survive in coach. He leaned into the aisle. "Miss? Hello?"

After a moment, the attendant appeared, bending over to whisper, "Yes, sir?"

"Another Scotch."

"Certainly." She turned away and within a minute, came to refill his cup.

"Leave the bottle," he said.

"I'm sorry, but—"

"I'll pay." He shifted to get his wallet. "How much is it?"

"We aren't allowed, sir. Are you all right? Do you need a barf bag?"

Beau grimaced, leaning away from her as if *she* were about to be sick. "I feel fine. I just don't—fly well." He flew all the time and had never had an issue. Beau took a too-big sip of his drink as the stewardess stood there. He needed a barf bag for his life. He wanted to tell her the story of how a gravely bad decision had rippled through his neatly-packaged world and turned it into shit. Not even thinking about his healthy bank account gave him comfort at that moment. *She* was a woman—maybe *she* could tell him what the fuck he didn't understand about the female gender.

Beau finished the drink and held out his cup. "One more. Then I can sleep."

She looked around the cabin, quiet except for one snoring idiot. She filled his drink to the brim and left.

What a magic trick Lola had pulled, disappearing into thin air, reappearing in the backwoods of Missouri. She couldn't run forever, though. At some point, she'd have to get a job, pay rent or a mortgage, charge things to her credit card like every other living, breathing American. He could wait in the wings, fading into one of her distant memories. He wouldn't pounce until she thought she was safe.

He didn't want to pounce, though, and he didn't want to be a memory. He could picture her now, sleeping next to him in bed, opening her eyes every few minutes as if to check he was still there. What was real, and what had she faked? Lola in his bed, wearing that piece-of-shit nightgown he passionately *hated*.

Beau thumped his head back against the leathery cushion. Everything began to spin. He tossed the magazine into the seat next to him and switched off the light, praying he wouldn't need that barf bag after all.

Face to face with the woman in New Orleans who was paying forward Lola's favor, Beau'd never felt more like he was standing in ruins he'd caused. Lola didn't want to be found. It wasn't that he thought he deserved her anymore. The opposite, in fact. But that'd never stopped him from pursuing anything. He'd negotiated business deals with men even more powerful than him and regularly took on entire boardrooms. Yet the girl in cat ears unraveled him. He would always be weak when it came to her.

This wasn't business. It wasn't a game. Lola wanted him out of her life and after the way he'd treated her, she had every right. The way to love her was to respect what she was telling him, not demand that she do things his way. The couple had paid it forward, and now it was his turn. He could sit and think up a million ways to make her happy, but it wouldn't matter, because she'd only actually left him one option—leave her alone.

The plane's engines hummed him a lullaby, his consciousness circling the drain. He glided his hand over the smooth surface of the seat's armrest. He could still appreciate her skin, the way she wore an evening gown, or had one ripped off. Thighs spread, tits pointed to the moon, firm but soft ass—and all this against the midnight hair on her head, between her legs.

Her eyelids would fall just as she'd catch her orgasm, never fully closing. She watched him watching her. Lola in her dresses, black and gold and peach. Turning her head over her shoulder and making eye contact with him. Smiling in the seat next to him at the theater, her polite applause. On the stage at Cat Shoppe, pirouetting around the pole in pink, arched ballet slippers, legs bowed, arms bent. A female audience member turned to him. "As we begin our descent, please make sure your seatbelt is securely fastened…"

Beau walked out of the strip club into a desert, sand

crunching under the soles of his dress shoes as he stepped over fat succulent plants. "Where am I?"

"Local time in Phoenix is 4:05 in the morning. The temperature is sixty degrees."

"I'm not supposed to be here."

"She knows that," said a female voice.

"Who?"

A camera shutter clicked, a light flashed. He squinted across a canyon at a young Lola, four or five years old, as she shielded her eyes from the sun. The horizon rippled.

"How could you not recognize her?" Lola's voice asked from behind him. "Your own daughter?"

He turned around. Lola stood in Beau's kitchen. A little girl clutched her leg. They both wore leotards and ballet slippers, fabric bunched at their ankles. The child's hair was as dark as her mother's, her cheeks flushed pink.

"My daughter?" he asked.

"Isn't that why you're here?" Lola sounded angry. "I don't think you're supposed to be here. You should leave."

"But I've been looking for you." She was trying to leave again. He lunged for her.

"Help," she screamed, backing into a refrigerator. "Somebody help. Hello? Sir?"

Beau woke up to blinding fluorescence. He blinked up at the flight attendant, whose eyebrows were wrinkled with concern. "Sir? Are you feeling okay? We've landed in Phoenix. If you have a connection to make, you should go now."

Beau sat up in his seat. He was sweating through his

suit, his hairline damp. Someone had taken his empty glass and raised his tray. He rubbed his face, his stubbly chin. When he blinked, the little girl was there in her bubblegum-colored outfit, a carbon copy of her mother.

He hadn't just lost Lola when he'd hurt her—he'd given up a life with her. Already, memories he'd never get were tormenting him. Beau stood and took his carryon from the overhead bin. The airport was midnight-quiet, Phoenix's dry desert air in his chest, his throat. Choking him.

Chapter Sixteen

Beau straightened his tie and exited the town car. Even through his sunglasses, the California sun seemed excessively bright. Or maybe it was because of the pulsing in his head. Partway up the sidewalk, a car door slammed behind him.

"You can wait here," Beau called back to Warner. "I'll only be a few minutes."

"I'd like to come with you."

Beau stopped and turned around, curious. Warner didn't 'like' to do things Beau hadn't asked him to—or at least, he never expressed it. "Why?"

Warner shifted from one foot to the other. "The same reason you're here instead of just sending me to pick Brigitte up. For support."

Beau walked back until he was face to face with Warner. He removed his sunglasses to look him in the eye. "Don't think I haven't noticed your behavior the past few weeks."

Warner's spine straightened as if trying to meet Beau's height. "Sir?"

"Defending her behavior to me. Sticking your nose where it doesn't belong. I should've suspected earlier. You've always been the only one who can stand to listen to her babble senselessly for hours."

"If you're suggesting I'm in love with your sister," Warner said, hesitating only a moment, "you'd be right."

"How long?"

"Years."

Beau pulled at the knot around his neck. The sun was unforgiving today. "You should tell her that."

"I did." He glanced away briefly. "While you were away. I needed to distract her the night you left for Missouri. She wasn't doing well."

"She never does while I'm away." Beau sighed, nodding back toward the doctor's office. "Is that why we're here?"

Warner nodded. "She came to me after your argument. Nothing unusual there, except this time when she tried to call and beg you not to go after Lola, I put my foot down."

Beau frowned at Warner, his employee who exhibited less emotion than a robot. "And how did that go?"

"She'd told me what you'd said about me having feelings for her, so I said it was true. And I asked her why she wanted to be second in your eyes when she was first in mine."

Beau couldn't remember Brigitte ever responding to romantic gestures, though he suspected she didn't care to share them with him. He almost didn't want to ask. "What'd she say?"

"We had an honest talk. She was young when she moved here and hadn't dealt with losing her mother the way a young girl should. She replaced one family with another before she ever had a chance to feel anything."

Warner was always in the background, but Beau hadn't realized how closely he must've been paying attention to them over the years. "She's terrified I'll leave her too," Beau said, "and she'll end up alone."

"She won't, and I told her so. Said she's always had two people who would never abandon her, she just needs help seeing that."

Beau gave Warner a heartfelt nod. He was grateful, for once, to have someone else looking out for Brigitte's best interest. "Let's go inside."

They walked side by side to the therapist's office, where they sat in the waiting room. Beau had nothing else to say to Warner. He kept quiet, wiped sweat from his temple with his shoulder sleeve.

His phone broke the silence, but he checked the screen and put it back in his pocket.

"You can take it," Warner said. "We have a few minutes."

Beau glanced at him and leaned his elbows on his knees. "It's fine." It rang again and didn't stop until Beau finally answered it. "What is it?"

"What do Texas, New Mexico and Arizona have in common?" Detective Bragg asked, sounding more joyful than Beau thought possible.

"A lot, actually," Beau said.

"They're all on the way back to Los Angeles. She should be on our turf by tomorrow."

Beau looked at the ground, bouncing his knee up and down. He'd learned his lesson—finally—when it came to assuming anything about Lola. Yet the promise he'd made himself to walk away was tenuous, something that could easily be broken if he wasn't careful. A memory nagged at him—*Texas, New Mexico, Arizona*—but he shook his head quickly to deflect it.

"You hear what I said?" Bragg continued. "She's coming home."

That was a blow. Lola might be coming back to California, but if she considered Beau her home, she wouldn't have left him this way. He massaged his forehead. "We decided to drop this."

"That was before I knew we were at the end."

"You were right, though. She wants to be…" It wasn't a memory nagging him—it was his dream from the airplane. The details were fuzzy, but he could clearly picture Lola in the desert with their daughter. He stilled his leg. "Did you say Arizona?"

"Got a pending motel charge in Tucson just now. That's why I called."

The doctor's office door opened, and a woman spoke. "See you in a few days, Brigitte?"

"I have to go," Beau said, pulling his phone away.

"Maybe I was wrong." Bragg cleared his throat. "About her not wanting to be found. Maybe I had it wrong."

Beau didn't think it could be that simple. "Congratulations on your second retirement, Bragg. Thanks for all your help."

He hung up the phone as Brigitte entered the waiting room and stopped when she saw them. She turned a balled-up tissue over in her hand, a watery smile on her face. "You both came."

Beau stood, and she went directly to him. She hugged him, melting against his body only a second before she pulled back. She narrowed her red-rimmed eyes. "You've been drinking."

"Not yet."

She shook her head. "Then you're wildly hungover."

"It's been a rough couple weeks."

Brigitte frowned, but for once it didn't alarm him, since it was purely concern. She looked about to speak but then closed her mouth. Beau had gotten off the airplane and had a voicemail from Brigitte—she was going into therapy, for real this time. Careful not to upset her, he hadn't yet mentioned any details about Lola or his trip, and Brigitte hadn't asked.

"Your big meeting with VenTech is tomorrow. Shouldn't you be at work prepping?"

Beau definitely should've been with his team, which was locked in a conference room surrounded by Subway sandwich wrappers. Things'd happened so quickly that the staff had been taking turns pulling all-nighters. Beau was having a hard time remembering why he needed VenTech so badly, though, and as a result, had been avoiding the office. That, and he was proud of Brigitte for finally making a good decision.

"I thought maybe my *soeurette* could use me more," he said. "And I wanted to congratulate you."

She shrugged. "It wasn't an easy decision, but with some urging from—"

"Not about that." He jerked his head fractionally in Warner's direction.

"Oh." She looked down between them, but it was hard to miss the pink flush of her pale skin. "I don't know where I was all these years. I must've been blinded by some—*thing*."

Beau nodded that he understood. In her reality, she and Beau were linked for life. Whether it was simply familial for her or something more, Beau'd never asked, in case he didn't like the answer. Her fear of loneliness was strong enough to shut out the truth. Beau was fine being pushed aside so Warner could take his place.

"We'll have to figure out a new arrangement," Beau said, loud enough for Warner to hear. "I'm not having my sister's boyfriend drive me around."

"Fire me."

Beau and Brigitte both turned to him. She disengaged from Beau to go hug Warner instead. "But, Brandon, darling, you love what you do."

Beau made a face. *Brandon?* He looked between them, suppressing his reflex to stop them from touching. He'd practically pushed Brigitte into Warner's arms, but seeing them together would take some getting used to.

"I can always do it somewhere else," Warner said. "At the end of the day, it's just a job."

Any other time, Beau might've scoffed at that—just a job? What else was there? But since Lola had disappeared, what he'd missed most was having someone to look forward to all day. He'd promised to make her a priority, but then he'd look up from his computer at some point to see afternoon had become evening, and he still hadn't finished. That was a mistake he was paying for dearly in the tender of regret. Maybe if he'd chosen her over work, like Warner was with Brigitte, Lola would've found a reason to stay.

Beau tuned out his thoughts and focused on Brigitte, who was relaying her session to them.

"At first, it wasn't too bad, mostly discussing what'll happen over the course of my therapy. Then she asked about the accident, and…" She stepped away from Warner to take Beau's hands. "And we talked about you. Me and you."

Beau wasn't looking forward to hearing whatever she said next, but he remained still despite his instinct to flee.

She must've noticed, because she held his hands more tightly. "Do you need to hear this from me? The doctor says I should tell you." She looked into his eyes. "You're a good brother. If I ever made you think otherwise, I'm sorry."

He shook his head. "I just want to see you healthy and happy."

"I'm not your responsibility. You don't have to take care of me."

Brigitte, on her own two feet, without him to support her? He couldn't picture it. "It's the nature of our relationship."

"Sometimes it's okay to let me fail or fall on my face. All I ask is that you're there to help me off the ground."

Beau had his complaints about Brigitte, and sometimes she made his life hard. But without her, who would he be? He didn't want to know, and he'd never wanted to be rid of her. Not completely, anyway. "I'm not going anywhere."

"I don't mean your money, Beau. Sometimes I just need you to be there when I call. That's the relationship I want us to have."

Beau's hands were clammy. He'd bent over backward his whole life to make sure Brigitte and his mom were comfortably set up, never without food, shelter or, of course, the finer things in life. "I thought we already had that."

"We don't. I've spent the last twenty years just

trying to get your attention, but nobody has your attention like your money."

Lola had said the same thing in different words. With a sharp pain in his chest, Beau briefly wondered if this on top of everything else was finally just going to kill him.

"Don't be upset," Brigitte said. "*I* know it's how you show affection. But it wasn't enough for Lola, and it's not enough for me anymore. I need a different kind of support from you now."

"So, what—I'm the bad guy all the time? For everyone?"

"No. Since we were together when our parents died, I thought we were connected on some supernatural level. But maybe that's a load of shit—at least, that's what the doctor seems to think. I've been a burden. You're not responsible for me—or your mom, for that matter. You're not the man of the house. We can't keep pulling you in different directions."

"I want to take care of both of you, but you guys make it difficult to do a good job."

"So don't do it anymore." She cleared her throat. "Take care of Lola instead."

Beau wanted his hands back, but Brigitte wouldn't let them go. "It's over," he said, subject closed, nothing else to say.

Brigitte looked down. "Ten years ago, you came home a complete mess because a *stripper* had turned down the money it'd taken you your whole life to earn. Remember that night?"

It was a rhetorical question. Of course Beau remembered every nuance of the hour he'd spent with

Lola, the way his heart had stabbed with every footstep he'd taken on his way out of the club. "What about it?"

"Tell me what happened."

"You already know the story—inside and out."

"Just tell me."

Beau sighed, glancing back at Warner. He'd also heard the story, so there wasn't one reason to tell it. "I gave up a lot for my first website, so when it sold for millions, it was surreal. The night I signed the papers, I was on a high. After years of having no social life, no women, I wanted someone that night. A beautiful girl to celebrate with. I walked into that strip club, and—" Beau paused, remembering how Lola had glistened and glittered from her shiny, black hair to her diamond bikini. "And there was no more beautiful woman than her. But she wouldn't have me, because she knew what she was worth. I tried to buy her for a night, but she didn't have a price."

Brigitte stared up at him, silent until Beau got uncomfortable. "What?" he asked.

With a disbelieving shake of her head, she said, "I've just never heard you tell it that way. It was always about what she'd done to you, or the pain she'd caused. You love her."

Beau took his hands away finally, wiping them on his slacks. "Not much I can do about it either way."

"What happened when you went to find her?"

"Nothing. Not a fucking thing." He shrugged. "By saying nothing, she's made herself clear."

"You're giving up?" She rushed the words out, bouncing once on the balls of her feet. She would have him all to herself again. "But you never give up on anything worth saving."

It took Beau a moment to register that she wasn't rooting against Lola. He cocked his head, glancing at Warner, whose lips were pressed together with a suppressed smile. "I'm not giving up. I figured it was time I start respecting her decision. Anyway, I wouldn't know where to find her."

Brigitte rolled her eyes as if the answer were obvious to everyone but Beau. "Stop acting like her opponent," she said, "and start thinking like her partner. What is she looking for? Where is she going to find it?"

Beau swallowed, looking away. Respect wasn't the only reason he had to let her go. Her name grated when he heard it aloud. He couldn't remember word for word the last thing she'd said to him. He would never tease her about seeing the ball of twine in person, as he hoped she had.

"We should go," he said, turning away from their raised eyebrows and craned necks.

Warner went by Brigitte's apartment first and walked her to the door. Beau watched them interact without a third party. When Warner leaned in to kiss her, she almost shied away. Warner wiped his forehead with the back of his hand. Beau doubted he and Warner suffered from the same kind of sweat, though. Beau looked out the other window to give them privacy.

"You never give up on anything worth saving."

"Stop acting like her opponent, and start thinking like her partner."

Beau asked himself when he'd ever *not* fought for anything in his life. Everything he owned, he had because he'd fought for it. He'd even fought *himself* countless times. He was tired. Thirty-seven years he'd been fighting without a break and carrying at least one person on his back. He looked at his watch, wondering how much longer he'd have to wait for a drink.

◆⊠◆⊠◆

Warner glanced at Beau in the rearview mirror for the third time in ten minutes. Beau'd insisted he'd take a taxi so Warner could stay with Brigitte, but Warner wouldn't have it. He pulled up to the curb in front of Beau's house and left the car idling.

Warner had been with Beau ten years. Their relationship had worked itself into a groove long ago. Beau took a stab at what was bothering Warner. "Should we discuss our new arrangement?"

"No need, sir. I'll start looking for a new employer in the morning."

Beau studied him. He seemed to have no problem making such a drastic change. Apparently, everyone around Beau was moving on, working toward becoming better people. "Let me do it," Beau said. "I only want you working for the best."

"Thank you, sir."

"You don't need to call me sir anymore."

Warner nodded once. "All right."

Beau hesitated. "About Brigitte. Do you think the counseling will help?"

"Yes. She's tried before, but this time, she actually wants things to change."

Beau hoped that was true. She certainly had never sought help on her own without Beau pushing her.

"Good." Beau reached for the handle.

"It may be selfish," Warner continued, "but I hope she doesn't change much. I want her to get better and somehow stay the same. Does that make sense?" He chuckled to himself, shaking his head. "She's a handful, but she grows on you."

Beau released the door and sat back in his seat. He smiled a little. "Just be careful what you wish for. Brigitte might mellow a bit, but her fire never burns out. No matter how many times I've wished it would."

"Better or worse, that fire's what I love about her," Warner said.

Beau looked at the floor. *Fire.* He missed Lola's fire most of all. The way she screamed at him, fought him, submitted to him, came for him, challenged him. *Fuck.* He needed a drink immediately before he lost it.

"Sir?" Warner asked. "Beau?"

Beau looked up. "Yes?"

Warner turned in his seat to look at him, went to speak. He shut his mouth, looking thoughtful. "I've been there from the beginning. That first night you picked Lola up at her house. I see how you are about her. I just—well, I know it hasn't been…if you need to talk—"

Beau held up his hand. "Not now. Definitely not now. Go home, Warner."

"Yes, sir."

Beau got out of the car, went inside and veered directly for his study. He poured himself a drink and took a sip. The burn was a poor substitute for Lola, but it was as close as he could get.

Brigitte wanted Beau to put himself in Lola's shoes. He was already in them, though, whether he wanted to be or not. He now knew the pain he'd caused her and understood how it'd driven her away. The question was why she was coming home. She had the money and motive to stay hidden. Maybe she thought Beau had given up on her. Or maybe she wasn't returning to Los Angeles at all.

Beau, a man who lived life on the top floor of whatever building he was in, had never felt smaller or more insignificant. Without Lola by his side, he was nothing. She'd left a hole in her place that'd grown into a canyon each day she was missing. Had she felt the same that morning she'd left his hotel room?

It'd been years since Beau had encountered a problem he couldn't buy his way out of. Once she was back in California, he could spend every dollar he had to track her down. He could fill her space with flowers or show up in a helicopter and take her to Paris for a night. He could build her a place to dance to her heart's content. Money was the only way he knew how to prove how much he loved her, but it wasn't right. Lola didn't deserve to be bought—he knew that better than anyone. He should've known that from the start.

She deserved a man who would fight for her. Lay down his life for her. Who would earn her love, no matter what it took, because he couldn't survive another day without it. A man who could give her the things money couldn't buy. Finally, Beau understood—he was that man. And he knew where she was headed.

Chapter Seventeen

Arizona had stretched-cotton clouds, blue skies and long-fingered cacti. Lola stuck her left arm out the window, opening her hand against the dry, mild air. It was cooler now that she'd passed Phoenix, and the desert was changing from sand to brittle grass, shrubs and trees.

She'd reached Tucson thinking it would be the last night of her road trip. Los Angeles was only seven or eight hours from there. But in the motel the night before, she'd lain on a hard-mattress bed, staring up at a dark ceiling, insomnia an overzealous friend. She didn't even know where she'd stop and park her car once she got home. That thought'd made her body heavy on the bed, as if she might risk driving right through the city if she didn't figure it out soon.

Back when she'd had nothing to lose, it'd been easy to slide behind the bar of Hey Joe. To insert herself into Johnny's life one toiletry at a time. To slip beside him in his bed. Things weren't so clear now. She only knew what she didn't want for herself or her baby—a life where things happened to her. She was capable of taking charge now. That was what she'd gained by choosing herself and driving away from something she loved.

She'd lain awake most of the night, memories of Beau gum-stuck to her no matter how hard she tried to clean them away. How he focused when he shaved. He didn't make coffee for himself, but he liked to leave her a fresh pot on the mornings he didn't see her, his version of a love note on his pillow. It was always too strong, the coffee. But what she remembered as clearly as those little things was the waiting. For the end. For him to come home. If Lola wasn't the woman Beau would leave work early for, then one didn't exist. By now, he would know it too, what he'd given up to stay on top.

Sometimes, though, he'd tried to make it right—most notably the evening they'd had coffee in his den and talked until the near dawn. After replaying that night's conversation about travel, she'd decided there'd be one more stop on her trip. It would be a way to pay homage to her time with Beau—and a place to seek answers. The earth had bottomed out from under her, but she was climbing her way back up. Where better to end this trip than a rift so deep, it could never be repaired?

Lola arrived at the Grand Canyon in the late afternoon. She waited in a line of cars to pay the entrance fee. The only money she carried now was a couple hundred dollars divided between her wallet and her suitcase. The rest was in a bank where it belonged. She passed through the cabin-esque, log-walled entrance, and drove to the parking lots. She circled them for fifteen minutes, hitting her brakes now and then for tourists in bunched-up socks and cameras around their necks. Everybody was arriving. Nobody seemed to be leaving.

Finally, she parked and got out, stretching her arms. The clear, cool sky was stark against its russet surroundings. A bus stopped at the curb of the Visitor's Center and a group spilled out. They wore more layers than she did and talked loudly about the impending sunset. She shoved her hands in her hoodie pockets and tried to weave through people, but they kept stopping to take pictures before they'd even made it to the canyon. She looped wide around the swarm. What she wouldn't miss about traveling was the crowds, lines, limited parking. People on top of people at every attraction.

She stopped first at the busiest spot, a fenced overlook. She leaned on a railing, gazing into the mouth of the canyon, wide open and the color of a bruise. It gave her a thrill. She scanned the canyon walls, a rust-rainbow of beiges that morphed into earthy purples and pinks as the sun lowered.

A man asked her to move out of a picture he was taking of his wife. Lola left to find a more secluded spot, her tennis shoes crunching along the path. Only Mather Point, where she'd just stood, was enclosed. The rest was open, the canyon ready to swallow anyone who might misstep. She walked the rim, the crowd thinning, and spotted a cliff where she could be alone.

She climbed off the path, down between two boulders. A whitewashed rock jutted out into the canyon and came to a square point. The thought of standing on the edge made her heart skip, but she hadn't come all this way to live life in the curtains. With slow, careful steps, she walked to the ledge. It was a straight drop down. Being so far up was physical, her stomach and legs prickling like being stabbed by hundreds of tiny pins. As a teenager, she'd get high trying to feel something akin to this. She shivered with a breeze, the hair on the back of her neck waking up.

"I'm ready for some answers," she said out loud,

her words expanding into nothing. She felt, inside, like the valley—deep, dangerous, beautiful. She had no idea how to be a mother. She didn't take it lightly, that responsibility, and it scared her. She needed to know how one night could've led to all this. One night, she'd looked over her shoulder and found Beau. One night, they hadn't used protection. "I don't know if I can do this by myself."

Nothing happened. The canyon was still. She wasn't going to find answers here. They were inside her, but they'd only come with time. She closed her eyes to take a mental picture, the wind light in her hair. She told herself she wasn't alone, that as much as it'd been forced on her, she'd also chosen this path. She wouldn't have been happy in that life with Beau, never having healed that wound he'd left, always being second place to his money.

That was where she stood, alone but steeped in hard-won peace, when he spoke from behind her.

"So this is where it ends."

Chapter Eighteen

Lola opened her eyes abruptly, her peacefulness shattering. Beau was so unexpected that her heart doubled in size and speed, fat and swollen, clambering up into her throat like a live fish trying to escape. She knew that voice, that unforgiving tone, as surely as she knew what would happen if she were to take one step forward.

"Turn the fuck around," Beau said.

The deeply-orange sun crested from behind a cloud, blinding her. She turned her head to the side, Beau in her peripheral vision. Closer than he should be. There was no one person she wanted to see least and most in that moment. She didn't want to explain herself, but she needed him to understand.

"Look me in the eye," he said. "You owe me that much."

She couldn't bring herself to do it. It was bad timing, being so close to the edge, vulnerable and unprepared for him. This wasn't on her terms like it was supposed to be.

But with the gravelly chew of his shoes, she turned quickly. She shielded her eyes, his shadow black and nebulous, blinking away the sun's neon imprint. "Wait," she said.

He'd already stopped, his feet apart, almost aggressively so. It reminded her of the beginning, the way he'd stood that first night on the Sunset Strip sidewalk, intruding on her moment alone. Just like then, he was perfectly put together in his suit, his dress shirt tucked in, his navy tie straight. Only his pants were wrinkled across the front, as if he'd been sitting in them for a long time. The day's last light illuminated his brown hair gold.

"What are you doing here?" she asked.

"What am *I*…?" He paused, running his hands up the sides of his nose. He inhaled a deep breath, made a fist, jammed a rigid finger into his chest. "You're asking me why *I'm* here? I'm doing the same thing I did in L.A., Missouri, New Orleans. I'm goddamn looking for you."

Lola wished for something to steady herself on—a gate, a fence, even a tall boulder. She checked over her shoulder—nothing but white-rock ledge. She pulled her shoulders up as she looked back at him. "I never asked you to do that."

"You turned my life upside down." He scrubbed his whiskered chin and shoved a hand in his hair, ruining it. It was too long and not as perfect as she'd thought. "More than once. Did you think I'd lie down and take that? You didn't think I'd fight back?" He'd said *fight* angrily, with a hard "F" and clipped "T".

Lola's heart beat a mile a minute, the tips of her fingers and toes tingling. "I don't want to fight with you, Beau," she said calmly. "I don't want to play. I just want the bullshit to end."

"It's over," Beau said. "Believe me. This game ended a long time ago."

"Then why are you here?"

"I think I'll ask the fucking questions, thank you." He took a step forward, and Lola instinctively moved back a little. "What happened to you that night?"

"I did what I had to do." She leveled her eyes on him. "What you *made* me do. You really thought I could love you after what you did to me?"

"Don't pretend you're innocent here, Lola." His nostrils flared. "Or do you go by Melody now?"

She kept her arms straight at her sides, caught off guard to hear her real name from his mouth. She hadn't thought he would remember that detail from the VIP room. "Is that how you found me?"

"That and a lot of money."

Her jaw tingled, saliva pooling in her mouth. She didn't know what answer she'd expected or hoped for with him. "Of course. Money."

"At first, yes," he continued. "But it only got me so far. After that, I had to figure it out on my own." He squinted, holding his arms out, nodding. "I'm a little late, but I made it. Not bad considering you left me with nothing to go on."

His words were bitter like his tone. He grabbed the knot of his tie and loosened it, leaving it crooked. There wasn't even a sliver of relief or happiness in his eyes.

Lola swallowed. "What are you going to do to me?"

"I've been asking myself the same thing." He took another step.

"I can't go through this again," she pleaded, shaking her head hard. "I've made peace with the pain."

"I haven't."

Lola glanced around without turning her head from him. There were only two exits from this situation—forward or backward.

"What was it all about?" he asked. "I want the

truth, so help me God. Don't bullshit me."

How could she explain what it'd been like to finally give in to her love for him after fighting it so hard, only to have him break her big, happy heart in half? And then—to have to pretend to worship him for weeks as she nursed her wounds in private? *That* was bullshit.

"That night," Lola started.

He jerked his head to the side. "Which one?

"In your hotel room, when we were planning how to leave Johnny. I'd never—it was the most—" Lola wiped her palms on the seat of her jeans. "You didn't ask. You just took. All of it. All of me."

"But you came back. You gave me another chance, and I did my best to make up for—"

"I *loved* you," she said, the word dropping like an axe between them.

They stood there a moment, two actors on an open stage, leaves rustling, voices distant, temperature dropping. A train horn echoed through the canyon.

"You don't anymore?" he asked.

Lola looked down at the ground. What did it say about her that she still loved him after everything he'd put her through? Her heart ached for him when he was right in front of her the way it had half a country away.

She looked up, keeping strength in her face, even though her body had begun to tremble. "My love hasn't gone anywhere. It's still in the garbage where you left it."

"I knew I was making a mistake that night. Even while I was doing it. But I'd gotten in too deep to pull myself out. Was it not enough punishment that I had to live with that? Knowing I loved you, but I could never truly make up for how badly I'd hurt you?"

"Knowing is one thing. You deserved—*deserve* to live the depth of your mistake."

"For how long?"

"That's for you to decide." She shrugged, limp and unconvincing. "It isn't something your assistant can add to your calendar. My forgiveness doesn't matter—you need your own."

"Where do you get off telling me what I need? Patronizing me? You have no idea what I've been through."

She shuffled back the last few inches, glancing behind her again. "Yes, I—"

"You don't know. You didn't care to," Beau continued, another step. "And I still have nothing. I don't know where you went from Cat Shoppe. How you got there. Why. If you laid beside me in my own bed, plotting against me."

Her throat thickened. She didn't respond. It didn't look as though he expected her to. He was in front of her now, and she was cornered. She dug her heels into the sand. If she screamed, would anyone hear? Would it even matter? Nobody was close enough to get to her in time. All she'd done was even the score. But maybe Beau didn't see it that way. Maybe to him, she had a debt that was too great to pay.

He reached up. "Even with all that—"

"Stop." Her heart hammered. She squeezed her eyes shut. Everything on her body was rigid except for her arms, curved gently over her stomach. "I'm p—"

"I forgive you," he said. "I forgive myself. And I surrender."

Her body shook, her breath stuttering out of her

mouth, wispy little butterflies. She balled a hand at her chin over her mouth, surprised to find it wet. She hadn't realized she'd been crying.

When she opened her eyes, his arms were spread as if to say it was all he had. She couldn't see anything but him and his hawk-like wingspan.

"I don't know if that's what you wanted, Lola, but you win."

Her chest deflated, relief and regret seeping through her. Surrender, forgiveness, victory. What was even left to win? What kind of prize was this to have fought so hard for? She shook her head. "That's not why I left."

"Then why?" He dropped his arms at his sides, his expression earnest, his thick eyebrows heavy in a different way than they just had been. "To escape? Or to get me to see?"

She shifted on her feet. "To see what?"

"I was stupid for you. You and I went deeper than anything, and I fought back out of fear. But I'm done making that mistake. My weapons are at my feet."

She waited, but he didn't continue. He hadn't moved back even an inch.

"That's it?" she asked. "That's your apology?"

"I'm sorry I hurt you. But I don't regret it. We wouldn't be here if I hadn't."

"Here?" Her hands still trembled. She closed them into two fists. "*This* is a good place to you?"

"It's where I should've been from the start. It was hell not knowing where you were. It opened my eyes, though, Lola. And like I said, now I finally see."

Lola tried to shut the words out. She believed him—tormenting him with her absence was the purpose of her plan. But his surrender wasn't, and it felt better than it should to hear he wasn't finished with her yet. "We both set out to destroy each other," she said. "How do I know that isn't what you're doing now?"

"Trust. Neither of us is good at it, but we each need it now. You know I love you—it's not a question of that. It's a question of if you'll let me. I do…love you."

She paused. It didn't shock her, but as his words registered, she realized that no matter how strongly she knew it in her gut, she'd thought she'd never hear him tell her he loved her. And that she'd somehow be okay with that. "I know you do. I always knew. You were the one who didn't."

"I do now. I get it. Put an end to this, Lola. I've repented. I've suffered. For you."

"How do I know? I wasn't there. I didn't see any of it."

"You chose not to. At least I looked you in the eye when I hurt you."

Her cheeks flushed. She wanted to be the only one who was justifiably angry, but he was right—and it embarrassed her. "So what? That makes it better?"

"There's no 'better' in this situation. We learn from our mistakes and move forward. I'm here to bring you home. To get the light back in my life."

The sun disappeared behind the rocky horizon. Lola had goose bumps everywhere and sweat along her hairline. These were things she thought she'd never hear. She jutted her palms between them. "Can you just step back? This is making me nervous."

He took her by the arm, his hand warm through her jacket, and pulled her closer to him.

Lola shrugged him off. "Not just the cliff."

He took some steps away without turning his back to her. In their relationship, she'd always been the one out on a ledge, expected to trust him blindly. To get into a stranger's limo, to uproot her life based on two nights.

"I've had a lot of time to think," Lola said, off the overhang now. "A lot of time alone. I came here for answers because…you said you got them here."

"Did you get them?"

She stuck a hand in her pocket, picked at some lint. "No."

"I never said I got answers, Lola. I said I came here looking for them. I don't like it here. It's so fucking bottomless, it just makes me feel like I have no control at all. But what I did get here was perspective. And I'm glad those answers never came, because it taught me a valuable lesson. Only one person makes things happen in my life."

"You."

He nodded. "So that's why I'm here. To do what it takes to fix this."

She lifted her chin. "I got some answers, Beau, just not here. This is my life, and I decide. You don't get to come here and tell me my trip is over and we're back together."

"I understand, but—"

"Don't interrupt me. I'm not going to make the same mistakes I did with Johnny."

Beau reeled back. "What's that supposed to mean?"

"I'm not coming back to L.A. because *you* say it's time. I'll do it when I decide it's right for me."

He worked his jaw side to side a moment. "I've told

you repeatedly, I'm not Johnny. Your happiness is my priority, and from now on, that's what drives my decisions. I'm here to take you home because I believe it's in your best interest."

"Why is it always what you say?" she asked, her voice rising. "When do *I* get to decide?"

He showed her his palms. "We're a team. You never have to be anything other than you when you're with me. You said it yourself that first night—I didn't choose you because I was looking for someone to roll over and take it."

Beau had always wanted Lola as she was—as long as it was on his terms. She shook her head, still uncomfortably close to the ledge. "It's not enough."

There was struggle in his face, his eyes, when he said, "It was once."

She nodded, remembering. *"I want you to know—to me, you are enough..."*

"I'm talking about all this." She gestured around them. "You can't just ask me to forgive you because you realize the mistakes you've made."

Beau inclined his head a little, squinting at her. "So what're you saying? This is just done?"

"Why'd you come here?"

"I couldn't walk away without knowing I'd tried."

"You tried, I'll give you that. But this is where it ends," she repeated his words back to him.

He shook his head. "I was talking about the torment, the pain, the games. All of that ends now." He gestured between them. "Not this."

Lola looked at Beau. He *was* trying, but she needed more. She needed all of him the way she'd been prepared to give him all of herself. He had to be exhausted by his love for her, because their child deserved that from both of them.

"This. Us," Lola said. "This is where *we* end."

"Don't." He shook his head. "You can't tell me you drove all that time and never thought of me. Never wished to be back in my arms, to be loved by me. That you—"

"You have no idea—"

"That you don't still love me—"

"Of course I do," Lola cried. Late nights clutching her pillow, wishing it was *him*. Driving for hours trying to think of anything but *him*. It wasn't fair that even when she hurt him, she hurt herself. She never got a break from the pain, and he had the nerve to come here and accuse her of otherwise. "You don't think this has been torture for me too? I fucking loved you with everything. You could've burned every last dollar—I wouldn't have cared. I loved the way you loved me, something nobody ever gave me. Fuck you," she said, reluctant tears flooding her eyes, "for thinking you suffered more than me."

"I broke your heart—fine. Mine broke every day I woke up and thought, 'Today I'll find her. Today I'll bring her home.' Now I have you—and you're going to tell me no?"

"You deserved everything you got."

"I did. I accept that. But don't keep punishing me."

"You don't even know what lies ahead," Lola said and resisted touching her stomach again. If there was an ounce of love in him for her, she could tear his heart out every day once he found out she was pregnant. But she'd be tearing her own heart out too and now, she actually needed it to raise this baby.

"I don't deserve this anymore," he said.

"You deserve it," she snapped. She breathed hard, curling her hands in and out of fists. She'd been holding the reins for weeks, and she didn't know how to loosen her grip. "You deserve all of it. For being a monster."

"I've learned my lesson. And I'm grateful for that, because now I know I can make you happy. You're more than enough, Lola—the money doesn't mean shit if you aren't by my side. I want to try to be enough for you."

"No. You had your chance, and you blew it. We're finished, and there isn't anything you can say to change my mind."

Slowly, he inclined his head forward. "You're serious about this?"

"I will not make the same mistakes again."

They stared at each other, him looking on the verge of speaking until he closed his mouth. "I don't know how else to get you to see—I thought…I thought—"

"You thought what? You'd never have to pay for treating people like this?"

He looked away from her, his eyes eventually drifting down to the ground. He blinked, his hand twitched. His eyebrows lowered. And she watched his every move, not knowing what she was hoping for, just that he wasn't giving it to her. He turned around.

"Where are you going?" Lola asked.

He stopped, looked back. "I don't know. I'm standing here, prepared to do whatever you ask, but you're asking me to do nothing."

"No," she said sharply. She jabbed a finger in his

direction. "*You* don't get to walk away. I do."

His eyebrows knit as he faced her again. "What?"

"Do you know how it feels to lay it all on the line only to have the person you love tear you apart?"

He nodded. "I do now."

"No, you don't. You said you loved me—but *I* was about to give you *everything* I had. You waited until I was at my most vulnerable to rip my heart out. I want to do the same to you, and then *I* get to walk away. Do you understand?"

"No. I—"

"I want to gut you of your dignity."

His face went smooth, his body still. Dignity, pride, ego, his and hers—that was how they'd gotten here. Neither of them wanted to give up those things. "I don't know what else to say." Beau's jaw clenched as he swallowed. "I love you. I want to make a life with you. That's my everything."

"Stand on the cliff," she said. "You stand there for once."

He glanced behind her. "What?"

She looked back at that enormous hole in the earth and pointed at the crag. "You need to know how it feels to be cornered for once. To have no control."

He walked toward. She held her breath as they passed each other and only let it go once they'd switched spots. He walked over to the ledge and looked down, but only for a brief second. He turned his back to it. "I never thought I could love anyone the way I love you."

"Did you hear that in a movie?" Lola asked.

He narrowed his eyes on her, rolling his lips inward. "It's true, Lola."

"It's not good enough."

"I don't understand. What do you want from me?"

"I want you to give me what I gave you. Every last thing you have. And when you're emptied out, and your heart is in the dirt? I'm going to walk away, Beau. I'm going to leave you standing here in your own mess. You will never see me again. So, come on. If you love me like you say, you'll give me the closure I deserve."

He stared at her, something miserable in his green eyes. It was almost enough to get her to call this off, but this was what she needed. Because nobody could hurt Beau's pride worse than himself. If he could go to that place for her, knowing it wouldn't win him anything in the end, then maybe Lola could trust in what he was trying to tell her.

She held her breath, waiting. For a minute, she worried he couldn't do it. He couldn't give himself up to save them.

He inhaled deeply through his nose. "I already told you I love you. How am I supposed to explain how deep it goes?"

"Try." Lola turned sideways. "If you can't, you can leave."

He continued to look at her, finally shaking his head. "I thought I'd find you here and all my questions would be answered. I knew we would fight. It's who we are, what we do to each other. We're both so angry. But I was going to take everything you had to give, and never once did I think that wouldn't be enough. In my gut, I knew—we'd leave here together."

"Both those nights, you let me live in a fantasy I thought was reality. Now it's your turn. Tell me all the details of this life you thought we would have. Where would we have gone from here?"

His put his hands in his pockets. It was ridiculous to see a man in a suit at a place like this, but it was his armor. His tie was still off center. "Don't make me do this."

She had done it, over and over, and in her experience—he had to know what he was losing in order to feel the full impact of its void. "Your plan was to come here and drive me off into the sunset? That isn't life," she said sharply. "Do it or leave. Go back to L.A."

"Back to L.A.," he repeated fast and loud, visibly tensing as though steeling himself. "That's where I would've taken you. Home, to the house—"

"I hated it there." It'd never felt like she'd belonged amongst the white carpets and polished wood. "That wasn't my home."

"Okay. I didn't know that," he said cautiously, grimacing. "So, then, I'd ask if you wanted to move to a different neighborhood, or if you'd found somewhere on your trip you liked better than L.A."

"You can't leave L.A."

He looked to the side, his eyebrows heavy, wrestling with something. "I could. It's not home anymore," he said distantly. "You are. Were."

Lola shifted on her feet. Beau was dedicated to that city even more than she was. "What about Bolt Ventures?"

"I would've given it up. Or worked remotely. Or started something new. At the end of the day, it's just a job." He smiled a little as he said it, like he was sharing an inside joke. But he looked back at her quickly, serious again. "I would've come home at five. I don't want to spend another evening without you. I hate it. I hate coming home to an empty house. Before, I didn't know the difference, but I do now. It's excruciating."

Lola's blood rushed loudly in her head. As angry as she was, she recognized his breakthrough for what it was. He was giving her the control by living out this dream he'd never get, by making himself vulnerable. While she'd been gone, getting her back had still been a possibility in his mind. But now, he knew no matter what he said, she was going to leave. He didn't have to say anything. He could walk away.

"I love you," he said. "So much that I went to see your mom. Once, to see if she knew where you were. Then again—yesterday morning, on my way to work. I stopped and spent an hour there, having coffee, talking to her whenever there was a lull between tables."

Lola leaned in as if she'd misheard him. She hadn't known about the second time, since it was after she'd spoken to Dina on the phone. "Did my mom tell you where to find me?"

"No. I didn't even ask."

"Then why'd you go?"

He shrugged one shoulder. "I missed you so fucking much, I didn't know what to do. I couldn't go to Hey Joe. My own home is hell, the stupidest shit reminds me of you. She was the only real connection I had left to you."

Lola tried to focus, but her mind had latched onto this one little thing—he hadn't just gone to see her mom. He'd taken an hour out of his workday to do it. And it wasn't to get anything or manipulate anyone. It was only to feel close to Lola. And she realized they were standing at the Grand Canyon at five-thirty on a Tuesday, when he should've been fifty stories above Los Angeles, ruling his empire.

Her heart squeezed. She'd needed that from him even more than she'd realized. And his words reverberated inside her—*'I missed you so fucking much. I missed you so fucking much.'*

"Beau—"

"I canceled a meeting to be here," he continued. "Not just any meeting—it was with VenTech."

Lola tilted her head, the name vaguely familiar.

"The company that bought my first website and made me a millionaire. It's struggling to stay afloat. Today, ten years after they destroyed all my hard work for my competitor's benefit, Bolt Ventures was going to make an embarrassingly low offer to acquire VenTech. Just so I could say I told you so as I sold it off in parts."

Lola touched her throat. So she wasn't the only other one Beau thought deserving of his wrath. She had to know, for her own sake, if he could still be that vindictive. "Tell me you aren't going through with it."

"I was. This morning would've been my first time facing the founder since I'd signed the contract at twenty-seven. But because there was the smallest chance I'd find you here today, I called off the deal last night. It wasn't worth it. None of this seems worth it anymore."

He'd been where she had, trying to find her, when he'd needed to be elsewhere. When he could've sent someone in his place. She'd been running away, living her life, and she'd also been his priority. And, like she'd planned all along, he'd learned his lesson. Canceling the acquisition was proof.

"Beau—"

"Wait. Before you go. I'm not finished." He doubled over, put his hands on his knees and took a deep breath as he stared at the ground. "I can't look at you for this part. I fucked things up, I know. But I had no idea how much I was throwing away. The reason I built all this, why I missed your dinners, was to make sure my family, whenever they came along, would have everything. It scares the fuck out of me to say this, but I thought that family would be with you, and I thought I'd worked hard enough, done enough, to deserve that." He squatted down, ran his hands over his face and looked up at her. "You're going to be a great mother, Lola. I've seen it."

She took two steps back, her hand on her stomach. There was only one way he could know about the baby. Dina's loyalty was to Lola, though—she had no reason to tell him. But he was as certain as she'd ever seen him. "What?"

"I'd hoped I'd be the one to give you that. I didn't even know I wanted it until…it doesn't matter. Fuck. It haunts me that someday you'll be the mother of someone else's child. But I have to live with that. So don't worry—I will get everything I deserve."

Tears streamed down her cheeks. He was almost on his knees, his chest opened, bleeding for her. All that, and he didn't even know she was carrying his child yet. It was enough. She put one hand over her mouth and sobbed into it while reaching out to him with the other. "Come here," she said. "Come home."

Chapter Nineteen

Beau was sure he'd heard wrong. That his mind was playing tricks on him. It wouldn't be a stretch—him, finally losing his sanity here on this ledge while Lola watched. He'd driven, literally, to the ends of the earth. He'd waited eight hours at the park's entrance for that red sports car to pull up, doubting himself, watching, watching, watching.

But it was worth it if he'd heard her correctly. Lola was crying into one hand, her other one outstretched to him. *"Come here. Come home."*

He couldn't move. As if getting into that position, kneeling at her feet on the edge of a cliff, had broken all his joints. It wasn't the abyss behind him that scared him but the idea of going on after seeing what could've been. Life had opened up to him, presenting him with all its beauty—he'd found her, and now he could make things right. Love her, marry her, give them both the child he'd dreamed about.

How could he miss it so much, something he'd never had?

He didn't blame Lola for breaking him down to this. It was the first time in his life he'd surrendered to someone else. Even the first two nights he'd spent with her, he'd given her just enough for them both to fall in love. But this wasn't love. It was something closer to death. A part of him had to die for Lola to know he wasn't the man she thought he was.

Beau eased from squatting to sanding, still unsure what she was offering him. Condolence? Pity? Something more? "But you said you were walking away."

She shook her head, removing her dampened hand to wipe her eyes. "Maybe I should, but I can't. I left to hurt you, hoping you'd regret what you'd given up, and I thought that would be it. I never planned to end up here."

Beau waited. He wanted to ask her if that meant she wasn't going to leave him there on the brink of his demise, but he was afraid one word from him might ruin it all.

"I'm happy in L.A., but I want to leave that house," she said. "I don't care where we go, it just has to have at least two bedrooms."

He stared at her, his heart rate increasing, unsure he could trust his ears. It sounded like she was saying she'd come home with him, but he didn't think he could take it if he was wrong yet again. He didn't know exactly what she was asking for, but he didn't care. "Consider the house gone. Whatever you want."

"I resented you." She paused. "For putting work first. I should've said it, but that would've meant I cared, and I didn't want to care. But I do now, so I'm saying it."

He nodded. Since she'd left, even he'd resented his work for what it'd cost him. "Work will always be a part of my life. I can't walk away completely."

"I don't want you to. It's your passion, but—"

"But it's not my priority. Not anymore. I will make changes, not because I have to, but because I have a reason to."

"That's not all," she said, eyeing him warily.

"I know it's not, but put me out of my misery. Please. Does this mean you're giving me a chance to earn you back?"

She reached out to him again, and this time, he went without hesitation. Those nights he'd had no idea where she was or if she was okay, he'd gone nearly mad, needing her back in his arms, the only place she was truly safe. Before he could put his hands on her, though, she took him by the wrist. Her long fingers wrapped around him, warming his chilled skin. She guided his hand to her waist, setting it there without letting him go. "You have nothing to earn," she said, looking into his eyes. "I see on your face what you've been through. When we were together, I know you never lied to me, never faked how you felt. I can forgive what you did because now that I understand you, I understand what drove you there. That Beau never would've stood where you just stood and willingly ripped his own heart out. I trust you."

Beau trusted her too, and he didn't question it. Hurting him was her way of fighting back. And she always would, he expected that from her. He loved that about her. But from now on, they'd be on the same side. "It's all I could've asked for from you. Forgive me. Love me."

"No," she said softly, shaking her head. "It's not all."

She readjusted her grip on his wrist—her palm was sweating. He glanced down. His hand wasn't actually flattened on her waist but her lower abdomen.

"When you said—" She paused, and he looked back at her face. Her expression had changed, her lips rolled inward with a frown. Her furrowed eyebrows lined her forehead with wrinkles. "Sometimes things don't really happen the way you plan—" She blew out a sigh and laughed in a strange, jittery way. "Obviously."

Beau lengthened his spine. Her demeanor had suddenly flipped, and he didn't need that. He didn't need to have the rug pulled out from under him again. Just a minute ago, she'd shoved her hand in his chest, taken hold of his heart, forced him to say *mercy*. Now, she could barely look him in the eye.

"What's wrong?" Beau asked. "Whatever it is, you can tell me. Nothing's going to change my—"

"I'm pregnant."

Beau jerked his head forward, his mouth and eyes wide open. They were both shaking—her body, his head side to side. They'd fucked a lot during the two nights of their arrangement, over and over. Him coming inside her, needing to own her in the quickest, most irrefutable way possible. He gulped some air, closed his mouth. "You're what? With—with me?"

She bit her bottom lip. "Yes. *We* are pregnant. I know it's not—what happened was, when my purse was stolen, my birth control was in there. When I moved in, we had those rules—I didn't think we'd—"

Beau squeezed his eyes shut for a brief second. He could barely hear her over the ringing in his ears. He was grateful he'd stepped away from the cliff. It came back to him all at once, his moment of weakness, taking her from behind against the bathroom counter. It'd nearly driven her away. He hadn't understood why then. It'd never occurred to him to ask about birth control.

That little girl in his dream, clutching Lola's leg, both of them otherworldly, divine. That was going to be his *reality*? After all the wrong he'd done, he was going to have that pureness in his life, that picture of perfection?

She was still talking. "And I know I signed that agreement—"

It was awkward handling her that way. He pulled his hand off her stomach and held it up. "Stop."

She blinked, her blue eyes sparkling more than usual, red and shiny with tears. By her quivering chin, she was trying not to cry. "You're not saying anything."

Already, he felt out of control. That's what children were—just a clusterfuck of disarray and irrational behavior. They couldn't be reasoned with.

Not his little girl, though. She'd be an angel.

Beau breathed hard through his nose, his insides running amuck. No, not his little girl, who was going to be as loved and revered as her mother.

He looked down at Lola, whose expression had morphed from anxious to horrified.

"What?" he asked. "Are you afraid of my reaction?"

Her face tightened up along with her jaw, her shoulders. "No." The wetness in her eyes evaporated. "You want this baby, Beau Olivier. Whether you know it or not."

He couldn't help his chuckle, even if it did sound a bit stiff. "I know it."

She opened her mouth.

Beau didn't let her speak. He dropped to his knees and slid up her top to expose her stomach. He cocked his head, examining the flawless, porcelain skin, the utter flatness of her abs. He glanced up at her. "You're sure?"

She nodded, slow but exaggerated. "Since before I even took the test."

Beau blinked lazily, feeling like he'd downed an entire bottle of his finest Scotch. "It's a girl."

Lola reared back a little, but he didn't let go of her. Her loud and sudden scoff skittered into a disbelieving laugh. "*Excuse* me?"

He got up again, brushing off his knees. "It's a girl. I've seen her."

She wrinkled her nose, pulling her head back. "Okay. You've finally…snapped."

He held her gaze, trying to stay serious, but he gave in and grinned. "That's possible. But if this is insanity, I like it here. Fuck, do I like it."

Her smile became hopeful, her face upturned to him like he was her sun. He knew without a doubt—he would never forget the beauty of this moment.

"You do?" she asked.

He took her face in his hands, felt her cheeks, her hair, ran the pad of his thumb over her bottom lip. "Is this too good to be real? Did I die in a plane crash on the way back from New Orleans?"

She took one of his hands and kissed his palm. "I'm so sorry I hurt you. Let me make it better. This is real. This is how it's supposed to be." She laced her fingers with his, watching them with a look of fascination. "Except you have one detail wrong. It's minor, really."

"What's that?"

"We're having a boy."

He arched an eyebrow, glancing down between them and back at her. "It's too early for you to know that."

"Call it a mother's instinct."

"Oh, mother's instinct. Right." He couldn't wait another second—he leaned down and kissed her on the lips once, a second time. She tasted a certain way—a certain way he'd missed. "What should we name her?"

"Him."

"Her."

"I'm positive," she said.

"I've never been more sure of anything," he said.

"I guess we'll see then, won't we?"

How could she even doubt him? Did she have any idea who she was dealing with? Once he described the details of his dream—the soft black curls of his daughter's hair, her giggle-drunk smile—Lola would see. Beau never ignored his instinct. After all, that was how they'd gotten there, on a cliff, on the brink of their lives, as night fell over the Grand Canyon. He'd seen a girl on a stage under a spotlight, and he'd known. *That one. I won't stop until I have* her.

TITLES BY JESSICA HAWKINS

LEARN MORE AT JESSICAHAWKINS.NET/BOOKS

WHITE MONARCH SERIES

VIOLENT DELIGHTS
VIOLENT ENDS
VIOLENT TRIUMPHS

RIGHT WHERE I WANT YOU

SOMETHING IN THE WAY SERIES

SOMETHING IN THE WAY
SOMEBODY ELSE'S SKY
MOVE THE STARS
LAKE + MANNING

SLIP OF THE TONGUE
THE FIRST TASTE
YOURS TO BARE

EXPLICITLY YOURS SERIES

POSSESSION
DOMINATION
PROVOCATION
OBSESSION

THE CITYSCAPE SERIES

COME UNDONE
COME ALIVE
COME TOGETHER

ABOUT THE AUTHOR

JESSICA HAWKINS is an Amazon bestselling author known for her "emotionally gripping" and "off-the-charts hot" romance. Dubbed "queen of angst" by both peers and readers for her smart and provocative work, she's garnered a cult-like following of fans who love to be torn apart...and put back together.

She writes romance both at home in the California desert and around the world, a coffee shop traveler who bounces from café to café with just a laptop, headphones, and coffee cup.

CONNECT WITH JESSICA

Stay updated & join the
JESSICA HAWKINS Mailing List
www.JESSICAHAWKINS.net/mailing-list

www.amazon.com/author/jessicahawkins
www.facebook.com/jessicahawkinsauthor
twitter: @jess_hawk

Printed in the USA
CPSIA information can be obtained
at www.ICGtesting.com
LVHW020730240824
789174LV00009B/194

9 780997 869156